The CHIMERA'S CURSE

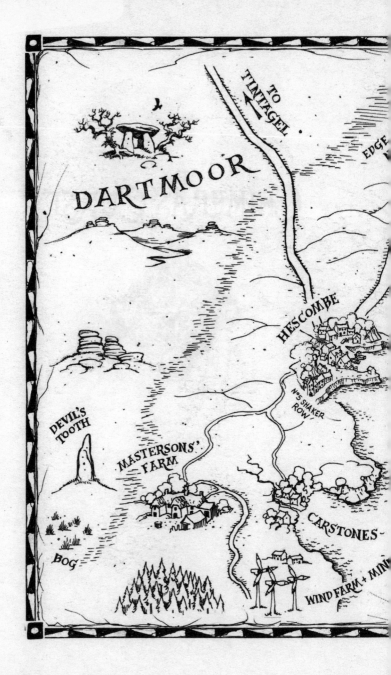

Also by Julia Golding

Secret of the Sirens—*Book One in the Companions Quartet*

The Gorgon's Gaze—*Book Two in the Companions Quartet*

Mines of the Minotaur—*Book Three in the Companions Quartet*

The Ship Between the Worlds

If you enjoy reading Julia's books, check out these two fun websites:

www.companionsclub.co.uk
www.juliagolding.co.uk

BOOK FOUR
THE COMPANIONS QUARTET

The CHIMERA'S CURSE

JULIA GOLDING

OXFORD
UNIVERSITY PRESS

For Lucy, Edward, and Toby

*With special thanks to Dr Nigel Pearson
for telling me about cobra bites*

OXFORD
UNIVERSITY PRESS

Great Clarendon Street, Oxford OX2 6DP

Oxford University Press is a department of the University of Oxford.
It furthers the University's objective of excellence in research, scholarship,
and education by publishing worldwide in

Oxford New York

Auckland Cape Town Dar es Salaam Hong Kong Karachi
Kuala Lumpur Madrid Melbourne Mexico City Nairobi
New Delhi Shanghai Taipei Toronto

With offices in

Argentina Austria Brazil Chile Czech Republic France Greece
Guatemala Hungary Italy Japan Poland Portugal Singapore
South Korea Switzerland Thailand Turkey Ukraine Vietnam

Oxford is a registered trade mark of Oxford University Press
in the UK and in certain other countries

British Library Cataloguing in Publication Data
Data available

ISBN 978-0-19-275463-9

3 5 7 9 10 8 6 4 2

Typeset in Garamond MT by TnQ Books and Journals Pvt. Ltd.,
Chennai, India

Printed in Great Britain by Cox & Wyman Ltd, Reading, Berkshire

Paper used in the production of this book is a natural, recyclable product made
from wood grown in sustainable forests. The manufacturing process conforms
to the environmental regulations of the country of origin.

Contents

1

Hunt

'Come to me, Universal. You know you are mine.'

Connie Lionheart stirred restlessly in her sleep. A hot wind whispered in the curtains, carrying the scent of the parched land. The breeze bore the sound of waves folding onto the beach. It was a sultry night and the sheet clung uncomfortably to her body.

'Come to the mark. Come to me. You know you must.'

Connie surfaced from sleep, struggling like a swimmer caught in weeds, thrashing to reach air. When she woke, she found the bedclothes twisted round her. She threw them off and sat up to gulp some water from the glass on her

1

bedside table, her hand shaking slightly. The voice had crept into her dreams again: the voice of Kullervo, the shape-shifter, her enemy—and her companion creature. He said the same thing each time, repeating the message again and again so that she could hear its echo during the daylight hours as well as in the stillness of the night. She knew where he wanted her to go: he wanted her to meet him at the mark he had made deep in her mind, the breach in the wall between her and his dark presence. But she would not give in to him.

'Sentinel!' Connie called out in thought. 'Help me! He's here again.'

Sentinel the minotaur, the creature appointed by the Trustees of the Society for the Protection of Mythical Creatures to guard the universal, sent his shadow-presence instantly to her side. He himself was hidden not far away in a cave in the cliffs, keeping watch, but he did not need to be with her in body when he could come to her through the bond between universal and creature. His presence burst into her mind, stamping out any residue of the dark creature that had visited her dreams. With bull head dipping from side to side, he gored and pierced the shadows, reducing the shape-shifter's presence to tatters and finally to nothing but a faint whisper of mocking

2

laughter. And then even that echo was snuffed out by the minotaur's bellow of anger. Satisfied all was now clear, shadow-Sentinel bowed to the universal, his hand clasped to his heart and his curved bull's horns lowered.

'He has gone,' he growled. 'You may sleep in peace.'

Too shaken to lie down immediately, Connie remained sitting and hugged her knees, her fear creeping back now she was alone again. It had been much easier to repel Kullervo before Argand, her golden dragon companion, grew too big to fit through her bedroom window. Each night they had curled up together and she had shared the dragonet's dreams, leaving no room for Kullervo to creep into her mind. But now Argand slept on the moors with the rest of her family and Connie was on her own.

She lifted her shaggy mane of black hair off her neck in a vain attempt to cool herself. She knew she was living on borrowed time: Kullervo would seek her out again. These night time visitations were just his way of teasing her: his real attack would come in some way she did not expect, and he would try to trick her into encountering him as he had done already three times in as many years. It was difficult to remain constantly alert. After all, she had a life to lead in Hescombe: she had to go to school, see her friends, have fun like any other ordinary teenager.

Connie shuddered. But, of course, she wasn't ordinary. As the only universal companion in existence, the only person who could bond with all mythical creatures, her life was never going to be conventional or safe. Kullervo would always hunt her because he needed her powers to achieve the destruction of humanity. The prospect paralysed her with fear. Connie rubbed her forearms, trying to drive away the tremors that set in when she thought of the threat hanging over her. Sometimes she wished she could forget what she knew. She clung on to the times when she could pretend to be normal, when she could relax and forget the burden and blessing of her gift. Like tomorrow, for example: tomorrow she was going for a picnic with her great-uncle, her brother Simon, and her friends, Jane and Anneena—none of them knew anything about mythical creatures so there was not a whiff of a creature encounter planned. She would seem to the world like an ordinary girl on her summer holidays, her extraordinary secret well hidden.

Holding on to this comforting image, Connie turned over and eventually drifted off to sleep.

* * *

Over at the Mastersons' Farm, Shirley's party was in full swing. Col was sitting on the front doorstep, can of Coke in hand, watching the dancers. The birthday girl's silky blonde hair swirled as she danced and she was laughing loudly among the crowds of young people. Col felt a twinge of envy at Shirley's ability to fit in so effortlessly with the non-Society friends she'd invited; he had to acknowledge that, recently, being a member of the Society had got in the way of how he would like normal people to see him. He feared that these days at his school no one would think him the least bit cool, not when his best friends, Connie and Rat, stood out for being strange.

Col crushed his empty can moodily. He wished it didn't matter to him but it did. Worse, he had no idea what to do about it. Only a few years ago he had been so confident in the class, easy in his skin; now he spent all his time worrying about how others saw him. He wouldn't dream of dropping his friends, but neither Rat nor Connie showed any sign of change so the problem wasn't going to be solved that way. But it just didn't feel right to spend most of his time embarrassed by their behaviour.

Col put his head in his hands and groaned. He was an idiot. He didn't deserve them. They were both extraordinarily gifted and Connie was unique. Perhaps he was the problem?

The song ended and some of the dancers drifted off the floor. With a jolt of surprise, Col noticed that Shirley was headed in his direction with a group of her school friends in tow. Long limbed, tanned, pretty, they were an intimidating sight. He suddenly felt very nervous: a pack of girls bearing down on him tended to have that effect. Assuming nonchalance he did not feel, he grabbed a fresh can from an ice-filled bucket and pulled the tag, letting it fizz on to the step.

'And this is Col,' Shirley said, sweeping her arm towards him. She quickly ran through the names of her friends. Pinned by their gaze, he felt as if they were silently marking him out of ten.

'Hi.' He managed a general greeting, giving himself zero for originality.

But it seemed to do the trick. On that signal, the girls clustered about him, giving him their full and very flattering attention. Slowly, he began to relax, thinking he was doing OK as they quizzed him about his school and his taste in music. That was until they started on his friendships.

'Shirley said you were friends with that girl, Connie Lionheart,' one dark-haired girl said sweetly.

Col swung round to her. 'Yeah. Do you know her then?'

'I've heard a lot about her.' The girl took a sip of her drink and exchanged a smile with Shirley. 'Didn't you both get stuck up a tree?'

'Er, yeah.' Col took a nervous gulp from his own can.

'Is she really your girlfriend?' The girl gave him an amused look, eyebrow arched in disbelief.

Col felt the blood rush to his cheeks. 'Of course she's not. Who gave you that idea?' It had to be Shirley, of course. He liked Connie; they were closer than he could explain, thanks to all that they had been through together, but girlfriend . . . !

'We didn't think so,' a second girl butted in. Clearly his love life had been much discussed even before they approached him. 'Everyone says she's so . . . so odd.'

Col knew he should speak up in defence of Connie. She was much more than this label of 'odd' that they had given her, but what could he say? He was acutely aware that Shirley's crowd would think badly of him if he said anything. He shouldn't care about their opinion, but he did.

'We're good friends,' he said lamely, letting the comment go, 'just good friends.'

Satisfied, Shirley indicated to her group that it was time to move on. 'Aren't you going to dance, Col?' she asked as they began to wander away.

'No,' he said bluntly, hating her for showing up his lack of loyalty to Connie, and cursing himself for succumbing to the pressure.

She gave him a triumphant smile. 'Fine. See you.'

The companion to weather giants returned to the dance floor and soon had her hands draped around the neck of a dark-eyed boy that Col recognized as Jessica Moss's selkie companion, a changeling creature that could transform into a seal. Jessica must have brought him, knowing that the boy could mingle inconspicuously with the other young people. Thinking about Jessica, Col spotted her sitting on her own on the bonnet of one of the cars in the yard. Freckle-faced, with a mass of reddish-brown curls, Jessica looked about as miserable as Col felt as she watched Shirley and her companion dancing. Getting up from his post by the front door, Col walked over, a fresh can of Coke in hand.

'Want something to drink, Jess?' he asked.

Jessica looked up at him with a grimace. 'Thanks, Col.' Taking the can, her eyes snapped back to the dance floor. 'Look at her. She's been longing to get her claws into Arran for ages and now she's succeeded.'

Col followed Jessica's gaze and saw that Shirley now had her head bent against the selkie's neck.

'Forget it.' Col slid onto the bonnet beside her. 'He'll soon work out she's not worth it.'

'I'm not jealous,' Jessica said quickly, though from the flash in her eyes Col doubted this was the case. 'But he's so green, so soft-hearted.'

Col kept his smile to himself. 'Don't worry. He'll not abandon his companion. It just doesn't work like that.'

Jessica sighed. 'I s'pose not. It's not very likely that he'll find a future with a weather giant companion, is it?'

'No chance. Too much rough water.'

Jessica relaxed, sitting back so that she leant against Col. 'Thanks. So, how are you?'

'Oh, I'm fine. Trying to put in the flying hours for my Grade Four exam.'

'I know what you mean.' Jessica yawned. 'I was up at the crackle of dawn for my swimming training.' She gazed at the rest of the crowd, her brow wrinkled. 'How come only you and I get invited to this party out of all of us in the Society?'

Col scanned the groups of dancers under the

flashing party lights, the knots of people by the drinks' table: he didn't know many of them well but he recognized the local in-crowd when he saw it. 'We're not the only ones. I was with the dragon twins earlier, but I think they left to go flying.'

'Still, what about Connie and Rat?'

Col gave a hollow laugh. 'Surely you know Shirley well enough, Jess, to know that she wouldn't invite them? Not Rat's kind of thing anyway.'

'S'pose not. But what about Connie?'

'Shirley didn't ask her. I don't know if it's because she's insanely jealous of our universal or because Connie's not cool enough for her friends from Chartmouth.' Col fell guiltily silent, remembering how he had just inadequately defended her only a few moments before.

'Oh.' Jessica wrinkled her nose in disgust. 'Well, I like Connie. Does that make me uncool?'

'I s'pect so—in Shirley's eyes at any rate.' Col noticed that Shirley now appeared to be kissing Arran's neck.

'Huh! You'll forgive me if I don't make her opinion the guide to what I like and don't like!' Jessica's eyes sparkled dangerously as she saw what was going on.

The song ended and at last the dancers broke apart. Arran looked in their direction and noticed

Col with his arm around Jessica. Immediately, the selkie abandoned Shirley and headed for them with a determined look on his face.

'Hello, Arran,' Col said levelly as the selkie came to stand in front of them. 'Enjoying the party?'

'Hello, Col,' said the selkie, his voice a snarl. Arran turned to his companion. 'I've had enough, Jess. Can we go now?'

Jessica sat up abruptly from leaning against Col and accepted Arran's hand to slide from the bonnet.

'Tired of your dance partner already?' she asked, swatting his arm. The selkie shuffled his feet awkwardly, looking down. If he had been in his seal shape, his whiskers would have drooped in shame. 'See you, Col,' Jessica said brightly, blowing him a kiss.

'Bye,' Col said out loud. 'See. Nothing to worry about,' he muttered as Jessica and Arran walked off hand in hand.

Getting up late the following morning, Col decided he'd hack across the moors to see Rat. He still felt annoyed with himself for how he'd behaved at Shirley's party. Being a member of the Society meant he spent much of his time hanging out with people who were frankly all a bit eccentric. This had never bothered him much before, but last night had brought home to him that he wanted to be . . . well . . . cool again.

Am I being a prat? he wondered, looking at himself in the mirror.

Probably, he admitted with a shamefaced grin. That's what Rat would say.

Rat's reaction he could handle, but why did he get tied up in knots any time someone mentioned Connie? He felt he should defend her, yet didn't; he wanted to be with her, but then felt embarrassed when she started doing things like talking to seagulls in public. He was in awe of her gift. She couldn't help it, but she always made him feel as if he was standing in her shadow. These days everyone saw the universal first and had no time for an insignificant pegasus companion. Indeed, why would they notice him? He'd done nothing worth mentioning.

Fetching his chestnut pony, Mags, from the stable, Col turned him towards the beach, planning a shortcut along the shore, hoping the ride would restore his good humour. On this route the only hazard they met were encampments of tourists marking out their territories with striped screens, sun-tents, deckchairs, buckets and spades.

'How much for a pony ride?' called a cheeky-faced boy of about seven or eight, popping out from behind a rock and running beside Col's stirrup for a few paces.

'Get lost!' grinned Col. But softening, he added, 'If you're still here when I come back, I'll give you a ride for nothing.'

'Done!' shouted the boy and zoomed off down the beach, arms outspread like an aeroplane, to splash into the scintillating water.

Col spurred Mags on. He was doing what he did best: riding. Surely nothing could go wrong with such glorious sunshine and not a cloud on the horizon?

Connie lay on the picnic rug, feeling full and deliciously lazy after an ample lunch. The picnickers had not gone far from her great-uncle's cottage, just up to the edge of the moor to a field where the Mastersons' flocks grazed the sun-bleached grass. Uncle Hugh snored gently in his folding chair, newspaper dangling precariously off his knees, sunhat slanting over his eyes. Her friends, Jane and Anneena, were talking in quiet voices not far away. Simon, her younger brother, was picking apart a strand of dry grass, and now started throwing bits onto his sister.

'Stop it, Si!' she said wearily, waving the nuisance away like a bothersome fly. 'Why don't you annoy someone else for a change?'

Simon continued to dribble bits of grass onto her, his short black hair bobbing about at the periphery of her vision as he stretched over.

'Do you have to do that to Connie, Simon?' came Anneena's voice from the other side of the picnic rug. Anneena was sitting up, fanning herself with her straw hat.

'Brothers can be such a pain,' said Jane grumpily. She had an older brother and was used to such tormenting.

'Look, why don't we go for a walk?' suggested Anneena. 'We could find some shade in the trees over there.'

'A walk?' groaned Connie. 'Surely not in this heat?'

'Yes. You shouldn't lie out in the sun: you'll burn.'

'OK. Let's go,' Connie said, sitting up, feeling momentarily dizzy as the world righted itself.

'I'm not coming. It'll be boring,' said Simon sullenly.

'Fine,' cut in Anneena. 'You stay here and clear up then.'

Simon got to his feet. 'I'm coming,' he said quickly.

The four of them headed towards the pine plantation, eager to reach the shade once they started walking in the glaring heat. Entering under the boughs, the contrast with the bright day could not have been greater: brown shadows clung to the tree trunks, obscuring the depths of the wood from view. A thick layer of pine needles muffled their footfalls, releasing the heady scent of resin as they were stirred. The air was stuffy, like a room that had been shut up for many years. Connie felt a prickle down her spine and shivered.

'I'm not sure it's any cooler in here,' said Jane doubtfully, taking a dislike to the place. 'Shall we go back?'

Anneena and Connie were ready to agree but Simon was standing very still, staring fascinated into the trees.

'No, I want to go further in,' he said firmly. His thick black eyebrows that almost met in the middle were set in a determined frown.

'Come on, Simon, let's get out into the fresh air again.' Connie pulled on his sleeve but he shook her off. Her skin was prickling; her body tense, on the verge of making a run for it. Anything to get out of this creepy wood.

'No,' he said angrily. 'You dragged me in here. It's not fair to make me go just because you've changed your mind.'

'He has a point,' said Jane. She brushed her fair hair off her face where it was sticking to her skin.

Connie now noticed that her brother was gazing into the shadows, a rapt expression on his face. She paused for a moment, focusing her thoughts on the creatures around her. Then she caught it too. There was something slinking through those trees—a creature whose presence she had never felt before—something dangerous.

'I think we'd better go back,' she said quietly, laying a hand on Simon's arm to try to convey to him that she understood.

He shook her off roughly. 'I'm going further in.'

'But it's not safe,' Connie said in a low voice, hoping Anneena and Jane would not hear. She did not want them to question her about her ability to sense mythical creatures.

'Not safe! It's not the Amazon jungle, you know. What do you think will get me in Hescombe—a particularly hacked-off squirrel? What'll it do: throw pine cones at me or something?'

Connie could have pointed out that dragons, stone sprites, minotaurs, and frost wolves were not unknown on the moors—to the Society members at least. But Simon was not a member of the Society and showed no interest in undergoing an assessment, though Connie had had

16

reason before today to suspect that he had a gift.

'I know,' she said, struggling to be reasonable as her instinct grew that they must retreat and quickly. 'But please trust me for once. It really isn't safe for anyone to go in there, not until we know *what it is*.' She held his gaze, trying to convey to him that she too sensed the creature in the shadows ahead.

'Know what what is?' asked Anneena intrigued by this exchange, looking eagerly from one to the other. 'Did you see something?'

Connie shook her head. 'No, I think Simon and I might've heard something moving about.'

She was saved further explanation by an ear-splitting whinny, a shout, followed by a thump, not far away to their right. They could all now hear something large crashing through the trees and Connie caught the glimpse of a long black tail disappearing into the undergrowth. Without hesitation, they all ran in the direction of the cry.

Simon was first to reach the scene. He found Col sitting on the ground, holding his head and groaning.

'Are you all right?' Connie pushed past her brother. 'What happened?'

'Mags threw me,' Col gasped, an astounding

17

statement from him as his riding skills were famous.

Connie gave a whistle and the chestnut pony galloped back into the clearing, eyes wide with fear. Mags nestled against her for comfort, skin quivering.

'How come you fell?' Simon asked. 'You never fall.'

'I dunno.' Col shook his head to clear it of the ringing in his ears. 'We were riding along, minding our own business when we . . . ' He stopped, suddenly remembering what he had seen. 'Connie, there's something loose on the moor. A big cat maybe. I saw its eyes in the bushes over there.' He gestured towards a thick tangle of fallen trees and new saplings. 'It leapt out, Mags reared, and I fell.'

'A big cat?' Anneena offered her hand to pull Col up from the ground. 'Are you sure?'

Col gave Connie an awkward look. Society members were sworn to keep mythical creatures secret and if this was one of them then he'd just made a monumental blunder. Anneena would never give up on such a tempting mystery. 'I'm not sure. Maybe it was just a deer or something.'

'It wasn't a deer,' Simon stated. 'I know it wasn't. Let's go look for it.'

Connie frowned at her brother. This was getting out of hand and she still felt they were in desperate danger. 'You can't go. You're forgetting that Col's hurt, aren't you Col?' she said, giving him a heavy hint.

On cue, Col clutched his ankle. 'Yeah. I think I've sprained it.'

'Let's go back to the cottage and get some ice for it. Simon, you'd better take one side, I'll take the other.' Forcing her brother to assume his part as one of Col's human crutches, Connie led the retreat, leaving two amber eyes watching her from the shadows.

2
Fire Imps

Ice pack in place, Col sat on a sun-lounger in the back garden of Rat's house, surrounded by the defunct engines sacrificed to Rat's father's hobby of car mechanics. Mr Ratcliff himself was asleep in the hammock slung where the washing line normally hung. Mrs Ratcliff was clattering in the kitchen, singing tunelessly, making what she called hedgerow jam and what her son and husband called 'Mam's Poisoned Spread'.

'It'd be OK if she just stuck to blackberries and things,' groaned Rat, 'but she will branch out—chuck in a bit of anything that catches her eye.'

'Like what?' asked Connie, plucking the petals off a daisy. 'He loves me, he loves me not,' she counted absent-mindedly.

'I dunno—like nettles and cow parsley—anything really.'

Connie threw the daisy aside and made a mental note to dispose quietly of the jar Mrs Ratcliff had given her great-uncle for Christmas.

Anneena had just finished running through what had happened in the plantation for Rat's benefit and was now speculating about the strange creature.

'It's not the first time, of course,' said Anneena, fanning herself with her sun hat. 'There've been reports of a beast on the moors for ages.'

'Oh?' said Connie guardedly. She had certainly never sensed the presence of this particular creature before and was still wondering what it was. It seemed so strange, so contradictory—dark and prowling like a big cat, snake-like in the way it slithered through the undergrowth, but also nimble, certainly fast enough to make a rapid escape.

'Yes. I saw a story from over Okehampton way last month about a flock of sheep being raided. Paw-prints everywhere, according to the farmer.'

'I don't think that was the same beast,' said Rat with a grin. He stretched out his thin, wiry body on the scrubby lawn dotted with bright yellow dandelions. His sharp profile twitched with suppressed laughter.

'Oh?' asked Anneena. 'Why not?'

Rat opened his mouth but was lost for words.

Col knew why: it must have been the frost wolf, Icefen, in one of his wilder moods. He wouldn't have been surprised if Rat hadn't encouraged him. Come to think of it, Rat might even have been riding him at the time.

'It's a long way from here, isn't it?' Col supplied for his friend who was notoriously bad at lying. Rat twisted over onto his belly and gave Col a grateful grin.

'But how many wild animals do you think there can be, Col?' asked Anneena dismissively.

Far more than you know, Col thought, but he shrugged for Anneena's benefit.

'Isn't it more likely that it's the same creature?' Anneena persisted. 'You can get all the way from here to Okehampton on open moor: it's unlikely to be spotted. Not unless someone's looking for it.'

Connie turned quickly to Anneena, hearing a familiar determined note in her friend's voice. Jane had picked up the same signal.

'Looking for it?' Jane asked slowly.

'Yes. Aren't you even the least bit interested to find out what's going on out there?' Anneena waved her slim hand vaguely in the direction of the moor. 'If a big cat's escaped from a zoo, it's got to be caught before it does any more harm.'

'Yes, but—' said Connie.

'And we know this area better than anybody. We could track it down.' Anneena had a dangerous glint in her eyes. They all knew that she liked nothing better than to have a project.

'I don't think it's a good idea,' said Connie firmly. 'It's too risky. You can't go tracking unknown wild animals, Anneena. You wouldn't stand a chance if you met it.'

'I don't want to meet it. I just want to gather as much information as I can about it. Once we've got a good idea of where it hunts, we can pass on the information to the proper authorities.'

'We?' asked Jane in a wary tone of voice.

Anneena looked around the unenthusiastic faces of her friends. 'Well, I hoped it would be "we". That creature is probably suffering out there—terrified and hungry. Can't be much fun surviving in this drought, can it?' She turned her large brown eyes to appeal to Connie. 'And if you met it, it'd probably just roll over and let you tickle its tummy.'

'Ha!' Connie gave a sceptical laugh. She knew too much about hostile mythical creatures to expect such a warm welcome.

'You didn't see it, Anneena,' Col warned. 'It's no pussy cat.'

'Oh, come on, you lot! What else have you got to do with your summer in any case?'

'I'll help you, Anneena,' said Rat to Col and Connie's surprise.

'Are you sure?' asked Connie doubtfully.

'Yeah. I've a good idea about the beast's habits already.' He winked at Connie. 'I know enough to keep Anneena occupied.'

'Rat!' Connie protested.

But Anneena cut in quickly, thinking that Connie was trying to undermine her idea: 'Thanks, Rat. I really appreciate your support.' She glared round at the others, saving her hardest stare for Connie.

'OK, OK,' said Jane, surrendering to the inevitable. 'I'll help.'

Anneena looked pointedly at Connie and Col.

Connie sighed. 'I will too. But you must trust me if I say it's too dangerous; you must promise to leave the moor immediately.'

'Don't take any notice of her,' chipped in Simon, who had been sitting forgotten, listening in on the conversation. 'She's just being a nag as usual. I'll help.'

Connie frowned at Simon but he was studiously avoiding her eye. Sibling relationships were definitely at an all-time low.

'Thanks, Simon,' said Anneena, somewhat surprised by this offer. Simon was normally to be found inside destroying aliens on his computer, not volunteering for a challenge outdoors.

Col spoke last. 'I'm with Connie on this. I'll only help if we follow her lead. We all know she's the one who understands animals.'

Simon snorted derisively. Col glared at him, making Simon swallow his comment.

'OK,' said Anneena, happy to have got her way. 'We'll start by looking up recent news reports of attacks and see if we can establish a pattern.' She looked around the circle. 'Any volunteers to come with me to the library in Chartmouth?'

'Libraries: not my thing, Anneena,' said Rat quickly.

Anneena must have agreed with him for she was now looking expectantly at Jane and Connie.

'OK. I can come on Monday morning,' admitted Connie.

'I'll come too,' volunteered Jane.

Connie and Jane shared a private, exasperated look. They both loved Anneena dearly, but sometimes being her friend could be taxing.

Astride Mags once more, Col trotted behind Connie as she pedalled her bike down the lanes bright with nodding summer flowers and grasses.

Since Col's father had married Connie's aunt last year, Col had been spending more time round at Shaker Row and it was becoming a second home to him. He had decided to go back with Connie to ask his father about the creature on the moors: as a member of the Society, Mack might have some ideas.

Col would also have liked to ask Connie for her opinion, but she did not seem disposed to talk at the moment. Instead, he watched in silence as butterflies fluttered in a circle over the universal's head, drifting in and out of formation like tiny ballroom dancers. Jane and Anneena were just in front, riding their bikes side by side, talking animatedly about the moorland beast.

Col turned his thoughts back to the scene in the plantation and shuddered. He hadn't caught a proper look at the animal but he remembered the wave of malevolence that accompanied its pounce. It had felt so powerful; he would put money on it being some kind of mythical creature. But which one? The Society had good relations with most of the beasts and beings on Dartmoor, except the mischievous creatures like the kelpies, horse-shaped sprites who liked to trick walkers and lead them into bogs. But that kind of harm was mostly a wicked play, rarely fatal; the creature in the plantation had been different. It had wanted blood.

Connie's thoughts were preoccupied not by the creature but by her brother's behaviour in its presence. She was relieved to leave Simon behind at her great-uncle's cottage on the headland where he was staying for the summer. They were definitely not getting on as well as they used to do. But she was going to have to grasp the nettle about his gift, talk to him about the Society at the very least, before he did something rash.

'So, what do you think?' Col asked her as soon as they waved farewell to Anneena and Jane on the outskirts of Hescombe.

'He's not himself,' she said.

'What?' Col had no idea what she was talking about.

'Simon: he definitely sensed the creature before I did, up in the plantation just now.'

'Oh,' said Col. This put a new spin on the whole adventure. 'D'you think—?'

'What else can it be?'

'Do you think he's another universal?'

Connie frowned, digging back in her memory to recall the other times she had been with her brother in the presence of animals. He had a special bond with her aunt's cat, he'd shown that long ago.

27

'I don't know. None of the mythical creatures have ever mentioned it to me and, in my own case, I know they sensed it without me having to ask them.'

'So what about entering him for an assessment?'

Connie shook her head. 'He's not interested. Both Evelyn and I have asked him before, but he's taken it into his head that the Society is my thing, so he hates it. And Mr Coddrington is still in place as the assessor for our region; I really couldn't face explaining the difficulty to the Society.' Though losing his post as Trustee and being almost universally disliked for his attempt to oust Connie from the Society, Mr Coddrington had clung on to his official role as an assessor at its London headquarters. Nothing had ever been proved against him so they couldn't sack him.

'Dr Brock then?' suggested Col.

'Yes, that's an idea. Or Horace Little. He's a friend of Uncle Hugh's so Simon might listen to him.'

They stopped outside the gate to Number Five.

'Do you want to come in?' Connie asked hesitantly, looking at him with her mismatched eyes, so like his, one green one brown. She was aware that there was a certain tension between them ever since she'd kissed him on the cheek a few months ago. Col no longer seemed easy in her presence. She now regretted doing it.

'Dunno,' said Col, glancing at his watch. He would like to stay, he really would. 'I'm not sure I've time. I did want a word—with Dad, that is . . . '

The decision was taken out of their hands by Mack Clamworthy. He had been on the watch for their return and spotted them hovering by the gate. He came striding down the path; a handsome man: fit, with spiky black hair, square jaw, and twinkling brown eyes. It was his Harley Davidson by the gate that Connie had just propped her bike against. She picked up the bicycle quickly, knowing how protective he was of his beloved motorcycle, though for once he seemed completely oblivious of his prized possession, not giving it a second glance.

'Col, Connie, just the people I want!' He threw the gate open and gave his son a bear hug, from which Col struggled to extricate himself. 'Come in, come in.' He made no attempt to hide that he was in an extremely good mood.

Col and Connie exchanged puzzled looks but there seemed nothing for it but to follow him inside. They trailed behind him down the garden path and round to the back door. The kitchen windows were wide open, the mobile of scavenged feathers and glass tinkling melodiously over the sink. The washing-up in the sink was piled high. Clearly no one had done any housework since breakfast, which was not unusual in this household. Mack strode into the hall and bellowed up the stairs.

'Evie, Connie and Col are back. Are you coming down?' He turned to grin at them. 'She's just having a rest. The heat got to her.' Rubbing his hands gleefully together, Mack paced across the stone floor, but said nothing more, waiting for his wife to arrive.

Col sat down at the table and tapped his fingers impatiently. He wished now he had slipped away and gone straight home. Connie, equally perplexed, helped herself to a glass of water at the sink, leant against the edge, and waited.

When Evelyn came in, with her long brown hair bundled up in a crimson scarf, Connie saw instantly that her aunt looked distinctly unwell. She poured a second glass of water and held it out to her.

'Here, have this. You don't look good.'

'Thanks, Connie,' said Evelyn, taking the water and gazing at it as if she would rather not drink it. 'I'm fine. Really, I'm fine.'

Connie took a step forward and put her hand to her aunt's forehead to see if she had a fever. She gave a small gasp.

'You're not . . . ?' Connie asked.

'I am,' said Evelyn with a weak smile. 'Feeling ghastly, but I am. How did you know?'

Col looked from one to the other. Connie at least now seemed to understand what was going on here but he was still in the dark. Was Evelyn seriously ill? Surely not?

'Will someone please tell me what's going on?' he demanded, feeling a sharp pang of concern.

Mack strode over to his son and clapped him on the shoulder. 'How would you like to hear that you are going to have a brother—'

'Or sister,' added Evelyn.

'—or sister. In March, we think.'

Col's jaw dropped. 'You're not . . . ?' he asked Mack.

'Yep. Going to have a baby. Well, Evie's going to have the baby. I'm just the proud father.' Mack went over to his wife and gave her a gentle squeeze.

'Poor kid,' said Col with a broad grin.

'So you're pleased?' Mack looked a little worried. Mack and Col both knew that he had not been the perfect father to Col, absent for much of the time.

'Course I'm pleased.' But for all his delight, Col couldn't help feeling jealous of the new baby. He or she would have Mack as a proper father, something Col had never been allowed.

31

Evelyn turned to Connie. 'And what do you think?' she asked her niece gently.

Connie had just been wondering if this new turn of events would mean that she was still welcome at Number Five. There wasn't much space and she had the attic bedroom, leaving just one for guests.

'It's great news. I'm really pleased.' How could she not be when it was so clearly what Evelyn and Mack wanted?

'So tell me, Connie, how did you know?' Evelyn was looking at her shrewdly with her bright green eyes.

Connie rubbed her throat. How could she explain? 'I felt him—or her,' she added quickly. 'I could feel another life.' She did not want to go on to say what else she knew. Why spoil the surprise with something that was for the moment only a suspicion?

When Col left the impromptu celebration in the kitchen, he found that Mags was not alone by the front gate. The boy he'd met hours earlier on the beach was waiting for him on the steps that led down to the shore, absent-mindedly brushing the sand from his feet, his nose red after a day of playing in the sun. He sprang up when he heard the gate clang shut and flashed a gappy-toothed grin at Col.

'See, I'm still here!' he said in an eager voice.

Col groaned inwardly. He would have very much preferred to head straight home so he could be alone with his thoughts about his father's news—but a promise was a promise.

'Where's your mum and dad?' Col asked, looking up and down the beach. It was deserted, the tide in, and the long, yawning shadows cast by the cliff making it far less inviting than it had appeared earlier in the day. The sea had lost its sparkle and now lapped with a dull grey sheen against the seaweed-strewn stones. A red light flushed the sky as the sun slipped beyond the horizon.

'They've gone back to the hotel,' said the boy, gesturing over his shoulder towards the harbour. 'They know I'm with you.'

That was a bit odd. The boy did not even know Col's name but had just assumed that he would keep his word and let him ride. And the boy's parents had let him stay out this late on his own? Col's grandmother would not have done the same at the boy's age.

'I can't give you a long ride because Mags here has been out all day and needs to get back to his stable.' Col patted his pony on the neck and gave him an apologetic look. Mags shook his mane, forgiving Col his foolish generosity. 'But I can take you for a quick trot on the beach. Have you ever ridden before?'

'Nope,' said the boy happily, already attempting to scramble onto Mags's back as if the pony were a climbing frame. Col grabbed him by the back of his T-shirt and pulled him down.

'Not like that,' he said, half-amused, half-irritated. 'Here, put this helmet on. Then put one foot in the stirrup and I'll help you up.'

Once the boy was safely in the saddle, Col shortened the stirrups and took Mags's halter. With a click of his tongue, he led the way down to the beach. Mags snorted in disgust as the boy bounced up and down, crowing with delight.

'Look, mate, he's got feelings, you know: he's not a pogo stick,' Col called up.

'Sorry!' said the boy, still laughing. 'This is great. I've always dreamed of riding a real horse.'

Col whispered something in Mags's ear and in unison they began to trot along the strand. The boy was now bouncing for real on the pony's back, clearly in seventh heaven. They reached the limit of the beach, forward progress cut off by the tide, and Col turned for home.

'What's that?' called the boy, pointing over Mags's head up in the air. Plumes of dark grey cloud were rising from the cliff top. Col caught the scent of smoke. He led the pony and rider into the shallows so he could get a better look. There was an orange glow above them, like a fringe of flaming hair on the brow of the hill.

'Some idiot's started a fire,' he answered. 'Shift up: we've got to call the fire brigade.' He swung up behind the boy and urged Mags forward, cursing himself for leaving his phone at home.

The boy was still staring with wonder at the fire.

'I can see people in the flames, dancing!' he said excitedly. 'Let's go up there!'

'No,' said Col sharply. 'There can't be—not in the fire.' However, he could see that there were shapes very like people leaping into the sky. But they were not human. The fire imps were rejoicing in the blaze. He wondered that the boy had seen them so quickly: most people just dismissed them as odd silhouettes in the flames.

'But I must!' the boy cried. His eyes shone with a fanatical gleam as he twisted round in the saddle to stare up at the fire. 'They're calling to me!' He began to slip from Mags's back as if he intended to scale the sheer cliff face in his desperation to reach the imps. Col gripped his arms firmly and yanked him back on.

'You're not going up there.' He kicked Mags

into a trot that swiftly turned into a gallop and the boy was forced to concentrate on staying on. Mags surged up the slope from the beach back to Number Five. Col dismounted, pulling the boy after him. 'You're coming with me.' He did not trust the boy on his own, being sure that he would run back to the fire the moment he was left alone.

'But—!' protested the boy, reluctantly allowing Col to propel him up the path to the back door, his eyes still fixed on the blaze.

Col banged the door open and pushed him into the kitchen, much to the astonishment of Connie and Mack who were just sitting down to supper. Evelyn had returned to bed, not feeling up to eating. Mack rose abruptly to his feet, chair clattering to the floor behind him.

'I've got to use your phone,' Col said. 'The headland's on fire.'

Mack chucked him the handset. 'And who's this?' Mack asked, looking the boy up and down. Col shrugged, having just got through to the emergency switchboard.

'I'm Liam,' said the boy defiantly, his chin tilted up to face the imposing figure of Mack Clamworthy.

'Sure you are,' said Mack with a grin, taking an instant liking to the lad. 'Sit down. Col won't be long.'

'Would you like something to drink, Liam?' Connie asked. She got to her feet and took a glass from the draining board. If she had been him, she knew she would not have liked being stared at by two strangers.

Liam, however, had other things on his mind than standing in an unfamiliar kitchen. 'There're people up there—dancing around in the flames!' he said excitedly. 'I saw them with my own eyes. I've got to get back to them.' He half-turned as if to make a dash for the door.

'Hey there!' Mack blocked the exit. 'Calm down!'

Connie paused, her hand gripping the cool glass at the tap. She closed her eyes and felt out to the cliff top, sensing the presence of the fire imps, darting in and out of the tongues of fire curling up from the bone-dry grass. When she opened them, she saw Col looking at her and he gave her a slight nod of confirmation.

'Didn't you hear them calling us to come and join them?' Liam asked Col. His grey-green eyes, the colour of smoke, were wide with a mixture of exhilaration and anger that no one seemed to understand or believe him.

Col shook his head. 'No. I didn't hear a thing.'

'But you must've done!' Liam said desperately, his fists clenched. 'Their voices were like . . . ' He

37

paused, struggling to find the right words. 'They sounded really clear to me like . . . '

'Like crackling twigs, hissing logs, and popping sparks,' said Connie softly. Liam turned to stare at her in amazement.

'You heard them then?' he asked.

'Yes, I've heard them,' said Connie. 'Now, Liam, what would you like to drink? You want a drink, don't you?'

'Yeah,' said Liam, licking his sunburnt lips and giving her a wary look. 'Have you got Coke?'

'Sorry, only water or orange juice.'

'Juice then.'

In the distance, the wail of a siren announced the arrival of the first firefighters on the cliff top. Connie handed Liam his drink and led him to a chair. The others were silent, content to let the universal deal with the situation. 'I know what you heard, Liam, but it's not safe to follow those voices until you know more about the creatures.'

'Creatures?' Liam was gazing at Connie as if he could not take his eyes off her. Col knew that there was something special about the effect Connie had on some people, those who were most sensitive to her gift, but seeing her with Liam made him realize afresh that there was a mesmerizing power within her. She contained a spring of energy that bubbled up and out to other living beings. He couldn't look away from her either.

'Yes, creatures.' Connie knelt beside Liam and put a hand on his arm. 'You've seen the fire imps tonight. Your companion species, I think. But you must keep it a secret from everyone until we've had a chance to talk to your parents. You see, we want to introduce you to other people—people like you.'

Mack gave a discreet cough. 'He's a bit young for an assessment, Connie,' he said. 'You-know-who'll never agree to do it.' He was right: Ivor Coddrington would not consider examining anyone under ten.

'It's a bit late for that, isn't it?' said Connie. She was no longer afraid of the assessor, her declared enemy within the Society. His opposition to the existence of a universal was now just a fact of life. 'Liam's seen them—he's heard them.'

'Yeah, you're right as usual,' Mack conceded.

'I'll take it to the Trustees if I have to. Anyway, perhaps it's not Mr Coddrington we need to ask. Liam, where do you live?'

'London,' said Liam, looking puzzled by the exchange he did not understand. 'Vauxhall.'

'That's near Brixton, isn't it?'

'Yeah.'

Connie smiled. Here was the answer: Horace and Antonia Little, her friends in Brixton, would help. Antonia was a member of the Company of the Elementals, creatures made of the four elements of water, earth, wind, and fire. And London had a different assessor. That meant she needn't approach Ivor Coddrington for help.

Col glanced up at the clock. It was half-past eight.

'We'd better get you home,' he said to Liam. 'Your mum and dad will be worried about you.'

'No they won't,' said Liam matter-of-factly, getting up to go. 'They'll be down the pub by now. As long as I'm in bed when they get back, they won't care.'

Col again swallowed his surprise that no one seemed to be looking out for Liam. 'Well, I've got to get back. My gran will be wondering where I am. Come on.'

Liam took a reluctant step to follow him. 'Can I come back tomorrow?' He looked to Connie as if he half-expected a rejection.

'I'm not here tomorrow,' Connie said. Liam's face fell.

'OK,' he said in a small but bitter voice. 'Fine.'

'But if you're still here on Tuesday, come by,' she added swiftly. Liam smiled.

Col grabbed a slice of garlic bread from the

table. 'But I'm here tomorrow. I'll look out for you on the beach. Perhaps Dad and I should try to meet your parents?'

His father got up and slung his jacket over his shoulder, keys jangling in its pockets.

'I was thinking of calling in at the Anchor to see if I can spot them tonight,' said Mack. 'I'll break the ice over a couple of beers. Let me walk you two back.'

Liam, who had been looking delighted by these invitations, now seemed worried. 'I'm not sure,' he said, biting his lip. 'They can be a bit weird my parents.'

Mack laughed. 'Don't worry, Liam. I do weird—ask anyone in Hescombe. I'm sure we'll get on like an imp on fire.'

Mack led the boys out of the house, leaving Connie to the now cold supper. In the silence as she ate, Connie let her thoughts stray to the hill-top. Had the fire really been an accident? She caught a whisper of a slinking presence and tasted sulphur at the back of her throat. It felt uncannily like the creature from the moor.

She got up to scrape the plates, trying to shake off the instinct that she was under threat. Whatever had started the fire, water was putting an end to the imps' party; their cries were rising up in indignant hisses as they were doused by hoses.

41

Their fragile bodies of flames were snuffed out leaving their spirits to wander on the wind until the next blaze ignited.

What did it mean, all this about Liam and the revelation of his gift? She had known the moment he had spoken, just as she had sensed Simon's bond with the mysterious creature of the moor. And then there was the baby in her aunt's womb. Her ability for divining the gifts of others was becoming more acute with each passing day. Not only could she now sense the presence of mythical creatures, she was coming to know their human companions, like an aerial buzzing with the transmissions of many radio stations. But the gift came at a price. It threatened to squeeze out her sense of self as she spent so much of her time resonating to the presence of others.

She thought back over her nights of disturbed sleep. If only she had the ability to tune out Kullervo's wavelength, perhaps then this gift would be more bearable, but there seemed no prospect of being able to do this. His presence was a current that flowed under all the others, wearing her down, engrained in her so deeply that she could not hope to block it out any more than she could turn the tide.

3
Devil's Tooth

Connie spooned the chocolate-coated froth off the top of her cappuccino, savouring the milky sweetness on her tongue. Anneena was bent over a pad, comparing notes with Jane after their session in Chartmouth library. Outside the air-conditioned coffee shop, the weather was cloudy but still hot and dry. A woman walked past with an elegant poodle mincing along at her high heels. Catching sight of Connie in the window, the poodle barked a greeting. Connie raised her little finger in a tiny wave.

'Now, this is really interesting.' Anneena's voice broke in upon Connie's daydream. 'There's an article on local wildlife in this drought. It says that many animals are being forced out of their normal habitats to find food and water. I bet that's what's happening to our creature.'

'Perhaps,' said Jane. 'It's been a funny year—hardly any rain since the beginning of July.'

Taking another sip off her spoon, Connie wondered what the weather giants made of it all. They were particularly angry at the changes brought to the climate by humans. Many of them had already gone over to Kullervo's side and he was urging them to take violent action. She wouldn't put it past them to be withholding the rain on purpose.

'The writer says the drought's down to global warming,' continued Anneena, reading off her handwritten notes.

'Maybe,' said Jane. 'But no one knows anything for sure. You should hear Dad on the subject.'

'I don't really think there's any doubt that we're doing the damage,' Connie said quietly, remembering what the mythical creatures had told her over the years.

'But no one's sure how much and how fast,' Jane explained. 'It really worries me.'

Anneena flipped her notebook closed. 'Me too. What about companies like Axoil pumping out all those greenhouse gases? They won't change unless someone makes them.'

'True,' said Jane, watching the cars growl by.

'But the rest of us don't live completely green lives either. I feel a fraud much of the time.'

Connie grimaced. She knew what Jane meant. It was easy to go on about the environment but much harder to do anything about it.

'So what else have we learnt about the beast of the moor?' Anneena asked, changing the subject. 'I've got a list here of recent sightings and attacks.'

Jane pulled out a map, opened it up on the table and pointed to each location. 'The pattern before July seemed fairly random and wide-ranging. But just before our sighting there was a report from a mile further on to the moor of a dark brown, catlike creature on the road—only seen in headlights and gone before the witness could get a second look.'

Anneena craned her head over the map. 'The plantation is the only place to hide in that area. It might well be living there for the moment. Why don't we keep watch for a few evenings to see if we can spot it moving about?'

Connie put her cup down abruptly. 'But I thought you didn't want to get too near it?'

Anneena shrugged. 'No good going on this old news. We've got to find out more about it ourselves. Perhaps even get a photo.' She shot a hopeful look at Jane. 'I don't want to stroke it or anything—just to see it.'

45

Connie was alarmed. This was all getting out of control. She couldn't understand why her friend had got so wrapped up in this mystery. 'Why, Anneena? There've been stories about a beast on the moor for years and you've never worried about it before.'

'But we almost saw it, Connie!' said Anneena as if she was astounded that her friend did not share her enthusiasm.

This was awful. Anneena had no idea what she was getting herself into.

'You know I don't like it, but if you're set on keeping watch for the creature, promise you'll take me with you,' said Connie firmly.

Anneena gave an offended laugh. The bracelets on her arms jangled as she stretched them above her head. 'That's a strange offer. First you say you don't want to go, then you say you've got to come along. But don't put yourself out: I'm sure I could get others to help. Your brother wanted to.'

That settled it. Connie knew she definitely had to be at hand if Simon was going near that creature again. 'I've got to be there. You don't understand, Anneena.'

'And you do?' her friend asked, irritated now. 'Yes.'

'In that case, why don't you share your *special* knowledge with the rest of us?' Anneena gathered up her things and thrust them in her bag. She flicked her long black hair off her shoulder in an angry gesture.

'Anneena.' Jane tugged at her friend's jacket, determined to prevent the row escalating. 'You know Connie's good with animals. You shouldn't turn down her help just because you're feeling a bit miffed.'

Anneena's annoyance dispersed as quickly as it had arisen. She put her bag down. 'Oh, you're right as usual. Sorry, Connie. Of course you have to be there. It's just that this beast thing is really getting to me. I have this weird feeling that we are fated to meet.'

Connie said nothing, hoping Anneena's instinct was for once way off target.

'Anneena's mad! We should keep as far as we can from that creature!' exclaimed Col.

Connie had just filled him in on her morning with Anneena and Jane in Chartmouth. They were walking through the Mastersons' yard on their way to their training sessions: Col to fly with Skylark and Connie to meet her mentor, Gard, the rock dwarf. The yard was buzzing with activity. Over by the barn, Dr Brock was talking intently to the two dragon companion twins. All

47

were dressed in their leather flying jackets, planning an evening expedition.

'Argand wants to see you, Connie,' Dr Brock called. His white hair, still ginger at the temples, shone in the late afternoon sunlight.

'Tell her I'll try to come out after my class,' called back Connie. 'I'll meet her in the usual place.'

'Don't keep her out late!' warned Dr Brock. 'Castanea was furious last time you two were out alone. She said that it was well past midnight before Argand came home.'

'You know Argand,' said Connie, pausing beside him for a moment. 'I wanted to go home much earlier but she insisted we stay out for the moonrise. She said she'd come and watch it on the beach in front of my house if I refused to remain on the moor with her.'

'Ah.'

'I thought that the family next door were probably not ready to see a dragon outside their front garden so I stayed.'

Dr Brock gave her a smile of understanding. Tom and Greg, the dragon twins, laughed sympathetically.

Tom, companion to one of Argand's siblings, commiserated. 'Castanea can be a bit fierce. I still bear the scars.'

'Always keep out of range of her tail, that's my motto,' added Greg.

'I'll try to remember that.' Connie gave them a rueful grin.

A crowd of young people from Sea-Snakes were just getting into a mini-bus for the trip down to a quiet cove they used for their training. Jessica and Arran greeted Col warmly, any bad feelings from Saturday night clearly forgotten. Then they both hugged Connie. The others Connie knew less well—a mermaid companion, a companion to the Nereids, as well as a stern-looking boy who was companion to Charybdis, the whirlpool sea-monster. Though the Sea-Snakes only knew Connie slightly, they all called out greetings to her, eager to catch the attention of the famous universal if only for a moment.

'We'd better get a move on or we'll be late,' said Col, picking up the pace, annoyed that he was being ignored again, though he knew he should be used to it by now. 'So what do you think's out there?'

Connie shrugged. 'I'm not sure. I can feel it's very wild—really dangerous.'

'Yeah, I could've told you that.'

'And it's not used to humans like one of our companion species would be. The problem is, I can't get a fix on its nature: one moment, it seems very catlike, then it slithers out of focus like a snake sliding under cover.' She paused, forehead wrinkled in a frown as she tried to sort out her confusion. It was no good: what she sensed would not settle into anything definite.

'If you don't know what it is, I'm not sure anyone would,' Col said loyally.

She shook her head. 'I hardly know anything, Col. There's so much to learn about being a universal. But Anneena's right about one thing: it's in that plantation, deep inside. I was thinking that maybe I could persuade Anneena to set out watch as far from it as possible. That way we probably won't see anything and, knowing her, she'll soon get bored. The only problem's Simon.'

'Simon? Why's he a problem?' asked Col, vaulting over a stile. Connie followed more slowly, jumping down on the other side.

'Well, if he can sense it too, he'll probably lead Anneena right to it.'

Col thought for a moment. 'Leave Simon to me. I'll see if I can't do something.'

'Thanks,' Connie said gratefully. 'That'd be a great help. If I say anything, he'll just do the opposite to annoy me.'

A strange warmth uncurled in the pit of Col's stomach. It felt good to have Connie's gratitude, to have her smiling at him as if he was the most wonderful friend she had. He only wished he deserved her admiration.

'Don't worry, Connie. You can count on me,' he said, swearing to himself that he'd prove it.

Connie's usual place for meeting Argand was up on the Devil's Tooth, an isolated outcrop of granite sticking out of the moor and the first tor reached after leaving the Mastersons' land. She could still see the roofs of the farm buildings below her as she made her way up the valley, though the farmhouse itself was swallowed up in the long shadows cast by the setting sun. Down in the darkness, she knew that the stocky black figure of Gard was watching her go, following her progress through her footfalls as she climbed up out of the mild valley onto the dry expanse of the moor. She waved to him.

'I'll be fine from here,' she told him, sending her thoughts diving down into the earth and along the granite rock bed under their feet. 'I can see the Devil's Tooth ahead of me now. You don't need to wait for me. Argand will be along any moment.'

'Be careful,' cautioned Gard. 'Call if you have need.'

'I will.'

Reaching the brow of the first rise, she paused to take a breath. A cattle-grid marked the beginning of the moor. A narrow ribbon of grey tarmac wound over the next hill, curling around the base of the Devil's Tooth. The tor jutted out of the top of a hillock like a fang gnawing at the sky. It was an eerie but beautiful sight, colours softened this evening by the wash of pinks and blues on the horizon. Clouds were fringed with intense shafts of flame as the sun set, dazzling Connie for a moment as she looked into the heart of the inferno. She stood back to let a Land Rover pass, its wheels juddering over the grid. The sheepdog in the back barked excitedly at her, scratching at the rear window in greeting. She laughed and waved but the car was soon out of view, heading back down into the valley for the evening. Overhead, three suspiciously dragon-shaped silhouettes flew high, heading out to sea. Dr Brock and the twins were airborne at last.

Balancing her way across the grid, Connie left the road to take a more direct route up to the tor. It wasn't far: she usually managed the climb in ten minutes or so, though she was slowed down tonight by the lingering heat of the day. Her brow was soon beaded with sweat and she wished she had thought to bring a bottle of water. Trying to distract herself from her thirst, she opened her mind to her surroundings. Having just come from a long session with Gard, she was alert to the nature of the earth she was treading on, probing down into the layers, passing through the thin covering of soil and grass to the bones of the moor below. A hot wind ruffled the parched grass at her feet. The normally emerald green moor was bleached in the sun, balding where the dry grass had been worn away by the passage of hoofs and feet. She could feel the vegetation crying out for relief, for the gift of a shower of refreshing rain, but the skies remained empty. She would have been grateful for a spot or two of rain herself just at that moment, she thought, running her tongue over her lips.

It was then that she felt it. There was a creature near her. *The* creature. Its presence flickered into her mind then darted out of perception, eluding her attempts to pin it down. Connie looked around, but could see nothing. The wind continued to rustle the grass. The brown bracken swayed slightly. Had that been the breeze or was something lurking in the cover of the waist-high stems?

Connie hesitated. Should she call Gard? To say what? That she was being stalked, for that was what it was doing, wasn't it? But surely she need not be afraid? If it thought it could trap a universal like this then it had another think coming: she had an appointment with a dragon; no beast would dare come near her once Argand arrived.

Picking up her pace, Connie clambered up the last few metres to the base of the Devil's Tooth. She quickly examined the stones, seeking out hand and footholds to take her to the top. If she got up there, no one could reach her without giving plenty of warning of their approach. Perhaps this was her chance to see the creature and find out what it was? Suffering a few scrapes along the way, she hauled herself up. Once on the crest, she was rewarded by a cooler gust of wind fanning her face.

From up here, she had the sensation she was on a grey ship looking down on the twilit sea. She did not like heights, and felt as if she was swaying on real waves, her head beginning to spin. She sat down to anchor herself against the stone. The granite still throbbed with the heat of the day, its cracks and crevices groaning as they contracted after hours of baking in the sun. Feeling more secure now she was seated, Connie gazed around for any sign of the creature. Nothing. Had she imagined it? After all, she had spent much of the day thinking about it: she had probably let her imagination run away with her.

Just then a flicker of flame between her and the road below caught her eye. Straining to make out what was happening in the gloom, she saw fire consuming a patch of bracken. Like a swarm of locusts, the sparks spread with voracious rapidity, cutting off her retreat back to the farm. A dark shadow slunk away from the blaze, slipping swiftly out of sight.

Connie grew suddenly conscious of her own exposure up on the Devil's Tooth. A moorland fire was an unpredictable thing; there was no doubt she was in danger if she stayed where she was for long. Fortunately the wind was blowing from behind her, driving the flames away from the tor. She had time.

'Argand!' Connie called, cupping her hands around her mouth. 'Help!' Surely the golden dragon was nearby? The sun had almost set: she should be here at any moment.

There was a shower of sparks to her left some distance from the original blaze. At first Connie thought that it was Argand sailing out of the sky to her aid, but then she realized a new fire had started. The grass surrendered to the flames without a struggle, expiring in a crackle of orange. Once again, Connie thought she glimpsed the prowling form of a creature, long tail whipping behind it as it leapt out of the way. Was it trying to flee the fire? Or was it starting the blaze? The acrid scent of smoke now came to her on the wind. Spinning round she saw that behind her a patch of flame had sprung into life, this one creeping towards her, driven by the wind. Desperate now, Connie looked out into the only expanse of darkness on her right and, sure enough, the rash of fire was ignited there too. The creature was trying to trap her in a ring of flame.

'Argand!' called out Connie. Trust her to be late when she was most needed! 'Gard!'

'Yes, Universal?' The presence of the rock dwarf was with her in an instant.

'I'm trapped. Fire on the moors! Get help!'

'We're coming. Stay where you are: I can sense another creature near you.' But Gard was over a mile away. He could do little on his own and would need time to find help from the other mythical creatures. All the dragons and pegasi were off flying. Who could reach her in time?

The fire was gaining a grip on the earth, a jewel-bright tide crawling over the surface like lava. Billows of choking smoke dotted with orange sparks whirled up into the air. Then came a subtle change in the wind, a shimmer on the horizon and Connie sensed the approach of the fire imps. From all directions their wispy bodies plummeted out of the sky like shadows of seabirds diving on a shoal of fiery herring. Once in contact with the heat, the imps ignited, their bodies bursting into joyous flame. Connie saw them writhing with delight, long hair flaring up to the heavens. They shook their pointed fingers defiantly at the sky, daring it to douse their celebration, but the sky was empty, having nothing to shed to quell this festival of fire. The hill on which the Devil's Tooth stood was now crowned with thorns of flame.

'Hurry up! Please!' Connie called out to Gard, her fear mounting. She could feel the heat on her cheeks and her eyes watered as the smoke stung them. A new presence, a dark tide, seemed to be rising in her mind. She began to feel dizzy and sick, fighting unconsciousness. Resting her head on her knees, she gasped and coughed.

A touch on the back of her neck made her sit up abruptly. Opening her eyes, she found herself looking into the fiery irises of the golden dragon. Argand crooned anxiously, her forked tongue flickering over her companion's cheek.

'Get me out of here,' croaked Connie. She threw her arms around the dragon's neck.

'But never carry before,' said Argand doubtfully. 'What if drop you?'

'No choice. Try. Please.' Connie could feel her lungs bursting for clean, fume-free air.

With a leap into space, the dragonet took off from the rock—and immediately plunged down into the flames, unable to support the weight of her companion.

'Hauberk!' the dragon screamed to Connie.

Just in time, Connie wrapped herself in her companion's unique protection against fire, donning it like a suit of golden mail against the shafts of flame. They thumped to the ground but Connie managed to cling on, gripping the fringe of scales that ran down Argand's neck. Blazing tongues now licked harmlessly round Connie's ankles. The fire imps shrieked in delight, whizzing around the universal and her dragon, releasing showers of sparks.

'Let's get out of here,' said Connie. 'Hop if you have to.'

With an ungainly shuffle, Argand began to jump forward, using her wings to help her. The wings acted like bellows, sending gusts of fire heavenwards with each downdraught. Connie was thankful that she had learned last year to use the hauberk; without it, she would have been a blackened crisp by now. With a final bound, Argand clattered down, her wings sagging like a collapsing golden marquee. She landed on the tarmac road, a firebreak stopping the flames at its very edge. Connie looked back up the hill and saw that the conflagration had reached the base of the Devil's Tooth. She had escaped just in time.

'What is that, Companion?' Argand asked curiously, pointing with one claw to the fiercest part of the blaze. Connie turned to look and saw with horror that there was a small figure, but not a fire imp, dancing hand in hand with those creatures.

'Oh no, it's Liam! You've got to save him!' She slid off Argand's back and pushed the dragon back towards the fire. 'He doesn't know about the imps yet.' He did not know how they could turn on you in an instant like a blaze fanned by a sudden change of wind, withdrawing their protection, the most fickle companion species.

'But how save him?' asked Argand, puzzled.

'He's only small. You might not be able to fly with me but I'm sure you'd be able to carry him for a short flight back. Please!' Connie's gaze was fixed desperately at the cavorting boy, willing the imps to keep their good humour a few more moments.

'I try,' agreed Argand.

The dragon took off and climbed into the sky to gain height for her rescue attempt. Every second that passed was agony for Connie, sure as she was that the imps would suddenly turn on their young companion. Judging her opportunity, the dragon swooped down, her claws held out in front, and scooped the unsuspecting Liam out of the fire. The imps screamed in fury, hissing and spitting at the dragon. Liam yelped: one of the sparks had scorched his bare legs.

Argand wheeled over Connie, spiralling down to earth, and dropped Liam at her feet. She landed a few metres away and began to preen her wings, the arch of her neck, the sly pleasure of the smile on her long narrow snout, radiating pride at her achievement. Liam stared in astonishment at the dragon and then looked up at Connie.

'Why did it do that?' he asked in a voice on the verge of tears. 'I was having fun!' He seemed more surprised by the abrupt end to his party than the fact that he had just been grabbed by a dragon.

'It wouldn't've lasted,' said Connie, putting her arm around him. 'How's your leg? Can you walk?'

Liam nodded.

'Good. We've got to get out of here. Let's go.'

The smoke was billowing across the road. The fire imps were shooting sparks in their direction. The creatures would punish them if only they could reach them.

'But can't I go back?' Liam protested.

'No,' said Connie firmly, steering the boy further from the blaze. 'Thanks, Argand. You were brilliant.' The dragon bobbed her head, accepting the praise as her due. 'I'll see you soon. You'd better get home too.'

Towing Liam down the hill, Connie had not gone far before she ran into a group of Society members, led by Gard, hurrying up from the farm. Bounding along behind them was Rat, perched on the back of Icefen, the frost wolf. Rat broke into a relieved grin when he saw Connie.

'So, you don't need us then?' he said, his eyes shifting curiously to the boy at her side.

'No, thanks to Argand. I'd've been toast by now if she hadn't pitched up just in time.' Connie felt numb. Though quite capable of functioning, even able to speak lightly of what had happened, she could not take in the fate she had so narrowly escaped.

Gard, usually so calm, was visibly shaken by the near miss. 'Are you unscathed, Universal?' he asked in a cracked voice.

'I'm fine.'

'I tried to find a winged beast, but there were none on the farm.' The polished facets of his coal-black face gleamed as if catching light from the glow of the flames behind Connie. 'All we could do was call the fire brigade and hope it was not too late.'

'Let's not talk about this now,' said Connie, with a shiver. 'Liam's injured. Let's get back.'

'Liam?' asked Rat.

Connie nodded to the boy who was holding tightly on to her hand and gazing fearfully at the strange collection of beasts and beings around him.

'Here, Liam, I'll give you a ride back to the farm,' said Rat cheerfully, holding out a hand to the boy.

Liam took one look at the slobbering jaws of the wolf and gave a whimper.

'It's fine. You can trust Rat,' Connie coaxed. She pushed him forward. Mr Masterson stepped out of the crowd and helped lift Liam up in front of Rat. 'I'll see you in a few minutes—I promise.'

With a whisk of his brush-like tail, Icefen bounded down the road. He took the shortest path back to the house, eager to put distance between himself and the punishing heat of the fire.

Gard turned to Connie. 'So, Universal? What happened?'

Mr Masterson gave Connie and Liam a lift back into Hescombe. They had to pull over several times to let the fire engines past—the second major incident for the fire service in as many days. Connie sat on the back seat with her arm around

62

the sleepy boy. She was feeling tired, having just had to relive the events up on the moor for Gard and other members of the Society. Her numbness was fading and her body began to tremble. She had almost died and had only herself to blame for she had dropped her guard, arrogantly assuming she could cope with anything, and had walked straight into danger. But what was it that wished her dead?

'Liam?' Connie said gently. 'What were you doing up on the moor?'

'Followed you,' yawned Liam, snuggling down against her. 'Followed Col out to that farm, then followed you.'

Connie was shocked. Liam was not a member of the Society yet but this meant he had seen many of their secrets.

'What did you see?'

'Oh, loads of brilliant creatures. I liked the dragons best—after the fire imps, of course.' He stretched like a cat settling itself to sleep on a welcoming lap.

'Did you see anything on the moor—when you followed me, I mean?'

'Nope.'

'Promise you won't tell anyone about what you saw today?'

'Course not. It's our secret, isn't it?'

'Yes, that's right. Our secret.'

Silence fell in the back of the car, broken only by the purr of the engine. She bent over Liam and could tell from his even breathing that he had fallen asleep. What were they going to do about him?

4

Bite, Burn, or Venom?

The next evening, Connie spent a long time sitting on her great-uncle's doorstep contemplating the plantation, trying to pick the safest spot away from the beast for Anneena's wildlife watch. Its presence was very faint tonight: if it was in the trees at all it was far away on the side fringing the open moor and nowhere near the cottages. If they camped near the wind farm they should have an uneventful night. But how was she to persuade Anneena and, more importantly Simon, to adopt this plan?

Anneena and Jane cycled up at eight o'clock. Anneena's front basket was weighed down with blood-stained white plastic bags. She brandished them triumphantly at Connie.

'Look, I got this from our restaurant kitchen! My uncle said the meat might lure a few foxes our way. It might attract something bigger, but I didn't tell him that.'

Jane was checking her camera, changing the lens for poor light conditions. 'Ready, Connie?' she asked with a commiserating smile.

Simon came out of the house with a rucksack on his back and a torch strapped to his belt. His eyes were shining with excitement.

'Uncle Hugh's packed some supplies for us—a flask and some chocolate,' he said. 'I'm so looking forward to this!'

'Where's Rat?' asked Anneena. 'Shall I go and get him?'

'No,' said Connie quickly. 'He's tied up tonight. He's sorry he can't make it.' Rat was on patrol with Icefen. The wolf and rider were currently hidden in the northern part of the plantation, watching the edge of the wood that was nearest to the sheep, thinking that this was the creature's most likely evening hunting ground. Col was doing an aerial sweep of the area on Skylark before coming along to join them later.

Anneena clucked her tongue in disappointment. 'I thought he was eager to help out. So no Rat and no Col.'

'Col's coming, just held up,' Connie added swiftly.

'Oh? He didn't tell me. He never said he had something else to do tonight.'

This gave Connie an idea. Here was her excuse. 'He has. But he'll've finished by eleven and said he'd meet us up by the wind farm. I said we'd start our watch there.'

'Is that a good idea?' said Jane. 'I mean, a wild creature will probably be spooked by those masts. We're not likely to see anything there.'

Shut up, Jane, thought Connie. Did her friend always have to be so clever? 'Oh, I don't know. Let's give it a few hours. Anyway, we've got Anneena's bait, haven't we? It might come out for that.'

Simon began to grumble his disagreement.

'Fine,' said Connie sharply. 'If you want to leave Col wandering around looking for us all night, then go ahead, choose another spot. I'm going to stay where I said we'd be.'

Faced with this ultimatum, the others had to agree. With no further arguments, they set out, past the humming transmission station, across the field under the wind turbines, arriving at the southerly edge of the plantation. It was already night under the closely grouped boughs of the pine trees.

'Where shall we set up camp?' asked Anneena.

Before Connie could speak, Simon jumped in. 'I think we should skewer the meat on sticks along the edge here, not far from these bushes. The creature'll want to feel he's got cover nearby if he's to come out.' He looked up into the sky, feeling for the wind. 'And the breeze is coming in off the sea. We should place ourselves downwind. What about by that fallen trunk there?' He pointed to one of the many trees that Connie had felled earlier in the year when she and Kullervo raised a whirlwind.

It was a good plan, thought Connie. Too good, for it had a chance of working. But, unfortunately, Anneena had also noticed that Simon knew what he was talking about.

'Great. Let's do that. Would you put out the bait for us, Simon?'

With a grin, glad to have his plan commended under the nose of his supposedly more experienced sister, Simon took the bag and proceeded to peg out the meat. The three girls took the rest of their stuff over to the trunk.

'I didn't know Simon was so bright,' Anneena said to Connie, 'you know, switched on to animals like you are.'

Connie did not share Anneena's obvious approval. In her eyes, her brother was being a complete pain, making her life even more difficult, but she bit her tongue, knowing that she would only make it worse by saying anything for the moment.

Simon jogged back to where they were hiding, wiping his bloodstained hands on his jeans.

'There, that's done. Not the best spot, but give it time, we might draw him out,' he said excitedly.

The four sat in silence, watching the night grow darker and darker. Wordlessly, Connie handed round mugs of coffee when an hour had passed. So far so good: no sign of anything. A rustle of wrappers as each broke into their chocolate and then silence again. Connie sat with her senses fully tuned to the presence of mythical creatures. Col and Skylark were patrolling the moor between here and the Devil's Tooth, just in case the creature decided to roam that way again. Gard was not far away, his presence felt through the soles of her feet. Sentinel waited alert just inside the entrance to the old tin mines over the hill. Icefen and Rat had become distracted: Connie could sense they had left their post and were now running through the flocks of sheep, Icefen unable to resist his instinct to give them a fright. And the creature? She was almost sure that the creature was waiting in its lair in the heart of the plantation. Connie allowed herself a small smile. Soon Col would be here to help.

Another hour crept past and the coffee was all drunk. Simon began to get restless.

'It's not working,' he said abruptly. 'He's never going to come so near to houses. Let's go in a bit further and see if we can lure him out.'

'No!' said Connie quickly. 'What about Col?'

'Oh, stuff Col,' said Simon. 'Why waste our evening's watch if he can't be on time? You stay here for him if you want. I'm going in.'

'You're right,' said Anneena, the boredom of watching nothing having got to her too. 'I'll come, Simon. Jane and Connie can wait for Col.'

'I think we should all wait here,' repeated Connie, but she knew she was losing the argument: Anneena and Simon were already on their feet. Jane looked torn, not wanting to be left behind if there was a chance of really seeing something. She fiddled with her camera strap.

'Look, if we don't go far, Connie can wait on her own for Col and then give us a shout when he gets here,' she suggested.

'Yeah. Give us a shout, Connie,' said Simon, hurrying off to pick up one of the meat lures to carry with him.

'But it's not fair!' protested Connie to her friends. 'You said you'd listen to me. It's not safe.'

'Don't be silly,' said Anneena in exasperation. 'The creature won't be interested in us if there's a ready supply of meat waiting for it.' She set off on the heels of Simon who, to Connie's horror, was already striding purposefully into the plantation as if he at least knew exactly which way to go. She'd lose him if she waited any longer.

And somewhere in the thicket of trees, the creature was on the move.

'You're not leaving me behind!' she called, stumbling along after the three of them. Simon laughed, already lost in the shadows ahead.

'I thought you'd change your mind if you saw there was any chance of you missing out on the fun!'

'Fun!' shouted back Connie with disgust. 'This isn't a joke, Simon!' She caught up with Anneena and Jane.

'Sssh!' hissed Anneena. 'You'll scare it off with all that racket.'

'Good,' Connie replied bitterly. But in her bones she knew that the creature was not frightened away: it was slinking closer and closer. 'We've got to get out of here. Where's Simon?'

But Simon had gone. The tall slim trunks of the pines stretched away on all sides like grey pillars in a dark hall. The darkness was almost tangible under the trees; Connie felt she was breathing it in with every intake so that it filled her lungs, drowning her.

Anneena was no longer so confident now they had lost the youngest member of their team. 'Simon!' she called out. 'Simon!' Her voice was swallowed up in one gulp by the night.

A tangle of bushes on their left rustled but there was no breeze under the trees. Connie felt an ominous presence drawing closer. What was it? Cat but not just cat.

'I don't like this,' said Jane in a small voice. 'It's creepy.'

Connie closed her eyes. If Simon had a gift, surely she should be able to sense where he was just as she could with other companions? As soon as she turned inwards, she heard Gard's voice in her head.

'It's near you, Universal. Get out of there!'

'Gard, quiet! I've got to find Simon.' A pause. Both of them sensed him, Gard through his footprints, Connie through his gift.

'Twenty paces ahead,' Gard confirmed. 'But the creature's moving swiftly: you've not got time.'

'But it's heading for him, isn't it? Not for me.' Connie began to run towards her brother. 'Simon!' she shrieked into the darkness. The stifling blanket of night seemed to muffle her call. Jane and Anneena were searching for Simon behind her. Not knowing that Connie knew exactly where he was, they had turned the other way. At least they were heading away from danger. 'Simon!'

She almost ran into her brother. He was standing stock-still with the pathetic meat lure held out in front of him.

'He's coming, isn't he?' he said triumphantly. 'You know it too, don't you?'

'Yes, I know,' she said, grabbing his arm. 'And we've got to get out of here.'

But it was too late.

Out of the trees bounded a huge lion-like creature, the size of shire horse, with a mangy black mane. Its muzzle was open in a roar, displaying a row of yellow-white teeth. Connie glimpsed the malevolent gleam of amber eyes and caught a whiff of its hot breath.

A chimera.

'Run!' she shrieked, dragging at Simon's arm, but he was still holding out the pitiful bait, no more than a cocktail snack for this giant. The creature swept it aside disdainfully, catapulting the stick into the air, and knocking Simon to the ground. It hesitated for a second, standing between the two of them, Connie on its right, Simon on its left. It seemed momentarily in doubt as to whom it should strike first, swinging its head to and fro, its whiskers twitching, its long black tail curling over its back like a scorpion's sting. Connie stumbled backwards, still screaming at Simon to move, but her brother was in a daze. He was even staring at the creature as if it was a vision of beauty rather than terror. She realized that he was held in the spell of seeing his companion creature for the first time.

'Simon, move! It's not trying to encounter you: it wants to kill us!'

Her shout seemed to decide the creature. It took a pace towards her, its jaws gaping in a hideous grin of anticipation. She turned and fled, but almost immediately tripped over a tree root in the dark and fell spectacularly onto her face, stunned as her head made sharp contact with the ground. The creature gave a yelp of pleasure. There was no need to hurry: this little prey could not escape the chimera's teeth, the nimble cloven goat's hooves of its hind legs, nor its serpent tail. Pulling herself up onto her knees, Connie could sense dimly that her friends in the Society were mobilized to come to her aid: Icefen was even now leaping back into the plantation; Sentinel was charging up from the mines; dragons had been sent on a sortie, but none were close enough to step between her and those jaws which must be mere inches from the back of her neck.

'Yah!' There was a yell behind her. Connie spun round to see Simon had jumped between her and the creature, brandishing a branch he had grabbed from the ground. 'Get back! Leave her alone!' he shouted at the beast. He whacked it over the nose, shattering his defence into scores of splinters. His intervention gave Connie the seconds she needed to get to her feet. She turned to face the creature and saw immediately that Simon's blow had riled it into madness. But it was not leaping on his throat: it was gathering itself for another kind of attack.

'Get behind me!' Connie cried, tugging at Simon. He resisted. 'Don't be an idiot! Get behind me.' As they scrambled away, she succeeded in pushing her brother so that she stood between him and the chimera.

Even as she did this she was diving deep into her mind, swiftly conjuring up the universal's shield. She raised it in front of her, the powerful mental tool taking shape in the air as a frail circle of silver mist. She had no idea if it would work against a physical attack, but it was either that or they would die. The chimera let out a roar of fury, releasing a lash of flame from deep in its throat. The fire licked at the shield, evaporating the mist in a hissing steam, but still Connie held it up. Her fingers could now feel the heat of the fiery breath battering against her protection, blistering the back of her hand.

Its fire resisted, the chimera drew breath, ending the outpouring of flame. It leapt forward and struck with its front paw, claws cutting into Connie's side and sending her spinning into the undergrowth. It jumped after her, pouncing before she had even hit the ground. Grabbing her by the back of her jacket, it bounded into the trees and away from the annoyance of the other human.

Dangling in its mouth, Connie could hear Simon's cries behind her and knew that he was following. She would have shouted at him to run for help, but she was nearly strangled by her own jacket. Her right side was in excruciating pain, bleeding freely from the deep scratches in her flesh. She knew she was going to die. Frozen with terror, she could not have cried out even if she had had the breath.

Then, as rapidly as the creature had carried her off, it dropped her onto the ground and rolled her over with its paw. She was staring up into the chimera's callous eyes, her senses almost overwhelmed by the reek of its breath. A heavy paw was placed in the centre of her chest, pinning her down. A second head darted into view: the hooded cobra that formed the tuft at the end of the chimera's whip-like black tail had come to gaze on its victim. A drop of venom dripped from its fangs and hissed like acid as it hit the ground by her ear. The paw pressed harder: Connie could now sense the presence of the creature trying to force its way into her mind. It wanted to encounter its prey. She let it in, thinking that this was her only hope of escape: perhaps if she bonded with it, she could turn it from its determination to kill?

As soon as the door in her mind opened, she regretted her decision. The attack in the physical world was terrifying enough, but now she was swept up into a vortex of stormy emotions. The three different natures of the chimera—lion, goat, and serpent—were in a constant battle with each other. But this was not like another conjoined creature she had encountered; not like the minotaur's formalized dance of man and bull: this was a chaotic frenzy of teeth, fang, and hoof. The ascendancy shifted second by second, giving the creature no stable identity. Connie cried out with pain as first she was filled with the fire of the lion, her appetite for blood voracious, tantalized by the delectable flesh of the goat that was for ever out of reach. Next she was squeezed into the writhing form of the snake, hungering to sink its fangs into the haunches of its own lion and goatskin, yet knowing that if it did so it would end its own life. Finally, she stretched into the agile form of the mountain goat, bounding in breathless haste from rock to rock, always desiring to flee the enemies that surrounded it front and rear, but unable ever to leave them behind. The creature was damaged, crazily divided against itself. Its only moments of calm came when all parts were joined in the hunt of another, a common focus for their hatred.

Connie heard its thoughts in her head. Each transition coming with a pain so exquisite she felt she was being torn apart.

'How shall we kill the universal?' asked the serpent, its tongue flickering between its teeth. 'Bite, burn, or venom?'

The lion head yawned, fire glowing at the back of its cavernous throat.

'Let's stamp on her then fly!' cried the goat hysterically.

The other two ignored this voice. 'Each will have his turn,' said the lion magisterially.

'Me first!' hissed the snake. 'It's my turn.'

The lion growled.

'You had your chance but you failed to burn her alive!' the serpent argued. 'You'll still have your turn. But it's no sport for me biting after you've had your way.'

'Please!' begged Connie, screaming to get her voice heard in this debate, but the three-natured creature kept slipping away from her, not interested in hearing any last-minute pleas from their quarry.

'Snake, then lion,' conceded the lion.

'Then me! Hooves after!' bleated the goat excitedly.

'Agreed,' said the lion, though with no more concern for the goat's wishes than it would have for the vultures that cleaned up after its kills.

The last thing Connie saw was the snake's head lashing down like a whip-stroke. Its bite felt as if hot needles had been driven into her neck. She grew rigid, her eyes misting over. With vague, dreamy relief, she knew that she was unlikely to be conscious when the next stage of the attack began. All went dark.

Col knew there was something seriously wrong as soon as he arrived at the deserted camp. He could hear screams and cries from in the trees. He plunged in, pushing his way through the branches in the direction of the loudest cries. After running for a few agonizing minutes he could see a torch flashing crazily ahead as someone sprinted at full speed towards the uproar.

'Connie!' he shouted. 'Wait for me!'

But the torch-carrier did not pause. With a sickening jolt, Col realized the screams had stopped. Finding this more unnerving than anything he had heard so far, he put on an extra burst of speed, arriving at Simon's shoulder as they both burst out of the trees into a clearing.

The chimera was standing over Connie, saliva dripping from its jaws as it licked its lips, preparing to bite. She lay stretched out on the bed of pine needles, still, white-faced, and deathlike, the only sign of a wound coming from the blood seeping from her side. Their entrance distracted the creature: it looked up, momentarily dazzled by the torch that Simon had the sense to shine full into its face. Then, on the other side of the clearing, a huge, white, rough-pelted wolf leapt from the trees. A small figure slid from its back as the frost wolf collided with the chimera, knocking it away from Connie. Simon and Col had to dive to one side as the two beasts rolled over in a furious knot of teeth and claws, kicking up twigs and cones in their frenzied struggle, snapping saplings off at the roots. The three boys dashed to Connie to drag her clear of the fight before the creatures rolled back and squashed her. Col tried to lift her from the ground but she hung limp in his arms.

'She's not dead, is she?' Simon sobbed, paying

no heed to the roars and growls as Icefen and the chimera crashed, clawed, and bit each other.

Col did not know what to answer.

'Let's get her out of here,' he said, half dragging her away.

There came the pounding of hooves behind them and Sentinel galloped onto the battlefield. Without a word, he scooped Connie from Col's arms and bounded away from the fighters.

'Follow me!' he called to the boys.

They had a hard job keeping up with the minotaur, even though he was the one carrying the burden. Col helped Simon along, realizing that the boy was close to collapse. After a nightmarish time of stumbling behind the fleet-footed creature, they reached the edge of the trees. The minotaur paused, snuffing the air. Connie dangled in his arms like a broken puppet. Sentinel laid her gently on the floor.

'Other humans approach. I leave the universal in your care. Fetch healers!' He plunged into the trees, heading back to where Icefen was still battling the chimera. He had no sooner disappeared than Jane and Anneena came running up, their torches darting over the leaf litter until they lit on Connie. Anneena let out a piercing scream.

'Shut up and do something!' said Col tersely.

He was dialling for an ambulance on his mobile. Jane bent over Connie feeling for any sign of life.

'She's bleeding from her side. She's quite cold, but I can definitely feel a pulse,' Jane said in a steady voice as she slipped off her sweater to cover her friend.

The competent touch of Jane's hand on her forehead roused Connie from her dark dreams. Her eyes flickered open, but her vision was blurred. Two Cols and two Janes swam in and out of focus.

'Col?' she murmured.

Col quickly knelt at her side. 'Yes?' he said urgently.

'Fetch Windfoal. Poison.' Her eyes closed again and she sank back into unconsciousness.

Col swallowed, feeling as though he had an apple-sized lump in his throat. Connie wanted the healing powers of the unicorn: but that was impossible. Windfoal must be far away at the moment. They would have to make do with non-mythical sources of help for the present.

'We've got to carry her down to the road,' Col said, getting a grip on himself now he had worked out what he must do first. 'Rat, help me with her head. Jane, Anneena: you take her legs.'

The awkward human stretcher bumped its way as quickly as it could down the field, passing under the slowly revolving blades of the wind turbines. Behind them, a loud roar from the plantation signalled that the battle of beasts had reached its climax. Col glanced nervously over at Rat.

'Icefen won,' Rat muttered back, his face taut with tension.

Jane and Anneena had also heard the commotion. 'It's the beast that got her, isn't it?' said Anneena, close to hysterical tears. 'It's all my fault. She told us not to go in!'

Col felt too angry with her to try to comfort her. Yes, it was her fault, he thought savagely.

'No, it's my fault,' sobbed Simon. 'I didn't understand. I thought I could speak to it. I never want to see it again. It's evil—wicked.'

Col hoped that the girls would put these disjointed sentences down to the ramblings of distress but clearly there was a problem for the Society here in the shape of Simon Lionheart.

They reached the road. At Jane's prompting, Simon ran on ahead to rouse his great-uncle. He had not been gone long when the blue flashing lights of an ambulance appeared at the head of the little valley. Jane waved her torch to show the driver where they were waiting and the white van came to a stop, headlights flooding the patch of road where Connie was lying. Uncle Hugh came panting up in his tartan dressing-gown and slippers, at the same moment as the paramedic jumped out of the vehicle. The Ratcliffs emerged from their house, anxious to find out what all the fuss was about.

'What happened?' gasped Hugh, seizing his niece's cold hand.

'Stand back, sir,' said the paramedic as he checked the pulse on her neck. She winced and moaned with pain, her eyes still shut. She raised her hand, trying to push the medic away from her throat, but he caught her wrist gently and laid her arm back by her side. Spotting the blood seeping through her clothing, he straightened up and turned to Hugh. 'We're taking her to hospital. I want someone who can tell me what has happened to ride along with me.'

'I'll come,' said Col quickly.

The paramedic's colleague appeared with a stretcher from the back of the ambulance. Together they lifted Connie on and wheeled her into the clinical white light of the treatment area. Col got in after them. The last thing he saw as the doors closed was Hugh comforting a sobbing Simon.

'I'm coming in the car!' Hugh called after him. 'Tell Connie I'm coming!'

Tell Connie? Just at the moment, Col could tell

her nothing: she was beyond his reach. He tried to stifle the terrifying thought that she might never return. He sat silently to one side watching the paramedic make his friend comfortable. The medic took out a pair of scissors and began to cut away the torn clothing so he could tend the wound in her side. Col flinched as he saw the four scratches scored into her skin.

The paramedic whistled through his teeth. 'What on earth did this?'

'Something big—a wild cat,' Col answered hoarsely.

'It must be a hell of a monster to do this much damage,' the man said. He bent closer. 'She's lucky: it doesn't look as if it went very deep. The jacket saved her, I'd say.'

Lucky? thought Col desolately. He wouldn't have called her that.

5
Unicorn

It was now three days since Connie had been admitted to Chartmouth hospital and the doctors were worried. At first, her injuries had not seemed life-threatening. Whatever it was that had attacked her in the wood—the theories in the local press ran from rabid fox, to stray dog, to escaped wild cat—had left deep scoring in her side but this had been successfully treated with stitches and was healing well. The burns on the back of her hands had been dressed, though quite where she got them remained a mystery. The problem was that she was still delirious, suffering from weakness of the limbs and neck, a strange lack of taste in her mouth and she was having trouble breathing. She surfaced only from her drowsy state for brief spells. The doctors decided she must have picked up a blood infection from the scratches but so far they had failed to isolate it in the samples they had taken. One keen-eyed junior from Nepal suggested that she showed the same characteristics as someone suffering with a venomous cobra bite, but when the consultant heard this theory he told the trainee bluntly to stop dreaming and keep his mind on his job. Cobras in England? Utter rubbish!

Conventional medicine having failed, the Society decided it was time to take matters into their own hands and send for Windfoal as Connie had requested. The unicorn was now waiting outside the hospital which was why Mack, Col, and Rat were walking down the long shining corridor armed only with a bunch of flowers and innocent smiles. Ignoring the nursing staff, Mack strode into the youth ward and scooped Connie off her bed before her room mates could protest. Connie groaned as he swung her up, just managing to hang on to consciousness.

'Just a quick trip to the car park and we'll bring her back unharmed, I promise,' Col assured the girls as he backed out of the ward on his father's heels.

'It's her horse, you see,' added Rat for good

measure. 'She'll never get better until she's satisfied it's OK, so we've brought it here.'

'Right, quick as we can!' said Mack once they were out in the main corridor. They made a dash for the lifts. 'Come on, come on!' He thumped the controls as the lift seemed to take ages to arrive. Mercifully it was empty when the doors opened. They entered, feeling relieved to have got this far without being stopped.

'Did you have to tell them about the horse?' Col asked Rat with exasperation, thinking that his friend was getting carried away.

'Course. We're parked right outside. I'll bet you any money they'll all be looking out of the window to see what we're doing.'

It was a good point. As a cover story it had its merits. Perhaps Rat wasn't as daft as he looked, conceded Col.

They reached the ground floor. Connie cradled in his arms, Mack marched determinedly through the crowds, out through the sliding doors and into the car park. Stationed in the '20 minutes only' slot by the entrance was the horsebox with Kira Okona, Windfoal's companion, leaning against it, checking her watch anxiously. Seeing them emerge from the hospital entrance, she opened the rear doors so Mack could carry Connie directly inside. Laying the universal gently on the hay, Mack stepped outside to leave her in Windfoal's care.

Five minutes later, Connie leant against the unicorn, resting after Windfoal had purged her blood of the illusive venom of the chimera. Her head was now clear: the unicorn's healing touch having burnt away the poison that had been gnawing at the bond between her and this world.

'You came just in time,' Connie whispered. 'I couldn't've held out much longer.'

Windfoal whickered her agreement, nuzzling her young friend affectionately. Her horn gleamed with a soft golden light in the darkness of the van, casting everything in a warm glow. Even Windfoal's normally silver-white coat seemed tinged with honeyed gold.

'I'd better go. I think everyone's in trouble because of me,' Connie said regretfully.

Windfoal pushed her towards the door with her velvety nose. 'Come and see me soon, Universal,' she said through their bond, 'so we will heal those scars as well.'

Connie nodded and slid the door open, reluctant to leave the peaceful haven of the horsebox. Col, Mack, and Rat were standing in a worried huddle, watching a posse of people headed in their direction. Kira started the engine. Three nurses, backed up by two uniformed security guards and a doctor, approached at a run. Col cheered up when he saw that Connie was on her feet.

'Let me handle this, OK?' she said to them. 'You'd better go.'

She walked over to meet her reception committee, reassured to hear the doors of the van slam behind her. The priority was to get Windfoal away before too many questions were asked.

'Connie!' exclaimed the staff nurse from her ward, 'what on earth are you doing? You're not well enough to be outside in naught but a night-dress! And no slippers!'

The van engine rumbled into life. The grit of the car park surface crackled as Kira pulled out of the parking slot.

'I'm fine. All I needed was a breath of fresh air,' said Connie.

The doctor, a young woman with short bleached hair and owlish glasses, came forward and took Connie's arm. 'I must say you do look much better,' she said, leading her back towards the hospital. 'I thought you were getting nowhere fast this morning when I checked you over, but now . . . Well, let's take you inside and see what's what.'

After a thorough examination, the doctor pronounced Connie miraculously improved.

'I don't know what you're on, Connie, but I wouldn't mind some of it,' the doctor said with a smile as she noted the healthy, almost golden, glow to her skin. 'Just the stitches to take out tomorrow and then you can go home.'

Connie was relieved to hear that she was to be discharged so quickly. Now she was returned to full consciousness, her memories of the terrifying night in the plantation had come flooding back. Uppermost in her mind was Simon: how was he? What was the Society to do about the disastrous revelation of his gift? And what about the chimera? Had Icefen mortally injured it or was it still out there, waiting for her?

That afternoon, she had two sets of visitors. First, a stricken Anneena and more composed Jane arrived bearing a bunch of roses. Anneena gave a muffled squeal of delight when she saw Connie sitting up, leafing through a magazine the girl in the bed opposite had lent her.

'Connie! I'm so, so sorry! But you're better! You look better than better: you look great.'

'Yes,' said Jane with a thoughtful expression, head cocked on one side, 'you do look well. What've they done to you?'

Connie smiled.

Anneena leant forward and took her friend's bandaged hand in hers. 'I'm really, really sorry, you know that, don't you?' Putting her other hand on her heart, she added, 'And I promise I won't go looking for that beast again.'

'I know,' said Connie, returning her friend's pressure on her fingers with difficulty through the bandages. 'Let's just hope it's the last we've seen of the . . . of it.'

Anneena sat back, satisfied and appearing more her old self. 'Oh, it's still out there unfortunately. There was no sign of it when they combed the plantation: lots of blood,' Anneena looked down as all of them were thinking that some of the blood must have been Connie's, 'but nothing. We don't know what drove it off and the ground was too dry for it to leave any tracks, but my dad says it'll have gone onto the moor to hide so it can lick its wounds.' She paused, her eyes sliding up to Connie's face. 'He's banned me from going up there again. I'm to stay in Hescombe until the creature's been caught and destroyed.'

'Me too,' said Jane. 'My parents are worried it may've got a taste for humans. What do you think your aunt will tell you?'

Connie shrugged. Her case was a bit more complicated. She had not yet considered what the fallout would be for her freedom to roam.

At that moment, her aunt and Dr Brock appeared in the doorway: Evelyn willowy and energetic, any hint of her previous queasiness now gone; Dr Brock stood at her shoulder, his lined face radiating pleasure at seeing Connie sitting up.

'Second shift,' said Jane, getting up to make room. 'See you when you get home, Connie.'

'Thanks for coming,' she called after them.

Evelyn waited until the girls had gone and then folded Connie into a tight hug. Connie again had the unnerving sensation of perceiving the little life inside her aunt.

'Connie, you look so much better. Windfoal's cured you then?' Evelyn said happily, not bothering to keep her voice down. The girl opposite, who had no visitors this afternoon, looked up curiously.

Dr Brock raised one brow in warning and bent over to kiss Connie on the cheek. 'Best not say too much about that just yet. Our companions, both big and little, send greetings, Connie.'

'Thank father and daughter for me,' said Connie smiling back at him, not without a pang of envy that he would be seeing Argand so soon and she was stuck inside for another day at least. 'So where is it now?' She could tell from their faces they both knew she was talking about the chimera. 'And how's Simon?'

Dr Brock sighed, taking a seat in the plastic chair Jane had vacated. 'Well, the two questions are linked, as you well know, because with you in here, only your brother can answer the first. The rock dwarves say they can't sense it—something to do with stone sprite interference. But Simon's not been seen by anyone except Hugh since the attack. He's been hiding away in his room.'

'You've got to talk to him, Connie,' said Evelyn. She angrily stuffed the roses into an empty vase on Connie's bedside table, snapping one from its stem. 'I'm afraid he's been damaged by what happened. He doesn't want to accept what he is—won't talk to any of us.'

'Of course I'll talk to him—as soon as I can.'

Dr Brock leaned forward and said in a confidential voice, 'The Trustees have convened an emergency assessment for him, and for that little boy Liam you identified. If you are well enough and can persuade Simon to come, it's to be held next week at the Society headquarters. And'—he dropped his voice even lower—'they also want to take counsel with you on the chimera. It's quite unheard of—a chimera in these parts. I have to admit that we're suspicious of the coincidence. Your brother a companion to it—you its quarry.'

Yes, thought Connie, put like that it did seem strange. If someone had known about Simon before she did and had wanted to create a trap for her, what would be better than using her brother to lure her into the mad creature's path? If they knew this much, they would have known that only she had the gift to sense the danger and would not abandon Simon to face it alone. But the creature itself gave no hint that it was doing anything but following its own crazed impulses.

'I see,' she said without committing herself to a comment on what Dr Brock had said, not wanting to speak her fears aloud. 'Of course, I'll try to persuade him. Simon owes me one.'

It was without much grace that Simon agreed to accompany his sister on the trip to London. He said he would go for her sake, but warned that he was doing so under protest. He wanted nothing more to do with his 'gift' as she insisted on calling it, nor did he want to see any more monsters, bull-headed or otherwise. Connie felt desperately sad for him: he was clinging on to the illusion that he could just pretend none of it had happened. He had even grown angry with her when she had forced him to admit to what he had seen and felt on that fateful night.

The visit coincided with Col's Grade Four theory examination, also to be held at the Society headquarters, and Connie was relieved to have his help in getting a reluctant Simon onto the train and for keeping up a light three-way conversation with her brother and Mack all the way to Paddington. She sat leaning against the window, feeling washed out; her right side still ached and was painfully sore when anything touched it. At night, Kullervo's voice still taunted and tempted her to join him at the mark. She had to wake repeatedly to drive him off with Sentinel's help, leaving her exhausted when dawn finally arrived. In a perfect world, she would have preferred to spend the day quietly at home. But it wasn't a perfect world and a meeting with the Trustees was not something she could miss.

'They've got absolutely no chance of winning the premiership,' Col was still arguing good-humouredly with Simon as they got out of the taxi onto the street outside Liam's home south of the Thames. Connie wrinkled her nose, smelling decay and neglect in the doorway of the low-rise block of flats. Col stopped teasing Simon about his team and gazed about him, also dispirited by what he saw. Black bags of rubbish were piled in a heap by the overflowing wheelie bins. Graffiti, pointlessly repeated initials, defaced the drab brick walls. A derelict car up on wooden blocks obstructed the entrance.

'Come on,' said Mack, the only one who seemed

unperturbed by their surroundings. He squeezed his way round the car. 'Let's go on up.'

They climbed two evil-smelling flights of concrete stairs and arrived at a landing. It ran down the front of the apartments like a pavement in the sky. It was less gloomy up here: bright window boxes decorated some of the homes. A little boy cycled past on a multi-coloured tricycle, ringing his bell happily. They stepped out of his path, and then moved aside quickly again as his dad jogged by in hot pursuit of his speeding toddler.

'It's Number Eighteen,' said Mack, checking a piece of paper. 'Last in the row.' He knocked. After a few moments, the door opened and a skinny woman, hair straggling on her shoulders, peered outside.

'What d'you want?' she asked. She took a drag on a thin white cigarette she held shakily in her right hand.

'Suzanne, it's me, Mack Clamworthy. We've come to take Liam out for the afternoon. Do you remember me calling you at the weekend about it?'

Suzanne lifted her tired pale eyes to him and a glimmer of recognition passed over her face. 'You'd better come in then.' She turned into the hallway, resting her hand to steady herself on the shiny wallpaper decorated with overblown roses. 'Liam, baby, your friends are here!'

The little boy erupted out of a door at the far end of the hall, hopping with delight.

'Great!' He sprinted towards them as if intending to leave there and then. But he wasn't ready. As neither Mack nor Suzanne said anything, Connie caught Liam gently by the shoulder.

'Shoes, Liam?' she asked, pointing to his bare feet.

He grinned up at her. 'Oops,' he said and ran back into the room he had come from.

Feet stuffed in tatty trainers, Liam breezed back into the hallway.

'See you later, Mum,' he called, nearly pushing Mack out of the door in his haste to be gone.

'Bye, baby,' she said, taking another drag on her cigarette.

'I'll bring him back around six,' Mack supplied for her when she forgot to ask. 'And you can reach me on my mobile.' He thrust a piece of paper into her hand, which she put absent-mindedly into her pocket.

'Fine. Have fun.'

6

Playing with Fire

Col glanced at his watch for the hundredth time as the taxi crawled slowly down the Strand.

'I'm going to be late!' he muttered. 'The test starts in five minutes.'

'You'll be there on time,' yawned Mack, turning the page of the newspaper he had brought with him. 'Anyway, I thought you said Grade Four would be a walkover for you and Skylark.' He gave Connie a wink. Simon and Liam looked up, their interest caught by a discussion they did not quite understand.

Col swallowed. His palms were sweaty but his throat dry. A flutter of nerves in his stomach made him feel sick. He was angry that his father as usual was failing to provide a sympathetic ear to his problems. Mack had never understood what it was like to be in his shoes.

'I said the practical exam will be a walkover, but the theory paper, that's different.'

'You'll be fine,' said Mack with annoying calm. 'When I was your age, I passed all my tests with top marks. Don't forget: you're a Clamworthy.'

'Shut up, Dad,' said Col.

Connie intervened before father and son could rub each other further up the wrong way. 'Give it another minute, Col, then you can always get out and go the rest of the way on foot if we're still stuck at these lights. We're almost there now.'

Col's hand hovered over the catch but at that moment the lights changed and the taxi grumbled on the final hundred yards, dropping them at the entrance to the alleyway leading to the Society headquarters. Col abandoned his father and the others, calling over his shoulder:

'See you later. I'll meet you in the foyer when I'm done.'

He disappeared into the dark tunnel of the alleyway, leaving them to follow more slowly.

'Connie, what's going to happen to me?' asked Liam, not as if he were afraid but as if he wanted to relish each exciting detail. Connie saw that

Simon, though pretending to be fascinated by the railings of the old houses they passed, was listening intently.

'Nothing bad. They'll do a test on you to make sure that I've got your gift right.'

'A test? What will I have to do? I can't read much yet.'

Connie gave him a reassuring smile. 'You won't need to do anything but follow a few simple orders and then answer some questions. You won't need to read anything.'

'And then?'

'Usually, after the test, you'll be given a mentor to help with the rest of your training—they'll teach you how to talk to your creature safely.'

Simon gave a sceptical snort. Connie knew what he was thinking: it was doubtful any training could teach you to encounter a crazed chimera without losing a limb. She had to admit she agreed with him.

Mack strode purposefully under the arch into the courtyard in front of the palatial headquarters of the Society for the Protection of Mythical Creatures. Its warm, caramel-coloured façade, decorated with ornate carvings depicting creatures from the four companies, glittered with three rows of high windows; the slate roof was topped with a lantern dome that sparkled like a lighthouse. The sun blazed on the cobbled forecourt, making the walls gleam like gold cliffs rising from a sparkling grey-blue sea. None of this splendour gave Mack a moment's pause, but both Liam and Simon stopped in their tracks.

'Are we allowed in?' asked Simon.

'Of course, or we wouldn't have brought you here,' said Connie, leading the way over the cobbles. She remembered very well how daunted she had felt on her first visit.

'What's this?' asked Simon, pointing up at the compass motif in the circular window over the doorway.

'It's the symbol of the universals,' said Connie briefly as she passed under it.

Simon gave her a sideways look. 'That's what you are, aren't you?' When she looked surprised, he added, 'I heard that minotaur call you—that name.'

This was the first time Simon had willingly referred to the events of the previous week. Connie nodded. 'That's right. That's my sign.'

Simon said nothing more, but Connie took heart from the fact that he was at least no longer trying to block out what he had seen and heard. The indisputably substantial presence of the Society headquarters appeared to be changing his mind. She only hoped this more co-operative mood would last.

Mack was waiting for them in the marble foyer, leaning against the porter's window, laughing with him about something.

'I've signed you all in,' he said loudly, his voice booming around the cavernous space. He chucked them each a badge, which Connie promptly dropped. Mack groaned.

'I should put her down for the England cricket team, shouldn't I?' he joked with the porter. 'She'd fit in with the current bunch.' Connie was forcibly reminded of his son: both Clamworthys had the ability to ignore atmospheres that would daunt others. She scooped her tag from the floor and saw that it had a silver compass next to her name.

'What are these for?' she asked. On her previous visits, she had only ever had to sign in.

'For the Chamber of Counsel,' said the porter. 'You're not allowed in there without one of those. Do you like yours? I got my wife to run that off the computer specially. Needless to say, we didn't have any in stock for you.'

Connie smiled shyly. 'Yes. Thank you—and thank your wife too.'

'Off you go then,' said the porter, waving them to the double doors opposite, which were nestled between the two curving flights of stairs leading up to the library above. 'The meeting's already started. You're the last to arrive.'

Mack led the way over to the entrance and pushed the doors open with a boom. Connie, who had never entered this chamber before, was astounded by what she saw. A huge room stretched before them, the same dimensions as the library on the floor above, but unlike that book-filled space, the walls here were lined with mirrors, reflecting themselves infinitely on all sides. It was like stepping inside a crystal ball—she felt momentarily giddy. Liam gasped. Simon moved closer to his sister.

The floor was of polished white marble, veined with blue-grey. In its centre was an inlaid four-pointed star made out of silver. As Connie approached, she recognized it as her sign. Looking straight ahead along the eastern point, she saw Storm-Bird perched on a golden rod suspended from the high ceiling. Its head was tucked under its wing but, as Connie's feet touched the centre of the compass, it awoke, croaking a greeting. A rumble of distant thunder rolled towards her as the giant crow-like bird fluttered to the floor. Seated cross-legged at Storm-Bird's feet was its companion, Eagle-Child, dressed in a tan suede jacket and trousers, his long black hair streaked with white. The front panels of his jacket were decorated with wings made from tiny blue and red stones. He raised his hand, palm outwards, in greeting to the universal. Glancing behind her, she heard the steady clip-clop of hooves on the marble. Windfoal, the unicorn, had stepped forward to take her stand at the western end of the Chamber of Counsel, her white coat making the marble dull by comparison. Her companion, Kira Okona, followed and took a seat on a wooden armchair by the unicorn's side. Kira was dressed in bright African cottons, her braided hair concealed today under a flamboyant blue and white headdress.

From the astounded expression on Simon's face as he stared to his right, Connie guessed he had spotted the ancient dragon, Morjik. His gnarled green hide seemed even rougher than Connie remembered it in contrast to the smooth stone floor. He looked like a volcanic island rising out of a sea of milk. His ruby eyes gleamed hotly, lit by the fire within. A tendril of smoke wound up from his snout, curling to the ceiling where it hung in an umbrella-shaped cloud over his head. His companion, Kinga Potowska, an elderly woman but still a formidable dragon-rider, looked up and smiled at Connie, her determined eyes glinting speculatively as she next turned her gaze on the two boys who trailed in the universal's wake.

Finally, Connie raised her sight to the northern-most point of the chamber to where the newest

Trustee pair was seated. The representatives of the Elementals, Chan Lee, a elderly Chinese man neatly dressed in a collarless black suit, and the rock dwarf, Jade, sat side by side, both still as stone. The rock dwarf, her body swathed in a green cloak, pushed back her hood to gaze on the universal. Connie was struck by her beauty: used as she was to Gard's craggy features, she had not expected this. Jade reminded Connie of an exquisitely carved chess queen she had once seen in a shop selling Far Eastern curios, wide almond eyes, long graceful neck, elegant fingers that lightly grasped a small silver mallet. But the most alluring thing about Jade was the beautiful polished sheen to her skin with its rich blue-green hue flecked with crystal.

'Greetings, Universal,' came Jade's voice, sliding through the veins of marble floor to the soles of Connie's feet. 'We meet at last.'

Connie bowed her head respectfully.

Kinga stood up and came a few paces forward, holding out her hand to the newcomers.

'On behalf of the Trustees for the Society for the Protection of Mythical Creatures, may I welcome you all into our circle,' she said, gesturing round at her colleagues. Connie, feeling exposed standing in the middle of the vast room with only the two boys beside her, looked round for Mack

106

and saw that he had gravitated instinctively to the southern end of the chamber and had seated himself on the far side of Morjik. She wished he hadn't abandoned her so quickly. His belief in her abilities often outstripped her own confidence in herself. She looked down shyly, noticing for the first time how her feet were in the very centre of the compass as if drawn to that spot like a magnet.

'Please, take a seat,' continued Kinga.

To Connie's surprise, Liam immediately headed off towards the rock dwarf and sat himself down at the hem of her robe. Connie saw Kinga look enquiringly over at the Trustee pair for the Elementals. Mr Chan nodded slightly and the rock dwarf gracefully rested her hand on Liam's hair and gave him an affectionate stroke.

'That is settled then,' said Kinga in a pleased voice. 'Liam is confirmed as a fire imp companion.'

Connie's face must have registered her astonishment for Eagle-Child laughed. 'There are more ways than one of carrying out an assessment, Universal, as you should remember from your own experience,' he said. 'When the candidate stands in the centre of all the Trustees, we do not need to resort to the substitutes used by the Society's assessors in our absence.'

107

Connie glanced across at Simon. He was still hovering in the middle of the room beside her, looking angry and confused. Why had it not worked for him then?

'Simon,' Connie asked softly, 'do you know which way you should go?'

Simon shook his head miserably; he bit his lip. Gazing round the circle, Connie noticed that the Trustees too now looked uncertain.

'Stand out of the circle, Connie,' said Kinga after a brief pause. 'Perhaps your presence is confusing us.'

Quickly, Connie moved towards Mack to a point as far away from the Trustees as she could go. The last thing she wanted to do was to mess up Simon's introduction to the Society, knowing how hostile he had been to the whole idea in the first place. Simon now stood alone in the centre. Her heart ached for him. She wished he would listen to the prompting of his gift and make up his mind.

'He is ours,' said Kira finally after a brief consultation with Windfoal.

'Surely not?' challenged Kinga.

'Ours,' growled Morjik.

Tension rippled in the air between the dragon and unicorn like a heat haze. Simon swayed. Connie feared he was going to make a run for it.

'He can not be in two places at once!' interrupted Mr Chan in a clipped, high-pitched voice. 'Honourable colleagues, one of you must be wrong.'

Mack stood up from where he had been lounging against the wall and scratched his head. 'Troublemakers, these Lionhearts,' he said to Connie, evidently amused to see the dispute amongst so august a company.

On another occasion, Connie might have made a tart response about the Clamworthys but she was too concerned for her brother. Then she had an idea.

'Let me stand with him,' she said coming forward. 'Let me see if I can confirm his gift.'

'What do you mean, Connie?' asked Kira.

'It's just a skill I seem to have gained. I can now sense where human companions are by their gift,' Connie said in a quiet voice, aware how strange this would sound to her listeners.

'But that is astounding, Connie,' said Kinga, looking up at Morjik then back at Connie as if the dragon had confirmed her thoughts. 'Why were we not told? How long have you been able to do this?'

'Since the beginning of the year. Since the shared bond.'

'You may, of course, try,' said Kinga. 'But we must talk further about this.'

Connie came to stand at her brother's side. 'I'm just going to put my hands on your shoulders, OK?' she said.

Simon shrugged. She could tell he was relieved to be no longer alone in the centre of that room. 'If you must,' he said in a falsely casual tone.

Connie ignored this. She closed her eyes, dipping into her mind to see the room through the bonds that filled it, rather than the physical presence of those gathered. Immediately, she could see the strong silver links of her own bond stretching out along all four points of the compass to the creatures, dragon, bird, unicorn, and dwarf. Then, less distinctly, she could make out the connections between creature and companion. Curiously, she turned her mind to Liam and saw that he was wrapped in a misty chain that, though it stretched to no creature in the room, was the same colour as the earthen links that connected Mr Chan to Jade. Confident now she knew what she was looking for, she rested her hands on Simon and turned her thoughts to his gift. Immediately, she saw it—or she should have said 'them'. Snaking out from his feet towards the Company of Sea-Creatures and Reptiles was an orange, swirling ribbon, but a second grass-green rope stretched straight towards the unicorn and the Company of Two and Four-legged Beasts and Beings.

'He's both,' she said simply on opening her eyes again. 'Like the chimera, he's both.'

'But that's impossible,' said Kira.

'No, it isn't,' Connie replied. 'I'm all four. What's impossible about my brother being bonded to two companies?'

'But you bond with all creatures, Connie,' said Kira. 'He's only a chimera companion.'

'Is he?' Connie asked, her eyes now turning to Morjik and Windfoal.

'The great snakes,' growled Morjik.

Windfoal whinnied. Kira said: 'The Amalthean goats and the Nemean lions.'

Simon's confusion had not lifted. 'What're they talking about, Connie?' he asked his sister anxiously.

'Simon, I don't think you are a chimera companion,' Connie said, her heart feeling lighter than it had since Simon first sensed the creature, 'at least, not just a chimera companion. You also bond with the creatures that produced the chimera—the Amalthean goats, the Nemean lions, and the great snakes.'

'My friend, you are unique, like your sister here,' said Eagle-Child, staring at Simon as if to read the secret of his strange powers. 'I have never heard of a companion bonding with more than one creature—other than the universal.'

'So what are we to do with him?' asked Kira, looking to Kinga and Morjik.

'What does the universal advise?' asked Kinga.

Connie found the answer came easily to her now the mystery was solved.

'Well, if Simon is happy, I think you should place him in the Company of the Two-Fours for now as two of his companions are in that group. You should mentor him on all three species. I don't think he wants to go any further with the chimera, do you, Simon?'

Simon shook his head dumbly, for once not arguing with something suggested by his sister.

'Then come,' said Kira, beckoning to the boy. 'Sit by Windfoal and me.'

With the first smile Connie had seen on his face for days, Simon nodded to his sister and went to sit at the western point of the chamber. As if the last piece of a puzzle had just been slotted into place, Connie sensed the energy in the room was once more in balance.

Mr Coddrington is just going to love this, she thought, watching Simon pat Windfoal's neck cautiously. She remembered how the assessor had resented her presence outside the normal four companies; now he had someone who was in two: it would mess up his filing system nicely.

'All that leaves,' said Connie aloud, looking round the room, 'is the question of where I should sit?'

Col doodled absent-mindedly on the test paper, reading through the answers he had written so far. All around him in the wood-panelled room, other candidates were scratching away at their responses. He could just see Jessica's curly head several rows away bent over her Grade Five sea-craft paper; Shirley was two rows to his right absorbed in her Grade Four storm-raising test, a lock of pale blonde hair dropping over her face, hiding her eyes. He wondered briefly what Grade Four consisted of for weather giant companions: light wind and rain? Short sharp showers? Minus points for brewing hurricanes? He hoped somebody had told the examiners about her taste for casting nasty lightning bolts and hail stones and would deduct points from her as a result. But as the only weather giant companion in Britain apart from Shirley was her mentor, Mr Coddrington, he supposed it was a done deal that she would get top marks.

His thoughts turned to Connie. She had looked really tired on the train, lacking her normal sparkle. He hoped the trustees weren't giving her a hard time about the chimera as none of it had been her fault. Ever since the attack, he'd been feeling guilty that he had failed to protect her. No one had. Despite its best efforts, the Society had proved unable to keep its universal safe. His pen nib punctured the question paper as he stabbed it in frustration. He couldn't bear it if anything happened to her.

But this train of thought wasn't going to get him through the exam.

With a deliberate effort to calm himself, Col turned back to his answer paper. Only thirty minutes to go but he was making good progress, having covered care and first aid, encounters, and intermediate manoeuvres. He had now reached the final section, which examined flying protocols, the rules of the airways.

Question Twenty: Name the circumstances in which you can use the Thessalonian Roll, and what safety precautions must always be observed?

Col had a sudden vivid recollection of Skylark plunging down towards the treetops of Mallins Wood with the Kullervo-pegasus on his tail, but he knew that this was not the answer the examiners were looking for. He put his pen to the blank sheet of paper before him.

The Thessalonian Roll should only be used after the pegasus and rider have passed their Grade Eight flying exam. It should only be done over water to reduce risk of serious injury if the rider falls off.

He looked down at the answer. What he had written was a load of rubbish. It was the technically correct answer as he had revised it, but it wasn't the truth. Behaviour like that wouldn't protect the universal when under attack. A spark of rebellion ignited in him as he remembered his confrontation in Mallins Wood and he picked up his pen again.

P.S. the roll also comes in useful when avoiding a more agile enemy, such as Kullervo, even if you've not got Grade Eight. In these circumstances, soft landings are unlikely to be available so you have to go ahead and do it anyway.

There, that should wake them up a bit.

'How was yours, Col?' Jessica asked him as the candidates poured out of the examination hall onto the landing near the library.

'OK,' said Col, not committing himself to a more definite answer. He didn't want to tempt fate by saying that he thought it had gone well. His only fear was that the examiner might deduct marks for his postscript about Kullervo. Perhaps he shouldn't have done that, he thought soberly, now the rebellious mood had passed. 'Yours?'

Jessica made a face. 'Much harder than Grade Four. Some of the questions were really tricky.'

'I'm sure you'll've done fine,' he said, glancing up at the clock again. 'I'll see you later.'

'OK,' said Jessica, a little surprised. 'But I was going to the café: don't you have time to come?'

Shirley Masterson arrived at Jessica's shoulder.

'Did someone say "café"?' she said. 'I'm dying of thirst. Shall we go?'

Jessica looked reluctant to be stuck with Shirley on her own.

'I was just asking Col if he had time,' she said, looking pleadingly at him and succeeding in making Col feel sorry for her.

'I'm supposed to be meeting the others.'

'Others?' enquired Shirley, looking around her to see who else was there from Hescombe.

'Dad, Connie, and a couple of new members you don't know.'

'Should've guessed you'd be meeting her,' muttered Shirley.

Col shrugged. 'I've gotta go. I might see you in the café later if Connie's still with the Trustees.' He was rather pleased to see Shirley's expression sour with envy as she heard that the universal was once again receiving VIP treatment. 'See you.' He bounded off down the stairs, taking them two at a time.

When he came into the foyer, he found Mack, Liam, and Simon waiting for him.

'There you are!' said Mack. 'How was the exam?'

'Fine. So, what happened? Where's Connie?' Col asked, looking at Simon. He was surprised to see that, though a bit dazed, Simon had cheered up since this morning.

'Connie's still talking to those Trustee people—and creatures,' Simon said, grappling with the new language of the Society.

'And?' prompted Col.

'I'm a fire imp companion!' said Liam, sparking with excitement.

'Well, we knew that, didn't we?' said Col, ruffling the boy's hair. 'That was stating the blindingly obvious, wasn't it?'

'And I'm a companion to the great snakes—' began Simon.

'Not the chimera?' interrupted Col too quickly.

'Let him finish,' growled Mack. 'You're going to like this.'

'—and the Nemean lions and Amalthean goats,' concluded Simon proudly, though he was still not quite sure what this all meant.

'No!' said Col, staring at Simon.

'Yeah,' said Mack. 'Connie found it out. Just as well, or Simon here would have been the rope in

117

a tug of war between the unicorn and the dragon. Both wanted him.'

'And Connie's still in there?'

'Yep. I said we'd meet her in the café. Horace and his granddaughter are waiting for us. They want to meet Liam, so does Liam's mentor. We'd better get along there before they give up on us.'

As Mack led the way to the south wing of the building to the café on the ground floor, Col followed behind with the two newest members of the Society. He couldn't quite believe what he had just heard: Simon, companion to more than one creature! It had been shock enough when he had first heard of Connie's gift, but at least universals were a known part of the Society's history. Simon seemed to be a wild departure from all established rules and practices.

The café was bright and airy, doors opening along the far wall onto the gardens that ran down to the banks of the Thames. The white-painted wrought-iron tables, laden with home-made cakes and tall cool drinks, lush pot-plants and striped awning over the patio gave the room a summery, celebratory feel. The place was buzzing as Col's fellow candidates toasted the end of their written papers for that year. Giving Shirley and Jessica a brief wave, Col accompanied his party to a table where Horace and Antonia Little were already seated. Horace, an elderly black man with grizzled white hair, stood up to greet them. His granddaughter, her hair braided in geometric plaits, had clearly also just finished her exam as she was gulping down her lemonade thirstily while looking back over her question paper. She gave Col a nod of recognition and then looked curiously at the other two boys. With the Littles was a small, bird-like lady with a headscarf. She had the olive-toned skin of someone from the Middle East and did not appear to understand much English when Horace tried to introduce her to the newcomers. Col began to wonder if this lady, Mrs Khalid, was really the best mentor for Liam the Society could've found.

'So, Liam,' said Horace genially, 'I hear you live near us. I hope you'll let us come and see you.'

Liam nodded eagerly, but his eyes kept straying to Mrs Khalid. Col had the impression that there was some communication going on between the two of them that did not need words.

'I'll introduce you to the other Elementals in our area,' said Antonia. 'There's no one exactly your age, but there's a couple of ten year olds.'

Suddenly, Mrs Khalid thrust her hand into the pocket of her baggy robe and pulled out a white candle in a stubby earthenware holder. The table fell silent.

'Lee-am,' she said softly. 'Watch.'

She struck a match and lit the flame expertly, cupping her hands around it to protect it from the breeze blowing in through the open doors. Abruptly, a little body of flame ignited, no bigger than a maple leaf, and began to dance in the heart of the candle flame. Mrs Khalid slid her finger into the fire and the creature jumped onto her knuckle and curled around it like a burning ring. She then removed her finger from the wick and held it pointing to the ceiling. The fire imp wound up to the tip of her finger and then danced on the very end, its little arms and legs flickering, sending out golden sparks with each stamp of foot and clap of hands.

'Wow!' breathed Liam. 'Can I have a go?' He leant forward as if to touch the creature but Mrs Khalid gently caught his hand in her free palm.

'Wait,' she cautioned. 'Watch what he do.'

After exhausting his delight at dancing on the fingertip, the fire imp turned a deeper shade of golden red. His tiny head turned from side to side as if looking for a new vent for his energies. Seeing nowhere to go from his position high in the air, away from any other objects, his tiny ember-bright eyes glittered with annoyance and he stamped his foot down on the finger that held him aloft.

'Ouch!' said Mrs Khalid with a wry smile. Col could tell that she had been expecting this and was not much hurt. She wagged her other index finger at the creature and made a noise that to Col's ears sounded like the spitting of damp wood on a campfire. 'Chtsh! Bad imp.'

Liam had been transfixed by these small events. 'He hurt you?' he asked Mrs Khalid with surprise.

She nodded.

'Why?'

'He not my pet. He not like to be kept in one place. Look, I send him back into air.' With a snap of her fingers, she quenched the flame on her fingertip.

Liam looked up as if he expected to see the creature hovering over their heads.

'Where's he gone?' he asked.

'To join brothers and sisters. He not come back unless I call,' said Mrs Khalid, leaning forward and blowing out the candle. With her hands resting on the table in front of her, Col noticed that they were a network of shiny red scars. Being a fire imp companion clearly took its toll on the body.

'So, can I call him?' Liam reached for the candle.

'Not yet. You learn about danger first. Start small with imps like my friend before dance with

121

big ones again.' Her eyes were serious as she held Liam's gaze in hers. 'You must read signs when mood about to change. Red glow is one, but there are others. I heard you needed golden dragon and universal to save you on your first encounter—'

'But I wasn't in danger!' protested Liam. 'We'd only just started dancing. It was great!'

'You in more danger than you know, Lee-am. The universal and her dragon will not always be there for you. You must learn to play safely with fire imps.'

Liam nodded, his face reflective as he absorbed this new perspective on his adventure. He did not look entirely convinced. Col sincerely hoped the lesson had sunk in. He hated to think that this might be the start of Liam's career as an arsonist as he sought bigger thrills and more danger than he could handle. Mrs Khalid appeared to have been thinking along the same lines.

'I have sons,' she said proudly, 'but not fire imp companions. Companions to the sylphs and the kelpies, yes, but not to fire imps. You be my fire imp son?'

'You'll teach me all this?' Liam asked Mrs Khalid, his face glowing as if she had conjured a fire inside him.

'I teach. You meet my sons. They are good

boys. Bigger than you. Twelve and fourteen. They look after you on streets when you come to my house. I send them for you. I live not far from you. Come have meal with us after school on Wednesdays. You learn then.'

'Brilliant!' said Liam.

Col smiled, a sudden image of Mrs Khalid cooking surrounded by fire imps popping into his mind. He had been wrong. The Trustees had clearly known exactly what they were doing when they chose Mrs Khalid as Liam's mentor. The boy now had a whole new surrogate family. With the Littles also close by, Liam had been attached to an extended network of friends; all of them would look out for the youngster: he need not worry about Liam any more.

7

Guy de Chauliac

Connie sat cross-legged in the centre of the compass in the Chamber of Counsel.

'If you are ready, Universal,' said Kinga, 'we will continue our discussions through the shared bond. All will then be able to take equal part.'

Connie nodded.

'You are still weak, Connie,' added the unicorn companion. 'The chimera's attack has taken more out of you than you realize. Windfoal says we must be careful. Signal when you are too tired to continue.'

'I will,' Connie said.

Kira looked to the other Trustees. 'First, let my companion heal the scars in the universal's side. She will be more comfortable after that.'

There was a brief pause while Windfoal and Connie bonded together in private. The stream of silver balm unwound from the tip of the unicorn's horn and twisted itself around Connie's waist like a bandage, easing the tightness and pain of the scars left by the stitches. Connie immediately felt better.

'I am ready for the bond,' she said aloud, and sat with head bowed as she waited for the three other mythical creatures to approach. With Morjik and Storm-Bird, she welcomed back old friends, but the encounter with Jade came with the thrill she always experienced on meeting a creature for the first time. The rock dwarf's presence stole up through the floor like a stream of liquefied emeralds, the slow creep of the rock-forming powers of the earth speeded up so Connie could sense the crystallization of Jade's thoughts in her head without waiting millennia. With his companion came the shy, neat presence of Chan Lee. The shadow Mr Chan bowed low, asking permission to enter the bond, which Connie immediately granted, and he took his place in the shadow Chamber of Counsel created in her mind. Finally she raised a silver image of herself to sit in the middle of the shadow-chamber, a focus for her thoughts and speech.

Now that the Trustees and universal could

all hear each other through the mediation of Connie, the discussion began in earnest.

'What shall we do about the chimera?' asked Eagle-Child. 'Was it hunting alone?'

'I don't know,' said Connie. 'I don't think I understood it properly. I've never met anything like it before. I think the creature's unstable, somehow driven into madness by fighting against itself.'

'It is the chimera's curse to be thus,' said Windfoal sadly, 'to be always divided in its own nature.'

'Like our world,' grunted Morjik. 'We are like the chimera, tearing each other apart.'

'Maybe,' said Windfoal, 'but the chimera has always been like this. We have not. We were once whole and healthy, living in balance. We can be so again. I do not know if any healing can be brought to this creature.'

Connie shook her head. 'I don't think it can ever be peaceful.'

'So,' said Kira, 'if the chimera is that disturbed, we cannot hope to turn it from its path by persuasion. We must find it and remove it to a safe place. We also need to find out if it was the agent of another. I for one do not believe its presence on Dartmoor was a coincidence. Chimeras are rarely found outside the Mediterranean.'

'I didn't sense anything other than the chimera

when it attacked me—' Connie stopped. She suddenly remembered how, during the fire up on the tor, at the point of losing consciousness, the dark tide she associated with the presence of Kullervo had swept upon her. As these thoughts could be sensed by those sharing the bond, she had no need to put them into words.

'He was there?' said Kinga.

'Perhaps. I don't know for sure.'

'It is probable, honourable colleagues. With brother to universal a companion,' said Mr Chan with a deferential bow to Connie, 'the shape-shifter does not need to do more than place chimera in locality and wait. Companion will seek out creature: we all know this.'

'I agree,' said Connie. 'But I don't understand why Kullervo would do this? To kill me or capture me?'

'I'd say he was trying to assassinate you,' said Kinga with a disgusted curl to her lip. 'That venom almost did the task.'

'But that would mean he's finally given up on turning me to his side,' said Connie. 'Which would mean—'

'Which would mean he found another universal. He not need you,' concluded Mr Chan.

'Revenge now on his mind,' said Jade in a silky voice.

The prospect of Kullervo finding another universal filled all of them with dread. The shadow chamber became obscured by a cold, damp fog as Connie could not contain her bewilderment at the new thought that Kullervo would now stop at nothing to eliminate her. The worst was not the fear for her life but his rejection of her: though she should not want him, he was still her companion. And if they did not find the other universal first, who knew what Kullervo would persuade him or her to do? She was also ashamed to feel a twinge of jealousy; she hated to think someone else shared that bond.

Stupid thought, she told herself, hoping the others had not sensed this traitorous feeling.

'Be comforted, Universal,' growled Morjik, dispelling the fog with his warm breath. 'Too many assumptions made. We do not know if there is another universal. We do not know that he wants to kill you. Scare, yes. Drive you to him, yes. But kill?'

'Morjik's right,' said Eagle-Child, 'the chimera may only have been following its nature. If our side had not intervened to save you, maybe Kullervo's plan was to come and get you at your weakest.'

Connie wasn't sure if this prospect was very comforting, but at least it wasn't a sentence of death.

'We need the chimera,' concluded Kira decisively. 'We have to take it away from the universal, but we also must ask it if it is working for Kullervo and what its orders were. That will answer many of our questions. But how can we catch it? Do you know where it is, Universal?'

'On the moor. But I don't know for certain. It eludes me, you see. I've never been able to pinpoint it until it's very close. I don't think I want to get that close again,' Connie added with a shudder that made the floor of the shadow chamber quake. 'Sorry.'

'Brothers and sisters, what would we do with it even if we did catch it?' asked Eagle-Child, looking round at his colleagues. 'It is not an easy beast to constrain even for a dragon or a giant.'

'Kullervo did so,' grunted Morjik.

'Yes,' said Kinga. 'If the creature is Kullervo's tool, we must assume that it is obedient to him part of the time. Kullervo must have found some inducement to make it bend to his will. If we knew what that was, perhaps we too could bring it under control long enough to make it safe and find out what we need to know.'

Eagle-Child shifted uneasily. Storm-Bird croaked. 'It is not the Society's way to capture and control,' the Native American said in a firm tone.

'That is the way of exploitative humans—and of Kullervo.'

'What do you suggest we do then?' asked Kinga. 'Allow it to run amok on the moor, trapping Connie in Hescombe because we cannot allow her out? You'll be caging *her* if you refuse to let us capture this creature.'

'You are right, Companion to Dragons,' said Eagle-Child fairly, his humility defusing any frustration that was building in the southern quarter of the room. 'I only ask that we make sure our means are not those of our enemies, even if our end is better.'

'We should find out more about the creature,' said Jade in a soft voice. 'Let us see what knowledge you have here in your British headquarters. If that fails us, we should send abroad to other great collections of the Society.'

'I'll summon the librarian,' said Kira, jumping to her feet.

'Er . . . ' said Connie, restraining the over-eager Trustee with a misty cord across the exit from her mind, 'hadn't I better end the encounter first before you leave?'

'Sorry, Connie,' laughed Kira. 'Yes, I remember what it was like to end the shared encounter too abruptly. I'd not like to experience that again.'

Slowly and calmly, Connie reeled in the links

that extended from her to the creatures, ending the shared bond for that time. All opened their eyes, blinking to find themselves back in the glittering surroundings of the real Chamber of Counsel.

'As I was saying,' said Kira with a warm smile at Connie, 'I'll fetch the librarian.'

Barely five minutes had passed before Kira returned with Mr Dove, the white-haired librarian Connie had met on her first visit to the head-quarters. He followed the Trustee, staggering under the weight of a large leather-bound volume. He almost toppled over with the combined hindrance of the book and his attempts to bow.

'Mr Dove has kindly agreed to help us in our search for knowledge,' said Kira to her colleagues. 'Here, why don't you put that book on this table?' She pulled forward a gilt-decorated, three-legged table that had been standing against the wall.

'Thank you,' said Mr Dove breathlessly, mopping his brow with a red silk handkerchief. 'Much obliged.' He glanced apprehensively over at Morjik, then darted a look at Storm-Bird, and took a swift sidelong survey of Jade. Connie dipped into her mind, glimpsing a hint of pale light dancing over his sparse crop of white hair. Yes, he was a companion to the will-o'-the-wisp: no wonder the large creatures disturbed him.

Lastly, Mr Dove's eyes fell on Connie, sitting hunched up on the centre of the compass. He gave her a respectful bow.

'Universal, a pleasure to meet you again.' His eyes crinkled in a smile. 'I should have guessed you would be here.'

'Mr Dove,' said Kinga, stepping forward, 'we would be grateful if you could tell us what stores of knowledge the library possesses on the subject of the chimera.'

Mr Dove reached in his top pocket and pulled out a pair of half-moon glasses which he perched on the end of his bony nose. With a slight cough, he addressed the company:

'This book is the index to all records we keep on the different mythical creatures. They are all listed alphabetically by name. If we have anything, it will be down here.' He opened the book, sending clouds of dust into the air as the boards thumped onto the tabletop. He ran a long, tapering finger down the list: 'Chaonian Bird, Charybdis, Chichevache . . . ah! Here it is— Chimera, or Chimaera, pronounced Kai-meer-a. The entry is very brief, I'm afraid, as you don't see many of those in England. In fact, this is the first one I've come across. Now, let me see.' He fell silent as he peered at the details once written down by quill. 'Should have all this on computer, I suppose,' he mused. 'I have a terrible time reading some of the handwriting, but, then, it somehow makes me feel more connected to my predecessors than a print-out.' Kinga coughed at his elbow to remind him of the urgency of their business. 'Yes, yes, here it is: we have one book on the subject. It is called *A Treatise on Conjoined Creatures and Multiple Monsters*, by Guy de Chauliac, translated by Edward Alleyne.' He sniffed. 'A rather offensive title if you ask my opinion. We would never call any creature a "monster" these days, but I suppose we have to make allowances as they were unenlightened days back then.'

'And where is it?' Kinga asked abruptly.

'Well,' said Mr Dove with a smile at Connie, 'normally, I would have to tell the reader that it was out of bounds, but you are in luck.'

'Why?' asked Kinga, beginning to pace as she restrained her urge to be rude to the long-winded old man.

'The book is in the universal's reading room. The young lady before us is the only one who can reach it.'

Kinga spun on her heel to face Connie. 'You remember the title, Connie?' Connie nodded. 'Then we would be grateful if you would make haste to read all you can in the time we have left. Morjik and Windfoal must leave under cover of darkness: their barge will be here at midnight so that gives you a few hours.'

'But the library closes at six!' protested Mr Dove, looking at his pocket watch whose golden hands showed that it was five o'clock already. Kinga looked hard at him and raised one of her dark eyebrows. Morjik released a puff of red smoke. 'But of course, we'll arrange special extended opening tonight,' Mr Dove added quickly, licking his dry lips.

'Good.' Kinga gave him a curt nod.

'But the universal is tired!' intervened Kira. 'We must not work her so hard.'

'I'm fine,' said Connie, suppressing a yawn. She was more eager than any of them to find out about the chimera if it could help them capture the creature. 'Could you please send a message to my brother and the Clamworthys that I might be some time? They'll probably want to take Liam home.'

'Of course,' said Kinga. 'I'll take care of that.'

'And we'll arrange for some refreshments for you,' added Kira.

Mr Dove was about to protest at the idea of food and drink in the library but one look at the pointed horn and ebony hooves of Windfoal made him think better of this.

* * *

Up in the universal's reading room, Connie took more time than usual to recover from the encounter with the great snake that guarded the entrance. The bite-like bond it demanded on each entry reminded her too vividly of the chimera's fangs and she felt sickened, her hand rising involuntarily to protect the place in her neck where the serpent had bitten her. Her skin seemed still to smart and there were two lumps under her fingers where the teeth had sunk in, throbbing slightly with remembered pain. To calm herself down, she poured a cup of coffee, took a mouthful of cheese sandwich and enjoyed chewing it under the disapproving nose of the doorward, which now lay curled up at the head of the winding stair, blue ribbon trailing from its mouth as it sucked on the golden key she had given it.

Time for her task.

Brushing the crumbs off the table, she got up to locate the book she wanted. She guessed it would not be filed under one of the four companies on the outer wall as the subject matter crossed the bounds of these categories. She therefore knelt down in front of the low circle of bookshelves devoted to subjects to do with the gift of the universal. She ran her finger down the spines of the books on which she had so far barely made any impression. So much knowledge for her to gain! Here her life's work was laid out before her. Hidden amongst the fat volumes filed under 'C' was the book she sought: a slim, handwritten manuscript bound in black leather. The pages crackled as she opened it, releasing the smell of dust and decay. At first she thought it was written in a foreign language as she could make out little on the page she had randomly selected. Laying it open on the table she saw that she was wrong. The language was English, but English as people seven hundred years ago would have spoken it.

She was about to give up in despair as she understood only two words in five, when she turned a page and found a bundle of yellowing notepaper slipped between the sheets. It was dated December 1940, and bore the name 'Reginald Cony'. Connie realized she had stumbled upon the notes made by the last British universal, the uncle that the Trustee Frederick Cony had told her about before his own death last year. She leafed through the pages. Reginald appeared to have been taking notes on behalf of a Society member and had addressed a letter to someone called George Brewer. But Reginald must have forgotten to take the notes with him, and the letter ended abruptly mid-sentence.

'Dear George' she read, 'I hope my last set of notes reached you safely through all the snow and ice. The griffin messenger said that the passage over the Arctic Circle was particularly hairy at the moment. I hope I can complete these today, but what with the frequent interruptions of the air-raids, I'm not confident. I got my call-up papers, as expected, so this will be my last opportunity to come here for some time. The lantern dome offers spectacular views of the bombers coming in from Germany but it isn't the safest place to be. We're moving as much as we can down to the basements but I'm afraid the universal's collection will just have to run the risk as I'm not going to try getting past the doorward with a bundle of books. I don't think it understands about human war.'

No, it wouldn't, agreed Connie, smiling to find that her predecessor had shared her mixed feelings about the guard.

'Now, as I wrote in my last, I fear de Chauliac spends most time on the chimera. I won't bore you with the details . . .'

Oh do, urged Connie, but it was hopeless: she was decades too late to influence this correspondence.

'But he does mention the shape-shifter a couple of times. It seems that Kullervo is able to calm the chimera's madness by turning into a chimera himself. This way the different parts of the chimera can communicate with their Kullervo-counterpart and he is able to persuade the creature to do his bidding. So if you run across a chimera up there, it's probably under Kullervo's sway and I'd advise you to steer clear.

'And here's something else that might interest you. I've just read the note made by the translator, one Edward Alleyne. He notes that Guy de Chauliac had made a special study of the conjoined creatures as a way to combat Kullervo—so you were on the right track there. He notes that both he and de Chauliac were fellow-universals. There were apparently ten identified ones in Europe alone in the 1340s! Can you imagine that! At the moment there's only poor old me and Miguel in Argentina, and you know that I can't speak a word of Spanish, nor he a word of English, so we're not much company for each other even when we do meet.

'De Chauliac, Alleyne, and their fellow universals had worked out that Kullervo was spreading the Black Death through rats. Over a third of the population in the known world had died by the time they figured this out and they knew that they had to act quickly. De Chauliac did do something—Alleyne said he "passyd oute of thys world by

138

the mark". So you were right: Kullervo does have to be challenged at the mark, but I think it is something only a universal can do, so I advise you to . . . '

Here the letter ended. So it had never been delivered to George Brewer, whoever he was. Connie supposed another bombing raid had sent Reginald scurrying to the basement and he had not returned to collect his letter. What had he been about to advise his friend to do? She leafed through the book to the note he referred to, wondering whether with his guide she could make anything of it.

'𝔊uy passyd oute of thys world by the mark and there was wepyng and dolour out of mesure. Our counsels are grievously lessened. But he defeated 𝔎ullervo for thys time.'

Well, that was clear enough. Whatever Guy de Chauliac had done—what had Reginald written? 'challenged him at the mark'—it had worked. She had the vivid image of a medieval Guy on horseback like some knight-errant of old, riding to face his opponent on the jousting field. But the challenge had cost him his life.

She closed the book and slipped the unfinished letter into her pocket, hoping the snake had not seen. She felt she might get away with taking the letter and the notes, but not the book. If ever there was a volume that she would like to smuggle out of the reading room, this was it, but she knew from past experience that was out of the question as far as the doorward was concerned. Picking up the remains of her picnic supper, she followed the snake down the winding stair, her mind still up in the lantern dome with Reginald and with Guy.

'So, now we know how Kullervo is controlling the chimera,' said Kinga, handing the notes back to Connie. 'Not a method we can use, I fear. None of us can change into a chimera.'

'Not so,' growled Morjik, his sulphury breath blooming around his nostrils in vibrant yellow flowers of smoke. 'There is a way.'

Connie had thought of it too, but had hoped no one else would.

'What do you mean?' asked Kira, her dark eyes bright with interest.

'He means,' said Connie wearily, 'that if we gather together a Nemean lion, a great snake, and an Amalthean goat, then through the shared bond they can communicate with the chimera. I can mediate.'

'Not only you,' said Jade softly.

This was the bit Connie had really hoped they would not think of, but she should have realized that the ageless rock dwarf and ancient dragon would have had many years in which to learn such secrets.

'Simon too,' she admitted reluctantly. 'But he's not even begun his training. You can't seriously expect him to help?' Her weariness was becoming almost unbearable; she was finding it increasingly difficult to master herself. The Trustees exchanged looks over Connie's head as she sat once more hugging her knees in their midst. 'Please, tell me you're not serious. He's only just turned twelve!'

'But you were only eleven the first time you faced Kullervo, Connie,' said Eagle-Child. 'Do not treat your brother as an infant. He is fast approaching manhood. In my tribe, he would soon be initiated as an adult.'

The unicorn companion was looking at her with a worried frown, sensing that the universal was exhausted.

'And as far as we know, the chimera is not instructed to kill him on sight. It would surely be safer to use his skills and train him for this task than risk putting you in the creature's path again?' said Kira calmly, moving towards her.

'No!' Connie leapt to her feet, swaying with tiredness. 'I can't let you do this. You don't understand what it's like!'

'No, we don't,' said Eagle-Child, 'but Simon will. It is his gift. You should not deny him this.'

'I'm not denying him anything. I'm just trying to stop you killing him in some stupid attempt to save me. I'm not exchanging my life for his!'

The room fell into stunned silence as Connie's last words echoed around the chamber. She had not meant to be so outspoken, but she stood by every word she had said.

Windfoal neighed and rippled her mane.

'Connie, you're tired and upset,' said Kira coming forward to lay a hand on her elbow. 'We've over-taxed you today. It is our fault. You should rest now.'

Connie was shaking slightly with a mixture of anger and fatigue. It would be unwise to say any more in her current condition, she knew that, but she had to make them understand! When would she have another chance to speak to the Trustees?

'You don't see it, do you? That letter isn't really about the chimera—that's just a sideshow. It's about Kullervo—this whole situation is about Kullervo. That's what Guy de Chauliac and Reginald Cony both realized. We should be talking about challenging him at the mark— about me challenging him at the mark—not about the chimera!'

The silence that followed turned icy. Connie could sense the Trustees thought she had gone too far. Kinga and Morjik were angry with her; Windfoal and Kira were afraid.

'What are you all looking at?' Connie asked with a defiant tilt to her head when no one spoke. 'Are you afraid to hear the truth?' Anger was making her feel quite a different person, not a shy teenager, but a universal, proud of her inheritance and ready to defend it.

Windfoal stamped her foot. 'We're not afraid of the truth, Universal,' said Kira sternly. 'We are afraid for you—and of you. It is you who does not know what she is talking about if you think the way to defeat Kullervo is to challenge him.'

'Connie, listen to yourself,' said Eagle-Child in a placatory voice. 'You do not even sound like yourself. You are talking about travelling a lonely path, repeating the same mistakes of the universals of the past.'

'But it wasn't a mistake,' said Connie beseechingly, turning to Eagle-Child. She could usually count on him to be on her side. It was very serious if even he did not agree. 'Look at what Guy de Chauliac did: it ended the Black Death, for heaven's sake!'

Eagle-Child shook his head. 'You have read only one account—a biased one by a friend of

143

his. By another universal. The histories in the libraries of the Society around the world tell how Guy de Chauliac failed in his challenge. He was taken by Kullervo before he could complete the ordeal. It is a horrible death you are talking about—a torture beyond your imagining.'

Connie was taken aback. They had already known about Guy, but what else did they know that she didn't?

'But Edward Alleyne said he succeeded,' she said miserably.

'He did. In part. He satisfied Kullervo's lust for destruction for that time. But Guy did not achieve his aim, which was to vanquish Kullervo once and for all. Do you want to pay that price? Your suffering as the sacrifice that will make Kullervo cease his attack for a brief time? And when he has exhausted you, thrown you aside, he'll come back for more—new victims, new forms of devastation.'

Connie sat down again, no longer wanting to be in the middle of the room, at the centre of everyone's attention, but she did not know where else to sit.

'But he knew there was a way to defeat him, didn't he?' she said, still stubbornly defending the memory of her predecessor like the sole fighter left after a hopeless siege. 'He was on to something.'

144

'He failed,' concluded Eagle-Child. He rose gracefully to his feet and came to sit cross-legged in front of her, his open, bronzed face smooth and calm. Only the flicker of fire in the depths of his eyes betrayed his anxiety. Connie's head was bowed so that he could not see her expression. He gently slid his hand under her chin to raise her face to his. Tears trickled down Connie's cheeks as she met his gaze. 'We forbid you to go any further down this path, Universal. Do you understand?'

Connie could feel the presences of all the mythical creatures snaking towards her, seeking to strengthen the prohibition of the Trustee for the Winged Beasts. She did not want them in her head; too much else was going on there just at the moment. In one swift move, she raised her shield against them, blocking entry, and jumped to her feet, knocking back Eagle-Child's hand.

'I understand,' she said bitterly. 'But I don't agree.' And, turning on her heels, she fled from the chamber.

8
Alone

Connie kept silent on the train journey home the following day. Col watched her out of the corner of his eye as she leafed through a book she had borrowed from the main section of the library—*The Early History of the Society, 1000–1500*. It looked a boring read to him: cramped, close-printed text with no illustrations. If she wanted to wade through tedious textbooks she only had to wait until school next week. She was probably just covering up her bad mood by pretending to be interested in it, he decided. It was what he would have done. He knew that she had fallen out with the Trustees, which he had to admit was pretty serious, but he did not know the details. Perhaps he should try to cheer her up and see if she wanted to talk about it?

'Hey, Connie, do you want a mint?' he asked, holding out a packet he kept in his pocket for Mags.

She shook her head mutely.

'Yeah, I'll have one!' said Simon, making a grab for the sweets. In complete contrast to his sister, Simon could not have been in better spirits.

'Hands off,' laughed Col, chucking him a single mint, which Simon caught.

'You show more promise as a fielder than your sister,' teased Mack, ruffling Connie's hair. She flinched away and Mack quickly withdrew his hand, which as usual had been stung by static. 'Why do I always forget about her defences?' Mack said ruefully, waving his fingers in the air to shake away the pain. He turned back to Simon, to whom he had been talking before Col offered round the sweets. 'And what did they tell you then?'

'They said I'm to be put on a fast-track training programme,' said Simon proudly. 'They've a special task for me.'

The Early History of the Society slid to the floor with a clunk.

'Yeah? What?'

'They want me to help capture the chimera so Connie can get out and about again.'

147

'That's cool,' said Col, glancing over at Connie who was bent forward, hair in a curtain around her face, as she picked up the book. Was this the problem? Did she not like being ordered to stay in Hescombe? Another thought struck him. Or was she jealous of Simon being given this special treatment? Surely not? You couldn't get more special than being a universal. Simon's gift, though unique, was not in the same league as hers.

'That's what I said when they told me.' Simon bubbled with enthusiasm. 'They're to make special arrangements with my school so I can carry on the training at the weekends. Apparently one of the teachers is a member of the Society—Mr Hawthorn, the science teacher—I'd never've guessed as he seems so normal. They're going to bring in a Nemean lion especially for me.'

'That's good, isn't it, Connie?' said Col, turning to her.

She paused, then said: 'I'm glad they're going to train Simon properly.'

Col sensed there was an unspoken reservation. 'But?'

She shut her book with a snap. 'But they shouldn't be using Simon to catch the chimera: it's too dangerous.'

'Oh, come on!' protested Simon. 'You're always trying to spoil my fun.'

Connie looked as though she felt like strangling her brother. 'Don't be so stupid.'

'Stupid!' Simon was riled now. 'You don't understand. You never understand.'

'Ha!' said Connie, getting up to push past Col who was blocking her path to the aisle. 'I think you'll find I'm the only one who understands. I'm going to get a coffee.' Grabbing her book from her seat, she disappeared in the direction of the buffet car.

Mack, Simon, and Col exchanged looks.

'Girls!' said Mack with a shrug. 'Hormones, mood-swings; Evie's the same.'

Simon nodded and returned to his account of what the Trustees had told him that morning. Col did not join in the conversation. Neither did he agree with Mack's diagnosis that Connie was merely being moody. She was normally one of the calmest people he knew. Something was up and he very much wanted to know what was going on. So, slipping out of his seat, he quietly followed Connie.

He found her standing with an untouched cup of coffee leaning against the grubby ledge that served inadequately as a table in the buffet car. Outside the rows of houses and industrial estates had given place to rolling green hills. They had escaped the coils of London and were heading home.

'Want anything else?' he asked, gesturing to her drink.

'No thanks. I don't recommend the coffee.'

Col bought himself an orange juice and came to lean beside her. They stood together in companionable silence watching the world pass by. He had the sudden strange sensation that the train was standing still and it was the trees and the cows that were being whisked away at great speed.

'So, what's the matter, Connie?'

She did not speak for a moment, biting her lip as she looked down at the plastic spoon she was fingering. It snapped in two.

'And don't say "nothing" for you and I both know each other better than that.'

She could not resist his sympathy. Yes, she could tell him. He would stand by her. She threw the splinters of the spoon into the bin and took the plunge.

'You know I had a . . . a disagreement with the Trustees yesterday?'

He nodded, keeping his eyes fixed on the distant hills in the hopes that it would be easier for her to speak if she did not feel under interrogation.

'Well, I think I've discovered a way, or an idea about a way of finally defeating Kullervo.'

Forgetting his resolution, he turned to stare

at her. 'That's great! Amazing! What is it?' He thought for a second longer. 'So, what's the problem with the Trustees?'

She tapped the spine of the book she had tucked under her arm. 'I'm not the first to find out about it. There've been other universals who've tried, but they've failed, or at least, only partially succeeded. That's what we argued about. The Trustees think it's too dangerous and won't work.'

Col's enthusiasm was dampened by her hints that it was a perilous path. 'So what is it?'

'I'm not sure exactly but it involves challenging Kullervo at the mark—the place where he enters our world. I think in the past this was a real place, but in my case, it's . . . well, you know where it is.'

He did indeed. He vividly remembered visiting Connie's mental wall of encounters and seeing the breach made by Kullervo: the dark void that whispered like waves on a distant sea.

'And what do you have to do in this challenge?'

'I'm not sure yet. I think the Trustees know as they told me those who failed were . . . ' She stopped and took a sip of her coffee, wrinkling her nose at the bitter taste.

'Were what?'

'Were tortured to death.'

151

Col choked on his mouthful of orange juice. 'Connie! No wonder they don't want you to have anything to do with this! And you were just telling Simon off for getting into danger! You must be crazy even to think of it.'

'Of course I don't want to get hurt!' she replied angrily, crumpling up an empty sugar sachet. 'I'm not stupid. But think what it would mean if I succeeded.'

'Yeah, right. And if you don't, as all the others have found out, you die a gruesome death. Good thinking, Connie.'

'I thought you'd understand,' she said in a small voice, turning her shoulder from him slightly.

'What? Understand your mad death wish? Sure, I understand,' he said in a voice laced with sarcasm. He couldn't believe she was really suggesting putting herself at such grave risk.

'It's not mad,' she said defiantly. 'Or if it is, it's only because I'm being driven mad by his voice in my head every night. I can't stand it. And if I can get rid of him for ever: think how many lives that would save!'

Col sighed. 'I'm sorry, Connie. I didn't know he was still bothering you.' He placed a hand on her arm. 'Look, it's just that none of us want to see you get hurt. We couldn't bear that—I couldn't bear that. Listen to the people you trust. You know they're only trying to do what's best for you. Don't go it alone on this one.'

'I don't want "to go it alone"—I want everyone's support for what I've got to do. I want to do this properly—avoid the mistakes made in the past.'

'Stop right there. You know I'm on your side, Connie, but I can't support you in such a suicidal plan. Don't even think about it. Anyway, the Trustees won't let you do it.' He could sense she was raw with pain so he put his arm around her and gave her a hug. 'You know it's not because we don't believe in you, don't you? You're an amazing person, Connie.' He had to get through to her. 'Promise me you'll not do anything stupid?'

Her voice, coming from the muffling centre of the hug, was close to a sob. 'I can't . . . promise.' She pushed him away and stood back to look into his eyes, her voice now firm. She would not allow even Col to stop her doing what she knew was right, even when it was so tempting to take the easy path of falling in line with his wishes. 'But thanks, Col. I know you're my friend—my best friend. And I'll promise I'll think over what you've said. Will that do?'

It would have to. 'OK,' said Col, still looking at her warily. 'Hadn't you'd better drink up? We're almost there.'

'Can't swallow the stuff,' she said, throwing her cup into the bin. 'Let's get back to the others.'

Connie's disagreement with the Trustees, which normally would have greatly concerned Evelyn, was overshadowed by two other rows. The first, Connie realized later, she should have foreseen. It arrived in the form of a telephone call from her parents that evening. If the handset could have given Connie warning of what was to come, it should have glowed throbbing red as she picked it up.

'WHAT IS ALL THIS!' bellowed her father. She held the receiver away from her ear. Her father was clearly attempting to get his voice heard from the other side of the world without the use of modern technology. 'Simon has just rung full of nonsense about joining that Society of yours!'

'Ah.'

'I can't stop him, of course,' he continued, 'not with you being a member.'

That was a shame, thought Connie. It would at least take away one problem if Simon wasn't allowed to train.

'But I blame you for this!'

'Me?' Connie was stung into a response at the

injustice of the accusation. 'What've I got to do with it?'

'What've you got to do with it! You only took him up there and enrolled him without our permission. I thought your aunt was bad enough, but I didn't think my own daughter would go against what you must have known would have been my express wishes. Why on earth have you involved your younger brother in that crazy society of yours? I expect your aunt's to blame too, but I can't tell her what I really think, not in her current condition. But I expected you to act more responsibly. Your mother agrees.'

'Yes, dear,' said Connie's mother, who appeared to have been listening in on the extension.

Connie was silent. What could she say? Here was another set of people who thought she was reckless. Join the club, she thought sourly.

'Are you there, Connie?' barked her father as the line crackled and hissed at him.

'Yes.'

'Well?'

'Well what?'

'What've you to say for yourself?'

'Nothing.'

'Nothing?'

'What do you want me to say?'

This question seemed to floor her father.

'That . . . that you're sorry for getting Simon mixed up with your bunch.'

'OK. I'm sorry for getting Simon mixed up in the Society.' That was partly true.

'And that you promise to try and keep him safe. Not let him do anything dangerous.'

Connie was silent. That was, of course, what she had already been trying to do.

'Connie?'

'I'll try.'

'I don't want any more early morning phone calls telling me one of my children has ended up in hospital with injuries from wild animals.'

'I'll see what I can do,' she said, trying hard to keep her bitterness to herself. It hadn't been her fault she'd ended up in Chartmouth's Accident and Emergency department. Her father hadn't shouted at Simon for leading her into the jaws of the chimera—not that he'd been told about that.

When she put the phone down, she found Evelyn watching her closely from the kitchen table where she was tucking into her fifth bacon sandwich of the day. Evelyn had developed a craving for bacon butties smothered in ketchup.

'Can he join?'

'Dad seems to think it's too late to stop him.'

'Are you OK?'

'Kind of.'

'That means no. Do you want to talk about it?'

Connie took a deep breath but at that moment, Mack stamped into the kitchen through the back door, holding up a pair of mud-splattered trainers.

'I thought we agreed,' he said tersely to Evelyn, 'that you're not to risk running on the moor with the banshees all alone.'

'We might've said something along those lines,' Evelyn replied awkwardly.

'Then what are these?'

'Obviously, they are my running shoes.'

'And why are they covered in mud?'

'Because I haven't cleaned them?'

'Evie!'

'OK. OK. Because I went running while you were in London. I changed my mind about the banshees.'

Mack swelled with rage like a bullfrog preparing to croak. 'But you know they're not good for the baby—not in the early months. All that spinning and wailing—think what you're doing to our child.'

'She fine,' said Evelyn patting her stomach. 'Isn't she, Connie?'

'Er . . . '

'Leave Connie out of this,' intervened Mack. 'This is between you and me, Evelyn Lionheart.'

Connie realized this was really not a good moment to be in the kitchen. She got up to go.

'Connie, we haven't had our chat yet,' said Evelyn, stalling for time as a full-blown row loomed on the horizon.

'It can wait,' said Connie, slipping her hand free of her aunt and moving to the door.

The following day, when Connie got out of bed and opened the curtains, it took her a moment or two to realize what she was seeing. The sky, which had been barren and dry for months, was clouding over from the west. Fat drops of rain were pattering onto the dusty road. The drought had broken.

When she entered the kitchen, she found Evelyn and Mack having a cosy breakfast together, harmony restored. Tactfully, she decided to leave them in peace and take hers back upstairs. Besides, she had some reading she wanted to get through before Gard arrived for her next training session. She sat cross-legged on her bed, balancing a cup of tea in one hand and *The History of the Society* in the other. The book had been recommended to her by Mr Dove, who had been overjoyed at her interest in the subject. On any other occasion, she would have been fascinated to read about the establishment and spread of the Society in its early years, but ever since she had

158

taken it out, she had been making her way slowly through the section on the later medieval period, trying to understand what it was the Trustees knew and she did not. So far, though she had learnt a lot, she had not discovered anything she might not have guessed herself. The Trustees were right that here was a very different account to that given by Edward Alleyne. The book contained a long and detailed chapter on the first major calamity to face the Society: the rat-borne Black Death, or bubonic plague, as the modern writer explained. This writer, however, did not regard Guy de Chauliac as a hero; indeed, the universals appeared to be the villains of the piece, after Kullervo.

The Company of Universals, he wrote, *acting against the wishes of the rest of the European members of the Society, dispatched their champion to challenge Kullervo to single-handed combat. This rash decision was opposed primarily because the other members thought that the reduction of the Company of Universals to only ten (already half of them had succumbed to the Black Death) meant that de Chauliac's life was too valuable to be risked in this way. They sensibly urged that other options be tried first. The membership also feared that if de Chauliac's will broke, he could become a tool of Kullervo, making the existing disaster seem only a rehearsal for something far more serious.*

Connie had now reached the part where Guy set out alone to confront Kullervo.

There were no witnesses to what happened so we have only the vaguest idea of what took place. We know this much: de Chauliac sailed into the Arctic Circle, to the edge of the glacier where Kullervo had entered our world at the mark.

Connie pictured the man in her imagination, striding across the glittering white icefield, feeling for him in his loneliness and fear. Whatever the majority thought, she considered him a brave man to choose to face Kullervo.

The foolhardy challenger is thought to have survived the first hour of combat, matching the universal's weapons to each metamorphosis of Kullervo's, but finally— inevitably—his defences were broken. But, clearly, Kullervo did not break his will for he did not join with him and no new disaster struck. As punishment, Kullervo took Guy and spent months exhausting him in the bonded encounter till the pain destroyed him.

Connie put the book down. Her memory had flitted back to the brief time she had spent in the air with Kullervo as he had shifted from shape to shape, spinning her, dancing with her. That had been a bonded encounter, but its memory was almost sweet. She had for one brief moment glimpsed something in Kullervo, a joy at the myriad forms of creation, that she could relate to and respect. Was this the torture Guy had experienced? How could it be? But then, if her time with Kullervo had proved anything to her, it was that everything he did had its dark side. It was not so difficult to imagine him turning this game into a torment as he forced his companion to inhabit each form with him. Connie remembered the pain of encountering the fractured mind of the chimera. This beast contained only three natures in contention with each other. Imagine what it would be like to encounter form after form, creature after creature, each more complex, more terrible than the last? It would drive you into madness even if it didn't kill you.

Connie returned to the book.

It has to be allowed that after the universal's failed attempt to defeat the shape-shifter once and for all, the intensity of the Black Death declined. Kullervo was successfully distracted from pushing his plan to its conclusion. Humanity survived. But so did the plague. It would return on many occasions, though never so virulent as this outbreak, as if Kullervo was taking a playful swipe at humans, reminding us that he is waiting only for the right occasion to finish us off.

Laying the book down on the bedside table, Connie stared out at the rain streaming down the window. Kullervo would find the occasion one day. The Society should not be complacent that because it had always managed to forestall disaster in the past that it could do so in the future. Kullervo was gaining in power. Almost all the weather giants had gone over to his side now. By its greed and carelessness, humanity was driving more and more creatures into his camp. The Society was losing touch with many of them, falling from its place of respect amongst the mythical creatures. She understood this even if the Trustees did not. She had heard the echoes of doubt and dissatisfaction in the minds of the creatures she had encountered. She'd heard them in her mind for that matter. At night, they came back to haunt her when Kullervo tempted her with her own uncertainties. If someone did not do something soon, it would be too late for the Society.

But do what? She was still no closer to understanding what it was she had to do to defeat Kullervo. She knew she could fight him for a time, like Guy had. Once or twice she had managed to wrong-foot him, but that had been mainly luck that she had caught him unprepared. He would be ready for her if she issued a formal challenge. She doubted she'd last even an hour under these circumstances. Guy had been a mature, fully trained universal; she barely knew anything. As Col had bluntly told her, to face him like this would be suicidal.

So, was there a way or not?

9
Testing Times

Mrs Clamworthy dropped Col and Simon at the Mastersons' on Saturday afternoon. The windscreen wipers of her old Fiesta could hardly keep up with the downpour.

'Good luck!' she called after her grandson as he slammed the door shut. 'I'll keep my fingers crossed for you.'

Simon squelched after Col through the thick mud of the farmyard, which was already churned up by the passage of pupils, their mentors and the examiners. He looked up at the sky, rain dripping off the end of his nose.

'They can't expect you to fly in this, surely?' he asked.

Col gave a hollow laugh. 'You don't know the Society very well if you think a bit of rain will put them off. They'd probably arrange a weather giant if nature did not oblige to make the test more "realistic", as my mentor puts it.'

'Oh,' said Simon. Most at home in front of his PlayStation, Simon was finding it hard to adjust to the outdoor life he had embarked on. 'OK, I s'pose I'd better wish you luck. See you later.' He splashed away into the barn to be introduced to his mentor for the Nemean lions. Col could hear the yawning roar of Simon's companion echoing in the rafters, which meant that the Society had finally succeeded in smuggling a lion into the country after some weeks of trying. He looked forward to hearing Simon's reaction later. He doubted if Simon would be worried about the wet weather once he'd met his companion for the first time.

'There you are, my boy!' Captain Graves strode across the yard and slapped him on the back. 'Pleased to see you are in good time for once. I suggest you go and warm up with Skylark. The examiners are just finishing lunch. I'll bring them out when they're ready.' The captain shook water droplets off his handlebar moustache, not much bothered by the rain that was streaming down his neck.

'OK,' said Col. 'Er . . . who are they this year?'

'Clare Ridley—you remember, the winner of the dressage?—and Sergeant Middleton, the champion in the steeplechase.'

Col remembered them very well. In the Society games earlier that summer, where he and Skylark had again won the junior competition, these two riders had impressed him with their skill. Looking at them with their mounts, he knew that, though he and Skylark were good, they weren't *that* good.

'Why've they both come?' Col asked, thinking it a strange coincidence that the Society's two best riders had come to Hescombe just to examine a Grade Four flying test.

Captain Graves smiled proudly. 'They've not said, of course, but my guess is they're talent-spotting for the inter-Society world championships next summer. You may be a bit on the young side, but you've shown talent—yes, indeed, you've shown talent—and I wouldn't mind a bet that there's a third place in the British squad waiting for a young rider with promise.'

Col swallowed. This was an honour he had not even dreamed of: to be invited to be part of the British squad at fourteen! Wow.

'But before you get carried away, young man,' said Captain Graves with an indulgent smile as he saw the look of wonder on his pupil's face, 'there's the little matter of impressing them in today's test. Hadn't you better go and get ready?'

'Yes, sir!' said Col, sprinting off to the stables.

'Skylark, you'll never guess!' burst out Col as soon as he found his companion.

The white-winged stallion ignored this and arched his neck proudly. 'How do I look?' he asked Col, showing off his groomed mane.

'You look great,' said Col quickly, knowing how vain Skylark was on such occasions. At least this time he hadn't asked Col to plait his tail with ribbons as he had at the competition. Col kept to himself the thought that all this gleaming mane would soon be wet and windswept in the rain outside.

'So, what won't I guess?' asked Skylark as Col vaulted onto his back.

'That we've only got Middleton and Ridley testing us. Captain Graves thinks they are talent-spotting for the British team!'

Skylark gave a shiver of delight. 'Well, we'll show them that they've come to the right place! We'll have to be on top form today, Col: focused and ruthless.'

Col felt his companion delve into his mind to explore their connection, deepening it so that their instincts were in harmony.

'What's this?' Skylark had stumbled across the

166

anxiety and irritation Col was currently feeling for Connie, plus something else that he could not put a name to yet.

Col hunched forward against the rain and urged Skylark into a warm-up trot. 'It's Connie. She thinks she's found a way to take on Kullervo and win.'

'And can she?' The pegasus picked up his pace to leap a fence. They did not land but circled up into the air together.

'Don't be daft. No one has ever defeated him.'

'Have you no faith in the universal?'

'Of course I do.'

'I think you are fooling yourself, Companion. You can't think straight when it comes to Connie; you never have.'

Col groaned. 'Skylark, this isn't a good time to discuss this.'

The pegasus snorted. 'When would it be a good time?'

A whistle blew from below. Skylark and Col spiralled down to land perfectly at Captain Graves's side. Firewings, Skylark's mentor, gave an approving snort at his pupil's elegant descent. Also with Captain Graves were two people dressed in the British squad's navy flying jacket with a gold pegasus on the back. Clare Ridley, an athletic woman with shoulder-length brown hair, gave Col a friendly nod. Her formidable-looking team mate, Sergeant Middleton, was inspecting Skylark closely, water dripping from his close-cropped head, his jaw jutting forward. Col knew already that the sergeant would stand no nonsense.

'Glad to see you've got high presentation standards,' Sergeant Middleton said to the horse, patting him on the shoulder before making a note in a leather-bound notebook.

Col looked down at his mud-splattered boots and then across at Sergeant Middleton's shining toecaps. He surreptitiously brushed at the dirt until he caught Mrs Ridley's eye. She was laughing at him, so he stopped and grinned back. She was right: it was too late to do anything about that now.

'Right,' barked Sergeant Middleton, 'on my signal, take off and go through the first three basic manoeuvres. At some point during this, I will make the signal for the emergency landing and I would like you both to descend as quickly and safely to the ground as possible, keeping yourselves under control at all times.' He blew his whistle.

Col did not even have to urge Skylark forward: his mount was already galloping into the rain for take off. Gaining height, Skylark began to go through the prescribed moves—both of them sharing a secret yawn at the pedestrian nature of what they were doing. Left turn. Right turn. Forward dive and recover. Just as they reached the top of their recovery, the whistle blew again.

'The mangy mule!' snorted Skylark, plunging down in a beautifully judged emergency dive. 'He waited till we were at the most difficult point!'

'Of course,' said Col, far from annoyed they had a chance to display their abilities in something more exciting than boring turns. They landed with a neat thud next to Sergeant Middleton who was looking smug as he enjoyed the trick he'd just played on them. Mrs Ridley came over to him to talk. Col and Skylark waited while the two champions whispered together.

'I think we've seen enough of the Grade Four moves to know what mark to award,' said Sergeant Middleton to Captain Graves. Col's mentor looked surprised: there were still many more moves that the examiners were supposed to test. 'We thought we'd give the candidates a chance to show us their full repertoire. I don't think we'll waste any more time on Grade Four. What do you say, Clamworthy?'

Col hesitated. Was this a trap? Were they testing him to see if he was going to break the rules by doing moves he was not qualified for?

'What repertoire?' he asked innocently.

Mrs Ridley smiled. 'Oh, you can't fool us into thinking that you and Skylark learned to fly as you do by never going beyond Grade Four, Col.'

'Careful,' said Skylark to Col in the privacy of their bond.

'Er . . . well . . . ' said Col, wishing Captain Graves would help him out of this spot.

'We think you're both quite ready to do what you do best: fly. No limitations. You have our permission to do whatever you feel you've mastered, just don't attempt anything you can't do safely. We want to see what you're made of.'

Captain Graves was struggling with his desire to allow Col and Skylark to show off before the British squad and his equally strong wish to stick to the rules. 'Anything, Clare?' he queried.

'Yes, anything, Michael. Oh, don't worry. It's all official. We got permission from Kira and Windfoal before we came out here. They told us Col and Skylark had used some impressive unconventional moves in operational circumstances. We want to see them for ourselves.'

'I suppose that's all right then,' said Captain Graves as if he doubted what he was saying.

'Off you go,' said Mrs Ridley.

Col urged Skylark forward. Though the rain continued to stream down, it no longer mattered to him.

'If they want the full repertoire,' said Col with a chuckle, 'they'll get the full repertoire. What do you say to Syracrusian Spiral, Athenian Dive, followed by Thessalonian Roll?' This was a little something he and Skylark had been working on in private. Theoretically, you couldn't do those three moves in sequence. He and Skylark were about to prove the theorists wrong.

'You're on!' said Skylark.

A good starting height was the secret to the success of the manoeuvre. They climbed up so that they were almost lost in the rain clouds.

'Careful to hold on, Col,' cautioned Skylark. 'Remember my back is very slippery in all this wet.'

'Get on with it, you old nag,' teased Col. 'Of course, I'll remember.'

With a kick of his rear legs, Skylark launched into the downward circle of the Syracrusian spiral, twisting with perfect loops over an imagined spot on the ground (they had chosen the head of a startled Captain Graves). They then moved fluidly into the Athenian dive, wings tucked in like an eagle plunging for the kill. Col clung close to Skylark's neck as his knees found little purchase on the pegasus's rain-slicked flanks. Both knew that they were at the point where the possible shaded into the impossible. So far, they had managed to

171

stay on the right side of that line but these weather conditions were threatening to push them over. Col braced himself for the final test. Just before they reached the level of the treetops, Skylark pulled away in a Thessalonian roll, flipping both himself and his rider over in a three hundred and sixty degree turn. Col's fingers slipped but he dug them deep into Skylark's rain-sodden mane. He kept his seat—just. Once righted, they glided down to land with barely a spray of mud in front of the judges. There was silence. Captain Graves was gaping: he had not known his pupil could do any of those moves, let alone do them together.

Finally, Clare Ridley spoke. 'When I said no limits, I was thinking more along the lines of a few Grade Six moves—not moves right out of the rule book entirely.'

Col's heart sank. Skylark's perky ears dropped back.

'Amazing,' breathed Sergeant Middleton. 'I'd've said you couldn't do that but I just saw it with my own eyes. Amazing.'

Col began to feel a bit more hopeful.

Mrs Ridley was recovering from her surprise. 'That's certainly given us plenty to think about. But don't try that again, will you, Col? Beginner's luck might run out.'

'Oh, we've been doing it for over a year now,'

said Col quickly. Seeing their shocked faces, he added, 'We had to do it when we were fighting Kullervo in Mallins Wood, which was how we discovered it was possible, you see?'

'I'm not sure what to make of that,' said Mrs Ridley. 'What do you think, Will?'

Sergeant Middleton scratched his chin. 'I think they should not do it again . . . ' (Col felt his heart sink—they had misjudged it) ' . . . unless they're at the world championships with us. That manoeuvre should wake up a few of our competitors, raise the bar on what we get up to.'

'Yes,' said Mrs Ridley, her uncertainty vanishing as he gave the answer she wanted to hear. 'Give us a few weeks and we'll be back in touch about your training for the squad. We might have a few problems with the age limit, but then . . . Anyway, that's our problem. Leave it with us.'

'Great!' Col grinned at Skylark. Neither could believe their luck.

Captain Graves stirred. The rain was relenting and the sun peeping through a break in the clouds. 'So what about their Grade Four practical?'

'It's a hard one,' said Sergeant Middleton with a smile warming his stern face, 'but I think they might just have scraped through. What do you think, Clare?'

'Scraped through with distinction, I'd say,' she replied, nodding at Col.

Connie and Gard had retreated to the front parlour for her training that weekend. No longer allowed to go to the Mastersons'—too near the moor and the chimera in the opinion of the Trustees—she and Gard had been forced to improvise a new routine. Today they were planning the next steps for her training. She had mastered the shield, sword, and helm—they were now second nature to her—and felt fairly confident with the hauberk. The lance and the quiver and arrows were next on the list.

'So,' grumbled Gard, leafing through the notes she had made in the universal's reading room some months ago, 'how is this quiver supposed to work?'

'I think,' said Connie, leaning over to check her notes as she sat beside him on the old sofa, 'it's a way of storing small bolts of energy from encounters to use later. It sounds quite vicious actually—one of the warrior tools. The example given in the book was gorgon darts—like cold paralysing stings. Not as powerful as the real thing, of course, but enough to take out an enemy for a few minutes. It said you could do the same with any other projectile power.'

Gard raised his craggy eyebrows at her. His dark eyes gleamed under the overhang of his jutting forehead. 'And the lance?' Sitting next to him like this, Connie could smell his breath, which carried a scent like that of a sooty chimney.

'The lance is more powerful. It comes from the powers of your companion. Unlike the sword, which the universal directs on his or her own, you guide it to the target together so it takes a bit of practice. It can't be stored up like the quiver and arrows. I think I did something like this with Storm-Bird the first time we met.'

'I see.' Gard got to his feet, creaking at the knees as his legs took his formidable weight. He walked to the fireplace and stood in front of the electric fire, deep in thought. 'Can I ask you a question, Universal?'

Connie could tell he was concerned about something. 'Of course.'

He turned so he could study her face. 'Why do you want to learn more warrior tools? Are there no defensive or healing tools that you could undertake first?'

She was not sure she wanted to admit the truth to Gard, knowing he would not approve. 'Oh, I'm just following the sequence of chapters in one of the books in the library. I thought that made sense.' The book did indeed run in this order but that was not why she was doing this.

'I had a long talk with Jade a few weeks ago,' said Gard, turning back to finger the marble figurine of a white horse on the mantelpiece. 'She told me you were talking about challenging Kullervo.'

'Oh?' said Connie, trying to keep her tone light as if the subject was not of such huge importance to her.

'You would not be thinking of training yourself with a mind to taking him on?' he asked, stroking the smooth back of the horse with a chipped fingertip.

'I thought there was no harm in being prepared. I've met him three times already—I can't believe he's going to leave me alone now.'

'No, he will not. But that is very different to seeking him out, as you well know.'

Connie said nothing and looked down at her rounded writing.

The quiver—deadly against smaller foes, useful delaying attack against larger creatures. A warrior universal should keep his quiver full at all times.

'Do not try to lie to me, Universal,' said Gard, tapping the horse as if to listen for flaws in the marble. 'The uppermost layer of your mind is seething with the idea. It is pouring through you like a lava flow.'

'I just thought . . . ' began Connie, 'I just wanted to understand. If there is a way of defeating Kullervo, surely I should do everything in my power to find it?'

'No!' said Gard sharply, the word ringing in the air. 'Do not be tempted to think your skills are a match for those of the shape-shifter. Others have thought that and suffered the consequences.'

'But—'

'There are no "buts", Connie. You should not be so quick to assume that as a universal you are always right. Instinct can lead you wrong. I remember Guy de Chauliac . . . '

Connie started with surprise, before she quickly reminded herself that the few hundred years separating her from her predecessor would seem but yesterday to the rock dwarf.

'I was serving as a Trustee with my companion at the time. Guy was headstrong. A loner. The universals under his leadership had stopped offering the shared bond to the Society, wanting to keep their powers to themselves. We were riven with petty feuds and rivalries as a result. I thought I understood him: I who do not like to mix with others out of my element believed I comprehended his desire to shut his mind away from everyone else. But I was wrong. He shut himself off because he was proud, too proud to share with others even the crumbs from the banquet of his gift.'

'I think he was brave,' said Connie boldly, not liking to hear another universal criticized so harshly.

'Oh yes, he was undoubtedly brave, I do not deny that. But was he right? We had other plans to combat the Black Death. Teams had been sent to places worst hit by plague to deal with the rats. We had begun to take action. It was not only thanks to Guy de Chauliac's foolish sacrifice that the plague was stemmed.'

'But, Gard, both he and Reginald Cony felt that there was a way to defeat Kullervo. Reginald told George Brewer in those notes I showed the Trustees.'

'Ah, George Brewer,' said Gard thoughtfully, 'now he was another one. Until today, I had forgotten that I knew him.' He moved to the other side of the fireplace and picked up the bronze statue of a bear rearing on its hind legs.

'Another what?'

'Another one who thought he knew what he was doing in the teeth of all advice. He also paid with his life.'

'So who was he?' asked Connie, determined to get as many clues as she could from the rock dwarf.

'Do you not know?' said Gard, looking round the room. 'We are surrounded by pictures of him, by his things,' he held out the statue, 'and you do not know?'

Connie gazed at the tarnished bear, unpolished over the decades since Sybil Lionheart passed away. A glimmer of the truth flickered into her mind. 'He was my great-uncle? Sybil's husband?' she asked tentatively.

Gard nodded. 'A companion to great bears. A good man in his way. Brave. Clever. Resourceful. He was the obvious choice to plan the evacuation from the Arctic Circle during the last big human war.'

'What evacuation?'

'Kullervo was using the chaos to feed his rebellion. Creatures were angry; they choked in the city smogs; they revolted at the cruel waste of lives as mankind slaughtered each other. We knew that the Earth cried out under the burden men had placed on her. Kullervo did not find it hard to find recruits to the army he was massing in the north. Those who would not join him had to flee. Amongst them were many of George Brewer's great bears. He helped them escape to Scandinavia and northern Canada.'

'So how did George die? How was Kullervo stopped?' Connie examined the picture of the young man holding her great-aunt's arm outside the church where they had just been married. His expression was purposeful, determined. She could see how he might have come to be chosen to wrestle with the most difficult challenges.

'He was a great friend of Reginald Cony, as you know. Reggie told me that George led a team to confront Kullervo to negotiate the release of the creatures still trapped behind Kullervo's lines. It appears he also thought they could win some of the creatures back to their side and defeat Kullervo.'

'And what happened?' Connie did not have a good feeling about the answer.

'They were all taken by Kullervo. Every single one. A useless sacrifice. It has gone down in the annals of the Society as our Charge of the Light Brigade into the enemy's guns. The creatures they had gone to save were released soon after: Kullervo has no desire to harm his fellow creatures, only humans.'

Only humans, thought Connie. A creature that relished all natural forms but one.

'And it seems from the notes you found that George Brewer had other ideas we did not know about. He was thinking of mounting a challenge himself and he not even a universal!' Gard put the statue back on the mantelpiece with a clunk.

'This house has already offered up one victim to Kullervo; I do not want to hear of a second.'

Connie shivered. She did not want to be a victim, but wasn't she that already? Kullervo had done enough damage to her over the last few years—invaded the most secret places in her mind; now he had sent the chimera to maim and kill her. If she just sat back as the Trustees advised and let others deal with the situation, she would be powerless to resist his next attack.

'But what if all of them—Guy, George, Reginald, Edward Alleyne—were on to something? Don't you think we should at least find out what it was?'

'They failed. They took grave risks and failed. Think no more about this, Universal.'

Connie felt something build in her chest. No one seemed to understand! Her gut instinct was that this was a trail worth following but every time she tried the Society erected barriers in her way. They were fighting a losing battle, support bleeding away as creatures lost confidence. Did the Society expect her to live out her life with Kullervo taunting her in her dreams, to be content like them to weaken bit by bit until she was no use to anyone? Kullervo wanted her to meet him at the mark. He expected her there.

'If he wants you there then that is all the more

reason for you not to go,' said Gard firmly. She had neglected to raise her shield and had forgotten that Gard had access to her superficial layers of thought at that moment. 'This is no joke, Universal. The Trustees have ruled on this. If you go against them, if you follow this path any further, there will be penalties.'

'What kind of penalties?'

'You will be banned from access to the universal's reading room. Your training will stop. You might even be suspended from membership of the Society.'

Connie gave a bleak laugh. 'Oh, we've been there before, Gard, or is everyone's memory so short?'

'Yes,' said Gard, his voice deadly serious, 'we remember. But then you were acquitted—you had been wrongly blamed for something you could not control. But this you do control. You are not a little child, Connie: you are old enough to take the consequences of your actions if you disobey the rules in this way.'

She made no reply but remembered this time to raise the shield so he could not hear the chorus of rebellious protests that had struck up in her head. If there was a way of defeating Kullervo, she had to find it. She could not live with his mark inside her for the rest of her life, threatening at any moment to swallow her up. The others may not see it, but this was a slow torture that would exhaust her as surely as Guy de Chauliac had been worn out by Kullervo all those years ago. Society rules or no Society rules, she was not going to stop asking questions. She would take the consequences when they came.

'So, shall we continue?' said Gard. He took her notebook and leafed through the pages. 'Why not study the portcullis? That looks a useful defence.'

Connie nodded mutely.

'Let us begin,' said Gard.

10
Candles

Autumn was passing swiftly. As the trees shed their leaves, becoming more ragged and skeletal each day, Connie found her mood becoming grimmer and more determined.

'What do you think, Connie?' Evelyn asked, levering open the can of paint in the middle of the empty guest room. This was about to be converted into a nursery.

Connie almost laughed when she saw the green paint Evelyn had picked out. It was exactly the same shade as the moor when the grass was lush and flourishing in spring. 'Very nice,' she said, returning to her task of scraping off the old wallpaper. 'What are you going to do about those?' She gestured to the cans of blue paint Mack had bought.

'Horrible colour, don't you think?' said Evelyn, sniffing disapprovingly at the tins. 'Not right for a baby.'

'Oh, I don't know,' said Connie lightly, 'the colour has a fresh, seaside feel to it.'

'But I'm sure the baby'll be much happier with some earthy greens,' said Evelyn with determination, dipping in her paint brush and letting the syrupy mixture drip back into the pot.

Connie could see that the nursery could quickly become a new battleground for Evelyn and Mack if she did not think of something.

'I think he's afraid you'll make the baby into a banshee companion if you have it all your way,' Connie said as tactfully as she could. 'That's why he's given you the blue.'

'What's wrong with being a banshee companion?' asked Evelyn sharply.

'Nothing,' Connie said quickly. 'But he wants to restore the balance. I wouldn't be surprised if he tries to get you to go swimming with the Kraken to even up the odds.'

'Funny you should say that.' Evelyn dropped the brush onto the paint tray. 'I refused, of course. I told him it was way too cold to go swimming, let alone go anywhere near the Kraken.' She seemed to be lost in thought for a moment, thinking about Mack and his perspective on their child. It seemed to Connie a good moment to suggest a compromise.

'Well, who said the room has to be one colour?' Connie asked. 'Isn't that a bit boring? Why not paint part of it green and part of it blue? You could do a moorland wall and a sea wall.'

If there was one thing Evelyn did not like, it was to be accused of being boring. 'You know, Connie, I think you're right. But you'll have to do the blue. The colour makes me feel seasick. I'll do the green.'

'It's a deal.'

They finished preparing the surfaces and began to paint. Connie enjoyed the soothing rhythm of wiping the brush up and down on the wall with Evelyn doing the same beside her. It was rather like tapping stones with a rock dwarf.

'Do you know anything about Aunt Sybil's husband?' she asked, her mind quick to circle back to the subject that had now consumed her for months.

If Evelyn was surprised by the sudden introduction of this subject, she did not show it. 'Oh, not much: he died long before I was born.'

'Didn't Sybil talk about him?' persisted Connie, thinking that if she could manage it without Evelyn and Mack noticing she would stencil a seagull over her waves to sneak in an element of the High Flyers.

'Of course. She had been very much in love with him but they were only married six months before he was killed.'

'How did he die? Did she say?'

Evelyn put down her brush. The temperature in the room seemed to have suddenly dropped a few degrees. 'I told you once. He was taken by Kullervo.'

'Is that all you know?' asked Connie, pretending not to notice her aunt's suspicious looks.

'Connie, why are you asking me all this?'

'I just want to know. I think it might be important.'

'How important?' Evelyn had still not resumed painting. She had her full attention on her niece.

'You know, don't you?' Connie replied, laying her brush down on the edge of the tin and wiping her hands on the old shirt she was wearing.

'Know what?'

'About my argument with the Trustees.' The words that had remained unspoken between them for months finally emerged.

Evelyn nodded.

'And you agree with them?'

Evelyn sat back on her heels, shifting the unaccustomed weight of the baby from her knees.

'I agree that you must not even think about challenging Kullervo, but . . . '

'But?' asked Connie eagerly.

'But I don't think you should be stopped from finding out all you can about defending yourself against him. You've had to fight him already and, though I hate to say it, will probably have to do so again.'

Connie felt a rush of gratitude towards her aunt. She wished she had spoken to her sooner. She should never have forgotten that Evelyn had been the first to defy the Trustees when the Society had expelled her last year.

'And you'll not stop me? Not report me?'

Evelyn smiled and picked up the brush again. 'Do you really think you live in a house where any of us will go running to the Society to tell tales? Even if I didn't agree with what you were doing, I'd never do that. I'd pack you off to your parents first. That'd keep you out of trouble.'

Connie grimaced. 'Thanks.'

'What's more, I want to help you. I'll give you all that I know about George Brewer if that's any use.'

'Brilliant! So what do you know?'

Evelyn took a bundle of old letters out from under her painting smock. 'I thought we might get round to discussing this today. If you hadn't raised it, I was going to. So I got these out for you.' She handed them over to Connie.

'Can I read them now?' asked Connie.

'They've waited over sixty years: they can wait a bit longer. We've got a room to prepare. But you can keep them as long as you need.'

'OK,' said Connie reluctantly, tucking them into her pocket. She turned back to the wall. Now where should she put the siren? Flying with the seagull or on the rock with the dragon?

Connie and Evelyn got quite carried away with the mural in the baby's room. By the end of the day it resembled nothing so much as a miniature version of the library in the Society's headquarters: a riot of creatures swimming, flying, and running. Evelyn was a bit scornful of the seascape at Connie's end, but Mack loved it. He thumped Connie enthusiastically on the back when he came in, making her spill paint all over his boots.

'And I left you the Kraken to do,' said Connie handing him the brush and a tin of black paint. 'There's a space in the centre.'

'Right!' said Mack, rolling up his sleeves. 'Time to watch the master at work.'

'Master!' protested Evelyn, gesturing at her

beautifully drawn circle of dancing banshees. 'So what's this?'

'The work of an inspired amateur,' replied Mack with a roguish grin.

Connie slipped upstairs. The letters had been burning a hole in her back pocket all day. She could wait no longer to read them.

Sitting on her bed, picking the speckles of paint off her arms absent-mindedly, Connie read her way through the small bundle of letters. Most of them were badly weathered as if they had passed through many a storm on their way from the Arctic to England. They smelt faintly of wood smoke. George's writing was how she pictured him: firm and resolute, commanding the reader's attention as it strode confidently across the paper. It was not until she reached the last letter sent from 'somewhere in the Arctic Circle' that she found something to justify her intrusion on the past.

Dearest Sybil,

I write this in the knowledge that it is possibly my last letter to you. Either because I will succeed and be back with you very soon or . . . well we both know what might happen to either of us during these terrible times.

I received a letter from Reggie with the first instalment of notes. I expect he told you about

*them before he was called up. I was right! It does
seem that the key to combating the cursed creature
is to survive the transformations until he adopts
one that is weak. If you last long enough, he's
bound to do this under the rules of the combat
that he laid down. In his pride, he has declared
that he has to keep changing form in answer to
every counter-attack. Surely, eventually one of
these will be something you can defeat?*

*I've been waiting for further information from
Reggie but I don't know where he is.*

Connie sat up: of course, the letter he was
waiting for had never been sent! It had been left
in the library.

*If I know the army, they've probably packed him
off to some training camp in the middle of
nowhere where he's completely out of touch with
the Society. Do you know where he is? We can't
wait much longer as Kullervo is on the move and
approaching our positions. We were thinking that
between us we should be able to keep him at bay
long enough. We have creatures and companions
from every company here. Bruin is eager to take
him on—you know what the bears are like!—and I
must say I feel the same. If we don't hear from
Reggie soon, we'll just have to do our best, even
without the advice of our universal.*

The griffin that carries this also brings my love.

It is a good show that love weighs nothing or he would not be able to fly with the extra burden! Keep safe.

Your loving husband,
George.

Connie could have wept as she put down the letter. Foolish, stupid, brave George: of course he didn't stand a chance. You can't keep Kullervo 'at bay' with only a few teeth and claws. The universal's mental tools were the only powers strong enough to keep him in check for any length of time. George had led others into a trap. Kullervo had probably crowed with delight as he saw them sledge their way to their deaths. Poor Sybil.

Moving to the window, Connie looked out into the darkness. She hoped she would never be so headstrong as to lead so many others to a pointless death. No, if she risked anything, it should be her own life and not that of her friends. Perhaps it was just as well that she was in this alone. It should be between her and Kullervo—no one else. But when had he ever transformed into anything weak? Had George really been right? He was hardly likely to turn into a beetle for her to stamp on, was he? If there was a way, this wasn't it. George had found that out at the cost of his life. In her plans to fight him, she had reached a dead end.

* * *

Connie was on her way back to London again, this time for Liam's birthday party. Unlike the hot sunny day when she had last been to the Society Headquarters, she was looking out of the train on a wet, chilly landscape. Not a proper winter's day, she thought to herself, no satisfying showers of snow, just a damp smudge of a day. Mack and Simon sat opposite her doing the end of year sports' quiz in the paper. But this time there was no Col to join in, no enthusiastic voice to shout out the answers and tease Simon that his team were in the relegation zone.

Connie traced his name on the window. She missed him badly. She wanted to tell him about her preparations even if he did disapprove, hear about his training, just be with him, but Col had barely been in Hescombe since joining the British team. The selection had changed Col, she thought. He had renewed confidence in himself, able to be more generous about other people's gifts, including her own, now he felt secure in his. The team was a very good thing for him—the only down side being that it had taken him away just at the time when she needed him. Not that she had ever plucked up the courage to admit it to him.

Before going to Liam's birthday party, the Lionhearts and Mack called in at the Headquarters to visit the library. Connie had a book to return and wanted to look up some new tools in the universals' reading room—'Before I'm banned,' she added under her breath. Simon did not mind the diversion as he was pleased by the fuss made over him by the porter.

'I've heard about you, son,' the porter said, holding out the book for Simon to sign. 'Two companies, eh? How many badges have they given you?'

Simon proudly showed off his horse and lizard badges, which he had pinned to the centre of his jumper.

'Treating you all right, are they, those Sea-Snakes?' the porter continued. 'If in doubt, you stick with us Two-Fours.'

A companion to the cerberi, the three-headed guard dog, Connie realized, the shadow of the porter's gift appearing in her mind's eye.

'Watch it, mate,' said Mack good-humouredly as he buffed up his own lizard badge.

The porter was now used to Connie's presence so made no comment as she signed herself in.

'You know where to go,' he said, waving them off. 'Upstairs. First floor.'

'I'll meet you in the café,' Connie said to her two companions. 'Give me an hour.'

She ran up the stairs two at a time and then pushed the door open to the library. The light seeped into the chamber from the lantern dome, giving the room an underwater feel, like a sea-grotto. This close to Christmas there were few readers. A couple of pale faces were raised on her entrance, blinking over their books at her like creatures disturbed from under their stone in a rock pool. Mr Dove was sitting at his desk in the centre of the room, nodding over a thick volume. Connie walked up to him and put *The History of the Society* softly on the desk in front of him. He started awake as if she had slammed it down and glared over the edge of the counter. Connie was for a brief moment reminded of the snake that guarded the universal's reading room. When he saw who it was, however, his expression changed and he smiled pleasantly at her.

'So sorry, Miss Lionheart. I should not have been asleep. You caught me unawares. Was this any good?' He held up the book she had just returned.

'Yes, very helpful, thank you.'

'Funny bunch, your lot, weren't they?' he asked conversationally as he checked the book back into the library records.

'My lot?'

'The universals. Got into a lot of hot water. A dangerous crowd, if you ask me. It's nice to have you with us, of course, but it's probably just as well there's only one of you.'

Here it was again: the prejudice against the universals. She had met it in its extreme form in Mr Coddrington, but she was surprised to hear it from the mild Mr Dove. But she wasn't here to pick an argument.

'The key, please,' she said, holding out her hand. It would be a relief to get away from all the other members. No wonder the universals had shut themselves away if they had to deal with critical comments like this all the time.

Then a thought struck her.

'Mr Dove, can I look up a creature in your index, please?' she asked.

'No,' he said, shaking his head, but added quickly when he saw her disappointment, 'only because I have to do that for you. It's the rules.'

'Rules?'

'Well, there are some restrictions on particular creatures, you know.'

'No, I didn't.'

'It's to stop unscrupulous companions taking advantage of prey, you see. For example, if you were a companion to the Scylla, we might want to ask why you were interested in finding out all there was to know about the selkies. Or a fire imp companion about a water sprite. Do you get the idea?'

Connie felt relieved. That was all right then.

'That wouldn't apply to me, surely?'

Mr Dove reached over for the volume she had seen once before when he had brought it before the Trustees. 'I suppose not. But rules are rules and even the universals are under some restrictions. What do you want to know?'

Connie cleared her throat. 'Are there any books about Kullervo?'

'Ah.' Mr Dove put the book back on the shelf behind him. 'We seem to have hit on one of those restrictions immediately.' When she said nothing, he added. 'I'm under instructions not to divulge that information to you at the present time.'

'Says who?' she asked angrily, though she already knew.

'I've an order here from the Trustees. The restriction is to last until—'

'Until they think I can be trusted,' Connie finished for him bitterly.

Mr Dove gave her a sympathetic nod and leaned forward over his desk to whisper to her. 'I personally do not approve of the decision—quite unfair to stop the spread of knowledge.' He glanced around to check they were not being overheard. 'But might I point out that the order does not say you cannot look at the books? Who's to say that you did not stumble across the right work quite by chance when you were look-ing in the central shelves of the universal's read-ing room under "C".' He gave her a ghost of a wink, sat back quickly and said more loudly, 'So you understand that I have absolutely no choice but to refuse to look that creature up for you.'

Connie gave him a grateful smile. 'I under-stand. Thank you.'

Mr Dove held out the universal's key on its blue ribbon. Connie was about to take it when the door to the library banged open, disturbing the centuries' thick layers of peace that had accu-mulated in this chamber.

'Stop!' shouted Mr Coddrington, striding purposefully across the room. The sleepy readers sat up, staring at the little group clustered around the central desk.

'Mr Coddrington!' protested the librarian. 'What is the meaning of this? How dare you burst in here like an ill-mannered great boar?'

Connie went cold, recognizing her enemy on the warpath again.

'Stop right there, Universal! Don't give her the key, Dove!' cried Mr Coddrington, thrusting himself between them.

'Whyever not? It's hers to take—it's her right,' said Mr Dove stubbornly. The key swayed in his grip like a pendulum. Connie was tempted to grab it and make a dash for her reading room. Mr Coddrington would not dare pursue her past the snake; he wouldn't be able to put a foot over the threshold.

Mr Coddrington swung round to glare at Connie as if he could guess her thoughts. His pale face was flushed with two bright spots high on his cheeks.

'Thank goodness that I found out she had slunk into the building. At least some of us are not lax about our duties!'

Mr Dove sniffed at the implied criticism. 'I had not heard that Miss Lionheart was to be denied entry, Assessor. I did not know that your zeal to persecute the universal had reached that height.'

Mr Coddrington turned back to the librarian. Connie noticed that most of the readers had left their places and come to stand in a ring around the desk. She met the gaze of one—an elderly woman with glasses dangling from a chain—and was dismayed to find that she was staring at her with a far from friendly expression.

Mr Coddrington dug inside his jacket pocket and pulled out a piece of paper which he brandished under Mr Dove's nose.

'Read this, Librarian. You'll find I have here an order, signed by all the Trustees, to ban the universal access to the reading room with immediate effect.'

Connie's heart plummeted.

'It took a lot of lobbying to get this much, I can tell you,' continued Mr Coddrington, addressing the audience of readers, 'but I managed finally to convince them after vividly representing the consequences of a lack of vigilance against her unguarded activities.'

Mr Dove gave Connie an apologetic glance and gingerly took the paper. He spread it out on the desk in front of him and bent over to read it.

'Well? You see I have the authority,' snapped Mr Coddrington, shooting Connie a triumphant look.

Mr Dove cleared his throat. 'It does appear to be as you say,' he admitted. He turned the paper over, paused, then smiled. 'But you seem to have forgotten something, Assessor. The paper has to be countersigned by the Senior Librarian. She is—unfortunately—away today and I am afraid I really do not feel that I have the *authority* to sign for her in her absence on so weighty a matter. It therefore would appear that the order has not yet come into effect.'

'But—!' spluttered Mr Coddrington.

'I know, Assessor, that you would be the first to recognize the importance of following such protocols to the letter,' continued Mr Dove, enjoying himself immensely. 'We have to observe the proper channels or where would we be, eh? I'm sure I've heard you talk on this subject numerous times in the past.' He held out the key to Connie.

'Damn the proper channels,' cursed the assessor, his face apoplectic with rage. He pointed an accusing finger at Connie. 'She's a danger to us all. She's got to be stopped.'

'But not by me—not until I have a direct order from my superior,' said Mr Dove calmly. 'And as far as I remember, the New Members' Department has no authority over the Library.' He placed the key in Connie's hand.

Seizing her chance, Connie shouldered her way through the murmuring crowd and fled for the safety of the snake-guarded stairwell before someone else tried to stop her. She had forgiven Mr Dove for his earlier slight against the universals. It was nice to know that she still had one or two allies in the Society.

Mrs Khalid had organized Liam's first ever birthday celebration, complete with games, presents, and cake. At home Liam was lucky if his parents remembered and they had never got round to inviting any of his friends over. When Mrs Khalid learned this, she had decided his eighth birthday would have to make up for all the ones he had missed in the past. Liam had made a surprising number of Society friends over the last four months and the room was packed.

Coming straight from the confrontation in the library, it took Connie a while to relax. She had not mentioned the scene to Mack or Simon, but after an hour she had begun to feel that here at least she was among people who liked her and did not fear her. Still, she felt too ashamed to admit to anyone that the Trustees had banned her from the reading room.

'Cake! Cake! Cake!' chanted Ahmed and Omar, Mrs Khalid's sons.

There was a burst of applause as Mrs Khalid emerged from the kitchen bearing aloft in triumph a three-tiered cake.

'Where are the candles?' called out Antonia from the corner next to Connie.

'Ah ha!' said Mrs Khalid, producing eight big candles from the inside of her robes like a magician pulling rabbits from a top hat.

'They're too big to go on the cake,' Antonia said to Connie.

'I don't think they're for the cake,' Connie replied with a smile.

Mrs Khalid placed her creation in the centre of the dining room table and then stuck the candles in eight holders around it.

'Omar, are you ready?' she asked her elder son, a tall, handsome boy with long black hair swept back from his face. He nodded. 'Lee-am, are you ready?' she said, turning to the pink-faced birthday boy.

'Yes!' he replied.

Mrs Khalid took a taper and lit each candle, hissing under her breath. 'Let game begin!' she said, stepping back.

Liam stood on a stool and cupped his hands round the first candle, a look of concentration on his face. When he took his hands away, Connie could see there was now a little fire imp dancing there. He swiftly moved round the table, summoning an imp to dance in each of the eight flames.

'Omar.' Mrs Khalid nodded to her son.

Omar stepped forward, flicking back his floppy fringe of dark hair. He hollowed his hands around his mouth and blew as if on an invisible horn. Connie sensed a rushing and tingling in the room. She looked up and saw the pale outline of a sylph, or wind sprite, burst into the room and circle overhead like a wheeling bird. Its body formed of nothing more than air, it shimmered against the ceiling, its long hair rippling out behind it. Ragged wings streamed like a tattered pennant in its wake. She nudged Antonia.

'Up there,' she said. Antonia looked up but could not spot it. 'Look for the ripples as it passes in front of something.'

'Ah yes. I see it now!' said Antonia, catching a glimpse of long legs brushing past the curtains.

The sylph darted down to the candles and blew hard at the first one Liam had lit. Connie could see the imp struggling in the wind, shaking its fist furiously at the sylph, red sparks shooting ineffectually against its enemy. In a blink of an eye, the fire imp puffed out of sight: its flame extinguished.

'No, I put out the candles, not you!' Liam was calling. The sylph, however, was too much for one boy to cope with and had extinguished half the candles by the time Liam had rekindled two. 'Connie! Help!' he appealed to the universal to come to his rescue.

'Go on, Connie!' said Antonia, pushing her up. 'You're needed.'

With a grin Connie waited for the sylph to fly near her. As it passed, she caught a puff of wind and stored it in her quiver. As the sylph dipped to the cake, Connie released her arrow. The sprite was blown off course to become entangled with the curtains. The audience cheered. The delay gave Liam enough time to relight his last candle.

'I win!' he shouted exultantly.

'You win,' conceded Omar, ruffling Liam's hair with brotherly affection.

The companion to the sylphs then strode up to Connie to congratulate her. He gave her a playful bow. 'Victory is yours, Universal. How did you do it?'

'Thanks. It was an arrow from the universal's quiver,' she explained. He raised one black eyebrow quizzically. 'A mental tool. I've been practising it recently. You catch some power and throw it back.'

'Let's sing so the birthday boy can blow out his candles,' roared Mack over the noise of the crowd.

When 'Happy Birthday' had died unmelodiously away, Liam stood on a stool, snapped his fingers and instantly all the imps disappeared, taking the flames with them.

'No need for wind as a fire imp companion,' he said proudly. Mrs Khalid applauded him enthusiastically from the kitchen door.

'Well done, Lee-am,' she called.

After slicing the cake into huge uneven slabs, Liam pushed his way through his guests to present Connie with the first slice.

'Here you are!' he said, thrusting it at her. 'Thanks for your help just now.'

'Any time,' she said, licking the icing off her fingers. 'I see your training is going well.'

'It's fantastic. Mamma Khalid says we can meet some of the big ones in spring. She wondered if we could come down your way to do it. Not enough space in her back garden, she says.'

'Of course. I'm sure Col and his grandmother can put you up,' Connie replied.

Simon came over. 'Well done, Liam. Those fire imps were cool.'

Liam glowed under the praise. 'How's the Athenian lion-goat-snake thing?' he asked.

'Nemean lion,' Simon corrected him. 'Very interesting. The Trustees think I might be ready to encounter the chimera soon. Can't keep Connie shut up in Hescombe much longer, can we?'

Liam looked up at Connie who had turned very pale. 'They've shut you up?'

'Not exactly. I'm not allowed out on the moor,' she explained. That familiar feeling of sick dread had returned. She looked at Simon's happy face and wondered how he could be so blasé about the prospect of encountering the chimera. But then, he did not know what he was letting himself in for, did he?

'What've you done wrong?' Liam asked.

'Nothing,' said Simon, 'there's just this great, dirty brute out there that wants to eat her.'

Liam looked shocked. 'Do you want me to set a fire imp on it for you, Connie?' he asked.

'Thanks, Liam. But not this time,' Connie said. She had to change the subject before she rowed with Simon again about what he was doing. 'Here, we've got you a present.' She dug in her bag and handed him a box. 'It's from all of us in Hescombe.' Liam ripped off the coverings and took out a mobile phone. 'Let us know when you need a top-up. 999 calls are free, I believe, if ever you need the fire brigade,' she added.

11
Portcullis

'I don't think I can get any further without practising,' said Connie to her mentor. 'I now know what to do in theory, but I've got to try it out on someone.'

'What about me, Universal?' suggested Gard, looking up from the notebook they had been studying together in the front parlour.

There was every chance that on the first few attempts she would fail to drop the portcullis in time and Connie knew she would very much prefer not to allow Gard through her defences. He might stumble upon the armoury she had been amassing in secret. In addition to the sword, shield, helm, and hauberk he knew about, she had added the quiver, bow and arrows, the lance, and most recently the mace—a crude tool she did not like using but she had to admit it was effective in smashing through most barriers. If he saw those, he would know in an instant that she had not obeyed the Trustees in abandoning the idea of challenging Kullervo.

'How about Sentinel?' she countered. 'He'd like that.' She could also trust the minotaur to guard the secrets of her mind labyrinth closer than she kept them herself.

Gard nodded. 'You are right. He would be a good subject for the test. Where is he now?'

Connie dipped into her mind and sensed the minotaur concealed in a cave along the cliff not far from Number Five. This was his favoured evening lookout post from where he could mount an effective watch over the universal, being within call. As the cave was so close to Hescombe, he had been disturbed on several occasions by unwary walkers on the beach but had so far managed to scare them away by menacing bellowing and stamping. Locally, the cave had gained the reputation of being haunted. The tourist information centre had even produced a leaflet on the subject that Sentinel had proudly tacked to the wall of his chamber in the abandoned tin mine.

'He's close by. Shall we go to him?'

209

'Yes. It would be good to get outdoors,' Gard agreed.

Connie went first, checking that the coast was clear. The dark January evening had deterred most people from leaving their warm houses: Hescombe had a cosy, battened-down-for-the-night feel to it. Lights shone in the houses along the quayside. There was no one around to see the rock dwarf slip down onto the beach and crunch his way along to the cave with Connie at his side.

'Sentinel?' Connie called into the chilly blackness of the cavern, a deep groove in the liver-red rock face where the sandstone had been worn away by the churning of the waves. After a few more decades of attack, the sea might well succeed in punching its way through to form an arch, but so far it had only hollowed out a small chamber—at low tide, a place of rock pools and slippery seaweed; at high tide, an ever-moving floor of foam. Fortunately, tonight the tide was out, though Connie knew the minotaur had spent many nights of devoted service standing up to his waist in the surge.

'Universal,' answered the minotaur, emerging at the mouth of the cave. His tawny hide matched the colour of the sandstone that surrounded him, acting as a further camouflage. He bowed low.

'I am at your command.' He then turned to the rock dwarf. 'Brother, you are welcome.'

Gard returned the minotaur's bow. 'We have come to ask you to assist the universal with her training. She needs to practise a new defence called the portcullis. Will you help?'

'Of course,' said Sentinel, gesturing to them to take seats on the fallen rocks that littered the entrance to his temporary abode. 'What is this portcullis?'

'It's a way of trapping an enemy when he has penetrated your first line of defence,' explained Connie. 'If I do it right, you should not be able to get beyond the entrance to my mind in an encounter and be caught there until I release you.'

Sentinel snorted, white plumes of hot breath puffing from his nostrils into the cold winter sky. 'Trap me? You think you are strong enough to contain a minotaur?'

Connie laughed. 'I've no idea. That's why I need to practise.'

'We should begin,' said Gard. 'The universal is cold.'

It was true. Her feet were frozen. A flake of snow fluttered out of the cloudy sky and settled on her knee.

'OK. Are you ready, Sentinel?' asked Connie. The minotaur nodded. In unison they closed their eyes to enter the shadow world of the encounter. Connie had hardly a moment to gather her thoughts before Sentinel came charging up to the portal to her mind and burst through.

'Not fair!' she exclaimed, breaking the encounter off quickly before he was able to enter too far into her thoughts. 'You gave me no time!'

Sentinel gave a bellow of laughter. 'An enemy does not wait for his adversary to be ready, Universal. Try again.'

She looked at him suspiciously. From the smug smile on his face, she guessed he had plenty more surprises in store.

'Again,' she agreed.

Closing her eyes, she rushed to be there first. On this occasion, the shadow-minotaur did not dash in; he stood waiting outside, pacing to and fro with his hands behind his back as if he had all the time in the world before making his move, his tail swishing lazily behind him. She knew what he was doing: he was waiting till she got bored or lost concentration. That would not do. She had a few tricks of her own up her sleeve that no one else knew about. It was time to play them.

'OK. Drawbridge,' she muttered. Mentally cranking on the winch that had appeared by the gate, she raised a heavy bridge out of the mists that surrounded the entrance, forcing the startled

Sentinel further in and cutting off his retreat. He made a dash for the gate. Connie had to abandon her drawbridge half-raised to cut the rope holding up the portcullis. It came crashing down, trapping Sentinel between the bridge and the strong lattice of the gate. The minotaur gave a bellow and charged back the way he had come, clambering nimbly up the sloping bridge and flinging himself over its lip to drop clear on the other side. Connie ended the encounter again.

'That was an improvement, Universal. The drawbridge was a clever move but you must be faster if you want to catch a minotaur,' Sentinel said, raising his curved horns proudly.

'Drawbridge?' asked Gard curiously.

'Er, just a little innovation of my own,' said Connie quickly. 'The two parts of the portcullis are hard to drop quickly enough to catch the attacker. Even with the bridge, I didn't manage it.' She could feel Gard's gaze on her but she looked down at her feet, refusing to meet his eye.

'One more attempt?' asked Sentinel, clearly relishing the challenge.

Connie nodded.

They were both ready swiftly this time. Sentinel had decided to play this one straight so charged at the portal. He crossed the threshold. Crash! Connie released the inner portcullis stopping any forward progress. Like lightning, Sentinel turned to retreat. Crash! The second gate clunked into place. She had trapped him. Undeterred, he threw himself at the gate to test its strength. It shivered, but held firm. He then charged the inner gate, horns lowered for maximum impact. The bull's head collided with the bars and a dull clang echoed around the gateway, but the portcullis stood firm.

'Very good, Universal,' the shadow-minotaur called out to his host. 'I let you catch me, of course, to see if I could break out.'

The gateway rumbled with teasing laughter. Sentinel rested against the iron-lattice, gazing in on the mindscape to which he had been barred entry.

'What are those?' he asked, pointing to the weapons Connie now had always ready by the entrance in case of need. She had forgotten they would be visible even from the gateway, arrayed in rows so that she could seize them quickly should she be attacked. Dismayed, she ended the encounter.

When she opened her eyes, she found Sentinel staring at her, his dark brown eyes reflecting the lights of Hescombe behind her. 'What did I see?' he asked her.

Connie felt uncomfortable under the scrutiny

of her two companions. 'That's my business, Sentinel. Can I have no secrets?'

He bowed. 'I will keep your secrets, but will you not explain them even to me?'

'What secrets?' asked Gard sharply.

Sentinel said nothing, ignoring the dwarf. Connie shook her head. 'Don't ask me, Gard.'

'But it is my duty to ask you,' Gard said, his fists clenched on his knees. She could tell he was angry with her and had guessed why she had chosen Sentinel to test her defences rather than him.

But it was too late to worry about his feelings. What about hers? Connie was sick of even her innermost thoughts being patrolled by the Society. Was nothing about her private? If she could not call her mind her own, she was nothing. 'Is there a rule that says that the universals have no right to their own thoughts?' she asked.

'No. But you know why I ask. If you will not tell me, I will have to ask our friend. Sentinel, did you see anything that suggests the universal is preparing to challenge Kullervo?'

Sentinel reared backwards in surprise. He had seen her armoury, of course, but had not realized she was amassing it for so serious a purpose. Connie turned pleading eyes to Sentinel, willing him not to fail her.

215

'I will not betray the secrets of the labyrinth,' he said finally but with evident reluctance.

'So you did see something?' Gard persisted.

'I say nothing.'

Gard stood up. 'Universal, this is most serious. After all our discussions, you know what will happen if I discover proof that you have gone against the will of the Trustees.'

'You have no proof,' said Connie quietly, hating that she was setting herself against him in this way.

'Then show me what the minotaur saw. Prove your innocence.'

'My mind and my thoughts are my own. You have no right to ask me that.'

'I have no right but, out of friendship, I ask you to do this, to put my mind at rest.'

She got to her feet and turned to face out of the entrance. 'Look, it's beginning to snow. I'd better get back. Thank you for your help, Sentinel. Thank you, Gard.' Quickly, she left the shelter of the cave and ran home along the high tide mark, the snow whirling around her like a swarm of white bees, melting as the flakes hit the salty pebbles. She felt terrible turning away from Gard like that but his mind would not have been 'put at rest', as he called it, by an encounter with her. No one should see what Sentinel had glimpsed tonight. Her refusal to clear herself might well mean she would incur further penalties from the Trustees. If she let any creature encounter her, she might well end up in even hotter water. There was nothing for it: she would have to keep herself to herself for a while and avoid all encounters.

When she reached home, she clattered through the kitchen, barely acknowledging Evelyn's and Mack's greetings, shouting something about needing to change into dry clothes. In the sanctuary of her room, she stripped off her outer layers and dived under her duvet, only now feeling safe from intrusion. Feet off the ground, Gard would not be able to follow her.

Noticing that in her hurry she had pushed her private notebook off the bed, she leaned over to pick it up. She had started keeping a second record of all the knowledge she knew she was not supposed to have. It contained her practice records on the forbidden weapons, as well as the notes she had taken in the universal's reading room on Kullervo on her last visit. She flicked through the pages to remind herself exactly why she was risking so much to follow this path and to bolster her resolve that she should, against her natural inclination, disappoint so many friends. The book Mr Dove had directed her to had confirmed her fears. She should not have

217

been surprised to find that Reginald Cony had been the author—of course, he would want to pass on the lessons his contemporaries had learned at such a heavy cost. The manuscript was not complete—it was a sketchy history of what was known about the shape-shifter, including a list of the known forms he adopted. From her own experience, she could add a few more. Reading it through, she realized that Reginald had been waiting in hope of hearing of one that could be defeated—some weakness in Kullervo's repertoire—but as far as Connie could see all of them were equally formidable. Indeed, what Reginald had missed (he had never confronted Kullervo, Connie reminded herself) was that Kullervo's real strength lay in his ability to shift between his forms. It was not a single shape that was strong, it was the sum of them.

Reginald's introduction which she had copied down confirmed her fears and justified her course of action to her:

While his shape is ever-changing, Kullervo remains constant in one thing. He will seek you out, my fellow universal. You must be prepared. He has attacked humanity throughout our history and I believe his next assault will come soon. Mercifully, Kullervo has never found me. I have been too well protected and maybe my powers are too weak to tempt him but even I in my old age must not be complacent. Perhaps it is safest for humanity if the universal gift does indeed die out as it seems to have done in my lifetime, but it goes against the grain to wish for the extinction of any creature. If anyone does read this account it means that the gift did not end with me. Be careful. Do not commit the same mistakes as I and my friends made. Be wise.

Wise? Connie put her notebook aside. The only thing she knew was that she knew very little.

Connie had not seen Col at all during the Christmas holidays and it was not until the day before they returned to school that she ran into him at Jerrard's, the bakery on the High Street. She'd been sent out to buy some bread; he was there stocking up on filled croissants before leaving for his training.

The bell rang as she entered the shop but Col did not look round as he was busy paying for his purchases.

'What'll you have today, love?' asked Mrs Jerrard, bustling forward to serve Connie.

'A sliced wholemeal, please,' Connie said. Col turned on hearing her voice, a full paper bag clutched under his arm. 'Hi, Col.'

'Connie! How are you?' He waited for her to

finish at the counter and followed her out. 'I've not seen you for ages.'

'No, you haven't. I know you've been busy.'

He looked guiltily pleased with himself. 'You could say that. It's been frantic.'

'I like the jacket.'

Col turned a little self-consciously to show off what only a Society member would recognize as his team strip. 'Thanks.'

'Tell me all about it.'

He glanced at his watch. He really should be going, but he hadn't had a chance to speak to her for so long he couldn't just walk away. Besides, he'd heard rumours that all was not well between her and Gard. He quickly filled in details of the rigorous schedule he and Skylark had been given, the weekends on Exmoor, the plans for a trip to the Alpine training at Easter.

'Sounds brilliant.' Connie felt a little sad that his new role was taking him away from Hescombe, but she wouldn't allow herself to feel envious. She only wanted what was best for him and this was clearly it.

'How about you, Connie?'

'Same old thing, you know.'

'Meaning?' He pulled her over to a bench in the bus shelter.

'Meaning everyone's convinced I'm reckless,

I'm grounded, not allowed out of Hescombe and I've been banned from my reading room.'

'What!'

'Mr Coddrington's doing, but the Trustees agreed.'

'Why?'

She shrugged.

Col ran through what she had said. There was only one explanation for the drastic action by the Trustees. 'You've not given up your idea of taking Kullervo on, have you?'

Connie rubbed her hand across her brow wearily. 'I'm not exactly seeking a battle if that's what you mean. I just want to be prepared.'

Col hated the idea of her facing Kullervo alone again. 'But you should let us look after you—keep you safe.'

'Yeah, like you did from the chimera?'

He swallowed. 'Yeah, well . . . '

'You see: it's going to come, isn't it? I've got to be able to defend myself.' She kicked a stone into the gutter. 'And you're hardly ever here, so what do you care?'

As soon as she said the words, she wished she could call them back. Her feeling of being abandoned by almost everyone had slipped out.

Col exploded. 'Care? Don't you dare say I don't care!'

She held up her hands. 'Sorry, I didn't mean it like that.'

But Col wasn't letting it go. 'You're getting so wrapped up in being a universal, Connie, you're not listening to others any more. Everyone's saying it. They're scared stiff you're going to do something stupid.'

'I won't.'

'I wouldn't bet on it.'

She turned to him. 'So you think they're right to stop me learning anything?'

Col sat stiffly, wondering how this conversation could have gone so wrong. 'Yeah, I think I do.'

Connie sprang to her feet and stalked off without even saying goodbye.

He couldn't let her go like that. He just wanted to make her see that she had to be safe. 'Connie!'

Her response was to break into a run, disappearing around the corner to the harbour. He ran to catch up, thinking he would find her and put his arguments properly, but when he reached the quayside, she had gone.

'Connie?' It was Dr Brock, not Col, who later found Connie hidden in the weather shelter, clutching a mangled loaf of bread. She had been crying but was attempting to hide this fact from him when he sat next to her.

'Having a hard time?' he asked gently.

'Just a bit,' she admitted, sniffing.

He passed her a large white handkerchief from his pocket. 'Want to talk about it?'

'Not really,' she said in a deadened tone of voice.

Dr Brock thought he could guess the cause of today's upset. He had heard rumblings amongst the senior members of the Society, complaints that the universal was going off the rails again, this time of her own volition. He knew that the Trustees were soon coming to Hescombe to confront her about her behaviour. Steps had already been taken against her which he knew must be painful.

'Well, if ever you do need to talk about it, remember I'm here for you,' he said kindly, patting her wrist.

'Thanks, but I don't think anyone can do anything.'

Dr Brock sat back, gazing out at the boats at anchor and the seagulls strutting along the quay-side. 'I wanted to talk to you about something, Connie.'

'What?' she asked, suspicious that he would lecture her on her deviations from her training agenda. It would be just like Gard to arrange for her to be taken to task by those she was closest to in hopes that they would get through to her.

'Have you felt anything odd recently? Anything out of the ordinary?'

This was not the question she had been expecting. 'Like what?'

'The dragons have sensed something strange going on up on the moor. The rock dwarves say they can't tell who's out there. Parts of it now seem almost always to be swathed in fog. It might, of course, just be thanks to this strange winter we've been having, but I'm not sure.' Dr Brock settled back on the seat beside her.

'I haven't been near the moor for ages. You know that. Not allowed.'

He turned his blue eyes on her. 'Indeed I do. But will you try for me now? Tell me what you sense from here?'

Connie closed her eyes and turned her thoughts to the moor. It was no good: at this distance, it was a confused babble of voices and presences like a badly tuned radio. She opened them again to find his gaze on her still. 'Sorry, I can't make anything out. It's beyond my range. And I think I've a headache coming.'

Dr Brock nodded in understanding. 'Oh well, it was worth a try. Don't break any rules now but you'll let me know if you sense anything, won't you?'

'I will.'

He got up to go. 'Don't stay out long, will you? It's too cold to sit here all day.'

She watched him walk away, erect and purposeful. A shadow passed over the pale sun, momentarily dimming his snowy hair. Connie looked up. For an instant, she could have sworn she saw the back of a weather giant pass over, hurrying westward, but now the mass of cloud had resolved itself into drifts of grey vapour. But the clouds were still moving west even though the breeze was against them.

12
Kelpies

March arrived in a series of howling storms, bringing trees down and flooding low-lying meadows. It seemed to Col that every day for the past few weeks he hadn't been able to go outside without waterproofs and boots and always returned soaked to the skin despite these precautions. His intensive training schedule had passed in a blur of wind, rain, and aching bones and he was relieved to have a weekend off for a change. Sometimes it was impossible to balance being a member of the Society and having normal friends. He felt torn but knew there was little he could do about it.

Worst of all, weeks had gone by and he had still not made it up with Connie. At school she'd been distant, almost as if she was purposely freezing him out, afraid he'd hurt her by probing too deeply into what she was thinking and feeling. She avoided Society meetings and stayed indoors as much as possible, a complete change from her usual behaviour. Gard was tight-lipped as to what he thought of his pupil's behaviour, but even Col, so rarely in Hescombe these days, could sense that things were coming to a head between the universal and the Society authorities.

With all that to worry about, Col decided he needed a hack on the moors with Mags. It would help him summon up the courage to corner Connie and sort things out.

'Glad to see the sun's out for once,' Col commented to his grandmother on his way out of the door.

Mrs Clamworthy looked out of the window despondently. Her water sprites loved the floods as it gave them more scope for their wanderings. 'Still, there's more rain forecast,' she said, brightening up at the thought. 'You've checked that the chimera's not about, I hope?'

'Of course. Simon says it's gone off further on to the moor.'

'Just stay near the cottages. I don't trust that creature to keep away.'

'OK. I shouldn't be back late,' he called as he splashed down the garden path to fetch Mags.

'Don't forget we're having tea with Liam!' she called.

'As if I would!' he replied, leaping the ditch.

Col guided Mags up the farm track leading out to the open countryside. New shoots were pushing through the soil in all directions. A clump of snowdrops, past their prime, had shrivelled and turned brown in the shade of a bank of daffodils. Birds sang in every hedge, declaring their territory.

Feeling both he and Mags would enjoy a good gallop over firm ground, he headed up the track towards the Devil's Tooth, now a small incisor on the horizon over the back of Masterson land. Hooves splashed through the deep puddles, spraying Col's jodhpurs with black speckles. Here and there, where the grass was still in the shade of a boulder or clump of bracken stalks, the frost lingered, dusting the ground like icing sugar, but the rest had melted away in the morning sunshine. Down in the hollows, mist lingered in thick swirls, making the high places of the moor look as though they were floating on clouds.

'Careful!' He checked Mags as he veered to the left towards some bright green grasses. That was boggy ground, home to the kelpies, the water horse tricksters. He knew better than to go down there.

But Mags would not stop fretting. Something was definitely spooking him. The mist swirled and gathered around them with unnatural speed, yet Col could see no other cause for alarm.

'What's the matter?' he crooned to the pony, patting his neck in reassurance. Mags side-stepped and tossed his head.

The air chilled a few degrees. Col could hear a strange clicking from close by. There was definitely something in the mist—lots of somethings. He pulled on the reins, thinking to make a quick retreat, but then an icy touch pinched the back of his neck. Mags reared and Col, already unconscious, tumbled from the saddle. In a panic, the pony bolted, leaving his rider out cold.

Mrs Clamworthy knocked on the door of Number Five and came in without waiting for an answer. She had interrupted the inhabitants as they relaxed in the aftermath of their supper. Mack was sitting with his feet up on the table, yawning, while watching Evelyn fuss around at the sink. His wife seemed to be unable to rest, refusing his pleas to take her considerable weight off her feet,

229

instead insisting that the sink needed cleaning. Connie had her head down over a pile of school books, pretending to do her homework, while really reading up her practice notes and running through her new tools in her head. She looked up when Mrs Clamworthy came in and immediately knew that something was wrong.

'Mum!' said Mack, leaping to his feet. 'Have a seat.'

'No, no, dear,' said Mrs Clamworthy in a fluster. 'I thought you had Gard with you. I was expecting Col back for tea—we've got Liam and the Khalids staying—but he's not come in yet. I thought Gard might be able to tell me where he is.'

Mack steered his mother further into the room but she shrugged off his attempts to remove her coat. 'Sorry, Gard's up at the Mastersons' as the Trustees have just arrived,' said Mack, not looking too concerned to hear his son was on walkabout.

Evelyn put her dishcloth down and crossed the kitchen to put an arm around her mother-in-law.

'Don't worry, Lavinia. Connie can summon Gard through that thing they do.' She looked expectantly at her niece. Connie put her pen on her pad.

'Of course,' Connie said hesitantly. Gard and she had not been speaking since the incident of

230

the portcullis and she was reluctant to let him into her mind when she knew it to be littered with evidence of her disobedience. But if Col was lost, she had to help him.

'Would you, dear?' said Mrs Clamworthy gratefully. 'It would take a great weight off my mind just to know where he is.'

'I'll do it right away,' Connie said, her hesitation vanishing. She went to the back door and planted her feet firmly on the stone path. 'Gard!' she called into the bedrock. 'Can you hear me?' There was no reply. Was he sulking or was he somewhere he really couldn't hear her? 'Gard, this is important.' Still no answer. It was not like Gard to fail to respond to a summons—whatever his feelings towards her at that moment. She went back into the kitchen.

'Sorry, he must be inside somewhere.'

Mack strode over to the phone and rang the Mastersons'. 'It's engaged,' he said, putting it back down.

'I know,' suggested Evelyn, 'why doesn't Mack drive you up to the Mastersons' and you can talk to Gard yourself? That would be better than sitting here worrying about things.'

Mack grabbed his jacket from the peg. 'Can I take your car, Evie? I don't think Mum's quite up to the back of the bike.'

Evelyn chucked him the keys to her little car. 'As long as you remember to treat my car like a lady and take the corners slowly. And be careful of the gears. They're tricky if you're not used to them.'

'Hah!' said Mack. 'There's not much I don't know about engines.'

Evelyn was about to protest but Mrs Clamworthy had no time for an argument. 'I won't keep him long, Evelyn,' she interjected. 'Why don't you sit down. You look all in.'

Evelyn gave a wan smile and patted her tummy. 'I will. When junior here stops kicking me to bits.'

'Ah, yes, Mack was just like that,' Mrs Clamworthy replied on her way to the door. 'Squirmed like a squid until the day he was born.'

'And why aren't I surprised?' Evelyn muttered.

'What was that?' asked Mack sharply.

'Go on,' scolded Evelyn, shooing him away with a wave of the hand.

The back door closed and the kitchen fell silent again. Evelyn winced as the sound of grating gears and an over-revved engine resounded in the lane. Connie tried to return to her work but it was no good. She kept turning over in her mind what might have happened to Col. Was he just out late and forgotten that he was due to have tea with Liam or had he had an accident? It then occurred to her that there was a way for her to find out without waiting around for Gard.

'Would it be OK if I went over to Uncle Hugh's?' she asked abruptly.

Evelyn gave her a shrewd look. 'Why? It's dark already.'

'Well, I thought if I got near enough to the moor, I might be able to sense Col through his gift. If I find out where he is, I can let you all know.'

Her aunt sighed and slumped into a chair, taking a breath against the discomfort of nine months' worth of baby thumping her in the ribs. 'I suppose it'll be OK. I'll send Mack to fetch you when he gets back from the Mastersons'. But they'll probably find Col first, or he'll have turned up of his own accord.'

'Probably. But, in that case, I still get to see Uncle Hugh and Simon, don't I?' said Connie, pulling on her outdoor clothes. 'Anyway, I've been meaning to check out what's happening on the moor for Dr Brock for a few weeks now. I could do that while I'm up there.'

'You're not to set one foot on the moor, Connie.'

'Of course not.' Connie dug her bike lights out of a drawer in the dresser. 'But I don't have to go any further than the field near the cottage to sense what's happening. I won't go on my own, I promise.'

When Connie reached Hugh's cottage she found it dark. This was highly unusual—not quite as strange as Col's disappearance but she could usually count on her great-uncle to be home at this time of night. She wondered where he was until she found a message for Simon tucked in a bottle on the back step. The note told Simon, who was expected back late from seeing Liam, to put himself to bed as 'the old man' had gone to a pub quiz in Hescombe with Horace Little and Dr Brock. Connie smiled as she read the name of the quiz team they had formed: the Old Dragons.

But there was someone else at the cottages always on the watch for her: Wolf, Rat's Alsatian, threw himself against the fence separating the two properties, making it shake alarmingly as he attempted to break through, barking fit to burst. The noise brought Rat outside.

'Hi, Connie,' he said. 'Thought it had to be you.'

Connie leant over the wooden panel and scratched Wolf on the head. He whined ecstatically. 'Hi, Rat. Have you seen Col?'

Rat shook his head. 'Nope. He's having tea with Liam, isn't he?'

'He was supposed to but he never showed up.'

Rat shrugged. 'Well, he's not here.'

Connie looked out over the dark fields leading up to the moor. The eight wind turbines revolved their ghostly white arms in the night. The plantation could only be seen as a darker shadow against the sky. A thin paring of moon peeped over the treetops, shedding little light. 'It's very late for him to still be on the moor. I thought I might be able to sense if he was out there. Will you come with me to the edge of the field? I've promised everyone I won't go any further, but I'll have a better chance of finding him if I'm as close as I can get.'

'OK,' said Rat. 'I'll just grab a torch.'

He came back a few moments later with the powerful lamp his dad used to fix cars. It acted like a small headlight as they made their way up past the wind farm. Connie led them up the far side of the field away from the plantation, not wanting to revisit that spot.

'Come on, let's get away from here,' she said, picking up the pace.

Rat nodded sympathetically.

They climbed until they reached a gate at the top of the field. Here the tidy farmland gave up its grip on the earth, leaving the moor to its own devices. Sheep bleated in the darkness. The grass hissed in the light breeze. Everything seemed normal. Rat switched off the light, understanding without being told that Connie's gift could see far better without this distraction.

Connie dipped into her mind, feeling out for the mythical creatures and their companions abroad at that moment. She had not opened up for some time, having chosen to remain closed away from others. But what was this? The moor was seething with presences—too many to distinguish. It was like turning over a stone and discovering an ants' nest bustling with activity. She opened her eyes and looked over at Rat who was leaning on the top bar of the gate, chewing peacefully on a stalk of grass.

'Rat, something's really not right. Where have all these creatures come from?'

'What creatures?' Rat asked, letting the stalk flutter to the ground.

'I've never felt so many up here before. Has the Society called a meeting I don't know about?'

'Not unless I don't know about it either. What's going on?'

Connie reached out into the darkness again but ended the attempt with a shake of her head. 'There's too many of them.' The hair on the back of her neck was on end. 'Something tells me that they're not friendly. We'd better warn Dr Brock.' She made a move to go.

'What about Col?' Rat snagged her jacket.

She had almost forgotten the reason for her visit in the shock of finding all those creatures congregating on the moor. 'I don't know if I'll be able to spot him in all this noise.'

'But what if one of those unfriendly creatures you're on about have got him?' Rat was craning his neck to see if he could make out anything in the twilight.

He was right. She could not give up now. Connie took a deep breath and tuned back into the presences humming away on the moor. Dragon. Banshee. Stone sprite. Kelpie. Hundreds of images flickered through her mind like a kaleidoscope. Concentrate. A companion to pegasi. A gold link amid the many. There: she had found him. He was not far or she would never have sensed him. In fact, he was only a short distance away, possibly just over the brow of the hill on the track up to the Devil's Tooth.

'He's almost within call,' she told Rat. 'A little to the north of us.'

Rat turned the torch back on and swung his leg over the gate. 'Come on. I'll need you to help me find him.'

Connie hung back, the promise to her aunt still fresh in her mind. The grass whipped at her legs in the stiff, rain-bearing breeze. 'But I'm not allowed on the moors!'

Rat jumped down the other side. 'Don't be pathetic: we're not going far. Or would you prefer Col to be attacked by one of these unknown mythical visitors?'

'Of course I wouldn't.' What did it matter if she got into more trouble with the Trustees if she could help Col? From the way he was so still, it was possible he had fallen and hurt himself. She clambered over the gate and set out in pursuit of Rat.

'This way!' she called to him as Rat veered off too far to the left, heading down towards the wet low-lying ground. 'It's dangerous down there—full of kelpies and will-o'-the-wisps. They'll lead you into the bog.' She ran to catch up with him. Rat gave her a grin.

'See, that's what I like about you, Connie,' he said, 'deep down, you don't care about the rules either.'

She wasn't sure if she should take this as a compliment, though it had clearly been intended as such. Guilt filled her as she thought what her aunt would be saying at this moment, sure that it would not be flattering. 'Let's get this done as quickly as possible,' she said. 'Follow me.'

She led them onto the track and turned right heading uphill. She was soon out of breath and had to pause to ease a stitch. Rat, who spent most of his time roaming on the moor, was unaffected by the climb; he took the opportunity to holler into the darkness, flashing his torch like a beacon. It picked out a body lying by the side of the track.

'Col!' Rat dashed forward and pulled Col's head and shoulders on to his lap.

'W-what?' Col said groggily.

Connie touched his hand: it was icy cold. 'How long have you been here?'

'I dunno.' He groaned and then flinched with the pain of aching muscles.

'What's the matter with him?' Rat asked Connie anxiously.

Col was still wearing his riding helmet. He didn't look as if he'd hurt himself. Connie ran her hands quickly over his forehead and neck, finding a tender patch of skin just below the hairline. Col flinched.

'Rat, shine the torch here a moment. I think a stone sprite must've touched him. I've seen marks like that before.' She had, on her own skin after touching one; only the universal's shield had held off their numbing attack.

'But I thought they lived in the ground. How could it reach his neck?'

239

'Good question.' Connie checked the surrounding area and again felt the hum of hundreds of creatures gathered not far away. 'But we don't have time. We've got to get off the moor. Can you walk, Col?'

'I think so.' He flexed his frozen feet.

'You missed tea,' Connie said gently, unbuckling his helmet.

Col gave an agonized groan. 'I bet Gran's worried sick.'

'Hadn't you better ring to tell her you're all right?'

Col's fingers were so cold by now that he fumbled his phone as he dragged it from his pocket and it fell on the stones with a crack. Rat picked it up for him and examined it in the torchlight. It was dead.

'Great,' said Col. 'It's really my day, isn't it?'

'Don't worry: you can use my phone.' Connie pulled hers out of her jacket pocket.

'On second thoughts, let me do that for you,' said Rat, intercepting the phone to dial up Col's home number.

'She might still be at the Mastersons',' Connie called out, helping Col to his feet. 'The number's in the address book.'

Rat nodded that he had understood.

'Mags,' Col murmured as his wits came back

to him. 'Is he all right?'

'I'll find him. Don't worry.' Connie whistled into the darkness but there was no response.

He stumbled a few paces, trying to bring the circulation back to his dead limbs.

'Mags!' he shouted hoarsely into the darkness. 'Mags!'

Rat joined them. 'Need the torch?' Col nodded. 'By the way, your gran says you're to go to bed when you get home and ordered us off the moor immediately.'

'Not without Mags,' said Col tersely. 'Shine your torch down there.'

Rat slowly moved the beam of light over the rough terrain, stopping each time it caught on a rock or horse-shaped tussock of grass. The moor was eerie in this half-light, a place of strange shapes and dark menace. Connie grabbed his arm.

'Look, there!' she said, pointing to three small silhouettes in the middle distance. 'He's wandered off with the Dartmoor ponies.'

With a preliminary pitter-patter, rain began to fall, building into a steady downpour. Rat turned his collar against the wet, having neglected to bring a coat.

'We'd better go and get him,' Connie said anxiously. 'I really don't like the moor tonight:

there's too much going on.' She dipped into her mind again to check for any activity near them and caught the tail of a slippery presence before it disappeared. 'In fact, we'd better make this quick: I think my friend is on the move.'

'Your friend?' asked Rat dimly.

A look of alarm flashed across Col's face. He shook himself out of his daze. 'The chimera.' He grabbed Connie's arm and pulled her along after him. 'Look, Connie, we'll get you on Mags and you can ride back to the cottages. You'll be safe there.'

Connie broke into a run. 'It's not just me I'm worried about,' she gasped. 'What about you and Rat?'

'Let's deal with one thing at a time,' said Col, though his mind was whirling. It would be the perfect end to the day to find himself face-to-face with the beast that had almost killed his friend. 'Where's Icefen?' he asked Rat.

'Miles away,' said Rat, running to keep up with him. 'No go.'

The boys exchanged a look, agreeing that their priority was to get the universal away from danger. They'd worry about themselves after.

Mags was cropping the grass with his new friends when they reached him. He did not protest when Col gave Connie a hand up onto his back, twittering to greet her. No sooner had she settled in the saddle than Mags snorted and reared in alarm as a new scent reached him on the breeze. Connie tumbled off backwards, her fall broken by Col who was still standing at the stirrup. Mags whinnied and would have bolted had not Rat made a grab for the reins in time.

'Mags!' cried Col. 'What's got into you?' His pony's eyes were rolling in their sockets, full of terror.

'He can't help it,' gasped Connie. Poor Mags: first stone sprites, now the chimera. She realized how lucky they were he had stayed near Col and not run for home.

With Col's aid, she scrambled back on. She did not need to dip into her mind to know that the chimera was loping towards them: the breeze also carried a triumphant roar of pleasure.

'You've got to get on!' she shouted. 'There's no time to run.'

'He'll be too slow with all of us,' said Col. His eyes fell on the ponies, which were still grazing, the scent and sound of the chimera not having disturbed them yet. The scraggy black-haired one perked his ears forward, as if listening for Col's voice, his eyes welcoming. The bay munched the grass as if nothing unusual was happening. 'We'll ride those! Come on, Rat.'

The two boys sprinted over to the ponies and leapt on their backs before the animals knew what had hit them.

'Yah!' yelled Col, grabbing a lock of tough black mane and spurring his mount forward. The pony gave a whinny of surprise and bounded away, closely followed by his brother and Mags. The three fled down the hill in an erratic career.

'Not that way!' cried Col as his beast turned to the right despite his rider's signals, relentlessly heading down to the marshy ground. Rat sped past, his mount putting on a burst of speed and tossing its head.

Connie pulled Mags up before he lost his footing in the boggy ground. 'Stop!' she cried. She had realized why those beasts had shown no signs of being alarmed by the chimera. 'Those aren't ponies!'

But it was too late. The creatures propelled their riders into the treacherous marsh and then vanished from beneath them, giving a whinny of laughter as they melted back into the mists. Col and Rat fell into the bog. The kelpies had ditched them.

13
Trap

'**R**un!' Col shouted at Connie while he floundered thigh-deep in thick, evil-smelling mud.

'No way! I'm not leaving without you!' Connie dismounted and stumbled to the edge of the mire, frantically trying to think of a way of saving them. She could see Rat thanks to the torch he was still holding: he was waist-deep and sinking.

Mags heard his master and had no hesitation in obeying his command. When Connie's back was turned, he gave a shrill whinny and bolted down the track, heading for the safety of the cottages.

'Mags!' Col shouted in warning, but Connie was too slow to catch the reins; her fingers made a snatch at thin air. She had to let him go; she could not spare any time to take off in pursuit: Col and Rat were inching closer to drowning.

'Stop moving!' she screamed at Rat, who in his panic was struggling against the irresistible suck of the bog.

'That all very well for you to say!' he yelled back.

'Spread your weight—lie flat!'

'I'm not putting my face any nearer this stuff,' Rat protested.

'Just do it!' growled Col, realizing Connie was right. Their sinking would be slowed if they tried to float on the surface. He spread-eagled himself, gagging on the foul gas that belched from the mud each time he stirred.

Looking up at Connie in the desperate hope she had come up with a plan, Col saw a flicker of flame appear in the darkness not far from her and then go out.

'Chimera!' he cried.

Connie spun round, just in time to see the chimera leaping down the hill towards them. Fleeing the only way left open, she took a leap onto a tussock of grass sticking like an island out of the bog. It sagged under her weight but remained firm. Out of the shadows loped the chimera, its lion's jaws open in an exultant grin, the black cobra head swishing excitedly. Then, catching a whiff of the stagnant air of the marsh, it stopped short at the edge and lowered its snout to sniff. The serpent darted to the lion's forepaws and fluttered its tongue on the mud-crusted surface, testing the ground. With a howl of disappointment it began to pace to and fro, its amber eyes glaring at Connie. It was calculating whether it could leap upon her and not tumble into the mud. When the lion's eyes met hers, they both knew it could not. But the chimera had other methods of attack.

And so do I, Connie thought to herself. Her armoury was prepared, her shield to hand.

'Col! Connie!' gasped Rat behind her. He was now up to his chest and could see nowhere to go but down.

The beast stopped on the edge of the firm ground closest to the universal and took a deep intake of breath. Swiftly, Connie delved into her mind and pulled out her shield to hold in front of her. A torrent of flame spouted from the lion's jaws. She knew from experience that the shield would hold for a short while. Steam hissed in the air as the silver vapour of the shield evaporated under the onslaught. With a quick sleight of hand, she made a grab at one of the tongues of fire licking at the edge of the dissipating shield. From where Col was lying, it looked as though

Connie was surrounded by a silver halo of cloud, battered by an intense flame. The fiery torrent ended as the chimera paused for breath. It ran its pink tongue over its flame-scorched lips, relishing the approaching moment of the kill. It knew the feeble protection was no match for a second bout of fire: the universal would be his.

Connie threw her shield aside.

'Connie!' yelled Col in dismay, seeing his friend standing unprotected only metres from the creature. He had no idea what she thought she was doing. It seemed pure madness to cast away the only barrier between her and the flames.

Almost instantaneously as the shield disappeared, in Connie's hands appeared a long bow, strung with gold. Reaching behind her, she pulled a single arrow from the glimmering quiver on her back, strung and fired. Her aim was true. The arrow, blazing with the chimera's own fire, flew through the air and pierced the flank of the goat. The terrified creature panicked at the sting of unaccustomed pain. It fled, forcing its bolder brethren of snake and lion with it as it hurtled off into the darkness, screaming with agony.

Col gave a feeble cheer, not wanting to move more than absolutely necessary as the mud lapped at his ears.

Connie turned on her tussock-island to face

him. 'Right.' She took off her shoulder-bag and threw one end to Col. The bag fell short. She tried again. This time as she threw it, Col took the gamble of lunging and grabbed it in his fingers. Connie knelt down to steady herself to pull him clear.

'No!' said Col. 'If you do that, we won't be able to reach Rat: he's too far in.' At that moment, the torchlight winked out, sunk beneath the bog.

'Rat!' Connie screamed. 'Are you still there?'

'Hurry!' came Rat's strangled voice as he spluttered on a mouthful of rancid water.

Col grappled at his waist, trying one-handed to remove his belt. He got it free, though every move he made pushed him deeper. He threw the end to Rat. Only Rat's head, forearm, and hand were still above the surface and he could not grip it unless it fell exactly in place. On the third throw, he caught it and took a firm grasp of the buckle.

'Pull, Connie,' said Col. 'Slowly!'

With hands slipping on the slimy mud that covered the strap, Connie began to heave her friends towards her. The effort was immense: two boys weighed down with the counterforce of the sucking mud were almost too much for her, but she dug deep and found the strength. After six heaves, Col was free, having reached the firm ground of the island. He passed the belt holding Rat to Connie and pulled himself out. Together they hauled Rat hand over hand out of the bog. He coughed and spluttered as he crawled onto dry land. The only problem now was that this left the three of them tottering on the frail refuge.

'Shall we stay here and wait for help?' Col asked, turning to Connie.

'No way,' said Rat. The brown water was creeping over his shoes as the island sank under their weight. 'I'm not going in there again.' He spat out a mouthful of mud. In the moonlight, the only part of him that shone white was the area around his nose and eyes: the rest of him was slimed in mud.

'The chimera?' Col asked Connie.

'It'll be back once the other two regain control from the goat. We've got to get to safety,' she said. There was no more she could do against the chimera. Surprise would work only once.

Over to the south, the roar of an angry creature reverberated in the air.

'Let's go then,' said Rat. Gathering himself for the leap, he jumped to the firm ground where the chimera had so recently stood, the grass blackened by its flame. Col followed him.

'Come on, Connie!' Col called holding out a hand to help her. It was as well he did for, without the benefit of a run at the jump, Connie fell a pace

250

short and was thigh-deep in the bog before he and Rat hauled her out.

'It's blocking our way to the cottages,' she panted, sliding in her shoes as she ran up the hill. She felt exhausted but knew she could not give in to tiredness now. 'Make for the Mastersons'.'

The three of them ran back the way they had come on the kelpies, hitting the track and making faster progress on the clear path. But they could not hope to outrun a chimera.

'Where are the dragons when you need them!' cursed Col, stumbling over a boulder he had not seen in the dark but managing to stay on his feet.

'I can't summon help on the move,' Connie gasped. 'Let's get to the Devil's Tooth. It'll buy us some time and I can call Gard from there.' The thought darted into her mind that after this she would be in serious trouble: ignoring warnings, going on the moor, using forbidden weapons. But that seemed the last of her worries just now.

With limbs like lead, Connie clambered up the hill to the base of the tor. Col gave her a leg-up onto the summit of the granite rock and pulled himself after her. Rat scrambled up the other side. The top of the Tooth formed a flat platform in the burnt-out patch of moor. It provided just enough room for the three of them to crouch.

All were silent while Connie concentrated on sending out her distress call.

'Gard! Help!'

Nothing.

'Please talk to me! Help!'

But there was no answer. There was going to be no second lucky escape from the Devil's Tooth.

'The stone sprites are blocking me,' she explained to the others. 'There's hundreds of them in the ground between us and the road. Even if we ran for it, they'd get us first.'

'Can they reach us here?' Col asked.

Connie nodded. 'Yes. But I think I can use my shield to stop them if you stick close to me.' Connie immediately found herself squeezed in the middle of a tight embrace from both boys. Rat was even stepping on her toes. 'But not that close!'

Rat gave a forced laugh and stepped back a little. 'Sorry,' he said, 'but just now you seem the only thing between me and my death.'

There was little anyone could say to that. Connie bowed her head, concentrating her energies on holding up the shield. Rat crouched down beside her. Despite everything, Col felt a surge of warmth just looking at his friends being so brave in the face of dire danger. It didn't matter what others thought of them; he knew there was no one else he'd prefer to be with in a crisis.

'So, we're trapped,' he said, his voice calm as he faced the truth. He found comfort in standing so near to his friends, to Rat and Connie. Particularly to Connie. If the end was coming, at least it was good to be with them. 'Is there no way of getting a message through?'

Connie shook her head. 'Not to Gard. Not unless someone comes close enough to hear me, but all I can sense are our enemies.'

'You forget we've got the technology,' said Rat, not yet downhearted. He pulled out Connie's phone from his hip pocket. It was wet and black with mud. He wiped it clean and punched the buttons. Nothing happened. 'But it broke.'

Col swore softly.

'But you've still got the universal with you,' Connie said determinedly. 'I'm not beaten yet.'

Col felt very proud of her at that moment. She was right. They were not giving up yet.

'What's the plan?' he asked, confident she would come up with something.

'I'm working on it.' Connie hunched forward, gazing over the edge of the platform.

Without warning, the chimera leapt out of the darkness. Connie screamed as it attempted to mount the tor, swiping at her with its razor-sharp claws. Moving with quick reactions, Col and Rat heaved her out of its path just in time. The chimera gave a deafening roar of disappointment and fell heavily back to the ground, its claws skittering on the bare granite. Col could feel Connie shaking like a leaf in his arms.

'I think the lion's back in charge,' said Rat grimly.

'But I don't think it can reach us up here,' Col added, looking hurriedly around to see where the beast had gone.

'But they can.' Rat pointed to the ground below.

Looking down, they saw movement in the rocky earth at the base of the Devil's Tooth. It seemed to be bubbling and seething like a hot spring. Bursting out of the surface of the rock were many pairs of long-fingered, emaciated hands. Creeping, crawling hands that made flesh shrink just to look at them.

'Stone sprites,' breathed Connie, her face creased in concentration. 'I'm keeping them off with my shield.'

The hands grew into long, spindly arms, flailing about in the air like misshapen plants in a gale. They seemed to be snatching, feeling for something. For warm flesh. Next, the crust of the rock split and rounded humps emerged, like the backs of whales rising above the sea. The rest of the sprites surfaced: heads slung low on scrawny chests, skeletal jaws and teeth, angular legs and arms. When they scuttled free of the rock, they looked like pale giant spiders, luminous body hanging down like some obscene cradle held up by four long limbs. Their joints clicked like pebbles grating on stone each time they moved.

'I guess we now know how they reached me on Mag's back,' Col said with a shudder.

Hundreds of these foul creatures scratched at the base of the tor, looking with hungry eyes up at the three warm bodies that Connie was keeping out of their range.

'Universal. Universal. We want the universal!' they chanted in thin, bloodless voices, battering on the shield, already damaged by the encounter with the chimera's fire.

Connie could also hear the hysterical voices of the chimera hissing, roaring and bleating against her defences.

'Come down!' the lion roared. 'Face us!'

'He wants you!' bleated the goat.

'It's you he's after,' hissed the snake.

'We'll take you to him,' growled the lion.

The three friends had reached a desperate dead-end. Connie was tired, at a loss how to save them from this trap. Without much hope, she wondered what words could do. She raised her hand for parley. Col and Rat, not privy to the dialogue in her mind, saw her lift her right hand and stand up straight. They looked at each other, wondering what was going on. In her mind, the voices of the creatures relented, giving her space to speak.

'Who wants me?' she asked, though she could guess the answer.

'Your companion. He has come to claim you,' tittered the snake.

Connie said nothing, ending the parley to think.

'Any ideas?' asked Col hopefully when he realized that Connie was back with them from the inner world of her gift.

'Yes, but you're not going to like it.'

'If it's better than being frozen or eaten, I'm listening,' said Rat.

'Yes, it's better than that.' Connie took a deep breath, knowing before she spoke that Col would refuse. But she was not going to lead them into a hopeless fight with creatures far more powerful than them. That was what George Brewer had done. 'We can make a deal.'

'That sounds good,' said Rat quickly.

'What kind of deal?' asked Col, his suspicions aroused. 'You don't mean—?'

'It's me they want. If I go down to them, they might let you go.'

'But they'll eat you alive, Connie! You can't do this.' Col grabbed hold of the back of her jacket as if she had been about to throw herself off the rock.

'They won't. They're working for Kullervo. They'll take me to him.'

Col let go of her and sat back. 'And that's better, is it?'

'I promise I won't let him take me over like last time. I'm prepared for him,' Connie pleaded, begging him to understand, to give her his support for what she was contemplating doing. She was finding it hard enough to stick to her purpose and had no energy to fight him too.

'But he'll kill you,' Col said in a monotone.

'He might. Or I might defeat him.'

A spark of understanding ignited in the depths of Col's eyes. 'You're not thinking of challenging him, Connie? You're not still thinking of that, surely?'

She said nothing. Rat stirred uneasily. Time was running out. They could not sit up here all night. Sooner or later, one of those creatures would break through the shield and get them.

'Col,' said Rat, 'listen to her. She's right: either she goes down and we get a chance to get away and find help, or we all get killed for sure.'

Col cursed and kicked the rock. He knew they

were telling the truth; he just didn't want to hear it. He grabbed Connie and pulled her towards him.

'Don't give in. Don't challenge him,' he whispered furiously in her ear. 'Just hold him off until we can get help.'

This was the signal she had been waiting for. Connie knew she had to go now while she still had the courage. She gave Col a wan smile, touched Rat on the arm in a gesture of farewell, and then slid her way down the rock. Seeing their quarry approach, the stone sprites scuttled to her side, following her like the rats after the Pied Piper. But none of them could touch her: her shield surrounded her now like a silver mist, placing her beyond their cold reach. Col watched her walk forwards to where the chimera was pacing, its tail flicking with an angry twitch. He realized that he was watching the bravest person he knew risk her life for him. The knowledge was almost unbearable.

Down among the stone sprites, Connie looked through the silver haze of her shield into the implacable eyes of the chimera.

'I'll come with you, if you let the others go free,' Connie said, her voice firm despite her fear.

'You will drop your shield?' yawned the lion, displaying its row of yellowed teeth and ridged red maw.

Connie nodded. 'Yes, I'll drop my shield. You'll be able to take me without a struggle. But you must promise to let my friends go free.'

The snake's head slithered forward to the edge of her shield and stared in at her, its eyes gleaming with malice in the silvery light. Slowly, the cobra nodded.

'You agree?' Connie asked.

The snake's head nodded again; the lion face smiled enigmatically.

Connie was not sure if she could trust this promise, but what choice did she have? With great reluctance, she dropped her shield, leaving herself unprotected within reach of the jaws of the chimera. Immediately her guard was down, the snake's head lashed round and struck her to the ground. Her head hit the earth, her mouth full of dirt. The chimera paced lazily forward and bent its lion's face to her. A rough tongue licked her bloodied cheek, its breath hot and reeking.

'You taste good,' the creature said.

Connie closed her eyes, anticipating the bite of teeth into her flesh. She nearly screamed, but she knew that the chimera fed on her fear and would be goaded into tormenting her further if she showed weakness. But it had no intention of eating her: it opened its jaws and once more Connie found herself in the grip of its mouth as it carried her away.

In the pale glow coming from the stone sprites, Col and Rat watched in horrified, impotent silence. Rat had to haul Col back as the chimera struck Connie.

'Don't be stupid!' he hissed. 'Don't waste the chance she's bought us!'

Once the chimera had disappeared into the darkness with their friend dangling from its mouth, the stone sprites in pursuit like an army of grey crabs, Col grabbed Rat.

'Let's run for it. Get help.'

A downdraught of wings hit Col as he was about to slide down the smooth-sided tor. Rat yelled. Looking up, Col saw Rat caught in the claws of a black dragon that had swooped in from the west. He cried out in protest, but then felt his own jacket pierced by talons and he was torn off the rock face. Above, he saw a white dragon. Its pink eyes glared down at him as if it considered him a very pitiful prey. Hanging limp in the clutch of the dragons, Col and Rat were carried away into the night sky.

14
Challenge

Connie thought the nightmare of the journey in the chimera's mouth would never end. The creature was running eastwards across open moor, jumping streams, clattering across roads, intent on reaching its goal. Each leap, each bound seemed to punch a little more air out of her struggling lungs and dig deeper bruises in her ribs. All Connie could tell was that they were heading towards Chartmouth. A flash of a car headlamp and the chimera cowered for a moment in the shelter of a hedge. Once the noise of the engine had faded, it leapt onto the tarmac and loped swiftly down the hill. To her right, Connie could hear the whisper of the trees in Mallins Wood.

'Help!' she cried out to any friendly wood sprite that might be listening but no answering voice met hers. Why was no one around to hear her?

The chimera's sharp sense of hearing sent it bounding into the shelter of the trees as another vehicle approached, this time a lorry grumbling its way slowly up the steep hill out of Chartmouth. Was the creature out of its senses? Connie wondered. It seemed to be intent on dragging her into the heart of a human settlement. Even the chimera, as insane and divided against itself as it was, must realize that it stood no chance in these surroundings. Connie felt a faint glimmer of hope that they would be spotted and she might be saved.

Once the lorry had gone, the chimera set off again, undaunted by any fears of being discovered. The hour was late. Traffic was light on the roads and the chimera slipped into the outskirts of Chartmouth unseen. It turned away from the houses onto the half-built industrial estate, deserted at this hour. Connie's hopes of being rescued faded as she realized it knew exactly where it was going. She was bumped along tarmac, her dangling hands grazed by the grit. Then the terrain changed: she was being dragged over weeds, half bricks, dirt and litter. Bounding along a perimeter fence, the chimera paused at a break in the wire, went down on its belly to squeeze through, trailing Connie on the ground as it did so.

'Gard!' begged Connie. But still no reply. A cold tide of stone sprites was flowing through the bedrock, freezing all communication.

The chimera loped across the empty car park to a huge white building, which was surrounded by storage tanks, ranging from turret-like cigar-shaped cisterns to two vast drum containers. The building itself was floodlit, gleaming against the night sky like the white castle of a modern giant. A gas flare burned perpetually in the sky above: a fiery flag marking the home of Axoil. The chimera had brought her to the oil refinery.

The chimera slipped in through an open door. Connie glimpsed a guard slumped in the shadows outside; his Alsatian whimpered pleadingly at her but there was nothing she could do to help. She could feel the material of her jacket beginning to split at the seams as the creature clattered up several flights of iron stairs, through some hanging plastic strips and into the central hall of the processing plant. It padded along a gantry, the steel structure ringing under the hooves of the goat, to drop Connie at the feet of Kullervo.

The shape-shifter had assumed his favourite shape of a midnight blue eagle and was perched on the gantry railing, his dark form a black void against the clinical white light bouncing off the walls. His shoulders were hunched as he brooded, hooked beak glinting like a scythe waiting to cut down anyone who came in reach.

Connie lay face down with a horrid sense of déjà vu, remembering how they had first met.

'You have hurt my companion.' Kullervo's voice echoed harshly in the cavernous room. 'How was this possible?'

Pleased by its successful labours for its master, the chimera sat on its haunches and licked its paws. Kullervo shifted shape, melting briefly into a dense dark mist before resolving into the form of a gigantic chimera, standing so that Connie was between his forepaws and could see in minute detail the ebony sharpness of his claws so close to her own skin. Watching the second chimera appear before it, Connie's abductor shivered with pleasure. The cobra-headed tail slithered to curl itself around its fellow, an intertwined knot of snakes. The lion-head sniffed the scent of its brother, recognizing the dominant male in its pride.

'She gave her word to drop her shield,' it purred subserviently.

'Ah. Being selfless no doubt. A human weakness,' Kullervo sneered.

Connie scrambled to her feet away from the

claws and raised her shield. It shone brightly even in this light, the four points of the universal's sign glittering like diamonds. With lightning swiftness, the chimera leapt away from Kullervo to block her escape, landing on the steel walkway with a clang.

'Well,' rumbled Kullervo in amusement, 'that promise did not last long.'

'I never promised how long.' Connie staggered backwards so that she was pressed against the railings. She stood between the chimerae, a mouse caught by two cruel cats intent on playing with her before the end. The Kullervo-chimera yawned and settled down on the gantry, rear hooves tucked to one side, snake tail undulating lazily over its back caressing its conjoined fellows. Kullervo raised a paw to his mismatched eyes and studied it.

'A most intriguing shape,' he mused. 'I like adopting this form: it has an enticing sense of danger as the three natures try to tear each other apart. Do you like it?' He turned his gaze to Connie. She said nothing. 'You've experienced an encounter with our friend here, I believe,' continued Kullervo. 'I was most jealous to hear about it. I would have enjoyed seeing you share this form. But there is still time for that.'

'Time?' said Connie, amazed to find she could

speak despite her terror. 'The Society will find out where I am. They'll come for me. Hadn't you better run before they get here?' But she knew her threats were hollow—and so did Kullervo. The refinery was the last place anyone would look for her even if Col and Rat did succeed in raising the alarm.

'Oh no, Universal. We have plenty of time. Your friends are busy fighting my army out on Dartmoor. Even as we speak the first clash of the dragons is taking place. They will have no chance to spare a thought for you—I have seen to that. They are hopelessly outnumbered and unprepared because, foolishly, they have not let their little universal near the moor to give them early warning of my massing forces.' Kullervo smiled, showing a row of white teeth.

'But the refinery—it can't be long before someone notices we're here!'

'Ah. You are right. Thank you for reminding me. I have a little diversion planned to keep the other humans busy too.' Kullervo nodded at the chimera. 'You know what to do. Bring our guests when you have finished.'

With a nimble leap, the chimera disappeared through the plastic screen and out of sight.

'What's it doing?' Connie asked fearfully, her thoughts going back to the guard she had glimpsed on her way in. Was the chimera going to attack anyone who came to the gate?

'Giving intruders a warm reception. This place has been doing its best to heat up the atmosphere: I thought it would be fitting if we hastened the process.'

'What do you mean?' Her shield wavered as she realized what was happening.

'Fire.' Kullervo shimmered fleetingly into the dark flickering form of a fire imp before taking shape as the eagle once more.

'But you'll kill us all!'

'Only the humans.' The eagle croaked as if pleased by her swiftness to grasp the situation. 'And not before you and I have concluded our business together. You, Companion, will survive if you do my bidding.'

Somewhere in the depths of the building a fire alarm began to ring.

'What business? You don't think you can persuade me to let you use my powers against humanity, do you? I'll never do that.'

The eagle took a pace nearer and lifted a talon towards the shield. 'This flimsy defence will not hold. You will be mine.'

'Never!' Connie gritted her teeth and clung on to the barrier. 'You'll have to kill me first.'

'Oh no, I'm not thinking of killing you. If you

refuse me again, it will be your friends' lives at stake.'

Connie heard footsteps behind her. She turned round quickly to see Col and Rat being pushed through the screen, the lion's jaws at Col's back, the snake hovering by Rat's neck.

'But our bargain!' Connie exclaimed to the chimera, her shield fading in shock.

'Never promised,' hissed the cobra in Connie's stunned mind. She raised her shield again and thrust the creature's presence from her.

Kullervo crowed with laughter. 'Never trust a two-faced creature, Companion. Bring him.' He pointed a claw at Col.

With a swipe of the lion's paw, Col was sent flying across the gantry, colliding with the railing before falling at Kullervo's feet.

'Careful,' the eagle chided the chimera, 'I do not want my guests to fall needlessly to their deaths. I have a far better use for them.'

The chimera growled, less compliant now that Kullervo was no longer in his chimera form.

Connie saw that Col was bleeding from many scratches. He raised his head; his eyes met hers; he seemed to be trying to apologize for having let her down, for having allowed himself to be captured.

'Oh yes, I will have great pleasure in killing

this troublesome one,' said Kullervo, turning his vicious eyes to Connie to see that she was hearing every word. 'If you don't agree to help me end once and for all the destruction brought by humanity, then I will have to find something to make you obey me. Perhaps I'll start with your friend. I have been feeling peckish.' He tapped his beak on Col's shoulder, rolling him over so that he was facing straight up at his captor. 'If you do not give in, I'll eat him. Where shall I begin?'

'No!' screamed Connie. She heard a scuffle behind her and a crack as Rat was knocked back by the snake as he had attempted to leap to his friend's aid. 'Don't you dare touch him!'

'So, you will be mine then?' asked the eagle gleefully, pawing at the meal before him with the talons of his right foot.

Col tried to push off Kullervo's hated touch but he was pinned to the floor. 'No, Connie. Don't give in!'

Overwhelmed with terror, Connie couldn't think straight. This wasn't how it was meant to be at all. When she had given herself up to the chimera, she had thought it was only her own life she was risking, but now she had the responsibility of her two friends to bear. Kullervo knew her too well: he had known she could be brave for herself, but not on behalf of others.

'I see you need more time to decide,' said Kullervo, beating his wings and shifting shape. The mist coiled and twisted, forming into a nine-headed hydra, black scales glowing like jet in the harsh light. 'Tie them up.' One head darted down to flicker its tongue over Col as if tasting his scent; another slid to Connie and grinned, ' . . . till dinner time.'

Suddenly, there was a deafening boom from outside; the ceiling-lamps went out and a wailing alarm echoed around the processing hall. The only light inside the building now came from the silver shimmer of the shield and the gleam of Kullervo's eighteen eyes. Beyond the windows danced the flicker of flame joined by the muffled noise of another explosion. Connie's eyes began to water as the air carried with it the trace of acrid fumes. Kullervo seemed very pleased with these signs of the progress of his plan. Two heads rose to look out of the window.

'Good, good,' he hissed. 'Very dangerous, oil fires. The fumes more harmful than the blaze itself. It will keep unwanted visitors away, but I advise you to decide quickly—or you all burn.'

He gave a spitting hiss into the shadows behind him, summoning more assistance, and Connie heard feet clanging on the stairs. Stone sprites scuttled into view with rope dangling in their teeth. Two went to Rat, two to Col, the remaining six surrounded Connie protected by her shield. She heard Rat cry out with shock as their cold pinching hands grasped his wrists.

'Don't hurt them!' she begged.

'Then I suggest you drop your shield and let my sprites tie you up like a good girl,' Kullervo laughed, the bubbles of foul gas bursting from the snake's head bobbing before her.

Reluctantly, Connie let the shield fade. The six creatures pounced on her, grabbing at her ankles and wrists. One had its freezing hands at her throat, constricting her breathing with its icy touch.

'Oh no, you are not to damage her,' said Kullervo, half-heartedly restraining his followers, unaware that Connie was secreting away some cold darts in her quiver beneath his very nose.

The stone sprites bound the three friends to the railings. They saved particular malice for the universal, lashing her so tightly she could barely move. Col and Rat were either side of her, out of reach but close enough for speech. The stone sprites scuttled off, their task done, the sound of their clicking joints disappearing into the shadows. Connie almost preferred it when she could see them: it was worse to imagine them waiting somewhere in the darkness to pounce.

The hydra slid over to Connie and curled in a half-moon around her.

'I will leave you to reflect on my offer,' Kullervo said with one of its many mouths. 'Offer! Offer!' echoed the others. 'Be sure to have your answer ready when I return. I will not be long. There is someone I want you to meet.'

The hydra reared up over the gantry railing and slithered down like a python hanging from a branch. Twisting around the walkway below, Kullervo slipped off into the darkness.

Left alone, the three friends felt the huge weight of the silence that had fallen between them. Col, shifting painfully on his scratched legs and back, knew that one of them must speak. He must help stiffen Connie's resolve to resist Kullervo, even if it meant condemning himself and Rat.

'Are you OK, Connie?' he whispered. A series of loud cracks and bangs exploded, indicating that another blaze had erupted outside. 'Sorry we couldn't get away.'

'It would've been no good,' she replied despondently, 'they're all busy fighting Kullervo's army. There's no one at the Mastersons'.'

'You know what?' said Rat, trying to sound cheerful, 'I'd've liked to have been in a decent battle with Icefen but . . . ' He couldn't finish the sentence.

'But now we're trussed up here like turkeys for Christmas,' said Col with a hollow laugh. Silence fell again.

'I'm scared, Col,' said Connie in a small voice. Col could see her sitting upright, straight-backed against the railing, her face deathly white.

'Me too,' Col replied, desperately trying to think of something to hearten her, some bright thought. 'But you must keep firm. This isn't about us two: it's about all of them out there. Think of all those beautiful, wonderful people you'll be saving—and the creatures who try to defend us. If you let him use you again, he'll destroy us all.'

Connie choked on her tears. 'I can't send you to your death. I just can't.'

'You must!' he growled.

Connie felt something crack inside her. 'I'm going to do it: I'm going to challenge him. It's the only way.'

'No!'

'I've said all along that it would come to this.' She was close to panic.

'But you've been forbidden to do so by the Trustees,' Col countered, wishing he could give her a hug as he could see her falling to pieces before his eyes. 'They had a good reason.'

'Stuff the Trustees, mate,' interrupted Rat.

'Shut up!' said Col. 'You don't know what you're asking her to do.'

'I'm only asking her not to feed me to that monster!' Rat shouted back. 'I don't want to die, even if you do.'

'Of course, I don't want to die!' Col yelled at him, wishing he had his hands free so he could throttle Rat for his stupidity, 'but we'll only die later if she can't hold out against him—and so will millions of others. That or he'll torture her to death.'

'Ah, that's what I like to hear,' hissed Kullervo, sliding back onto the gantry and writhing past Col to stop before Connie. He seemed to swell in size in the presence of their argument. 'Friend at war with friend—my favourite human trait.'

Col and Rat both shut up abruptly, neither of them wanting to give Kullervo the satisfaction of hearing them disagree.

'So, have you decided, Companion?' asked Kullervo.

Connie nodded, keeping her eyes on the floor. She wasn't brave. She was a coward.

'And what is your decision?' the hydra asked, its tongues like black ticker tape fluttering in the air above her in celebration.

274

Connie raised her head and looked briefly across at Col, her interior struggle evident on her face. Col shook his head but she turned her gaze on the nearest head of the hydra.

'Meet me at the mark. I challenge you to single-combat.'

15
Voice from the Past

'No, Connie!' cried Col, straining at his bonds to reach her, to stop her doing this, but she ignored him.

'But I want a proper bargain this time. No tricks. They must be set free first.' She gestured with her head to Rat and Col. 'And all the other humans you've got trapped here. I want to see them walking out to safety. Then,' her voice almost disappearing, 'I'm all yours.'

Kullervo dissolved and reformed into the shape of a great bear, thick blue-black fur shining in the light coming through the high windows. He moved towards Connie, the gantry groaning under the weight of his vast bulk. He raised a sharp-clawed paw in the air. Connie closed her eyes, not wanting to see her death approaching. She felt the rush in the air as the claws passed close to her neck, the soft pelt brushing her cheek. The ropes that bound her fell to the ground.

'Very well,' growled Kullervo. 'They go free. The stone sprites will drag the other humans clear of the fire to a place where they can be found. I would have made them walk away like you ask, but unfortunately, they are all out cold.' The bear growled with laughter.

'They're not dead?' she asked.

'Not yet—and thanks to you, it looks as though they will live another day.' His snout nuzzled the top of her head. 'Just one more day before you surrender to me. We both know that you have only bought them a temporary reprieve.'

'Temporary or not—I'm taking it,' said Connie with determination, getting to her feet and away from him. Even upright, she did not reach the thigh of the great bear.

How can she possibly hope to defeat that? Col marvelled.

But she doesn't expect to win, another voice in his head whispered. She's going to sacrifice herself to let you survive.

'Connie, it's not too late. Please change your mind,' Col urged her.

Kullervo turned to him. 'I am getting tired of the bleating of this little one. I will be pleased to get rid of him.' He raised his paw. Connie shrieked, unable to stop herself, fearing he was about to strike.

The bear swung his head towards her. 'Do not be concerned, Companion. Our bargain will hold for a little longer.' He cut through Col's bonds. 'Run, boy. You are free. Take your chance. But you'd better hurry: the chimera is on the prowl outside and, though I command it in most things, I cannot be answerable for how it chooses to satisfy its appetite.'

Col scrambled to his feet, dodged past the massive forepaws of the bear and ran to Rat. He swiftly untied the knots holding Rat to the railing and hauled him to his feet. The moment Rat felt his bonds loose, he made a dash for the exit. Col hesitated and glanced at Connie, who was standing so still as she watched her two friends escape. No way could he just run. He sprinted back to her and swept her into a tight hug.

'If we get out of this,' he whispered in her ear, 'there's something I want to ask you.'

'I'll look forward to it,' she said bravely, though without much hope. 'Give my love to . . . to the others.'

Col felt a paw push on his back.

'Get away from my companion. She is mine now,' growled Kullervo.

With a final desperate hug, Col turned and ran after Rat, each step costing him worse pain than anything he had experienced so far that night.

Bursting out of the side door, he was pulled up short by Rat who had pressed himself against the wall.

'Stone sprite!' Rat warned.

To their left, Col could see the pale outline of a sprite dragging a man away. An Alsatian barked and snapped at the creature, but its teeth made no impression on rock.

'At least Kullervo's keeping his part of the bargain,' muttered Col as they watched the stone sprite pull the man into a warehouse, separate from the refinery building. 'They should be OK in there.'

In contrast, the refinery itself was clearly in grave danger. Between the boys and the main entrance a fire now raged. The battlements of the oil castle were under siege. Great billows of black smoke belched into the air, lashed by red tongues of flame from burning cisterns. A wall of fire separated them from the emergency vehicles that had rushed to the scene. The boys could hear the wail of sirens in the night but they had no chance of reaching help that way.

'We need to get out,' said Col.

Rat jerked on his sleeve and nodded over to their right. The dark form of the chimera was slinking between the two big drum containers, scorching their metal sides with bursts of its flame. Fortunately for Col and Rat, it was too preoccupied by its game to notice them. With stone sprites on their left, a chimera and a wall of fire on their right, they had no choice but to make a dash straight ahead to see if they could find a way through the high fence.

'On three,' breathed Col, waiting for a moment when the chimera had its back turned, 'One, two, three!'

The boys burst from their hiding place and sprinted across the car park, hitting the fence with a clatter.

'Look, there's a gap!' cried Rat, dragging Col through the entrance used by the chimera.

The boys paused on the other side of the fence, at a loss for a moment what they should do.

'Shall we go to the police?' Col asked, knowing the idea sounded ridiculous. What could even the whole Devon and Cornwall constabulary do against Kullervo?

Rat nodded. 'We've got to give it a try.'

It seemed miles running around the perimeter of the refinery. Stumbling in the dark over weeds, bits of masonry, and an abandoned supermarket trolley that had been left in the no-man's land of the industrial estate, they finally made their way onto the access road. In contrast to the desert they had just left, this was teeming with people. Seven fire engines were parked as close to the fires as they could, hoses trained on the blaze. Firefighters with blackened, sweaty faces jogged by carrying more equipment, jostling the boys out of the way.

'What the hell are you doing here?' A policeman strode over from his car and clamped a firm hand on the shoulders of both. 'The order to evacuate the area was given half an hour ago—and that includes you two.'

'But—!' protested Col, trying to wriggle free as the burly policeman pulled them away.

'No buts,' said the policeman.

'But we were in there,' Rat shouted at him, trying to get it through the man's thick skull that there was another emergency for him to deal with. 'Our friend's in there.'

Rat's words had started a completely new train of thought in the policeman's head. 'You were in there?' He dropped his hold on Col and began to pat Rat's pockets, checking for matches. 'Not indulging in a little bit of arson, were you?'

This wasn't going well. If the policeman had

his way they would be spending the rest of the night answering questions at the local police station.

Col caught Rat's eye. Rat understood.

'Now!' yelled Col.

With a twist to equal Skylark's Syracrusian Spiral, Rat slipped free from the policeman's hand and ran off to the left. Col darted to the right.

Rat had had plenty of practice dodging the police so he knew back-up would be after them. Catching a glimpse of Col sprinting parallel to him through a depot belonging to the local dairy, he made a dash across the road and pulled Col into the darkness of an unlit alleyway.

'Keep still,' he hissed.

A police car zipped past, heading away from the refinery, blue lights flashing.

'We need to reach help,' panted Col, 'but it's going to take too long on foot.'

Rat pulled out Connie's phone but it was still dead.

'Remember, she said everyone would be up on the moor,' said Col.

'Not everyone—what about your dad? You can't get the Kraken up onto the moor.'

'You're right. And Evelyn will be home, even if he's not.'

'And what about the Khalids? Aren't they

staying at your house? I doubt the Society will have sent them up there—at least not the boys.'

Col nodded. 'Let's split up: you go to my house; I'll fetch Dad. He'll know what to do.' Col felt a sudden powerful desire to see his father, to hand over responsibility for tonight's mess to someone he could trust to have Connie's best interests at heart. Mack had fought to save Connie last year; he would do the same now.

'But we're still miles from Hescombe. We need transport—the police'll pick us up in an instant if they find us running down the road.'

Col gazed around him for inspiration. The answer was obvious. 'I wouldn't normally suggest this but . . . '

Rat was quick to catch on. 'We'll need to get the keys.' Without pausing for further thought, Rat picked up the metal lid of an old milk churn lying in the passage and chucked it through the window behind them. An alarm bell began to sound inside the dairy, but all the workers had been evacuated and there was no one, not even a night guard, to stop the two boys climbing in and ransacking the garage until they found the keys.

'Here, put these on too,' said Rat, throwing an overall and cap to Col. 'You look a mess.'

Col gave a grunt of laughter for they both knew that Rat looked, if anything, worse.

The boys dashed over to one of the milk floats standing idle in the yard. The evacuation had come as the dairy workers were halfway through loading up for the morning's deliveries. The van was stacked with crates of milk and orange juice. Rat grabbed a couple of packets from the back before slipping onto the seat beside Col.

'Let's go,' he commanded, ripping open a carton of orange and downing it thirstily.

The engine whined into life and purred out onto the roadway. Slowly but steadily they made their way along the road leading out of the industrial estate. Col had to pull over a couple of times as more fire engines and six ambulances passed in convoy.

'They must've found the workers in the warehouse,' Col noted grimly. They looked at each other, both wondering what had happened to Connie by now. Was she still alive?

A police car slowed beside them, the driver peering curiously at the milk float making its way as fast as it could away from the refinery. Col pulled his cap low over his eyes. Rat put his feet up on the dashboard and began to whistle cheerfully. The policewoman lowered her window.

'You do know you were supposed to have evacuated an hour ago?' she called to them.

'Yes, officer,' called Rat politely. 'We're just on

our way now. My brother here said we couldn't let our customers down, you see.'

'Well,' said the policewoman tersely, 'if you're making deliveries anywhere downwind of the refinery, you'll find all your customers have gone.'

'No, no, we're on our way to Hescombe.'

The policewoman gave a curt nod. 'Then hurry on out of here. But I'll be complaining to your bosses at . . . ' she glanced at the side of the van, 'at the Sunnyside Dairy that you didn't get out quicker.'

'Er . . . yeah, sorry.'

'On your way, then,' she said at last, deciding that, what with the fire and the evacuation, there were too many other things to worry about to waste her time on them.

Col breathed a sigh of relief and put his foot down on the accelerator. The police car sped past, leaving them following slowly in its wake.

Once Col and Rat had left, Connie felt a huge weight of responsibility lift from her shoulders. She thought she could bear to face anything that might happen to her, but she could not have watched Kullervo torture them before her eyes. There was silence between Connie and the shape-shifter as they listened to the boys' footsteps clattering away on the stairs.

'Satisfied, Companion?' grunted the bear, ambling over to her on four paws and nuzzling her again with his velvety black snout. Connie felt a shudder of revulsion and dodged away. The creature did not seem deterred by her rejection of his touch.

'I am certain you will not be like the others, Universal. None of them understood me like you do. They all fought to the end—their end—but not you. You will be different.'

Connie said nothing, still standing straight-backed against the railing.

'Those men from the Society were proud crea-tures, all of them. They only thought of me as a monster to be destroyed. They did not realize, as I know you do, that humanity is the monster that must be wiped out.'

'So you killed them all—Guy de Chauliac, George Brewer, and I don't know how many countless others,' said Connie bitterly.

The bear settled down at her feet, throwing out an arm to hook her away from the edge so she came to rest between his forepaws like a tiny cub. His warm breath, scented of honey, stirred her hair as he growled softly above her. 'Yes, there were many. But that is nature's way. The weak perish; the strong survive. You should not blame me for being what I am.' Connie sat tensely in his embrace, trying to control her terror. 'And you will find that even I can be merciful. I did not kill them all.'

Surprised, Connie turned her head to gaze up at him to see if he was telling the truth. His blazing eyes were shadowed by no lie that she could detect. 'Are you telling me that you did not kill Guy de Chauliac?'

The bear grunted. 'Oh no, I killed the universal. He was a feast that could not be resisted. No, I kept alive one who offered only a mouthful, who had no powers for me to consume.' He raised his snout and growled a low rumbling summons into the shadows. 'Come forward, Companion to Great Bears.'

Connie heard the tap of a walking stick and the wheeze of halting breath. Out of the darkness stepped an old man, bent over under the weight of long years of suffering. He limped forward, trailing a dirty fur cloak on the ground. Several of the fingers that grasped his staff had lost their tips as if he had once been severely frostbitten. He came to a halt by the bear and bowed.

'Master,' he said hoarsely. He then raised his grey-skinned face, deeply scored with lines, to peer at Connie. 'I am honoured to meet you, great-niece.'

16
Human Companion

Col dropped Rat at the top of the High Street, leaving him to dash to the Clamworthys' house while he puttered on to Shaker Row. The milk float seemed to be going infuriatingly slowly—only twenty miles an hour downhill—and he was on several occasions tempted to abandon it to continue on foot. But he knew that in his exhausted state it was quicker to remain where he was.

The milk bottles rattled and clanked as he turned into the Row. He saw that Evelyn's car was not parked outside. His heart sank: it looked as if his father was not there. But he had come all this way: he had to check. Leaving the float outside

Mr and Mrs Lucas's gate, he clattered round to the back door.

'Dad! Dad!' he yelled, bursting into the kitchen.

'Col! Thank God!' It was not his father who answered but Evelyn.

Col could not see her at first. 'Evelyn? Where are you?'

Evelyn gave a long agonized groan. Col now spotted her doubled up on the floor by the empty fireplace. 'It's the baby. It's coming. I've tried the hospital . . . ' She stopped, another wave of pain hitting her. Col ran over to kneel at her side. 'But all the ambulances are at some fire. They've called the midwife, but she's been evacuated from her home. They said they'd try to send a doctor . . . aargh!' She swore again, waiting for the agony to fade.

Col did not know what to do first. 'Where's Dad?' he asked quickly.

'I don't know,' she said, panting hard, 'he's not come back. But there's no time for that. I think it's almost here. You've got to help.'

'I'll be with you in a minute,' Col said frantically. He dialled his home. There was no answer. He dialled the Mastersons' and Shirley picked up the phone.

'Yes?'

'Is my dad there?' he asked without even giving

289

his name. But Shirley knew full well who was speaking.

'Get off the line, Col,' she said angrily. 'Don't you realize there's an emergency on the moor? I'm running headquarters as everyone else is out there.'

'Even my dad?'

'No, not your dad. He left with your gran before the alarm. Now put the phone down.'

'Forget the moor, Shirley,' he hissed so Evelyn would not hear. 'Kullervo's got Connie at the refinery—that's the real emergency. Get a message to the others.'

Col slammed the phone down as Evelyn gave a groan. Glancing between the door and his stepmother, Col struggled with what to do next. Really, there was only one thing he could do. He couldn't abandon Evelyn, not now.

Many anxious minutes later, Col was the first one to pick up the baby from the cocoon of towels, feeling its warm wetness and beating of the tiny heart in its chest. Just as he handed it to Evelyn with shaking hands, the back door flew open and the doctor rushed into the kitchen carrying a heavy black bag.

'Sorry I wasn't here sooner, Evelyn,' she said, rushing to her patient's side. 'The hospital switchboard was in chaos—they only just got through to me.' Assuming that Col would know where everything was, she dispatched him to fetch fresh clothes for Evelyn and the romper suit that had been set aside for the infant. After a few false starts, Col dug out one of his father's nightshirts for Evelyn and then went through to the nursery. Turning on the light, he stood for a moment in silent admiration. Winged horses revolved with dragons in a mobile over the baby's cradle. The Kraken writhed darkly in the centre of the wall. Banshees and wood sprites circled in endless dances across a green field. The room reminded him of nothing more than Connie's wall of encounters.

Connie.

Grabbing a pile of clothes, he leapt down the stairs two at a time and back into the kitchen.

'You'll be OK now, won't you?' said Col, dumping the clothes beside the startled doctor and dashing to the door. 'I'm off to find Dad.'

Evelyn smiled up contentedly over the black hair of her baby. 'Yes, your brother and I will be fine. Thanks, Col.'

When Col ran out of Number Five, he thought he would have no choice but to drive the milk float back to Chartmouth, though the chances of getting there in time to be of any help were remote.

But fortunately there was a much swifter means of transport waiting for him. He felt a prickle at the back of his neck before he heard the clatter of hooves landing on the tarmac behind him.

'Skylark!' he cried, never having felt so relieved to see the pegasus in his life. 'You've come in the nick of time!'

Skylark trotted forward a few paces so his companion could mount him. 'Where've you been, Col?' the pegasus asked, relief replacing the cold anxiety that had gripped him all night. 'I've been looking for you all over the moor! It's a nightmare out there—casualties being ferried back to the Mastersons', reinforcements arriving from all over the country—I couldn't get a word of sense out of anyone. Finally, I found Mags and all he would tell me was that you'd been attacked.'

'We were, but there's no time to explain. Let's get going.'

'Where to?' asked Skylark as he began to gallop down Shaker Row to reach take-off speed.

'To the refinery.' The bumpy ride was replaced with smooth strokes of wings as Skylark's hooves left the ground. 'Kullervo's got Connie there—or he had a couple of hours ago.' Col could not bring himself to imagine what might have happened since. 'I think Rat, Dad, and the others set off earlier. I hope Shirley passed the message on to the rest of the Society members. The attack on the moor's a diversion.'

Skylark neighed, shaking damp droplets from his white mane. He had been flying all night scouring each valley and hilltop for his friend and was exhausted but he found new strength hearing of the threat to the universal. 'Perhaps she did. I saw Dr Brock and Argot heading towards Chartmouth some time ago. I wondered what they were up to. But the Trustees and our volunteers were still trying to hold back Kullervo's army. I feared that he might have you with his forces.'

'How are we doing?'

'We're paying a high price—the dragon twins were both injured by that renegade weather giant, Hoo; at least one of the dragons is dead. Six of the rock dwarfs were attacked by stone sprites and have been reduced to rubble—it's terrible. I couldn't see any more but I know that scores are being treated by Kira and Windfoal at the farm. They could do with the universal's help right now.'

'Connie can't help—she might not even be alive. Oh, Skylark!' Col said no more, his thoughts choked off by the grip of fear.

They were now flying over Mallins Wood. Before them, Col could see great plumes of black smoke rising into the grey dawn sky. The blue and red lights of the emergency vehicles flashed below: there were at least twenty vehicles parked haphazardly in front of the fire. A fringe of gold flame blazed on the tops of the two drum containers like twin volcanoes on the verge of erupting.

'Where can we land?' wondered Skylark, looking down at all the humans scurrying like ants around a burning nest.

'In no-man's land,' said Col, steering him around the curtain of cloud. 'There's another way in. I bet that's where Rat would've taken everyone.'

Col was right. When they landed not far from the hole in the fence, they found a small knot of people and creatures gathered outside the perimeter. All looked grim. Mack was talking earnestly to Rat, Col's grandmother, Mrs Khalid, and Liam; Dr Brock was huddled in the middle of a group of four that included Simon, a Nemean lion, an Amalthean goat, and a great snake. Omar Khalid was standing just inside the fence, arms raised like a conductor, directing the activities of six sylphs who were busy keeping the smoke wall intact to hide their presence, as well as blowing the poisonous fumes away. Argot stood guard in front of Omar, his emerald eyes fixed on the prowling presence of the chimera, which was striding in the middle of the empty car park, jaws open in a mad grin, ready to pounce on anyone who tried to reach the door. Not that any human could have survived in there now: smoke, accompanied by the occasional belch of flame, issued from the building. Col felt sick: he could see at a glance that there was no sign of Connie amongst the little of band of Society members.

Everyone looked up when they spotted Skylark circling down from overhead. Mack strode over and gave his son a clumsy embrace as Col dismounted. 'Are you all right, son? What kept you?'

Mrs Clamworthy swooped on her grandson and gave him a trembling hug.

'I'll tell you later,' said Col quickly to Mack. This did not seem the moment to break the news of the new arrival. 'What's the plan?'

Mack sighed. He looked wrung out with anxiety. 'There's been no sign of Connie or Kullervo. The stone sprites scuttled away about ten minutes ago—they were blocking our way too and we hadn't worked out a way past them. Now we've just got the chimera to deal with. And the fire.' He added as an afterthought, 'And Kullervo.'

Col was on the verge of asking if Mack thought there was any hope, but he bit his tongue, knowing it was pointless. They had to continue as if there was still a chance Connie could be saved. Instead he asked, 'So, what first?'

'The chimera,' replied Mack. He turned to Dr Brock. 'Ready?' The doctor nodded and, steering Simon by the arm, ducked through the wire mesh. The three companions followed: the lion, a magnificent tawny giant with a mane of black fur; the goat who was of a size to match the lion, with a fleece white and silky and great curling horns; the snake, as thick as a tree trunk and at least twenty metres long by the time it had unfurled to wriggle through the fence. Dr Brock said some final words to Simon. He nodded and took five paces forward. The three companions closed ranks around him, the snake coiling protectively around his feet, the lion at his right shoulder, the goat at his left. The chimera stopped prowling and gathered itself for a roar of challenge. Who were these who dared to invade its territory? No one in the little group of four companions flinched, though Col had put his hands over his ears at the deafening, hated sound of that creature's voice. Simon closed his eyes—the last thing Col would have wanted to do standing within an easy bound of the chimera—and raised his arms to touch the silky fleece of the goat and the rough pelt of the lion. The snake's tongue flickered across his shoes.

Slowly, Simon then removed his right hand and pointed it directly at the chimera.

With a start as though it had just been struck, the chimera leapt backwards and gave an angry bellow. The attempt to bond with it seemed to send it further into madness. Horrified, fearful for Simon's safety, Col watched the chimera shake its lion-head in agony, the snake tail lashing, hooves sparking on the tarmac like flashes from flint. Desperate to end the voices now speaking in its head, commanding its obedience, the creature leapt towards Simon, attempting to silence by force the source of this suffering. With reflexes of lightning, the Nemean lion pounced to intercept, knocked the chimera sideways, and came to rest with his two great paws on the chimera's chest. At the same instant, the great snake slid forwards and swiftly curled itself around the chimera's tail before it could sink its fangs into the lion. Joining the melee, the Amalthean goat galloped forward and stamped on the kicking, struggling hooves. The creature now pinioned, Simon walked calmly to the head of the beast.

'Don't forget its fire!' Col breathed, while he stood watching, amazed at Simon's courage.

But Simon was not concerned that he would receive a blast of flames for his trouble: he sensed, as no one else could, the change within his companion creature. It had recognized the superior strength of the king of lions; the tail was curled in fraternal embrace with a far greater snake; even the goat stopped struggling hysterically as it realized that neither flight nor fight would save it.

'Be at peace,' commanded Simon, laying a hand on the chimera's mane and stroking it. The chimera shivered. Even from where Col was standing, he could hear the deep rumbling that now came from its throat: it was purring. Simon stood up and nodded to Mack.

'Good,' said Mack, ducking his head as he came through the fence. On this signal, the others followed him. 'Now for the fire.'

Kullervo left George Brewer alone with his great-niece, pacing off to see the progress of the fire he had started. The firefighters were making little impression. Every time they thought they had begun to gain control over a blaze a new one erupted in a quite different part of the refinery. The fire had now reached the staff canteen and the building itself was aflame.

'Magnificent, isn't he?' said George Brewer watching the great bear stalk off into the night. He turned and sat down beside Connie, groaning as he lowered his worn out limbs to the floor. 'I didn't understand, you see? I didn't understand what he was really like when I attacked him.'

Connie did not want to hear praise of Kullervo. She hadn't yet recovered from the shock of seeing a dead man come back to life. 'So why did you let everyone believe you were dead? Why didn't you come home?'

'I wanted to at first,' said George, gazing up at the flames flickering outside the windows, his face drawn with the memory of the early years in Kullervo's service. 'Until I saw that his way was better. He thought you might come along.'

'What? How could he know?' She hugged her knees, resting her head on them, wishing she was anywhere else but here.

'The eyes, my dear: the mark of the families to which universals are born. You've all had them, you know, all you universals. Sometimes the universal gift can lie fallow for many generations, but the eyes remind us that the bloodline persists to be discovered again one day. Your great-aunt Sybil had them too, you know, showing that the Lionhearts still carried the gift.'

'He knew about her eyes?' Connie asked in a hollow tone of voice. 'How?'

'I admit he did extract that from me.' George

shuddered as if the memory was painful. 'When he found that out, he said he would spare me because I might be useful to him one day. And so I am, it would seem.' He gave Connie a feeble grin. He'd lost most of his front teeth—Connie wondered if they had been knocked out; his hands and face bore many scars. Pity stirred in her.

'Useful? How so?' she asked gently.

'To explain to you, my great-niece, that it is no good fighting him. I should know: I watched many good men die at his hands.'

'And you still serve him!' exclaimed Connie, now in disgust.

George shook his head. 'You don't understand. It was we who attacked him—it was I who led them to their deaths. I have paid for my error ever since. Don't fight him, my girl.'

'I am not your girl. You're not even my proper uncle.' Connie got up to distance herself from him. 'You left my great-aunt thinking she was a widow. You never cared about what happened to her, did you?'

'Oh, I cared,' George said sadly, and Connie knew he was speaking the truth. 'But he wouldn't let me go. He calls me his pet human.' He gave a humourless laugh.

'Better to have died than live like that!'

'Do you really think so?' he asked as if giving serious thought for the first time to her suggestion. 'I would've preferred to die at the beginning. That was until I realized his way was right. I have been living in the north all these years with nothing to do but watch as humans heated up the world. It seemed to me that our reckless, greedy burning of fuel was like that of a sailor on a wooden raft setting light to his own vessel just to keep warm, paying no heed to the consequences. My disgust and hatred of my own kind grew as I watched the ice melt, the polar bears lose their habitat, the creatures being driven closer to the edge of extinction and I found I no longer thought my own life was of any value. It no longer mattered if I lived or died: only if they survived. And they will only survive if you help him.' He raised his scrawny hand to clasp her sleeve. 'Join with him. Help Kullervo save the world from humanity.'

Connie could see the mad gleam in George Brewer's eyes as he looked up at her. His years of isolation in the snowy wastes of the Arctic had unhinged him. If he could say those words and mean them, then he must have forgotten what it was to love another human. Having felt nothing but fear for the past few hours, Connie was flooded with the comforting warmth of the most powerful emotion she knew. She realized she had not forgotten for one moment what it was to love—not only other creatures but her own imperfect fellow humans; what she felt for brave, proud Col; for daft, vibrant Rat; for argumentative, grumbling Simon; for complex, caring Evelyn; for her loving yet disapproving parents; for Jane and Anneena, innocent of knowledge of any of this; even for brash, courageous Mack; and for all her other friends. Yes, they were worth dying for. That was her greatest strength.

'I will not join with him. But I won't fight him. He'll have to kill me,' Connie said, surprised to find her voice quite firm as she spoke.

An angry growl rumbled in the darkness. The gantry creaked as Kullervo-great bear bounded back in. He took a swipe—Connie instinctively ducked but the blow was not aimed at her. George Brewer was flung the full length of the walkway, smashing into the far wall. 'You failed me!' snarled Kullervo. 'All these years of waiting, and you failed me! You are a pathetic, useless human!'

'Sorry, master,' George whispered, as he slid to the floor. He did not move again.

Kullervo turned back to Connie, his rage now deadly cold. 'So, you are going to refuse me after all? Just like the other universals I had to kill?'

'I have no choice,' she whispered. 'I'm not a murderer.'

'You had a choice and you chose to die. You chose not to save your fellow creatures just to protect your own kind. I despise you for that. You are not worthy to be my companion.' He sniffed her hair, the saliva from his jaws dripping on her shoulder. 'I will have great pleasure in exhausting your powers. Though young, you have proved stronger than many of the others and will make a good meal for me. Shall I start now?'

Connie took a pace backwards and faced him, raising her shield so that the compass etched on its surface blazed into his eyes. She saw herself mirrored there—sharp and clear in the light of the shield. It gave her an idea.

She took a breath. 'Not so fast, Companion. I challenged you to meet me at the mark.'

Kullervo gave a growl of delight. 'So you are going to fight after all? If I must kill, then I prefer my prey to resist. The hunt is no fun without a chase.'

'Meet me at the mark,' Connie replied tersely.

Learning the lesson the minotaur had taught her that an enemy will not wait, Connie closed her eyes and dashed to arrive first at the wall of encounters, the place deep in her mind where all the creatures with whom she had bonded had left their mark and where Kullervo's dark void was found. She could hear the hiss and suck of his presence just through the wall, so close that it was hard to say where her mind ended and his began. But she was not going to let him in this time to take her over; nor was she going to exhaust her weak armoury in a futile defence of the barrier. She was going to do what no other universal had done: she was going through.

Abandoning the shield that she still held in her hand, Connie launched herself through the mark, diving like a seabird from a cliff. The wall of encounters crumbled and collapsed behind her. Her shadow-body lost its form once it was in the black void on the other side. She became a waterfall of silver tumbling down to meet him. She was in a place she had never been before—inside the shape-shifter's very being. The mind of Kullervo stretched away on all sides with seemingly no beginning or end, appearing to her like a starless sky over a dark blue sea. But the waters were alive with potential, poised to shift into a new shape in the blink of an eye. Though starless, the sky was not without light. Flickering shapes like the patterns cast over the North Pole by the Aurora Borealis etched themselves briefly across the heavens before winking out. As she fell towards the waters below, she saw that these patterns were reflected beneath her, the forms that Kullervo had mastered rippling in the sea, an endless stream of possibilities, bodies to inhabit, powers to assume.

But there was one possibility Kullervo had never anticipated: his waters were about to receive a new form in the shape of an uninvited guest.

Kullervo had no time to prepare himself for the unexpected attack from the girl he thought he had subdued. The meeting of the two tides—the powers of the universal and of the shape-shifter—was like the meeting of two oceans at the continental cape. They crashed together, mingling, creating great shock waves.

'I challenge you—you must take my form,' Connie urged the darkness. 'You must.' She brought the imprint of herself into him in the very collision that sent his water soaring into the air. She wanted to give him knowledge of the human form—its wonders, its limitations, its strengths. But she received only rejection in return.

The dark waters fled from the silver tide that swept through them. Even so, they could not escape mingling with the weak creature that they hated more than any other: a human.

'No!' stormed Kullervo. He fought back but he could no longer assault the frail mind of the universal as he had done in the past. Connie had totally abandoned herself to him and had left nothing behind for him to attack. She could not go back now even if she tried. She had become him and he had to become her. Kullervo rose up into the form of a weather giant to blow the silver waves away, but the tide of the universal twisted round him, pulling the nascent form back into the sea. He writhed into the many-armed shape of the Kraken to cast her aside, but he could get no hold on the illusive being that slid through his grasp like quicksilver.

'I'll crush you!' cursed Kullervo. 'I'll stamp out every trace of your being, you foul creature, you monster!' Images of rampaging creatures flickered across the sky like flashes of lightning.

'Take my form,' the universal challenged him again. 'Defeat me that way if you must.'

Then the silver waters rose to the surface and began to close in around Kullervo's darkness like a glove enveloping a hand, squeezing him into the tight confines of the form of a young girl.

'Find out what it is to be human,' she urged him. 'We may be weak. We may be destructive. But we are part of this world too. Acknowledge this and I'll let you go. I'll become whatever you want.'

'Never!' howled Kullervo, battering against the prison of the shape he most despised and had always resisted adopting. He was not going to succumb to this trial she had thrust upon him.

She sensed his resistance and sought for a way to soften it. If only they could be brought to understand each other, she thought, maybe they could find peace? She was prepared to risk it, but would he?

'You see, I can love even you, Kullervo—what we could have been—what we could still be. Remember—you once showed me.' A shared memory crackled between them like an electric current as they relived the dance in the air—she had tumbled and twisted in the cloud of his being as he turned into dragon, phoenix, griffin. The silver water diverted from the human form it had been trying to take and assumed the form of each creature as they remembered together their dangerous game. But Connie had made a perilous concession. Kullervo took advantage of this lull in her onslaught and continued to play through the changes—fire imp, great bear, eagle. The shifts were coming faster and faster—Connie could not wrench him back on the path to take the human form. Instead she found herself being spun into more and more shapes—stretched into a great snake, sprouting the wings of a siren, heads of a cerberus, tail of a salamander. Hydra. Chimera. It was agony.

'I take you, Universal!' roared Kullervo, exulting in her pain as he forced her to assume shape after shape. 'But this is even better than before, better than any of the others I have encountered. I have you here, inside me, you'll never be exhausted, never escape. This game can go on for all eternity!'

'No!' gasped Connie, suddenly aware of the terrible danger she was in, scrambling to escape the kaleidoscope of shapes he was shifting her through. 'I challenged you to take my form. By the rules of the combat, you cannot refuse!'

Rock dwarf, wood sprite, kelpie, gorgon. Kullervo cackled with glee as he dragged her through more shapes, delighting in displaying the endless variety of his repertoire. Connie was drowned in pain beyond anything she had ever felt or imagined. She could feel her sense of self beginning to disintegrate under the onslaught; the silver tide was in danger of dispersing and being mingled for ever with his darkness.

What was it like to be human? She could no longer remember. She could not even recall what she looked like. Just let the pain stop, she cried. But she knew it would not.

Nemean lion, cyclops, pegasus.

Suddenly she remembered—not her own face, but that of Col, the companion to pegasi.

Then came Rat, her aunt, Mack, Anneena, Jane—images of all the people she loved were seared into her mind with a power that only death could extinguish. The pegasus dissolved and out of the waters rose a silver Col, laughing as he flew on Skylark. Beside him, Rat emerged from the waves, chewing calmly on a piece of straw—Anneena waving her arms enthusiastically—Jane reading quietly—Simon grumbling about something—Evelyn dancing with Mack. Everywhere she looked she saw the silver shape of the people she loved rising out of Kullervo's waters, down to her parents who appeared watching the scene with characteristically shocked expressions.

'What are these abominations?' screamed Kullervo, striking at the human shapes with clawing waves.

Finally out of the water rose a silver girl—amongst her friends once more, Connie could remember herself. The silver shapes joined hands with her in their midst, forming an unbreakable circle.

'Will you not learn to love this form too?' she asked Kullervo. 'We could be joined together as equals—live in peace.'

'Never,' he cursed her. 'I reject your way utterly.'

'Then, my friends, let us complete the challenge,' Connie said to her circle.

On her signal, they dived down into the dark waters that so hated them, taking into the very heart of Kullervo their knowledge of what it was to be human. His darkness and hate fought back but he could not resist the transforming power of Connie's love. Used to invading the minds of others and bending them to his will, he discovered he was bound to hers for he and his companion were equals: there was no force in him that could break her grip when she carried the challenge to him. Her love for humanity transfused like fire into his soul. It was a power beyond anything he knew. The universal whispered to him that if he embraced it too, he might find there something to satisfy the emptiness inside him, the void that drove him to assume the shape of others. But he rejected her offer, attempting to dash the knowledge away as if it were a poisoned chalice she held to his lips.

As the silver radiance shone ever brighter, penetrating the darkest corners of his being, burning it away, Kullervo had nowhere to run from the searching light of the universal, no dark shadows he could twist to his purposes. His whole being was now ablaze as the elements disintegrated—water burned.

'Never equals! Not on your terms!' he howled, his voice frail now like ash blown away on the wind.

'Then I take you. You are mine,' the universal said sorrowfully. 'For ever.'

The silver girl stood alone on the barren rock. The dark tide had been consumed in the fire. Nothing remained but her.

17
Return to the Elements

Connie opened her eyes. She was sitting propped up against the gantry railing. The heat in the room had built unbearably since she had last been conscious. She coughed—the air reeked of oil fumes. Raising her head, she saw that Kullervo had gone; the great bear that had towered before her had disappeared. She corrected herself. No he hadn't, he was still here, with her—

He now was her.

She clambered slowly to her feet and held out her hands. They glowed in the darkness with a strange silvery sheen as though they had been dipped in starlight. Taking a breath, she thought of a new form, a different shape, a sylph. Her body dissolved into a silver mist and then reshaped into the long-limbed, flowing form of a sylph before swiftly slipping back to be a girl again.

A faint round of applause—clap, clap, clap—came from the place where George Brewer had fallen. Reminded of the danger they were both still in, Connie dropped her hands and ran to his side.

'Uncle George, let me help you,' she said, easing an arm under his head.

The old man coughed. 'No, my dear, you've done enough. I've seen what you've become—and it's beautiful. Sybil would be proud.' He patted her on the arm. 'Do you know . . . ' His voice sank to a whisper, 'I think your way was best . . . after all.' His last breath came in a soft hiss and Connie knew that his broken body had released its spirit.

A cloud of smoke belched from the stairwell. She had to get out. But what could she do with the body of a man everyone thought had died years ago?

A fire imp whizzed into the hall overhead and ignited a pile of printouts stacked by a computer. The plastic casing of the machinery began to sag and melt like candle wax.

'Leave him to us!' sang the fire imp. 'His spirit is gone: we'll return his body to the four elements.'

Yes, that was the way it should be, thought

Connie, laying the old man's head gently on the floor. Nature should get back what we had borrowed.

No longer afraid of the blazing room around her, Connie walked along the gantry towards the exit. This stairwell was also on fire; the plastic screen dripped molten droplets onto the floor. No one—or nearly no one—could escape that way.

With a silver-shimmer like a heat haze, Connie dissolved into the flickering form of a fire imp and passed through the flames.

The chimera tamed, Mack beckoned Mrs Khalid and Liam forward. With a protective hand around the boy's shoulders, Mrs Khalid stepped across the car park and past the creature. It made no attempt to stop them, its eyes now closed as if it had fallen into sleep. Mrs Khalid led Liam towards the heart of the fire: the two drum containers, burning fifty metres away, the heat so intense even at this distance that Liam's brow was shining with sweat. Deciding they were close enough, Mrs Khalid leant down and pointed Liam to the one on the right, then turned to the other. With a quick confirmatory glance at his mentor, Liam raised his hands to the sky as if cupping the hot draught of wind in his palms. In unison, two great tongues of fire ignited with an echoing whoosh. The flames leapt into the sky from the top of each drum. But they did not go out: they remained, flickering and dancing, taking the shape of two fire imps. They were as tall as skyscrapers, a vivid angry red, waving their long spiky fingers in gestures of rude defiance at the thin jets of fire suppressant aimed at them from the engines on the other side of the wall of smoke.

Mrs Khalid turned back to her charge. 'Remember, Lee-am, though bigger, they are the same.'

Liam nodded, his tongue sticking out between his teeth in concentration. On Mrs Khalid's signal, the fire imp companions called to their creatures. Distracted from their game with the firefighters, the imps looked down on the two tiny humans below and held out tapering limbs of flame towards them as if inviting them to the party. Mrs Khalid shook her head, though for a moment Liam looked tempted.

'Now!' she called out.

The fire imp companions clicked their fingers together. The fire imps were snuffed out, leaving curling plumes of smoke rising to the sky.

At the same moment, a tongue of strangely silvery flame issued from the stairwell directly in front of Mrs Khalid and Liam, darted into the air and disappeared. Even before the smoke cleared, Col was running across the open space between him and the rear door to the refinery. He dashed past Liam and plunged into the building with not a clue what he was going to do. He just knew he had to reach Connie. He would have continued recklessly on into the smouldering stairwell if a hand had not grabbed his belt and pulled him up short.

'You weren't thinking of going in there again, were you?' asked a familiar voice. 'Because I wouldn't recommend it.'

Col was speechless. He grabbed hold of the arm that was restraining him to check it was real.

'Let's get away from this smoke,' coughed Connie.

In a daze, Col stumbled after her. Once outside, he grabbed her to stop her running further and stared into her face.

'You're alive,' he said at last.

'So it would seem,' said Connie faintly. Her hair seemed to glisten in the dawn-light as if it had been dusted with silver.

'But, Connie, what about Kullervo?' He glanced behind as if he expected to see the shape-shifter bound from the building.

He did not get an answer as a tidal wave of people hit them. Mack enfolded Connie in a bear hug; Rat squirmed through to give her a slap on the back; Simon hung onto his sister round the waist; Liam was hopping up and down to touch any available inch of skin; Dr Brock kissed her on the cheek once Mack had allowed her to surface for air; Mrs Clamworthy squeezed her hand as if she would never let go. Even Omar Khalid waited his turn to give her a relieved embrace.

Finally, Connie pushed her friends away gently. 'Sorry to have kept you all waiting,' she said calmly as if she was merely late for dinner. 'Hadn't we better go?' She nodded to the thinning smoke screen.

Mack grinned, coming to himself. 'Yeah, we'd better get out of here. Explanations can wait.'

'But Kullervo?' asked Dr Brock urgently.

'He's . . . gone,' she said, meeting his eyes. 'For ever.'

'I can't believe it, but if you're here it must be true.' Stunned, Dr Brock gazed at her in wonder. 'Connie, I want to know exactly what happened but there's no time now. We must get the news to the Trustees and stop the battle.' Argot rose to his feet and snorted to his companion. Dr Brock sprinted across the tarmac and vaulted onto his back. 'We must spread the message to Kullervo's forces. See you at the Mastersons', Connie!' the doctor shouted as the red dragon propelled himself up into the air.

317

Mack turned to his son, still standing in a daze a few metres away. 'Col, you'd better get Skylark out of here before he's spotted. Simon, you and your companions lead that monster to the farm across the moor—but hurry! Connie, Rat, Liam—let's go before we're arrested.'

Simon was about to dash away when Connie caught his arm. She gave her brother a hug just for him. 'Great job, Companion to Chimera,' she said in a low voice, nodding over at the sleeping beast. 'I'm proud of you.'

Simon smiled back but felt too choked to say anything.

'Well, what're you waiting for?' smiled Connie. 'Don't spoil it all now by getting caught!' She pushed him away. He stumbled off, but not without turning once or twice to look back at his sister as if to check she was really there.

Col knew how he felt. He had not recovered from his surprise at seeing her walk out of the burning building. No one should have been able to survive in there—let alone walk away from Kullervo.

'Col, are you going to stand there all day?' bellowed his father, spotting that his son was still rooted to the spot.

Realizing the answers were not going to be given just then, Col shook himself out of his stupor. There was another event he had witnessed this night and it was about time he shared it. He jogged over to catch up with his father. Blocking the gap at the moment was Simon astride the Nemean lion. Once on the other side, the three creatures, lion, goat, and snake, led the chimera into the grey shadows of the dawn, cutting across no-man's land to reach the open moor.

'Congratulations, Dad,' Col said when he came alongside Mack.

Mack threw an arm around his shoulders. 'It was nothing, son. The others did most of it, as you saw.'

'I know,' said Col with a grin. 'But it's not every day you become a father for the second time.'

Connie gasped. Mack froze. Col could have sworn he heard the cogs in Mack's brain grind as they adjusted to this new piece of information. 'What?'

'Yes. An hour or so ago. At home. Mother and baby are fine.' Col could see Connie smiling broadly on the far side of his father.

Without another word, Mack broke into a sprint, pushed Omar and Rat out of the way as he dived through the fence and raced off into the twilight. A moment later, the sound of grating gears and a screaming engine indicated that Mack was making a fast getaway in Evelyn's Citroën.

Mrs Clamworthy put her hands on her hips. 'Typical!' she said in exasperation with her son. 'We've got seven people to get home and he takes one of the cars without so much as a single passenger!'

'It's all right, Gran. I can take someone on Skylark,' said Col, looking hopefully towards Connie.

The universal shook her head slightly, refusing his unspoken offer. 'Mrs Clamworthy, you take Liam and the Khalids with you. Rat can go with Col,' she said, guiding Mrs Clamworthy over the rough ground to where the old lady's Fiesta stood waiting.

'I can't do that. What about you?' protested Mrs Clamworthy.

'Oh, I'll be fine. I just need a little time to myself to get used to . . . to recover. I'll find my own way home.' Mrs Clamworthy gave her a questioning look but Connie smiled and shook her head again. 'It's no good asking: I'm not going to explain. You'd better go.'

'If you insist,' said Mrs Clamworthy, giving in to the new-found authority in Connie's voice. No one listening to her could doubt that she would get home safely.

'See you later.' Connie turned from them and began to walk off across no-man's land, following the route taken by her brother and his companions. Her slight form was soon swallowed up by the shadows except perhaps for the faint glimmer of silver in the half-light.

Skylark neighed, reminding Col there were only a few minutes left of semi-darkness for them to make their escape unseen. Col leapt onto his back as the Fiesta stuttered into life. Rat scrambled up behind him and hung onto Col.

'What do you think happened?' Rat asked once they were airborne.

'I don't know,' mused Col. 'And I'm not sure we're ever going to find out. Connie's different. She seemed older somehow—more mysterious.'

'She was cool,' pronounced Rat, squirming in his seat to get a parting look at the smouldering refinery.

'Yeah, she was cool,' agreed Col.

Connie was lying on her bed, supposedly resting, when she heard footsteps on the path. At first she did not move. She was still reliving the events of the past few hours, concluding with her flight home in the form of a silver pegasus. Col would like that one, she thought with a smile. But so much had happened, she was so different, she did not know where to begin. She felt like a tiny stream swollen suddenly with a flash flood: all she could do was wait for the torrent to pass so she could absorb what had taken place. She was a universal still—yes, she could sense her powers within her—but she now also had Kullervo's gift, the imprint of his nature, mingled with her deepest self. If anyone visited her mental landscape today, they would find a vast ocean of silver lapping peacefully at their feet, waiting to curl itself into new forms.

'Connie!' Mack called up the stairs. 'Jane and Anneena are here.'

Raising herself from her pillow, Connie brushed down her clothes, checked in the mirror that she had resumed her shape properly, and hurried downstairs. She found her friends in Mack and Evelyn's room bending over the cradle where the new baby was sleeping, an awed expression on their faces.

'He's so tiny,' whispered Anneena, putting the tip of her little finger in the clasp of one of his curled hands. He gripped it instinctively and shifted in his sleep, mouth feeding on air.

'Look, he's dreaming of milk!' said Jane softly. 'Let's leave him in peace.'

They tiptoed down to the kitchen. Evelyn was sitting with her feet up by the fireside; Mack was washing up at the sink: he looked distinctly shell-shocked. Connie hoped the excitement of last night had not been too much for him.

'Is Mack OK?' she asked her aunt quietly as Jane and Anneena fetched their presents. 'He looks a bit . . . a bit odd. He's not still worried about what happened at the refinery, is he? And the battle on the moor—that's over now, isn't it?'

Evelyn smiled sadly. 'Oh yes. I think we're both feeling a bit mixed up. It's strange to be grieving for those who died during the battle while feeling so happy to have a new life in the family. It feels all wrong somehow.' Evelyn sighed and closed her eyes. 'At least Kullervo's sudden disappearance meant that the Society avoided a slaughter at the hands of his supporters. It could have been much, much worse. We all realize that.'

Connie braced herself. 'Tell me who we lost.'

'Three dragons, six rock dwarves, two pegasi, a great boar—I'm afraid the list goes on. Ten human companions were injured, two seriously so.'

'And Kullervo's supporters?'

'I don't know. They must have suffered losses too. They retreated in confusion, led by that weather giant, Hoo. You remember him, I think.'

Oh yes, she remembered him. He had abused his position as a Trustee and allowed Kullervo to invade her last year.

'Kullervo may be gone, but the weather giants will not give up,' added Evelyn.

Connie sighed. 'You're right. We've given them too much cause to hate us humans. The world's gone mad. I sometimes think it's like the chimera. We shouldn't be fighting these creatures—we should be doing what we can to keep the Earth fit for us all to live in.'

They sat together in silence. Inside Connie's head, a wail of grief reverberated. She felt the urge to shift into a banshee to spin out her misery in their mind-numbing dance. It seemed the only way open to her to dull the pain of being part of this world.

Upstairs, George Clamworthy let out a cry in his sleep. Instinctively, Connie rose to comfort him but the baby had settled again before she could reach the door.

Evelyn patted the chair beside her. 'Sit down for a moment. I want to tell you something. You have to realize that you are not to blame for these losses. You cannot be everywhere and save everyone. You conquered Kullervo: that is enough—more than enough.'

Connie knew her aunt was right. She had had no choice last night. But still so many had died.

'Life is full of the bitter as well as the sweet. Your victory—our little George—these are what you should be thinking about now.' Evelyn held Connie's gaze, trying to fathom what was going on behind her niece's eyes. 'Something's happened to you—I can tell. I wasn't the only one to become someone different last night.'

'How do you mean?'

'I became a mother. I think the change has been as great for you, maybe greater. Am I right?'

Connie shivered: that was exactly how it felt— she had shed the skin of her old life and transformed into something new.

'Yes, I've changed. But I can't explain it.'

'I understand. I can't tell you yet what it's like to be a parent. It's as if my centre of gravity has shifted into that baby—it'll take me a while to regain my balance.'

Further discussion was prevented as Anneena came back carrying a magnificent bunch of flowers for Evelyn. Jane followed with several bags piled high with boxes of food.

'Here's your lunch—thanks to Anneena's mum,' said Jane. 'So, tell us, Connie, what were you doing last night when all this excitement was going on—the baby, the fire, the evacuation— don't tell me you missed out on it all?'

Connie felt pincered between the fascinated gaze of her aunt and Mack, neither of whom had yet heard any details of what had gone on inside the refinery and both of whom had been itching to ask.

'I . . . er . . . I was somewhere else,' she said.

'Oh? Where?' persisted Jane.

'Somewhere new. A place I'd never been before. Nature-watching.'

'Didn't you notice the fire from there?' asked Anneena, sensing there was something strange in their friend's answer.

'Yes, but I didn't think much about it, I was too caught up in . . . in other things.'

Anneena gave an exasperated tut. 'Typical! It's just like you, Connie, to go about with eyes only for badgers or something when half of Devon is on fire! You always seem to miss out on the real excitement. Remember how you slept through that tornado last year?'

'I remember.' How could she forget?

'It's a good job Jane and I keep our eyes peeled for you. You stick with us, we'll see you don't miss out on the next adventure.'

'Er . . . thanks. I'll do that.'

18
The Company of the Universals

The defeat of Kullervo and his supporters could not be allowed to pass without marking it with the biggest event the Society had ever organized. First, in a simple ceremony out on the moors, the Trustees honoured the dead and wounded from the battle. Connie saw for herself that the fight had been intense as many members gathered bore the marks of fresh scars. Kullervo's supporters had been merciless towards the creatures they believed had betrayed them by allying with humans in the Society.

'To them, we are the monsters,' Connie thought sadly. Anger washed inside her like a tide as she stood with the others in the chill breeze to say farewell to their friends and comrades. She felt she could not bear the pain of it.

If this was what it was like for you, Kullervo, she told the shape-shifter inside her, I can understand how part of you was driven to violence to silence this agony.

She barely felt like taking part in the celebration of her victory but everyone expected her there. It took her some time to shake off the melancholy mood that had settled on her out on the moors. She wandered about the Mastersons' farm aimlessly, watching the preparations and avoiding conversation when she could. The farm had been commandeered by the Trustees for the event and mythical creatures and their companions continued to pour in from all over Britain. A huge bonfire had been lit in the paddock and dragons were already warming up for the most magnificent fireworks display in their history, breathing out practice sparks of silver over the upturned heads of the crowd. Dr Brock and Argot flew over, blasting the barn roof with emerald flame that lingered on the ridge like a crown for a few moments before disappearing, leaving no trace of its passage. The crowd cheered, neighed, whistled, stamped and made every other noise known to animal-kind, entreating the Sea-Snakes to start the entertainment for real.

'Later!' shouted Dr Brock from Argot's shoulder. 'It's time to eat!'

Volunteers with flushed faces were manning the barbecues and tables, all of which groaned with food to suit every palate: sides of meat, bowls of creamy desserts, stacks of cakes, and pyramids of fruit and vegetables. The platters of gleaming fish were surrounded by a crowd of enthusiastic selkies—Arran in their midst with his arm draped around Jessica's shoulders. He was balancing a herring on his nose and making everyone laugh and clap with appreciation of his skill. With a flick of his neck, the herring sailed into the air, Arran stood beneath with mouth wide open— only to find his supper intercepted by Argand who flew over and took it in one gulp.

Rat was ecstatic because he and Icefen had been given express permission to use the wolf's breath to wipe the memory of any humans that came across the gathering. Connie, standing with Sentinel at her side to keep off the crowds of Society members, was a still spot in the swirling masses that surrounded her. She watched Rat and Icefen bound off into the night on the trail of a small group of paratroopers who had been so unwise as to exercise on the moor that night. They did not stand a chance, thought Connie— the soldiers, that is.

Rat's mentor, Erik Ulvsen, turned up five minutes later on an even bigger wolf than Icefen.

'Off hunting?' Erik asked delightedly when Connie informed him where his pupil had gone. 'Excellent.' Frost wolf and rider took off after Rat.

Liam slipped under Sentinel's guard and shyly took Connie's hand. Simon, who was keeping an eye on him for Mrs Khalid, gave his sister a hug.

'That looks fun,' said Liam, watching the frost wolves bounding over the fields. 'Do you think Rat'll let me have a go?'

'He'd love to,' said Connie, her spirits lifting a little when she saw Liam's look of delight.

'Perhaps I could come along for the ride on Rex?' suggested Simon. When Connie and Liam looked blank, he added, 'The Nemean lion. I'm sure he could carry two—would you like to come, Connie?'

'I might later. But I'll make my own arrangements for a ride.' It was Simon's turn to look puzzled. 'There's something I've got to tell you . . . ' She stopped, sensing the approach of someone from behind. She knew without turning that it was the soft-footed companion to Storm-Bird.

'Universal, the Trustees would like to speak to you,' said Eagle-Child.

'Tell me later,' said Simon as he and Liam stood back to allow the Trustee to guide Connie

330

into the stillness of the barn. Sentinel followed at a discreet distance.

Connie had known this moment would come—the moment when she would have to account for the conquest of Kullervo. But what could she say when even she did not understand everything that had happened? As she had discovered today, it was going to take her a long time to get used to her new gift and she had a shrewd suspicion it would take others even longer. Over the last few years, she had been brought face-to-face with the prejudice against the universals in the Society: what would they do when they discovered that she had become even more unusual, placed herself further beyond the stretch of their understanding.

Indeed, what had she become?

Walking into the centre of the circle of Trustees, Gard sitting alongside Jade next to Mr Chan, Connie sensed that emotion in the room was running high. Morjik crouched in the shadows like a rough-hewn rock of green granite. Only the glitter of his ruby eyes showed that he was glowing hot with life. Kinga was sitting between his forepaws, his ancient head resting on her lap. Storm-Bird croaked once from the rafters, seen in the darkness as a blacker shadow in the night. Windfoal gleamed with snowy purity at the western side of the barn, her long mane sparkling like

331

the froth of a waterfall tumbling over her powerful shoulders. Kira, dressed in an orange and yellow kikoi, brought a vibrant dash of colour into the room, making an exotic contrast to her companion. The Trustees for the Elementals, both past and present, sat still like pieces from a chess game in which the sides had been mixed up: Gard's northern solidity, a king from the Isle of Lewis set, pitched against Mr Chan and Jade, both strays from an antique Chinese board, lines fluid and graceful as willows. Despite the silence that reigned in the room, Connie perceived that the Trustees were at once delighted and wary: overjoyed that Kullervo appeared to have been defeated at long last, but afraid of the one who had achieved it.

Without pausing to be asked, Connie threw out the links of the shared bond and waited for them to come to her.

'Greetings, Universal,' said Gard, stomping through the portal to her mind, stopping on the threshold to take a curious look at the silver ocean that now lapped there.

'Hello,' she said simply. Rising from the waves, she conjured an image of herself to stand with him, head bowed.

The other Trustees joined them, paddling ankle-deep in the water, bemused by the change that had come over her mind. Morjik stirred it with a claw, sending concentric waves rippling off into infinity. He growled in recognition, seeing for the first time the ocean that he had sensed in her long ago.

When it was clear she was going to say no more, Gard spoke again. 'You took a terrible risk in challenging Kullervo.'

'Yes, it was terrible.'

'Will you tell us what happened?'

'I'm not sure I can explain. I took him at his weakest and . . . and now he's no longer a threat to us. That's all I can say.'

'So is he gone?'

'Yes—and no.'

'You speak in riddles, Universal.'

'Only because I've become a riddle, even to myself.'

There was silence as the Trustees pondered her words.

'You broke the rules, Universal,' said Kinga finally. 'We should expel you for that.' But she was smiling at her.

'Are you going to?' asked Connie, not much worried by this threat. 'In that case, I should mention that I had the unanimous support of the Company of the Universals. I was acting on their behalf.'

Eagle-Child laughed, his voice echoing from the waters. 'We have agreed that you can stay in the Society this time.'

'The universals always were a law unto themselves,' grunted Gard. He rubbed his brow, still pondering the new landscape she had revealed.

'Thank you,' said Connie, 'I'd like to stay in the Society—that's if you think you can cope with me.'

'Oh,' said Kira, splashing her toes in the warm water as if it were the Indian Ocean, 'I think we're used to you now.'

Oh no, you're not, thought Connie to herself.

With a slight nod of her shadow-head, Connie raised a soft bed of silver sand under Kira's toes, glistening with shells, to honour the Trustee's holiday mood. Kira gave an astonished gasp, bent down and pulled out a curved conch shell. Putting it to her ear, she smiled at the universal: 'I can hear the waves of my home!'

Eagle-Child was crouched on the very portal, looking gravely at the water. Connie shivered and around him sprung up tall prairie grass, hissing softly in the wind. He stroked his hand across the tops of the grasses and began to hum a song of his people. Storm-Bird swirled overhead, flying in the clouds that raced across the silver sky. Flashes of lightning scored the canopy with sharp gashes of light.

334

'What is happening, Universal?' marvelled Gard.

Connie shook her head slightly, denying him words of explanation, instead she sent him a stream of molten rock, curling it around him like a climbing rose and letting it set in a fantastical rock sculpture. He stepped away, leaving the stone flowers suspended delicately like an arch. Jade and Mr Chan moved closer to examine it, wondering at its fragile beauty.

'This goes beyond explanations,' said Kinga as Connie now turned her attention to the Trustees for the Sea Snakes, surrounding them with a sudden growth of thick primeval forest. Kinga ran her hand over the rough bark of an oak, its roots nestled on a bed of moss. Turning to her fellow Trustees, Kinga added, 'The universal has become something we've never seen before in a human companion.'

'I think, Universal, you are now one of us,' growled Morjik. 'A mythical creature. Or should I say: you are all of us.'

Connie laughed softly. 'Yes, that's it. You're all here, and always will be, part of me.'

Kinga shook her head. 'Something wonderful has happened to the universal—we can all see that and we must understand it. But I do not think this is a matter that will be grasped in one visit. Let us enjoy her victory for we still have many battles to fight if we are to save the world for all creatures. The universal's task is far from over.'

Connie ended the encounter. They returned to the present in the barn, feeling relaxed and peaceful.

'I know,' said Connie. 'The threat from Kullervo may be gone but his army is still out there. There are many more Axoils and many angry creatures who would want to punish humanity for our greed.' She looked around the circle, feeling a great tie of love binding her to each of these marvellous creatures. 'I feel as if my work has only just begun.'

Col waited outside the barn in trepidation. He knew that Connie was closeted with the Trustees but he was not worried about that: what could they do to the Society's hero, the girl who had beaten Kullervo? No, he was worried for himself and for what he was going to say. In the last twenty-four hours, he had gone from not understanding what love was, to seeing it in action as Connie sacrificed herself for him and Rat. She had opened his eyes to his own feelings and he did not want to let this moment slip away. And Skylark, relieved that his companion had finally come to his senses, had sworn he would not speak to him again unless he did something about it.

336

Connie came out with Sentinel, looking happy. She spotted Col through the throngs of people and began to push her way towards him, greatly assisted by Sentinel who took his bodyguard duties very seriously. She had almost reached him when Omar Khalid intercepted her. She turned aside to speak to him. Col watched as Omar bent low over his friend talking intently. With a pang of jealousy, Col saw Omar raise his hand to stroke Connie's arm. She was blushing. If Col didn't do something quickly, it would be too late—for him. He pushed through the crowd and broke in upon the private conversation.

'Sorry to interrupt,' he lied cheerfully. 'Omar, do you mind if I borrow Connie for a moment?'

Omar clearly did mind, but was too polite to say so. 'Of course,' he said, graciously. 'I hope I'll see you later, Connie.'

Not if I have anything to do with it, Col vowed silently.

'Can we go somewhere I can speak to you on your own?' asked Col.

Connie nodded and let him lead her away. She expected that he wanted an explanation and she knew he deserved one. If there were anyone in the world that she would tell the whole story to, it would be Col.

His determined attempt to get her on her own

337

almost failed as Mr Coddrington arrived in their path. Sentinel snorted with anger. Connie placed a restraining hand on the minotaur's sinewy forearm to prevent him charging.

'Miss Lionheart—Connie, if I may be so bold—may I say how delighted I am to see you safe and sound?' said Mr Coddrington smarmily, reaching out to shake her hand. Connie snatched her hand away, leaving him grasping air. The assessor frowned.

Connie looked with distaste at the companion to weather giants, remembering all the pain he had caused her. And now he had the nerve to pretend he was her friend! A wave of silver-blue anger welled up inside her, tempting her to shift shape, to crush the insignificant creature before her. It was time he got what he deserved.

'Mr Coddrington,' she said with a dangerous edge to her voice as she struggled to contain her anger. It was frighteningly difficult to stop herself lashing out. 'Let me be frank: no, you may not call me "Connie". You've never been my friend and never will be.'

'Miss Lionheart,' protested Mr Coddrington, bristling defensively at her tone, 'don't think that just because you are a universal you can get away with such impertinence to a senior member of the Society!'

'And don't think you can get away with bullying me any more, Mr Coddrington, or you'll find you've picked a fight you've no hope of winning. Keep out of my way in future or else.' Connie began to walk away. Col gaped at this new side to her character but hurried to follow.

'Or what?' shouted Mr Coddrington at her back. 'You can't do anything against me!'

'Can't I?' said Connie calmly. With an action so quick that Col could barely make out what she was doing, Connie conjured the universal's bow into her hands, strung and fired it. An arrow, bearing a sharp cold sting of stone sprite whistled through the air and slapped Mr Coddrington on the cheek. He was instantly frozen to the spot, a look of horrified indignation on his face. 'Come on, Col.'

Col tripped after her, dumbfounded at what she had done. 'Will he be all right? I'm not worried about him but, I mean, won't you get into trouble?'

Connie shrugged, though she was still shaking. She had for a moment felt something inside, a presence that goaded her into attacking. The balance of power between her and the part of her that was Kullervo was a delicate one: she had almost lost it.

'He'll be fine. It'll wear off in a few minutes. Anyway, I'm in trouble enough already.' She left this comment hanging as an invitation to Col to find out more. While walking the knife edge of her new nature, she would have liked to confide in him. Would he—would the others—think her a monster? That was her greatest fear. But Col was too preoccupied by something else and did not take up her invitation to ask more.

They escaped the crowds and left Sentinel guarding the pathway to the stables. Col turned to her.

'Connie, do you remember what I said last night—that I had something to ask you?'

Connie nodded. 'Yes, I do.'

In the darkness away from the party, Col could have sworn she still glistened with that strange silver sheen he had noticed earlier.

'I've been a complete idiot waiting so long, but last night helped me see you properly for the first time.'

She gave him a strange look. 'There's more to me than you think.'

Col grinned. 'I know that. You're the girl that beat Kullervo: how could I forget?' He was bright red now and not meeting her eyes. 'I realized that I want to spend my time with you—no one else, apart from Skylark, of course, but that's different.' He laughed nervously. 'So I just wondered, would it spoil things if . . . if I asked you to go out with me?'

This was the last question Connie had been

expecting but she already knew what her answer would be—the answer she would have given him months ago if it had crossed his mind to ask her.

'No, I ... er ... don't think it would spoil things.'

'So, will you?'

'Yes—but you might be getting more than you bargained for.' It was only fair to warn him, she thought. 'I've changed since last night.'

Col felt relieved that she agreed. He had been a fool not to ask her before. It had taken a close shave with death to understand his feelings at last. 'Last night changed me too so I'm not worried about that,' he said, finally getting the hug he had missed out on that morning. He ruffled his fingers through her hair. 'Look, no sparks.' He laughed and hugged her close.

Connie smiled, feeling more completely happy than she had ever done in her life. She would tell him about Kullervo—but not yet. This moment was too perfect to spoil.

When Connie and Col emerged back into the party, arm in arm, they found that their presence had hardly been missed. Mack and Evelyn had arrived, Mack bearing the baby in his arms triumphantly, holding him up like the World Cup. Argand flew around them, breathing joyous golden flames into the sky, forming a glowing circle of fire to mark the little one's arrival. Spotting his older son, Mack skilfully avoided the elderly lady members who had come to coo over the child and dumped the baby on him.

'You know what my greatest achievement is, Col?' Mack asked him as he put his hand on his shoulder.

'No,' said Col, not really wanting to hear about his father's exploits just then.

'It's having two smashing sons. Thanks for what you did last night. I know I don't say this enough, but I love you.' He would have enfolded his son in an embrace had not the baby started crying at that point, feeling the squeeze of his over-enthusiastic father. Evelyn rushed over, but not out of concern as Col was doing fine, nursing the baby on his shoulder like a pro.

'See,' she said proudly to Connie, 'he cries like a banshee already!'

'George swam like a fish when I bathed him,' said Mack, giving Connie a wink.

Connie looked up at the circle of fire and then down at the little bundle sniffing on Col's shoulder. George Clamworthy blinked back at her with his mismatched eyes, one green, one brown. Her instinct had been right. She was no longer alone: the Company of the Universals had a new member.

JULIA GOLDING grew up on the edge of Epping
Forest. After reading English at Cambridge, she
joined the Foreign Office and served in Poland. Her
work as a diplomat took her from the high point of
town twinning in the Tatra Mountains to the low of
inspecting the bottom of a Silesian coal mine.

On leaving Poland, she joined Oxfam as a lobbyist
on conflict issues, campaigning at the United
Nations and with governments to lessen the impact
of war on civilians living in war zones. She now
works as a freelance writer.

Married with three children, she lives in Oxford.
The Chimera's Curse is the final part of the glorious
'Companions Quartet'. It follows *Secret of the Sirens*,
The Gorgon's Gaze and *Mines of the Minotaur*.

www.juliagolding.co.uk

Object Properties toolbar (Other *displays related dialog box*)

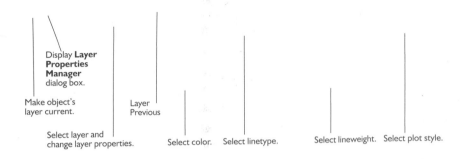

Display **Layer Properties Manager** dialog box.

Make object's layer current.

Layer Previous

Select layer and change layer properties.

Select color.   Select linetype.

Select lineweight.   Select plot style.

Layer Manager icons (*Click headers to change sort order.*)

Name	On	Freeze in all VP	Lock	Color	Linetype	Lineweight	Plot Style	Plot	Current VP Freeze	New VP Freeze
0	♀	☼	⊟	■ White	Continuous	— Default	Normal	🖨	🗗	🗗
Layer1	♀	❋	🔒	■ Magenta	DOT	— 0.35 mm	Style 1	🖨	🗗	🗗

Name
On/ off
Thaw/ freeze
Unlock/ lock
Color
Linetype
Lineweight
Plot style
Plot/ don't plot
Freeze/thaw in current viewport
Freeze/thaw in new viewports

Status Bar buttons (*Right click for menu.*)

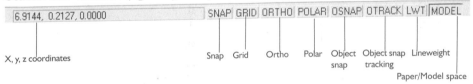

| 6.9144, 0.2127, 0.0000 | | SNAP GRID ORTHO POLAR OSNAP OTRACK LWT MODEL |

X, y, z coordinates

Snap   Grid   Ortho   Polar   Object snap   Object snap tracking   Lineweight

Paper/Model space

Command Line keystrokes

Enter or ▭	Executes or repeats command.
←	Moves cursor back to the left.
Home	Places cursor at the beginning of the line.
End	Places cursor at the end of the line.
→	Moves cursor forward to the right.
Insert	Toggles insertion mode on and off.
Delete	Deletes character to the right of the cursor.
↑	Displays previous line in command history.
↓	Displays next line in command history.
Ctrl + V	Pastes text from Clipboard to command line.

Acad.Exe switches

/b — Run script file.

/c — Path to alternative hardware configuration file.

/nologo — Supress AutoCAD logo.

/p — User-defined profile.

/r — Restore default pointing device.

/s — Path to support folders.

/t — Template filename.

/v — Display named view.

The
Illustrated AutoCAD® 2002
Quick Reference

Ralph Grabowski

autodesk Press

THOMSON
™
LEARNING   Australia • Canada • Mexico • Singapore • Spain • United Kingdom • United States

autodesk Press

The Illustrated AutoCAD® 2002 Quick Reference
Ralph Grabowski

Business Unit Director:
Alar Elken

Executive Editor:
Sandy Clark

Acquisitions Editor:
James DeVoe

Development Editor:
John Fisher

Editorial Assistant:
Jasmine Hartman

Executive Marketing Manager
Maura Theriault

Executive Production Manager:
Mary Ellen Black

Channel Manager:
Mary Johnson

Book Design and Typesetting:
Ralph Grabowski

Production Manager:
Larry Main

Production Editor:
Tom Stover

Art/Design Coordinator:
Mary Beth Vought

Marketing Coordinator:
Karen Smith

Library of Congress
Cataloging-in-Publication
Data
ISBN 0-7668-3849-8

About This Book

The Illustrated AutoCAD 2002 Quick Reference presents concise facts about all commands found in AutoCAD 2002 and earlier. The clear format of this reference book demonstrates each command, starting on its own page, illustrated by over 500 figures, plus these exclusive features:

- All variations of commands, such as the **View**, **-View**, and **+View** commands.
- Scores of AutoCAD 2002 commands not documented by Autodesk.
- A dozen "Quick Start" mini-tutorials that help you get started quicker.
- Over 100 definitions of acronyms and hard-to-understand terms.
- Nearly 1,000 context-sensitive tips.
- All system variables in Appendix A, including those not listed by the **SetVar** command.
- Obsolete commands that no longer work in AutoCAD 2002 in Appendix B.

The name of each command is in mixed upper and lower case to help you understand the name, which is often condensed. For example, the name of the **VpClip** command is short for "ViewPort CLIP." Each command includes all alternative methods of command input:

- Alternate command spelling, such as **Donut** and **Doughnut**.
- ' (the apostrophe prefix) indicating transparent commands, such as **'Blipmode**.
- All aliases, such as **L** for the **Line** command.
- Pull-down menu picks, such as **Draw ⅏ Construction Line** for the **XLine** command.
- Control-key combinations, such as **CTRL+E** for the **Isoplane** toggle.
- Function keys, such as **F1** for the **Help** command.
- Alt-key combinations, such as **ALT+TE** for the **Spell** command.
- Table menu coordinates, such as **M2** for the **Hide** command.

The brief command description notes when the command is *renamed* from an earlier release of AutoCAD, or is a command *undocumented* by Autodesk.

The version or release number indicates when the command first appeared in AutoCAD, such as **V. 1.0**, **Rel. 14**, or **2000i**. This is useful when working with older versions of AutoCAD. See Appendix B for the list of commands removed from every release of AutoCAD.

Each command includes one or more of the following: command line options, dialog box options, shortcut menu options, related commands, related toolbar icons, and related system variables.

Many commands include one or more tips that help you use the command more efficiently or warn you of the command's limitations. Numrerous commands include a list of definitions of acronyms and jargon words.

Special thanks to Randall Rath for his helpful technical editing, and to Stephen Dunning for his keen copy editing.

Ralph Grabowski
Abbotsford, British Columbia, Canada
June 15, 2001
Contact: **ralphg@xyz.press.com**

Contents

A

▦ Indicates the command is new to AutoCAD 2000i.

▦ Indicates the command is new to AutoCAD 2002.

' Indicates the command is transparent.

Italics Indicate the command is undocumented.

B

C

E

I

J

L

N

O

P

V

W

X

Z

3

Appendices

'About

Rel.12 Displays the AutoCAD version, serial number, and copyright notice.

Command	Alias	Ctrl+	F-key	Alt+	Menu Bar	Tablet
'about	...	...	...	HO	Help	...
					⌐About	

Command: **about**
Displays dialog box:

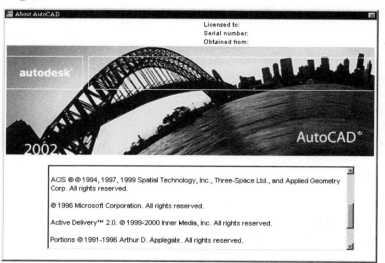

DIALOG BOX OPTION

x   Dismisses dialog box.

RELATED COMMANDS

Status   Displays information about the drawing and environment.
Stats   Displays information about the rendering environment.

RELATED SYSTEM VARIABLES

_PkSer   The AutoCAD software serial number.
_Server   Network authorization code.

AcisIn

Rel.13 Imports an SAT file (*short for "save as text," an ASCII-format ACIS file*) into the drawing; then creates 3D solids, 2D regions, and bodies (*an ACIS command*).

Command	Alias	Ctrl+	F-key	Alt+	Menu Bar	Tablet
acisin	...	...	...	IA	Insert ⌐ACIS File	...

Command: **acisin**
Displays dialog box:

DIALOG BOX OPTIONS

Cancel   Dismisses the dialog box.
Open   Opens the SAT file.

RELATED COMMANDS

AcisOut   Exports ACIS objects — 3D solids, 2D regions, and bodies — to a SAT file for import into other ACIS-aware CAD software.

AmeConvert   Converts AME v2.0 and v2.1 solid models and regions into ACIS solids.

RELATED FILE

*.SAT   The ASCII format of ACIS model files.

TIPS

- **ACIS** is the solids modeling technology from the Spatial Technologies division of Dassault Systemes, and is used by AutoCAD and other 3D CAD packages.

- "Acis" comes from first names of the original developers, as in "Andy, Charles, and Ian's System." In Greek mythology, Acis was the lover of the goddess Galatea; when Acis was killed by the jeolous Cyclops, Galatea turned the blood of Acis into a river.

AcisOut

Rel.13 Exports AutoCAD 3D solids, 2D regions, and bodies to a SAT file (*an ACIS command*).

Command	Alias	Ctrl+	F-key	Alt+	Menu Bar	Tablet
acisout	...	...	...	FE	File	...
				⌐ACIS	⌐Export	
					⌐ACIS	

```
Command: acisout
Select objects: [pick]
Select objects: ENTER
```
Displays dialog box:

DIALOG BOX OPTIONS

Cancel   Dismisses the dialog box.

Save   Saves the selected objects as a SAT file.

RELATED COMMANDS

AcisIn   Imports a SAT file, and creates 3D solids, 2D regions, and bodies.

StlOut   Exports ACIS solid models in STL format for use by stereolithography devices.

3dsOut   Exports ACIS solid models as 3D faces for import into 3D Studio software.

RELATED FILE

*.SAT   The ASCII format of ACIS model files; short for "save as text."

TIPS

■ **AcisOut** export objects that are 3D solids, 2D regions, and bodies only.

■ SAT files can be read by other ACIS-based CAD programs.

'AdcClose

2000 Exits the AutoCAD DesignCenter.

Command	Alias	Ctrl+	F-key	Alt+	Menu Bar	Tablet
'adcclose	...	2	...	TA	Tools	X12
					⌐AutoCAD DesignCenter	

Command: **adcclose**

COMMAND LINE OPTIONS
None.

RELATED COMMANDS
AdCenter   Opens the AutoCAD DesignCenter window.
Close   Closes the current drawing.

TIPS
■ The **AdcClose** command does not display a prompt.

■ As an alternative to typing 'adcclose', click the small **x** button in the upper-right corner of the AutoCAD DesignCenter window, which closes it.

■ **Ctrl+2** is a toggle keystroke: it opens and closes AutoCAD DesignCenter each time you press it.

'AdCenter

2000 Opens the AutoCAD DesignCenter window.

Command	Alias	Ctrl+	F-key	Alt+	Menu Bar	Tablet
'adcenter	adc	2	...	TA	Tools	X13
	content				⬐AutoCAD DesignCenter	

Command: **adcenter**

Displays window:

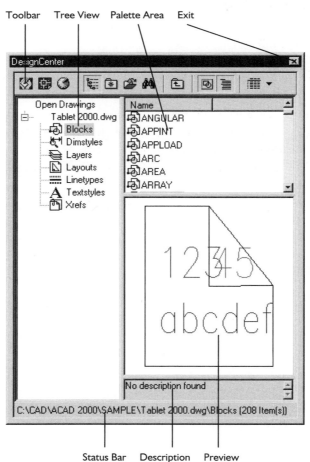

TOOLBAR OPTIONS

Desktop   Displays the folders and files of your computer's drives.

Open Drawings Displays the drawings currently open in this session of AutoCAD.

Custom Content(*Optional*) Displays proxy data, if the associated ObjectARX application is running.

History   Displays the last 120 documents viewed by DesignCenter.

Tree View Toggle

Hides and displays the Desktop and Open Drawings tree views.

Favorites   Displays the files in the *Windows**Favorites**Autodesk* folder.

Load   Displays the **Load DesignCenter Palette** dialog box; allows you to open a drawing, including drawings from the Internet.

Find   Displays the dialog box; allows you to search for a drawing.

Up   Moves the tree view up by one level.

Preview   Toggles the display of the preview image; previews DWG and raster files.

Description   Toggles the display of the description area.

View   Changes the display format of the palette area.

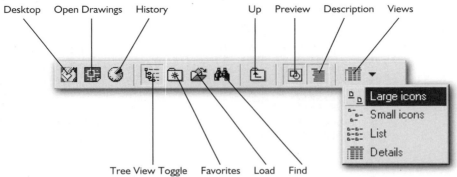

RELATED COMMANDS

AdcClose   Closes the AutoCAD DesignCenter window.

AdcNavigate   Specifies the initial path for AutoCAD DesignCenter.

TIPS

- Use the AutoCAD DesignCenter to keep track of drawings and parts of drawings, such as block libraries.

- You can drag blocks and other drawing parts from the AutoCAD DesignCenter into the drawing.

- The DesignCenter window can switch between floating and docked by right-clicking and selecting the option from the menu.

- As an alternative to typing **adcclose**, you may click the small **x** button in the upper-right corner to close the AutoCAD DesignCenter.

- **Ctrl+2** is a toggle keystroke; it opens and closes the AutoCAD DesignCenter each time you press it.

AdcNavigate

2000 Specifies the initial path for the AutoCAD DesignCenter to display files.

Command	Alias	Ctrl+	F-key	Alt+	Menu Bar	Tablet
adcnavigate	...	...	...	...	...	...

```
Command: adcnavigate
Enter pathname <>:
```

COMMAND LINE OPTION

Enter pathname   Type a path, such as *c:\program files\acad2002\sample*.

RELATED COMMAND

AdCenter   Opens the AutoCAD DesignCenter window.

TIPS

■ AutoCAD uses the path specified by AdcNavigate to locate files displayed by DesignCenter's Desktop option.

■ This command also opens the DesignCenter window, if closed.

■ You can enter the path to a file, folder, or network location:

Example of a folder path:	c:\program files\autocad 2002\sample
Example of a file path:	c:\design center\welding.dwg
Example of a network path:	\\downstairs\project

Ai_xxx

A variety of undocumented commands used by AutoCAD in menu files.

Ai_Box

Draws a 3D box as a surface object.

Command	Alias	Ctrl+	F-key	Alt+	Menu Bar	Tablet
ai_box	...	...	...	...	...	...

```
Command: ai_box
Specify corner point of box: [pick]
Specify length of box: [pick]
Specify width of box or [Cube]: [pick]
Specify height of box: [pick]
Specify rotation angle of box about the Z axis or [Reference]:0
```

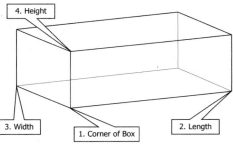

COMMAND LINE OPTIONS

Corner of box Specifies the initial corner of the box.
Length   Specifies the length of one side of the box.
Cube   Creates a cube based on the **Length**.
Width   Specifies the width of the box.
Height   Specifies the height of the box.
Rotation angle Specifies the angle the box rotates about the z-axis.

TIPS

■ This command creates a 3D surface object; the **Box** command creates a 3D solid model.

■ The **Ai_box** command creates rectangular boxes and cubes.

■ When specifying the **Width** and **Height**, move the cursor back to the **Corner of box** point; otherwise the box may have a different size than you expect.

■ The box is made of a single polymesh; using **Explode** converts each side to an independent 3D face object.

■ The base of the box is drawn at the current setting of the **Elevation** system variable.

Ai_CircTan

Draws a circle tangent to three points.

Command	Alias	Ctrl+	F-key	Alt+	Menu Bar	Tablet
ai_box	...	...	...	...	...	...

```
Command: ai_circtan
Enter Tangent spec: [pick]
Enter second Tangent spec: [pick]
Enter third Tangent spec: [pick]
```

A circle drawn tangent to three lines (left) and three circles (right).

COMMAND LINE OPTION

Enter Tangent spec

Pick an object to which the circle should be tangent to.

TIPS

■ This command is meant for use in toolbar and menu macros.

■ If the circle cannot be drawn, the command complains, "Circle does not exist."

■ This command is an alternative to the **Circle** command with the **3P** option.

Ai_Cone

Draws a 3D cone as a surface object.

Command	Alias	Ctrl+	F-key	Alt+	Menu Bar	Tablet
ai_box	...	...	...	...	...	...

```
Command: ai_cone
Specify center point for base of cone: [pick]
Specify radius for base of cone or [Diameter]: [pick]
Specify radius for top of cone or [Diameter] <0>: ENTER
Specify height of cone: [pick]
Enter number of segments for surface of cone <16>: ENTER
```

```
4. Height          3. Radius of Top
5. Number of Segments
                   2. Radius of Base
1. Base Center Point
```

COMMAND LINE OPTIONS

Base center point Specifies the center point of the cone's base.
Diameter of base Specifies the diameter of the base.
Radius of base Specifies the radius of the base.
Diameter of top Specifies the diameter of the top of the cone.
Radius of top Specifies the radius of the top of the cone; 0 = cone with a point.
Height Specifies the height of the cone.
Number of segments
Specifies the number of "lines" that define the curved surface of the cone; default = 16.

TIPS

■ The **Ai_Cone** command creates "pointy" and truncated cones; see figure.

■ The base of the cone is drawn at the current setting of the **Elevation** system variable.

(Ai_Deselect)

Deselects all selected objects.

Command	Alias	Ctrl+	F-key	Alt+	Menu Bar	Tablet
ai_box	...	...	...	...	...	...

Command: **(ai_deselect)**
Everything has been deselected.

COMMAND LINE OPTIONS

None.

TIPS

- This command is meant for use in menu macros and toolbars.

- The command must be used with parentheses.

- The opposite command to select all is **Ai_SelAll.**

AiDimPrec

Changes the precision displayed by existing dimensions.

Command	Alias	Ctrl+	F-key	Alt+	Menu Bar	Tablet
ai_box	...	...	...	...	...	...

```
Command: aidimprec
Enter option [0/1/2/3/4/5/6] <4>: 1
Select objects: [pick]
Select objects: ENTER
```

*Before (left) and after (right) applying **AiDimPrec = 1** to a decimal dimension.*

*Before and after applying **AiDimPrec = 1** to a fractional dimension.*

COMMAND LINE OPTIONS

Enter option Specify the precision (number of decimal places, or fractional equivalent); enter a number between 0 and 6.

Select objects Select one or more dimensions.

TIPS

- This command allows you retroactively to change the precision displayed by selected dimensions. It is meant for use by menu and toolbar macros.

- You can specify between zero to six decimal places. Fractional units are rounded to the nearest fraction:

AiDimPrec	Architectural Units
0	Rounded to the nearest unit.
1	1/2"
2	1/4"
3	1/8"
4	1/16"
5	1/32"
6	1/64"

- *Caution!* Since the **AiDimPrec** command rounds off dimensions, it can create false dimensions. For example, the dimension line below measures 3.4375", but setting **AiDimPrec** to 0 causes the dimension text to be rounded down to three inches.

*Applying **AiDimPrec = 0** to a 3 $^7/_{16}$" dimension.*

AiDimStyle

Saves and applies one of six preset dimension styles.

Command	Alias	Ctrl+	F-key	Alt+	Menu Bar	Tablet
ai_box	...	...	...	...	...	...

```
Command: aidimstyle
Enter option [1/2/3/4/5/6/Other/Save] <1>:
Select objects: [pick]
Select objects: ENTER
```

COMMAND LINE OPTIONS

Enter option   Specify predefined dimension style numbered 1 through 6.
Other   Apply a named dimension style to selected dimension(s).
Save   Save the style of the selected dimension(s).
Select objects   Select one or more dimensions.

Other option:

```
Enter option [1/2/3/4/5/6/Other/Save] <1>: o
```
      Displays dialog box:

```
Select objects: [pick]
Select objects: ENTER
```

Save option:

```
Enter option [1/2/3/4/5/6/Other/Save] <1>: s
```
      Displays dialog box:

O K   Saves style to the selected dimension style name. AutoCAD warns:

```
Select objects: [pick]
Select objects: ENTER
```

TIPS

■ This command quickly applies and saves dimensions styles; it is meant for macros.

■ *Caution!* The **Save** option overwrites existing dimstyles; it does not create new style names.

Ai_Dim_TextAbove

Moves dimension text above the dimension line.

Command	Alias	Ctrl+	F-key	Alt+	Menu Bar	Tablet
ai_box	...	...	...	...	...	...

```
Command: ai_dim_textabove
Select objects: [pick]
Select objects: ENTER
```

*Before (left) and after (right) applying **Ai_Dim_TextAbove** .*

COMMAND LINE OPTION

Select objects Select one or more dimensions.

TIPS

- This command allows you quickly to make dimensions compliant with the JIS (*Japan Industrial Standard*) dimensioning.

- This command moves the dimension text to the left of the dimension line on vertical dimensions.

- The **DimTEdit** command aligns text to the left, center, or right on horizontal dimensions.

Ai_Dim_TextCenter

Centers dimension text vertically on the dimension line.

Command	Alias	Ctrl+	F-key	Alt+	Menu Bar	Tablet
ai_box	...	...	...	...	...	...

```
Command: ai_dim_textcenter
Select objects: [pick]
Select objects: ENTER
```

Before (left) and after (right) applying **Ai_Dim_TextCenter**.

COMMAND LINE OPTION

Select objects Select one or more dimensions.

TIPS

■ This command works with all types of dimensions; it is meant for use in macros.

■ This command centers text vertically on the dimension line, but not horizontally. To center dimension text horizontally, use the **Ai_Dim_TextHome** command.

■ As an alternative, you can use the **DimTEdit** command to align text to the left, center, or right on dimensions.

Ai_Dim_TextHome

Centers dimension text horizontally on the dimension line.

Command	Alias	Ctrl+	F-key	Alt+	Menu Bar	Tablet
ai_box	...	...	...	...	...	...

```
Command: ai_dim_texthome
Select objects: [pick]
Select objects: ENTER
Select objects: ENTER
```

*Before (top) and after (bottom) applying **Ai_Dim_TextHome**.*

COMMAND LINE OPTION

Select objects Select one or more dimensions.

TIPS

- This command works with all types of dimensions.

- This command centers text horizontally on the dimension line, but not vertically. To center text vertically, use the **Ai_Dim_TextCenter** command.

- The **DimTEdit** command aligns text to the left, center, or right on horizontal dimensions.

AiDimTextMove

Moves the location of dimension text.

Command	Alias	Ctrl+	F-key	Alt+	Menu Bar	Tablet
ai_box	...	...	...	...	...	...

```
Command: aidimtextmove
Enter option [0/1/2] <2>: 2
Select objects: [pick]
Select objects: ENTER
```

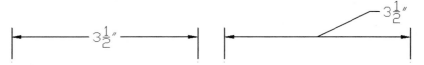

*Before (left) and after (right) applying **AiDimTextMove = 0** to dimension text.*

*Before and after applying **AiDimTextMove = 1** to dimension text.*

*Before and after applying **AiDimTextMove = 2** to dimension text.*

COMMAND LINE OPTIONS

Enter option   Specify the style of text movement:

Option	Meaning
0	Moves text with dimension line.
1	Adds a leader to the moved text.
2	Moves text anywhere without leader line (default).

Select objects Select one or more dimensions.

TIPS

- This command allows you retroactively to change the position of dimension text. It is meant for use in menu and toolbar macros.

- Although the command allows you to select more than one dimension, it operates on the first-selected dimension only.

Ai_Dish

Draws a 3D half-sphere as a surface model.

Command	Alias	Ctrl+	F-key	Alt+	Menu Bar	Tablet
ai_box	...	...	...	...	...	...

```
Command: ai_dish
Specify center point of dish: [pick]
Specify radius of dish or [Diameter]: [pick]
Enter number of longitudinal segments for surface of dish
    <16>: ENTER
Enter number of latitudinal segments for surface of dish
    <8>: ENTER
```

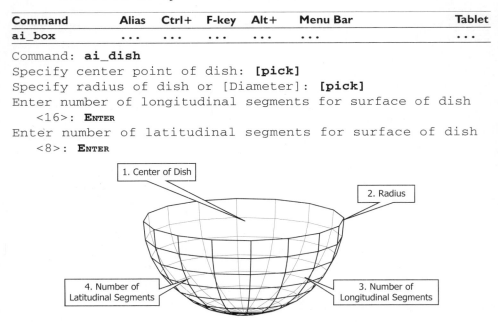

COMMAND LINE OPTIONS

Center of dish Specifies the center of the dish's base.

Diameter Specifies the diameter of the dish.

Radius Specifies the radius of the dish.

Number of longitudinal segments
Specifies the number of "lines" that define the curved surface, in the vertical direction; default = 16.

Number of latitudinal segments
Specifies the number of "lines" that define the curved surface, in the horizontal direction; default = 8.

TIPS

■ The **Ai_Dish** command draws the bottom half of a sphere.

■ The "base" of the dish is drawn at the current setting of the **Elevation** system variable; the dish is drawn downward (in the negative z direction).

Ai_Dome

Draws a half-sphere as a surface model.

Command	Alias	Ctrl+	F-key	Alt+	Menu Bar	Tablet
ai_box	...	...	...	...	...	...

```
Command: ai_dome
Specify center point of dome: [pick]
Specify radius of dome or [Diameter]: [pick]
Enter number of longitudinal segments for surface of dish
    <16>: ENTER
Enter number of latitudinal segments for surface of dish
    <8>: ENTER
```

4. Number of Latitudinal Segments

3. Number of Longitudinal Segments

2. Radius

1. Center of Dome

COMMAND LINE OPTIONS

Center of dome Specifies the center of the dome's base.

Diameter Specifies the diameter of the dome.

Radius Specifies the radius of the dome.

Number of longitudinal segments
Specifies the number of "lines" that define the curved surface, in the vertical direction; default = 16.

Number of latitudinal segments
Specifies the number of "lines" that define the curved surface, in the horizontal direction; default = 8.

TIPS

- The **Ai_Dome** command draws the upper half of a sphere.

- The "base" of the dome is drawn at the current setting of the **Elevation** system variable; the dome is drawn upward (in the positive z direction).

Ai_Fms

Switches to layout mode, then to floating model space.

Command	Alias	Ctrl+	F-key	Alt+	Menu Bar	Tablet
ai_box	. . .	. . .	. . .	. . .	. . .	. . .

Command: **ai_fms**
Switches to layout mode, then to the first floating model viewport.

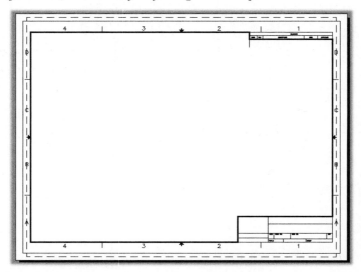

The heavy border indicates the currently active floating viewport in model space.

COMMAND LINE OPTIONS
None.

TIPS

■ This command combines two commands: **Layout** followed by **MSpace**.

■ The command is meant for use with menu and toolbar macros.

Ai_Mesh

Draws a non-planar mesh as a surface model.

Command	Alias	Ctrl+	F-key	Alt+	Menu Bar	Tablet
ai_box	. . .	. . .	. . .	. . .	. . .	. . .

```
Command: ai_mesh
Specify first corner point of mesh: [pick]
Specify second corner point of mesh: [pick]
Specify third corner point of mesh: [pick]
Specify fourth corner point of mesh: [pick]
Enter mesh size in the M direction:  [specify a number]
Enter mesh size in the N direction:  [specify a number]
```

4. Fourth Corner

5. Mesh M Size

6. Mesh N Size

3. Third Corner

1. First Corner

2. Second Corner

COMMAND LINE OPTIONS

First corner Specifies the location of the mesh's first corner.
Second corner Specifies the location of the mesh's second corner.
Third corner Specifies the location of the mesh's third corner.
Fourth corner Specifies the location of the mesh's last corner.
Mesh M size Specifies the number of horizontal "lines" that define the mesh's surface.
Mesh N size Specifies the number of vertical "lines" that define the mesh's surface.

TIP

■ Use the **.xy** filter first to specify the x,y coordinate, followed by the z coordinate, as follows:

```
First corner:.xy
of [pick]
need Z: 2
```

Ai_Molc

Changes the current layer to one belonging to the selected object (*short for "make object layer current"*).

Command	Alias	Ctrl+	F-key	Alt+	Menu Bar	Tablet
ai_box	...	...	...	...	...	...

Command: **ai_molc**
Select object whose layer will become current: **[pick]**
0 is now the current layer.

COMMAND LINE OPTION
Select object   Selects a single object.

RELATED COMMANDS
Layer   Displays the **Layer Properties Manager** dialog box.
LayerP   Reverts to the previous layer.
MatchProp   Matches the properties of one object to other objects.

RELATED SYSTEM VARIABLE
CLayer   Holds the name of the current layer.

Ai_Pyramid

Draws a 3D pyramid as a surface model.

Command	Alias	Ctrl+	F-key	Alt+	Menu Bar	Tablet
ai_box	...	...	...	...	...	...

```
Command: ai_pyramid
Specify first corner point for base of pyramid: [pick]
Specify second corner point for base of pyramid: [pick]
Specify third corner point for base of pyramid: [pick]
Specify fourth corner point for base of pyramid or
    [Tetrahedron]: t
```

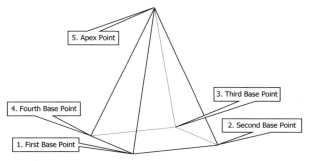

COMMAND LINE OPTIONS

First base point   Specifies the location of the pyramid's first base point.
Second base point Specifies the location of the pyramid's next base point.
Third base point   Specifies the location of the pyramid's third base point.
Tetrahedron   Draws a triangular pyramid with equal-sized sides.
Fourth base point Specifies the location of the pyramid's last base point.
Ridge   Specifies a ridge-top for the pyramid; see figure below.
Top   Specifies a flat-top for the pyramid; see figure below.
Apex point   Specifies a point for the pyramid's top.

TIPS

■ To draw a 2D pyramid, enter no z coordinate for the **Ridge**, **Top**, and **Apex point** options.

■ Use the **.xy** filter to specify the z coordinate for the **Ridge**, **Top**, and **Apex** point option:

```
Apex point:.xy
of [pick]
need Z: 3
```

Ai_SelAll

Selects all objects in the drawing.

Command	Alias	Ctrl+	F-key	Alt+	Menu Bar	Tablet
ai_box	...	A	...	...	...	...

```
Command: ai_selall
Selecting objects...done.
```

COMMAND LINE OPTIONS
None.

TIPS

■ This command is meant for use in menu macros and toolbars.

■ As of AutoCAD 2002, you can use **Ctrl+A** to select everything; prior versions of AutoCAD used **Ctrl+A** to toggle group mode.

■ The opposite command to un-select all is **(ai_deselect)**.

Ai_Sphere

Draws a 3D sphere as a surface model.

Command	Alias	Ctrl+	F-key	Alt+	Menu Bar	Tablet
ai_box	...	...	...	...	...	...

```
Command: ai_sphere
Specify center point of sphere: [pick]
Specify radius of sphere or [Diameter]: [pick]
Enter number of longitudinal segments for surface of sphere
    <16>: ENTER
Enter number of latitudinal segments for surface of sphere
    <16>: ENTER
```

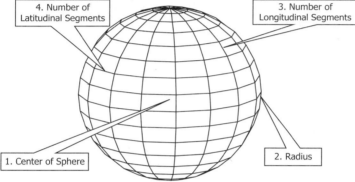

4. Number of Latitudinal Segments

3. Number of Longitudinal Segments

1. Center of Sphere

2. Radius

COMMAND LINE OPTIONS

Center of sphere Specifies the center point of the sphere.
Diameter Specifies the diameter of the sphere.
Radius Specifies the radius of the sphere.
Number of longitudinal segments
  Specifies the number of "lines" that define the curved surface, in the vertical direction; default = 16.
Number of latitudinal segments
  Specifies the number of "lines" that define the curved surface, in the horizontal direction; default = 16.

Ai_Torus

Draws a 3D torus as a surface model.

Command	Alias	Ctrl+	F-key	Alt+	Menu Bar	Tablet
ai_box	...	...	...	...	...	...

```
Command: ai_torus
Specify center point of torus: [pick]
Specify radius of torus or [Diameter]: [pick]
Specify radius of tube or [Diameter]: [pick]
Enter number of segments around tube circumference <16>: ENTER
Enter number of segments around torus circumference
    <16>: ENTER
```

4. Segments Around Tube

5. Segments Around Torus

3. Radius of Tube

1. Center of Torus

2. Radius of Torus

COMMAND LINE OPTIONS

Center of torus   Specifies the center point of the torus.
Diameter of torus   Specifies the diameter of the torus.
Radius of torus   Specifies the radius of the torus.
Diameter of tube   Specifies the diameter of the tube.
Radius of tube   Specifies the radius of the tube.
Segments around tube circumference <16>
                Specifies the number of "lines" defining the curved surface;
                default = 16.
Segments around torus circumference <16>
                Specifies the number of "lines" defining the curved surface;
                default = 16.

TIPS

■ The **Ai_Torus** command draws donut shapes.

■ The tube diameter cannot exceed the torus radius.

Ai_Wedge

Draws a 3D wedge as a surface model.

Command	Alias	Ctrl+	F-key	Alt+	Menu Bar	Tablet
ai_box	...	...	...	...	...	...

Command: **ai_wedge**
Specify corner point of wedge: **[pick]**
Specify length of wedge: **[pick]**
Specify width of wedge: **[pick]**
Specify height of wedge: **[pick]**
Specify rotation angle of wedge about the Z axis: **0**

```
                    ┌──────────┐
                    │ 4. Height │
                    └──────────┘




        ┌──────────┐        ┌──────────────────┐        ┌───────────┐
        │ 3. Width  │       │ 1. Corner of Wedge │       │ 2. Length  │
        └──────────┘        └──────────────────┘        └───────────┘
```

COMMAND LINE OPTIONS

Corner of wedge
　　　　　Specifies the corner of the wedge's base.
Length　　　Specifies the length of the wedge's base.
Width　　　Specifies the width of the wedge's base.
Height　　　Specifies the height of the wedge.
Rotation angle Specifies the angle the box rotates about the z-axis.

TIPS

■ The point you pick for the **Corner of wedge** determines the higher end of the wedge.

■ When specifying the **Width** and **Height**, move the cursor back to the **Corner of wedge** point; otherwise the wedge may have a different size than you expect.

■ You can use the .xy point filter to specify the height.

The following applies to the Ai_ surface model commands:

RELATED SYSTEM VARIABLES

SurfU   Surface mesh density in the m-direction.
SurfV   Surface mesh density in the n-direction.

TIPS

■ You *cannot* perform Boolean operations (such as intersect, subtract, and union) on 3D surface objects.

■ You cannot convert 3D surface objects into 3D solid objects.

■ To convert 3D solid objects into 3D surface objects, export with **3dsOut**; then import with the **3dsIn** command.

■ Variants of 3D objects drawn by the **Ai_** series of commands:

Command	Variant
Ai_Box	Rectangular box, cube.
Ai_Cone	Pointy cone, truncated cone.
Ai_Pyramid	Pyramid, truncated pyramid, tetrahedron, truncated tetrahedron, roof shape.
Ai_Torus	Torus or donut.
Ai_Wedge	Wedge.

■ Mesh m- and n-sizes are limited to values between 2 and 256.

■ Each of these surface shapes is made of a single polymesh; use the **Explode** command to convert each facet to independent 3Dface objects.

■ The base of box, cone, dish, dome, mesh, and pyramid is drawn at the current setting of the **Elevation** system variable — unless you specify a z-coordinate. The center of sphere and torus at the current elevation.

■ You can use the **Hide**, **Shade**, and **Render** commands on these surface model shapes.

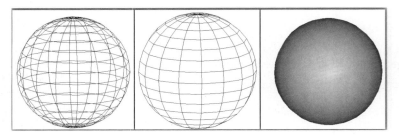

Align

Rel.12 Moves, transforms, and rotates objects in three dimensions.

Command	Alias	Ctrl+	F-key	Alt+	Menu Bar	Tablet
align	al	...	...	M3L	Modify	X14
					↳3D Operation	
					↳Align	

```
Command: align
Select objects: [pick]
Select objects: ENTER
Specify first source point: [pick]
Specify first destination point: [pick]
Specify second source point: [pick]
Specify second destination point: [pick]
Specify third source point or <continue>: [pick]
Specify third destination point: [pick]
```

COMMAND LINE OPTIONS

First point Moves object in 2D or 3D when one source and destination point are picked.

Second point Moves, rotates, and scales object in 2D or 3D when two source and destination points are picked.

Third point Moves, rotates, and scales object in 3D when three source and destination points are picked.

Continue option:

```
Scale objects based on alignment points? [Yes/No] <N>:
```
The distance between the first and second destination points is used for the reference length by which to scale the object.

RELATED COMMANDS

Mirror3d Mirrors objects in three dimensions.

Rotate3d Rotates objects in three dimensions.

TIPS

■ Enter the first pair of points to define the move distance:

```
Specify first source point: [pick]
Specify first destination point: [pick]
Specify second source point: ENTER
```

■ Enter two pairs of points to define a 2D (or 3D) transformation, scaling, and rotation:

Points	Alignment Defined
First	Base point for alignment.
Second	Rotation angle.
Third	Scale based on distance between first and second destination points.

■ The third pair defines the 3D transformation.

AmeConvert

Converts solid models and regions created by AME v2.0 and v2.1 (*from AutoCAD Release 11 and 12*) into ACIS solids models.

Command	Alias	Ctrl+	F-key	Alt+	Menu Bar	Tablet
ameconvert	...	...	...	...	...	...

```
Command: ameconvert
Select objects: [pick]
Processing Boolean operations.
```

COMMAND LINE OPTION

Select object Selects AME objects to convert; ignores non-AME objects, such as the ACIS solids produced by AutoCAD Release 13, Release 14, and 2000.

RELATED COMMAND

AcisIn Imports ACIS models from an SAT file.

TIPS

- After conversion, the AME model remains in the drawing in the same location as the ACIS model. Erase, if necessary.
- AME holes may become blind holes in ACIS.
- AME fillets and chamfers may be placed higher or lower in ACIS.
- Once the **AmeConvert** command converts a Release 12 PADL drawing into an AutoCAD 2002 ACIS model, it cannot be converted back to PADL format.
- This command ignores objects that are neither an AME solid nor a region.
- Old AME models are stored in AutoCAD as an anonymous block reference.

DEFINITIONS

ACIS The name of the solids modeling technology in AutoCAD since R13.

AME Short for "Advanced Modeling Extension," the name of the solids modeling module used by AutoCAD in Release 10 through 12.

PADL Short for "Parts and Description Language," the solids modeling technology used in AutoCAD Release 10 through 12.

'Aperture

V. 1.3 Sets the size, in pixels, of the object snap target height, or box cursor.

Command	Alias	Ctrl+	F-key	Alt+	Menu Bar	Tablet
'aperture	...	...	...	...	...	...

```
Command: aperture
Object snap target height (1-50 pixels) <10>:
```

Aperture size = 1 (left), 10 (center), and 50 pixels (right).

COMMAND LINE OPTION

Height   Specify the height of the object snap cursor's target.

RELATED COMMANDS

Options   The **Drafting** tab allows you to set the aperture size interactively.

RELATED SYSTEM VARIABLE

Aperture   Contains the current target height, in pixels:

Aperture	Meaning
1	Minimum size.
10	Default size, in pixels.
50	Maximum size.

TIPS

- This box cursor appears only during object snap selection; to change the size of the pick cursor, use the **Pickbox** command.

- Use the **Options** command to change the size of the aperture visually.

AppLoad

Rel.12 Creates a list of LISP, VBA, ObjectDBX, and ObjectARx applications
to load (*short for APPlication LOADer*).

Command	Alias	Ctrl+	F-key	Alt+	Menu Bar	Tablet
appload	ap	...	...	TL	Tools	V10
					↳Load Applications	

Command: **appload**
Displays dialog box:

DIALOG BOX OPTIONS

Look in   Lists drives and folders.

File name   Specifies the name of the file to load.

Files of type   Displays list of file types:

Filetype	Meaning
ARX	ObjectARX
DVB	Visual Basic for Applications (VBA)
DBX	ObjectDBX
FAS	Fast Load AutoLISP
LSP	AutoLISP
VLX	Visual Lisp Executable

Load   Loads all or selected files into AutoCAD.

Loaded Applications
    Displays the names of applications already loaded into AutoCAD.

History List   Displays the names of applications previously saved to this list.

Add to History   Adds the file to the history tab.

Unload   Unloads all or selected files out of AutoCAD.

Close   Exits the dialog box.

Startup Suite options:

Contents Displays the **Startup Suite** dialog box:

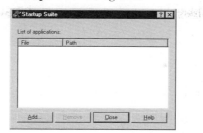

List of applications
  Lists the file name and path of applications automatically loaded each time AutoCAD starts.

Add Displays the **Add File to Startup Suite** dialog box; allows you to select one or more application files.

Remove Removes the application from the list.

Close Returns to the **Load/Unload Applications** dialog box.

RELATED COMMANDS

Arx Lists ObjectARX programs currently loaded in AutoCAD.

VbaLoad Loads VBA applications.

RELATED AUTOLISP FUNCTIONS

(load) Loads an AutoLISP program.

(autoload) Predefines commands to load related AutoLISP programs.

TIPS

■ Use **AppLoad** when AutoCAD does not automatically load a command.

■ ObjectARX, VBA, and DBX applications are loaded immediately; FAS, LSP, and VLX files are loaded when this dialog box is closed.

■ This command was a transparent command in earlier versions of AutoCAD.

■ You can drag files from Windows Explorer into the **Loaded Applications** list.

■ The *Acad2000Doc.Lsp* file establishes autoloader and other utility functions, and is loaded automatically each time a drawing is opened; the *Acad2000.Lsp* file is loaded only once per AutoCAD session. Use the **AcadLspAsDoc** system variable to control loading these files.

■ To load LISP code into every drawing, add the code to *AcadDoc.Lsp*.

Arc

V. 1.0 Draws a 2D arc of less than 360 degrees, by eleven methods.

Command	Alias	Ctrl+	F-key	Alt+	Menu Bar	Tablet
arc	a	...	...	DA	Draw ↳Arc	R10

```
Command: arc
Specify start point of arc or [CEnter]: [pick]
Specify second point of arc or [CEnter/ENd]: [pick]
Specify end point of arc: [pick]
```

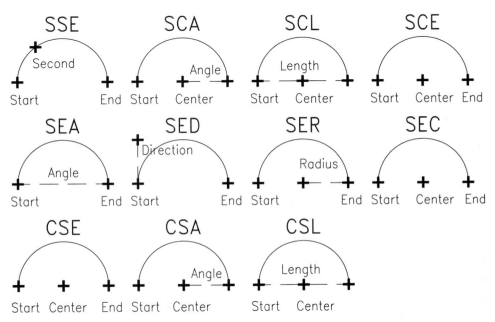

COMMAND LINE OPTIONS

SSE arc options:

Start point   Indicates the start point of a three-point arc (*see figure*).
Second point   Indicates a second point anywhere along the arc.
Endpoint   Indicates the endpoint of the arc.

SCE, SCA, and SCL arc options:

Start point   Indicates the start point of a two-point arc.
Center   Indicates the arc's enter point.
Angle   Indicates the arc's included angle.
Length of chord Indicates the length of the arc's chord.
Endpoint   Indicates the arc's endpoint.

SEA, SED, SER, and SEC arc options:

Start point Indicates the start point of a two-point arc.
End Indicates the arc's end point.
Center point Indicates the arc's center point.
Angle Indicates the arc's included angle.
Direction Indicates the tangent direction from the arc's start point.
Radius Indicates the arc's radius.

CSE, CSA, and CSL arc options:

Center Indicates the center point of a two-point arc.
Start point Indicates the arc's start point.
Endpoint Indicates the arc's end point.
Angle Indicates the arc's included angle.
Length of chord
  Indicates the length of the arc's chord.

Continued arc option:

ENTER Continues arc tangent from endpoint of last-drawn line or arc.

RELATED TOOLBAR ICONS

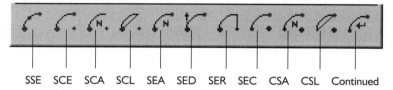

SSE SCE SCA SCL SEA SED SER SEC CSA CSL Continued

RELATED COMMANDS

Circle Draws an "arc" of 360 degrees.
Ellipse Draws elliptical arcs.
Polyline Draws connected polyline arcs.
ViewRes Controls the roundness of arcs.

RELATED SYSTEM VARIABLE

LastAngle Saves the included angle of the last-drawn arc (read-only).

TIPS

■ To start an arc precisely tangent to the endpoint of the last line or arc, press **Enter** at the 'Specify start point of arc or [CEnter]:' prompt.

■ You can drag the arc only during the last-entered option.

■ Specifying an x,y,z coordinate as the starting point of the arc draws the arc at the z elevation.

- In some cases, it may be easier to draw a circle and use **Break** and **Trim** to convert the circle into an arc.
- When the chord length is positive, the minor arc is drawn counterclockwise from the start point; when negative, the major arc is drawn counterclockwise.
- The components of an AutoCAD arc:

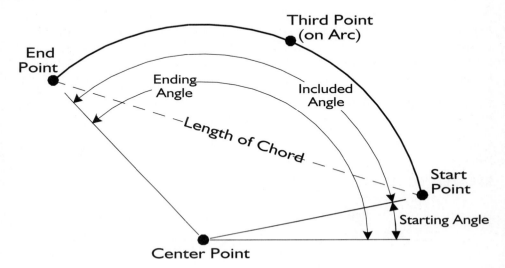

Area

V. 1.0 Calculates the area and perimeter of areas, closed objects, and polylines.

Command	Alias	Ctrl+	F-key	Alt+	Menu Bar	Tablet
area	aa	. . .	. . .	TQA	Tools	T7
					↳Inquiry	
					↳Area	

```
Command: area
Specify first corner point or [Object/Add/Subtract]: [pick]
Specify next corner point or press ENTER for total: [pick]
Specify next corner point or press ENTER for total: [pick]
Specify next corner point or press ENTER for total: ENTER
Area = 1.8398, Perimeter = 6.5245
```

COMMAND LINE OPTIONS

First point	Indicates the first point to begin measurement.
Object	Indicates the object to be measured.
Add	Switches to add-area mode.
Subtract	Switches to subtract-area mode.
Enter	Indicates the end of the area outline.

RELATED COMMANDS

Dist	Returns the distance between two points.
Id	Lists the x,y,z coordinates of a selected point.
MassProp	Returns surface area, etc. of solid models.

RELATED SYSTEM VARIABLES

Area	Contains the most recently-calculated area.
Perimeter	Contains the most recently-calculated perimeter.

TIPS

- At least three points must be picked to calculate an area; if necessary, AutoCAD automatically "closes the polygon" before measuring the area.

- You can specify 2D x,y coordinates or 3D x,y,z coordinates.

- The **Object** option returns the following information:

Object	Measurement Returned
Circle, ellipse	Area and circumference.
Planar closed spline	Area and circumference.
Closed polyline, polygon	Area and perimeter.
Open objects	Area and length.
Region	Area of all objects in region.
2D Solid	Surface area.

- The area of a wide polyline is measured along its centerline; closed polylines must have one closed area only.

- This command does not measure the area of solid objects; use the **MassProp** command.

⊞ Array

V. 1.3 Creates a 2D rectangular or polar array of objects.

Command	Alias	Ctrl+	F-key	Alt+	Menu Bar	Tablet
array	ar	...	...	MA	Modify	V18
					⌊Array	

Command: **array**
Displays dialog box:

DIALOG BOX OPTIONS

Rectangular Array
        Displays the options for creating a rectangular array.
Polar Array   Displays the options for creating a polar array.
Select objects Temporarily dismisses the dialog box, so that you can select the objects in
        the drawing:
               Select objects: **[pick]**
               Select objects: ENTER
        Press ENTER or right-click to return to the dialog box.
Preview   Temporarily dismisses the dialog box so that you can see what the array
        will look like; see **Preview** dialog box.

Rectangular Array options:

Rows   Specifies the number of rows; minimum=1, maximum=100,000.
Columns   Specifies the number of columns; minimum=1, maximum=100,000.
Row offset Specifies the distance between rows; use negative number to draw rows in
        the negative x-direction (to the right).
Column offset Specifies the distance between columns; use negative number to draw rows
        in the negative y-direction (downward).
Angle of array Specifies the angle of the array, which "tilts" the array.

Polar Array options:

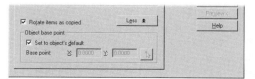

Center point Specifies the center of the polar array.
Method Specifies the method by which the array is constructed:
   • Total number of items and angle to fill.
   • Total number of items and angle between items.
   • Angle to fill and angle between items.
Total number of items
   Specifies the number of objects in array; minimum=2.
Angle to fit Specifies angle of "arc" to construct the array; min=1 deg; max=360 deg.
Angle between items
   Specifies the angle between each object in the array.
Roate items as copied
   Yes: Objects are rotated so that they face the center of the array.
   No: Objects are not rotated.
More Displays additional options for constructing a polar array.

More dialog box:

Set to the object's default:
   No: Allows you to specify the base point.
   Yes: Uses the default base point of the object, as follows:

Object	Default base point
Arc, circle, ellipse	Center point
Polygon, rectangle	First vertex
Line, polyline, 3D polyline, ray, spline	Start point
Donut	Start point
Block, mtext, text	Insertion point
Xline	Midpoint
Region	Grip point

Preview dialog box:

Accept   Accepts the array settings, exits the **Array** command, and draws the array.
Modify   Returns to the **Array** dialog box, so that you can modify the parameters.
Cancel   Exits the **Array** command, and does not draw the array.

-ARRAY COMMAND

```
COmmand: -array
Select objects: [pick]
Select objects: ENTER
```

Rectangular options:

```
Enter the type of array [Rectangular/Polar] <R>: r
Enter the number of rows (---) <1>: [enter number]
Enter the number of columns (|||) <1>: [enter number]
Enter the distance between rows or specify unit cell (---):
    [specify distance]
Specify the distance between columns (|||): [specify distance]
```

Polar options:

```
Rectangular or Polar array (R/P): p
Specify center point of array: [pick]
Enter the number of items in the array: [enter number]
Specify the angle to fill (+=ccw, -=cw) <360>: [enter angle]
Rotate arrayed objects? [Yes/No] <Y>:
```

COMMAND LINE OPTIONS

R   Creates a rectangular array of the selected object.
P   Creates a polar array of the selected object.
Center point Specifies the center point of the array.
Rows   Specifies the number of horizontal rows.
Columns   Specifies the number of vertical columns.
Unit cell   Specifies the vertical and horizontal spacing between objects.

RELATED COMMANDS

3dArray   Creates a rectangular or polar array in 3D space.
Copy   Creates one or more copies of the selected object.
MInsert   Creates a rectangular block array of blocks.

RELATED SYSTEM VARIABLE

SnapAng   Determines the angle of a rectangular array.

TIPS

■ To create a rectangular array at an angle, use the **Rotation** option of the **Snap** command to set the angle of rotation.

■ Rectangular arrays are drawn upward in the positive x direction, and rightward in the positive y direction; to draw the array in the opposite directions, specify negative row and column distances.

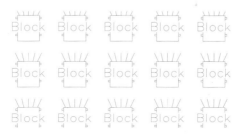

A 3-row by 5-column rectangular array:

■ Polar arrays are drawn counterclockwise; to draw the array clockwise, specify a negative angle.

■ In polar arrays, you can choose to have the objects rotated as they are copied.

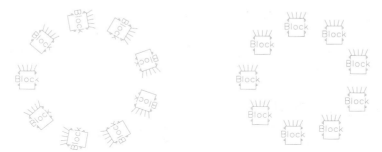

Nine-item polar arrays — rotated (left) and unrotated (right).

■ Use the **Divide** or **Measure** command to create a linear array along a path.

Arx

Displays information regarding currently loaded ObjectARX programs.

Command	Alias	Ctrl+	F-key	Alt+	Menu Bar	Tablet
arx	...	...	...	...	...	...

```
Command: arx
Enter an option [?/Load/Unload/Commands/Options]: o
Enter an option [Group/CLasses/Services]:
```

COMMAND LINE OPTIONS

?	Lists names of currently loaded ObjectARX programs.
Load	Loads the ObjectARX program into AutoCAD.
Unload	Unloads the ObjectARX program out of memory.
Commands	Lists the names of command associated with each ObjectARX program.

Options options:

CLasses	Lists the class hierarchy for ObjectARX objects.
Groups	Lists the names of objects entered into the "system registry."
Services	Lists names of services entered in the ObjectARX "service dictionary."

RELATED COMMAND

AppLoad   Loads LISP, VBA, ObjectDBX, and ObjectARX programs via dialog box.

RELATED AUTOLISP FUNCTIONS

(arx)	Lists currently loaded ObjectARX programs.
(arxload)	Loads an ObjectARX application.
(autoarxload)	Predefines commands that load the ObjectARX program.
(arxunload)	Unloads an ObjectARX application.

RELATED FILE

*.ARX   ObjectARX program files.

TIPS

■ Use the **Load** option to load external commands that do not seem to work.

■ Use the **Unload** option of the **Arx** command to remove ObjectARX programs from AutoCAD to free up memory. These are some of the largest programs (250KB or more):

ObjectArx	Meaning
Acmted.Arx	MText text editor.
Ase.Arx	AutoCAD SQL extension.
Asilisp.Arx	AutoCAD SQL interface LISP functions.
Ism.Arx	The **Image**-related commands.
Render.Arx	The rendering commands.

REMOVED COMMANDS:

ASE-related commands were removed from AutoCAD 2000: **AseAdmin**, **AseExport**, **AseLinks**, **AseRows**, **AseSelect**, and **AseSqlEd**. Use **DbConnect** instead.

AttachURL

Rel.14 Attaches a hyperlink to an object or an area (*an undocumented command*).

Command	Alias	Ctrl+	F-key	Alt+	Menu Bar	Tablet
attachurl	...	...	...	...	...	...

```
Command: attachurl
Enter hyperlink insert option [Area/Object] <Object>: o
Select objects: [pick]
1 found Select objects: ENTER
Enter hyperlink <Current drawing>: http://www.upfrontezine.com
```

COMMAND LINE OPTIONS

Area Creates a 2D hyperlink by specifying two corners of a rectangle.
Object Creates a 1D hyperlink by selecting one or more objects.
Enter hyperlink
  Allows you to enter a valid hyperlink.

Area options:

First corner Picks first corner of rectangle.
Other corner Picks second corner of rectangle.

RELATED COMMANDS

Hyperlink Displays a dialog box for adding a hyperlink to an object.
SelectUrl Selects all objects with attached hyperlinks.

TIPS

■ The hyperlinks placed in the drawing can link to *any* other file: another AutoCAD drawing, an office document, or a file located on the Internet.

■ See **Hyperlink** for tutorial on attaching hyperlinks to objects in the drawing.

■ Autodesk recommends that you use the following URL formats:

File Location	Example URL
Web Site	http://*servername*/*pathname*/*filename*.**dwg**
FTP Site	ftp://*servername*/*pathname*/*filename*.**dwg**
Local File	file:///*drive*:/*pathname*/*filename*.**dwg**
o r	file:////*localPC*/*pathname*/*filename*.**dwg**
Network File	file://*localhost*/*drive*:/*pathname*/*filename*.**dwg**

■ The **Area** option creates a layer named URLLAYER with the default color of red, and places a rectangle object on that layer; do not delete layer URLLAYER.

■ The URL or hyperlink is stored as follows:

Attachment	URL
One object	Stored as xdata (extended entity data).
Multiple objects	Stored as xdata in each object.
Area	Stored as xdata in a rectangle object on layer URLLAYER.

Assist

<u>**2000i**</u> Opens the Active Assistance window, which provides real-time assistance.

Command	Alias	Ctrl+	F-key	Alt+	Menu Bar	Tablet
assist	...	...	...	HA	Help ᐳActive Assistance	...

Command: **assist**
Displays window:

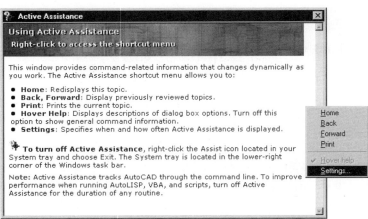

COMMAND LINE OPTIONS
None.

SHORTCUT MENU OPTIONS

Home	Displays the "home" page.
Back	Displays the previous topic.
Forward	Displays the next topic, if the **Back** option has been used.
Print	Prints the topic.
Hover Help	Displays help for items in dialog boxes in the **Active Assistance** window.
Settings	Displays the **Active Assistance Settings** dialog box.

Settings dialog box:

Show on start Launches **Active Assistance** automatically when AutoCAD starts.

Hover Help	Toggles hover help for items in dialog boxes.
Activation	Determines when **Active Assistance** displays its help topics:

- **All commands** displays assistance for all commands.
- **New and enhanced commands** displays assistance for commands new to AutoCAD and for commands that have changed since the last release.
- **Dialogs only** displays assistance for dialog boxes only.
- **On demand** displays assistance only when you click the icon on the Windows taskbar.

RELATED COMMAND

Help	Displays static help in a window.

TIPS

- To turn off Active Assitance, turn off the **Show on Start** option in the **Active Assistance Settings** dialog box.

- Not all commands are supported by Active Assistance:

- To access Active Assistance on-demand, double-click the icon found on the Windows taskbar, or right-click and select an option from the shortcut menu:

Active Assistance icon

⬦ AttDef

V. 2.0 Defines attribute modes and prompts (*short for ATTribute DEFinition*).

Command	Alias	Ctrl+	F-key	Alt+	Menu Bar	Tablet
attdef	att	...	...	DKD	Draw	...
	ddattdef				⬦Block	
					⬦Define Attributes	
-attdef	-att					

Command: **attdef**
Displays dialog box:

DIALOG BOX OPTIONS

Mode options:

Invisible	Makes the attribute text invisible.
Constant	Uses constant values for the attributes.
Verify	Verifies the text after input.
Preset	Presets the variable attribute text.

Attribute options:

Tag	Identifies the attribute.
Prompt	Prompts the user for input.
Value	Sets the default value for the attribute.

Insertion Point options:

Pick point	Picks insertion point with cursor.
X	Specifies the x coordinate insertion point.
Y	Specifies the y coordinate insertion point.
Z	Specifies the z coordinate insertion point.

Text *options:*

Justification   Sets the justification.
Text style   Selects a style.
Height   Specifies the height.
Rotation   Sets the rotation angle.

Align   Places the text automatically below the previous attribute.

-ATTDEF COMMAND

Command: **-attdef**
Current attribute modes: Invisible=N Constant=N Verify=N
    Preset=N
Enter an option to change [Invisible/Constant/Verify/Preset]
    <done>: ENTER
Enter attribute tag: **[enter tag]**
Enter attribute prompt: **[enter prompt]**
Enter default attribute value: **[enter value]**
Specify start point of text or [Justify/Style]: **[pick]**
Specify height <0.200>: ENTER
Specify rotation angle of text <0>: ENTER

COMMAND LINE OPTIONS

Attribute mode Selects the mode(s) for the attribute:
            I: Toggles visibility of attribute text in drawing (short for Invisible).
            C: Toggles fixed or variable value of attribute (short for Constant).
            V: Toggles confirmation prompt during input (short for Verify).
            P: Toggles automatic insertion of default values (short for Preset).
Start point Indicates the start point of the attribute text.
Justify Selects the justification mode for the attribute text.
Style Selects the text style for the attribute text.
Height Specifies the height of the attribute text; not displayed if the style specifies a height other than 0.
Rotation angle Specifies the angle of the attribute text.

RELATED COMMANDS

AttDisp   Controls the visibility of attributes.
EAttEdit   Edits the values of attributes.
EAttExt   Extracts attributes to disk.
AttRedef   Redefines an attribute or block.
Block   Binds attributes to objects.
Insert   Inserts a block and prompts for attribute values.

RELATED SYSTEM VARIABLES

AFlags   Contains the value of modes in bit form:

AFlags	Meaning
0	No attribute mode selected
1	Invisible
2	Constant
4	Verify
8	Preset

AttDia   Toggles use of dialog box during **Insert:**

AttDia	Meaning
0	Uses command-line prompts
1	Uses dialog box

AttReq   Toggles use of defaults or user prompts during **Insert:**

AttReq	Meaning
0	Assumes default values of all attributes
1	Prompts for attributes

TIPS

■ Constant attributes cannot be edited.

■ Attribute tags cannot be null (have no value); attribute values may be null.

■ You can enter any characters for the attribute tag, except a space or an exclamation mark. All characters are converted to uppercase.

■ When you press **Enter** at 'Attribute Prompt,' AutoCAD uses the attribute *tag* as the prompt.

■ 'Attribute Prompt' and 'Default Attribute Value' are not when displayed when constant mode is turned on. Instead, AutoCAD prompts 'Attribute Value.'

■ When you press **Enter** at the 'Starting point:' prompt, **AttDef** automatically places the next attribute below the previous one.

*Block with attribute **value** (left) and attribute **tags** (right).*

'AttDisp

V. 2.0 Controls the display of all attributes in the drawing (*short for ATTribute DISPlay*).

Command	Alias	Ctrl+	F-key	Alt+	Menu Bar	Tablet
'attdisp	...	...	...	VLA	View ⌐Display ⌐Attribute Display	L1

Command: **attdisp**
Enter attribute visibility setting [Normal/ON/OFF] <Normal>:
Regenerating drawing.

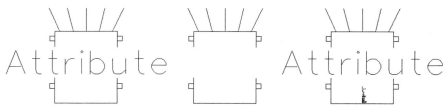

Attribute display **Normal** *(left),* **Off** *(center), and* **On** *(right).*

COMMAND LINE OPTIONS

Normal	Displays attributes according to **AttDef** setting.
ON	Displays all attributes, regardless of **AttDef** setting.
OFF	Displays no attributes, regardless of **AttDef** setting.

RELATED COMMANDS

AttDef	Defines new attributes, including their default visibility.
DdAttDef	Defines new attributes via dialog box.

RELATED SYSTEM VARIABLE

AttMode   Contains current setting of **AttDisp**:

AttMode	Meaning
0	Off: no attributes are displayed.
1	Normal: invisible attributes are not displayed.
2	On: all attributes are displayed.

TIPS

- If necessary, use **Regen** after **AttDisp** to see change to attribute display.

- When you define invisible attributes, use **AttDisp** to view them.

- Use **AttDisp** to turn off the display of attributes, which helps increase display speed and reduce drawing clutter.

AttEdit

V. 2.0 Edits attributes in a drawing (*short for ATTribute EDIT*).

Command	Alias	Ctrl+	F-key	Alt+	Menu Bar	Tablet
attedit	ate	...	...	MOAS	Modify	Y20
					⤷Object	
	atte				⤷Attribute	
					⤷Single	
-attedit	-ate			MOAG	Modify	
					⤷Object	
					⤷Attribute	
					⤷Global	

Command: **attedit**
Select block reference: **[pick]**
Displays dialog box:

Edit Attributes	
Block name:	direct
Light Name	asdf
Look-at Y	1
Light Intensity	2
"not used"	3
"not used"	-1
Depth Map Size	3
Light Color (RGB)	4,5,6
Look-at Z	2

OK | Cancel | Previous | Next | Help

DIALOG BOX OPTIONS

Block Name   Names the selected block.
Attribute prompt
            Allows you to change the attribute value.
O K   Accepts the changes and closes the dialog box.
Cancel   Discards the changes and closes the dialog box.
Previous   Displays the previous list of attributes.
Next   Displays the next list of attributes.

-ATTEDIT COMMAND
Command: **-attedit**

One-at-time *attribute editing options:*
Edit attributes one at a time? [Yes/No] <Y>: ᴇɴᴛᴇʀ
Enter block name specification <*>: ᴇɴᴛᴇʀ
Enter attribute tag specification <*>: ᴇɴᴛᴇʀ
Enter attribute value specification <*>: ᴇɴᴛᴇʀ
Select Attributes: **[pick]**
1 found Select Attributes: ᴇɴᴛᴇʀ
1 attributes selected.
Enter an option [Value/Position/Height/Angle/Style/Layer/
    Color/Next] <N>:

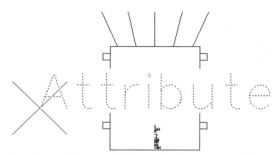

During single attribute editing, **AttEdit** *marks the current attribute with an 'X'.*

Global *attribute editing options:*
Edit attributes one at a time? [Yes/No] <Y>: **n**
Performing global editing of attribute values.
Edit only attributes visible on screen? [Yes/No] <Y>: ᴇɴᴛᴇʀ
Enter block name specification <*>: ᴇɴᴛᴇʀ
Enter attribute tag specification <*>: ᴇɴᴛᴇʀ
Enter attribute value specification <*>: ᴇɴᴛᴇʀ
Select Attributes: **[pick]**
1 found Select Attributes: ᴇɴᴛᴇʀ
1 attributes selected.
Enter string to change: **[enter existing string]**
Enter new string: **[enter new string]**

COMMAND LINE OPTIONS

Value	Changes or replaces the value of the attribute.
Position	Moves the text insertion point of the attribute.
Height	Changes the attribute text height.
Angle	Changes the attribute text angle.
Style	Changes the text style of the attribute text.
Layer	Moves the attribute to a different layer.
Color	Changes the color of the attribute text.
Next	Edits the next attribute.

RELATED SYSTEM VARIABLE

AttDia	Toggles use of **AttEdit** during **Insert** command.

RELATED COMMANDS

AttDef	Defines an attribute's original value and parameter.
AttDisp	Toggles an attribute's visibility.
AttRedef	Redefines attributes and blocks.
Explode	Reduces an attribute to its tag.

TIPS

- Constant attributes cannot be edited with **AttEdit**.

- You can only edit attributes parallel with the current UCS.

- Unlike other text input to AutoCAD, attribute values are case-sensitive.

- To edit null attribute values, use **-AttEdit**'s global edit option and enter \ (backslash) at the 'Enter attribute value specification' prompt.

- The wildcard characters ? and * are interpreted literally at the 'Enter string to change' and 'Enter new string' prompts.

- When selecting attributes for global editing, you may pick the attributes, or use the following selection modes: Window, Last, Crossing, BOX, Fence, WPolygon, or CPolygon.

- To edit the different parts of an attribute, use the following commands:

Command	Edit Attribute
Attedit	Non-constant attribute *values* in one block.
-AttEdit	Attribute *values* and *properties* (such as position, height, and style) in one block or in all attributes.

AttExt

V. 2.0 Extracts attribute data from the drawing to a file on disk (*short for ATTribute EXTract*).

Command	Alias	Ctrl+	F-key	Alt+	Menu Bar	Tablet
attext	...	...	...	FE	File	...
				⌐DXX	⌐**Export**	
					⌐**DXX Extract**	

-attext

Command: **attext**
Displays dialog box:

```
┌─ Attribute Extraction ──────────────── [?] [X] ┐
│  ┌─ File Format ─────────────────────────────┐ │
│  │  (•) Comma Delimited File (CDF)            │ │
│  │  ( ) Space Delimited File (SDF)            │ │
│  │  ( ) DXF Format Extract File (DXX)         │ │
│  └───────────────────────────────────────────┘ │
│                                                 │
│    [ Select Objects < ]   Number found:  0      │
│    [ Template File... ]   [                  ]   │
│    [ Output File...   ]   [ Drawing1.txt     ]   │
│                                                 │
│        [   OK   ]   [ Cancel ]   [  Help  ]      │
└─────────────────────────────────────────────────┘
```

DIALOG BOX OPTIONS

File Format options:
Comma Delimited File (CDF)
    Creates a CDF text file, where commas separate fields.
Space Delimited File (SDF)
    Creates an SDF text file, where spaces separate fields.
DXF Format Extract File (DXX)
    Creates an ASCII DXF-format file.

Select Objects Returns to the graphics screen to select attributes for export.
Template File Specifies the name of the TXT template file for CDF and SDF files.
Output File Specifies the name of the attribute output file: **TXT** for CDF and SDF formats; **DXX** for DXF format.

-ATTEXT COMMAND

Command: **-attext**

Enter extraction type or enable object selection
   [Cdf/Sdf/Dxf/Objects] <C>: ᴇɴᴛᴇʀ

*Displays the **Select Template File** and **Create Extract File** dialog boxes.*

n records in extract file.

COMMAND LINE OPTIONS

Cdf	Outputs attributes in comma-delimited format.
Sdf	Outputs attributes in space-delimited format.
Dxf	Outputs attributes in DXF format.
Objects	Selects objects from which to extract attributes.

RELATED COMMAND

AttDef   Defines attributes.

RELATED FILES

*.TXT	Required extension for template file; extension for CDF and SDF files.
*.DXX	Extension for DXF extraction files.

TIPS

■ **CDF** is short for "Comma Delimited File"; it has one record for each block reference; a comma separates each field; single quote marks delimit text strings.

■ **SDF** is short for "Space Delimited File"; it has one record for each block reference; fields have fixed width padded with spaces; string delimiters are not used.

■ **DXF** is short for "Drawing Interchange File"; it contains only block reference, attribute, and end-of-sequence DXF objects; no template file is required.

■ Before you can specify the SDF or CDF option, you must create the template file.

■ CDF files use the following conventions:
   • Specified field widths are the maximum width.
   • Positive number fields have a leading blank.
   • Character fields are enclosed in ' ' (single quotation marks).
   • Trailing blanks are deleted.
   • Null strings are " (two single quotation marks).
   • Uses spaces; do not uses tabs.
   • Use the C:DELIM and C:QUOTE records to change the field and string delimiters to another character.

■ To output the attributes to the printer, specify:

Logical Filename	Meaning
CON	Displays on text screen
PRN *or* **LPT1**	Prints to parallel port 1
LPT2 *or* **LPT3**	Prints to parallel port 2 or 3

'AttRedef

Rel.13 Redefines blocks and attributes *(short for ATTribute REDEFinition)*.

Command	Alias	Ctrl+	F-key	Alt+	Menu Bar	Tablet
'attredef	at	...	...	...	...	...

```
Command: redefine
Name of Block you wish to redefine: [enter name]
Select objects for new Block...
Select objects: [pick]
Select objects: ENTER
Insertion base point of new block: [pick]
```

COMMAND LINE OPTIONS

Name of Block you wish to redefine
> Enters the name of the block to be redefined.

Select objects Selects objects for new block.

Insertion base point of new block
> Picks the new insertion point.

RELATED COMMANDS

AttDef	Defines an attribute's original value and parameter.
AttDisp	Toggles an attribute's visibility.
EAttEdit	Edits the attribute's values.
Explode	Reduces an attribute to its tag.

TIPS

■ Existing attributes retain their values.

■ Existing attributes not included in the new block are erased.

■ New attributes added to an existing block take on default values.

AttSync

2002 Updates blocks with current attributes (*short for ATTribute SYNChronization*).

Command	Alias	Ctrl+	F-key	Alt+	Menu Bar	Tablet
attsync	...	...	...	...	...	...

Command: **redefine**
Enter an option [?/Name/Select] <Select>: ENTER
Select a block: **[pick]**
ATTSYNC block name? [Yes/No] <Yes>: ENTER

COMMAND LINE OPTIONS

?	Lists names of all blocks in the drawing.
Name	Enters the name of the block.
Select	Selects a single block with the cursor.

RELATED COMMANDS

AttDef	Defines an attribute.
BattMan	Edits the attributes in a block definition.
EAttEdit	Edits the attributes in block references.

TIPS

■ The order in which this command would be used is:

1. **AttDef** and **Block** defines the attributes and attaches them to the block.

2. **Insert** inserts the block and gives values to the attributes.

3. **EAttEdit** changes the attribute values in a specific block.

4. **AttSync** reverts the attribute values to their original.

5. **BattMan** changes the attributes in the original block definition.

6. **AttSync** updates the attributes to the new definition.

■ This command does not operate if the drawing lacks blocks with attributes. AutoCAD complains, "This drawing contains no attributed blocks."

Audit

<u>Rel.11</u> Examines a drawing file for structural errors.

Command	Alias	Ctrl+	F-key	Alt+	Menu Bar	Tablet
audit	...	...	...	FUA	File ⇩Drawing Utilities ⇩Audit	...

Command: **audit**
Fix any errors detected? [Yes/No] <N>: **y**

Sample output:
```
 2          Blocks audited
Pass 1 24       objects audited
Pass 2 24       objects audited
Total errors found 0 fixed 0
```

COMMAND LINE OPTIONS
N   Reports errors found; does not fix errors.
Y   Reports and fixes errors found in the drawing file.

RELATED COMMANDS
Save   Saves a recovered drawing to disk.
Recover   Recovers a damaged drawing file.

RELATED SYSTEM VARIABLE
AuditCtl   Controls the creation of the ADT audit log file:

AuditCtl	Meaning
0	No log file is written
1	ADT log file is written to drawing directory

RELATED FILE
*.ADT   Audit log file reports the progress of the auditing process.

TIPS
- The **Audit** command is a diagnostic tool for validating and repairing the contents of a DWG file.

- Objects with errors are placed in the Previous selection set. Use an editing command, such as **Copy**, to view the objects.

- If **Audit** cannot fix a drawing file, use the **Recover** command.

Background

Rel.14 Places a solid color, linear gradient, raster image, or the current view in the background of a rendering.

Command	Alias	Ctrl+	F-key	Alt+	Menu Bar	Tablet
background	...	...	...	VEB	View ↳Render ↳Background	Q2

Command: **background**
Displays dialog box:

DIALOG BOX OPTIONS

Solid options:

Colors　　　Specifies a color from the RGB (red, green, blue) or HLS (hue, lightness, saturation) slider bars.

Select Custom Color
　　　Displays the Windows **Color** dialog box.

AutoCAD Background
　　　Uses the current AutoCAD background color (default = white).

Gradient options:

Top　　　Specifies the top color for two- and three-color gradients.

Middle　　　Specifies the middle color for three-color gradients.

Bottom　　　Specifies the bottom color for two- and three-color gradients.

Horizon　　　Determines the center of the gradient as a percent of the viewport's height.

Height　　　Determines the start of the second color of a three-color gradient; automatically set to 0 for two-color gradients.

Rotation　　　Rotates the angle of the gradient.

Image options:

Image Name	Specifies the name of the raster file to use as the background image
Find File	Displays file dialog box; allows selection of a BMP (Windows bitmap), GIF, JPG (JPEG), PCX (PC Paintbrush), TGA (Targa), or TIFF file.
Adjust Bitmap	Adjusts the position of a raster image; displays the **Adjust Background Bitmap Placement** dialog box.

Environment options:

Environment	Allows reflection and refraction effects on objects: mirror effect with the Photo Real renderer; or raytracing with the Photo Raytrace renderer.
Use Background	
	Specifies that objects reflect the background, whether a color, gradient, image, or merged image.

Merge options:
None.

Adjust Background Bitmap Placement dialog box

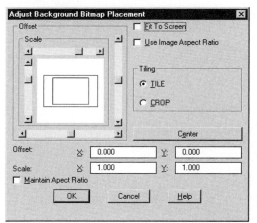

Offset	Uses the slider bars to position the image in the viewport.
Fit to Screen	Stretches the image to fit the viewport.
Use Image Aspect Ratio	
	Ensures the image is not distorted.
Tiling	Adjusts the size of the image when the image does not fit the viewport:
	• **Tile**: Repeats the image.
	• **Crop**: Cuts off the edges from the image to make it smaller.
Center	Centers the image in the viewport.
X,Y Offset	Changes the position of the image.
X,Y scale	Changes the size of the image.

RELATED COMMANDS

Fog	Creates a fog-like effect.
ImageAttach	Loads a raster image as an xref file.
Render	Renders 3D objects in the drawing.
Replay	Displays a raster image in the current viewport.

TIPS

- Gradient backgrounds are useful for simulating a sunset (cyan-pink-orange) or underwater view (green-blue-black).

- To create a 2-color gradient, set **Height** to 0.

- Image backgrounds are useful for placing the 3D rendered model in its environment, such as a rendered house on its building site.

- AutoCAD includes some background images in the *acad 2002\textures* folder.

- The four types of background:

*Top: The **Solid** option displays a uniform color (left); **Gradient** option displays a 2- or 3-color linear gradient (right).*

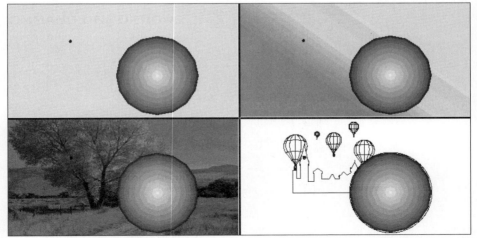

*Bottom: **Image** option displays a raster image (left); **Merge** option displays the current AutoCAD viewport (right).*

'Base

<u>V. 1.0</u>   Changes the 2D or 3D insertion point of the current drawing, located by default at (0,0,0).

Command	Alias	Ctrl+	F-key	Alt+	Menu Bar	Tablet
'base	...	...	...	DKB	Draw	...
					⌐Block	
					⌐Base	

Command: **base**
Enter base point <0.0000,0.0000,0.0000>: **[pick]**

COMMAND LINE OPTION
Enter base point
> The x,y,z coordinates of the new insertion point.

RELATED COMMANDS
Block   Allows you to specify the insertion point of a new block.
Insert   Inserts another drawing into the current drawing.
Xref   References another drawing.

RELATED SYSTEM VARIABLE
InsBase   Contains the current setting of the drawing insertion point.

TIPS
■ Use this command to shift the insertion point of the current drawing.

■ This command does not affect the current drawing. Instead, it comes into effect when you insert it or xref it into another drawing.

BAttMan

<u>2002</u>   Edits all aspects of attributes in a block; works with one block at a time
(*short for Block ATTribute MANager*).

Command	Alias	Ctrl+	F-key	Alt+	Menu Bar	Tablet
battman	...	...	...	MOAB	Modify	...
					⬐Object	
					⬐Attribute	
					⬐Block Attribute Manager	

Command: **battman**
When drawing contains no blocks with attributes, displays error message:
This drawing contains no attributed blocks.

When drawing contains at least one block with attributes, displays dialog box:

DIALOG BOX OPTIONS

Select block	Dismisses the dialog box and prompts, "Select a block:".
Block	Lists the names of blocks in the drawing; displays the name of the selected block.
Sync	Changes the attributes in block insertions to match the changes made here.
Move Up	Moves attribute tag up; constant attributes cannot be moved.
Move Down	Moves attribute tag down.
Edit	Displays the **Edit Attribute** dialog box (see the **EAttEdit** command).
Remove	Removes the attribute tag and related data from the block; does not operate when the block contains a single attribute.
Settings	Displays the **Settings** dialog box.
Apply	Apply the changes to the block definition.

Settings dialog box

Display in list options:

Prompt	Toggles (turns on and off) display of the column of attribute prompts.
Default	Toggles the display of the attribute's default value.
Modes	Toggles the display of the attribute's modes: invisible, constant, verify, and/or preset.

Style	Toggles the display of the attribute's text style name.	
Justification	Toggles the display of the attribute's text justification.	
Height	Toggles the display of the attribute's text height.	
Rotation	Toggles the display of the attribute's text rotation angle.	
Width Factor	Toggles the display of the attribute's text width factor.	
Oblique Angle	Toggles the display of the attribute's text obliquing angle (slant).	
Layer	Toggles the display of the attribute's layer.	
Linetype	Toggles the display of the attribute's linetype.	
Color	Toggles the display of the attribute's color.	
Lineweight	Toggles the display of the attribute's lineweight.	
Plot style	Toggles the display of the attribute's plot style name (available only when plot styles are turned on).	
Select All	Selects all display options.	
Clear All	Clears all display options, except tag name.	

Emphasize duplicate tags

> **On**: Highlights duplicate attribute tags in red.
> **Off**: Does not highlight duplicate tags.

Apply changes to existing references

> **On**: Applies changes to all block instances that reference this definition in the drawing.
> **Off**: Only newly inserted-blocks take on the new attribute definitions.

RELATED COMMANDS

AttDef	Defines attributes.
Block	Binds attributes to a symbol.
Insert	Inserts a block, then allows you to specify the attribute data.

TIPS

■ Use this command to edit and remove attribute definitions, as well as change the order in which attributes appear.

■ The **Sync** option does not change the values you assigned to attributes.

■ When an attribute has a mode of Constant, it cannot be moved up or down the list.

■ An attribute definition cannot be changed to Constant via the **Edit Attribute** dialog box.

■ The **Remove** option does not work when the block contains a single attribute.

■ Turning on all the options displays a lot of data. To see all the data columns, you can stretch the dialog box.

With the cursor, grab the edge of the dialog box to make it larger and smaller.

BHatch

__Rel.12__ Automatically applies an associative hatch pattern object within a boundary (*short for Boundary HATCH*).

Command	Alias	Ctrl+	F-key	Alt+	Menu Bar	Tablet
bhatch	bh	...	...	DH	Draw	P9
	h				ᵗⁱHatch	

-bhatch

Command: **bhatch**
Displays dialog box:

![Boundary Hatch dialog box. Quick tab selected with Advanced tab. Type: Predefined. Pattern: ANSI31. Swatch showing diagonal hatching. Custom pattern (grayed). Angle: 0. Scale: 1.0000. Relative to paper space checkbox. Spacing: 1.0000 (grayed). ISO pen width (grayed). Right side buttons: Pick Points, Select Objects, Remove Islands, View Selections, Inherit Properties. Double checkbox. Composition: Associative (selected), Nonassociative. Bottom buttons: Preview, OK, Cancel, Help.]

DIALOG BOX OPTIONS

Pick Points Detects a boundary, which will be filled with the hatch pattern.
Select Objects Selects objects for hatching.
Remove Islands Removes islands from the hatch pattern selection set.
View Selections Views hatch pattern selection set.
Inherit Properties
 Select the hatch pattern parameters from an existing hatch pattern.
Double **Yes:** Hatch is applied a second time at 90 degrees to the first pattern.
 No: Hatch is applied once.
Composition Determines the associativity of the hatch pattern:
 • **Associative**: Hatch is automatically updated when boundary or properties are modified; pattern is created as a hatch object.
 • **Nonassociative:** Hatch cannot be updated; pattern is created as a block.
Preview Displays a preview of the hatch pattern.

Quick tab:

Type   Selects the pattern type:

Type	Meaning
Predefined	Hatch patterns predefined by AutoCAD; patterns stored in Acad.Pat and AcadIso.pat files.
User Defined	Hatch pattern defined by you.
Custom	Hatch pattern defined by PAT files added to AutoCAD's search path.

Pattern   Selects hatch pattern.

...   Displays **Hatch Pattern Palette** dialog box showing sample pattern types:

Swatch   Displays a non-scaled preview of the hatch pattern; click to display the **Hatch Pattern Palette** dialog box.

Custom Pattern   Lists the custom patterns, if any are available.

Angle   Specifies hatch pattern angle; default = 0 degrees.

Scale   Specifies hatch pattern scale; default = 1.0.

Relative to Paper Space

                  Specifies the scale of the hatch pattern relative to paper space units; available only in layout mode.

Spacing   Specifies the spacing between lines of a user-defined hatch pattern.

ISO Pen Width   Scales pattern according to pen width.

Advanced Options tab:

Advanced

Island detection style

◉ Normal   ○ Outer   ○ Ignore

Object type
[Polyline ▾]   □ Retain boundaries

Boundary set
[Current viewport ▾] ⬚ New

Island detection method
◉ Flood
○ Ray casting

Island Detection Style

- **Normal:** Alternate areas are hatched; text is not hatched.
- **Outer:** Only the outermost areas are hatched; text is not hatched.
- **Ignore:** Everything within the boundary is hatched; text is hatched.

Object Type Constructs the boundary from either a polyline object; or a region object.

Retain Boundaries

Yes: The boundary created during the hatching process is kept after **BHatch** finishes.

No: The boundary is discarded.

Boundary Set Defines the objects analyzed for defining a boundary; not available when **Select Objects** is used to define the boundary (default = current viewport).

New Creates a new boundary set.

Island Detection Method

- **Flood** includes islands as boundary objects.
- **Ray Casting** runs an imaginary line from the pick point to the nearest object, then traces the boundary in a counter clockwise direction; excludes islands.

Hatch Pattern Palette dialog box:

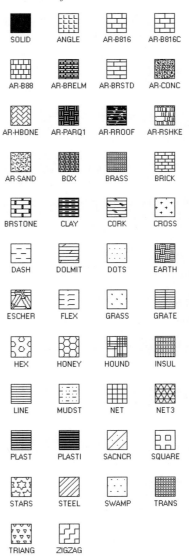

Other Predefined Patterns:

ANSI Patterns:

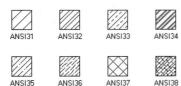

ISO Patterns:

-BHATCH COMMAND

Command: **-bhatch**
Current hatch pattern: ANSI31
Specify internal point or [Properties/Select/Remove
  islands/Advanced]: **[pick]**

COMMAND LINE OPTIONS

Internal point option:
[pick]   Creates a boundary based on the point you pick.

Property options:
Enter a pattern name or [?/Solid/User defined] <ANSI31>: **[Enter]**
Specify a scale for the pattern <1.0000>: **[Enter]**
Specify an angle for the pattern <0>: **[Enter]**

Enter a pattern name
                Allows you to enter the name of the hatch pattern.
?   Lists the names of available hatch patterns.
Solid   Floods the area with a solid fill in the current color.
User defined Creates a simple, user-defined hatch pattern.
Specify a scale Specifies the hatch pattern angle (default = 0 degrees).
Specify an angle Specifies the hatch pattern scale (default: = 1.0).

Select option:
Select objects: **[pick]**
1 found Select objects: **[Enter]**
Select objects Selects one or more objects to fill with hatch pattern.

Remove islands options:
Select island to remove: **[pick]**
<Select island to remove>/Undo:
Select island to remove
                Selects the island to remove, which is not filled with the hatch pattern.
Undo   Adds the removed island.

Advanced *options:*
Enter an option [Boundary set/Retain boundary/Island detection/
Style/Associativity]:
Boundary set Defines the objects **BHatch** analyzes when defining a boundary from a
                specified pick point.
Retain boundary
                Yes: The boundary created during the hatching process is kept after **BHatch**
                finishes.
                No: The boundary is discarded.

Island detection

        Yes: Objects within the outermost boundary are used as boundary objects.

        No: All objects within outermost boundary are filled.

Style   Selects the hatching style: ignore, outer, or normal.

Associativity   **Yes**: Hatch pattern is associative.

        No: Hatch pattern is not associative.

RELATED COMMANDS

Boundary	Traces a polyline automatically around a closed boundary.
Convert	Converts Release 13 (and earlier) hatch patterns into Release 14 format.
Hatch	Creates a nonassociative hatch.
HatchEdit	Edits the hatch pattern.
PsFill	Floods a closed polyline with a PostScript fill pattern.

RELATED SYSTEM VARIABLES

DelObj   Toggles whether boundary is erased after hatch is placed:

DelObj	Meaning
0	Boundary is retained.
1	Boundary is deleted (default).

HpAng   Indicates the current hatch pattern angle (default = 0).

HpBound   Indicates the hatch boundary object:

HpBound	Meaning
0	Polyline object.
1	Region object (default).

HpDouble   Indicates single or double hatching:

HpDouble	Meaning
0	Single hatch (default).
1	Double hatch.

HpName   Indicates the current hatch pattern name (up to 31 characters long):

HpName	Meaning
ANSI31	Default pattern name.
""	No current pattern name.
"."	Eliminate current pattern name.

HpScale   Indicates the current hatch pattern scale factor (default = 1).

HpSpace   Indicates the current hatch pattern spacing factor (default = 1).

PickStyle   Controls the selection of hatch patterns:

PickStyle	Meaning
0	Neither groups nor hatches selected.
1	Groups selected (default).
2	Associative hatches selected.
3	Both selected.

SnapBase   Starting coordinates of hatch pattern (default = 0,0).

RELATED FILES

Acad.Pat   ANSI and other hatch pattern definition file.
AcadIso.Pat   ISO hatch pattern definition file.

TIPS

- The **BHatch** command first generates a boundary, then hatches the inside area.

- Use the **Boundary** command to create just the boundary.

- **BHatch** stores hatching parameters in the pattern's extended object data.

'Blipmode

V. 2.1 Turns the display of pick-point markers, known as "blips," on and off.

Command	Alias	Ctrl+	F-key	Alt+	Menu Bar	Tablet
'blipmode	...	...	...	...	...	...

```
Command: blipmode
Enter mode [ON/OFF] <OFF>: on
```

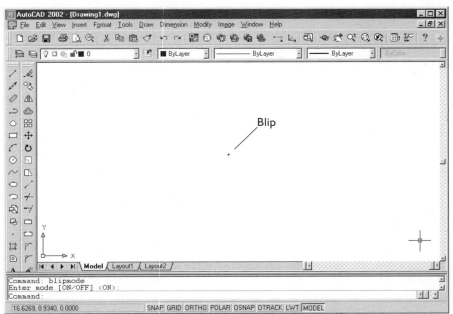

A blipmark at the center of the screen.

COMMAND LINE OPTIONS

ON	Turns on display of pick-point markers.
OFF	Turns off display of pick-point markers.

RELATED COMMANDS

Options	Allows blipmode toggling via a dialog box.
Redraw	Cleans blips off the screen.

RELATED SYSTEM VARIABLE

Blipmode	Contains the current blipmode setting.

TIPS

- You cannot change the size of the blipmark.

- Blipmarks are erased by any command that redraws the view, such as **Redraw**, **Regen**, **Zoom**, and **Vports**.

Block

V. 1.0   Defines a group of objects as a single named object; creates symbols.

Command	Alias	Ctrl+	F-key	Alt+	Menu Bar	Tablet
block	b	...	...	DKM	Draw	N9
	bmake				↳Block	
					↳Make	
-block	-b					

Command: **block**

Displays dialog box:

DIALOG BOX

```
Block Definition

Name:  [_____]

┌ Base point ──────────┐   ┌ Objects ──────────────────┐
│  [ ] Pick point       │   │  [ ] Select objects   [ ] │
│                       │   │                  QuickSelect
│  X:  0.0000           │   │  ○ Retain                 │
│  Y:  0.0000           │   │  ● Convert to block       │
│  Z:  0.0000           │   │  ○ Delete                 │
│                       │   │  ⚠ No objects selected    │
└───────────────────────┘   └───────────────────────────┘

┌ Preview icon ─────────────────────────────────┐
│  ○ Do not include an icon                      │
│  ● Create icon from block geometry             │
└────────────────────────────────────────────────┘

Insert units:  [Inches                    ▼]
Description:   [                           ]
               [                           ]

[ Hyperlink... ]

        [ OK ]    [ Cancel ]    [ Help ]
```

DIALOG BOX OPTIONS

Name   Names the block (*maximum = 255 characters*).

Base point *options:*

Pick point   Picks the block's insertion point from the drawing.

X,Y,Z   Specifies the x,y,z coordinates of the insertion point.

Objects *options:*

Select objects   Picks the objects that make up the block from the drawing.
- **Retain:** Leaves objects in place after block is created.
- **Convert to Block:** Erases objects making up the block, and replaces them with the block.
- **Delete:** Erases the objects making up the block; block is stored in drawing.

Quick Select   Displays the **Quick Select** dialog box; see the **QSelect** command.

Preview icon options:

Do not include an icon

> Does not create an icon.

Create icon from block geometry

> Creates a preview image of the block.

Insert units   Selects the units for the block when dragged from AutoCAD DesignCenter.

Description   Allows you to enter a description of the block.

Hyperlink   Displays the **Insert Hyperlink** dialog box; see the **Hyperlink** command.

-BLOCK COMMAND

```
Command: -block
Enter block name or [?]: [type name]
Specify insertion base point: [pick]
Select objects: [pick]
```

COMMAND LINE OPTIONS

Block name   Allows you to enter the name of the block.

?   Lists the names of blocks stored in the drawing.

Insertion base point

> Specifies the x,y coordinates of the block's insertion point.

Select objects   Selects the objects and attributes that make up the block.

RELATED COMMANDS

Explode   Reduces a block its original objects.

Insert   Adds a block or another drawing to the current drawing.

Oops   Returns objects to the screen after creating the block.

WBlock   Writes a block to a file on disk as a drawing.

XRef   Displays another drawing in the current drawing.

RELATED SYSTEM VARIABLES

InsName   Default block name.

InsUnits   Drawing units for blocks dragged from AutoCAD DesignCenter:

InsUnits	Meaning	InsUnits	Meaning
0	Unitless	12	Nanometers
1	Inches	13	Microns
2	Feet	14	Decimeters
3	Miles	15	Decameters
4	Millimeters	16	Hectometers
5	Centimeters	17	Gigameters
6	Meters	18	Astronomical Units
7	Kilometers	19	Light Years
8	Microinches	20	Parsecs
9	Mils		
10	Yards		
11	Angstroms		

RELATED FILE

*.DWG   All drawing files can be inserted as blocks.

TIPS

■ A block consists of these parts:

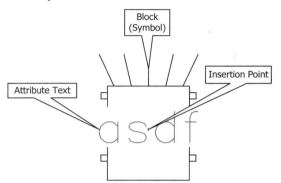

■ A block name has up to 255 alphanumeric characters, including $, -, and _.

■ Use the **INSertion** object snap to select the block's insertion point.

■ A block created on a layer other than layer 0 is always inserted on that other layer.

■ A block created on layer 0 is inserted on the current layer.

■ AutoCAD 2002 has five types of blocks:

Block	Meaning
User block	A named block created by the user.
Nested block	A block inside another block.
Unnamed block	A block created by AutoCAD.
Xref	An externally-referenced drawing.
Dependent block	A block in an externally-referenced drawing.

■ AutoCAD creates the following unnamed blocks, also called "anonymous blocks":

Name	Meaning
*An	Group.
*Dn	Associative dimension.
*Un	Created by AutoLISP or ObjectARx app.
*Xn	Hatch pattern.

■ AutoCAD automatically purges unreferenced anonymous blocks when the drawing is first loaded.

■ You cannot place an anonymous block with **Insert**.

BlockIcon

2000 Creates a preview images for all blocks, created with Release 14 or earlier, in the drawing.

Command	Alias	Ctrl+	F-key	Alt+	Menu Bar	Tablet
blockicon	...	...	...	...	...	...

```
Command: blockicon
Enter block names <*>: [Enter]
n blocks updated.
```

COMMAND LINE OPTION

Enter block names

Specifies the blocks for which to create icons; press **Enter** to add icons to all blocks in the drawing.

RELATED COMMANDS

Block   Creates new blocks, as well as their icons.

AdCenter   Displays the icon created by this command:

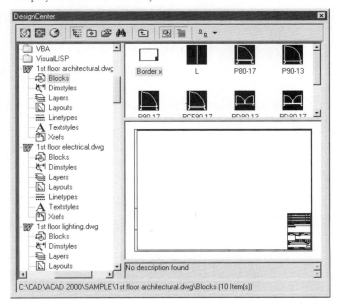

BmpOut

Rel.13 Exports the current viewport to a BMP file.

Command	Alias	Ctrl+	F-key	Alt+	Menu Bar	Tablet
bmpout	...	...	...	FE	File	...
				⌐BMP	⌐Export	
					⌐BMP	

Command: **bmpout**
Displays **Create BMP File** *dialog box.*

DIALOG BOX OPTION
Save   Saves the drawing as a BMP file.

RELATED COMMANDS
CopyClip   Copies selected objects to the Clipboard in several formats.
WmfOut   Exports selected objects to a WMF file.

RELATED WINDOWS COMMANDS
PrtScr   Saves screen to the Clipboard.
Alt+PrtScr   Saves the topmost window to the Clipboard.

TIPS
- BMP is short for "bitmap," the raster file standard for Windows.

- The **BmpOut** command exports all objects visible in the current viewport.

- This command creates a compressed BMP file, which cannot read by most Windows programs.

Boundary

Rel.12   Creates a boundary as a polyline or 2D region.

Command	Alias	Ctrl+	F-key	Alt+	Menu Bar	Tablet
boundary	bo	...	...	DB	Draw	Q9
	bpoly				⁴⁴Boundary	
-boundary	-bo					

Command: **boundary**
Displays dialog box::

DIALOG BOX OPTIONS

Object Type   Boundary is constructed from:
- Polyline object.
- Region object.

Boundary Set   Defines the objects analyzed for defining a boundary; not available when **Select Objects** is ued to define the boundary (default = current viewport).

New   Creates a new boundary set.

Island Detection Method
- **Flood:** Includes islands as boundary objects.
- **Ray Casting:** Runs an imaginary line from the pick point to the nearest object, then traces the boundary in a counter clockwise direction; excludes islands.

Pick Points   Picks point inside of closed area.

-BOUNDARY COMMAND

Command: **-boundary**

Specify internal point or [Advanced options]: **a**

Enter an option [Boundary set/Island detection/Object type]:

COMMAND LINE OPTIONS

Internal Point option:

[pick]   Creates a boundary based on the point you pick.

Advanced Options options:

Boundary set   Defines the objects **BHatch** analyzes when defining a boundary from a specified pick point: a new set of objects, or all objects visible in the current viewport.

Island detection

       Yes: Objects within the outermost boundary are used as boundary objects.

       No: All objects within outermost boundary are filled.

Object type   Selects polyline or region as the boundary object.

RELATED COMMANDS

PLine   Draws a polyline.

PEdit   Edits a polyline.

Region   Creates a 2D region from a collection of objects.

RELATED SYSTEM VARIABLE

HpBound   Object used to create boundary:

HpBound	Meaning
0	Draw as region.
1	Draw as polyline (default).

TIPS

■ Use **Boundary** together with the **Offset** command to help create poching.

■ Although the **Boundary Creation** dialog box looks similar to the **BHatch** command's **Advanced Options** dialog box, be aware of differences.

 # Box

Rel.13 Draws a 3D box as a solid model (*an external command in Acis.Dll*).

Command	Alias	Ctrl+	F-key	Alt+	Menu Bar	Tablet
box	...	...	...	DIB	Draw ⬐Solids ⬐Box	J7

```
Command: box
Specify corner of box or [CEnter] <0,0,0>: [pick]
Specify corner or [Cube/Length]: [pick]
Specify height: [pick]
Second point: [pick]
```

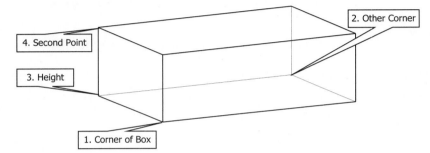

COMMAND LINE OPTIONS

Corner of box	Specifies one corner for the base of box.
Center	Draws the box about a center point.
Cube	Draws a cube box — all sides are the same length.
Length	Specifies the x, y, z lengths.
Height	Specifies the height of the box.

RELATED COMMANDS

Ai_Box	Draws a 3D wireframe box.
Cone	Draws a 3D solid cone.
Cylinder	Draws a 3D solid tube.
Sphere	Draws a 3D solid ball.
Torus	Draws a 3D solid donut.
Wedge	Draws a 3D solid wedge.

RELATED SYSTEM VARIABLES

DispSilh   Displays 3D objects as silhouettes after hidden-line removal and shading.
IsoLines   Number of isolines on solid surfaces:

IsoLines	Meaning
0	No isolines; minimum.
4	Default value.
12 *or* 16	Reasonable values.
2047	Maximum.

⊡ Break

V. 1.4 Removes a portion of an object.

Command	Alias	Ctrl+	F-key	Alt+	Menu Bar	Tablet
break	br	...	...	MK	Modify ⌐Break	W17

```
Command: break
Select object: [pick]
Specify second break point or [First point]: f
Enter first point: [pick]
Enter second point: [pick]
```

1. First Point	2. Second Point

Breaking a line at two points.

COMMAND LINE OPTIONS

Select object Selects one object to break; pick point becomes first break point, unless the **F** option is used at the next prompt.

Specify second break point
Selects the second break point.

First point Specifies the first break point.

@ Uses the first break point's coordinates for the second break point.

RELATED COMMANDS

Change Changes the length lines.

PEdit Removes and relocates vertices of polylines.

Trim Shortens the lengths of open objects.

TIPS

■ Use this command to convert a circle into an arc.

■ This command can erase a portion of an object, as shown in the figure, or remove the end of an open object.

■ The second point does not need to be on the object; AutoCAD breaks the object nearest to the pick point.

■ The **Break** command works on the following objects: lines, arcs, circles, polylines, ellipses, rays, xlines, and splines, as well as objects made from polylines, such as donuts and polygons.

Browser

Launches a Web browser (*an external command in AcBrowse.Arx*).

Command	Alias	Ctrl+	F-key	Alt+	Menu Bar	Tablet
browser	...	...	...	HD	Help	Y8
					↳Autodesk On The Web	

```
Command: browser
Enter Web location (URL) <http://www.autodesk.com>: ENTER
```
Launches browser:

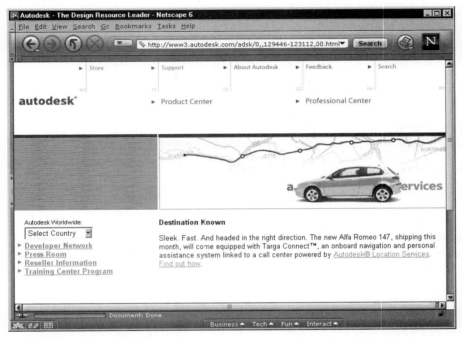

COMMAND LINE OPTION

Enter Web location
Specifies the URL; see **AttachURL** command for information about URLs.

RELATED SYSTEM VARIABLE

InetLocation   Contains the name of the last-accessed URL.

TIPS

■ **URL** is short for "uniform resource locator," the universal file-naming system used on the Internet; also called a link or hyperlink.

■ An example of a URL is http://www.autodeskpress.com, the Autodesk Press Web site.

■ Many file dialog boxes also give you access to the Web browser; see the **Open** command.

'Cal

Rel.12 Command-line algebraic and vector geometry calculator (*short for CALculator*).

Command	Alias	Ctrl+	F-key	Alt+	Menu Bar	Tablet
'cal	...	...	...	...	...	...

Command: **cal**
\>\>Expression:

COMMAND LINE OPTIONS

( )	Grouping of expressions.
[ ]	Vector expressions.
+	Addition.
–	Subtraction.
*	Multiplication.
/	Division.
^	Exponentiation.
&	Vector product of vectors.
sin	Sine.
cos	Cosine.
tang	Tangent.
asin	Arc sine.
acos	Arc cosine.
atan	Arc tangent.
ln	Natural logarithm.
log	Logarithm.
exp	Natural exponent.
exp10	Exponent.
sqr	Square.
sqrt	Square root.
abs	Absolute value.
round	Round off.
trunc	Truncate.
cvunit	Converts units using *Acad.Unt*.
w2u	WCS to UCS conversion.
u2w	UCS to WCS conversion.
r2d	Radians-to-degrees conversion.
d2r	Degrees-to-radians conversion.
pi	The value PI.
xyof	x,y coordinates of a point.
xzof	x,z coordinates of a point.
yzof	y,z coordinates of a point.
xof	x coordinate of a point.
yof	y coordinate of a point.
zof	z coordinate of a point.

rxof	Real x coordinate of a point.
ryof	Real y coordinate of a point.
rzof	Real z coordinate of a point.
cur	x,y,z coordinates of picked point.
rad	Radius of object.
pld	Point on line, distance from.
plt	Point on line, using parameter *t*.
rot	Rotates point through angle about origin.
ill	Intersection of two lines.
ilp	Intersection of line and plane.
dist	Distance between two points.
dpl	Distance between point and line.
dpp	Distance between point and plane.
ang	Angle between lines.
nor	Unit vector normal.
Esc	Exits Cal mode.

RELATED COMMANDS
All.

RELATED SYSTEM VARIABLES
UserI1 — UserI5   User-definable variables, which can be used to store integers.
UserR1 — UserR5   User-definable variables, which can be used to store real numbers.

TIPS
■ Since **'Cal** is a transparent command, it can be used to perform a calculation in the middle of another command.

■ To use **Cal**, type an expression at the >> prompt. For example:

   Expression >> **(1.2^2)*pi**   *(area of a circle with radius = 1.2 units)*
   4.52389

■ **Cal** understands the following prefixes:
   *   Scalar product of vectors.
   &   Vector product of vectors.

■ And the following suffixes:
   r   Radian (degrees is the default).
   g   Grad.
   '   Feet (unitless distance is the default).
   "   Inches.

Camera

Sets the camera and target coordinates to create a 3D viewpoint.

Command	Alias	Ctrl+	F-key	Alt+	Menu Bar	Tablet
camera	...	...	...	...	...	...

```
Command: camera
Specify new camera position <7.6386,4.5000,21.1085>:
Specify new camera target <7.6386,4.5000,0.0000>:
Regenerating model.
```

COMMAND LINE OPTIONS

Specify new camera position
>   Specifies the x,y,z coordinates for the "look from" point.

Specify new camera target
>   Specifies the x,y,z coordinates for the "look at" point.

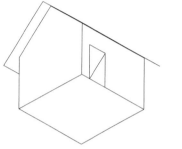   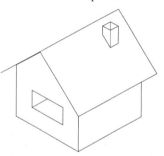

Camera position: 1,1,1   *Camera position: -1,-1,-1*
Camera target: -1,-1,-1   *Camera target: 1,1,1*

RELATED COMMANDS

DView   The **CAmera** option interactively sets a new 3D viewpoint.
VPoint   Sets a 3D viewpoint through x,y,z coordinates or angles.
3dOrbit   Sets a new 3D viewpoint interactively.

TIPS

■ Following the **Camera** command, you may need to use **Zoom Extents** to see the model.

■ Use **Hide** to check whether you are looking at the model from above or below.

Chamfer

V. 2.1   Bevels the intersection of two lines, all vertices of a 2D polyline, and the faces of a 3D solid model.

Command	Alias	Ctrl+	F-key	Alt+	Menu Bar	Tablet
chamfer	cha	...	...	MC	Modify ↳Chamfer	W18

```
Command: chamfer
(TRIM mode) Current chamfer Dist1 = 0.5000, Dist2 = 0.5000
Select first line or [Polyline/Distance/Angle/Trim/
   Method]: [pick]
Select second line: [pick]
```

COMMAND LINE OPTIONS

Select first line Selects the first line, arc, face, or edge.
Select second line
    Selects the second line, arc, face, or edge.

Polyline option:
```
Select 2D polyline: [pick]
n lines were chamfered
```
2D polyline   Chamfers *all* segments of a 2D polyline; if the polyline is not closed with the **Close** option, the first and last segments are not chamfered.

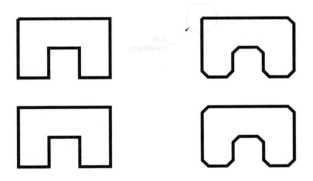

Distance options:
```
Specify first chamfer distance <0.5000>:
Specify second chamfer distance <0.5000>:
```
First distance Specifies the chamfering distance along the line picked first.
Second distance
    Specifies the chamfering distance along the line picked second.

Angle options:
```
Specify chamfer length on the first line <1.0000>:
Specify chamfer angle from the first line <0>:
```
Chamfer length Specifies the chamfering distance along the line picked first.
Chamfer angle Specifies the chamfering angle by an angle from the line picked first.

Trim option:
```
Enter Trim mode option [Trim/No trim] <Trim>: n
```
Trim   Lines, edges, and faces are trimmed after chamfer.
No trim   Lines, edges, and faces are not trimmed after chamfer.

Intersecting lines before (at right) and after a no-trim chamfer (at left).

Method option:
```
Enter trim method [Distance/Angle] <Angle>:
```
Distance   Chamfer is determined by the two specified distances.
Angle   Chamfer is determined by the specified angle and distance.

Chamfering a 3D Solid: **EDGE MODE**
```
Command: chamfer
(TRIM mode) Current chamfer Dist1 = 0.5000, Dist2 = 0.5000
Polyline/.../<Select first line>: [pick 3D solid]
Select base surface:
Next/<OK>: ENTER
Enter base surface distance <0.5000>: ENTER
Enter other surface distance <0.5000>: ENTER
Loop/<Select edge>: [pick]
Loop/<Select edge>: ENTER
```

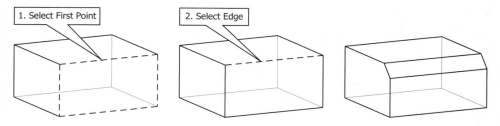

Chamfering a 3D Solid: **LOOP MODE**

```
Command: chamfer
(TRIM mode) Current chamfer Dist1 = 0.5000, Dist2 = 0.5000
Polyline/.../<Select first line>: [pick 3D solid]
Select base surface:
Next/<OK>: ENTER
Enter base surface distance <0.5000>: ENTER
Enter other surface distance <0.5000>: ENTER
Loop/<Select edge>: l
Edge/<Select edge loop>: [pick]
Edge/<Select edge loop>: ENTER
```

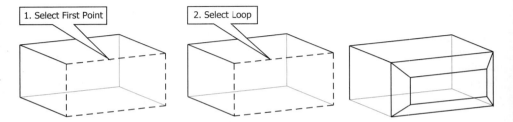

COMMAND LINE OPTIONS

Select first line Selects the 3D solid.

Next   Selects the adjacent face or press **Enter** to accept face.

Enter base surface distance
      Specifies the first chamfer distance (default = 0.5).

Enter other surface distance
      Specifies the second chamfer distance (default = 0.5).

Loop   Selects all edges of the face.

Select edge Selects a single edge of the face.

RELATED COMMANDS

Fillet	Rounds the intersection with a radius.
SolidEdit	Edits the faces and edges of solids.

RELATED SYSTEM VARIABLES

ChamferA	First chamfer distance (default = 0.5).
ChamferB	Second chamfer distance (default = 0.5).
ChamferC	Length of chamfer (default = 1).
ChamferD	Chamfer angle (default = 0).
ChamMode	Toggles chamfer measurement:

ChamMode	Meaning
0	Chamfer by two distances (default).
1	Chamfer by distance and angle.

TrimMode   Determines whether lines/edges are trimmed after chamfer:

TrimMode	Meaning
0	Do not trim selected edges.
1	Trim selected edges (default).

TIPS

■ *Caution!* The associativity of a hatch pattern is only maintained when the pattern boundary is a polyline; when the pattern boundary consists of lines, associativity is lost.

■ When **TrimMode** is set to 1 and when lines do not intersect, **Chamfer** extends or trims the lines to intersect.

■ When the two objects are not on the same layer, **Chamfer** places the chamfer line on the current layer; the chamfer line takes on the layer or current color and linetype.

Change

V. 1.0   Modifies the color, elevation, layer, linetype, linetype scale, lineweight, plot style, and thickness of most objects, and certain other properties of lines, circles, blocks, text, and attributes.

Command	Alias	Ctrl+	F-key	Alt+	Menu Bar	Tablet
change	-ch	...	...	...	...	...

```
Command: change
Select objects: [pick]
Select objects: ENTER
Specify change point or [Properties]: p
Enter property to change [Color/Elev/LAyer/LType/ltScale/
    LWeight/Thickness/Plotstyle]: [enter an option]
```

COMMAND LINE OPTIONS

Change point Selects an object to change:
[pick line]   Indicates the new length of a line.
[pick circle] Indicates the new radius of a circle.
[pick block] Indicates the new insertion point or rotation angle of a block.
[pick text]   Indicates the new location of text.
[pick attribute] Indicates an attribute's new text insertion point, text style, height, rotation angle, text, tag, prompt, or default value.

ENTER   Changes the insertion point, style, height, rotation angle, and text of a text string.

Properties options:
Color   Changes the color of the object.
Elev   Changes the elevation of the object.
LAyer   Moves the object to a different layer.
LType   Changes the linetype of the object.
ltScale   Changes the scale of the linetype.
LWeight   Changes the lineweight of the object.
Thickness   Changes the thickness of any object, except blocks and 3D solids.
Plotstyle   Changes the plotstyle of the object; available only when plotstyles are turned on.

RELATED COMMANDS

AttRedef   Changes a block or attribute.
ChProp   Contains the properties portion of the **Change** command.
Color   Changes the current color setting.
Elev   Changes the working elevation and thickness.
LtScale   Changes the linetype scale.
Properties   Changes most aspects of all objects.
PlotStyle   Sets the plot style.

RELATED SYSTEM VARIABLES

CeColor	Sets the current color setting.
CeLType	Sets the current linetype setting.
CelWeight	Sets the current lineweight.
CircleRad	Contains the current circle radius.
CLayer	Contains the name of the current layer.
CPlotstyle	Contians the names of the current plot style.
Elevation	Contains the current elevation setting.
LtScale	Contains the current linetype scale.
TextSize	Contains the current height of text.
TextStyle	Contains the current text style.
Thickness	Contains the current thickness setting.

TIPS

■ The **Change** command cannot change the size of donuts, the radius or length of arcs, the length of polylines, or the justification of text.

■ Use this command to change the endpoints of a group of lines to a common vertex:

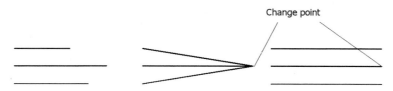

Change with ortho mode turned off (center) and ortho mode turned on (at left).

■ Turn on ortho mode to extend or trim a group of lines, without needing a cutting edge (as would the **Extend** and **Trim** commands).

■ The **PlotStyle** option is not displayed when plotstyles are not turned on.

CheckStandards

<u>2001</u> Checks the drawing for adherence to standards previously specified by the **Standards** command.

Command	Alias	Ctrl+	F-key	Alt+	Menu Bar	Tablet
checkstandards ...	...	...	...			

Command: **checkstandards**

*When the **Standards** command has not set up standards for the drawing, displays error message:*

When standards have been set up for the drawing, displays dialog box:

DIALOG BOX OPTIONS

Problem   Describes the property in the drawing that does not match the standard; this dialog box displays one problem at a time.

Replace With Lists linetypes, text styles, etc. found in the DWS standards file.

Fix   Replaces the non-standard property with the selected standard; the color checkmark icon means a fix is available.

Mark this problem as ignored

                  Ignores non-standard property, and marks it with the user's login name; some errors are ignored by AutoCAD, such as layer 0 and DefPoints.

Next   Displays the next non-standard property.

Settings   Displays the **Check Standards - Settings** dialog box.

Check Standards - Settings dialog box

Automatically fix non-standard properties

                  On: Fixes properties not matching the CAD standard automatically .

                  Off: Allows you to step manually through the properties not matching the CAD standard.

Show ignored problems

                  On: Displays problems marked as ignored.

                  Off: Does not display ignored problems.

Preferred standards file to use for replacements

                  Selects the default DWS file.

RELATED COMMANDS

Standards   Selects the DWS standards file.

LayTrans   Translates layers.

RELATED SYSTEM VARIABLES

None.

RELATED PROGRAM

DwgCheckStandards.Exe

The Batch Standards Checker program checks one or more drawings at a time.

RELATED FILES

*.DWS	Drawing standards file; stored in DWG format.
*.CHX	Standard check file; stored in XML format.

TIPS

■ While this dialog box is open, you can use the following shortcut keys:

Shortcut	Meaning
F4	Fix problem
F5	Next problem

■ AutoCAD includes a single drawing standards file, **MKMStds.Dws** found in the **Support** folder.

ChProp

Rel.10 Modifies the color, layer, linetype, linetype scale, lineweight, plot style, and thickness of most objects.

Command	Alias	Ctrl+	F-key	Alt+	Menu Bar	Tablet
chprop	...	...	...	...	...	...

```
Command: chprop
Select objects: [pick]
Select objects: ENTER
Enter property to change [Color/LAyer/LType/ltScale/
    LWeight/Thickness/Plotstyle]: [enter an option]
```

COMMAND LINE OPTIONS

Color	Changes the color of the object.
LAyer	Moves the object to a different layer.
LType	Changes the linetype of the object.
ltScale	Changes the linetype scale.
LWeight	Changes the lineweight of the object.
Thickness	Changes the thickness of any object, except blocks.
Plotsytle	Changes the plotstyle of the object; available only when plotstyles are turned on.

RELATED COMMANDS

Change	Allows changes to lines, circles, blocks, text and attributes.
Color	Changes the current color setting.
Elev	Changes the working elevation and thickness.
LtScale	Changes the linetype scale.
LWeight	Sets the lineweight options.
Properties	Changes most aspects of all objects.
PlotStyle	Sets the plot style.

RELATED SYSTEM VARIABLES

CeColor	Sets the current color setting.
CeLType	Sets the current linetype setting.
CelWeight	Sets the current lineweight.
CLayer	Contains the name of the current layer.
CPlotstyle	Contains the names of the current plotstyle.
LtScale	Contains the current linetype scale.
Thickness	The current thickness setting.

TIPS

- Use the **Change** command to change the elevation of an object.
- The **Plotstyle** option is not displayed when plotstyles are not turned on.

Circle

V. 1.0   Draws 2D circles by five different methods.

Command	Alias	Ctrl+	F-key	Alt+	Menu Bar	Tablet
circle	c	...	...	DC	Draw ⌐Circle	J9

```
Command: circle
Specify center point for circle or [3P/2P/Ttr (tan tan
   radius)]: [pick]
Specify radius of circle or [Diameter]: [pick]
```

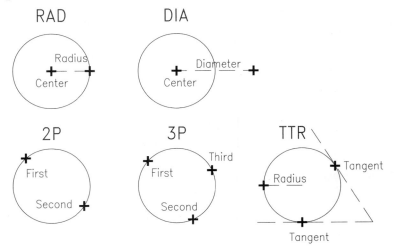

COMMAND LINE OPTIONS

Center and Radius or Diameter circle options:
```
Specify center point for circle or [3P/2P/Ttr (tan tan
   radius)]: [pick]
Specify radius of circle or [Diameter] <0.5000>: d
Specify diameter of circle <0.5000>: [pick]
```

Center point   Indicates the circle's center point.
Radius   Indicates the circle's radius.
Diameter   Indicates the circle's diameter.

3P (three-point) circle options:
```
Specify first point on circle: [pick]
Specify second point on circle: [pick]
Specify third point on circle: [pick]
```

First point   Indicates first point on the circle.
Second point   Indicates second point on the circle.
Third point   Indicates third point on the circle.

2P (two-point) circle options:
```
Specify first end point of circle's diameter: [pick]
Specify second end point of circle's diameter: [pick]
```

First end point Indicates first point on circle.
Second end point
> Indicates second point on circle.

TTR (tangent-tangent-radius) circle options:
```
Specify point on object for first tangent of circle: [pick]
Specify point on object for second tangent of circle: [pick]
Specify radius of circle <0.5000>: ENTER
```

First tangent Indicates first point of tangency.
Second tangent
> Indicates second point of tangency.

Radius Indicates first point of radius.

RELATED TOOLBAR ICONS

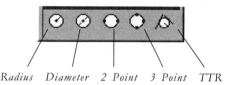

> *Radius   Diameter   2 Point   3 Point   TTR*

RELATED COMMANDS

Ai_CircTan	Draws a circle tangent to three objects.
Arc	Draws an arc.
Donut	Draws a solid-filled circle or donut.
Ellipse	Draws an elliptical circle or arc.
Sphere	Draws a 3D solid ball.
ViewRes	Controls the visual roundness of circles.

RELATED SYSTEM VARIABLE

CircleRad Specifies the current circle radius.

TIPS

- The 3P (three-point) circle defines three points on the circle's circumference.

- When drawing a TTR (tangent, tangent, radius) circle, AutoCAD draws the circle with tangent points closest to the pick points; note that more than one circle placement is possible.

- Selecting **Draw | Circle | Tan, Tan, Radius** from the menu bar automatically turns on the TANgent object snap.

- Giving a circle thickness turns it into a cylinder.

Close

<u>**2000**</u> Closes the current drawing.

Command	Alias	Ctrl+	F-key	Alt+	Menu Bar	Tablet
close	...	F4	...	FC	File	...
					⌐Close	

Command: **close**
Displays dialog box if the drawing has not been saved since the last change:

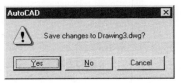

DIALOG BOX OPTIONS

Yes   Displays the **Save Drawing As** dialog box, or saves the drawing if it has been previously saved.

No   Exits the drawing without saving it.

Cancel   Returns to the drawing.

RELATED COMMANDS

Quit   Exits AutoCAD.

Open   Opens additional drawings, each in its own window.

CloseAll Closes all drawings.

TIP

■ To close the drawing, you can click the **x** button on the title bar:

CloseAll

Closes all drawings; does not exit AutoCAD.

Command	Alias	Ctrl+	F-key	Alt+	Menu Bar	Tablet
closeall	...	...	...	WL	Window	...
					⬉Close All	

Command: **closeall**
Displays dialog box if the drawings have not been saved since last changed:

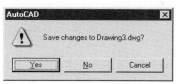

DIALOG BOX OPTIONS

Yes   Displays the **Save Drawing As** dialog box, or saves the drawing if it has
             been previously saved.
No   Exits the drawing without saving it.
Cancel   Returns to the drawing.

RELATED COMMANDS

Quit   Exits AutoCAD.
Open   Opens additional drawings, each in its own window.
Close   Closes the current drawing only.

'Color or 'Colour

V. 2.5 Sets the new working color.

Command	Alias	Ctrl+	F-key	Alt+	Menu Bar	Tablet
'color	ddcolor	...	...	OC	Format	U4
'colour	col				⌐Color	
'-color	...	...	...	...	...	...

Command: **color**
Displays dialog box:

DIALOG BOX OPTIONS

Standard Colors *options:*
> Selects one of the nine colors hues, #1 through #9.

Gray Shades *options:*
> Selects one of the six gray shades, #250 through #255.

Logical Colors *options:*
Bylayer   Sets color to BYLAYER.
Byblock   Sets color to BYBLOCK.

Full Color Palette *options:*
> Selects one of the 240 other colors, #10 through #249.

Color   Sets the color by number or name.

-COLOR COMMAND

Command: **-color**

Enter default object color <BYLAYER>:

COMMAND LINE OPTIONS

BYLAYER   Sets working color to color of current layer.

BYBLOCK   Sets working color of inserted blocks.

Color Number   Sets working color using number (*1 through 255*), name, or abbreviation:

Color Number	Color Name	Abbreviation
1	Red	R
2	Yellow	Y
3	Green	G
4	Cyan	C
5	Blue	B
6	Magenta	M
7	White	W
8 - 249	Other colors	...
250 - 255	Greys	...

RELATED COMMANDS

Change   Changes the color of objects via command line.

ChProp   Changes the color via command line in fewer keystrokes.

Properties   Changes the color of objects via a dialog box.

RELATED SYSTEM VARIABLES

CeColor   The current object color setting:

CeColor	Meaning
1	Red; minimum value.
7	White (default value) on black background or black on white background.
255	Maximum value.

TIPS

■ 'BYLAYER' means that objects take on the color assigned to that layer.

■ 'BYBLOCK' means objects take on the color in effect at the time the block is inserted.

■ White objects display as black when the background color is white.

■ When more than one method is used to assign color to objects in a block, unpredictable results occur when the block is inserted or has its color changed.

■ Color "0" cannot be specified; AutoCAD uses that color internally as the background color.

Compile

Compiles SHP shape, SHP font, and PFB font files into SHX format.

Command	Alias	Ctrl+	F-key	Alt+	Menu Bar	Tablet
compile	...	...	...	...	...	...

Command: **compile**
*Displays **Select Shape or Font File** dialog box.*

DIALOG BOX OPTIONS

Open   Opens the SHP or PFB file for compiling.

RELATED COMMANDS

Load   Loads a compiled SHX shape file into the current drawing.
Style   Loads SHX and TTF font files into the current drawing.

RELATED SYSTEM VARIABLE

ShpName   The current SHP filename.

RELATED FILES

*.SHP   AutoCAD font and shape source files.
*.SHX   AutoCAD compiled font and shape files.
*.PFB   PostScript Type B font file.

TIPS

■ As of AutoCAD Release 12, **Style** converts SHP font files on-the-fly; it is only necessary to use the **Compile** command to obtain an SHX font file.

■ As of Release 14, AutoCAD no longer supports PostScript font files. Instead, use the **Compile** command to convert PFB files to SHX format.

■ TrueType fonts are not compiled.

Cone

Rel.11 Draws a 3D ACIS cone with a circular or elliptical base (*an ACIScommand*).

Command	Alias	Ctrl+	F-key	Alt+	Menu Bar	Tablet
cone	...	...	...	DIO	Draw	M7
					⌐Solids	
					⌐Cone	

Command: **cone**

Cone with circular base:
Current wire frame density: ISOLINES=4
Specify center point for base of cone or [Elliptical]
   <0,0,0>: **[pick center point]**
Specify radius for base of cone or [Diameter]: **[specify
   radius or type D]**
Specify height of cone or [Apex]: **[specify height]**

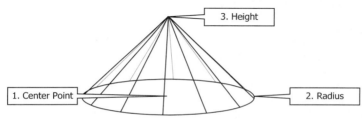

Cone with elliptical base and apex:
Specify center point for base of cone or [Elliptical]
   <0,0,0>: **e**
Specify axis endpoint of ellipse for base of cone or
[Center]: **[pick]**
Specify second axis endpoint of ellipse for base of cone:
   [pick]
Specify length of other axis for base of cone: **[pick]**
Specify height of cone or [Apex]: **[specify height]**

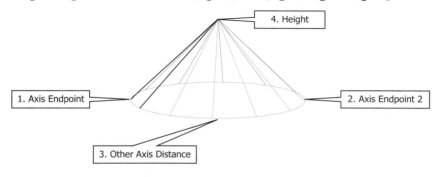

COMMAND LINE OPTIONS

Elliptical   Draws a cone with an elliptical base.
Center point   Specifies the center point of the cone's base.
Axis endpoint Picks the endpoint of the axis defining the elliptical base.
Center of ellipse
                     Picks the center of the elliptical base.
Height   Specifies the height of the cone.
Apex   Determines the height and orientation of the cone's tip.

RELATED COMMANDS

Ai_Cone   Draws a 3D wireframe cone.
Box   Draws a 3D solid box.
Cylinder   Draws a 3D solid tube.
Sphere   Draws a 3D solid ball.
Torus   Draws a 3D solid donut.
Wedge   Draws a 3D solid wedge.

RELATED SYSTEM VARIABLES

DispSilh   Toggles display of 3D objects as silhouettes after hidden-line removal and shading.
IsoLines   Specifies the number of isolines on solid surfaces:

IsoLines	Meaning
0	Minimum; no isolines.
4	Default.
12 *or* 16	A reasonable value.
2047	Maximum value.

TIPS

■ You define the elliptical base in two ways: by the length of the major and minor axes, or by the center point and two radii.

■ To draw a cone at an angle, use the **Apex** option.

CHANGED COMMAND

The **Config** command now displays the **Options** dialog box; see the **Options** command.

Convert

Converts 2D polylines and associative hatches to optimized formats.

Command	Alias	Ctrl+	F-key	Alt+	Menu Bar	Tablet
convert	...	...	...	...	...	...

```
Command: convert
Enter type of objects to convert [Hatch/Polyline/All] <All>:
Enter object selection preference [Select/All] <All>:
n hatch objects converted.
n 2D polyline objects converted.
```

COMMAND LINE OPTIONS

Hatch   Converts associative hatch patterns from anonymous blocks to hatch objects; displays warning dialog box:

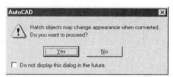

Yes: Converts hatch patterns to hatch objects.
No: Does not convert hatch patterns.
Polyline   Converts 2D polylines to Lwpolyline objects.
All   Converts all polylines and hatch patterns.
Select   Selects the hatch patterns and polylines to convert.

RELATED COMMANDS

BHatch   Creates associative hatch patterns.
PLine   Draws 2D polylines.

RELATED SYSTEM VARIABLE

PLineType   Determines whether pre-R14 polylines are converted in AutoCAD 2002.

PlineType	Meaning
0	Not converted; **PLine** creates old-format polylines.
1	Not converted; **PLine** creates lwpolylines.
2	Converted; **PLine** creates lwpolylines (default).

TIPS

- When a R13 or earlier drawing is opened in AutoCAD 2002, it automatically converts most (not all) 2D polylines to lwpolylines; hatch patterns are not automatically updated.

- A hatch pattern is automatically updated the first time the **HatchEdit** command is applied, or when its boundary is changed.

- Polylines are not converted when they contain curve fit segments, splined segments, extended object data in their vertices, or 3D polylines.

- System variable **PLineType** affects: **Boundary** (when a polyline), **Donut**, **Ellipse** (**PEllipse** = 1), **PEdit** (converts a line or arc), **Polygon**, and **Sketch** (**SkPoly** = 1).

ConvertCTB

Converts a plot style file from CTB color-dependent format to STB named format (*short for CONVERT Color TaBle*).

Command	Alias	Ctrl+	F-key	Alt+	Menu Bar	Tablet
convertctb	...	...	...	...	...	...

Command: **convertctb**
*Displays **Select File** dialog box.*
*1. Select a CTB file and click **Open**. AutoCAD displays the **Create File** dialog box.*
*2. Specify the name of an STB file and click **Save**.*
When AutoCAD has completed the conversion, displays dialog box:

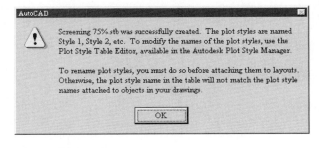

DIALOG BOX OPTIONS
Open   Opens the CTB file.
Save   Saves as an STB file.

RELATED COMMANDS
ConvertPStyles Converts a drawing between color-dependent and named plotstyles.
PlotStyle   Sets the plotstyle for a drawing.

RELATED FILES
*.CTB   Color-dependent plot style table file.
*.STB   Named plot style table.

TIPS
■ "Color-dependent plot styles" was used by older versions of AutoCAD, where the color of the object controlled the pen selection.

■ "Named plot styles" is the alternative introduced with AutoCAD 2000, which allows plotter-specific information to be assigned to layers and objects.

ConvertPStyles

2001 Converts a drawing between color-dependent and named plotstyles (*short for Convert Plot STYLES*).

Command	Alias	Ctrl+	F-key	Alt+	Menu Bar	Tablet
convertpstyles ...	...	...	...	...	...	...

Command: **convertpstyles**
Displays warning dialog box:

When AutoCAD has completed the conversion, displays message:
Drawing converted from Named plot style mode to Color Dependent mode.

DIALOG BOX OPTIONS

O K Proceeds with the conversion.
Cancel Prevents the conversion.

RELATED COMMANDS

ConvertCTB Converts a plot style file from CTB color-dependent format to STB named format.
PlotStyle Sets the plot style for a drawing.

TIPS

■ "Color-dependent plot styles" was used by older versions of AutoCAD, where the color of the object controlled the pen selection.

■ "Named plot styles" is the alternative introduced with AutoCAD 2000, which allows plotter-specific information to be assigned to layers and objects.

Copy

V. 1.0   Creates one or more copies of an object.

Command	Alias	Ctrl+	F-key	Alt+	Menu Bar	Tablet
copy	co	...	...	MY	Modify	V15
	cp				⌐Copy	

```
Command: copy
Select objects: [pick]
Select objects: ENTER
Specify base point or displacement, or [Multiple]: [pick]
Specify second point of displacement or <use first point as
    displacement>: [pick]
```

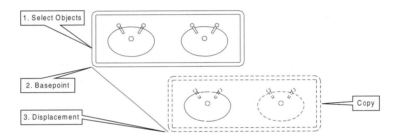

COMMAND LINE OPTIONS

Base point   Indicates the starting point.
Multiple   Allows the object(s) to be copied more than once.
Second point   Indicates the point to move to.
Displacement   Uses the selection point as the base point when you press **Enter**.
Esc   Cancels multiple object copying.

RELATED COMMANDS

Array   Draws a rectangular or polar array of objects.
MInsert   Places an array of blocks.
Move   Moves an object to a new location.
Offset   Draws parallel lines, polylines, circles, and arcs.

TIPS

■ Use the **M** (*multiple*) option to place quickly several copies of the original object.

■ Inserting a block multiple times is more efficient than placing multiple copies.

■ Turn on ortho mode to copy objects in a precise horizontal and vertical direction; turn snap mode on to copy objects in precise increments; use object snap modes to copy objects precisely from one geometric feature to another.

■ To copy an object by a known distance, enter 0,0 as the 'Base point.' Then enter the known distance as the 'Second point.'

CopyBase

Copies selected objects to the Clipboard with a specified base point (*short for COPY with BASEpoint*).

Command	Alias	Ctrl+	F-key	Alt+	Menu Bar	Tablet
copybase	...	...	...	EB	Edit	...
					⤷Copy with Basepoint	

```
Command: copybase
Specify base point: [pick]
Select objects:  [pick]
1 found Select objects: ENTER
```

COMMAND LINE OPTIONS

Specify base point
> Specifies the base point.

Select objects Selects the objects to copy to the Clipboard.

RELATED COMMANDS

CopyClip Copies selected objects to the Clipboard without a specified basepoint.

PasteBlock Pastes from the Clipboard into the drawing as a block.

PasteClip Pastes from the Clipboard into the drawing.

TIPS

■ The purpose of this command is to allow you to place the copied objects with the **PasteClip** command.

■ When **PasteClip** pastes objects selected with the **CopyBase** command, it prompts you 'Specify insertion point' and pastes the objects as a block with a name similar to A$C7E1B27BE.

■ When specifying the **All** option at the 'Select objects' prompt, **CopyBase** selects all objects visible only in the current viewport.

CopyClip

Copies selected objects from the drawing to the Clipboard (*short for COPY to CLIPboard*).

Command	Alias	Ctrl+	F-key	Alt+	Menu Bar	Tablet
copyclip	...	C	...	EC	Edit ⇘Copy	T14

```
Command: copyclip
Select objects: [pick]
Select objects: ENTER
```

The Clipboard Viewer shows an object copied from AutoCAD to the Clipboard.

COMMAND LINE OPTION

Select objects Selects the objects to copy to Clipboard.

RELATED COMMANDS

CopyBase	Copies objects to the Clipboard with a specified basepoint.
CopyHist	Copies Text window text to the Clipboard.
CopyLink	Copies current viewport to the Clipboard.
CutClip	Cuts selected objects to the Clipboard.
PasteBlock	Pastes from the Clipboard into the drawing as a block.
PasteClip	Pastes from the Clipboard into the drawing.

RELATED WINDOWS COMMANDS

PRTSCR	Copies the entire screen to the Clipboard
ALT+PRTSCR	Copies the topmost window to the Clipboard.

TIPS

- Contrary to the AutoCAD *Command Reference*, text objects are *not* copied to the Clipboard in text format; instead, text is copied as an AutoCAD object.

- When the **All** option is specified at the 'Select objects' prompt, **CopyClip** selects objects visible only in the current viewport.

CopyHist

<u>Rel.13</u>   Copies Text window text to the Clipboard (*short for COPY HISTory*).

Command	Alias	Ctrl+	F-key	Alt+	Menu Bar	Tablet
copyhist	...	...	...	EH	Edit	...
					⌐Copy History	

Command: **copyhist**

COMMAND LINE OPTIONS
None.

RELATED COMMAND
CopyClip   Copies selected text from the drawing to the Clipboard.

RELATED WINDOWS COMMAND
ALT+PRTSCR   Copies the Text window to the Clipboard in graphics format.

TIPS
- To copy a selected portion of Text window text to the Clipboard, highlight the text first, then select **Edit | Copy** from the Text window's menu bar.

- To paste text to the command line, select **Edit | Paste to Cmdline** from the menu bar. However, this only works when the Clipboard contains text — not graphics.

- As an alternative, you can right-click in the Text window to bring up the cursor menu:

Getting the right Clipboard result

You can use the Clipboard to display AutoCAD drawings in other Windows applications, such as word processing, desktop publishing, and paint programs. AutoCAD has two primary commands for copying objects from the drawing to the Clipboard: **CopyLink** and **CopyClip**. The result of using these commands, however, may surprise you, since each command produces a different result, depending on whether AutoCAD is in model or layout mode.

- **CopyClip** (**Edit | Copy**) copies selected objects from the drawing, as follows:

      Command: **copyclip**
      Select objects: **all**
      Select objects: ENTER

Warning: when you select **All** objects, AutoCAD selects only those object visible in the current viewport.

- **CopyLink** (**Edit | Copy Link**) copies everything visible in the current viewport. Use this command to capture a layout view with *all* viewports.

The two commands take on different meanings, as described below.

MODEL MODE

In *model mode*, AutoCAD copies only objects visible in the current viewport. If the drawing contains more than one viewport, you must select the correct viewport before copying objects to the Clipboard. **CopyClip** and **CopyLink** have the same effect:

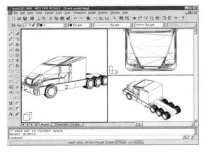

AutoCAD viewports in model mode. *Drawing pasted in Word after either* **CopyClip** *or* **CopyLink**.

LAYOUT MODE

In layout mode's **PAPER** space, **CopyClip** copies objects drawn only in paper space — *nothing* drawn in model space is copied to the Clipboard, even if it is visible.

CopyLink copies *all* visible objects, whether drawn in paper space or model space. Notice that this command also copies the margin lines and gray background.

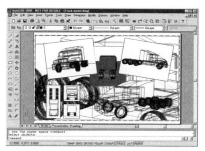

AutoCAD in layout mode's PAPER space.

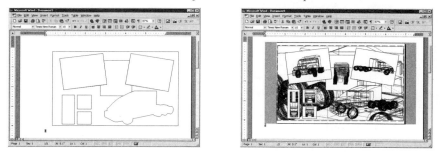

*Result in Word after using AutoCAD's **ClipClip** (left) and **CopyLink** (right).*

In layout mode's **MODEL** space, AutoCAD copies only objects drawn in model space that are visible in the selected viewport. **CopyClip** and **CopyLink** produce the same result when pasted in Word and other Windows applications.

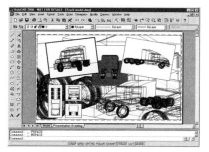

A viewport in layout mode's MODEL space.

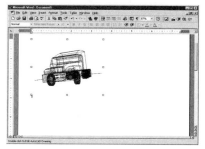

Drawing pasted in Word after either ***CopyClip** or **CopyLink**.*

CopyLink

<u>Rel.13</u>   Copies the current viewport to the Clipboard; optionally allows you to link the drawing back to AutoCAD.

Command	Alias	Ctrl+	F-key	Alt+	Menu Bar	Tablet
copylink	...	...		EL	Edit ⤷Copy Link	...

Command: **copyclip**

COMMAND LINE OPTIONS
None.

RELATED COMMANDS
CopyClip	Copies selected objects to the Clipboard.
CopyEmbed	Copies selected objects to the Clipboard.
CopyHist	Copies Text window text to the Clipboard.
CutClip	Cuts selected objects to the Clipboard.
PasteClip	Pastes from the Clipboard into the drawing.

RELATED WINDOWS COMMANDS
PRTSCR	Copies the entire screen to the Clipboard
ALT+PRTSCR	Copies the topmost window to the Clipboard.

TIPS
- In the other application, use the **Edit | Paste Special** commands to paste the AutoCAD image into the document; to link the drawing back to AutoCAD, select the **Paste Link** option.

- AutoCAD does not let you link a drawing to itself.

- This command copies everything in the current viewport (if in model space) or the entire drawing (if in paper space).

- **CopyEmbed** is identical to **CopyLink**, except that **CopyEmbed** prompts you to select objects.

Customize

<u>2000i</u> Creates and changes toolbars, toolbar macros and icons, and keyboard shortcuts.

Command	Alias	Ctrl+	F-key	Alt+	Menu Bar	Tablet
customize	toolbar	...	...	TC	Tools	T13
					↳Customize	

Command: **customize**
Displays dialog box:

DIALOG BOX OPTIONS

Close   Closes the dialog box, and saves the changes.

Commands tab:

Categories   Lists names of primary menu items.

Commands   Lists command names and related icons, if any; drag a command name out of the dialog box to start creating a new toolbar.

Show image and name

          Yes: Lists all command names and related icons.

          No: Lists only icons; commands without an icon are shown as a gray square.

Toolbars tab:

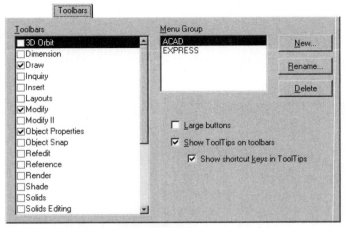

Toolbars	Lists the names of predefined toolbars, and toggles their visibility.
Menu Groups	Lists the names of menu groups loaded in AutoCAD.
New	Creates a new toolbar; displays **New Toolbar** dialog box, which prompts you to select the menu group to which the new toolbar should be added.
Rename	Changes name of selected toolbar; displays **Rename Toolbar** dialog box.
Delete	Deletes the selected toolbar; displays a warning dialog box: "Are you sure you want to delete the toolbar from the menu group?"

Large buttons

Yes: Toolbar buttons and icons are displayed at a larger size for better visibility on very-high resolution screens, or for visually-impared users (40 pixels wide).

No: Toolbar buttons and icons displayed at standard size (24 pixels wide).

Normal buttons (left) and large buttons (right).

Show tooltips on toolbars

Yes: Displays a small yellow tag with the command name.

No: Does not display tooltips.

Show shortcut keys in Tooltips

Yes: Displays shortcut keystrokes, such as **CTRL+N**, in the tooltip.

No: Does not display shortcut keystrokes.

Tooltip with shortcut key ***CTRL+N***.

Properties tab:

When you first click the **Properties** *tab, AutoCAD prompts:*

Tip: Select a toolbar item to view or modify its properties.

Click any toolbar button; AutoCAD displays the **Button Properties** *tab:*

Button Properties	
Name:	Insert Hyperlink
Description:	Attaches a hyperlink to a graphical object or modifies an existing hyperlink: HYPERLINK
Macro associated with this button:	
^C^C_hyperlink	

Button Image

Edit...

Apply   Reset

Name　　　　　　Specifies the wording for the tooltip.
Description　　　　Specifies the help text displayed on the status line.
Macro associated with this button
　　　　　　　　　　Specifies the macro executed when the button is clicked.
Edit　　　　　　　Edits the icon; displays the **Button Editor** dialog box.

Keyboard tab:

Categories	Allows you to select the name of a toolbar, menu item, or all AutoCAD commands.
Commands	Lists the commands, as specified by **Categories**.
Menu Group	Lists the names of menu groups loaded in AutoCAD.
Current Keys	Lists the shortcut key(s) assigned to the command; this option appears to not work with pre-assigned keys, such as **CTRL+N**.

Press new shortcut key

Selects the shortcut key: hold down **CTRL** or **CTRL+SHIFT**, plus a letter or number key between A and Z, and 1 and 0.

Assign	Assigns the shortcut keystroke to the command.
Remove	Removes the shortcut keystroke from the command.
Show All	Lists all assigned shortcut keys; displays the **Shortcut Keys** dialog box.

Button Editor dialog box:

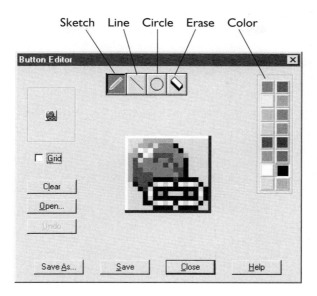

Sketch Line Circle Erase Color

Grid	**Yes**: Displays a grid in the icon drawing area. **No**: Hides the grid.
Clear	Erases the icon.
Open	Opens a BMP (bitmap) file, which can be used as an icon.
Undo	Undoes the last operation.
Save As	Saves the icon as a BMP (bitmap) file.
Save	Saves the changes to the icon in AutoCAD's internal storage.
Close	Closes the dialog box.

Shortcut Key dialog box:

Accelerator	Command	Group	Category
Alt+F11	Visual Basic Editor	ACAD	Tools Menu
Alt+F8	Macros	ACAD	Tools Menu
Ctrl+1	Properties	ACAD	Standard Toolbar
Ctrl+2	AutoCAD DesignCenter	ACAD	Standard Toolbar
Ctrl+6	dbConnect	ACAD	Tools Menu
Ctrl+A	Select All	ACAD	Edit Menu
Ctrl+B	Toggles Snap		AutoCAD Internal
Ctrl+C	Copy to Clipboard	ACAD	Standard Toolbar
Ctrl+D	Toggles coordinate display		AutoCAD Internal
Ctrl+E	Cycles through isometric planes		AutoCAD Internal
Ctrl+F	Toggles running object snaps		AutoCAD Internal
Ctrl+G	Toggles Grid		AutoCAD Internal
Ctrl+H	_setvar;pickstyle;$M=	ACAD	AutoCAD Commands
Ctrl+J	Executes last command		AutoCAD Internal
Ctrl+K	Insert Hyperlink	ACAD	Standard Toolbar
Ctrl+L	^O	ACAD	AutoCAD Commands
Ctrl+N	New	ACAD	Standard Toolbar
Ctrl+O	Open	ACAD	Standard Toolbar
Ctrl+P	Plot	ACAD	Standard Toolbar
Ctrl+R	^V	ACAD	AutoCAD Commands
Ctrl+S	Save	ACAD	Standard Toolbar
Ctrl+T	Toggles Tablet mode		AutoCAD Internal

OK

OK   Closes the dialog box.

RELATED COMMANDS

BmpOut   Exports selected objects in the current view to a BMP file.
MenuLoad   Loads partial menus into AutoCAD.
-Toolbar   Opens and closes toolbars via the command line.

TIP

■ Elements of a toolbar:

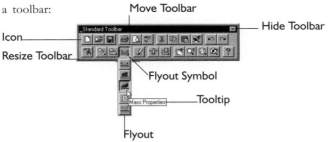

CutClip

Rel.12 Cuts the selected objects from the drawing to the Clipboard (*short for CUT to CLIPboard*).

Command	Alias	Ctrl+	F-key	Alt+	Menu Bar	Tablet
cutclip	...	X	...	ET	Edit ⌐Cut	T13

```
Command: cutclip
Select objects: [pick]
Select objects: ENTER
```

COMMAND LINE OPTION

Select objects Selects the objects to cut to Clipboard.

RELATED COMMANDS

BmpOut   Exports selected objects in the current view to a BMP file.
CopyClip   Copies selected objects to the Clipboard.
CopyHist   Copies Text window text to the Clipboard.
CopyLink   Copies current viewport to the Clipboard.
PasteClip   Pastes from the Clipboard into the drawing.
WmfOut   Exports selected objects to a WMF file.

RELATED WINDOWS COMMANDS

PRTSCR   Copies the entire screen to the Clipboard
ALT+PRTSCR   Copies the topmost window to the Clipboard.

TIPS

■ When the **All** option is specified at the 'Select objects:' prompt, **CutClip** selects all objects only visible in the current viewport.

■ In the other application, use the **Edit | Paste** or **Edit | Paste Special** commands to paste the AutoCAD image into the document; the **Paste Special** command lets you specify the pasted format.

■ You can use the **Undo** command to return the "cut" objects to the drawing.

⬢ Cylinder

Rel.12 Draws a 3D ACIS cylinder with a circular or elliptical cross section (*an ACIS command*).

Command	Alias	Ctrl+	F-key	Alt+	Menu Bar	Tablet
cylinder	...	...	...	DIC	Draw	L7
					⌐Solids	
					⌐Cylinder	

```
Command: cylinder
Current wire frame density:  ISOLINES=4
Specify center point for base of cylinder or [Elliptical]
   <0,0,0>: [pick]
Specify radius for base of cylinder or [Diameter]:[pick]
Specify height of cylinder or [Center of other end]: [pick]
```

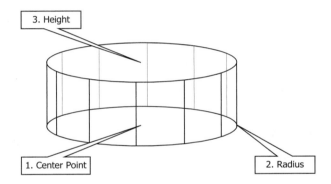

3. Height

1. Center Point

2. Radius

COMMAND OPTIONS

Center point Specifies the center point of the cylinder's base.
Radius Specifies the cylinder's radius.
Diameter Specifies the cylinder's diamter.
Height Specifies the cylinder's height.
Center of other end
   Specifies the z orientation of the cylinder.

Elliptical options:
```
Specify axis endpoint of ellipse for base of cylinder
   or [Center]: [pick]
Specify second axis endpoint of ellipse for base of
   cylinder: [pick]
Specify length of other axis for base of cylinder: [pick]
Specify height of cylinder or [Center of other end]: [pick]
```

Axis endpoint Specifies one end of the ellitical axis.
Center   Specifies the center point of the elliptical base.
Second axis endpoint
                    Specifies the other end of the axis.
Length of other axis
                    Specifies the length of the other elliptical axis.

RELATED COMMANDS

Box	Draws a 3D solid box.
Cone	Draws a 3D solid cone.
Elevation	Turns a circle into a wireframe cylinder.
Extrude	Creates a cylinder with an arbitrary cross-section and sloped walls.
Sphere	Draws a 3D solid ball.
Torus	Draws a 3D solid donut.
Wedge	Draws a 3D solid wedge.

RELATED SYSTEM VARIABLES

DispSilh   Displays 3D objects as silhouettes after hidden-line removal and shading.
IsoLines   Determines the number of isolines on solid surfaces:

IsoLines	Meaning
0	Minimum (no isolines).
4	Default.
12 *or* 16	A reasonable value.
2047	Maximum value.

TIPS

- The **Ellipse** option draws a cylinder with an elliptical cross-section.

- Use the **Intersect** command remove solid portions from the cylinder; use the **Union** command to add solid portions to the cylinder.

DbcClose

2000 Closes the **dbConnect Manager** window.

Command	Alias	Ctrl+	F-key	Alt+	Menu Bar	Tablet
dbcclose	...	6	...	TD	Tools	...
					dbConnect	

Command: **dbcclose**

COMMAND LINE OPTIONS
None.

RELATED COMMANDS
DbConnect   Opens the **dbConnect Manager** window.
Close   Closes the current drawing.
AdcClose   Closes the **DesignCenter** window.

TIP
■ Pressing **CTRL+6** toggles on and off the display of the **dbConnect Manager** window; see **DbConnect** command.

DbConnect

<u>**2000**</u>   Opens the **dbConnect Manager** window to connect objects with external database tables (*short for Data Base CONNECTion*).

Command	Alias	Ctrl+	F-key	Alt+	Menu Bar	Tablet
dbconnect	dbc	6	...	TD	Tools ↳dbConnect	W12

Command: **dbconnect**
Displays window:

TOOLBAR OPTIONS

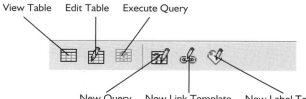

View Table   Opens an external database table in *read-only* mode; select a table, link template, or label template to make this button available.

Edit Table   Opens an external database table in *edit* mode; select a table, link template, or label template to make this button available.

Execute Query   Executes a query; select a previously-defined query to make this button available.

New Query   Displays the **New Query** dialog box when a table or link template is selected; displays the **Query Editor** when a query is selected.

New Link Template
Displays the **New Link Template** dialog box when a table is selected; displays the **Link Template** dialog box when a link template is selected; not available for link templates with links already defined in a drawing.

New Label Template
Displays the **New Label Template** dialog box when a table or link template is selected; displays the **Label Template** dialog box when a label template is selected.

View Table and Edit Table Windows

*The **View Table** and **Edit Table** windows are identical, with the exception that **View Table** is read-only; hence all text in the columns is grayed-out.*

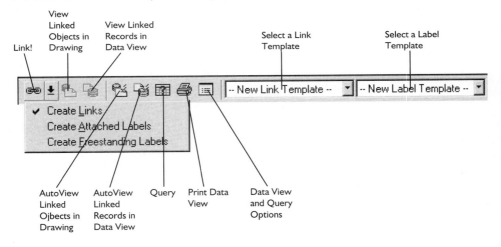

TOOLBAR OPTIONS (Data View)

Link!   Creates a link or a label; click the drop list to select an option:
- **Create Links:** Turns on link creation mode.
- **Create Attached Labels**: Turns on attached label creation mode.
- **Create Freestanding Labels:** Turns on freestanding label creation mode.

View Link Objects in Drawing
   Highlights objects linked to selected records.

View Linked Records in Data View
   Highlights records linked to selected objects in the drawing.

AutoView Linked Objects in Drawing
  Automatically highlights objects linked to selected records.
AutoView Linked Records in Data View
  Highlights records linked to selected objects in the drawing.
Query Displays the **New Query** dialog box.
Print Data View
  Prints the data in this window.
Data View and Query Options
  Displays the **Data View and Query Options** dialog box.
Select a Link Template
  Lists the names of previously-defined link templates.
Select a Label Template
  Lists the names of previously-defined label templates.

New Query dialog box:

New query name
  Specifies the name of the query.
Existing query names
  Uses an existing query.
Continue Displays the **Query Editor** dialog box.

Query Editor dialog box:
Execute Executes the query.
Close Closes the dialog box.
Store Saves the settings.
Options Displays the **Data View and Query Options** dialog box.

Quick Query tab:

Field   Select a field name.
Operator   Specifies a conditional operator:

Operator	Meaning
= Equal	Exactly match the value (default).
<> Not equal	Does not match the value.
> Greater than	Greater than the value.
< Less than	Less than the value.
>= Greater than or equal	Greater than or equal to the value.
<= Less than or equal	Less than or equal to the value.
Like	Contain the value; use the **%** wild-card character (equivalent to * in DOS).
In	Matches two values separated by a comma.
Is null	Does not have a value; used for locating records that are missing data.
Is not null	Has a value; used for excluding records that are missing data.

Value   Specifies the value for which to search.
Look up values Displays a list of existing values:

Range Query tab:

Field	Lists the names of fields in the current table.
From	Specifies the first value of the range.
Look Up Values	Displays the **Column Values** dialog box.
Through	Specifies the second value of the range.

Indicate Records in Data View

Highlights records that match the search criteria in the **Data View** window (default = on).

Indicate Objects in Drawing

Highlights objects that match the search criteria in the drawing (default = on).

Query Builder tab:

(	Groups search criteria with parentheses; up to four sets can be nested.
Field	Specifies a field name; double-click the cell to display the list of fields in the current table.
Operator	Specifies a logical operator; double-click to display the list of operators.
Value	Specifies a value for the query; click **...** to display a list of current values.
)	Specifies a closing parenthesis.
Logical	Specifies an **And** or **Or** operator; click once to add **And**; click again to change to **Or**.

Fields in table Displays the fields in the current table; when no fields are selected, the query displays all fields from the table; double-click a field to add it to the list.

Show fields Specifies the fields displayed by the **Data View** window; drag the field out of the list to remove it.

Add Adds a field from the **Fields in table** list to the **Show fields** list.

Sort By Specifies the sort order: the first field is the primary sort; to change the sort order, drag the field to another location in the list; press **Delete** to remove a field from the list.

Add Adds a field from the **Fields in table** list to the **Sort by** list (default = ascending).

A ∀ Reverses the sort order.

Indicate Records in Data View
Highlights records that match the search criteria in the **Data View** window (default = on).

Indicate Objects in Drawing
Highlights objects that match the search criteria in the drawing (default = on).

SQL Query tab:

Table Lists the names of all database tables available in the current data source.

Add Adds the selected table to the SQL text editor.

Fields Displays a list of field names in the selected database table.

Add Adds the selected field to the SQL text editor.

Operator Specifies the logical operator, which is added to the query (default = Equal).

Add Adds the selected operator to the SQL text editor.

Values Specifies a value for the selected field.

Add Adds the value to the SQL text editor.

... Lists available values for the field.

Indicate Records in Data View
Highlights records that match the search criteria in the **Data View** window (default = on).

Indicate Objects in Drawing
Highlights objects that match the search criteria in the drawing (default = on).

Data View and Query Options dialog box:

AutoPan and Zoom options:

Automatically Pan Drawing

Causes AutoCAD to pan the drawing automatically to display associated objects (default = on).

Automatically Zoom Drawing

Causes AutoCAD to zoom the drawing automatically to display associated objects (default = off).

Zoom Factor

Specifies the zoom factor as a percentage of the viewport area:

Zoom Factor	Meaning
20	Minimum.
50	Default.
90	Maximum.

Query Options options:

Send as Native SQL

Makes queries to database tables in:

On: The format of the source table.

Off: SQL 92 format (default).

Automatically Store

Automatically stores queries when they are executed (default = off).

Record Indication Settings options:

Show Only Indicated Records

Displays the records associated with the current AutoCAD selections in the Data View window (default).

Show All Records, Select Indicated Records

Displays all records in the current database table.

Mark Indicated Records

Colors linked records to differentiate them from unlinked records.

Marking Color Specifies the marking color (default = yellow).

Accumulate Options options:

Accumulate Selection Set in Drawing

> **Yes**: Adds objects to the selection set as data view records are added.
>
> **No**: Replaces the selection set each time data view records are selected (default).

Accumulate Record Set in Data View

> **Yes**: Adds records to the selection set as drawing objects are selected.
>
> **No**: Replaces the selection set each time drawing objects are selected (default).

New Link Template dialog box:

New link template name

> Specifies the name of the link template.

Start with template

> Reuses an existing template.

Continue   Displays the **Link Template** dialog box.

Link Template dialog box:

Key Fields   Selects one field name; you may select more than one field name, but AutoCAD warns you that too many key fields may slow performance.

New Label Template dialog box:

New label template name
> Specifies the name of the label template.

Start with template
> Reuses an existing template.

Continue   Displays the **Label Template** dialog box.

Label Template dialog box:

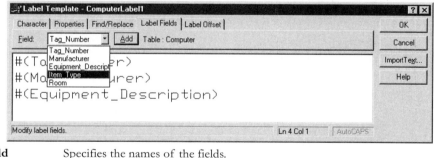

Field   Specifies the names of the fields.
Add   Adds the field to the label.
Label Offset Displays the **Label Offset** tab:

| Start: | 4⊳ Middle Center MC ▾ | Leader offset X: 1.0 Y: 1.0 | Tip offset X: 0.0 Y: 0.0 |

#(Tag_Number)
#(Manufacturer)

Modify label offset.   Ln 3 Col 1   AutoCAPS

Start   Specifies the justification of the label starting point.
Leader offset Specifies the x,y distance between the label's starting point and the leader line.
Tip offset   Specifies the offset distance to the leader tip or label text.
> *See **MText** command for the other tabs.*

RELATED COMMANDS

AttDef   Creates an attribute definition, akin to an internal database.

AttExt   Exports attributes.

TIPS

- Query searches are case sensitive: "Computer" is not the same as "computer".

- OLE DB v2.0 must be installed on your computer before you use the **dbConnect Manager**.

- Leaders must have a length; to get rid of a leader, use a freestanding label.

- SQL is short for "structured query language."

- The properties of a link template can only be edited if it contains no links, and if the drawing is fully loaded (cannot be partially loaded).

- AutoCAD 2002 includes a sample UDL file called *jet_dbsamples.udl*. It uses Microsoft Jet v3.51 OLE DB Provider.Install MDAC v2.0 by running *mdac_typ.exe* in the *data* folder of the AutoCAD 2002 CD-ROM.

- Autodesk notes that AutoCAD 2002 "may experience a performance impact when accessing a table using an SQL Server 7.0 in Windows 98."

- Before you can edit a record with an SQL Server table, it must have a primary key defined.

QUICK START TUTORIAL:

Constructing your first query

Step 1:

From the **Tools** menu, select **dbConnect**. AutoCAD adds the **dbConnect** item to the menu bar.

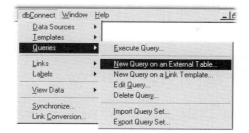

Step 2:

From the **dbConnect** menu, select **Queries | New Query on an External Table**. AutoCAD displays the **Select Data Object** dialog box.

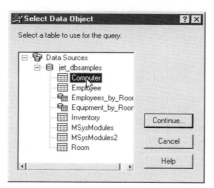

Step 3:

Select a table, then click **Continue**. AutoCAD displays the **New Query** dialog box.

Step 4:

Enter a name for the query in **New query name** text field, or select an existing name.

Step 5:

Click **Continue**. AutoCAD opens the **Query Editor** dialog box.

Step 6:

Ensure the **Quick Query** tab is showing. Also, make sure that **Indicate records in data view** and **Indicate objects in drawing** are both checked.

Step 7:

Select a field name from the **Field** list by highlighting it.

Step 8:

Select an operator from the **Operator** list. For example, to match a value, select **= Equal**.

Step 9:

Enter a value in the **Value** field, or click **Look up values** and select a value from the list of values already in the database.

Step 10:

Click **Store** to save the query for reuse in the future.

Step 11:

Click **Execute** to run the query. AutoCAD closes the dialog box, then displays the records that match your selection in the **Data View** window.

DblClkEdit

2000i Determines whether objects can be edited with a double-click of the mouse button (*short for DouBLe CLicK EDITing*).

Command	Alias	Ctrl+	F-key	Alt+	Menu Bar	Tablet
dblclkedit	...	...	...	...	...	...

Command: **dblclkedit**
Enter double-click editing mode [ON/OFF] <ON>: **off**

COMMAND LINE OPTIONS

ON   Enables double-click editing.
OFF   Disables double-click editing for compatibility with earlier versions of AutoCAD.

RELATED COMMANDS

[Right-click]   Displays a shortcut menu with editing commands.
Properties   Displays the **Properties** dialog box.

TIPS

- When this command is turned on, double-clicking an object is the equivalent of entering a command, which displays a dialog box:

Object	Dialog Box	Equivalent Command
Attribute	Edit Attribute	DdEdit or EAttEdit
Block	Reference Edit	RefEdit
Hatch	Hatch Edit	HatchEdit
Leader	Multiline Text Editor	MtEdit
Mline	Multiline Edit Tools	MlEdit
Mtext	Multiline Text Editor	MtEdit
Text	Edit Text	DdEdit
Xref	Reference Edit	RefEdit

- In all other cases, double-clicking an object displays the **Properties** window, and highlights the object with grips:

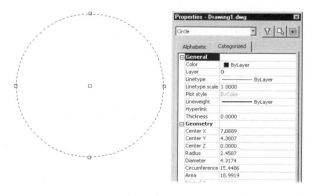

DbList

V. 1.0 Lists information on all objects in the drawing (*short for Data Base LISTing*).

Command	Alias	Ctrl+	F-key	Alt+	Menu Bar	Tablet
dblist	...	...	...	...	...	...

Command: **dblist**

Sample listing:

```
        LINE        Layer: 1
                    Space: Model space
    from point, X=    3.7840   Y=    4.7169   Z=    0.0000
      to point, X=    4.1440   Y=    4.7169   Z=    0.0000
  Length =   0.3600,   Angle in X-Y Plane =        0
  Delta X =   0.3600, Delta Y = 0.0000, Delta Z = 0.0000

        ARC         Layer: 2
                    Space: Model space
    center point, X=    2.1000   Y=    7.0000   Z=    0.0000
    radius     1.2000
     start angle       0
      end angle      180
```

COMMAND LINE OPTIONS

ENTER	Continues display after pause.
ESC	Cancels database listing.

RELATED COMMANDS

Area	Lists the area and perimeter of objects.
Dist	Lists the 3D distance and angle between two points.
Id	Lists the 3D coordinates of a point.
List	Lists information about selected objects in the drawing.

REMOVED COMMANDS

DdAttDef was removed from AutoCAD 2000; it was replaced by **AttDef**.
DdAttE was removed from AutoCAD 2000; it was replaced by **AttEdit**.
DdAttExt was removed from AutoCAD 2000; it was replaced by **AttExt**.
DdChProp was removed from AutoCAD 2000; it was replaced by **Properties**.
DdColor was removed from AutoCAD 2000; it was replaced by **Color**.

DdEdit

Rel.11   Edits a single line of text; launches the text editor for editing multiline text (*short for Dynamic Dialog EDITor*).

Command	Alias	Ctrl+	F-key	Alt+	Menu Bar	Tablet
ddedit	ed	...	...	MOTE	Modify ↳Object ↳Text ↳Edit	Y21

Command: **ddedit**
Select an annotation object or [Undo]: **[pick text]**
For single-line text placed by the **Text** *and* **DText** *commands, displays* **Edit Text** *dialog box.*
For paragraph text placed by **MText** *command, displays* **Multiline Text Editor** *dialog box.*

COMMAND LINE OPTIONS
Undo   Undoes editing.
Esc   Ends the command.

DIALOG BOX OPTIONS
Edit Text dialog box:

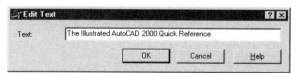

Text   Displays the selected text; editing options:

Keystroke	Meaning
Left or Up	Moves cursor one character left.
Right or Down	Moves cursor one character right.
Home	Moves cursor to beginning of line.
End	Moves cursor to end of line.
Delete	Erases character to right of cursor.
Backspace	Erases character to left of cursor.

OK   Accepts editing changes, and dismisses dialog box.
Cancel   Ignores editing changes, and dismisses dialog box.

Multiline Text Editor dialog box:

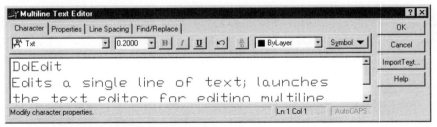

*See **MText** command for **Multiline Text Editor** options.*

RELATED COMMANDS

AttEdit	Edits all text attributes connected with a block.
MtEdit	Edits paragraph text.
Properties	Edits all text *properties*, including the text itself.

RELATED SYSTEM VARIABLE

MTextEd   Specifies the name of the text editor used for editing multiline text.

TIPS

■ **DdEdit** automatically repeats; press **Esc** to cancel the command.

■ As of AutoCAD 2000, this command no longer edits attribute text; use **AttEdit** instead.

REMOVED COMMANDS

DdGrips was removed from AutoCAD 2000; replaced by the **Selection** tab of the **Options** command.

DDim was removed from AutoCAD 2000; it was replaced by **DimStyle**.

DdInsert was removed from AutoCAD 2000; it was replaced by **Insert**.

DdModify was removed from AutoCAD 2000; it was replaced by **Properties**.

'DdPtype

Rel.12 Sets the style and size of points (*short for Dynamic Dialog Point TYPE*).

Command	Alias	Ctrl+	F-key	Alt+	Menu Bar	Tablet
'ddptype	...	...	...	OP	Format ⮫Point Style	U1

Command: **ddptype**
Displays dialog box:

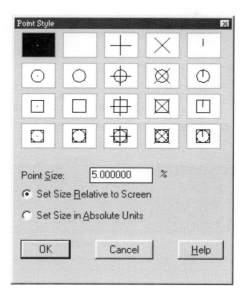

DIALOG BOX OPTIONS
Point size   Sets the size in percent or pixels.
Set Size Relative to Screen
        Sets the size as a percentage of total viewport height.
Set Size in Absolute Units
        Sets the size in pixels.

RELATED COMMANDS
Divide   Draws points along an object.
Point   Draws points.
Measure   Draws points a measured distance along an object.
Regen   Displays the new point format with a regeneration.

RELATED SYSTEM VARIABLES

PdMode   Determines the look of a point:

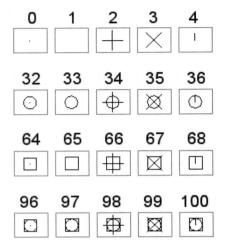

PdSize   Contains the size of the point:

PdSize	Meaning
0	Point is 5% of viewport height (default).
positive	Absolute size in pixels.
negative	Percentage of the viewport size.

REMOVED COMMANDS

DdEModes was removed from AutoCAD Release 14; it was replaced by the **Object Properties** toolbar.

DdLModes was removed in AutoCAD 2000; is was replaced by **Layer**.

DdLtype was removed in AutoCAD 2000; it was replaced by **Linetype**.

DdRename was removed from AutoCAD 2000; it was replaced by **Rename**.

DdRModes was removed from AutoCAD 2000; it was replaced by **DSettings**.

DdSelect was removed from AutoCAD 2000; it was replaced by the **Selection** tab of the **Options** command.

DdUcs and **DdUcsP** have been removed from AutoCAD 2000; they have been replaced by **UcsMan**.

DdUnits was removed from AutoCAD 2000; it was replaced by **Units**.

DdView was removed from AutoCAD 2000; it was replaced by **View**.

DdVPoint

Rel.12 Changes the viewpoint of drawings via a dialog box (*short for Dynamic Dialog ViewPOINT*).

Command	Alias	Ctrl+	F-key	Alt+	Menu Bar	Tablet
`ddvpoint`	`vp`	...	...	V3I	View ↳3D Views ↳Viewpoint Presets	N5

`Command: **ddvpoint**`

Displays dialog box:

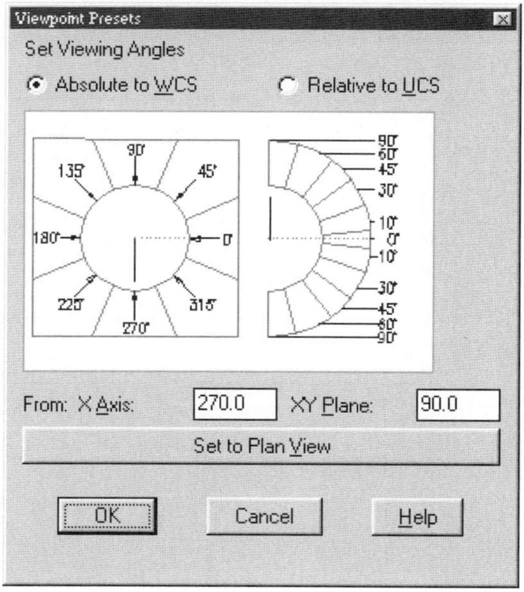

DIALOG BOX OPTIONS

Set Viewing Angles options:

Absolute to WCS
Sets the view direction relative to the WCS.

Relative to UCS Sets the view direction relative to the current UCS.

From X Axis Measures view angle from the x axis.

From XY Plane Measures view angle from the x,y plane

Set to Plan View
Changes view to plan view.

RELATED COMMANDS

VPoint Adjusts the viewpoint from the command line.

3dOrbit Changes the 3D viewpoint interactively.

RELATED SYSTEM VARIABLE

WorldView   Determines whether viewpoint coordinates are in WCS or UCS.

TIPS

- After changing the viewpoint, AutoCAD performs an automatic **Zoom** extents.

- In the image tile, the black arm indicates the new angle.

- In the image tile, the red arm indicates the current angle.

- WCS is short for "world coordinate system."

- UCS is short for "user-defined coordinate system."

- To select an angle with your mouse:

For fine angle control, click an angle in the inner region of the circle or half-circle.

For less-precise angle control, click the outer regions.

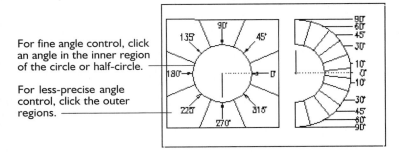

'Delay

<u>v. 1.4</u> Delays the next command, in milliseconds.

Command	Alias	Ctrl+	F-key	Alt+	Menu Bar	Tablet
'delay	...	...	...	...	...	...

Command: **delay**
Delay time in milliseconds: **[enter a number]**

COMMAND LINE OPTION

Delay time   Specifies the number of milliseconds by which to delay the next command.

RELATED COMMAND

Script   Initiates a script

TIPS

- Use **Delay** to slow down the execution of a script file.
- The maximum delay is 32767, just over 32 seconds.

DetachURL

Rel.14 Removes a URL from an object or an area (*undocumented command*).

Command	Alias	Ctrl+	F-key	Alt+	Menu Bar	Tablet
detachurl	...	...	...	...	...	...

```
Command: detachurl
Select objects: [pick]
Select objects: ENTER
```

COMMAND LINE OPTION
Select objects Selects the objects from which to remove URL(s).

RELATED COMMANDS
AttachUrl   Attaches a hyperlink to an object or an area.
Hyperlink   Attaches and removes hyperlinks via dialog box.
SelectUrl   Selects all objects with attached hyperlinks.

TIPS
- When you select a hyperlinked area to detach, AutoCAD reports:

```
1.  hyperlink ()
Remove, deleting the Area.
1 hyperlink deleted...
```

- When you select an object with no hyperlink attached, AutoCAD reports nothing.

- A URL (short for "uniform resource locator") is the universal file naming convention of the Internet; also called a link or hyperlink.

Dim

<u>**V. 1.2**</u> Changes the prompt from 'Command' to 'Dim'; allows access to AutoCAD's old dimensioning commands (*short for DIMensions*).

Command	Alias	Ctrl+	F-key	Alt+	Menu Bar	Tablet
dim	...	...	...	...	...	...

```
Command: dim
Dim: [enter a dimension command from the list below]
```

COMMAND LINE OPTIONS

Aliases for the dimension commands are shown in UPPERCASE.

ALigned — Draws linear dimension aligned with object (*first introduced with AutoCAD version 2.0*); replaced by **DimAligned**.

ANgular — Draws angular dimension measuring an angle (*ver. 2.0*); replaced by **DimAngular**.

Baseline — Continues a dimension from a basepoint (*ver. 1.2*); replaced by the **QDim** and **DimBaseline** commands.

CEnter — Draws a + mark on circle and arc centers (*ver. 2.0*); replaced by **DimCenter**.

COntinue — Continues a dimension from the previous dimension's extension line (*ver. 1.2*); replaced by the **QDim** and **DimContinue** commands.

Diameter — Draws diameter dimension on circles, arcs, and polyarcs (*ver. 2.0*); replaced by the **QDim** and **DimDiameter** commands.

Exit — Returns to 'Command' prompt from 'Dim' prompt (*ver. 1.2*).

HOMetext — Returns dimension text to its original position (*ver. 2.6*); replaced by the **DimEdit** command's **Home** option.

HORizontal — Draws a horizontal dimension (*ver. 1.2*); replaced by **DimLinear**.

LEAder — Draws a leader (*ver. 2.0*); replaced by the **Leader** and **QLeader** commands.

Newtext — Edits text in associative dimensions (*ver. 2.6*); replaced by the **DimEdit** command's **New** option.

OBlique — Changes the angle of extension lines in associative dimensions (*rel. 11*); replaced by the **DimEdit** command's **Oblique** option.

ORdinate — Draws x- and y-ordinate dimensions (*Rel. 11*); replaced by the **QDim** and **DimOrdinate** commands.

OVerride — Overrides the current dimension variables (*Rel. 11*); replaced by **DimOverride**.

RAdius — Draws radial dimension on circles, arcs, and polyline arcs (*ver. 2.0*); replaced by the **QDim** and **DimRadius** commands.

REDraw — Redraws the current viewport (*same as* **'Redraw;** *ver. 2.0*).

REStore — Restores dimension to the current dim style (*Rel. 11*); replaced by the **-DimStyle** command's **Restore** option.

ROtated — Draws a linear dimension at any angle (*ver. 2.0*); replaced by **DimLinear**.

SAve — Saves the current setting of dimension styles (*Rel. 11*); replaced by the **-DimStyle** command's **Save** option.

STAtus — Lists the current settings of dimension variables (*ver. 2.0*); replaced by the **-DimStyle** command's **Status** option.

STYle — Sets a style for the dimensions (*ver. 2.5*); replaced by **DimStyle**.

TEdit — Changes location and orientation of text in associative dimensions (*Rel. 11*); replaced by **DimTEdit**.

TRotate	Changes the rotation of text in associative dimensions (*Rel. 11*); replaced by the **DimTEdit** command's **Rotate** option.
Undo	Undoes the last dimension action (*ver. 2.0*); replaced by the **Undo** command.
UPdate	Updates selected associative dimensions to the current dimvar setting (*ver. 2.6*); replaced by the **-DimStyle** command's **Apply** option.
VAriables	Lists value of variables associated with a dimension style, *not* dimvars (*Rel. 11*); replaced by the **-DimStyle** command's **Variables** option.
VErtical	Draws vertical linear dimensions (*ver. 1.2*); replaced by **DimLinear**.

RELATED DIM VARIABLES

Dimxxx	Specifies system variables for dimensions; see **DimStyle** command.
DimAso	Determines whether dimensions are drawn associatively.
DimScale	Determines the dimension scale.

TIPS

■ The 'Dim' prompt dimension commands are included for compatibility with AutoCAD Release 12 and earlier.

■ Only transparent commands and dimension commands work at the 'Dim' prompt. To use other commands, you must exit the 'Dim' prompt and return to the 'Command' prompt with the **Exit** command.

■ Most dimensions consist of four basic components, as shown below:

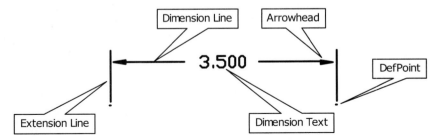

■ The defpoint (short for "definition point") is used by earlier versions of AutoCAD to locate the extension lines. Defpoints appear as a small dot on the **DefPoints** layer. When stretching a dimension, make sure you include the defpoints,;otherwise the dimension will not be updated automatically.

■ As of AutoCAD 2002, defpoints are not used when **DimAssoc**=2 (the default); dimensions are attached directly to objects instead.

■ All the components of an *associative dimension* are treated as a single object; components of a nonassociative dimension are treated as individual objects.

■ When changing dimension text, AutoCAD recognizes the <> metacharacters as representing the dimension text. For example, if AutoCAD measures a dimension as 25.4, then **<>mm** means 25.4mm.

Dim1

V. 2.5 Executes a single dimensioning command, and returns to the 'Command' prompt (*short for DIMension once*).

Command	Alias	Ctrl+	F-key	Alt+	Menu Bar	Tablet
dim1	...	...	...	...	...	...

```
Command: dim1
Dim: [enter a dimension command]
```

COMMAND LINE OPTIONS

All "old" dimension commands; see **Dim** *command for complete list.*

RELATED COMMANDS

DimStyle   Displays dialog box for setting dimension variables.
Dim   Switches to "old" dimensioning mode and remains there.

RELATED DIM VARIABLES

DimAso   Determines whether dimensions are drawn associatively.
DimTxt   Determines the height of text.
DimScale   Determines the dimension scale.

TIP

■ Use **Dim1** when you need to use just a single "old" dimension command.

DimAligned

Rel 13 Draws linear dimensions aligned with an object.

Command	Alias	Ctrl+	F-key	Alt+	Menu Bar	Tablet
dimaligned	dal	...	...	NG	Dimension	W4
	dimali				⌐Aligned	

```
Command: dimaligned
Specify first extension line origin or <select object>: ENTER
Select object to dimension: [pick]
Specify dimension line location or [Mtext/Text/Angle]: [pick]
Dimension text = nnn
```

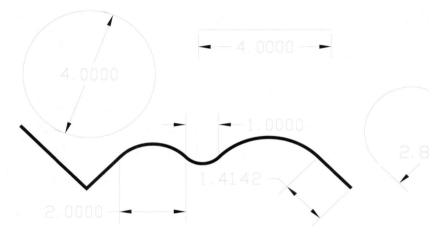

COMMAND LINE OPTIONS

Specify first extension line origin
> Picks a point for origin of the first extension line.

Specify second extension line origin
> Picks a point for origin of the second extension line.

Select object Selects an object to dimension after pressing ENTER.

Select object to dimension
> Picks a line, arc, polyline, etc.; the individual segments of a polyline are dimensioned.

Specify dimension line location
> Picks a point to locate the dimension line and text.

Mtext Changes the wording of the dimension text.

Text Changes the position of the text.

Angle Changes the angle of dimension text.

RELATED DIM COMMAND

DimRotated Draws an angular dimension line with perpendicular extension line.

Editing dimensions with grips

Dimensions may be edited directly without first invoking an editing command. Click the dimension once to display grips (small blue squares). Double-click the dimension to display the **Properties** window; see the **Properties** command.

LINEAR DIMENSIONS

Grips change the location of the dimension line, text, and extension lines.

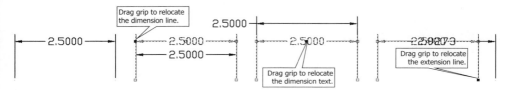

ALIGNED DIMENSIONS

Grips change the location of the dimension line, text, and angle of entire dimension.

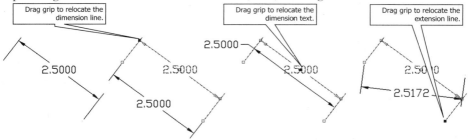

ANGULAR DIMENSIONS

Grips change the location of the dimension line, text, arrowhead location, and extension lines.

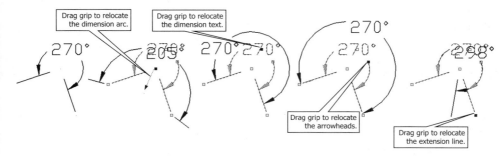

DIAMETER AND RADIUS DIMENSIONS

Grips change the location of the dimension line, text, and centermark.

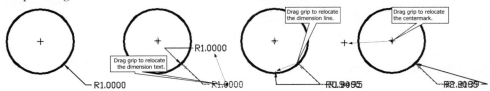

ORIDINATE DIMENSIONS

Grips change the location of the ordinate line, text, and endpoint.

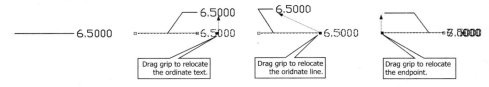

LEADER DIMENSIONS

Grips allow you to change the location of the dimension line, text, and extension lines.

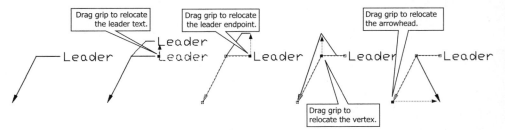

DimAngular

Rel 13 Draws a dimension that measures an angle.

Command	Alias	Ctrl+	F-key	Alt+	Menu Bar	Tablet
dimangular	dan	...	...	NA	Dimension	X3
	dimang				⌖Angular	

```
Command: dimangular
Select arc, circle, line, or <specify vertex>: [pick]
Specify dimension arc line location or [Mtext/Text/
    Angle]: [pick]
Dimension text = nnn
```

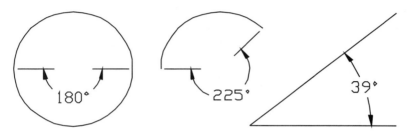

COMMAND LINE OPTIONS

Select arc   Measures the angle of the arc.
Circle   Prompts you to pick two points on the circle.
Line   Prompts you to pick two lines.
Specify vertex   Prompts you to pick points to make an angle.

Specify dimension arc/line location
                     Specifies the location of the angular dimension.
Mtext   Changes the wording of the dimension text.
Text   Changes the position of the text.
Angle   Changes the angle of the dimension text.

RELATED DIM COMMANDS

DimCenter   Places a centermark at the center of an arc or circle.
DimRadius   Dimensions the radius of an arc or circle.

DimBaseline

Rel 13 Draws linear dimension from the previous starting point.

Command	Alias	Ctrl+	F-key	Alt+	Menu Bar	Tablet
dimbaseline	dba	...	...	NB	Dimension	...
	dimbase				⸂Baseline	

```
Command: dimbaseline
Specify a second extension line origin or [Undo/Select]
   <Select>: [pick]
Dimension text = nnn
Specify a second extension line origin or [Undo/Select]
   <Select>: Esc
```

COMMAND LINE OPTIONS

Specify a second extension line origin

Positions the extension line of the next baseline dimension.

Select Prompts you to select the originating dimension.

Undo Undoes the previous baseline dimension.

[Esc] Exits the command.

RELATED DIM COMMANDS

Continue Continues linear dimensioning from last extension point.

QDim Creates a continuous or baseline dimension quickly.

RELATED DIM VARIABLES

DimDli Specifies the distance between baseline dimension lines.

DimSe1 Suppresses the first extension line.

DimSe2 Suppresses the second extension line.

DimCenter

Rel 13 Draws centermarks and lines on arcs and circles.

Command	Alias	Ctrl+	F-key	Alt+	Menu Bar	Tablet
dimcenter	dce	...	...	NM	Dimension	X2
					↳Center Mark	

```
Command: dimcenter
Select arc or circle: [pick]
```

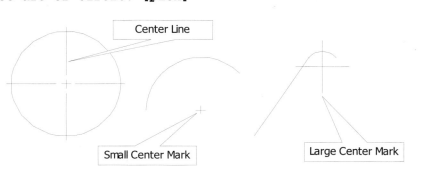

Center Line

Small Center Mark

Large Center Mark

COMMAND LINE OPTION

Select arc or circle

Places the centermark at the center of the selected arc, circle, or polyarc.

RELATED DIM COMMANDS

DimAngular Dimensions arcs and circles.
DimDiameter Dimensions arcs and circles by diameter value.
DimRadius Dimensions arcs and circles by radius value.

RELATED DIM VARIABLE

DimCen Size and type of the center mark:

DimCen	Meaning
negative value	Draws center marks and lines.
0	No center mark or center lines drawn.
positive value	Draws center marks.
0.09	Default value.

⊞ DimContinue

<u>Rel 13</u> Continues a dimension from the second extension line of the previous dimension.

Command	Alias	Ctrl+	F-key	Alt+	Menu Bar	Tablet
dimcontinue	dco	...	...	NC	Dimension	...
	dimcont				⤷Continue	

```
Command: dimcontinue
Specify a second extension line origin or [Undo/Select]
   <Select>: [pick]
Dimension text = nnn
Specify a second extension line origin or [Undo/Select]
   <Select>: Esc
```

|← 2.5000 →|← 1.5000 →|← 1.5000 →|

Original Dimension   Continued Dimension   Continued Dimension

COMMAND LINE OPTIONS

Specify a second extension line origin
Positions the extension line of the next continued dimension.

Select   Prompts you to select the originating dimension.

Undo   Undoes the previous continue dimension.

[Esc]   Exits the command.

RELATED DIM COMMANDS

DimBaseline   Continues dimensioning from first extension point.

QDim   Creates a continuous or baseline dimension quickly.

RELATED DIM VARIABLES

DimDli   Sets the distance between continuous dimension lines.

DimSe1   Suppresses the first extension line.

DimSe2   Suppresses the second extension line.

DimDiameter

Draws a diameter dimension on arcs, circles, and polyline arcs
(formerly the Dim:Diameter command).

Command	Alias	Ctrl+	F-key	Alt+	Menu Bar	Tablet
dimdiameter	ddi	...	...	ND	Dimension	X4
	dimdia				⌂Diameter	

```
Command: diameter
Select arc or circle: [pick]
Dimension text = nnn
Specify dimension line location or [Mtext/Text/Angle]: [pick]
```

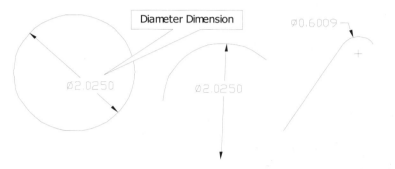

Diameter Dimension

COMMAND LINE OPTIONS

Select arc or circle
    Selects an arc, circle, or polyarc.
Specify dimension line location
    Specifies the location of the angular dimension.
Mtext   Changes the wording of the dimension text.
Text   Changes the position of the text.
Angle   Changes the angle of dimension text.

RELATED DIM COMMANDS

DimCenter   Marks the center point of arcs and circles.
DimRadius   Draws the radius dimension of arcs and circles.

TIP

■ To include the diameter symbol, use the **%%d** code or the Unicode **\U+2205** .

DimDisassociate

<u>2002</u>   Converts associative dimensions to non-associative (*the AutoCAD command that's most difficult to spell correctly*).

Command	Alias	Ctrl+	F-key	Alt+	Menu Bar	Tablet
dimdisassociate	...	...	...	...	...	...

```
Command: dimdisassociate
Select dimensions to disassociate...
Select objects: all
58 found.
4 were on a locked layer.
18 were not in current space.
Select objects: ENTER
36 disassociated.
```

COMMAND LINE OPTION

Select objects Selects dimensions to convert to non-associative type.

RELATED DIM COMMANDS

DimReassociate
　　　　Converts dimensions from non-associative to associative.
DimRegen   Makes all dimensions associative automatically.

RELATED SYSTEM VARIABLE

DimAssoc   Determines whether newly created dimensions are associative:

DimAssoc	Meaning
0	Dimension is created "exploded," where each part (such as dimension line, arrowheads) is an individual, ungrouped object.
1	Dimension is created as a single object, but is not associative.
2	Dimension is created as a single object, and is associative (default).

TIPS

■ As you select objects, this command ignores non-dimensions, dimensions on locked layers, as well as those not in the current space (model or paper).

■ The command displays a report of filtered and disassociated dimensions.

■ The effect of this command can be reversed with the **U** and the **DimReassociate** commands.

DimEdit

<u>Rel 13</u> Applies editing changes to the dimension text.

Command	Alias	Ctrl+	F-key	Alt+	Menu Bar	Tablet
dimedit	ded	...	...	NQ	Dimension	Y1
	dimed				↳Oblique	

Command: **dimedit**
Enter type of dimension editing [Home/New/Rotate/Oblique]
    <Home>: **ENTER**
Select objects: **[pick]**
n found, *n* total Select objects: **ENTER**

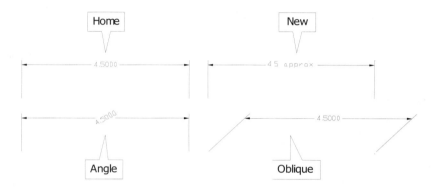

COMMAND LINE OPTIONS

Angle   Rotates the dimension text.
Home   Returns the dimension text to original position.
Oblique   Rotates the extension lines.
New   Allows editing of the dimension text.

RELATED DIM COMMANDS
All.

RELATED DIM VARIABLES
Most.

TIPS

■ When you enter dimension text with the **DimEdit** command's **New** option, AutoCAD recognizes the <> metacharacters represent the existing text.

■ Use the **Oblique** option to angle dimension lines by 30 degrees, suitable for isometric drawings; use the **Style** command to oblique text by 30 degrees. See the **Isometric** command.

■ **DimEdit** operates differently when used on the command line versus from the menu bar; the **Oblique** option is the default when selected from the menu bar.

⊞ DimLinear

<u>Rel 13</u> Draws horizontal dimensions.

Command	Alias	Ctrl+	F-key	Alt+	Menu Bar	Tablet
dimlinear	dli	...	...	NL	Dimension	W5
	dimlin				⌙Linear	

```
Command: dimlinear
Specify first extension line origin or <select object>:
[pick]
Specify second extension line origin: [pick]
Specify dimension line location or
    [Mtext/Text/Angle/Horizontal/Vertical/Rotated]: [pick]
Dimension text = nnn
```

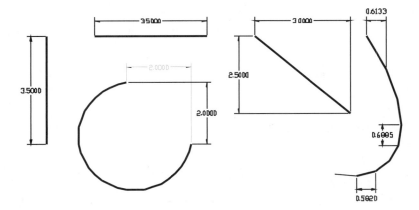

COMMAND LINE OPTIONS

Specify first extension line origin
           Specifies the location of the origin for the first extension line.
Select object   Dimensions a line, arc, or circle automatically.

Specify dimension line location
           Specifies the location of the angular dimension.
Mtext   Displays the **Multiline Text Editor** dialog box, which allows you to modify the dimension text; see the **MText** command.
Text   Prompts you to replace the dimension text on the command line: 'Enter dimension text <*nnn*>'.
Angle   Changes the angle of dimension text: 'Specify angle of dimension text:'.
Horizontal Forces dimension to be horizontal.
Vertical   Forces dimension to be vertical.
Rotated   Forces dimension to be rotated.

RELATED DIM COMMANDS

DimAligned Draws linear dimensions aligned with objects.
QDim   Dimensions an object quickly.

DimOrdinate

__Rel 13__ Draws an x or y ordinate dimension.

Command	Alias	Ctrl+	F-key	Alt+	Menu Bar	Tablet
dimordinate	dor	...	...	NO	Dimension	W3
	dimord				⌐Ordinate	

```
Command: dimordinate
Specify feature location: [pick]
Specify leader endpoint or [Xdatum/Ydatum/Mtext/Text/
   Angle]: [pick]
Dimension text = 10.5904
```

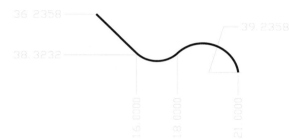

COMMAND LINE OPTIONS

Xdatum	Forces x ordinate dimension.
Ydatum	Forces y ordinate dimension.
Mtext	Displays the **Multiline Text Editor** dialog box, which allows you to modify the dimension text; see the **MText** command.
Text	Prompts you to replace the dimension text on the command line: 'Enter dimension text *<nnn>*'.
Angle	Changes the angle of dimension text: 'Specify angle of dimension text:'.

RELATED DIM COMMANDS

Leader	Draws leader dimensions.
Tolerance	Draws geometric tolerances.

RELATED TOOLBAR ICONS

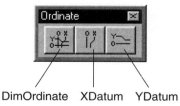

DimOrdinate   XDatum   YDatum

TIP

- AutoCAD misuses the term "ordinate," which by definition is the distance from the x axis only.

DimOverride

<u>Rel 13</u> Overrides the currently-set dimension variables.

Command	Alias	Ctrl+	F-key	Alt+	Menu Bar	Tablet
dimoverride	dov	...	...	NV	Dimension	Y4
	dimover				⌐Override	

Command: **dimoverride**
Enter dimension variable name to override or [Clear overrides]: **[enter dimension variable name]**
Enter new value for dimension variable <*nnn*>: **[enter new value]**
Select objects: **[pick]**
Select objects: Enter

COMMAND LINE OPTIONS

Dimension variable to override
          Requires you to enter the name of the dimension variable.
Clear   Removes the override.
New Value   Specifies the new value of the dimvar.
Select objects Selects the dimension objects to which the change should apply.

RELATED DIM COMMAND
DimStyle   Creates and modifies dimension styles.

RELATED DIM VARIABLES
All dimension variables.

DimRadius

Draws radial dimensions on circles, arcs, and polyline arcs.

Command	Alias	Ctrl+	F-key	Alt+	Menu Bar	Tablet
dimradius	dra	...	...	NR	Dimension	X5
	dimrad				⌂Radius	

```
Command: dimradius
Select arc or circle: [pick]
Dimension text = nnn
Specify dimension line location or [Mtext/Text/
    Angle]: [pick]
```

COMMAND LINE OPTIONS

Select arc or circle
> Selects the arc, circle, or polyarc to dimension.

Specify dimension line location
> Specifies the location of the angular dimension.

Mtext
> Displays the **Multiline Text Editor** dialog box, which allows you to modify the dimension text; see the **MText** command.

Text
> Prompts you to replace the dimension text at the command line: "Enter dimension text <*nnn*>".

Angle
> Changes the angle of dimension text, and prompts: "Specify angle of dimension text:".

RELATED DIM COMMANDS

DimCenter Draws center mark on arcs and circles.
DimDiameter Draws diameter dimensions on arcs and circles.

RELATED DIM VARIABLE

DimCen Determines the size of the center mark.

DimReassociate

2002 Associates dimensions with objects.

Command	Alias	Ctrl+	F-key	Alt+	Menu Bar	Tablet
dimreassociate	...	...	...	NN	Dimension	X4
					↳Reassociate Dimensions	

```
Command: dimreassociate
Select dimensions to reassociate...
Select objects: all
58 found. 4 were on a locked layer.
18 were not in current space.
Select objects: ENTER
Specify first extension line origin or [Select object]: [pick]
Select are or circle <next>: [pick or ENTER]
```

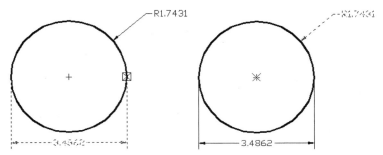

The boxed X indiactes that the linear dimension is associated with the circle; the X indicates the radius dimension is not associated.

COMMAND LINE OPTIONS

Select objects Selects the dimensions to reassociate.

Specify first extension line origin
> Picks a point to which the dimension should be associated.

Select are or circle
> Picks a circle or arc to which the dimension should be associated.

Next Goes to the next circle or arc.

RELATED DIM COMMANDS

DimDisassociate
> Converts dimensions from associative to non-associative.

DimRegen Makes all dimensions associative automatically.

TIPS

■ As you select objects, this command ignores non-dimensions, dimensions on locked layers, as well as those not in the current space (model or paper).

■ AutoCAD displays a boxed X to indicate the object to which the dimension is associated; an unboxed X indicates an unassociated dimension. The markers disappear when a wheelmouse performs a zoom or pan.

DimRegen

Updates the locations of associative dimensions.

Command	Alias	Ctrl+	F-key	Alt+	Menu Bar	Tablet
dimregen	...	...	...	...	...	...

Command: **dimregen**

COMMAND LINE OPTIONS
None.

RELATED DIM COMMANDS
DimDisassociate
> Converts dimensions from associative to non-associative.

DimReassociate
> Converts dimensions from non-associative to associative.

TIPS
■ This command is meant for use after three conditions:

- The drawing has been edited by a version of AutoCAD prior to 2002.

- The drawing contains externally-referenced dimensions, and the xref has been edited.

- The drawing is in layout mode, model space is active, and a wheelmouse has been used to pan or zoom.

DimStyle

Rel 13 Creates and edits dimstyles (*short for DIMension STYLEs; formerly the **DDim** command*).

Command	Alias	Ctrl+	F-key	Alt+	Menu Bar	Tablet
dimstyle	d	...	...	NS	Dimension	Y5
	dst				⌐Style	
	dimsty			OD	Format	
	ddim				⌐Dimension Style	
-dimstyle	...	...	...	NU	Dimension	
					⌐Update	

```
Command: dimstyle
```
Displays dialog box:

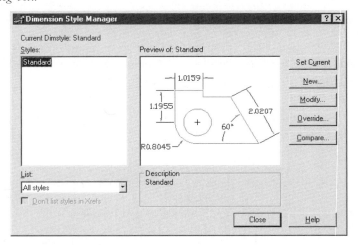

DIALOG BOX OPTIONS

Styles Lists the names of dimension styles in the drawing.

List Modifies the style names listed under **Styles**: **All styles** or **Styles in use**.

Don't list styles in Xrefs
On: Dimension styles found in externally-referenced drawings are not listed.
Off: Xref dimension styles are listed under **Styles** (default).

Preview Displays a preview of the elements of the current dimension style.

Description Names the current dimstyle; shows changes to dimension variables, if any.

Set Current Sets the selected style as the current dimension style.

New Creates a new dimension style via **Create New Dimension Style** dialog box.

Modify Modifies an existing dimension style; displays **Modify Dimension Style** dialog box.

Override Allows temporary changes to a dimension style; displays **Override Dimension Style** dialog box.

Compare Lists the differences between dimension variables of two styles; displays the **Compare Dimension Styles** dialog box.

CURSOR MENU OPTIONS

Right-click a dimension style name under **Styles:**

Set Current   Sets the selected dimension style as the current style.

Rename   Renames the dimensions style name.

Delete   Erases the dimension style from the drawing; you cannot erase the STANDARD style, or styles that are in use.

Create New Dimension Style dialog box:

When creating a new dimension style, you typically make changes to an existing style.

New Style Name
     Specifies the name of the new dimension style.

Start With   Lists the names of the current dimension style(s), which are used as the template for the new dimension style.

Use for   Creates a substyle that applies to a specific type of dimension type: linear, angular, radius, diameter, ordinate, leaders and tolerances.

Continue   Continues to the next dialog box, **New Dimension Style**.

Cancel   Dismisses this dialog box, and returns to the **Dimension Style Manager** dialog box.

New Dimension Style dialog box:

O K   Records the changes made to dimension properties, and returns to the **Dimension Manager** dialog box.

Cancel   Cancels the changes, and returns to the **Dimension Manager** dialog box.

Lines and Arrows tab:

Sets the format of dimension lines, extension lines, arrowheads, and center marks.

Dimension Lines section

Color Specifies the color of the dimension line; select **Other** to display the **Select Color** dialog box (stored in dimension variable **DimClrD**; default = ByBlock).

Lineweight Specifies the lineweight of the dimension line (**DimLwD**; default = ByBlock).

Extend beyond ticks
Specifies the distance the dimension line extends beyond the extension line; used with oblique, architectural, tick, integral, and no arrowheads (**DimDlE**; default = 0).

Baseline spacing
Specifies the spacing between the dimension lines of a baseline dimension (**DimDlI**; default = 0.38).

Suppress Suppresses the first and second dimension lines when outside the extension lines (**DimSd1** and **DimSd1**; default = off).

Extension Lines section:

Color Specifies the color of the extension line; select **Other** to display the **Select Color** dialog box (stored in dimension variable **DimClrE** ; default=ByBlock).

Lineweight Specifies the lineweight of the extension line (**DimLwE**; default=ByBlock).

Extend beyond dim lines
Specifies the distance the extension line extends beyond the dimension line; used with oblique, architectural, tick, integral, and no arrowheads (**DimExe**; default = 0.18).

Offset from origin

Specifies the distance from the origin point to the start of the extension lines (**DimExO**; default = 0.0625).

Suppress   Suppresses the first and second extension lines (**DimSe1** and **DimSde1**; default = off).

Arrowheads options:

1st   Specifies the name of the arrowhead to use for for the first end of the dimension line (**DimBlk1**; default = closed filled).

➤ Closed filled
▷ Closed blank
⇨ Closed
● Dot
✓ Architectural tick
╱ Oblique
⇒ Open
⦵ Origin indicator
⦵ Origin indicator 2
→ Right angle
⇉ Open 30
◆ Dot small
⊸ Dot blank
○ Dot small blank
⊲ Box
◀ Box filled
◁ Datum triangle
◀ Datum triangle filled
ʃ Integral
None

To use a custom arrowhead, select **User Arrow** to display the **Select Custom Arrow Block** dialog box:

2nd   Specifies the arrowhead for the second dimension line; select **User Arrow** to display the **Select Custom Arrow Block** dialog box (**DimBlk2**; default = closed filled).

Leader   Specifies the arrowhead for the leader; select **User Arrow** to display the **Select Custom Arrow Block** dialog box (**DimLdrBlk**; default = closed filled).

Arrow Size   Specifies the the size of arrowheads (**DimASz**; default = 0.18).

Center Marks for Circles options:

Type   Specifies the type of center mark (**DimCen**; default = 0.09):

Type	Meaning
Mark	Places a center mark (**DimCen** > 0).
Line	Places a center mark and centerlines (**DimCen** < 0).
None	Places no center mark or centerline (**DimCen**=0).

Size   Specifies the size of the center mark or centerline (**DimCen**; default = 0.09).

Text tab:

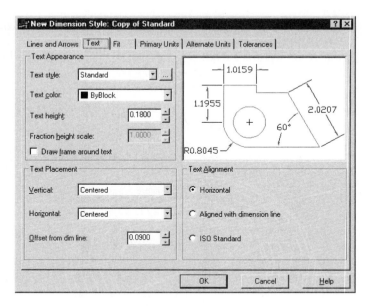

Text Appearance *options:*

Text style Specifies the text style name for dimension text (**DimTxSty**; default = Standard).

... Displays the **Text Style** dialog box; see the **Style** command.

Text color Specifies the color of the dimension line; select **Other** to display the **Select Color** dialog box (**DimClrT**; default = ByBlock).

Text height Specifies the height of the dimension text, when the height defined by the text style is 0 (**DimTxt**; default = 0.18).

Fraction height scale
Scales fraction text height relative to dimension text; AutoCAD multiples this value by the text height (**DimTFac**; default = 1.0).

Draw frame around text
Draws a rectangle around dimension text; when on, dimension variable **DimGap** is set to a negative value (**DimGap**; default = off).

Text Placement *options:*

Vertical Specifies the vertical justification of dimension text relative to the dimension line (**DimTad**; default = 1):

Vertical	Meaning
Centered	Centers dimension text in the dimension line (**DimTad** = 0).
Above	Places text above dimension line (**DimTad** = 1).
Outside	Places text on the side of the dimension line farthest from the first defining point (**DimTad** = 2).
JIS	Places text in conformity with JIS (**DimTad**= 3).

Horizontal   Specifies the horizontal justification of dimension text along the dimension and extension lines (**DimJust**; default = 0):

Horizontal	Meaning
Centered	Centers dimension text along the dimension line between the extension lines (**DimJust** = 0).
1st Extension Line	Left-justifies the text with the first extension line (**DimJust** = 1).
2nd Extension Line	Right-justifies the text with the second extension line (**DimJust** = 2).
Over 1st Extension Line	Places the text over the first extension line (**DimJust** = 3).
Over 2nd Extension Line	Places thje text over the second extension line (**DimJust** = 4).

Offset from dimension line

Specifies the text gap, the distance between dimension text and the dimension line (**DimGap**; default = 0.09).

Text Alignment options:

Horizontal   Forces dimension text to be always horizontal (**DimTih** = on; **DimToh** = on).

Aligned with dimension line

Forces dimension text to be aligned with the dimension line (**DimTih** = off; **DimToh** = off).

ISO Standard Forces text to be aligned with dimension line when inside the extension lines; forces text to be horizontal when outside the extension lines (**DimTih** = off; **DimToh** = on).

Fit tab:

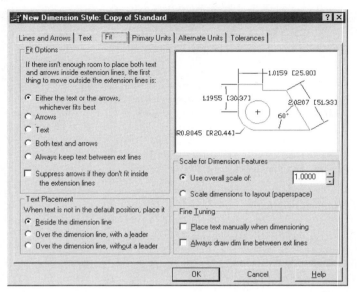

Fit Options options:

If there isn't enough room to place both text and arrows inside extension lines, the first thing to move outside the extension lines is:

- **Either the text or the arrows, whichever fits best:** Places dimension text and arrowheads between the extensions lines when space is available; when space is not available for both, the text or the arrowheads are placed outside the extension lines, whichever fits best; if there is room for neither, both are placed outside the extension lines (**DimAtFit** = 3; default).

- **Arrows:** places arrowheads between extension lines when there is not enough room for arrowheads and dimension text (**DimAtFit** = 2).

- **Text:** places text between extension lines when there is not enough room for arrowheads and dimension text (**DimAtFit** = 1).

- **Both text and arrows:** places both outside the extension lines when there is not enough room for dimension text and arrowheads (**DimAtFit** = 0).

- **Always keep text between ext lines:** forces text between the extension lines (**DimTix**; default = off).

Suppress arrows if they don't fit inside the extension lines

Suppresses arrowheads when there is not enough room between the extension lines.

Text Placement:

- **Beside the dimension line:** places dimension text beside the dimension line (DimTMove = 0; default).
- **Over the dimension line, with a leader:** draws a leader when dimension text is moved away from the dimension line (DimTMove = 1).
- **Over the dimension line, without a leader:** does not draw a leader when dimension text is moved away from the dimension line (DimTMove = 2).

Scale for Dimension Features :

- **Use overall scale of:** specifies the scale factor for all dimensions in the drawing; affects text and arrowhead sizes, distances, and spacings (**DimScale**; default = 1.0).
- **Scale dimension to layout (paper space):** determines the scale factor of dimensions in layout mode; based on the scale factor between the current model space viewport and the layout (**DimScale** = 0; default = off).

Fine Tuning options:

Place text manually when dimensioning

Places text at the position picked at the 'Dimension line location' prompt (**DimUpt**; default = off).

Always draw dim line between ext lines

Forces the dimension line between the extension lines (**DimTofl**; default = off).

Primary Units tab:

Linear Dimensions options:

Unit Format Specifies the linear units format; does not apply to angular dimensions
(**DimLUnit**; default = Decimal):

DimLUnit	Meaning
1	Scientific.
2	Decimal (default).
3	Engineering.
4	Architectural.
5	Fractional.
6	Windows desktop setting.

Precision Specifies the number of decimal places (or fractional accuracy) for linear
dimensions (**DimDec**; default = 4).

Fraction Format

Specifies the stacking format of fractions (**DimFrac**; default = 0):

DimFrac	Meaning
0	Horizontal stacked: $\frac{1}{2}$ (default).
1	Diagonal stacked: ½
2	Not stacked: 1/2.

Decimal Separator

Specifies the separator for decimal formats (**DimDSep**; default = .).

Round Off Specifies the format for rounding dimension values; does not apply to
angular dimensions (**DimRnd**; default = 0).

Prefix	Specifies a prefix for dimension text (**DimPost**; default = nothing); you can use the following control codes to show special characters:

Control Code	Meaning
%%nnn	Character specified by ASCII number nnn.
%%o	Turns on and off overscoring.
%%u	Turns on and off <u>underscoring</u>.
%%d	Degrees symbol (°).
%%p	Plus/minus symbol (±).
%%c	Diameter symbol (Ø).
%%%	Percentage sign (%).

Suffix   Specifies a suffix for dimension text (**DimPost**; default = nothing); you can use the control codes listed above to show special characters.

Measurement Scale *options:*

Scale factor   Specifies a scale factor for linear measurements, except for angular dimensions (**DimLFac**; default = 1.0); use this, for example, to change dimension values from imperial to metric.

Apply to layout dimensions only

Specifies that the scale factor is applied only to dimensions created in layout mode or paper space (stored as a negative value in **DimLFac**; default = off).

Zero Suppression options:

Leading   Suppresses leading zeros in all decimal dimensions (**DimZin** = 4).
Trailing   Suppresses trailing zeros in all decimal dimensions (**DimZin** = 8).
0 Feet   Suppresses zero feet of feet-and-inches dimensions (**DimZin** = 0).
0 Inches   Suppresses zero inches of feet-and-inches dimensions (**DimZin** = 2).

DimZin	Meaning
0	Suppresses zero feet and precisely zero inches (default).
1	Includes zero feet and precisely zero inches.
2	Includes zero feet and suppresses zero inches.
3	Includes zero inches and suppresses zero feet.
4	Suppresses leading zeros in decimal dimensions.
8	Suppresses trailing zeros in decimal dimensions .
12	Suppresses leading and trailing zeros.

Angular Dimensions *options:*

Units Format   Specifies the format of angular dimensions (**DimAUnit**; default = 0):

DimAUnit	Meaning
0	Decimal degrees (default).
1	Degrees/minutes/seconds.
2	Gradians.
3	Radians.

Precision   Specifies the precision of angular dimensions (**DimADec**; default = 0).

Zero Suppression *options:* same as for linear dimensions (**DimAZin**; default = 0).

Alternate Units tab:

Display alternate units
     Adds alternate units to dimension text (**DimAlt**; default = off).

Alternate Units options:
Unit Format   Specifies the alternate units formats (**DimAltU**; default = Decimal).
Precision   Specifies the number of decimal places or fractional accuracy (**DimAltD**; default=2).
Multiplier for alt units
     Specifies the conversion factor between primary and alternate units (**DimAltF**; default = 25.4).
Round distances to
     Specifies the format for rounding dimension values; does not apply to angular dimensions (**DimAltRnd**; default = 0.0000).
Prefix   Specifies a prefix for dimension text (**DimAPost**; default = nothing); you can use control codes to show special characters.
Suffix   Specifies a suffix for dimension text (**DimAPost**; default = nothing).

Zero Suppression options:
Leading   Suppresses leading zeros in all decimal dimensions (**DimAltZ** = 4).
Trailing   Suppresses trailing zeros in all decimal dimensions (**DimAltZ** = 8).
0 Feet   Suppresses zero feet of feet-and-inches dimensions (**DimAltZ** = 0).
0 Inches   Suppresses zero inches of feet-and-inches dimensions (**DimAltZ** = 2).

Placement:
    • **After primary units:** places alternate units behind the primary units (**DimAPost**).
    • **Below primary units:** places alternate units below the primary units.

Tolerances tab:

Tolerance Format options:

Method Specifies the tolerance format:
- **None** does not display tolerances (**DimTol** = 0; default).
- **Symmetrical** places a ± after the dimension (**DimTol**=0; **DimLim**=0).
- **Deviation** places + and − symbols (**DimTol** = 1; **DimLim** = 1).
- **Limits** places maximum over minimum value (**DimTol**=0; **DimLim**=1):
  Maximum value = dimension value + upper value.
  Minimum value = dimension value - lower value
- **Basic** boxes the dimension text (**DimGap**=negative value).

Precision Specifies the number of decimal places for tolerance values (**DimTDec**; default=4).

Upper value Specifies the upper tolerance value (**DimTp**; default = 0).

Lower value Specifies the lower tolerance value (**DimTm**; default = 0).

Scaling for height
  Specifies the scale factor for tolerance text height (**DimTFac**; default = 1.0).

Vertical position
  Specifies the vertical text position for symmetrical and deviation tolerances (**DimTolJ**; default = 1):

Vertical	Meaning
Top	Aligns the tolerance text with the top of the dimension text (**DimTolJ** = 2).
Middle	Aligns the tolerance text with the middle of the dimension text (**DimTolJ** = 1).
Bottom	Aligns the tolerance text with the bottom of the dimension text (**DimTolJ** = 0).

Zero Suppression *options:*

Leading   Suppresses leading zeros in all decimal dimensions (**DimTZin** = 4).

Trailing   Suppresses trailing zeros in all decimal dimensions (**DimTZin** = 8).

0 Feet   Suppresses zero feet of feet-and-inches dimensions (**DimTZin** = 0).

0 Inches   Suppresses zero inches of feet-and-inches dimensions (**DimTZin** = 2).

Alternate Unit Tolerance *options:*

Precision   Specifies the precision — the number of decimal places — of tolerance text (**DimAltTd**; default = 2).

Zero Suppression *options:* the same as for tolerance format; stored in **DimAltTz.**

Modify Dimension Style dialog box:
This dialog box is identical to the **New Dimension Style** *dialog box.*

Override Dimension Style dialog box:
This dialog box is identical to the **New Dimension Style** *dialog box.*

Compare Dimension Styles dialog box:
The list is blank when AutoCAD finds no differences. When **With** *is set to* **<none>** *or the same style as* **Compare**, *AutoCAD displays all dimension variables.*

Compare   Displays the name of one dimension style.

With   Displays the name of the second dimension style.

Copy to Clipboard

    Copies the style comparison text to the Clipboard, which can be pasted in another Windows application.

Description   Describes the dimension variable.

Variable   Names the dimension variable.

Close   Closes the dialog box.

-DIMSTYLE COMMAND

Command: **-dimstyle**
Current dimension style: Standard
Enter a dimension style option
[Save/Restore/STatus/Variables/Apply/?] <Restore>: **V**
Current dimension style: Standard
Enter a dimension style name, [?] or <select dimension>:
   ENTER
Select dimension: **[pick]**
Current dimension style: Standard

COMMAND LINE OPTIONS

Save	Saves current dimvar settings as a named dimstyle.
Restore	Sets dimvar settings from a named dimstyle.
STatus	Lists dimvars and current settings.
Variables	Lists dimvars and their current settings.
Apply	Updates selected dimension objects with current dimstyle settings.
?	Lists names of dimstyles stored in drawing.

INPUT OPTIONS

~dimvar	(*Tilde*) Lists the differences between current and selected dimstyle.
ENTER	Lists the dimvar settings for selected dimension object.

RELATED DIM COMMANDS

DDim	Changes dimvar settings.
DimScale	Determines the scale of dimension text.

RELATED DIM VARIABLES

All
DimStyle   Contains the name of the current dimstyle.

TIPS

■ At the 'Dim' prompt, the **Style** command sets the text style for the dimension text and does *not* select a dimension style.

■ Dimstyles cannot be stored to disk, except in a drawing.

■ Read dimstyles from other drawings with the **XBind Dimstyle** command.

■ Dimstyles stored in prototype drawings:

Dimension Style	Drawing File
AutoCAD default	Acad.Dwg
American architectural	Us_Arch.Dwg
American mechanical	Us_Mech.Dwg
ISO	AcadIso.Dwg
JIS architectural	Jis_Arch.Dwg
JIS mechanical	Jis_Mech.Dwg

DimTEdit

Rel 13   Dynamically changes the location and orientation of text in dimensions.

Command	Alias	Ctrl+	F-key	Alt+	Menu Bar	Tablet
dimtedit	...	...	...	NX	Dimension ⃔Align Text	Y2

```
Command: dimtedit
Select dimension: [pick]
Specify new location for dimension text or [Left/Right/
    Center/Home/Angle]: [pick]
```

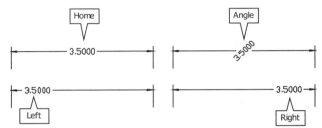

COMMAND LINE OPTIONS

Select dimension
                Selects the dimension to edit.
Angle   Rotates dimension text.
Center   Centers the text on the dimension line.
Home   Returns dimension text to original position.
Left   Moves dimension text to the left.
Right   Moves dimension text to the right.

RELATED DIM VARIABLES

DimSho   Dimension text is updated dynamically while dragged.
DimTih   Dimension text is drawn horizontally or aligned with dimension line.
DimToh   Dimension text is forced inside dimension lines.

RELATED TOOLBAR ICONS

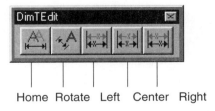

Home Rotate Left Center Right

TIPS

■ This command works only with associative dimensions; use the **DdEdit** command to edit text in non-associative dimensions.

■ An angle of 0 returns dimension text to its default orientation.

'Dist

V. 1.0 Lists the 3D distances and angles between two points (*short for DISTance*).

Command	Alias	Ctrl+	F-key	Alt+	Menu Bar	Tablet
'dist	di	...	...	TYD	Tools ⬑Inquiry ⬑Distance	T8

```
Command: dist
Specify first point: [pick]
Specify second point: [pick]
```

Example result:
```
Distance=17.38, Angle in XY Plane=358, Angle from XY Plane=0
Delta X = 16.3000, Delta Y = -7.3000,  Delta Z = 0.0000
```

COMMAND LINE OPTIONS

Specify first point
> Determines start point of distance measurement.

Specify second point
> Determines end point.

RELATED COMMANDS

Area	Calculates the area and perimeter of objects.
Id	Lists the 3D coordinates of a point.
Length	Reports the length of open objects.
List	Lists information about selected objects.

RELATED SYSTEM VARIABLE

Distance   Last calculated distance.

TIPS

- Use object snaps to measure precisely between two geometric features.

- When the z-coordinate is left out, **Dist** assumes the current elevation for z.

Divide

V. 2.5 Places points or blocks at equally-divided distances along an object.

Command	Alias	Ctrl+	F-key	Alt+	Menu Bar	Tablet
divide	div	...	...	DOD	Draw	V13
					⌐Point	
					⌐Divide	

```
Command: divide
Select object to divide: [pick]
Enter the number of segments or [Block]: [enter a number]
```

Polyline (left) divided by ten points (right).

COMMAND LINE OPTIONS

Select object to divide
> Selects a single open or closed object.

Enter the number of segments
> Specifies the number of segments; must be a number between 2 and 32767.

Block options:
```
Enter name of block to insert: [enter name of block]
Align block with object? [Yes/No] <Y>:
Enter the number of segments: [enter a number]
```
Enter name of block to insert
> Specifies the name of a block in the current dawing.

Align block with object
> Aligns the block's x axis with the object.

RELATED COMMANDS

Block	Creates the block to use with the **Divide** command.
Insert	Places a single block in the drawing.
MInsert	Places an array of blocks in the drawing.
Measure	Divides an entity into measured distances.

RELATED SYSTEM VARIABLES

PdMode	Sets the style of point drawn.
PdSize	Sets the size of the point, in pixels.

TIPS

■ The first dividing point on a closed polyline is its initial vertex; on circles, the first dividing point is in the 0-degree direction from the center.

■ The points or blocks are placed in the **Previous** selection set, so that you can select them with the next 'Select Objects' prompt.

◎ Donut or Doughnut

V. 2.5   Draws solid circles with a pair of wide polyline arcs.

Command	Alias	Ctrl+	F-key	Alt+	Menu Bar	Tablet
donut	do	. . .	. . .	DD	Draw	K9
					↳Donut	
doughnut						

```
Command: donut
Specify inside diameter of donut <0.5000>: [enter number]
Specify outside diameter of donut <1.0000>: [enter number]
Specify center of donut or <exit>: [pick]
Specify center of donut or <exit>: ENTER
```

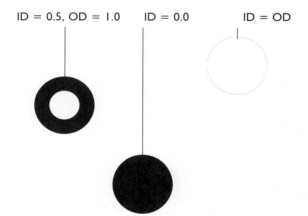

ID = 0.5, OD = 1.0   ID = 0.0   ID = OD

Default donut (left), solid donut (center), and polyline circle (right).

COMMAND LINE OPTIONS

Inside diameter Indicates the inner diameter by entering a number or picking two points.

Outside diameter

Indicates the outer diameter.

Center of donut

Indicates the donut's centerpoint by entering coordinates, or by picking a point.

exit   Exits the **Donut** command.

RELATED COMMAND

Circle   Draws a circle.

RELATED SYSTEM VARIABLES

DonutId   Specifies the current donut internal diameter.
DonutOd   Specifies the current donut outside diameter.
Fill   Toggles the filling of the donut.

TIP

■ Command automatically repeats itself until cancelled.

'Dragmode

V. 2.0 Controls the display of objects during dragging operations.

Command	Alias	Ctrl+	F-key	Alt+	Menu Bar	Tablet
'dragmode	...	...	...	...	...	...

```
Command: dragmode
Enter new value [ON/OFF/Auto] <Auto>:
```

Highlight image (center) and drag image (right).

COMMAND LINE OPTIONS

ON	Enables dragging display only with the **Drag** option.
OFF	Turns off all dragging displays.
Auto	Allows AutoCAD to determine when to display drag image.

COMMAND MODIFIER

Drag   Displays drag image when **DragMode** = on.

RELATED SYSTEM VARIABLES

DragMode   Current drag setting:

DragMode	Meaning
0	No drag image.
1	On if required.
2	Automatic.

Drag1   Drag regeneration rate (default = 10).
Drag2   Drag redraw rate (default = 25).

TIP

■ Turn off **DragMode** and **Highlight** in very large drawings to help speed up editing.

DrawOrder

Rel. 14 Controls the display of overlapping objects.

Command	Alias	Ctrl+	F-key	Alt+	Menu Bar	Tablet
draworder	dr	...	...	TO	Tools ↳Display Order	T9

```
Command: draworder
Select objects: [pick]
n found, n total Select objects: ENTER
Enter object ordering option [Above object/Under object/
    Front/Back] <Back>: a
Select reference object: [pick]
Regenerating model.
```

Illus   nce   Illustrated Quick Reference

*Text **under** solid (left) and text **above** solid (right).*

COMMAND LINE OPTIONS

Select objects Selects the objects to be moved.

Above object Forces selected objects to appear above the reference object.

Under object Forces selected objects to appear below the reference object.

Front Forces selected objects to the top of the display order.

Back Forces selected objects to the bottom of the display order.

Select reference object
Selects the object above or below which to place objects.

TIPS

■ When you pick more than one object for reordering, AutoCAD maintains the relative display order of the selected objects.

■ The order in which you select objects has no effect on drawing order.

■ *Caution!* AutoCAD has been known to not maintain the display order correctly.

'DSettings

2000 Controls the most-common settings for drafting operations (*short for Drafting SETTINGS; replaces the **DdRModes** command*).

Command	Alias	Ctrl+	F-key	Alt+	Menu Bar	Tablet
'dsettings	ds	...	...	TF	Tools	W10
	se				⬏Drafting Settings	
	ddrmodes					

+dsettings

Command: **+dsettings**
Tab Index <0>:

COMMAND LINE OPTION

Tab Index   Displays the **Drafting Settings** dialog box, with the associated tab:

Tab Index	Meaning
0	Displays the **Snap and Grid** tab (default).
1	Displays the **Polar Tracking** tab.
2	Displays the **Object Snap** tab.

Command: **dsettings**
Displays dialog box:

DIALOG BOX OPTIONS

Options	Displays the **Options** dialog box; see **Options**.
OK	Saves the changes to settings, and closes the dialog box.
Cancel	Discards the changes to settings, and closes the dialog box.

Snap and Grid tab:

```
┌─ Snap and Grid ┐
│  ☐ Snap On (F9)                    ☐ Grid On (F7)
│  ┌─Snap──────────────────┐  ┌─Grid──────────────────┐
│  │ Snap X spacing:  [0.5000]│  │ Grid X spacing:  [0.5000]│
│  │ Snap Y spacing:  [0.5000]│  │ Grid Y spacing:  [0.5000]│
│  │ Angle:           [0     ]│  └──────────────────────┘
│  │ X base:          [0.0000]│  ┌─Snap type & style────┐
│  │ Y base:          [0.0000]│  │  ⦿ Grid snap          │
│  └──────────────────────┘  │    ⦿ Rectangular snap   │
│  ┌─Polar spacing─────────┐  │    ○ Isometric snap     │
│  │ Polar distance [13.0000]│  │  ○ Polar snap          │
│  └──────────────────────┘  └──────────────────────┘
```

Snap On (F9)   Turns on and off snap mode (setting is stored in system variable **SnapMode**; default = off).

Snap options:
Snap X spacing   Specifies the snap spacing in the x direction (**SnapUnit**; default = 0.5).
Snap Y spacing   Specifies the snap spacing in the y direction (**SnapUnit**; default = 0.5).
Angle   Specifies the snap rotation angle (**SnapAng**; default = 0).
X base   Specifies the x coordinate for the snap origin (**SnapBase**; default = 0).
Y base   Specifies the y coordinate for the snap origin (**SnapBase**; default = 0).

Polar spacing options:
Polar distance   Specifies the snap distance, when **Snap type & style** is set to **Polar snap**; when 0, the polar snap distance is set to the value of **Snap X spacing** (**PolarDist**; default = 13).

Grid On (F7)   Turns on and off the grid display (**GridMode**; default = off).

Grid options:
Grid X spacing   Specifies the spacing of grid dots in the x direction; when 0, the grid spacing is set to the value of **Snap X spacing** (**GridUnit**; default = 0.5).
Grid Y spacing   Specifies the spacing of grid dots in the y direction; when 0, the grid spacing is set to the value of **Snap Y spacing** (**GridUnit**; default = 0.5).

Snap type & style options:
Grid snap   Specifies non-polar snap (**SnapType**; default = on).
Rectangular snap Specifies rectangular snap (**SnapStyl**; default = on).
Isometric snap Specifies isometric snap mode (**SnapStyl**; default = off).
Polar snap   Specifies polar snap (**SnapType**; default = on).

SnapType	SnapStyl	Meaning
0 (off)	0 (off)	Rectangular snap.
0 (off)	1 (on)	Isometric snap.
1 (on)	0 (off)	Polar snap.

Polar Tracking tab:

Polar Tracking On (F10)
> Turns on and off polar tracking (**AutoSnap**; default = off).

Polar Angle Settings *options:*

Increment angle
> Specifies the increment angle displayed by the polar tracking alignment path; select one of the preset angles — 90, 60, 45, 30, 22.5, 18, 15, 10, or 5 degrees — or type any value (**PolarAng**).

Additional angles
> Allows additional polar tracking angles to be displayed (**PolarMode**; default=off).

New
> Allows you to add up to ten polar tracking alignment angles (**PolarAddAng**; default = 0;15;23;45).

Delete
> Deletes additional angles.

Object Snap Tracking Settings *options:*

Track orthogonally only
> Displays orthogonal tracking paths when object snap tracking is on (**PolarMode**).

Track using all polar angle settings
> Tracks cursor along polar angle tracking path when object snap tracking is turned on (**PolarMode**).

Polar Angle Measurement *options:*

Absolute   Forces polar tracking angle along the current user coordinate system (UCS).

Relative to Last Segment
> Forces polar tracking angles on the last-created object.

Object Snap tab

| Object Snap |

☑ Object Snap On (F3)   ☐ Object Snap Tracking On (F11)

Object Snap modes

☐ ☐ Endpoint	⟓ ☐ Insertion		Select All
△ ☐ Midpoint	∟ ☐ Perpendicular		Clear All
○ ☐ Center	♡ ☐ Tangent		
⊠ ☐ Node	✕ ☐ Nearest		
◇ ☐ Quadrant	⊠ ☐ Apparent intersection		
✕ ☐ Intersection	∕∕ ☐ Parallel		
⋯ ☐ Extension			

To track from an Osnap point, pause over the point while in a command. A tracking vector appears when you move the cursor. To stop tracking, pause over the point again.

Object Snap On (F3)

    Turns on and off running object snaps (**OsMode**; default = off).

Object Snap Tracking On (F11)

    Turns on and off object snap tracking (**AutoSnap**; default = on).

Object Snap modes *options:*

ENDpoint   Snaps to the nearest endpoint of a line, multiline, polyline segment, ray, arc, and elliptical arc; and to the nearest corner of a trace, solid, and 3D face.

MIDpoint   Snaps to the midpoint of a line, multiline, polyline segment, solid, spline, xline, arc, ellipse, and elliptical arc.

CENter   Snaps to the center of an arc, circle, ellipse, and elliptical arc.

NODe   Snaps to a point.

QUAdrant   Snaps to a quadrant point (90 degrees) of an arc, circle, ellipse, and elliptical arc.

INTersection   Snaps to the intersection of a line, multiline, polyline, ray, spline, xline, arc, circle, ellipse, and elliptical arc; edges of regions; does not snap to the edges and corners of 3D ACIS solids.

EXTension   Displays an extension line from the endpoint of objects; snaps to the point where two objects would intersect if they were infinitely extended; does not work with the edges and corners of 3D ACIS solids; automatically turns on intersection mode (do not turn on apparent intersection at the same time as extended intersection).

INSertion   Snaps to the insertion point of text, block, attribute, or shape.

PERpendicular   Snaps to the perpendicular of a line, multiline, polyline, ray, solid, spline, xline, arc, circle, ellipse, and elliptical arc; snaps from a line, arc, circle, polyline, ray, xline, multiline, and 3D solid edge; in which case deferred perpendicular mode is automatically turned on.

TANgent   Snaps to the tangent of an arc, circle, ellipse, or elliptical arc; deferred tangent snap mode is automatically turned on when more than one tangent snap is required.

NEArest   Snaps to the nearest point on a line, multiline, point, polyline, spline, xline, arc, circle, ellipse, and elliptical arc.

APParent intersection

Snaps to the apparent intersection of two objects that do not actually intersect but appear to intersect in 3D space; works with a line, multiline, polyline, ray, spline, xline, arc, circle, ellipse, and elliptical arc; does not work with edges and corners of 3D ACIS solids.

PARallel   Snap to a parallel point when AutoCAD prompts for a second point.
Clear All   Turns off all object snap modes.
Select All   Turns on all object snap modes.

RELATED COMMANDS

Grid   Sets the grid spacing and toggles visibility.
Isoplane   Selects the working isometric plane.
Ortho   Toggles orthographic mode.
Snap   Sets the snap spacing and isometric mode.

RELATED SYSTEM VARIABLES

AutoSnap   Controls AutoSnap, polar tracking, and object snap tracking.
GridMode   Indicates the current grid visibility:

GridMode	Meaning
0	Off (default).
1	On.

GridUnit   Indicates the current grid spacing (default = 0.0).
OsMode   Holds the current object snap modes:

OsMode	Meaning
0	NONe
1	ENDpoint
2	MIDpoint
4	CENter
8	NODe
16	QUAdrant
32	INTersection
64	INSertion
128	PERpendicular
256	TANgent
512	NEArest
1024	QUIck
2048	APParent Intersection
4096	EXTension
8192	PARallel

PolarAddAng   Specifies user-defined polar angles, separated by semicolons.
PolarAng   Specifies the increments of the polar angle.
PolarDist   Specifies the polar snap distance.

| PolarMode | Holds settings for polar and object snap tracking: |

PolarMode	Meaning
0	Measures polar angles based on current UCS (absolute); tracks orthogonally; doesn't use additional polar tracking angles; and acquires object tracking points automatically.
1	Measures polar angles from selected objects (relative).
2	Uses polar tracking settings in object snap tracking.
4	Uses additional polar tracking angles (via **PolarAng**).
8	Acquires object snap tracking points when **SHIFT** is pressed.

SnapAng	Current snap rotation angle (default = 0).
SnapBase	Base point of snap rotation angle (default = 0,0).
SnapIsoPair	Current isoplane:

SnapIsoPair	Meaning
0	Left isoplane (default).
1	Top isoplane.
2	Right isoplane.

SnapMode	Current snap mode setting.
SnapStyl	Snap style setting:

SnapStyl	Meaning
0	Standard (default).
1	Isometric (default).

SnapUnit	Current snap spacing (default = 1,1).

TIPS

- Use snap to set the cursor movement increment.

- Use the grid as a visual display to help you better gauge distances.

- Use object snaps to draw precisely to geometric features.

- Use these CTRL and function keys to change modes during a command:

Mode	Ctrl Key	Function Key
Grid	CTRL+G	F7
Isoplane	CTRL+E	F5
Object Snap	CTRL+F	F3
Object Snap Tracking	...	F11
Ortho	CTRL+L	F8
Polar Tracking	...	F10
Snap	CTRL+B	F9

DsViewer

Rel.13 Displays the bird's-eye view window; provides real-time pan and zoom (*short for DiSplay VIEWer*).

Command	Alias	Ctrl+	F-key	Alt+	Menu Bar	Tablet
dsviewer	av	...	...	VW	View ↳Aerial View	K2

Command: **dsviewer**
*Displays **Aerial View** window:*

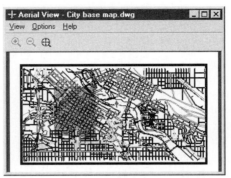

MENU BAR OPTIONS

View options:
Zoom In   Increases centered zoom by a factor of 2.
Zoom Out   Decreases centered zoom by a factor of 2.
Global   Displays entire drawing in Aerial View window.

Options options:
Auto Viewport Updates the **Aerial View** automatically with the current viewport.
Dynamic Update
              Updates the **Aerial View** automatically with editing changes in the current viewport.
Realtime Zoom Updates the drawing in real time as you zoom in the **Aerial View** window.

TOOLBAR ICONS

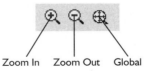

Zoom In   Zoom Out   Global

RELATED COMMANDS

Pan   Moves the drawing view.
View   Creates and displays named views.
Zoom   Makes the view larger or smaller.

TIPS

- The purposes of the **Aerial View** are to let you see the entire drawing at all times, and zoom and pan without entering the **Zoom** and **Pan** commands, or selecting items from the menu.

- The parts of the Aerial View:

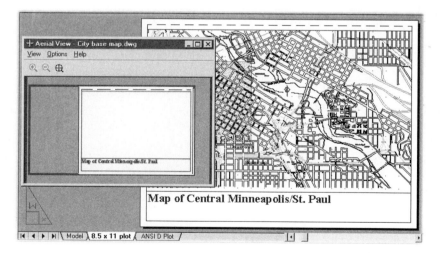

Greyed-out icon.

Drawing extents.

Current view.

Pan window.

- To switch quickly between **Pan** (default) and **Zoom** modes, click the **Aerial View** window.

- *Warning!* When in paper space, the **Aerial View** window shows only paper space objects.

Map of Central Minneapolis/St. Paul

REMOVED COMMAND

DText was removed from AutoCAD 2000; it was combined with **Text**.

DView

Rel.10 Dynamically zooms and pans 3D drawings, and turns on perspective mode (*short for Dynamic VIEW*).

Command	Alias	Ctrl+	F-key	Alt+	Menu Bar	Tablet
dview	dv	...	...	...	...	...

```
Command: dview
Select objects or <use DVIEWBLOCK>: [pick or ENTER]
Enter option
[CAmera/TArget/Distance/POints/PAn/Zoom/TWist/CLip/Hide/
   Off/Undo]:
```

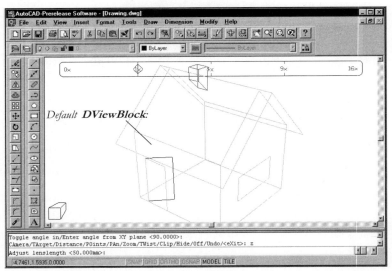

Default **DViewBlock:**

COMMAND LINE OPTIONS

CAmera	Indicates the camera angle relative to the target.
Toggle	Switches between input angles.
TArget	Indicates the target angle relative to the camera.
Distance	Indicates the camera-to-target distance; turns on perspective mode.
POints	Indicates both the camera and target points.
PAn	Pans the view dynamically.
Zoom	Zooms the view dynamically.
TWist	Rotates the camera.

CLip options:
  Back clip options:

ON	Turns on the back clipping plane.
OFF	Turns off the back clipping plane.
Distance from target	
	Indicates the location of the back clipping plane.

Front clip options:

Eye   Positions the front clipping plane at the camera.

Distance from target

          Indicates the location of the front clipping plane.

Off   Turns off view clipping.

Hide	Removes hidden lines.
Off	Turns off the perspective view.
Undo	Undoes the most recent **DView** action.
eXit	Exits **DView**.

RELATED COMMANDS

Hide	Removes hidden-lines from a non-perspective view.
Pan	Pans a non-perspective view.
VPoint	Selects a non-perspective viewpoint of a 3D drawing.
Zoom	Zooms a non-perspective view.
3dOrbit	Creates a 3D view interactively.

RELATED SYSTEM VARIABLES

BackZ	Specifies back clipping plane offset.
FrontZ	Specifies front clipping plane offset.
LensLength	Specifies perspective view lens length, in millimeters.
Target	Specifies UCS 3D coordinates of target point.
ViewCtr	Specifies 2D coordinates of current view center.
ViewDir	Specifies WCS 3D coordinates of camera offset from target.
ViewMode	Specifies perspective and clipping settings.
ViewSize	Specifies height of view.
ViewTwist	Specifies rotation angle of current view.

RELATED SYSTEM BLOCK

DViewBlock   Alternate viewing object during **DView**.

TIPS

- The view direction is from camera to target.

- Press **Enter** at the 'Select objects' prompt to display the DViewBlock house.

- You can replace the house block with your own by redefining the **DViewBlock** block.

- To view a 3D drawing in one-point perspective, use the **Zoom** option.

- Menus and transparent zoom and pan are not available during **DView**.

- Once the view is in perspective mode, you cannot use **Sketch**, **Zoom**, and **Pan**.

Two- and 3-point perspective

In two-point perspective, the camera and the target are at the same height. Vertical lines remain vertical. In three-point perspective, the camera and target are at different heights.

Step 1: TWO-POINT PERSPECTIVE

1. Start **DView** and select all objects:

        Command: **dview**
        Select objects: **all**
        1 found Select objects: ᴇɴᴛᴇʀ

Step 2: PLACE CAMERA AND TARGET

1. The **POints** option combines the **TArget** and **CAmera** options into one step:

        CAmera/TArget/Distance/POints/.../Undo/<eXit>: **po**

2. Use the **.xy** filter to pick the target point on the floorplan:

        Enter target point <0.4997, 0.4999, 0.4997>: **.xy**
        of **[pick target point]**

3. Enter a number for your eye height, such as 5'10" or 180cm:

        (need Z): **[type height]**

4. Use the **.xy** filter to pick the camera point:

        Enter camera point <0.4997, 0.4999, 1.4997>: **.xy**
        of **[pick camera point]**

5. Type the same z coordinate for the camera height:

        (need Z): **[enter same height]**

Step 3: TURN ON PERSPECTIVE MODE

1. The **Distance** option turns on perspective mode:

        CAmera/TArget/Distance/POints/.../Undo/<eXit>: **d**

2. In perspective mode, the UCS icon becomes a perspective icon. Use the slider bar to set the distance while in **Distance** mode:

        New camera/target distance <1.0943>: **[move slider bar]**

Slider bar: ⎯⎯⎯⎯⎯

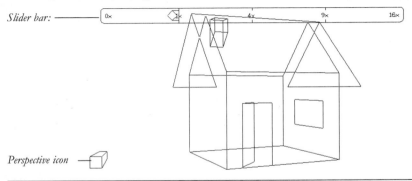

Perspective icon ⎯⎯⎯

Step 4: THREE-POINT PERSPECTIVE

- In three-point perspective, the target and camera heights differ. Most commonly, the camera is higher than the target, so that you look down on the 3D scene.

1. Follow the earlier steps, but change the camera and target heights, as follows:
   ```
   Command: dview
   Select objects: all
   1 found Select objects: ENTER
   CAmera/TArget/Distance/POints/.../Undo/<eXit>: po
   ```

2. For target height, enter the height of an object you are looking at, such as a window or table:
   ```
   Enter target point <0.4997, 0.4999, 0.4997>: .xy
   of [pick target point]
   (need Z): [enter a height]
   ```

3. For the camera height, enter your eye height or a larger number for a bird's-eye view:
   ```
   Enter camera point <0.4997, 0.4999, 1.4997>: .xy
   of [pick camera point]
   (need Z): [enter a greater height]
   CAmera/TArget/Distance/POints/.../Undo/<eXit>: d
   New camera/target distance <1.0943>: [adjust distance]
   ```

4. Use the **Hide** option to create a hidden-line view:
   ```
   CAmera/TArget/Distance/POints/.../Hide/Off/Undo/<eXit>: h
   ```

Hidden-line view in three-point perspective mode.

Step 5: EXIT DVIEW

1. Exit **DView**:
   ```
   CAmera/TArget/Distance/POints/.../Undo/<eXit>: ENTER
   ```

- The view remains in perspective mode. While in perspective mode, the **Zoom**, **Pan**, and **DsViewer** commands and scroll bars do not work.

2. To exit perspective mode, use the **Plan** command.

DwfOut

Rel.14   Exports the current drawing in DWF format *(short for Drawing Web Format OUTput; an undocumented command)*.

Command	Alias	Ctrl+	F-key	Alt+	Menu Bar	Tablet
dwfout	...	...	...	...	...	...

```
Command: dwfout
NOTE: The DWFOUT command has been deprecated, and will not be
supported in future versions of AutoCAD. It is provided here
for limited backward compatibility only. Please refer to the
User's Guide for a complete discussion of the new, powerful
features of DWF ePlot.
Enter filename <C:\filename.dwf>: [type filename]
Enter Format [ASCII/Binary] <Binary>: ENTER
Enter Precision [Low/Medium/High] <Medium>: ENTER
Compress file? [No/Yes] <Yes>: ENTER
Include layer information? [No/Yes] <Yes>: ENTER

Please wait.  DWF options are being passed to the PLOT command.
Effective plotting area:  5.34 wide by 9.60 high
Plotting viewport 2.
```

COMMAND LINE OPTIONS

Enter filename Specifies the name of the file; AutoCAD adds the DWF extension.

Enter Format **ASCII**: file can be read by humans but takes up more file space.

Binary: filesize is smaller (default).

Enter Precision **Low**: 16-bit precision; creates smaller file size.

Medium: 20-bit precision; the default (default).

High: 24-bit precision; meant for drawings with fine details.

Compress file **Yes**: Compresses file; file size is smaller, but file might not be readable by some applications (default).

No: Does not compress file; file size is larger.

Include layer information

Yes: Layer information is retained (default).

No: Objects are not separated in layers.

TIPS

- For a better image, zoom in. Also, consider the effect of the **ViewRes**, **FaceTRes**, **DispSilh**, and **Hide** commands on image quality.

- DWF is strictly 2D; set the 3D viewpoint before making a DWF file of 3D objects.

- The DWF file uses the same background color as the current AutoCAD setting.

REMOVED COMMAND

DwfOutD was removed from AutoCAD 2000; it was combined with **DwfOut**.

DwgProps

Records information about the drawing (*short for DraWinG PROPertieS*).

Command	Alias	Ctrl+	F-key	Alt+	Menu Bar	Tablet
dwgprops	...	...	...	FI	File	...
					↳Drawing Properties	

Command: **dwgprops**
Displays tabbed dialog box.

DIALOG BOX OPTIONS
OK   Records the changes, and exits the dialog box.
Cancel   Discards the changes, and exits the dialog box.

General tab:
Displays information about the drawing obtained from the operating system:

File Type   Indicates the type of the file.
Location   Indicates the location of the file.
Size   Indicates the size of the file.

MS-DOS Name Indicates the MS-DOS filename; usually truncated to eight characters.
Created   Indicates the date and time the file was first saved.
Modified   Indicates the date and time the file was last saved.
Accessed   Indicates the date and time the file was last opened.

Attributes options:
Read-Only   Indicates the file cannot edited or erased.
Archive   Indicates the file has be changed since it was last backed up.
Hidden   Indicates the file cannot be seen in file listings.
System   Indicates the file is a system file; DWG drawing files never have this attribute turned on.

Summary tab:

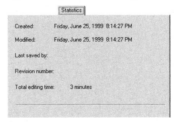

Title	Specifies a title for this drawing; is usually different from the filename.
Subject	Specifies a subject for this drawing.
Author	Specifies the name of the drafter of this drawing.
Keywords	Specifies keywords used by the operating system's **Find** command to locate the drawing.
Comments	Specifies comments about this drawing.
Hyperlink Base	Specifies the base address for relative links in the drawing, such as http://www.autodeskpress.com; may be an operating system path name, such as *C:\acad 2002*, or a network drive name. Stored in system variable **HyperlinkBase**.

Statistics tab:

Displays information about the drawing obtained from the drawing:

Created	Indicates the date and time the drawing was first opened, as stored in system variable **TdCreate**.
Modified	Indicates the date and time the drawing was last opened or modified, as stored in system variable **TdUpdate**.
Last saved by	Indicates, by the name stored in the **LoginName** system variable, who last accessed this drawing file.
Revision number	
	Indicates the revision number; usually blank.
Total editing time	
	Indicates the total amount of time that the drawing has been open, as stored in system variable **TdInDwg**.

Custom tab:

Custom Properties *options:*

Name   Specifies the name of a customized field.
Value   Specifies the value of the customized field.

RELATED COMMANDS

Properties   Lists information about objects in the drawing.
Status   Lists information about the drawing.

TIP

■ Use the **Find** button in **DesignCenter** to search for drawings containing values in the **Custom Properties** tab.

Dxbin

V. 2.1 Imports a DXB-format file into the current drawing (*short for Drawing eXchange Binary INput*).

Command	Alias	Ctrl+	F-key	Alt+	Menu Bar	Tablet
dxbin	...	...	...	IE	Insert	...
					↳Drawing Exchange Binary	

Command: **dxbin**
*Displays **Select DXB File** dialog box.*

DIALOG BOX OPTION
Open   Opens the DXB file and inserts it in the drawing.

RELATED COMMANDS
DxfIn   Reads DXF-format files.
Plot   Writes DXB-format files when configured for ADI plotter.

TIPS
■ Configure AutoCAD with the ADI plotter driver to produce a DXB file.

■ This command was created for an early Autodesk software product called CAD/camera, which converted raster scans into the DXB vector format.

Dxfin

V. 2.0   Reads a DXF-format file into a drawing (*short for Drawing interchange Format INput; an undocumented command*).

Command	Alias	Ctrl+	F-key	Alt+	Menu Bar	Tablet
dxfin	...	...	...	FO	File	...
				⬐DXF	⬐Open	
					⬐DXF	

Command: **dxfin**
*Displays **Select File** dialog box.*

DIALOG BOX OPTION
Open   Opens the DXF file.

RELATED COMMANDS
DxbIn   Reads a DXB-format file.
DxfOut   Writes a DXF-format file.

TIPS
- DXF files come in two styles: *complete* and *partial*. A complete DXF file contains all data required to reproduce a complete drawing file; a partial DXF file must be imported into an existing drawing.

- To load a complete DXF file, AutoCAD requires the current drawing to be empty.

- To create an empty drawing, use **New** with the **Start from Scratch** option.

- When you try to import a complete DXF file but the drawing is not new, some versions of AutoCAD complain, "DXFIN requires a new drawing."

- If you need to import the complete DXF file into a non-empty drawing (named, for example, "*First.Dwg*"), take these steps:

Step 1. Use **DxfIn** to import the complete DXF file into an empty drawing.

Step 2. Save the drawing with the **SaveAs** command, using the name of, for example, "Second.Dwg."

Step 3. Open the non-empty First.Dwg drawing, and use the **Insert** command with the ***** option to place the contents of the Second.Dwg.

- A partial DXF file can be imported into any drawing, empty or not.

DxfOut

V. 2.0 Writes a DXF-format file of part or all of the current drawing (*short for Drawing interchange Format OUTput; an undocumented command*).

Command	Alias	Ctrl+	F-key	Alt+	Menu Bar	Tablet
dxfout	...	...	...	FA	File	...
				⌐DXF	⌐Save As	
					⌐DXF	

Command: **dxfout**
Displays **Save Drawing As** *dialog box.*

DIALOG BOX OPTIONS

Save   Saves the drawing as a DXF file.
Files of type   Creates a DXF file compatible with earlier versions of AutoCAD:
  - AutoCAD 2000, as well as 200i.
  - AutoCAD Release 14, AutoCAD LT 98 and 97
  - AutoCAD Release 13, AutoCAD LT 95
  - AutoCAD Release 12, AutoCAD LT Release 2

From the **Save Drawing As** *dialog box's toolbar, select* **Tools | Options:**

Format options:
ASCII   Creates a file in text format, which is human-readable and importable by most applications (default).
Binary   Creates a binary file with a smaller filesize, but it cannot be read by all applications.

Select objects Select objects to export, instead of the entire drawing.
Save thumbnail preview image
      Includes a preview image in the DXF file.
Decimal places of accuracy (0 to 16)
      Specifies the decimal places of accuracy.

RELATED COMMANDS

DxfIn	Reads a DXF-format file.
AcisOut	Saves the drawing in ACIS-comaptible SAT format.
Save	Writes the drawing in DWG format.

TIPS

- Use the ASCII DXF format to exchange drawings with other CAD and graphics programs.

- A binary DXF file is much smaller, and is created much faster than an ASCII binary file; few applications, however, read a binary DXF file.

- The AutoCAD Release 12 dialect of DXF is the most compatible with other applications.

- Drawing files created by AutoCAD 2000 are compatible with AutoCAD 2000i and 2002.

- *Caution!* AutoCAD 2002 erases or converts Release 13- and Release 14-specific objects into simpler objects.

EAttEdit

2002 Edits attribute values and properties in a selected block *(short for Enhanced ATTribute EDITor)*.

Command	Alias	Ctrl+	Key	Alt+	Menu Bar	Tablet
eattedit	...	...	...	MOAS	Modify ⌐Object 　⌐Attribute 　　⌐Single	...

Command: **eattedit**
Select a block: **[pick]**
Displays dialog box.

DIALOG BOX OPTIONS

Select block   Selects another block for attribute editing.

Apply   Applies the changes to the attributes.

Attribute tab:

Value   Modifies the value of the selected attribute; neither the tag nor the prompt can be modified by this command.

Text Options tab:

Text Style   Selects a text style name from the list; text styles are defined by the **Style** command; default is Standard.

Justification   Selects a justification mode from the list; default is left justification.

Height	Specifies the text height; can be changed only when height is set to 0.0 in the text style.
Rotation	Specifies the rotation angle of the attribute text; default = 0 degrees.
Backwards	Displays the text backwards.
Upside Down	Displays the text upside-down.
Width Factor	Specifies the relative width of characters; default = 1.
Oblique Angle	Specifies the slant of characters; default = 0 degrees.

Properties tab:

Properties

Layer: ASHADE

Linetype: Continuous

Color: ■ Red   Lineweight: — ByLayer

Plot style: ByLayer

Layer	Selects a layer name from the list; layers are defined by the **Layer** command.
Linetype	Selects a linetype name from the list; linetypes are loaded into the drawing with the **Linetype** command.
Color	Selects a color from the list; to select from the full 255 spectrum, select **Other**.
Lineweight	Selects a lineweight from the list; to turn on the display of lineweights, click **LWT** on the status bar.
Plot style	Selects a plot style name from the list; available only if plot styles are enabled in the drawing.

RELATED COMMANDS

AttDef	Creates attribute definitions.
Block	Attaches attributes to objects.
BAttMan	Manages attributes.
EAttExt	Extracts attributes to a file.

TIPS

■ This command edits only attribute values and their properties; to edit all aspects of an attribute, use the **BAttMan** command.

■ If you select a block with no attributes, AutoCAD complains, "The selected block has no editable attributes."

■ When you select an object that isn't a block, AutoCAD complains, "Error selecting entity."

EAttExt

<u>2002</u>   Extracts attribute data to file via a step-by-step guide procedure *(short for Enhanced ATTribute EXTraction)*.

Command	Alias	Ctrl+	Key	Alt+	Menu Bar	Tablet
eattext	...	...	...	...	...	...

Command: **eattext**
*Displays **Attribute Extraction** dialog box.*

DIALOG BOX OPTIONS

Back   Goes back to the previous step.
Next   Proceeds to the next step.
Cancel   Exits the dialog box.
Help   Displays helpful information.

Select Drawing step 1:

Drawings   Specifies the location of the blocks containing attributes:

- **Select objects:** Selects the specific blocks in the current drawing.
- **Current drawing:** Selects all blocks containing attributes in the current drawing.
- **Select drawings:** Selects drawings located on your computer or network.

Drawing Files Lists the names of drawing files from which attributes will be extracted.

Settings step 2:

Include xrefs   Specifies that attributes in xrefs should be extracted.

Include nested blocks

Specifies that *nested blocks* (blocks within blocks) should be searched for attribute data.

Use Template step 3:

- **No template**: you will specify the data output format.
- **Use template**: AutoCAD uses the existing output format, previously stored in an BLK file.

Use Template   Displays the **Open** dialog box; select a Block Template File (BLK). AutoCAD does not include any BLK files; you can create one later during the **Save Template** step.

Select Attributes step 4:

List of Blocks Found in Drawing(s)   List of Attributes for each Block

☑ *or* ☐	Click the box next to each block (in lefthand column) and each attribute (in righthand column) either to include or exclude each.
Check All	Selects all blocks or attributes.
Uncheck All	Unselects all blocks or attributes.
Alias	Allows you to enter an alias for each block and attribute; an *alias* is an alternative name.

Block Information	Attribute Information
Block Name	Attribute
Block Alias	Attribute Value
Number	Alias

View Output step 5:

Alternate view 1: Block Name, Count, and attribute data.

Alternate view 2: Block Name, Count, and block data.

Block Name   Lists the name of each block; block names prefixed with *X are hatch patterns created by AutoCAD. Click the header to list block names in alphabetical order.

Count   Specifies the number of times the block appears.

Alternate View   This stage displays the data in two formats:
- Information about each block.
- Information about each attribute.

Alternate View 1	Alternate View 2
Block Name	Block Name
Count	Count
Attribute	X, Y, Z Insertion
Attribute Value	Layer
	Orient
	X, Y, Z scale
	X, Y, Z Extrusion
	User Defined

Note: This step can take a long time to display on slow computers with drawings containing a large number of blocks.

Copy to Clipboard

Copies the displayed data to the Windows Clipboard in tab-delimited format (each field is separated by a tab), which can be pasted into a spreadsheet or document with the **Edit | Paste** (**CTRL+V**) command.

Save Template step 6:

Save Template Saves the block and attribute selections (made in the **Select Attributes** step) to a BLK (Block template) file; this BLK file can be reused during the **Use Template** step.

Export step 7:

File Name	Specifies the name of the file that holds the extracted attribute data.
File Type	Selects the format of the data:

• **CSV** (comma separated values) separates fields with a comma.
• **TXT** (tab delimited values) separates fields with a tab.
• **XLS** (Excel spreadsheet format) saves the data in a proprietary format.

Finish	Completes the attribute data extraction process.

RELATED COMMANDS

AttExt	Exports to DXF format, as well as comma- and tab-delimited formats; an older method of attribute extraction.
AttDef	Creates attribute definitions.
Block	Attaches attributes to objects.
BAttMan	Manages attributes.

TIPS

■ This command does not export attribute data in DXF format; if you require this format, use the **AttExt** command.

■ When the attribute data has been exported, you may open the file in another program, such as WordPerfect (word processing), Lotus 1-2-3 (spreadsheet), or Access (database).

■ A drawing (and its xrefs) can contain many attributes. For example, the 1st Floor.dwg sample drawing contains nearly a thousand blocks, which take up nearly 8,000 rows in a spreadsheet.

■ You can use this command to create a crude BOM (bill of material). During the **View Output** step, click the **Copy to Clipboard** button, and paste the data in the AutoCAD drawing.

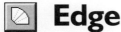

Edge

Rel.12 Toggles the visibility of 3D faces.

Command	Alias	Ctrl+	F-key	Alt+	Menu Bar	Tablet
edge	...	...	...	DFE	Draw ↳Surfaces ↳Edge	...

```
Command: edge
Specify edge of 3dface to toggle visibility or [Display]: d
Enter selection method for display of hidden edges
   [Select/All] <All>: s
Select objects: [pick]
Specify edge of 3dface to toggle visibility or [Display]: Esc
```

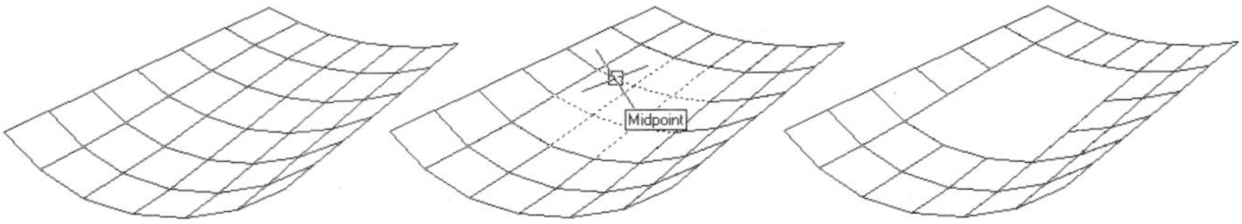

*3d faces (left), edges selected with **Edge** (center), and invisible edges (right).*

COMMAND LINE OPTIONS

Specify edge Selects edge to make invisible.

***Display** options:*

Select Highlights invisible edges.

All Selects all hidden edges and regenerates them.

RELATED COMMAND

3dFace Creates 3D faces.

RELATED SYSTEM VARIABLE

SplFrame Toggles visibility of 3D face edges.

TIPS

- Make edges invisible to make 3D objects look better.
- **Edge** applies only to objects made of 3d faces; it does not work with polyface meshes or solid models.
- Use the **Explode** command to convert meshed objects into 3D faces.
- Re-execute **Edge** to display an edge that has been made invisible.
- Command repeats itself until you press **Enter** or **Esc** at the 'Specify edge of 3dface to toggle visibility or [Display]:' prompt.

EdgeSurf

Rel.10 Draws a 3D polygon mesh as a Coons surface patch between four boundaries (*short for EDGE-defined SURFace*).

Command	Alias	Ctrl+	F-key	Alt+	Menu Bar	Tablet
edgesurf	...	...	...	DFD	Draw	R8
					↳Surfaces	
					↳Edge Surface	

```
Command: edgesurf
Current wire frame density:  SURFTAB1=6   SURFTAB2=6
Select object 1 for surface edge: [pick]
Select object 2 for surface edge: [pick]
Select object 3 for surface edge: [pick]
Select object 4 for surface edge: [pick]
```

Edge 1
Edge 4
Edge 2
Edge 3

Surftab1=6
Surftab2=6

Surftab1=6
Surftab2=20

Surftab1=20
Surftab2=20

COMMAND LINE OPTION
Select object   Picks an edge.

RELATED COMMANDS
3dMesh   Creates a 3D mesh by specifying every vertex.
3dFace   Creates a 3D mesh of irregular vertices.
PEdit   Edits the mesh created by **Edgesurf**.
TabSurf   Creates a tabulated 3D surface.
RuleSurf   Creates a ruled 3D surface.
RevSurf   Creates a 3D surface of revolution.

RELATED SYSTEM VARIABLES
SurfTab1   The current m-density of meshing.
SurfTab2   The current n-density of meshing.

TIPS
■ The Coons surface created by **EdgeSurf** is an interpolated bi-cubic surface.

■ The four boundary edges can be made from lines, arcs, and open 2D and 3D polylines; the edges must meet at their endpoints.

■ The maximum mesh density is 32767.

'Elev

V. 2.1 Sets elevation and thickness of extruded 3D objects (*short for ELEVation*).

Command	Alias	Ctrl+	F-key	Alt+	Menu Bar	Tablet
'elev	...	...	...	...	...	...

```
Command: elev
Specify new default elevation <0.0000>: [enter value]
Specify new default thickness <0.0000>: [enter value]
```

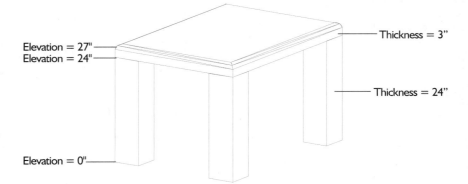

Elevation = 27"
Elevation = 24"
Thickness = 3"
Thickness = 24"
Elevation = 0"

COMMAND LINE OPTIONS

Elevation   Changes the base elevation from z = 0.
Thickness   Extrudes new 2D objects in the z-direction.

RELATED COMMANDS

Change   Changes the thickness and z coordinate of objects.
Move   Moves objects, including in the z direction.
Properties   Changes the thickness of objects.

RELATED SYSTEM VARIABLES

Elevation   Stores the current elevation setting.
Thickness   Stores the current thickness setting.

TIPS

- The current value of elevation is used whenever a z coordinate is not supplied.

- Thickness is measured up from the current elevation in the positive z direction.

 # Ellipse

V. 2.5 Draws an ellipse — by four different methods — and elliptical arcs and
isometric circles.

Command	Alias	Ctrl+	F-key	Alt+	Menu Bar	Tablet
ellipse	el	...	...	DE	Draw ⌐Ellipse	M9

Command: **ellipse**
Specify axis endpoint of ellipse or [Arc/Center]: **[pick]**
Specify other endpoint of axis: **[pick]**
Specify distance to other axis or [Rotation]: **[pick]**

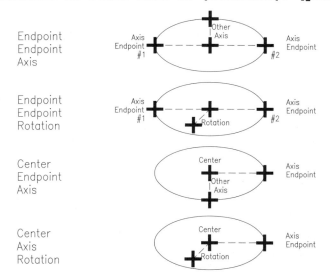

Endpoint
Endpoint
Axis

Endpoint
Endpoint
Rotation

Center
Endpoint
Axis

Center
Axis
Rotation

COMMAND LINE OPTIONS

Specify axis endpoint of ellipse
Indicates the first endpoint of the major axis.
Specify other endpoint of axis
Indicates the second endpoint of the major axis.
Specify distance to other axis
Indicates the half-distance of the minor axis.

Arc options:
Specify axis endpoint of elliptical arc or [Center]: **[pick]**
Specify other endpoint of axis: **[pick]**
Specify distance to other axis or [Rotation]: **[pick]**
Specify start angle or [Parameter]: **[pick]**
Specify end angle or [Parameter/Included angle]: **[pick]**

Specify start angle

> Indicates the starting angle of the elliptical arc.

Specify end angle

> Indicates the ending angle of the elliptical arc.

Parameter   Indicates the starting angle of the elliptical arc; draws arc with this formula:

$$p(u) = \mathbf{c} + (\mathbf{a}*\cos(u)) + (\mathbf{b}*\sin(u))$$

Parameter	Meaning
a	Major axis.
b	Minor axis.
c	Center of ellipse.

Included angle

> Indicates an angle measured relative to the start angle, rather than 0 degrees.

Center *option:*

`Specify center of ellipse:` **[pick]**

Specify center of ellipse

> Indicates the center point of the ellipse.

Rotation *option:*

`Specify rotation around major axis:` **[pick]**

Specify rotation around major axis

> Indicates a rotation angle around the major axis:

Rotation	Meaning
0 degrees	Minimum rotation: creates a round ellipse, like a circle.
89.4 degrees	Maximum rotation: creates a very thin ellipse.

Isocircle *options:*

Note: this option appears only when ***SnapStyl*** *is set to 1 (isometric snap mode).*

`Specify axis endpoint of ellipse or [Arc/Center/Isocircle]:` **i**
`Specify center of isocircle:` **[pick]**
`Specify radius of isocircle or [Diameter]:` **[pick]**

Specify center Indicates the center point of the isocircle.
Specify radius Indicates the radius of the isocircle.
Diameter   Indicates the diameter of the isocircle.

RELATED COMMANDS

IsoPlane   Sets the current isometric plane.
PEdit   Edits ellipses (when drawn with a polyline).
Snap   Controls the setting of isometric mode.

RELATED SYSTEM VARIABLES

PEllipse   Determines how the ellipse is drawn:

PEllipse	Meaning
0	Draw ellipse with the ellipse object (default).
1	Draw ellipse as series of polyline arcs.

SnapIsoPair   Current isometric plane:

SnapIsoPair	Meaning
0	Left (default).
1	Top.
2	Right.

SnapStyl   Regular or isometric drawing mode:

SnapStyl	Meaning
0	Standard (default).
1	Isometric.

TIPS

- Previous to AutoCAD Release 13, **Ellipse** constructed the ellipse as a series of short polyline arcs.

- When **PEllipse** = 1, the **Arc** option is not available.

- Use ellipses to draw circles in isometric mode. When **Snap** is set to isometric mode, **Ellipse**'s isocircle option projects a circle into the working isometric drawing plane. Use **CTRL+E** to toggle isoplanes.

- The **Isocircle** option only appears in the option prompt when **Snap** is set to isometric mode.

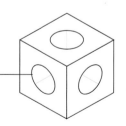

These isometric circles were drawn with the **Ellipse** command's **Isocircle** option.

REMOVED COMMAND

End was removed from AutoCAD Release 14; it was replaced by **Quit**.

EndToday

2000i Closes the AutoCAD Today window.

Command	Alias	Ctrl+	Key	Alt+	Menu Bar	Tablet
endtoday	...	...	...	...	...	...

Command: **endtoday**

COMMAND LINE OPTIONS
None.

RELATED COMMAND
Today   Opens the AutoCAD Today window.

TIPS
■ Keep the AutoCAD Today window closed for faster AutoCAD startups, and more screen real estate.

■ As an alternative, you can close the AutoCAD Today window by clicking the small x in the upper-right corner of the window:

Erase

V. 1.0 Erases objects from the drawing.

Command	Alias	Ctrl+	Key	Alt+	Menu Bar	Tablet
erase	e	...	Del	ME	Modify ⁹Erase	V14
					Edit ⁹Clear	U14

```
Command: erase
Select objects: [pick]
Select objects: ENTER
```

COMMAND LINE OPTION
Select objects Selects the objects to erase.

RELATED COMMANDS
Break	Erases a portion of a line, circle, arc, or polyline.
Oops	Returns the most-recently erased objects to the drawing.
Trim	Cuts off the end of a line, arc, and other objects.
Undo	Returns the erased objects to the drawing.

TIPS

■ The **Erase L** command combination erases the last-drawn item visible in the current viewport.

■ **Oops** brings back the most-recently erased objects; use **U** to bring back other erased objects.

■ *Warning!* The **Erase All** command erases all objects in the drawing, except on locked, frozen, and off layers.

eTransmit

Transmits the current drawing and all related files as an email message *(short for Electronic TRANSMITtal).*

Command	Alias	Ctrl+	Key	Alt+	Menu Bar	Tablet
etransmit	...	...	...	FT	File	...
					⤷eTransmit	

-etransmit

Command: **etransmit**

If the drawing has not been saved, displays error dialog box:

O K	Saves drawing and displays **Create Transmittal** dialog box.
Cancel	Cancels **eTransmit** command.

DIALOG BOX OPTIONS

General tab:

Notes Allows you to enter a note for the recipient of the transmittal.

Type   Selects how the files will be bundled:
- In a folder (set of files).
- In a self-extracting executable program (*.exe).
- In a Zip file (*.zip).

Password   Displays the **Set Password** dialog box.

Location   Specifies the drive and folder to place the transmittal files.

Browse   Displays the file dialog box for selecting the drive and folder.

Convert drawings to

    Yes: Converts the drawings to earlier versions of AutoCAD.

    No: Keeps the drawings in AutoCAD 2000i format.
- AutoCAD 2000/LT 2000 Drawing Format
- AutoCAD R14/LT 98/ LT 97 Drawing Format

Preserve directory structure

    Yes: Keeps the folder structure; useful when the destintation computer has the same folder structure as the sending computer.

    No: Collects files into a single folder.

Remove paths from xrefs and images

    Yes: Strips the path name from externally-referenced drawings and attached images.

    No: Preserves the paths.

Send email with transmittal

    Yes: Starts up the Windows Messaging software.

    No: Does not start the mail software.

Make Web page files

    Yes: Generates a Web page (found in the \My Documents folder), which can be used to download the transmittal with a Web browser.

    No: Does not generate a Web page.

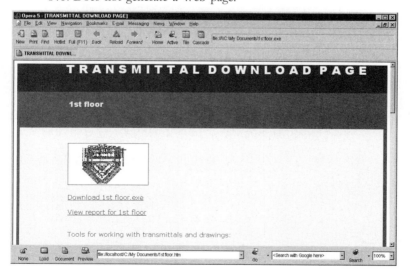

Files tab:

Add File   Displays the file dialog box so that you can select additional files to
                  include with the transmittal.

Include fonts **Yes**: Includes SHX (AutoCAD) and TTF (Microsoft) font files with the
                  transmittal.

                  No: Does not include fonts.

Report tab:

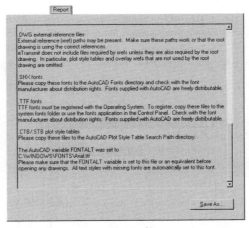

Save As   Saves the report as a text (TXT) file.

-ETRANSMIT COMMAND

Command: **-etransmit**

Transmittal type [Folder/self-extracting Executable/Zip/
   Report only]: **z**

Transmittal note: **[enter text]**

ENTER

Include fonts? [Yes/No] <Yes>:

Convert all drawings? [No/R14(LT98/LT97)/2000(LT2000)]
   <No>: **ENTER**

Preserve directory structure? [Yes/No] <No>: **ENTER**

Remove xref and image paths? [Yes/No] <Yes>: **ENTER**

Make web page files? [Yes/No] <No>: **ENTER**

Password (press ENTER for none): **ENTER**

Transmittal created: C:\filename.zip.

COMMAND LINE OPTIONS

Folder   Saves the drawing and related files in a folder (subdirectory).

self-extracting Executable
     Saves the drawing and related files in a compressed self-extracting file (.exe).

Zip   Saves the drawing and related files in a compressed PkZIP file (.zip).

Report only Saves the report to a TXT file.

Transmittal note
     Allows you to include a note to the recipient; press **ENTER** twice to end the note function.

Include fonts? Includes SHX (AutoCAD) and TTF (Microsoft) fonts.

Convert all drawings?
     Converts the drawings to AutoCAD 2000 or Release 14 format.

Preserve directory structure?
     Preserves the folder structure, so that files are restored into the same folders.

Remove xref and image paths?
     Removes the path from externally-referenced drawings and attached images.

Make web page files?
     Generates a Web page for accessing the transmittal by Web browser.

Password   Specifies the password to prevent unauthorized opening of the transmittal; press **ENTER** for no password.

RELATED COMMANDS

DwfOut   Saves the drawing as a DWF file.

PublishToWeb Saves the drawing as an HTML file.

TIPS

■ The **eTransmit** command is an expanded version of the **Pack'n Go** command, a bonus command first included with AutoCAD Release 14.

■ The **Password** button is *not* available when you select the **Folder** option.

■ Including a TrueType font (TTF) is a touchy issue, because sending a copy of the file might infringe on its copyright. All SHX and TTF files included with AutoCAD may be transmitted. For this reason, the dialog box has the **Include Fonts** option, which you should turn off when the fonts cannot be copied legally, or when the recipient already has the fonts. In addition, not including the fonts can save a significant amount of file space; recall that a smaller file takes less time to transmit via modem.

■ "Self-extracting executable" means that the files are compressed into a single file with the .exe extension. The email recipient double-clicks the file to extract (uncompress) the files. The benefit is that the recipient does not need to have a copy of the PkUnzip or WinZip utilities on their computer; the drawback is that a virus could hide in the EXE file.

■ The benefit to converting the drawing to AutoCAD 2000 or Release 14 format is that clients with older versions of the software can read the file; the drawback is that R2000-specific objects are either erased or modified to a simpler format. Two problems that can occur include: (1) lineweights are no longer displayed (lineweights are restored when the drawing is opened again in AutoCAD 2002); and (2) database links and freestanding labels are converted to Release 14 links and displayable attributes.

■ The **Make Web page files** options is useful when the recipient does not have email access; for example, when out in the field, or when you want the transmittal available on a public basis (the file can be locked via the password, if necessary).

■ If your computer cannot compress the files (or if your recipient cannot uncompress them), you are probably lacking the software needed to uncompress the ZIP file. (Do not confuse ZIP files with Iomega's ZIP disk drive; the two having nothing in common, except the name.) You can obtain the PkUnzip and WinZIP utilities as freeware or shareware.

■ Files occasionally become corrupted when sent by email; the transmittal may need to be resent. If you continue to have problems, you may need to change a setting in your email software. Try changing the attachment encoding method from BinHex or Uuencode to MIME.

Explode

V. 2.5 Explodes a polyline, block, associative dimension, hatch, multiline, 3D solid, region, body, or polyface mesh into its constituent objects.

Command	Alias	Ctrl+	F-key	Alt+	Menu Bar	Tablet
explode	x	...	...	MX	Modify ⮡Explode	Y22

```
Command: explode
Select objects: [pick]
Select objects: ENTER
```

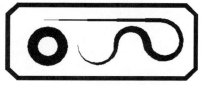 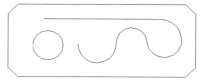

Polylines (at left) exploded into lines and arcs (at right).

COMMAND LINE OPTION

Select objects Selects the objects to explode.

RELATED COMMANDS

Block	Recreates a block after an explode.
PEdit	Converts a line into a polyline.
Region	Converts 2D objects into a region.
Undo	Reverses the effects of explode.
Xplode	Provides control over the explosion process.

RELATED SYSTEM VARIABLE

ExplMode Toggles whether non-uniformly scaled blocks can be exploded:

ExplMode	Meaning
0	Does not explode (R12-compatible).
1	Explodes (default).

TIPS

■ As of Release 13, you *can* explode blocks inserted with unequal scale factors, mirrored blocks, and blocks created by the **MInsert** command.

■ You cannot explode xrefs and dependent blocks, which are blocks from an xref drawing.

■ Parts making up exploded blocks and associative dimensions may change their color and linetype, most commonly to color White (or black when the background color is white) and linetype Continuous.

■ Resulting objects become the previous selection set.

■ The **Explode** command reduces:

Object	Exploded Into
Block	Constituent parts.
Circle within a non-uniform scaled block	Ellipse.
Arc within a non-uniform scaled block	Elliptical arc.
Associative dimension	Lines, solids, and text.
2D polyline	Lines and arcs; width and tangency information is lost.
3D polyline	Lines.
Multiline	Lines.
Polygon mesh	3D faces.
Polyface mesh	3D faces, lines, and points.
3D solid	Regions and bodies.
Region	Lines, arcs, ellipses, and splines.
Body	Single bodies, regions, and curves.

Export

Rel.13 Saves the drawing in formats other than DWG or DXF.

Command	Alias	Ctrl+	F-key	Alt+	Menu Bar	Tablet
export	...	...	...	FE	File	W24
					⌐Export	

Command: **export**
Displays dialog box:

DIALOG BOX OPTIONS

Save in	Selects the folder (subdirectory) and drive to which to export the file.
Back	Returns to the previous folder (**ALT+1**).
Up One Level	Moves up one level in the folder structure (**ALT+2**).
Search the Web	
	Displays a simple Web browser that accesses the Autodesk Web site (**ALT+3**).
Delete	Erases the selected file(s) or folder (**DEL**).
Create New Folder	
	Creates a new folder (**ALT+5**).
Views	Displays files and folders in a list or with details.
Tools	Lists several additional commands, including the **Options** dialog box — available only with encapsulated PostScript; see the **PsOut** command.
File name	Specifies the name of the file, or accepts the default.
Save as type	Selects the file format in which to save the drawing.
Save	Saves the drawing.
Cancel	Dismisses the dialog box, and returns to AutoCAD.

RELATED COMMANDS

AttExt	Exports attribute data in the drawing in CDF, SDF, or DXF formats.
CopyClip	Exports the drawing to the Clipboard.
CopyHist	Exports text from the text screen to the Clipboard.
Import	Imports several vector and raster formats.
LogFileOn	Saves the command line text as ASCII text in the *Acad.Log* file.
MassProp	Exports the mass property data as ASCII text in an MPR file.
MSlide	Exports the current viewport as an SLD slide file.
Plot	Exports the drawing in a many vector and raster formats.
SaveAs	Saves the drawing in AutoCAD DWG format.
SaveImg	Exports the rendering in TIFF, Targa, or BMP formats.

TIPS

■ The **Export** command acts as a "shell" command; it launches other AutoCAD commands that perform the actual export function, as noted below.

■ The **Export** command exports the current drawing in the following formats:

Extension	Meaning
3DS	3D Studio file: **3dsOut** command.
BMP	Device-independent bitmap file: **BmpOut** command.
DWG	AutoCAD drawing file : **WBlock** command.
DWF	Drawing Web format file: **DwfOut** command.
DXF	AutoCAD drawing interchange file: **DxfOut** command.
DXX	Attribute extract DXF file: **AttExt** command.
EPS	Encapsulated PostScript file: **PsOut** command.
SAT	ACIS solid object file: **AcisOut** command.
STL	Solid object stereo-lithography file: **StlOut** command.
WMF	Windows metafile: **WmfOut** command

REMOVED COMMAND

The **ExpressTools** command was removed from AutoCAD 2002, known as "bonus CAD tools" in earlier versions of AutoCAD. Many of the bonus tools, such as **QLeader** and **BattMan**, have been included as commands in AutoCAD.

Extend

V. 2.5 Extends the length of a line, ray, open polyline, arc, or elliptical arc to a boundary.

Command	Alias	Ctrl+	F-key	Alt+	Menu Bar	Tablet
extend	ex	...	...	MD	Modify ⌐Extend	W16

```
Command: extend
Current settings: Projection=UCS Edge=None
Select boundary edges ...
Select objects: [pick]
Select objects: ENTER
Select object to extend or [Project/Edge/Undo]: [pick]
Select object to extend or [Project/Edge/Undo]: ENTER
```

Line, arc, and variable-width polyline before (right) and after being extended to dotted line.

COMMAND LINE OPTIONS

Select objects Selects the objects to be used for the extension boundary.
Select objects to extend
          Selects the objects that will be extended.
Undo   Undoes the most recent extend operation.

Project options:
```
Enter a projection option [None/Ucs/View] <Ucs>: ENTER
```

None   Extends objects to boundary (Release 12-compatible).
Ucs   Extends objects in the x,y-plane of the current UCS.
View   Extends objects in the current view plane.

Edge options:
```
Enter an implied edge extension mode [Extend/No extend]
   <No extend>: e
```

Extend   Extends to implied boundary.
No extend Extends only to actual boundary (Release 12-compatible)..

RELATED COMMANDS

Change	Changes the length of lines.
Lengthen	Changes the length of open objects.
SolidEdit	Extends the face of a solid object.
Stretch	Stretches objects wider or narrower.
Trim	Reduces the length of lines, polylines and arcs.

RELATED SYSTEM VARIABLES

EdgeMode   Toggles boundary mode for the **Extend** and **Trim** commands:

EdgeMode	Meaning
0	Use actual edges; Release 12 compatible (default).
1	Use implied edge.

ProjMode   Toggles projection mode for the **Extend** and **Trim** commands:

ProjMode	Meaning
0	None; Release 12 compatible.
1	Current UCS (default)
2	Current view plane.

TIPS

■ The following objects can be used as a boundary:

2D polyline	Line
3D polyline	Ray
Arc	Region
Circle	Spline
Ellipse	Text
Floating viewport	Xline

■ When a wide polyline is the edge, **Extend** extends to the polyline's centerline.

■ Pick the object a second time to extend it to a second boundary line.

■ Circles and other closed objects are valid edges: the object is extended in the direction nearest to the pick point.

■ Extending a variable-width polyline widens it proportionately; extending a splined polyline adds a vertex.

Extrude

Rel.11   Creates a 3D solid by extruding a 2D object, with optional tapered sides (*an ACIS command*).

Command	Alias	Ctrl+	F-key	Alt+	Menu Bar	Tablet
extrude	ext	...	...	DIX	Draw	P7
					⌐Solids	
					⌐Extrude	

```
Command: extrude
Select objects: [pick]
Select objects: ENTER
Specify height of extrusion or [Path]: [enter value]
Specify angle of taper for extrusion <0>: ENTER
```

Extrusion ——————

Tapered extrusion

Extrusion along a path

COMMAND LINE OPTIONS

Select objects   Selects the 2D objects to be extruded.
Specify height of extrusion
           Specifies the extrusion height.
Specify angle of taper for extrusion
           Specifies the taper angle; ranges from -90 to +90 degrees.

Path option:
Select extrusion path
           Specifies the path for the extrusion.

RELATED COMMANDS

Revolve   Creates a 3D solid by revolving a 2D object.
Elev   Gives thickness to non-solid objects to extrude them.

TIPS

■ You can extrude the following objects:
> Circle
> Ellipse
> Donut
> Closed polyline
> Polygon
> Closed spline
> Region

■ You *cannot* extrude polylines with less than 3 or more than 500 vertices; similarly, you cannot extrude crossing or self-intersecting polylines.

■ Objects within a block cannot be extruded; use the **Explode** command first.

■ The taper angle must between 0 (default) and 90 degrees.

■ Positive angles taper in from base; negative angles taper out.

■ This command does not work when a taper angle is less than -90 degrees or more than +90 degrees.

■ **Extrude** also does not work if the combination of angle and height makes the object's extrusion walls intersect.

■ You can use the following objects as an extrusion path:
> Line
> Polyline
> Arc
> Elliptical arc
> Circle
> Ellipse

FileOpen

Rel.12 Opens a drawing file without a dialog box (*an undocumented command*).

Command	Alias	Ctrl+	F-key	Alt+	Menu Bar	Tablet
fileopen	...	...	...	...	...	...

Command: **fileopen**
Enter name of drawing to open <filename.dwg>: **[enter filename]**

COMMAND LINE OPTIONS

Enter name of drawing
Specifies the name of the DWG file to open.

RELATED COMMANDS

Close   Closes the current drawing.
Open   Opens multiple drawing files.

RELATED SYSTEM VARIABLES

DbMod   Detects whether the drawing was changed since being opened.
SDI   Allows only one drawing to be open in AutoCAD at a time.

TIPS

■ Use this command in menu and toolbar macros to open a drawing file when you don't want a dialog box displayed.

■ This command can only be used in SDI (single drawing interface) mode; if you use this command when two or more drawings are open, AutoCAD complains, "The SDI variable cannot be reset unless there is only one drawing open. Cannot run FILEOPEN if SDI mode cannot be established."

■ Use **QSave** before using **FileOpen**; otherwise, **FileOpen** displays the following dialog box:

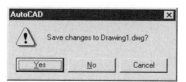

When you click **Yes**, AutoCAD closes the current drawing, and displays the **Select Drawing File** dialog box.

REMOVED COMMAND

The **Files** command was removed from Release 14. In its place, use Windows Explorer.

'Fill

V. 1.4   Toggles wide objects — traces, multilines, solids, and polylines — to be displayed and plotted as solid-filled or as outlines.

Command	Alias	Ctrl+	F-key	Alt+	Menu Bar	Tablet
'fill	...	...	...	...	...	...

```
Command: fill
Enter mode [ON/OFF] <ON>: off
Command: regen
Regenerating model.
```

Fill on (left) and off (right) with a wide polyline, donut, and 2D solid.

COMMAND LINE OPTIONS

ON   Turns on fill after the next regeneration.
OFF   Turns off fill after the next regeneration.

RELATED SYSTEM VARIABLE

FillMode   Current setting of fill status:

FillMode	Meaning
0	Fill mode is off.
1	Fill mode is on (default).

RELATED COMMAND

Regen   Changes the display to reflect the current fill or nofill status.

TIPS

- The state of fill (or no fill) does not come into effect until the next regeneration.

- Traces, solids, and polylines are not filled when the view is *not* in plan view, regardless of the setting of **Fill**.

- Since filled objects take longer to regenerate, redraw, and plot, consider leaving fill off during editing and plotting. During plotting, use a wide pen for filled areas.

- **Fill** affects objects derived from polylines, including donut, polygon, rectangle, and ellipse when created with **PEllipse** = 1.

- **Fill** does *not* affect TrueType fonts, which have their own system variable — **TextFill** — that toggles their fill-no fill status.

- **Fill** does not toggle in rendered mode.

Fillet

V. 1.4 Joins two intersecting lines, polylines, arcs, circles, or 3D solids with a radius.

Command	Alias	Ctrl+	F-key	Alt+	Menu Bar	Tablet
fillet	f	...	...	MF	Modify ⌐Fillet	W19

```
Command: fillet
Current settings: Mode = TRIM, Radius = 0.5000
Select first object or [Polyline/Radius/Trim]: [pick]
Select second object: [pick]
```

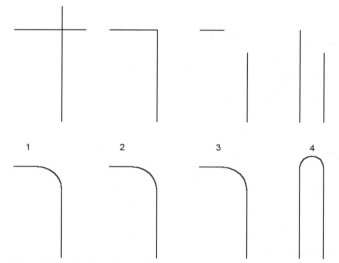

*Lines before (top) and after (bottom) applying the **Fillet** command:*
1. Crossing lines.   2. Touching lines.   3. Non-intersecting lines.   4. Parallel lines.

COMMAND LINE OPTIONS

Select first object
> Selects the first object to be filleted.

Select second object
> Selects the second object to be filleted.

Polyline option:
```
Select 2D polyline: [pick]
n lines were filleted
```
Select 2D polyline
> Fillets all vertices of a 2D polyline; a 3D polyline cannot be filleted.

Radius *option:*
Specify fillet radius <0.5000>: **[enter value]**
Specify fillet radius
        Signifies the filleting radius.

Trim *option:*
Enter Trim mode option [Trim/No trim] <Trim>: **n**
Trim   Trims objects when filetted.
No trim   Does not trim objects.
When a 3D solid is selected:
Select an edge or [Chain/Radius]: **[pick]**
Select an edge or [Chain/Radius]: E<small>NTER</small>
n edge(s) selected for fillet.

Box before (left) and after (right) applying **Fillet** *and* **Render** *to a 3D solid.*

Edge option:
Select an edge or [Chain/Radius]: **[pick]**
Select edge   Selects a single edge.

Chain *option:*
Select an edge chain or [Edge/Radius]:   **[pick]**
Select an edge chain
        Selects all tangential edges.

Radius *option:*
Enter fillet radius <1.0000>: **[enter value]**
Enter fillet radius
        Specifies the fillet radius.

RELATED COMMANDS

Chamfer   Bevels intersecting lines or polyline vertices.

SolidEdit   Edits 3D solid models.

RELATED SYSTEM VARIABLES

FilletRad   Specifies the current filleting radius.

TrimMode   Toggles whether objects are trimmed.

TIPS

■ Pick the end of the object you want filleted; the other end will remain untouched.

■ The lines, arcs, or circles need not touch.

■ As a faster substitute for the **Extend** and **Trim** commands, use the **Fillet** command with the radius of zero.

■ If the lines to be filleted are on two different layers, the fillet is drawn on the current layer.

■ The fillet radius must be smaller than the length of the lines. For example, if the lines to be filleted are 1.0m long, the fillet radius must be less than 1.0m.

■ Use the **Close** option of the **PLine** command to ensure a polyline is filleted at all vertices.

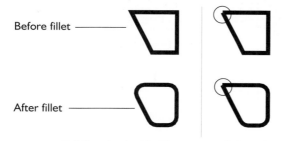

*Polyline closed with **Close** option (left) and without (right).*

■ You cannot fillet polyline segments from different polylines.

■ Filleting a pair of circles does not trim them.

■ As of AutoCAD Release 13, the **Fillet** command fillets a pair of parallel lines; the radius of the fillet is automatically determined as half the distance between the lines.

'Filter

Rel.12 Creates a filter list, which can be applied to selection sets.

Command	Alias	Ctrl+	F-key	Alt+	Menu Bar	Tablet
'filter	fi	...	...	...	...	...

Command: **filter**
Displays dialog box:

```
┌─ Object Selection Filters ──────────────────────────── ✕ ─┐
│  ┌──────────────────────────────────────────────────────┐ │
│  │                                                        │ │
│  │                                                        │ │
│  └──────────────────────────────────────────────────────┘ │
│  ┌─Select Filter──────────┐   ┌─Edit Item─┬─Delete─┬─Clear List─┐ │
│  │ Arc Center        ▼│ Select...│                              │ │
│  │                        │   ┌─Named Filters─────────────┐   │ │
│  │  X: │= ▼│ 0.0000    │   │ Current: │*unnamed       ▼│   │ │
│  │  Y: │= ▼│ 0.0000    │   │                            │   │ │
│  │  Z: │= ▼│ 0.0000    │   │ Save As: │            │   │ │
│  │  Add to List   Substitute │   │ Delete Current Filter List │   │ │
│  │  Add Selected Object <     │   │ Apply   Cancel   Help      │   │ │
│  └────────────────────────┘   └───────────────────────────┘   │
└────────────────────────────────────────────────────────────┘
```

```
Applying filter to selection.
Select objects: [pick]
n found n were filtered out.
Select objects: ENTER
Exiting filtered selection.
```
AutoCAD highlights filtered objects with grips.

DIALOG BOX OPTIONS

Select Filter options:

Select   Displays all items of the specified type in the drawing.
X, Y, Z   Specifies object's coordinates.
Add to List   Adds the current select-filter option to the filter list.
Substitute   Replaces a highlighted filter with the selected filter.
Add Selected Object
                      Selects the object to be added from the drawing.

Edit Item   Edits the highlighted filter item.
Delete   Deletes the highlighted filter item.
Clear list   Clears the entire filter list.

Named Filter options:

Current   Selects the named filter from the list.
Save As   Saves the filter list with a name and the .NFL extension.
Delete Current Filter List
                      Deletes the named filter.
Apply   Closes the dialog box, and applies the filter operation.

COMMAND LINE OPTION

Select options Selects the objects to be filtered; use the **All** option to select all non-frozen objects in the drawing.

RELATED COMMANDS

Any AutoCAD command with a 'Select objects' prompt.

QSelect   Creates a selection set quickly, via a dialog box.

Select   Creates a selection set via the command line.

RELATED FILE

*.NFL   Named filter list.

TIPS

- The selection set created by **Filter** is accessed via the **P** (previous) selection option.

- Alternatively, **'Filter** is used transparently at the 'Select objects' prompt.

- **Filter** cannot find objects when color is set to BYLAYER and linetype is set to BYLAYER.

- Save selection sets by name to an NFL (short for *named filter*) file on disk for use in other drawings or editing sessions.

- **Filter** uses the following grouping operators:

**Begin OR	*with*	**End OR
**Begin AND	*with*	**End AND
**Begin XOR	*with*	**End XOR
**Begin NOT	*with*	**End NOT

- **Filter** uses the following relational operators:

Operator	Meaning
<	Less than.
< =	Less than or equal to.
=	Equal to.
! =	Not equal to.
>	Greater than.
> =	Greater than or equal to.
*	All values.

Filtering a selection set

To erase, for example, all construction lines from a drawing:

Step 1: Start the **Erase** command then call the **Filter** command transparently:

```
Command: erase
Select objects: 'filter
```

Notice that AutoCAD displays the **Object Selection Filters** dialog box:

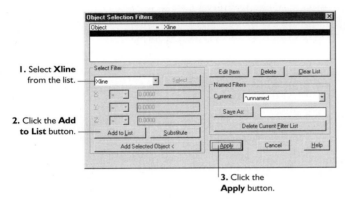

1. Select **Xline** from the list.

2. Click the **Add to List** button.

3. Click the **Apply** button.

Step 2: In the **Select Filter** section, select **Xline** from the drop list.

Step 3: Click the **Add to List** button.

Step 4: Click **Apply**. Notice that the **Filter** command continues by displaying prompts on the command line:

```
Applying filter to selection.
```

Step 5: Specify that **Filter** should search the entire drawing with the **All** option:

```
Select objects: all
n found n were filtered out.
```

Step 6: Exit the **Filter** command by pressing ENTER:

```
Select objects: ENTER
Exiting filtered selection.  <Selection set: 7>
n found
```

Step 7: AutoCAD resumes the **Erase** command. Press ENTER to end it:

```
Select objects: ENTER
```

AutoCAD uses the selection set created by the **Filter** command to erase the xlines.

 # Find

2000 Finds and, optionally, replaces text in the drawing..

Command	Alias	Ctrl+	F-key	Alt+	Menu Bar	Tablet
find	...	...	...	EF	Edit ⬐Find	X10

Command: **find**
Displays dialog box:

```
┌─ Find and Replace ──────────────────────────────── ? X ┐
│  Find text string:              Search in:              │
│  [plate mirror            ▼]    [Entire drawing  ▼] ⬚ │
│  Replace with:                                          │
│  [                        ▼]    [ Options.. ]          │
│  Search results:                                        │
│  ┌─ Context ──────────────┐   ┌──[ Find Next ]──┐      │
│  │ PLATE MIRRORED         │      [ Replace ]            │
│  │                        │      [ Replace All ]        │
│  │                        │      [ Select All ]         │
│  │                        │      [ Zoom to ]            │
│  └────────────────────────┘                            │
│  ┌───────────────────────────────────────┐            │
│  │                                         │            │
│  └───────────────────────────────────────┘            │
│              [ Close ]        [ Help ]                  │
└────────────────────────────────────────────────────────┘
```

DIALOG BOX OPTIONS

Find text string Specifies the text find; enter text or click the down arrow to select one of the most recent lines of text searched for.

Replace with Specifies the text to be replaced (only if replacing found text); enter text or click the down arrow to select one of the most recent lines of text searched for.

Search in Indicates:
Current Selection: searches the current selection set for text; click the **Select objects** button to create a selection set, if necessary.
Entire Drawing: searches the entire drawing.

Select objects Allows you to select objects in the drawing; press **Enter** to return to the dialog box.

Options Displays the **Find and Replace Options** dialog box.

Search results options:
Context Displays the found text in its context.
Find Next Finds the text entered in the **Find text string** field.
Replace Replaces a single found text with the text entered in the **Replace with** field.
Replace All Replaces all instances of the found text.

Select All	Selects all objects containing the text entered in the **Find text string** field; AutoCAD displays the message "AutoCAD found and selected *n* objects that contain "..."".
Zoom to	Zooms in to the area of the current drawing containing the found text.

Find and Replace Options dialog box:

Include options:
Block Attribute Value
> Finds text in attributes.

Dimension Annotation Text
> Finds text in dimensions.

Text (Mtext, DText, Text)
> Finds text in paragraph text placed by the **MText** command, and single-line text placed by the **Text** command.

Hyperlink Description
> Finds text in the description of a hyperlink.

Hyperlink	Finds text in a hyperlink.
Match case	Finds text that exactly matches the uppercase and lowercase pattern; for example, when searching for "Quick Reference," AutoCAD would find "Quick Reference" but not "quick reference."

Find whole words only
> Finds text that exactly matches whole words; for example, when searching for "Quick Reference," AutoCAD would find "Quick Reference" but not "Quickly Reference."

RELATED COMMANDS

AttDef	Creates attribute text.
DdEdit	Edits text.
Dim*xxx*	Creates dimension text.
Hyperlink	Creates hyperlinks and hyperlink descriptions.
MText	Creates paragraph text.
Properties	Edits selected text.
QSelect	Finds text objects.
Text	Creates single-line text.

Fog

Rel.14 Creates a fog-like effect in renderings to add visual distance cues to suggest the apparent distance of the objects from the camera.

Command	Alias	Ctrl+	F-key	Alt+	Menu Bar	Tablet
fog	...	...	...	VEF	View	P2
					⁀Render	
					⁀Fog	

Command: **fog**

Displays dialog box:

```
┌─ Fog / Depth Cue ─────────────────────────────── ⊠ ┐
│  ☑ Enable Fog          ☐ Fog Background             │
│                                                      │
│   Color System:  ┌RGB ──────────────────────┐▼      │
│   Red:           ┌0.50┐  ◄│   _│    │►              │
│   Green:         ┌0.50┐  ◄│   _│    │►              │
│   Blue:          ┌0.50┐  ◄│   _│    │►              │
│   ┌────────┐     ┌───────────────────────────┐      │
│   │        │     │   Select Custom Color...   │      │
│   │        │     ├───────────────────────────┤      │
│   └────────┘     │   Select from ACI...       │      │
│                  └───────────────────────────┘      │
│                                                      │
│   Near Distance:     ┌0.00┐ ◄│_        │►           │
│   Far Distance:      ┌1.00┐ ◄│         │►│          │
│                                                      │
│   Near Fog Percentage:   ┌0.00┐ ◄│_        │►       │
│   Far Fog Percentage:    ┌1.00┐ ◄│        │►│       │
│                                                      │
│      ┌─── OK ───┐   ┌─ Cancel ─┐   ┌─ Help ─┐       │
└──────────────────────────────────────────────────── ┘
```

DIALOG BOX OPTIONS

Enable Fog   Turns fog effect on; allows turning fog off without affecting parameters.

Fog Background
Applies fog effect to background; see the **Background** command.

Colors   Selects the color of the fog by either RGB (red, green blue) or HLS (hue, lightness, saturation) methods.

Near Distance Defines where the fog effect begins; value is the percent distance between camera and the back clipping plane.

Far Distance Defines where the fog effect ends.

Near Fog   Specifies percentage of fog effect at near distance; ranges between 0 and 100%.

Far Fog   Specifies percentage of fog effect at the far distance; ranges between 0 and 100%.

RELATED COMMAND

Render   Creates a rendering with optional fog effect.

TIPS

- The fog can be any color:

Color	RGB	HLS	Effect
White	1,1,1	0,1,0	Fog.
Black	0,0,0	0,0,0	Distance.
Green	0,1,0	0.33,0.5,0	Alien mist.

- The effect of using White as the fog color:

- It can be tricky getting the fog effect to work. Use the **3dOrbit** command to set the back clipping plane at the back of the model or where you want the fog to have its full effect. Then use **Fog** to set up the following parameters:

  Near distance: 0.70
  Far distance: 1.00
  Near fog percentage: 0.00
  Far fog percentage: 1.00

REMOVED COMMAND

GiffIn was removed from Release 14. In its place, use **Image**.

'GotoUrl

Goes to the hyperlink contained by an object (*an undocumented command*).

Command	Alias	Ctrl+	F-key	Alt+	Menu Bar	Tablet
'gotourl	...	...	...	...	...	...

```
Command: gotourl
Select objects: [pick]
n found Select objects: ENTER
browser Enter Web location (URL) <http://www.autodesk.com>:
    [enter URL]
```
AutoCAD launches your computer's default Web browser.

COMMAND LINE OPTIONS

Select objects Selects one or more objects containing a hyperlink.
Enter Web location (URL)
            Specifies the name of the hyperlink.

RELATED COMMANDS.

Browser   Launches the Web browser.
Hyperlink   Attaches, edits, and removes hyperlinks from objects.

TIPS

■ This command is meant for use by macros and menus.

■ AutoCAD uses this command for the shortcut menu's **Hyperlink | Open** option.

'GraphScr

V. 2.1 Switches the text window back to the graphics window.

Command	Alias	Ctrl+	F-key	Alt+	Menu Bar	Tablet
'graphscr	...	...	F2	...	...	...

Command: **graphscr**

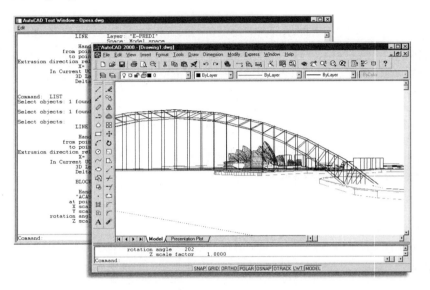

Text window (underneath) and graphics windows (on top).

COMMAND LINE OPTIONS
None.

RELATED COMMANDS
CopyHist   Copies text from the Text window to the Clipboard.
TextScr   Switches from the graphics window to the Text window.

RELATED SYSTEM VARIABLE
ScreenMode   Indicates whether current screen is in text or graphics mode:

ScreenMode	Meaning
0	Text window.
1	Graphics window (default).
2	Dual screen displaying both text and graphics.

TIP
- The Text window appears to be frozen when a dialog box is active. Click the dialog box's **OK** or **Cancel** buttons to regain access to the Text window.

'Grid

<u>V. 1.0</u> Displays a grid of reference dots within the currently set limits.

Command	Alias	Ctrl+	F-key	Alt+	Status Bar	Tablet
'grid	...	G	F7	...	GRID	...

```
Command: grid
Specify grid spacing(X) or [ON/OFF/Snap/Aspect] <0.5000>:
```

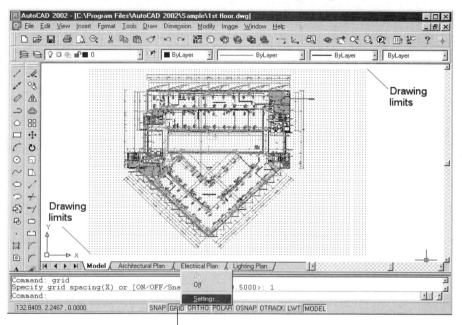

*Click **GRID** to toggle the grid display; right-click for menu.*

COMMAND LINE OPTIONS

Specify grid spacing(X)

Sets the x and y direction spacing; an X following the value sets the grid spacing to a multiple of the current snap setting.

ON   Turns on grid markings.

OFF   Turns off grid markings.

Snap Makes the grid spacing the same as the snap spacing.

Aspect options:

```
Specify the horizontal spacing(X) <0.0000>: [enter value]
Specify the vertical spacing(Y) <0.0000>: [enter value]
```

Horizontal Sets the spacing in the x direction.

Vertical   Sets the spacing in the y direction.

RELATED COMMANDS

Options	Sets the grid via a dialog box.
Limits	Sets the limits of the grid in WCS.
Snap	Sets the snap spacing.

RELATED SYSTEM VARIABLES

GridMode   Current grid visibility:

GridMode	Meaning
0	Grid is off (default).
1	Grid is on.

GridUnit	Specifies the current grid x,y-spacing.
LimMin	Specifies the x,y coordinates of the lower-left corner of the grid display.
LimMax	Specifies the x,y-coordinates of the upper-right corner of the grid display.
SnapStyl	Displays a normal or isometric grid:

SnapStyl	Meaning
0	Normal (default)
1	Isometric grid.

TIPS

- The grid is most useful when set to the snap spacing, or to a multiple of the snap spacing.

- When the grid spacing is set to 0, it matches the snap spacing.

- You can set a different grid spacing in each viewport and a different grid spacing in the x and y directions.

- Rotate the grid with the **Snap** command's **Rotate** option.

- The **Snap** command's **Isometric** option displays an isometric grid.

- If a very dense grid spacing is selected, the grid will take a long time to display; press **Esc** to cancel the display.

- AutoCAD will not display a grid that is too dense and returns the message, "Grid too dense to display."

- Grid markings are not plotted; to create a plotted grid, use the **Array** command to place an array of points.

Group

Rel.13 Creates a named selection set of objects.

Command	Alias	Ctrl+	F-key	Alt+	Menu Bar	Tablet
group	g	...	...	...	...	X8
-group	-g					

Command: **group**
Displays dialog box:

Object Grouping

Group Name	Selectable
BUILDINGS	Yes
QUICKREFERENCE	Yes
STREETS	Yes

Group Identification
Group Name: QUICKREFERENCE
Description: All objects in opera house
[Find Name <] [Highlight <] □ Include Unnamed

Create Group
[New <] ☑ Selectable □ Unnamed

Change Group
[Remove <] [Add <] [Rename] [Re-Order...]
[Description] [Explode] [Selectable]

[OK] [Cancel] [Help]

DIALOG BOX OPTIONS

Group Name   Lists the names of groups in the drawing.

Group Identification options:
Group Name   Displays the name of the current group.
Description   Describes the group; may be up to 64 characters long.
Find Name   Lists the name(s) of group(s) that a selected object belongs to.
Highlight   Highlights the objects included in the current group.
Include Unnamed
              Lists unnamed groups in the dialog box.

Create Group options:
New   Selects objects for the new group.
Selectable   Toggles selectability: picking one object picks the entire group.
Unnamed   Creates an unnamed group; AutoCAD gives the name ***A**n, where n is a number that increases with each group.

Change Group options:
Remove   Removes objects from the current group.
Add   Adds objects to the current group.
Rename   Renames the group.

Re-order	Changes the order of objects in the group; displays the **Order Group** dialog box.
Description	Changes the description of the group.
Explode	Removes the group description; does not erase group members.
Selectable	Toggles selectability.

Order Group dialog box:

Group Name	Lists the names of groups in the current drawing.
Description	Describes the selected group.

Remove from position (0 - *n*)

    Selects the object to move.

Replace at position (0 - *n*)

    Moves group name to a new position.

Number of objects (1 - *n*)

    Lists the number of objects to reorder.

Re-Order	Applies the order changes.
Highlight	Highlights the objects in the current group.
Reverse Order	Reverses the order of the groups.

-GROUP COMMAND

Command: **-group**
[?/Order/Add/Remove/Explode/REName/Selectable/Create]
  <Create>: **ENTER**

COMMAND LINE OPTIONS

?	Lists the names and descriptions of currently-defined groups.
Order	Changes the order of objects within the group.
Add	Adds objects to the group.
Remove	Removes objects from the group.
Explode	Removes the group definition from the drawing.
REName	Renames the group.
Selectable	Toggles whether the group is selectable.
Create	Creates a new named group from the objects selected.

RELATED COMMANDS

Block	Creates a named symbol from a group of objects.
Select	Creates a selection set.

RELATED SYSTEM VARIABLE

PickStyle   Toggles whether groups are selected by the usual selection process:

PickStyle	Meaning
0	Groups and associative hatches are not selected.
1	Groups are included in selection sets.
2	Associate hatches are included in selection sets.
3	Both are selected (default).

TIPS

- As of AutoCAD 2002, you can no longer toggle groups on and off with the **CTRL+A** shortcut keystroke.

- Consider a group as a named selection set; unlike a regular selection set, a group is not "lost" when the next group is created.

- Group descriptions are up to 64 characters long.

- Anonymous groups are unnamed; AutoCAD refers to them as ***A**n.

Hatch

V. 1.4 Draws a non-associative crosshatch pattern within a closed boundary.

Command	Alias	Ctrl+	F-key	Alt+	Menu Bar	Tablet
hatch	-h	...	...	...	...	...

```
Command: hatch
Enter a pattern name [?/Solid/User defined] <ANSI31>:
   [enter a pattern name]
Specify a scale for pattern <1.0000>: ENTER
Specify an angle for pattern <0>: ENTER
Select objects to define hatch boundary or <direct hatch>,
Select objects: [pick]
n found Select objects: ENTER
```

COMMAND LINE OPTIONS

Enter a pattern name

Specifies the valid name of a hatch pattern; include one of the following optional, undocumented style parameters, such as:

```
Enter a pattern name [?/Solid/User defined]: ansi31,o
```

Style	Meaning
N	Hatches alternate boundaries (Normal).
O	Hatches only outermost boundary (Outermost).
I	Hatches everything within outermost boundary (Ignore).

Specify a scale Specifies the hatch pattern scale.

Specify an angle

Specifies the hatch pattern angle.

Select objects Selects the objects that make up the hatch pattern boundary.

Pattern name options:

?   Lists the hatch pattern names: 'Enter pattern(s) to list <*>:'.

Solid   Specifies a solid fill drawn at the current color.

User defined options:

```
Specify angle for crosshatch lines <0>: ENTER
Specify spacing between the lines <1.0000>: ENTER
Double hatch area? [Yes/No] <N>: ENTER
Select objects to define hatch boundary or <direct hatch>,
Select objects: [pick]
1 found Select objects: ENTER
```

Direct Hatch options:
*Press **ENTER** at the first 'Select objects' prompt.*

```
Select objects: ENTER
Retain polyline boundary? [Yes/No] <N>:
Specify start point: [pick]
```

```
Specify next point or [Arc/Close/Length/Undo]: [pick]
Specify next point or [Arc/Close/Length/Undo]: [pick]
Specify next point or [Arc/Close/Length/Undo]: c
Specify start point for new boundary or <apply hatch>: ENTER
```

Retain polyline boundary?

> **Yes**: leaves boundary in place after hatch is complete.
> **No**: erases boundary after hatch is complete.

Specify start point

> Begins drawing the hatch boundary.

Specify next point

> Draws straight line.

Arc   Draws an arc hatch boundary; prompts 'Enter an arc boundary option
         [Angle/ CEnter/CLose/Direction/Line/Radius/Second pt/Undo/
         Endpoint of arc] <Endpoint>"; see the **Arc** command.

Close   Closes the hatch boundary.

Length   Continues the boundary by a specified distance; prompts 'Specify
         length of line.'

Undo   Undoes the last-drawn segment

RELATED COMMANDS

BHatch   Places automatic, associative hatching.
Boundary   Automatically creates polyline or region boundary.
Explode   Reduces hatch pattern to its constituent lines.
Snap   Changes the hatch pattern's origin.

RELATED SYSTEM VARIABLES

HpAng   Specifies the current hatch pattern angle.
HpDouble   Specifies doubled hatch pattern.
HpName   Specifies the current hatch pattern name.
HpScale   Specifies the current hatch pattern scale.
HpSpace   Specifies the current hatch pattern spacing.
SnapBase   Controls the origin of the hatch pattern.
SnapAng   Controls the angle of the hatch pattern.

RELATED FILES

Acad.Pat   Hatch pattern definition file for ANSI.
AcadIso.Pat   Hatch pattern definition file for ISO.

TIPS

■ The **Hatch** command draws non-associative hatch patterns; the pattern remains in place when its boundary is edited.

■ For complex hatch areas, you may find it easier to outline the area with a polyline — using object snap — or with the **Boundary** or **BHatch** commands.

■ To create the hatch as lines, precede the pattern name with * (asterisk).

HatchEdit

Rel.13   Edits associative hatch objects.

Command	Alias	Ctrl+	F-key	Alt+	Menu Bar	Tablet
hatchedit	he	...	...	...	Modify	Y16
					⌐Hatch	

-hatchedit

Command: **hatchedit**
Select associative hatch object: **[pick]**
Displays dialog box:

DIALOG BOX OPTIONS

Most options are grayed-out because they are unavailable.

Preview   Dismisses the dialog box temporarily, so that you can see the effect of the
                  editing changes on the hatch pattern.

Inherit Properties
                  Allows you to pick another hatch pattern whose properties will apply to
                  the selected hatch pattern.

Quick tab:

Pattern Type Selects the source of the hatch pattern:

Source	Meaning
Predefined	Acad.Pat (default).
User-defined	Create hatch pattern on the fly.
Custom	Select hatch from another PAT file.

Pattern	Selects a pattern name from the drop list.
...	Selects a pattern from tabbed dialog box.
Custom Pattern	Names the custom hatch pattern.
Scale	Specifies the hatch pattern scale.
Angle	Specifies the hatch pattern angle.
Spacing	Specifies the spacing between pattern lines.

Advanced tab:

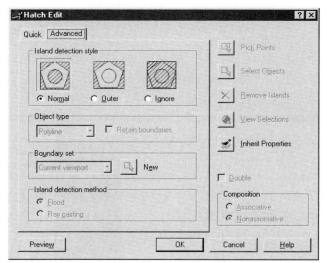

Island Detection Style

- **Normal** hatches the alternate boundaries (default).

- **Outer** hatches only the outermost boundary.

- **Ignore** hatches everything within the outermost boundary.

-HATCHEDIT COMMAND

Command: **-hatchedit**
Select associative hatch object: **[pick]**
Enter hatch option [Disassociate/Style/Properties]
    <Properties>: **[enter option]**

COMMAND LINE OPTIONS

Select   Selects a single associative hatch pattern.
Disassociate Removes associativity from hatch pattern.

Style options:
Enter hatching style [Ignore/Outer/Normal] <Normal>:

Normal   Hatches alternate boundaries (default).
Outer   Hatches only outermost boundary.
Ignore   Hatches everything within outermost boundary.

Properties options:
See **Hatch** *command.*
Pattern name Specifies the name of a valid hatch pattern.
?   Lists the available hatch pattern names.
Solid   Replaces the hatch pattern with solid fill.
User defined Creates a new on-the-fly hatch pattern.
Scale   Changes the hatch pattern scale.
Angle   Changes the hatch pattern angle.

RELATED COMMANDS

BHatch   Applies associative hatch patterns.
Explode Explodes a hatch pattern block into lines.

RELATED SYSTEM VARIABLES

HpAng   Specifies the current hatch pattern angle.
HpDouble Specifies doubled hatch pattern.
HpName   Specifies the current hatch pattern name.
HpScale   Specifies the current hatch pattern scale.
HpSpace   Specifies the current hatch pattern spacing.
SnapBase Controls the origin of the hatch pattern.
SnapAng   Controls the angle of the hatch pattern.

TIPS

- **HatchEdit** only works with associative hatch objects.

- To select a solid fill, click the outer edge of the hatch pattern, or use a crossing window selection on top of the solid fill.

- Even though the **Hatch Edit** dialog box looks identical to the **BHatch** dialog box, many options are not available in the **Hatch Edit** dialog box.

? 'Help *and* '?

V. 1.0 Lists text screens of information for using AutoCAD's commands.

Command	Alias	Ctrl+	F-key	Alt+	Menu Bar	Tablet
'help	'?	...	F1	HH	Help ↳Help	Y7

Command: **help**
Displays window:

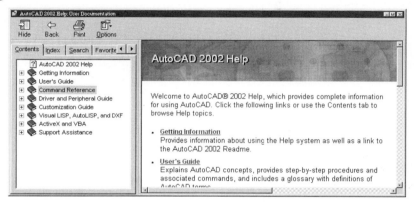

RELATED COMMANDS
All.

RELATED FILE
Acad.Chm   AutoCAD help file.

TIP
■ Since **'Help**, **?**, and **F1** are transparent commands, you can use them during another command to get help on the command's options.

Hide

V. 2.1 Removes hidden lines from 3D drawings.

Command	Alias	Ctrl+	F-key	Alt+	Menu Bar	Tablet
hide	hi	...	...	VH	View ↳Hide	M2

```
Command: hide
Regenerating drawing.
Removing hidden lines: 25
```

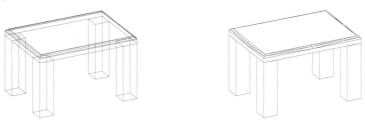

3D object without (left) and with hidden lines removed (right).

COMMAND LINE OPTIONS
None.

RELATED COMMANDS
MView	Removes hidden lines during plots of paper space drawings.
Plot	Removes hidden lines during plots of 3D drawings.
Regen	Returns the view to wireframe.
Render	Performs realistic renderings of 3D models.
ShadeMode	Performs quick renderings and quick hides of 3D models.
VPoint	Selects the 3D viewpoint.
3dOrbit	Removes hidden lines of perspective in 3D views.

RELATED SYSTEM VARIABLES
HaloGap Specifies the distance to shorten "haloed" lines; expressed as a percent of 1". A *halo* creates a gap in a line when it passes under another object in hidden-line views.

ObscuredColor Specifies the color for hidden (obscured) lines:

ObscuredColor	Meaning
0	Hidden lines are not displayed
1	Hidden lines displayed in red
2	Yellow
3	Green
4	Cyan
5	Blue
6	Magenta
7	Black (white)
8	Dark gray
9	Light gray
10 - 255	Other colors

ObscuredLtype Specifies the linetype for hidden lines:

ObscuredLtype	Meaning
0	Hidden lines are not displayed
1	Solid
2	Dashed (traditional Hidden)
3	Dotted
4	Short Dash
5	Medium Dash
6	Long Dash
7	Double Short Dash
8	Double Medium Dash
9	Double Long Dash
10	Medium Long Dash
11	Sparse Dash

TIPS

■ This command considers the following objects as opaque: circle, 2D solid, trace, wide 2D polyline, 3D face, polygon mesh, any object with thickness, regions, and 3D solids.

■ For a faster hide, use the **ShadeMode** command's **Hide** option.

■ Use **MSlide** (or **SaveImg**) to save the hidden-line view as a SLD (or TIFF, TGA, or GIF) file. View the saved image with **VSlide** or **Replay**.

■ Freezing layers speeds up the hide process, since **Hide** ignores objects on frozen layers.

■ **Hide** does not consider the visibility of text and attributes.

■ To create a hidden-line view when plotting in paper space, select the **HidePlot** option of the **MView** command.

■ To view the hidden lines, use the **ObscuredColor** and **ObscuredLtype** system variables (new to AutoCAD 2002) to specify the color and linetype of hidden lines. Both system variables must be non-zero for this feature to work; non-hidden lines are forced to black. Settings are local to drawings; linetype scale cannot be controlled by **LtScale**.

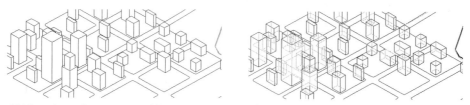

Either obscured system variable set to 0 (at left); both obscured sysvars turned on (at right).

REMOVED COMMAND

HpConfig was removed from AutoCAD 2000; it was replaced by the **Plot** command.

⬛ Hyperlink

<u>2000</u> Attaches a hyperlink (or URL) to objects in the drawing.

Command	Alias	Ctrl+	F-key	Alt+	Menu Bar	Tablet
hyperlink	...	K	...	IH	Insert ⤷Hyperlink	...

-hyperlink

Command: **hyperlink**
Select objects: **[pick]**
Select objects: ENTER
Displays dialog box:

COMMAND LINE OPTION

Select objects Selects the objects to which to attach the hyperlink.

DIALOG BOX OPTIONS

Existing File or Web Page options:

Text to display Describes the hyperlink; the description is displayed by the tooltip; when blank, the tooltip displays the URL.

Type the file or Web page name
        Specifies the hyperlink (URL) to associate with the selected objects; the hyperlink may be any file on your computer, on any computer you can access on your local network, or on the Internet.

Or select from list
        • Recent files
        • Browsed pages
        • Inserted links

File   Opens the **Browse the Internet - Select Hyperlink** dialog box.

Web Page	Starts up a simple Web browser.
Path	Displays the full path and filename to the hyperlink; only the filename appears when **Use relative path for hyperlink** is checked.
Target	Specifies a location in the file, such as a target in an HTML file, a named view in AutoCAD, or a page in a spreadsheet document. Displays **Select Place in Document** dialog box.
Use relative path for hyperlink	
	Toggles use of the path for relative hyperlinks in the drawing; when "" (null), the drawing paths stored in **AcadPrefix** are used.
Remove link	Removes the hyperlink from the object; this button appears only if you select an object that already has a hyperlink.

View of This Drawing option:

Select a view of this

Selects a layout, named view, or named plot.

Email Address option:

Email address Specifies the email address; the *mailto:* prefix is added automatically.

Subject Specifies text that will be added to the Subject: line.

Recently used e-mail addresses

Lists the email addresses you may have recently entered.

Select Place in Document option:

Select an existing place in the document

Selects a named locatation.

-HYPERLINK COMMAND

Command: **-hyperlink**
Enter an option [Remove/Insert] <Insert>: **ENTER**
Enter hyperlink insert option [Area/Object] <Object>: **o**
Select objects: **[pick]**
n found Select objects: **ENTER**
Enter hyperlink <current drawing>: **[enter hyperlink address]**
Enter named location <none>: **ENTER**
Enter description <none>: **ENTER**

COMMAND LINE OPTIONS

Remove   Removes a hyperlink from selected objects or areas.
Insert   Adds a hyperlink to selected objects or areas.
Select objects   Selects the object to which the hyperlink will be added.
Enter hyperlink
                  Specifies the filename or hyperlink address.
Enter named location
                  (*Optional*) Specifies a location within the file or hyperlink.
Enter description
                  (*Optional*) Specifies a description of the hyperlink.

RELATED COMMANDS

HyperlinkOptions
                  Toggles the display of the hyperlink cursor, shortcut menu, and tooltip.
HyperlinkOpen
                  Opens a hyperlink (URL) via the command line.
HyperlinkBack Returns to the previous URL.
HyperlinkFwd Moves forward to the nexxt URL; works only when the HyperlinkBack command was used; otherwise AutoCAD complains, "** No hyperlink to navigate to **".
HyperlinkStop Stops the display of the current hyperlink.
GoToUrl   Displays a specific Web page.
PasteAsHyperlink
                  Pastes a hyperlink to the selected objects.

RELATED SYSTEM VARIABLE

HyperlinkBase Specifies the path for relative hyperlinks in the drawing; when "" (null), the drawing paths stored in **AcadPrefix** are used.

TIPS

■ If the drawing has never been saved, AutoCAD is unable to determine the default relative folder. For this reason, the **Hyperlink** command prompts you to save the drawing.

■ By using hyperlinks, you can create a *project document* consisting of drawings, contacts (word processing documents), project timelines, cost estimate (spreadsheets pages), and architectural renderings. To do so, create a "title page" of an AutoCAD drawing with hyperlinks to the other documents.

■ To edit a hyperlink with **Hyperlink**, select object(s), make editing changes, and click **OK**.

■ To remove a hyperlink with **Hyperlink**, select the object, then click **Remove Link**.

■ An object can have just one hyperlink attached to it; more than one object, however, can share the same hyperlink.

■ The alternate term for hyperlink is *URL*, which is short for "uniform resource locator," and is the universal file naming system used by the Internet.

HyperlinkOpen, Back, Fwd, Stop

2000   Control the display of hyperlinked pages (*undocumented commands*).

Command	Alias	Ctrl+	F-key	Alt+	Menu Bar	Tablet
hyperlinkopen	...	...	...	...	...	...
hyperlinkback						
hyperlinkfwd						
hyperlinkstop						

Command: **hyperlinkopen**
Enter hyperlink <current drawing>: **www.autodesk.com**
Enter named location <none>: **ENTER**
Displays the specified Web page or file, if possible.

Command: **hyperlinkback**
Returns to the previous hyperlinked page.

Command: **hyperlinkstop**
Stops displaying the Web page.

Command: **hyperlinkfwd**
Hyperlinks to the next page; can be used only after the **HyperLinkBack** *command.*

COMMAND LINE OPTIONS

Enter hyperlink Enters a URL (uniform resource locator) or a filename.
Enter named location
Enters a named view or other valid target.

RELATED COMMANDS

Hyperlink   Attaches a hyperlink to objects.
HyperlinkOptions
Specifies the options for hyperlinks.
GoToUrl   Displays a specific Web page.

RELATED TOOLBAR ICONS

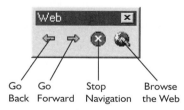

Go   Go   Stop   Browse
Back   Forward   Navigation   the Web

Go Back   Goes to the previous hyperlink; executes the **HyperlinkBack** command.
Go Forward   Goes to the next hyperlink; executes the **HyperlinkFwd** command.
Stop Navigation Stops loading the current hyperlink file; executes **HyperlinkStop** command.
Browse the Web Displays the Web browser; executes the **Browser** command.

HyperlinkOptions

<u>**2000**</u>   Toggles the display of the hyperlink cursor, shortcut menu, and tooltip (*the longest command name in AutoCAD*).

Command	Alias	Ctrl+	F-key	Alt+	Menu Bar	Tablet
hyperlinkoptions ...	...	...	...	...	

Command: **hyperlinkoptions**
Display hyperlink cursor and shortcut menu? [Yes/No] <Yes>:
Display hyperlink tooltip? [Yes/No] <Yes>:

Hyperlink cursor and tooltip (at left); hyperlink shortcut menu (at right).

COMMAND LINE OPTIONS

Display hyperlink cursor and shortcut menu
> Toggles the display of the hyperlink cursor and shortcut menu.

Display hyperlink tooltip
> Toggles the display of the hyperlink tooltip.

CURSOR MENU OPTIONS

Select an object containing a hyperlink; then right-click to display the cursor menu.
Hyperlink options:

Open "url"   Launches the appropriate applications and loads the file referenced by the URL.

Copy Hyperlink
> Copies hyperlink data to the Clipboard; use the **PasteAsHyperlink** command to paste the hyperlink to selected objects.

Add to Favorites
> Adds the hyperlink to the favorites list.

Edit Hyperlink
> Displays the **Edit Hyperlink** dialog box; see the **Hyperlink** command.

RELATED COMMANDS

Hyperlink   Attaches a hyperlink to objects.
Options   Determines options for most other aspects of AutoCAD.

RELATED SYSTEM VARIABLE

HyperlinkBase Specifies the path for relative hyperlinks in the drawing; when "" (null), the drawing paths stored in **AcadPrefix** are used.

'Id

V. 1.0 Identifies the 3D coordinates of a picked point (*short for IDentify*).

Command	Alias	Ctrl+	F-key	Alt+	Menu Bar	Tablet
'id	...	...	...	TYI	Tools ⌐Inquiry ⌐Id Point	U9

```
Command: id
Specify point: [pick]
```

Example output:
```
X = 1278.0018     Y = 1541.5993     Z = 0.0000
```

COMMAND LINE OPTION
Specify point   Pick a point.

RELATED COMMANDS
List   Lists information about a picked object.
Point   Draws a point.

RELATED SYSTEM VARIABLE
LastPoint   The 3D coordinates of the last picked point.

TIPS
- The **Id** command stores the picked point in the **LastPoint** system variable. Access that value by entering *@* at the next prompt for a point value.

- Use the **Id** command to set the value of the **LastPoint** system variable, which can be used as relative coordinates in another command.

- The z-coordinate displayed by **Id** is the current elevation setting; if you use **Id** with an object snap, then the z-coordinate is the object-snaped value.

Image

Rel.14 Controls the attachment of raster images.

Command	Alias	Ctrl+	F-key	Alt+	Menu Bar	Tablet
image	im	...	...	IM	Insert	T3
					⬐Image Manager	
-image	-im					

Command: **image**

Displays dialog box:

DIALOG BOX OPTIONS

Attach   Displays the **Attach Image File** dialog box; see the **ImageAttach** command.

Detach   Erases the image from the drawing.

Reload   Reloads the image file into the drawing.

Unload   Removes the image from memory without erasing the image.

Save Path   Describes the drive and subdirectory location of the file.

Browse   Searches for the image file; displays the **Attach Image File** dialog box.

Details   Describes the technical details of the images; displays dialog box.

Image File Details dialog box:

-IMAGE COMMAND

Command: **-image**

Enter image option [?/Detach/Path/Reload/Unload/Attach]
    <Attach>: **ENTER**

COMMAND LINE OPTIONS

?	Lists currently-attached image files.
Detach	Erases the image from the drawing.
Path	Lists the names of images in the drawing.
Reload	Reloads the image file into the drawing.
Unload	Removes the image from memory without erasing the image.
Attach	Displays the **Attach Image File** dialog box; see the **ImageAttach** command.

RELATED SYSTEM VARIABLE

ImageHlt   Toggles whether the entire image is highlighted:

RELATED COMMANDS

ImageAdjust   Controls the brightness, contrast, and fading of the image.
ImageAttach   Attaches an image in the current drawing.
ImageClip   Creates a clipping boundary on an image.
ImageFrame   Toggles display of the image's frame.
ImageQuality Toggles display between draft and high-quality mode.
Transparency Changes the transparency of the image.
Xref   Attaches a DWG drawing as an externally-referenced file.

TIPS

■ The **Image** command handles raster images of these color depths:

Depth	Colors
Bitonal	Black and white (monochrome).
8-bit gray	256 shades of gray.
8-bit color	256 colors.
24-bit color	16.7 million colors.

■ AutoCAD can display one or more images in any viewport.

■ There is no theoretical limit to the number and size of images.

ImageAdjust

Rel.14 Controls brightness, contrast, and fading of the attached raster image (*an external command in AcIsmUi.Arx*).

Command	Alias	Ctrl+	F-key	Alt+	Menu Bar	Tablet
imageadjust	iad	...	...	MOIA	Modify	X20
					⮡Object	
					⮡Image	
					⮡Adjust	

-imageadjust

Command: **imageadjust**
Select image(s): **[pick]**
Select iamge(s): **ENTER**
Displays dialog box:

DIALOG BOX OPTIONS

Brightness options:

Dark   Reduces the brightness of the image when values are closer to 0.
Light   Increases the brightness of the image when values are closer to 100.

Contrast options:

Low   Reduces the image contrast when values are closer to 0.
High   Increases the image contrast when values are closer to 100.

Fade options:

Min   Reduces the image fading when values are closer to 0.
Max   Increases the image fading when values are closer to 100.

Reset   Resets the image to its original parameters; default values are:

Parameter	Original Setting
Brightness	50
Contrast	50
Fade	0

-IMAGEADJUST COMMAND

Command: **-imageadjust**
Select image(s): **[pick]**
Select image(s): ENTER
Enter image option [Contrast/Fade/Brightness] <Brightness>:

COMMAND LINE OPTIONS

Contrast option:
Enter contrast value (0-100) <50>: **[enter value]**
Enter contract value

Adjusts the contrast between 0% contrast and 100% contrast (*default = 50*).

Fade option:
Enter fade value (0-100) <0>: **[enter value]**
Enter fade option

Adjusts the fading between 0% faded and 100% faded (*default = 0*).

Brightness option:
Enter brightness value (0-100) <50>: **[enter value]**
Enter brightness value

Adjusts the brightness between 0% bright and 100% bright (*default = 50*).

RELATED SYSTEM VARIABLES

None.

RELATED COMMANDS

Image   Controls the loading of raster image files in the drawing.
ImageAttach   Attaches an image in the current drawing.
ImageClip   Creates a clipping boundary on an image.
ImageFrame   Toggles display of the image's frame.
ImageQuality Toggles display between draft and high-quality mode.
Transparency Changes the transparency of the image.

TIPS

■ **Brightness** ranges from 0 (*left*) to 50 (*center*) and 100 (*right*).

■ **Contrast** ranges from 0 (*left*) to 50 (*center*) and 100 (*right*).

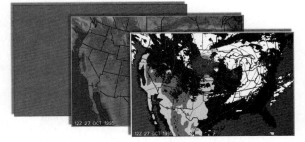

■ **Fade** ranges from 0 (*left*) to 50 (*center*) and 100 (*right*).

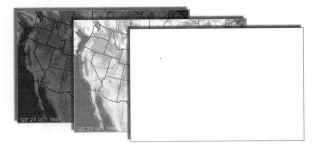

ImageAttach

<u>Rel.14</u> Selects a raster file to attach to the current drawing.

Command	Alias	Ctrl+	F-key	Alt+	Menu Bar	Tablet
imageattach	iat	...	...	II	Insert ⇘Raster Image	...

Command: **imageattach**
Displays file dialog box:

*Selecting an image and clicking **Open**, displays dialog box:*

DIALOG BOX OPTIONS

Name   Selects name from a list of previously-attached image names.

Browse   Selects file; displays **Select Image File** dialog box.

Retain Path   Saves the path to the image file.

Insertion point options:
Specify On-Screen

           Specifies the insertion point of the image in the drawing, after the dialog box is dismissed.

X, Y, Z Specifies the x, y, z coordinates of the lower-left corner of the image.

Scale options:

Specify on-screen

Specifies the scale of the image (relative to the lower-left corner) in the drawing after the dialog box is dismissed.

Scale Specifies the scale of the image; positive value enlarges the image, while negative values reduce the image.

Rotation options:

Specify on-screen

Specifies the rotation angle of the image about the lower-left corner in the drawing, after the dialog box is dismissed.

Angle Specifies the angle to rotate the image; positive angles rotate the image counterclockwise.

Details Expands the dialog box to display information about the image:

```
              OK          Cancel        Help        Details <<

  ┌ Image Information ─────────────────────────────────────────────
  │
  │  Resolution:                      Current AutoCAD unit:
  │    Horizontal:  240.00 per AutoCAD unit    Inches
  │    Vertical:    240.00 per AutoCAD unit
  │
  │  Image size in pixels:            Image size in units:
  │    Width:   240                     Width:   1
  │    Height:  441                     Height:  1.8375
```

RELATED COMMANDS

Image Controls the loading of raster image files in the drawing.
ImageAttach Attaches an image in the current drawing.
ImageClip Creates a clipping boundary on an image.
ImageFrame Toggles the display of the image's frame.
ImageQuality Adjusts the quality of the image.
Transparency Changes the transparency of the image.

RELATED SYSTEM VARIABLE

InsUnits Specifies the drawing units for the inserted image.

TIPS

- For a command-line version of the **ImageAttach** command, use the **-Image** command's **Attach** option.

- This dialog box no longer selects units from the **Current AutoCAD Unit** list box; as of AutoCAD 2000, use the **InsUnits** system variable.

■ ImageClip

Rel.14 Clips a raster image.

Command	Alias	Ctrl+	F-key	Alt+	Menu Bar	Tablet
imageclip	icl	...	...	MCI	Modify ⌐Clip ⌐Image	X22

```
Command: imageclip
Select image to clip: [pick]
Enter image clipping option [ON/OFF/Delete/New boundary] <New>:
```

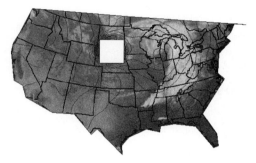

COMMAND LINE OPTIONS

Select image   Selects one image to clip.
ON   Turns on a previous clipping boundary.
OFF   Turns off the clipping boundary.
Delete   Erases the clipping boundary.

New Boundary options:
```
Enter clipping type [Polygonal/Rectangular] <Rectangular>:
```

Polygonal   Creates a polygonal clipping path.
Rectangular   Creates a rectangular clipping boundary.

Polygonal options:
```
Specify first point: [pick]
Specify next point or [Undo]: [pick]
Specify next point or [Undo]: [pick]
Specify next point or [Close/Undo]: [pick]
Specify next point or [Close/Undo]: c
```

Specify first point
   Specifies the start of the first segment of the polygonal clipping path.
Specify next point
   Specifies the next vertex.
Undo   Undoes the last vertex.
Close   Closes the polygon clipping path.

Rectangular *options:*

Specify first corner point: **[pick]**
Specify opposite corner point: **[pick]**

Specify first corner point
> Specifies one corner of the rectangular clip.

Specify opposite corner point
> Specifies the second corner.

When you select an image with a clipped boundary, AutoCAD prompts:

Delete old boundary? [No/Yes] <Yes>: **y**

Delete old boundary
> **Yes**: Removes previously-applied clipping path.
> **No**: Exits command.

RELATED COMMANDS

Image Controls the loading of raster image files in the drawing.
ImageAdjust Controls the brightness, contrast, and fading of the image.
ImageAttach Attaches an image in the current drawing.
ImageFrame Toggles the display of the image's frame.
ImageQuality Toggles the display between draft and high-quality mode.
Transparency Changes the transparency of the image.
XrefClip Clips a DWG drawing attached as an external reference file.

TIPS

■ You can use object snap modes on the image's frame, but not on the image itself.

■ To clip a hole in the image, create the hole, then double back on the same path:

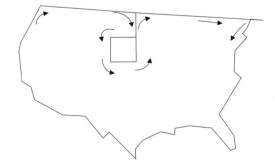

■ For a rounded clipping path, apply the **PEdit** command.

ImageFrame

Rel.14 Toggles the display of the frame around the image.

Command	Alias	Ctrl+	F-key	Alt+	Menu Bar	Tablet
imageframe	...	...	...	MOIF	Modify	...
					↳Object	
					↳ Image	
					↳ Frame	

```
Command: imageframe
ON/OFF/<on>: off
```

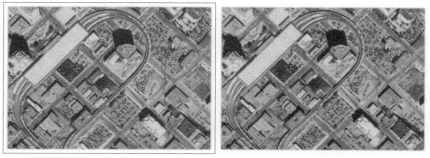

Image frame turned on (left) and turned off (right).

COMMAND LINE OPTIONS

ON Turns on display of image frame (default).

OFF Turns off display of image frame.

RELATED SYSTEM VARIABLE

ImageHlt Toggles whether entire image is highlighted:

ImageHlt	Meaning
0	Highlights image frame.
1	Highlights entire image (default).

RELATED COMMANDS

Image Controls the loading of raster image files in the drawing.

ImageAdjust Controls the brightness, contrast, and fading of the image.

ImageAttach Attaches an image in the current drawing.

ImageClip Creates a clipping boundary on an image.

ImageQuality Toggles the display between draft and high-quality mode.

Transparency Changes the transparency of the image.

TIPS

■ *Warning!* When **ImageFrame** is turned off, you cannot select the image.

■ The frame is turned on (or off) in all viewports.

■ The image frame is plotted.

ImageQuality

Rel.14 Toggles the quality of the image between draft and high quality.

Command	Alias	Ctrl+	F-key	Alt+	Menu Bar	Tablet
imagequality	...	...	...	MOIQ	Modify ↳Object ↳Image ↳Quality	...

Command: **imagequality**
Enter image quality setting [High/Draft] <High>: **d**

COMMAND LINE OPTIONS

High	Displays image at its highest quality.
Draft	Displays image at a lower quality.

RELATED COMMANDS

Image	Controls the loading of raster image files in the drawing.
ImageAdjust	Controls the brightness, contrast, and fading of the image.
ImageAttach	Attaches an image in the current drawing.
ImageClip	Creates a clipping boundary on an image.
ImageFrame	Toggles the display of the image's frame.
Transparency	Changes the transparency of the image.

TIP

■ High quality displays the image more slowly; draft displays the image more quickly.

⌗ Import

Rel.13 Imports vector and raster files into the current drawing.

Command	Alias	Ctrl+	F-key	Alt+	Menu Bar	Tablet
import	imp	...	...	...	...	T2

Command: **import**
Displays dialog box:

DIALOG BOX OPTIONS

Look in	Selects the folder (*subdirectory*) and drive from which to import the file.
File name	Specifies the name of the file, or accepts the default.
File of type	Selects the file format in which to import the file.
Open	Imports the file.
Cancel	Dismisses the dialog box, and returns to AutoCAD.
Find File	Displays the **Find File** dialog box, which lets you search for a filename.
Options	Displays the **Options** dialog box; content varies with filetype.
Locate	Searches the paths for the file.

RELATED COMMANDS

AppLoad	Loads AutoLISP, VBA, and ObjectARX routines.
DxbIn	Imports DXB file.
Export	Exports the drawing in several vector and raster formats.
Load	Imports SHX shape objects.
Insert	Places another drawing in the current drawing as a block.
InsertObj	Places an OLE object in the drawing via the Clipboard.
LsLib	Imports landscape objects.
MatLib	Imports rendering material definitions.
MenuLoad	Loads menu files into AutoCAD.
Open	Opens AutoCAD (any version) DWG and DXF files.
PasteClip	Pastes objects from the Clipboard.

PasteSpec	Pastes or links object from the Clipboard.
Replay	Displays rendering in TIFF, Targa, or GIF format.
VSlide	Displays SLD slide files.
XBind	Imports named objects from another DWG file.
XRef	Displays another DWG file in the current drawing.

TIPS

■ The **Import** command acts as a "shell" command; it launches other AutoCAD commands that perform the actual import function. Other options may be available with the actual command, such as insertion point and scale.

Format	Meaning
Metafile	Windows metafile WMF; executes the **WmfIn** command.
ACIS	ASCII SAT; executes the **AcisIn** command.
Encapsulated PS	Encapsulated PostScript; executes the **PsIn** command.
3D Studio	3D Studio 3DS format; executes the **3dsIn** command.

■ To import a DXF file, use the **Open** command.

■ To import an XML file, use the **Insert** command.

REMOVED COMMANDS

INetCfg was removed from AutoCAD 2000; it was replaced by Windows 98/NT's Internet configuration.

INetHelp was removed from AutoCAD 2000; it was replaced by AutoCAD's standard online help.

Insert

V. 1.0   Inserts a previously-defined block into the drawing; imports XML files.

Command	Alias	Ctrl+	F-key	Alt+	Menu Bar	Tablet
insert	i	...	...	IB	Insert	T5
	inserturl				⌐Block	
-insert	-i					

Command: **insert**
Displays dialog box

[Insert dialog box]

Name:
Path:
Insertion point — ☑ Specify On-screen X: 0.0000 Y: 0.0000 Z: 0.0000
Scale — ☐ Specify On-screen X: 1.0000 Y: 1.0000 Z: 1.0000 ☐ Uniform Scale
Rotation — ☐ Specify On-screen Angle: 0
☐ Explode   OK   Cancel   Help
Browse...

DIALOG BOX OPTIONS

Name   Selects from a list of previously-inserted blocks.

Browse   Displays file dialog box to select the block in one of the following formats:
- **Drawing (*.dwg)** AutoCAD drawing file.
- **DXF (*.dxf)** drawing interchange file.
- **DesignXML (*.xml)** extended markup language (new to AutoCAD 2002).

Insertion point options:

Specify On-Screen
   Specifies the insertion point in the drawing, after the dialog box is dismissed.

X, Y, Z   Specifies the x, y, z coordinates of the lower-left corner of the block.

Scale options:

Specify on-screen
   Specifies the scale of the block (relative to the lower-left corner) in the drawing, after the dialog box is dismissed.

X, Y, Z   Specifies the x,y,z scale of the block; positive values enlarge the block, while negative values reduce the block.

Uniform Scale Forces the y and z scale factors to be the same as the x scale factor.

Rotation options:

Specify on-screen
   Specifies the rotation angle of the block (about the lower-left corner) in the drawing after the dialog box is dismissed.

Angle   Specifies the angle to rotate the block; positive angles rotate the block counterclockwise.

Explode   Explodes the block upon insertion.

-INSERT COMMAND

```
Enter block name or [?]: [enter name]
Specify insertion point or [Scale/X/Y/Z/Rotate/PScale/PX/PY/
   PZ/PRotate]: [pick]
Enter X scale factor, specify opposite corner, or
   [Corner/XYZ] <1>: ENTER
Enter Y scale factor <use X scale factor>: ENTER
Specify rotation angle <0>: ENTER
```

COMMAND LINE OPTIONS

Block name Specifies the name of the block to be inserted.

?   Lists the names of blocks stored in the drawing.

Specify insertion point
                Specifies the lower-left corner of the block's insertion point.

P   Supplies predefined block name, scale, and rotation values.

X scale factor Indicates the x scale factor.

Corner   Indicates the x and y scale factors by pointing on the screen.

XYZ   Displays the x, y, and z scale submenu.

INPUT OPTIONS

In response to the 'Block Name' prompt, you can enter:

Option	Meaning
~	Display a dialog box of drawings stored on disk: Block name: **~**
*	Insert block exploded: Block name: ***filename**
=	Redefine existing block with a new block: Block name: **oldname=newname**

In response to the 'Insertion point' prompt, you can enter:

Option	Meaning
Scale	Specify x, y, and z-scale factors.
PScale	Preset the x, y, and z-scale factors.
XScale	Specify x scale factor.
PxScale	Preset x scale factor.
YScale	Specify y scale factor.
PyScale	Preset y scale factor.
ZScale	Specify z scale factor.
PzScale	Preset the z scale factor.
Rotate	Specify the rotation angle.
PRotate	Preset the rotation angle.

RELATED COMMANDS

Block	Creates a block of a group of objects.
Explode	Reduces inserted blocks to their constituent objects.
MInsert	Inserts a block as a blocked rectangular array.
Rename	Renames blocks.
WBlock	Writes blocks to disk.
XRef	Displays drawings stored on disk in the drawing.

RELATED SYSTEM VARIABLES

ExplMode Toggles whether non-uniformly scaled blocks can be exploded:

ExplMode	Meaning
0	Cannot explode; AutoCAD Release 12 compatible.
1	Can be exploded (default).

InsBase	Specifies the name of the most-recently inserted block.
InsUnits	Specifies the drawing units for the inserted block.

TIPS

- You can insert any other AutoCAD drawing into the current drawing.

- A *preset* scale factor or rotation means the dragged image is shown at that scale, but you can enter a new scale when inserting.

- Drawings are normally inserted as a block; prefix the filename with an * (*asterisk*) to insert the drawing as separate objects.

- Redefine all blocks of the same name in the current drawing by adding the = (*equal*) suffix after its name at the 'Block name' prompt.

- Insert a mirrored block by supplying a negative x- or y-scale factor, such as:

```
X scale factor: -1
```

- AutoCAD converts a negative z scale factor into its absolute value, which makes it always positive.

- As of AutoCAD Release 13, you can explode a mirrored block and a block inserted with different scale factors when the system variable **ExplMode** is turned on.

- AutoCAD 2002 (and 2000i with the DesignXML extension) uses the **Insert** command to import drawings in XML format. Use the **WBlock** command to export the drawing in XML format.

InsertObj

Rel.13 Places an OLE object as a linked or embedded object (*short for IN-SERT OBJect*).

Command	Alias	Ctrl+	F-key	Alt+	Menu Bar	Tablet
insertobj	io	...	...	IO	Insert	T1
					⅋OLE Object	

Command: **insertobj**
Displays dialog box:

DIALOG BOX OPTIONS

Create New   Creates a new OLE object in another application, then embeds the object in the current drawing.

Create from File Selects a file to embed or link in the current drawing.

Object Type   Selects an object type from the list; the related application automatically launches if you select the **Create New** option.

Display As Icon
Displays the object as an icon, rather than as itself.

RELATED COMMANDS

OleLinks   Controls the OLE links.

PasteSpec   Places an object from the Clipboard in the drawing as a linked object.

RELATED WINDOWS COMMANDS

Edit | Copy   Copies an object to the Clipboard in another Windows application.

File | Update Updates an OLE object from another application.

REMOVED COMMAND

InsertUrl was removed from AutoCAD 2000; it was replaced by the **Insert** command's **Browse | Search the Web** option.

Interfere

Rel.11 Determines the interference of two or more 3D solid objects; creates a 3D solid body of the volumes in common (*an ACIS command*).

Command	Alias	Ctrl+	F-key	Alt+	Menu Bar	Tablet
interfere	inf	...	...	DII	Draw	...
					↳Solids	
					↳Interference	

```
Command: interfere
Select first set of solids:
Select objects: [pick]
Select objects: [Enter]
Select second set of solids:
Select objects: [pick]
Select objects: ENTER
Comparing 1 solid against 1 solid.
Interfering solids (first  set): 1
                    (second set): 1
Interfering pairs            : 1
Create interference solids? [Yes/No] <N>: y
```

A pair of interfering solids (left) and the interference (right).

COMMAND LINE OPTIONS

Select objects Checks all solids in a single selection set for interference with each other.
Create interference solids
       Creates a solid representing the volume of interference.

RELATED COMMANDS

Intersect	Creates a new volume from the intersection of two volumes.
Section	Creates a 2D region from a 3D solid.
Slice	Slices a 3D solid with a plane.

TIP

■ When more than two solids interfere, AutoCAD prompts, "Highlight pairs of interfering solids?"

⬤ Intersect

Rel.II Creates a 3D solid of 2D region via Boolean intersection of two or more solids or regions (*an ACIS command*).

Command	Alias	Ctrl+	F-key	Alt+	Menu Bar	Tablet
intersect	in	...	...	MNI	Modify ⮑Solids Editing ⮑Intersect	X17

```
Command: intersect
Select objects: [pick]
Select objects: [pick]
Select objects: ENTER
```

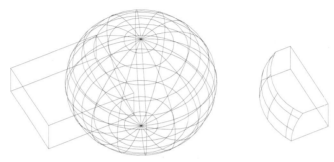

Two intersecting solids (left) and the resulting intersection (right).

COMMAND LINE OPTION

Select objects Selects two or more objects to intersect.

RELATED COMMANDS

Interfere	Creates a new volume from the interference of two or more volumes.
Subtract	Subtracts one 3D solid from another.
Union	Joins 3D solids into a single body.

TIPS

■ You can use this command on 2D regions and 3D solids.

■ The **Interference** and **Intersect** command may seem similar. Here is the difference between the two:

> **Intersect** *erases* all of the 3D solid parts that do not intersect.
> **Interfere** *creates a new object* from the intersection; it does not erase the original objects.

'Isoplane

V. 2.0 Switches the crosshairs and grid pattern among the three isometric drawing planes.

Command	Alias	Ctrl+	F-key	Alt+	Menu Bar	Tablet
'isoplane	...	E	F5	...	...	...

```
Command: isoplane
Enter isometric plane setting [Left/Top/Right] <Top>: ENTER
Current isoplane: Top
```

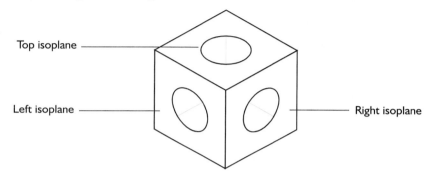

COMMAND LINE OPTIONS

Left	Switches to the left isometric plane.
Top	Switchs to the top isometric plane.
Right	Switches to the right isometric plane.
Toggle	Switches to the next isometric plane in the order of: left, top, right.

RELATED COMMANDS

Options	Displays a dialog box for setting isometric mode and planes.
Ellipse	Draws isocircles.
Snap	Turns on isometric drawing mode.

RELATED SYSTEM VARIABLE

SnapIsoPair	Contains the current isometric plane.
GridMode	Current grid visibility:

GridMode	Meaning
0	Grid is off (default).
1	Grid is on.

GridUnit	Current grid x,y spacing.
LimMin	X,y coordinates of the lower-left corner of the grid display.
LimMax	X,y coordinates of the upper-right corner of the grid display.
SnapStyl	Displays a normal or isometric grid:

SnapStyl	Meaning
0	Normal (default).
1	Isometric grid.

Creating isometric dimensions

AutoCAD's dimensions must be modified for isometric drawings so that the dimension text looks "correct" in isometric mode. This involves two steps — (1) creating isometric text styles and (2) changing dimension variables — repeated three times, once for each isoplane.

Step 1: CREATE ISO TEXT STYLES

1. From the menu bar, select **Format | Text Style**.

2. When the **Text Style** dialog box appears, click **New**.

3. Enter **isotop** for the name of the new text style, which is used for text in the top isoplane.

4. Click **OK**.

5. When the **Text Style** dialog box reappears, select *Simplex.Shx* from **Font Name**.

6. Change the **Oblique Angle** to **-30**.

7. Click **Apply**.

8. Create text styles for the other two isoplanes:

Style Name	Font Name	Oblique Angle
IsoTop	*Simplex.Shx*	-30
IsoRight	*Simplex.Shx*	30
IsoLeft	*Simpelx.Shx*	30

Enter these values into the **Text Style** dialog box, and click **Apply;** then **Close**.

Step 2: CREATING ISOMETRIC DIMENSION STYLES

1. Create the dimension styles for the three isoplanes by selecting **Format | Dimension Styles** from the menu bar. These dimension variables must be changed:

2. Create a new dimension style:

   - Click **New**.
   - Enter **IsoLeft** in the **New Style Name** field.
   - Click **Continue**.

2. Force dimension text to align with the dimension line:

   - Select the **Text** tab.
   - Select **Aligned with dimension line** in the **Text Alignment** section.

3. Specify text style for dimension text:

   - Select **ISOLEFT** from the **Text Style** list box.
   - Click **OK**.

5. One of the three needed dimension styles has been created. Create dimstyles for all isoplanes using these parameters:

Dimstyle Name	Text Style
Isotop	IsoTop
Isoright	IsoRight
Isoleft	IsoLeft

6. Click **Close** to exit the **Dimension Style Manager** dialog box.

Step 3: PLACING ISOMETRIC DIMENSIONS

To place linear dimensions in an isometric drawing, you must use the **DimAligned** command, because it aligns the dimension along the isometric axes: place all dimensions in one isoplane, then switch to the next isoplane.

1. Press **F5** to switch to the appropriate isoplane, such as **Top**.
2. Use the **DimStyle** command to select the associated dimension style, such as **IsoTop**.
3. Place the dimension with **DimAligned**; it is helpful to use INTersection object snaps.
4. Use the **DimEdit** command's **Oblique** option to skew the dimension by 30 or -30 degrees, as follows:

IsoPlane	DimStyle	Oblique Angle
Top	IsoTop	30
Left	IsoLeft	30
Right	IsoRight	-30

Aligned dimension text before (left) and after applying **DimEdit**'s **Oblique** *option (right).*

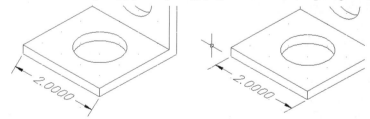

5. To place a leader, use the **Standard** dimstyle and **Standard** text style.

2001 Changes the justification of text.

Command	Alias	Ctrl+	F-key	Alt+	Menu Bar	Tablet
justifytext	...	...	...	MOTJ	Modify ⌐Object ⌐Text ⌐Justify	...

```
Command: justifytext
Select objects: [pick]
Select objects: ENTER
Enter a justification option
[Align/Fit/Center/Middle/Right/TL/TC/TR/ML/MC/MR/BL/BC/BR]
   <Left>: [enter option]
```

COMMAND LINE OPTIONS

Select objects	Select one or more text objects in the drawing.
Align	Aligns the text between two points with adjusted text height.
Fit	Fits the text between two points with fixed text height.
Center	Centers the text along the baseline.
Middle	Centers the text horizontally and vertically.
Right	Right-justifies the text.
TL	Justifies to top-left.
TC	Justifies to top-center.
TR	Justifies to top-right.
ML	Justifies to middle-left.
MC	Justifies to middle-center.
MR	Justifies to middle-right.
BL	Justifies to bottom-left.
BC	Justifies to bottom-center.
BR	Justifies to bottom-right.

RELATED COMMANDS

Text	Places text in the drawing.
DdEdit	Edits text.
ScaleText	Changes the size of text.
Style	Defines text styles.

TIPS

■ This command works with text, mtext, leader text, and attribute text.

■ When the justification is changed, the text does not move.

'Layer

V. 1.0 Controls the creation and visibility of layers.

Command	Alias	Ctrl+	F-key	Alt+	Menu Bar	Tablet
'layer	la	...	...	OL	Format	U5
	ddlmodes				⌐Layer	
-layer	-la					

Command: **layer**
Displays dialog box:

```
Layer Properties Manager                                                    ? X
┌─ Named layer filters ──────────────────────────────┐      [   New   ] [  Delete  ]
│ Show all layers            ▼  ...   □ Invert filter.│
│                                 □ Apply to Object Properties toolbar.  [ Current ] [ Show details ]
Current Layer: 0                                              [ Save state... ] [ Restore state... ]

Name              On Freeze in all VP Lock Color   Linetype           Lineweight   Plot Style              Plot
1st floor plan|Hatch     ♀    ☼     ⚐  ■ 15    Continuous     ── Default  PLAN_Hatch              ☖
1st floor plan|Interior Walls ♀ ☼   ⚐  ■ White  Continuous     ── 0.30 mm  PLAN_Interior Walls     ☖
1st floor plan|Partitions ♀  ☼     ⚐  ■ White  Continuous     ── 0.30 mm  PLAN_Partitions         ☖
1st floor plan|Pillars   ♀   ☼     ⚐  ■ 30     Continuous     ── Default  PLAN_Pillars            ☖
1st floor plan|Title Block ♀ ☼     ⚐  ■ White  Continuous     ── Default  LAYOUT_Title Block      ☖
1st floor plan|Viewports ♀   ☼     ⚐  ■ White  1st floor plan|Solid ── Default  LAYOUT_Viewports   ☖
3                        ♀   ☼     ⚐  □ Green   Continuous     ── Default  LAYOUT_3                ☖
Border                   ♀   ☼     ⚐  ■ Blue    Continuous     ── Default  LAYOUT_Border           ☖
Defpoints                ♀   ☼     ⚐  ■ White   Continuous     ── Default  Normal
Electrical Diagram       ♀   ☼     ⚐  ■ 200     Continuous     ━━ 0.70 mm  LAYOUT_Electrical Diagram ☖
HP                       ♀   ☼     ⚐  ■ Magenta Continuous     ── Default  LAYOUT_HP               ☖
Nodes                    ♀   ☼     ⚐  □ 82      Continuous     ── Default  LAYOUT_Nodes            ☖
PORM-2                   ♀   ☼     ⚐  ■ White   Continuous     ── Default  Normal                  ☖
PORM-6                   ♀   ☼     ⚐  ■ White   Continuous     ── Default  Normal                  ☖
Symbols                  ♀   ☼     ⚐  ■ Blue    Continuous     ── Default  LAYOUT_Symbols          ☖
Title block              ♀   ☼     ⚐  ■ White   Continuous     ── Default  LAYOUT_Title Block      ☖
Title block text         ♀   ☼     ⚐  ■ White   Continuous     ── Default  LAYOUT_Title Block Text ☖
TXT                      ♀   ☼     ⚐  ■ Blue    Continuous     ── Default  LAYOUT_TXT              ☖
Viewports                ♀   ☼     ⚐  ■ White   Continuous     ── Default  Normal                  ☖
Xref_Architectural       ♀   ☼     🔒 ■ White   Continuous     ── Default  Normal                  ☖

60 Total layers   60 Layers displayed

                                              [   OK   ] [ Cancel ] [  Help  ]
```

DIALOG BOX OPTIONS

Named layer filters

Displays the following groups of layers:

- **Show all layers** displays all layers defined in the current drawing.
- **Show all used layers** displays any layer with content.
- **Show all xref dependent layers** displays layers in externally-referenced drawings.

... Displays **Named Layer Filters** dialog box.

Invert filter Inverts the display of layer names; for example, when **Show all used layers** is selected, the **Invert filter** option causes all layers with no content to be displayed.

Apply to Object Properties toolbar

Applies the filter to the names of the layers displayed by the **Object Properties** toolbar.

New Creates a new layer.

Current Sets the selected layer as the current layer.

Save state	Displays the **Layer States Manager** dialog box.
Delete	Purges the selected layer; some layers cannot be deleted, as described by the warning dialog box:

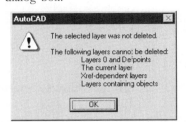

Show Details Displays the **Details** portion of the **Layer Properties Manager** dialog box.
Restore state Displays **Layer States Manager** dialog box.

Details options:

Name	Names the selected layer; if the name cannot be edited, the field is grayed out.
Color	Selects the color; click **Other** to display the **Select Color** dialog box.
Lineweight	Selects the lineweight.
Linetype	Selects the linetype.
Plot style	Selects the plot style.

Off for display Turns off the display of the layer.
Lock for editing Locks this layer; it is seen but cannot be edited.
Do not plot Prevents the layer from being plotted.
Freeze in all viewports
 Freezes the layer; the current layer cannot be frozen.
Freeze in active viewport
 Freezes the layer when **TileMode** = 0 (off); grayed out in model mode.
Freeze in new viewport
 Freezes the layer when a new viewport is created and when **TileMode** = 0; grayed out in model mode.

Named Layer Filters dialog box:

Filter name	Names the filter.
Add	Adds the name to the list of filters; note that these names are also available in the **Layer Properties Manager** dialog box's **Named layer filters** list.
Delete	Removes a name.
Reset	Resets all filters to their default values.

See wildcard metacharacters below:

Layer name	Specifies the names of layers to filter.
On/Off	Selects the layers that are on, off, or both.
Freeze/Thaw	Selects the layers that are frozen, thawed, or both.
Active viewport	Selects the layers that are frozen, thawed, or both in the current viewport.
New viewport	Selects the layers that are frozen, thawed, or both in the new viewport.
Lock/Unlock	Selects the layers that are locked, unlocked, or both.
Plot	Selects the layers that plot, do not plot, or both.
Colors	Selects the layers of a specific color.
Lineweight	Selects the layers with a specific lineweight.
Linetype	Selects the layers with a specific linetype.
Plot style	Selects the layers with a specific plot style.

Save Layer States dialog box
New to AutoCAD 2000i:

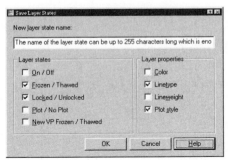

New layer state name
> Specifies the name of the layer state.

Layer states   Specifies the layer states that will be saved.

Layer properties
> Specifies the layer properties that will be saved.

Layer States Manager dialog box
New to AutoCAD 2000i:

Layer states   Lists the names of layer states that can be restored.

Restore   Restores the listed layer states.

Edit   Displays the **Edit Layer States** dialog box, identical to the **Save Layer States** dialog box.

Rename   Renames the selected layer state.

Delete   Deletes the selected layer state.

Import   Imports an LAS (layer state) file; layer states can be shared among drawings.

Export   Exports the selected layer state to an LAS file.

Close   Closes the dialog box.

SHORTCUT MENU OPTIONS

*Right-click a layer name in the **Layer Properties Manager:***

Make Current Makes the selected layer current.
New Layer   Creates a new layer with the default name of **Layer1**.
Select All   Selects all layers.
Clear All   Deselects all layers.
Select all but current
                Selects all layers, except the current layer; this allows you easily to freeze
                all layers except the current layer, which cannot be frozen.
Invert selection
                Inverts the selection of layer names.
Invert layer filter
                Inverts the layer names displayed by the current filter.

Layer filters options:
Show all layer Displays all layers defined in the current drawing.
Show all used layers
                Displays any layer with no content.
Show all xref dependent layers
                Displays layers in externally-referenced drawings.

Xref Filters   Displays names of xref'ed drawings to display only their layers.
Save Layer States
                Displays **Save Layer States** dialog box.

LIST OF LAYERS

Click a header to sort alphabetically (A-Z); click a second time for reverse-alphabetical sort (Z-A):

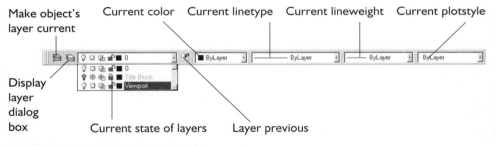

Name	Lists the names of layers in the current drawing.	
On	Toggles the layer between on and off.	
Freeze in all VP	Toggles the layer between thawed and frozen in all viewports.	
Lock	Toggles the layer between unlocked and locked.	
Color	Specifies the color for all objects on the layer.	
Linetype	Specifies the linetype for all objects on the layer.	
Lineweight	Specifies the lineweight for all objects on the layer.	
Plot Style	Specifies the plot style for all objects on the layer.	
Plot	Toggles the layer between plot and no-plot.	

OBJECT PROPERTIES TOOLBAR

Make object's layer current   Current color   Current linetype   Current lineweight   Current plotstyle

Display layer dialog box

Current state of layers   Layer previous

WILDCARD METACHARACTERS

Char	Meaning
*	Matches any one or more characters.
?	Matches any single character.
@	Matches any alphabetic character (A - Z).
#	Matches any numeric digit (0 - 9).
.	Matches any non-alphanumeric character (!@#$%^&*, etc.)
~	Matches anything but the pattern of characters.
[ ]	Matches any one enclosed character.
[~]	Matches any character not enclosed.
[-]	Matches a range of characters.
`	Allows literal use of metacharacters.

-LAYER COMMAND

Command: **-layer**
Current layer: "0"
Enter an option
[?/Make/Set/New/ON/OFF/Color/Ltype/LWeight/Plot/Freeze/
    Thaw/LOck/Unlock]: **[enter option]**

COMMAND LINE OPTIONS

Color	Indicates the color for all objects drawn on the layer.
Freeze	Disables the display of the layer.
LOck	Locks the layer.
Ltype	Indicates the linetype for all objects drawn on the layer.
LWeight	Specifies the lineweight.
Make	Creates a new layer, and makes it the current layer.
New	Creates a new layer.
OFF	Turns off the layer.
ON	Turns on the layer.
Plot	Specifies the plot style.
Set	Makes the layer the current layer.
Thaw	Unfreezes the layer.
Unlock	Unlocks the layer.
?	Lists the names of layers created in the drawing.

RELATED COMMANDS

LayerP	Returns to the previous layer.
Change	Moves objects to a different layer via command line.
Properties	Moves objects to a different layer via dialog box.
LayTrans	Translates layer names.
Purge	Removes unused layers from the drawing.
Rename	Renames layers.
VpLayer	Controls the visibility of layers in paper space viewports.

RELATED SYSTEM VARIABLE

CLayer	Contains the name of the current layer.

RELATED FILE

*.LAS	Layer state file; uses DXF format.

TIPS

- Layer **Defpoints** is a non-plotting layer.

- To create more than one new layer at a time, use commas to separate layer names.

- For a new layer to automatically take on the properites of an existing layer, select the layer before clicking **New**.

- If layer names appear to be missing, they have been filtered from the list.

LayerP

Undoes changes made to layer settings *(short for LAYER Previous)*.

Command	Alias	Ctrl+	F-key	Alt+	Menu Bar	Tablet
layerp	...	...	...	...	...	...

Command: **layerp**
Restored previous layer status

COMMAND LINE OPTIONS
None.

RELATED COMMANDS
LayerPMode   Toggles layer previous mode on and off.
Layer   Creates and set layers and modes.

RELATED SYSTEM VARIABLE
CLayer   Specifies the name of the current layer.

TIPS
■ This command acts like an "undo" command for changes made to layers only, such as changes to the layer's color or lineweight.

■ **LayerPMode** command must be turned on for the **LayerP** command to work.

■ The **LayerP** command does not undo the renaming of a layer, the deleting or purging a layer, and creating new layers.

LayerPMode

2002 Turns on and off layer previous mode *(short for LAYER Previous MODE).*

Command	Alias	Ctrl+	F-key	Alt+	Menu Bar	Tablet
layerpmode	...	...	...	...	...	...

Command: **layerpmode**
Enter LAYERP mode [ON/OFF] <ON>: **off**

COMMAND LINE OPTIONS
Enter LAYERP mode
> **On**: Turns on layer previous mode.
> **Off**: Turns off layer previous mode.

RELATED COMMANDS
LayerP   Returns the drawing to the previous layer.
Layer   Creates and sets layers and modes.

RELATED SYSTEM VARIABLES
None.

TIP
- When layer previous mode is on, AutoCAD tracks changes to layers.

Layout

<u>2000</u>   Creates and deletes paper space layouts on the command line.

Command	Alias	Ctrl+	F-key	Alt+	Menu Bar	Tablet
layout	lo	...	...	IL	Insert ↳Layout	...

-layout

Command: **layout**
Enter layout option [Copy/Delete/New/Template/Rename/
    SAveas/Set/?] <set>: **[enter option]**

COMMAND LINE OPTIONS

Copy	Copies a layout to create a new layout.
Delete	Deletes a layout; the **Model** tab cannot be deleted.
New	Creates a new layout tab, automatically generating the name for the layout (default = Layout1), which you may override.
Template	Displays the **Select File** dialog box, which allows you to select a DWG drawing or DWT template file to use as a template for a new layout. If the file has layouts, it displays the **Insert Layout(s)** dialog box.
Rename	Renames a layout.
SAveas	Saves the layouts in a drawing template (DWT) file. The last current layout is used as the default for the layout to save.
Set	Makes a layout current.
?	Lists the layouts in the drawing in a format similar to the following:

    Active Layouts:
    Layout: Architectural Plan Block name: *Paper_Space.
    Layout: Electrical Plan Block name: *Paper_Space1.
    Layout: Lighting Plan Block name: *Paper_Space0.

SHORTCUT MENU
Right-click any layout tab:

New layout
From template...
Delete
Rename
Move or Copy...
Select All Layouts
Page Setup...
Plot...

|◄ ◄ ► ►| \ Model / Architectural Plan / Electrical Plan / Lighting Plan /

New layout   Creates a new layout with the default name of **ENTER**.
From template Displays the **Select File** and **Insert Layout** dialog boxes.

Delete   Deletes the selected layout; displays a warning dialog box:

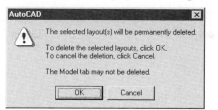

Rename   Displays the **Rename Layout** dialog box:

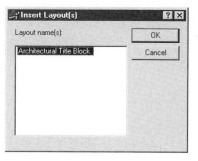

Move or Copy Displays the **Move or Copy** dialog box.
Select All Layouts
                  Selects all layouts.
Page Setup   Displays the **Page Setup** dialog box; see the **PageSetup** command.
Plot   Displays the **Plot** dialog box; see the **Plot** command.

Insert Layout(s) dialog box:

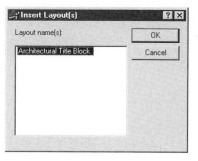

Layout names(s)
                  Lists the names of layouts found in the selected drawing; you may select
                  more than one layout at a time by holding down the **CTRL** key.
O K   Adds the selected layouts to the current drawing.
Cancel   Dismisses the dialog box and cancels the command.

Move or Copy dialog box:

Move or Copy

Move or copy selected layouts

Before layout:

Layout1
Layout2
Layout3
Layout4
Architectural Plan
(move to end)

[ ] Create a copy

OK
Cancel

Before layout Selects a layout to appear before the current layout.
Move to end Moves the current layout to the end of layouts.
Create a copy Makes a copy of the layout.

RELATED COMMAND

LayoutWizard Creates and deletes paper space layouts via wizard.

TIPS

■ "Layout" is the new name for paper space as of AutoCAD 2000.

■ A layout name can be up to 255 characters long; the first 32 characters are displayed in the tab.

■ The **Model** tab cannot be deleted, renamed, moved, or copied.

■ To switch between layouts, click the tab located below the drawing:

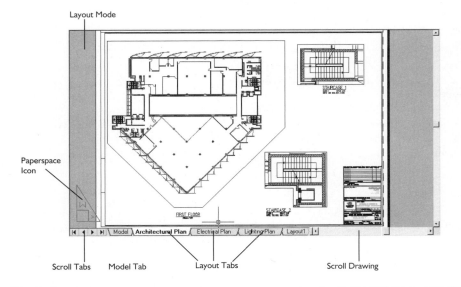

LayoutWizard

2000 Creates and deletes paper space layouts via wizard.

Command	Alias	Ctrl+	F-key	Alt+	Menu Bar	Tablet
layoutwizard	...	...	...	ILW	Insert ↳Layout ↳Layout Wizard	...
				TZC	Tool ↳Wizards ↳Create Layout	

Command: **layoutwizard**
Displays dialog box:

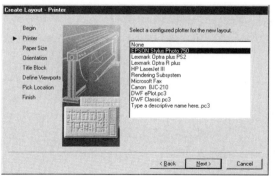

DIALOG BOX OPTIONS

Enter a name Specifies the name for the layout.
Back Displays the previous dialog box.
Next Displays the next dialog box.
Cancel Cancels the command.

Select a configured plotter
Selects a printer or plotter to which to output the layout.

Select a paper size
> Selects a size of paper supported by the output device.

Enter the paper units
- **Millimeters** meansures paper size in metric units.
- **Inches** measures paper size in Imperial units.
- **Pixels** measures paper size in dots per inch.

Select the orientation
- **Portrait** plots the drawing vertically.
- **Landscape** plots the drawing horizontally.

Select a title block
> Specifies a title border for the drawing as a block or an xref.

Specify the viewport type

- **None** creates no viewport.
- **Single** creates a single paper space viewport.
- **Std. 3D Engineering Views** creates top, front, side, and isometric views.
- **Array** creates a rectangular array of viewports.

Viewport scale

- **Scaled to Fit** fits the model to the viewport.
- **m:n** specifies a scale factor, ranging from 1:1 to 1/128":1'0".

Rows   Specifies the number of rows for arrayed viewports.

Columns   Specifies the number of columns for arrayed viewports.

Spacing between rows

Specifies the vertical distance between viewports.

Spacing between columns

Specifies the horizontal distance between viewports.

Select location Specifies the corners of a rectangle holding the viewports.

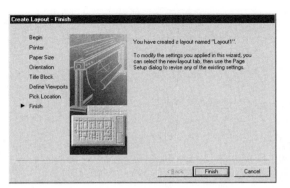

| Finish | Exits the dialog box and creates the layout. |

RELATED COMMANDS

| Layout | Creates a layout on the command line. |

RELATED SYSTEM VARIABLES

| CTab | Contains the name of the current tab. |

LayTrans

Translates layer names *(short for LAYer TRANSlation).*

Command	Alias	Ctrl+	F-key	Alt+	Menu Bar	Tablet
laytrans	...	...	...	TSL	Tools	...
					⌄CAD Standards	
					⌄Layer Translator	

Command: **laytrans**
Displays dialog box:

[Layer Translator dialog box]

DIALOG BOX OPTIONS

Translate From *options:*

Translate From

Lists the names of layers in the current drawing; icons indicate whether the layer is being used (is being referenced):

≣ TXT • **Green** icon: the layer contains at least one object.

≣ Unused layer • **White** icon: the layer contains no objects, and can be purged.

Selection Filter Specifies a subset of layer names; see **Wildcard Metacharacters** in the **Layer** command.

Select Highlights the layer names that match the selection filter.

Map Maps the selected layer(s) in the **Translate From** column to the selected layer in the **Translate To** column.

Map same Maps layers automatically with the same name.

Translate To *options:*

Translate To Lists layer names in the drawing opened with the **Load** button.

Load Accesses the layer names in another drawing via the **Select Drawing File** dialog box.

New Creates a new layer via the **New Layer** dialog box.

Layer Translation Mappings options:

Edit   Edits the linetype, color, lineweight, and plot style settings via the **Edit Layer** dialog box; identical to the **New Layer** dialog box.

Remove   Removes the selected layer from the list.

Save   Saves the matching table to a DWS (drawing standard) file.

Settings   Specifies translation options via the **Settings** dialog box.

Translate   Changes the names of layers, as specified by the **Layer Translation Mappings** list.

New Layer dialog box:

Identical to the **Edit Layer** *dialog box.*

Name   Specifies the name of the layer, up to 255 characters long.

Linetype   Selects a linetype from those available in the drawing.

Color   Selects a color; or, select **Other** for the **Select Color** dialog box.

Lineweight Selects a lineweight.

Plot style Selects a plot style from those available in the drawing; this option is not available if plot styles have not been enabled in the drawing.

Settings dialog box:

Force object color to Bylayer
       Forces every translated layer to take on color Bylayer.

Force object linetype to Bylayer
       Forces every translated layer to take on linetype Bylayer.

Translate objects in blocks
       Forces objects in blocks to take on new layer assignments.

Write transaction log

Writes the results of the translation to a LOG file, using the same filename as the drawing. When command is complete, AutoCAD reports:

`Writing transaction log to filename.log.`

Show layer contents when selected

Lists the names of selected layers only in the **Translate From** list.

RELATED COMMANDS

Standards   Creates the standards for checking drawings.
CheckStandards
                Checks the current drawing against a list of standards.
Layer   Creates and sets layers and modes.

RELATED FILES

DWS   Drawing standard file; saved in DWG format.
LOG   Log file recording layer translation; saved in ASCII format.

RELATED SYSTEM VARIABLES

None.

TIPS

- You can purge unused layers (those prefixed by a white icon) from within the **Layer Translator** dialog box:

  1. Right click any layer name in the **Translate From** list.

  2. Select **Purge Layers**. The layers are removed from the drawing.

- You can load layers from more than one drawing file; duplicate layer names are ignored.

Leader

Rel.13 Draws a leader line with one or more lines of text.

Command	Alias	Ctrl+	F-key	Alt+	Menu Bar	Tablet
leader	lead	...	...	...	...	R7

```
Command: leader
Specify leader start point: [pick]
Specify next point: [pick]
Specify next point or [Annotation/Format/Undo]
    <Annotation>:[pick]
Specify next point or [Annotation/Format/Undo]
    <Annotation>: ENTER
Enter first line of annotation text or <options>: [enter text]
Enter next line of annotation text: ENTER
```

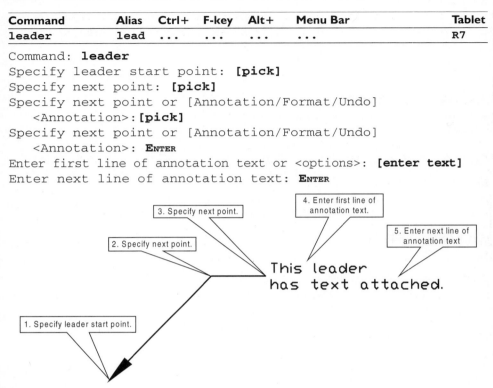

COMMAND LINE OPTIONS

Specify start point
　　　　　Specifies the location of the arrowhead.
Specify next point
　　　　　Positions the leader's vertex.
Undo　　　Undoes the leader line to the previous vertex.

Format options:
```
Enter leader format option [Spline/STraight/Arrow/None] <Exit>:
```
Spline　　Draws the leader line as a NURBS (short for non uniform rational Bezier spline) curve.
STraight　Draws the straight leader line (default).
Arrow　　Draws the leader with an arrowhead (default).
None　　Draws the leader with no arrowhead.

Annotation *options:*

```
Enter first line of annotation text or <options>: ENTER
Enter an annotation option [Tolerance/Copy/Block/None/
   Mtext] <Mtext>: [enter option]
```

Enter first line of annotation text
                             Specifies the leader text.

Tolerance	Places one or more tolerance symbols; see the **Tolerance** command.
Copy	Copies text from another part of the drawing.
Block	Places a block; see the **-Insert** command.
None	Specifies no annotation.
MText	Displays the **Multiline Text Editor** dialog box; see the **MText** command.

RELATED DIM VARIABLES

DimAsz	Specifies the size of the arrowhead and the hookline.
DimBlk	Specifies the type of arrowhead.
DimClrd	Specifies the color of the leader line and the arrowhead.
DimGap	Specifies gap between hookline and annotation; gap between box and text.
DimScale	Specifies the overall scale of the leader.

TIPS

■ This command was replaced by the **QLeader** command.

■ The text in a leader is an mtext (multiline text) object.

■ Use the \P metacharacter to create line breaks in leader text.

■ This command can draw several types of leader:

Lengthen

Rel.13 Lengthens and shortens open objects by four methods.

Command	Alias	Ctrl+	F-key	Alt+	Menu Bar	Tablet
lengthen	len	...	...	MG	Modify ↳Lengthen	W14

Command: **lengthen**
Select an object or [DElta/Percent/Total/DYnamic]: **[pick]**
Current length: *n.nnnn*

COMMAND LINE OPTIONS

Select an object Displays length and included angle; does not change object.

DElta option:
Enter delta length or [Angle] <0.0000>: **[enter value]**
Specify second point: **[pick]**
Select an object to change or [Undo]:
Enter delta length
    Changes the length by an incremental amount.

Percent option:
Enter percentage length <100.0000>: **[enter value]**
Select an object to change or [Undo]: **[pick]**
Enter percent length
    Changes the length by a percentage of the original length.
Undo   Undoes the most-recent lengthening operation.

Total option:
Specify total length or [Angle] <1.0000)>: **[enter value]**
Select an object to change or [Undo]: **[pick]**
Specify total length
    Changes the length by an absolute value.
Angle   Changes the angle by an absolute value.
Undo   Undoes the most-recent lengthening operation.

DYnamic option:
Select an object to change or [Undo]: **[pick]**
Specify new end point: **[pick]**
Specify new end point
    Changes the length dynamically by dragging.
Undo   Undoes the most-recent lengthening operation.

TIPS

- **Lengthen** command only works with open objects, such as lines, arcs, and polylines; it does not work with closed objects, such as circles, polygons, and regions.

- **DElta** option changes the length or angle using the following measurements: (1) the distance from endpoint of the selected object to the pick point; or (2) the incremental length measured from the endpoint of the an.

Light

Rel.12 Places four types of lights for use by **Render**.

Command	Alias	Ctrl+	F-key	Alt+	Menu Bar	Tablet
light	...	...	...	VEL	View	O1
					⌁Render	
					⌁Light	

Command: **light**
Displays dialog box:

DIALOG BOX OPTIONS

Lights	Lists the currently-defined lights in the drawing.
Modify	Modifyies an existing light in the drawing; displays **Modify Light** dialog box.
Delete	Deletes the selected light.
Select	Selects a light from the drawing.
New	Creates a new point, spot, or direct light; displays **New Light** dialog box.
North Location	Selects the direction for North; displays **North Location** dialog box.

Ambient Light option:
Ambient Light Intensity
> Adjusts intensity of ambient light from 0 (dark) to 1.0 (bright).

Color options:
Red	Adjusts the level of red from 0 (black) to 1.0 (full red).
Green	Adjusts the level of green from 0 (black) to 1.0 (full green).
Blue	Adjusts the level of blue from 0 (black) to 1.0 (full blue).

Select Custom Color
> Displays Windows' **Color** dialog box.

Select from ACI
> Displays AutoCAD's **Select Color** dialog box.

North Location dialog box:

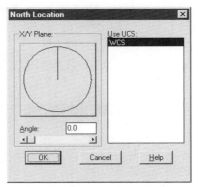

XY Plane *options:*
Angle   Selects angle from icon; enter a number, or drag the slider bar.
Use UCS   Selects a named UCS (user-defined coordinate system).

New Point Light dialog box:
Point lights must be positioned, and they radiate light in all directions.

Light Name   Names the light; maximum = 8 characters, no spaces.
Intensity   Specifies the intensity of the light, from 0 (turned off) to 31.33.

Attenuation *options:*
None   Specifies a light that does not diminish in intensity with distance.
Inverse Linear Specifies a light whose intensity decreases with distance.
Inverse Square Specifies a light whose intensity decreases with the square of the distance.

Position *options:*

Modify　　　Changes the location of the light.

Show　　　Displays **Show** dialog box.

Shadows *options:*

Shadows On　Turns on shadow casting.

Shadow Options

Displays **Shadow Options** dialog box.

Shadow Options dialog box:

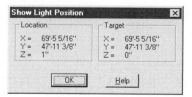

Shadow Volumes/Raytrace Shadows

Creates volumetric shadows; raytracer creates ray-traced shadows; disables shadow map.

Shadow Map Size

Specifies the size of one side of the shadow map; ranges from 64 to 4096 pixels; larger values give more accurate shadows.

Shadow Softness

Specifies the number of pixels at the shadow's edge blended with the underlying image; ranges from 1 to 10.

Shadow Bounding Objects

Selects objects to clip the shadow maps.

Color　　　Selects a color for the light.

Show Light Position dialog box:

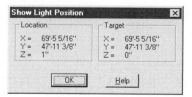

New Distant Light dialog box:

Distant lights must be positioned, and they radiate light in parallel rays in specified directions.

Name	Names the light; maximum = 8 characters.
Intensity	Specifies the intensity of the light; 0 is off.
Color	Specifies the color of the light.
Shadows	Creates shadows.
Azimuth	Sets light's position between -180 and 180 degrees.
Altitude	Sets an angle for the light between 0 and 90 degrees.

Light Source Vector options:

X	Specifies the vector x coordinate ranges from -1.0 to 1.0.
Y	Specifies the vector y coordinate ranges from -1.0 to 1.0.
Z	Specifies the vector z coordinate ranges from -1.0 to 1.0.
Modify	Changes the position of the light.

Sun Angle Calculator

Displays **Sun Angle Calculator** dialog box.

Sun Angle Calculator dialog box:

This calculator eliminates the need to specify the azimuth, altitude, and light source vectors for a distant light.

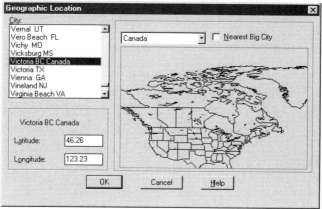

Date	Displays today's date or any date of the year.
Clock Time	Displays the current time or any time of day.
Latitude	Displays the latitude on earth.
Longitude	Displays the longitude.
Geographic Locator	
	Displays dialog box.

Geographic Locator dialog box:

City	Selects the name of a city.
Latitude	Displays the latitude of the city.
Longitude	Displays the longitude of the city.
Nearest Big City	
	Selects a city from its list closest to your pick point.

New Spotlight dialog box:
Spotlights radiate a cone of light, from the light to a spot centered on the target position.

Light Name	Names the light; maximum = 8 characters, no spaces.
Intensity	Specifies the intensity of the light, from 0 *(turned off)* to 31.33.

Attenuation options:
None	Specifies that the light does not diminish in intensity with distance.
Inverse Linear	Specifies that the light's intensity decreases with distance.
Inverse Square	Specifies that the light's intensity decreases with the square of the distance.

Position options:
Modify	Changes the location of the light.
Show	Displays **Show Light Position** dialog box.

Shadows options:
Shadows On	Turns on shadow casting.
Shadow Options	Displays the **Shadows Options** dialog box.
Color	Specifies the color of the light.

RELATED COMMANDS

Render	Renders the drawing.
Scene	Specifies tje lights and view to use in rendering.

RELATED FILES

In \Acad 2002\Support subdirectory:
Direct.Dwg Direct light block
Overhead.Dwg Overhead drawing block.
Sh_Spot.Dwg Spotlight drawing block.

Direct (left), Overhead (center), and Spotlight (right).

TIPS

■ When you use the **Render** command with no lights defined, AutoCAD assumes ambient light.

■ While it is not necessary to define any lights to use the **Render** command, a light must be included in a **Scene** definition for the **Render** command to make use of the light.

■ In a spotlight, the light beam travels from the *light location* (light block placement) to the *light target*.

■ Ambient light ensures every object in the scene has illumination; ambient light is an omnipresent light source.

■ Set ambient light to 0 to turn off for night scenes.

■ Place one distant light to simulate the Sun; distant lights have parallel light beams with constant intensity.

■ Place several point lights as light bulbs (*lamps*); a point light beams light in all directions, with inverse linear, inverse square, or constant intensity.

■ Spotlights beam light in a cone.

■ Intensity of 0 turns light off.

DEFINITIONS

Constant light   Attenuation is 0; default intensity is 1.0.

Inverse linear light

   Light strength decreases to ½-strength two units of distance away, and ¼-strength four units away; default intensity is ½ extents distance.

Inverse square light

   Light strength decreases to ¼-strength two units away, and $1/_8$-strength four units away; default intensity is ½ the square of the extents distance.

Extents distance   Distance from minimum lower-left coordinate to the maximum upper-right coordinate.

RGB color   The three primary colors — red, green, blue — shaded from black to white.

HLS color: Changes each color by hue (color), lightness (more white or more black), and saturation (less gray).

Hotspot   The brightest cone of light; beam angle ranges from 0 to 160 degrees (default: 45 degrees).

Falloff   The angle of the full light cone; field angle ranges from 0 to 160 degrees (default: 45 degrees).

'Limits

V. 1.0 Defines the 2D limits in the WCS for the grid markings and the **Zoom All** command; optionally prevents drawing outside of limits.

Command	Alias	Ctrl+	F-key	Alt+	Menu Bar	Tablet
'limits	...	...	...	OA	Format ↳Drawing Limits	V2

```
Command: limits
Reset Model space limits:
Specify lower left corner or [ON/OFF] <0.0000,0.0000>: [pick]
Specify upper right corner <12.0000,9.0000>: [pick]
```

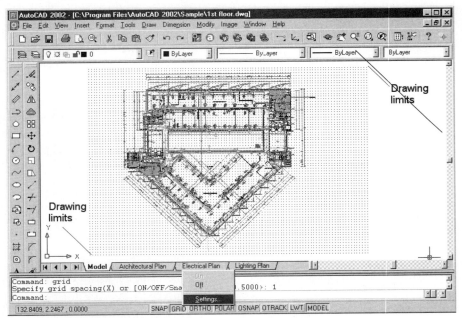

COMMAND LINE OPTIONS
OFF Turns off limits checking.
ON Turns on limits checking.
ENTER Retains limits values.

RELATED COMMANDS
Grid Displays grid dots, which are bounded by limits.
Status Lists the current drawing limits.
Zoom Displays the drawing's extents or limits with the **All** option.

RELATED SYSTEM VARIABLES
LimCheck Toggle for limit's drawing check.
LimMin Lower-right 2D coordinates of current limits.
LimMax Upper-left 2D coordinates of current limits.

Line

V. 1.0 Draws straight 2D and 3D lines.

Command	Alias	Ctrl+	F-key	Alt+	Menu Bar	Tablet
line	l	...	...	DL	Draw ⏷Line	J10

```
Command: line
Specify first point: [pick]
Specify next point or [Undo]: [pick]
Specify next point or [Undo]: [pick]
Specify next point or [Close/Undo]: [pick]
Specify next point or [Close/Undo]: ENTER
```

Single Segment Line:

From Point

To Point
and press Enter

Multi Segment Line:

From Point

To Point

To Point

To Point
and press Enter

Closed, MultiSegment Line:

From Point

To Point

To Point and
Press C

COMMAND LINE OPTIONS

Close   Closes the line from the current point to the starting point.

Undo   Undoes the last line segment drawn.

ENTER   Continues the line from the last endpoint at the 'From point' prompt; terminates the **Line** command at the 'To point' prompt.

RELATED COMMANDS

MLine	Draws up to 16 parallel lines.
PLine	Draws polylines and polyline arcs.
Trace	Draws lines with width.
Ray	Creates a semi-infinite construction line.
XLine	Creates an infinite construction line.

RELATED SYSTEM VARIABLES

Elevation	Distance above (or below) the x,y plane a line is drawn.
Lastpoint	Last-entered coordinate triple (x,y,z-coordinate).
Thickness	Determines thickness of the line.

TIPS

- To draw a 2D line, enter x,y coordinate pairs; the z coordinate takes on the value of the **Elevation** system variable.

- To draw a 3D line, enter x,y,z coordinate triples.

- When system variable **Thickness** is not zero, the line has thickness, which makes it a plane perpendicular to the current UCS.

'Linetype

V. 2.0 Loads linetype definitions into the drawing, creates new linetypes, and sets the working linetype.

Command	Alias	Ctrl+	F-key	Alt+	Menu Bar	Tablet
'linetype	lt	...	...	ON	Format	U3
	ltype				⁵Linetype	
	ddltype					
-linetype	-lt					
	-ltype					

Command: **linetype**
Displays dialog box:

![Linetype Manager dialog box showing Linetype filters with "Show all linetypes" selected, Invert filter checkbox, Load, Delete, Current, Hide details buttons. Current Linetype: ByLayer. A list showing Linetype, Appearance, Description columns with ByLayer, ByBlock, CENTER (selected), CONTINUOUS (Continuous). Details section with Name: CENTER, Description, Use paper space units for scaling checkbox, Global scale factor: 1.0000, Current object scale: 1.0000, ISO pen width: 1.0 mm. OK, Cancel, Help buttons.]

DIALOG BOX OPTIONS

Linetype filters

Displays the following groups of linetypes:
- **Show all linetypes** displays all linetypes defined in the current drawing.
- **Show all used linetypes** displays all linetypes being used.
- **All xref dependent linetypes** displays linetypes in externally referenced drawings.

Invert filter   Inverts the display of layer names; for example, when **Show all used linetypes** is selected, the **Invert filter** option displays all linetypes not used in the drawing.

Loads   Displays the **Load or Reload Linetypes** dialog box.

Current   Sets the selected layer as the current layer.

Delete   Purges the selected linetypes; some linetypes cannot be deleted, as described by the warning dialog box:

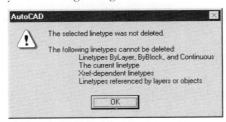

Show Details   Displays the **Details** portion of the **Linetype Properties Manager** dialog box.

Details options:

Name   Names the selected linetype.

Description   Displays the description associated with the linetype.

Use paper space units for scaling

Specifies that paper space linetype scaling is used, even in model space.

Global scale factor

Specifies the scale factor for all linetypes in the drawing.

Current object scale

Specifies the individual object scale factor for all subsequently-drawn linetypes, multiplied by the global scale factor.

ISO pen width

Applies standard scale factors to ISO linetypes.

Load or Reload Linetypes dialog box:

File   Names the LIN linetype definition file.

SHORTCUT MENU
Right-click any linetype name in the Linetype Manager:

Select All
Clear All

Select All   Selects all linetypes.
Clear All   Selects no linetype.

-LINETYPE COMMAND
Command: **-linetype**
?/Create/Load/Set: **[enter option]**

COMMAND LINE OPTIONS
Create   Creates a new user-defined linetype; see *Quick Start Tutorial.*
Load   Loads a linetype from an LIN linetype definition file.
Set   Sets the working linetype.
?   Lists the linetypes loaded into the drawing.

RELATED COMMANDS
Change   Changes objects to a new linetype; changes linetype scale.
ChProp   Changes objects to a new linetype.
LtScale   Sets the scale of the linetype.
Rename   Changes the name of the linetype.

OBJECT PROPERTIES TOOLBAR

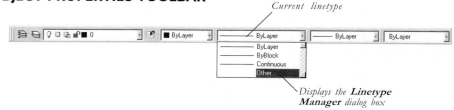

Current linetype

Displays the **Linetype Manager** *dialog box*

RELATED SYSTEM VARIABLES
CeLtype   Specifies the current linetype setting.
LtScale   Specifies the current linetype scale.
PsLtScale   Specifies the linetype scale relative to paper scale.
PlineGen   Controls how linetypes are generated for polylines.

TIPS
■ The only linetypes defined initially in a new AutoCAD drawing are:

• **Continuous**: unbroken line.

• **Bylayer**: linetype is specified by the layer setting.

• **Byblock**: linetype is specified by the block definition.

- Linetypes must be loaded from LIN definition files before being used in a drawing.

- When loading one or more linetypes, it is faster to load all linetypes, then use the **Purge** command to remove the linetype definitions that have not been used in the drawing.

- As of AutoCAD Release 13, objects can have independent linetype scales.

RELATED FILE

- The following standard linetypes are in *Acad 2002**Support**Acad.Lin*:

ACAD_ISO02W100	ISO dash __ __ __ __ __ __ __ __ __ __ __ __
ACAD_ISO03W100	ISO dash space __ __ __ __ __ __ __
ACAD_ISO04W100	ISO long-dash dot ____ . ____ . ____ . ____ . _
ACAD_ISO05W100	ISO long-dash double-dot ____ .. ____ .. ____ .
ACAD_ISO06W100	ISO long-dash triple-dot ____ ... ____ ... ____
ACAD_ISO07W100	ISO dot . . . .
ACAD_ISO08W100	ISO long-dash short-dash ____ __ ____ __ ____ _
ACAD_ISO09W100	ISO long-dash double-short-dash ____ __ __ ____
ACAD_ISO10W100	ISO dash dot __ . __ . __ . __ . __ . __ .
ACAD_ISO11W100	ISO double-dash dot __ __ . __ __ . __ __ . __
ACAD_ISO12W100	ISO dash double-dot __ . . __ . . __ . . __ . .
ACAD_ISO13W100	ISO double-dash double-dot __ __ . . __ __ . .
ACAD_ISO14W100	ISO dash triple-dot __ . . . __ . . . __
ACAD_ISO15W100	ISO double-dash triple-dot __ __ . . . __ __ .
BATTING	Batting SSSSSSSSSSSSSSSSSSSSSSSSSSSSSSSSSSSSSSS
BORDER	Border __ __ . __ __ . __ __ . __ __ .
BORDER2	Border (.5x) __.__.__.__.__.__.__.__.__.
BORDERX2	Border (2x) ____ ____ . ____ ____ . ____
CENTER	Center ____ _ ____ _ ____ _ ____
CENTER2	Center (.5x) ____ _ ____ _ ____ _ ____ _ __
CENTERX2	Center (2x) _____ __ _____ __ _____
DASHDOT	Dash dot __ . __ . __ . __ . __ . __ .
DASHDOT2	Dash dot (.5x) __.__.__.__.__.__.__.__.__.
DASHDOTX2	Dash dot (2x) ____ . ____ . ____ . __
DASHED	Dashed __ __ __ __ __ __ __ __ __ __ __ __
DASHED2	Dashed (.5x) _ _ _ _ _ _ _ _ _ _ _ _ _ _ _
DASHEDX2	Dashed (2x) ____ ____ ____ ____ ____
DIVIDE	Divide ____ . . ____ . . ____ . . ____ . . ____
DIVIDE2	Divide (.5x) __.__.__.__.__.__.__.__.__._
DIVIDEX2	Divide (2x) _____ . . _____ . . _
DOT	Dot . . . .
DOT2	Dot (.5x) . . . .
DOTX2	Dot (2x) . . . .
FENCELINE1	Fenceline circle ----O-----O-----O-----O----O---
FENCELINE2	Fenceline square ----[]-----[]----[]-----[]----
GAS_LINE	Gas line ----GAS----GAS----GAS----GAS----GAS---
HIDDEN	Hidden __ __ __ __ __ __ __ __ __ __ __ __
HIDDEN2	Hidden (.5x) _ _ _ _ _ _ _ _ _ _ _ _ _ _
HIDDENX2	Hidden (2x) ____ ____ ____ ____ ____ ____
HOT_WATER_SUPPLY	Hot water supply ---- HW ---- HW ---- HW ----
PHANTOM	Phantom ____ __ __ ____ __ __ ____
PHANTOM2	Phantom (.5x) ____ __ __ ____ __ __ ____ __ __
PHANTOMX2	Phantom (2x) _____ ____ ____ _
TRACKS	Tracks -l-l-l-l-l-l-l-l-l-l-l-l- -l-l-l-l
ZIGZAG	Zig zag /\/\/\/\/\/\/\/\/\/\/\/\/\/\/\/

QUICK START TUTORIAL
Create a custom linetype

You can create a custom linetype on-the-fly. This method does not work for complex linetypes that include shapes or text:

Step 1: Enter the **-Linetype** command and use the **Create** option:

```
Command: -linetype
Current line type:  "ByLayer"
Enter an option [?/Create/Load/Set]: c
```

Step 2: Name the linetype in three steps:

- First, the linetype name:
  Enter name of linetype to create: **[enter up to 31 characters]**

- Second, the LIN filename. When you select *Acad.Lin*, AutoCAD appends your new linetype description to *Acad.Lin*; when you enter a new filename, AutoCAD creates a new LIN file.

- Third, describe the linetype:
  Descriptive text: **[enter up to 47 characters]**

Step 3: Define the linetype pattern by using five codes:

- Positive number for dashes; for example, **0.5** is a dash 0.5 units long.
- Negative number for gaps; for example, **-0.25** is a gap 0.25 units long.
- Zero for dots: **0** is a single dot.
- An **A** forces the linetype to align between two endpoints; linetypes always start and stop with a dash.
- Commas (**,**) separate values.

  Example:
  *DASHDOT,__ . __ . __ . __ . __ . __ . __ .
  A,.5,-.25,0,-.25 [Enter]

Step 4: Press **Enter** to end the linetype definition.

Step 5: Use the **-Linetype** command's **Load** option to load the pattern into the drawing.

Enter linetype(s) to load: **[enter name]**

Step 6: Use the **Set** option to set the linetype.

New object linetype (or ?) <>: **[enter name]**

Alternatively, use the **Properties** command to change objects to the new linetype.

 # List

V. 1.0   Lists information about selected objects in the drawing.

Command	Alias	Ctrl+	F-key	Alt+	Menu Bar	Tablet
list	li	...	...	TYL	Tools	U8
	ls				↳Inquiry	
					↳List	

```
Command: list
Select objects: [pick]
Select objects: ENTER
```

Example output:

```
        LINE        Layer: 36
                    Space: Model space
          Color: BYLAYER      Linetype: CCNTINUOUS
          Handle = 24A6
     from point, X=  10.0000  Y=   6.0000  Z=   0.0000
       to point, X=   9.0000  Y=   4.0000  Z=   0.0000
 Length =   2.2361,   Angle in X-Y Plane =     243
 Delta X =  -1.0000, Delta Y =   -2.0000, Delta Z =   0.0000
```

COMMAND LINE OPTIONS

ENTER	Continues the display.
ESC	Cancels the display.
F2	Returns to graphics screen.

RELATED COMMANDS

Area	Calculates the area and perimeter of some objects.
DbList	Lists information about all objects in the drawing.
Dist	Calculates the 3D distance and angle between two points.
MassProp	Calculates the properties of 2D regions and 3D solids.

TIPS

■ **List** is a faster alternative to **Dist** and **Area** for finding lengths and areas of objects.

■ The **List** command does *not* list *all* information about the selected objects. The following information is only listed under certain conditions:

Information	Condition
Color	When not set BYLAYER.
Linetype	When not set BYLAYER.
Thickness	When not 0.
Elevation	When z coordinate is not 0.
Extrusion direction	When z axis differs from current UCS.

■ Object handles are described by hexadecimal numbers.

REMOVED COMMAND

ListURL was removoved from AutoCAD 2000; it was replaced by **-Hyperlink**.

Load

V. 1.0 Loads SHX-format shape files into the drawing via a dialog box.

Command	Alias	Ctrl+	F-key	Alt+	Menu Bar	Tablet
load	...	...	...	...	...	...

Command: **load**
*Displays **Load Shape File** dialog box.*

COMMAND LINE OPTIONS
None.

RELATED AUTOCAD COMMAND

Shape   Inserts shapes into the current drawing.

TIPS

- Shapes are more efficient than blocks, but are harder to create.

- The **Load** command cannot load SHX files that are meant for fonts. AutoCAD complains, "D:\ACAD 2002\support\gdt.shx is a normal text font file, not a shape file."

RELATED FILES

*.SHP   Source code for shape files.
*.SHX   Compile shape files.

In \Acad 2002\Support subdirectory:
Gdt.Shx, Gdt.Shp
        Geometric tolerance shapes (used by the **Tolerance** command).
LtypeShp.Shx, LtypeShp.Shp
        Linetype shapes (used by the **Linetype** command).

LogFileOff

Rel.13 Closes the Acad.Log file.

Command	Alias	Ctrl+	F-key	Alt+	Menu Bar	Tablet
logfileoff	...	Q	...	...	...	...

Command: **logfileoff**

COMMAND LINE OPTIONS
None.

RELATED AUTOCAD COMMAND
LogFileOn   Turns on the recording of 'Command' prompt text to file *Acad.Log*.

RELATED SYSTEM VARIABLE
LogFileMode   Text window written to log file:

LogFileMode	Meaning
0	Text not written to file (default).
1	Text written to file.

TIP
■ AutoCAD places a dashed line at the end of each log file session.

LogFileOn

Opens *Acad.Log* file and records 'Command' prompt text to the file.

Command	Alias	Ctrl+	F-key	Alt+	Menu Bar	Tablet
logfileon	...	Q	...	...	...	...

Command: **logfileon**

COMMAND LINE OPTIONS
None.

RELATED AUTOCAD COMMANDS
CopyHist   Copies all command text from the Text window to the Clipboard.
LogFileOff   Turns off recording 'Command' prompt text to file *Acad.Log*.

RELATED SYSTEM VARIABLES
LogFileMode   Text window written to log file:

LogFileMode	Meaning
0	Text not written to file (default).
1	Text written to file.

LogFileName   Name of the log file (default = *acad.log*).

RELATED FILE
■ **Acad.Log**   Default filename for log file.

TIPS
■ If log file recording is left on, it resumes when AutoCAD is next loaded.

■ AutoCAD places a dashed line at the end of each log file session.

■ *Historical note*: In some early versions of AutoCAD, **Ctrl+Q** meant "quick screen print" and output the current screen display to the printer. In AutoCAD Release 14, **Ctrl+Q** reappeared to record command text to a file; the shortcut keystroke no longer works with AutoCAD 2002.

■ You can give the log file a different name with the **Preferences** command's **Files** tab or with system variable **LogFileName**.

LsEdit

Rel.14 Edits the properties of a landscape object *(short for LandScape EDIT)*.

Command	Alias	Ctrl+	F-key	Alt+	Menu Bar	Tablet
lsedit	...	...	...	VEE	View	...
					↳Render	
					↳Landscape Edit	

Command: **lsedit**
Select a Landscape Object: **[pick]**
Displays dialog box:

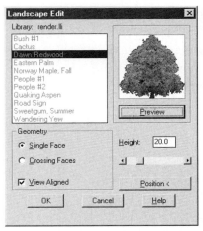

DIALOG BOX OPTIONS

Height Changes height of the object, by entering a new value or moving the slider bar.

Position Moves the object to another position in the drawing.

Geometry options:
Single Face Renders faster, but is less realistic.
Crossing Face Produces more realistic ray-traced shadows.
View Aligned Forces object always to face the camera.

RELATED COMMANDS

LsLib Lets you add and remove raster images from the *Render.Lli* file.
LsNew Places a landscape object in the drawing.
Render Renders the landscape object.

TIP

■ Landscape objects are rendered only when using the **Render** command's photoreal or photo ray trace options.

LsLib

Rel.14 Maintains a library of landscape objects (*short for LandScape LIBrary*).

Command	Alias	Ctrl+	F-key	Alt+	Menu Bar	Tablet
lsedit	...	...	...	VEC	View	...
					⌖Render	
					⌖Landscape Library	

Command: **lslib**
Select a Landscape Object: **[pick]**
Displays dialog box:

DIALOG BOX OPTIONS

Library	Indicates current LLI landscape library filename; selects a landscape object.
Modify	Changes the properties of a landscape object; displays **Landscape Library Edit** dialog box.
New	Assigns defaults values to a landscape object; displays **Landscape Library New** dialog box.
Delete	Removes a landscape object from library.
Open	Opens a landscape library file; displays the **Open Landscape Library** dialog box.
Save	Saves landscape objects to LLI file; displays dialog box:

Landscape Library Edit dialog box:

Default Geometry *options:*
Single Face   Renders faster, but is less realistic.
Crossing Face Produces more realistic ray-traced shadows.
View Aligned   Forces the object always to face the camera.

Preview   Previews the landscape image.

Name   Names the landscape object.
Image File   Specifies the type of raster file: BMP, GIF, JPG, PCX, TGA, PNG, or TIF.
Opacity Map File
                   Names the raster file that provides opacity.
Find File   Finds the file; displays the **Find Image File** dialog box.

Landscape Library New dialog box:
Options are identical to those found in the ***Landscape Library Edit*** *dialog box.*

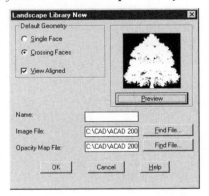

RELATED COMMANDS
LsEdit   Edits the properties of a landscape object.
LsNew   Places a landscape object in the drawing.
MatLib   Provides a library of surface textures.

LsNew

<u>Rel.14</u>   Places a landscape object in the drawing *(short for LandScape NEW)*.

Command	Alias	Ctrl+	F-key	Alt+	Menu Bar	Tablet
lsnew	...	...	...	VEN	View	...
					⌐Render	
					⌐Landscape New	

Command: **lsnew**
Displays dialog box:

DIALOG BOX OPTIONS

Preview   Views the raster image.

Height   Changes the height of the object by entering a new value or moving the slider bar.

Position   Moves the object to another position in the drawing.

Geometry *options:*
Single Face   Renders faster, but is less realistic.
Crossing Face   Produces more realistic ray-traced shadows.
View Aligned   Forces the object always to face the camera.

RELATED COMMANDS

LsLib   Lets you add and remove raster images from the *Render.Lli* file.
LsEdit   Edits the properties of a landscape object.
Render   Renders the landscape object.

TIPS

- A *landscape object* is defined as a **Plant** object in the AutoCAD database.

- Turn on **View Aligned** when you want the landscape object — such as a tree — always to face the camera.

- Turn off **View Aligned** when you want to fix the orientation of the landscape object, such as a store front.

A landscape object with ***crossing faces*** *(left) and* ***single face*** *(right).*

- Although AutoCAD's standard grip commands — stretch, move, scale, and rotate — work on landscape objects, the grips at the base, top, and corners have special meaning:

Grip	Meaning
Top	Changes the object's height.
Bottom corner	Rotates (if not view aligned) and scales the object.
Base	Moves the object.

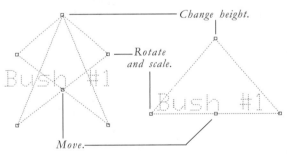

- An *opacity map* determines which part of a raster image is opaque and which is transparent.

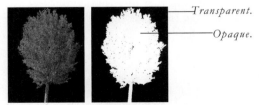

- The opacity map should be a bi-color (*black and white*) image file.

'LtScale

V. 2.0 Sets the global scale factor of linetypes (*short for Line Type SCALE*).

Command	Alias	Ctrl+	F-key	Alt+	Menu Bar	Tablet
'ltscale	lts	...	...	...	...	...

```
Command: ltscale
Enter new linetype scale factor <1.0000>: [enter factor]
Regenerating drawing.
```

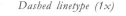

Dashed linetype (1x)   Dashed2 linetype (0.5x)   DashedX2 linetype (2x)

COMMAND LINE OPTION

Enter new linetype scale factor
> Changes the global scale factor of all linetypes in the drawing.

RELATED COMMANDS

ChProp   Changes the linetype scale of one or more objects.
Properties Changes the linetype scale of objects.
Linetype   Loads, creates, and sets the working linetype.

RELATED SYSTEM VARIABLES

LtScale   Contains the current linetype scale factor.
PlineGen   Controls how linetypes are generated for polylines.
PsLtScale Specifies that the linetype scale is relative to paper space.

TIPS

- If the linetype scale is too large, the linetype appears solid.

- If the linetype scale is too small, the linetype appears as a solid line that redraws very slowly.

- In addition to setting the scale with the **LtScale** command, the *Acad.Lin* file contains each linetype in three scales: normal, half-size, and double-size.

- You can change the linetype scaling of individual objects, which is then multiplied by the global scale factor specified by the **LtScale** command.

REMOVED COMMAND

MakePreview was removed from AutoCAD Release 14.

LWeight

<u>**2000**</u>   Sets the current lineweight (*display width*) of objects.

Command	Alias	Ctrl+	Status Bar	Alt+	Menu Bar	Tablet
lweight	lw	...	LWT	OW	Format	W14
	lineweight				↳Lineweight	
-lweight						

Command: **lweight**
Displays dialog box:

DIALOG BOX OPTIONS

Lineweights   Lists lineweight values.

Units for Listing

Specifies the units of lineweights:
* **Millimeters (mm)** specifies lineweight values in millimeters.
* **Inches (in)** specifies lineweight values in inches.

Display Lineweight

Toggles the display of lineweights; when checked, lineweights are displayed.

Default   Specifies the default lineweight for layers (default = 0.01" or 0.25 mm).

Adjust Display Scale

Controls the scale of lineweights in the **Model** tab, which displays lineweights in pixels.

SHORTCUT MENU OPTIONS

Right-click LWT on status bar to display shortcut menu:

On
Off
Settings...

NAP | GRID | ORTHO | POLAR | OSNAP | OTRACK | LWT | MODEL

On   Turns on lineweight display.
Off   Turns off lineweight display.
Settings   Displays **Lineweight Settings** dialog box.

-LWEIGHT COMMAND

Command: **-lweight**

Enter default lineweight for new objects or [?]: **[enter number]**

COMMAND LINE OPTIONS

Enter default lineweight

Specifies the current lineweight; valid values include Bylayer, Byblock, and Default.

? Lists the valid values for lineweights:

ByLayer	ByBlock	Default			
0.000"	0.002"	0.004"	0.005"	0.006"	0.007"
0.008"	0.010"	0.012"	0.014"	0.016"	0.020"
0.021"	0.024"	0.028"	0.031"	0.035"	0.039"
0.042"	0.047"	0.055"	0.062"	0.079"	0.083"

RELATED SYSTEM VARIABLES

LwDefault Specifies the default linewidth; default = 0.01" or 0.25 mm.

LwDisplay Toggles the display of lineweights in the drawing.

LwUnits Determines whether lineweight is measured in inches or millimeters.

TIPS

■ To create custom lineweights for plotting, use the **Plot Style Table Editor**.

■ A lineweight of 0 plots the lines at the thinnest width of which the plotter is capable, usually one pixel or one dot wide.

MassProp

Rel.11 Reports the mass properties of a 3D solid model, body, or 2D region (*short for MASS PROPerties; an ACIS command*).

Command	Alias	Ctrl+	F-key	Alt+	Menu Bar	Tablet
massprop	...	...	...	TYM	Tools	U7
					↳Inquiry	
					↳Mass Properties	

Command: **massprop**
Select objects: **[pick]**
Select objects: **[Enter]**

Example output of a solid sphere:

```
————————  SOLIDS  ————————
Mass:                     12.6241
Volume:                   12.6241
Bounding box:          X: 4.7910  —  10.7826
                       Y: -1.0540  —  4.9376
                       Z: -2.9958  —  2.9958
Centroid:              X: 7.7868
                       Y: 1.9418
                       Z: 0.0000
Moments of inertia:    X: 828.9818
                       Y: 7233.2389
                       Z: 7657.9057
Products of inertia:   XY: 1702.9437
                       YZ: 0.0000
                       ZX: 0.0000
Radii of gyration:     X: 2.7130
                       Y: 8.0140
                       Z: 8.2459
Principal moments and X-Y-Z directions about centroid:
                       I: 404.3150 along [1.0000 0.0000 0.0000]
                       J: 404.3150 along [0.0000 1.0000 0.0000]
                       K: 404.3150 along [0.0000 0.0000 1.0000]
Write analysis to a file? [Yes/No] <N>: y
```

COMMAND LINE OPTIONS

Select objects Selects the ACIS objects — 2D regions, 3D solids, and bodies — to analyze.
Write to a file Yes: Writes mass property report to an MPR file.
                    No: Doesn't write report to file.

RELATED COMMAND

Area   Calculates area and perimeter of non-ACIS objects.

RELATED FILE

*.MPR   **MassProp** writes its results to an MPR (mass properties report) file.

TIPS

- This command can be used with 2D regions as well as 3D ACIS solids; it cannot be used with 3D surface models.

- As of Release 13, AutoCAD's solid modeling no longer allows you to apply a material density to a solid model. All solids and bodies have a density of 1.

- AutoCAD only analyzes regions coplanar (laying in the same plane) to the first region selected.

DEFINITIONS

Area Total surface area of the selected 3D solids, bodies, or 2D regions.

Bounding Box The lower-right and upper-left coordinates of a rectangle enclosing the 2D region; the x,y,z coordinate triple of a 3D box enclosing the 3D solid or body.

Centroid The x,y,z coordinates of the center of the 2D region; the center of mass for 3D solids and bodies.

Mass Equal to the volume since density = 1; not calculated for regions.

Moment of Inertia
For 2D regions = **Area** * **Radius**^{2}
For 3D solids and bodies = **Mass** * **Radius**^{2}

Perimeter Total length of inside and outside loops of 2D regions; not calculated for 3D solids and bodies.

Product of Inertia
For 2D regions = **Mass** * **Distance** (of centroid to y,z axis) * **Distance** (of centroid to x,z axis).
For 3D solids and bodies = **Mass** * **Distance** (of centroid to y,z axis) * **Distance** (of centroid to x,z axis)

Radius of Gyration
For 2D regions and 3D solids = (**MomentOfInertia** / **Mass**)$^{1/2}$

Volume 3D space occupied by a 3D solid or body; not calculated for regions.

MatchProp *and* Painter

Rel.14 Matches the properties between selected objects (*short for MATCH PROPerties*).

Command	Alias	Ctrl+	F-key	Alt+	Menu Bar	Tablet
matchprop	ma	...	...	MM	Modify	Y14
					⌐Match Properties	
painter						

```
Command: matchprop
Select source object: [pick]
Current active settings:  Color Layer Ltype Ltscale Lineweight
Thickness PlotStyle Text Dim Hatch
Select destination object(s) or [Settings]: [pick]
Select destination object(s) or [Settings]: ENTER
```

COMMAND LINE OPTIONS

Select source object

Gets property settings from the source object.

Select destination object(s)

Passes property settings to the destination objects.

Settings Displays dialog box:

DIALOG BOX OPTIONS

Basic Properties options:

Color Specifies the color for the destination object; not available when an OLE object is selected.

Layer Specifies the layer name for the destination object; not available when an OLE object is selected.

Linetype Specifies the linetype for the destination object; not available when an attribute, hatch pattern, mtext, OLE object, point, or viewport has been selected.

Linetype Scale Specifies the linetype scale for the destination object; not available when an attribute, hatch pattern, mtext, OLE object, point, or viewport has been selected.

Lineweight Specifies the lineweight for the destination object.

Thickness Specifies the thickness for the destination object; available only for objects that can have a thickness: arc, attribute, circle, line, mtext, point, 2D polyline, region, text, and traces.

Plot Style Specifies the plot style; not available when **PStylePolicy** = 1 (color-dependent plot style mode) or when an OLE object is selected.

Special Properties options:

Dimension Changes the dimension style of dimension, leader, and tolerance objects.

Text Changes the text style of text and mtext objects.

Hatch Changes the hatch pattern of hatched objects.

RELATED SYSTEM VARIABLE

PStylePolicy Determines if the **PlotStyle** option is available.

RELATED COMMAND

Properties Changes most aspects of one selected object.

TIP

- In AutoCAD LT, this command is called **Painter**; in other Windows applications, this command is known as **Format Painter**.

MatLib

Rel.13 Imports and exports material-look definitions for use by the **RMat** command (*short for MATerial LIBrary*).

Command	Alias	Ctrl+	F-key	Alt+	Menu Bar	Tablet
matlib	...	...	...	VEY	View ⌐Render ⌐Materials Library	Q1

Command: **matlib**
Displays dialog box:

[Materials Library dialog box shown with Current Drawing "GLOBAL", Preview (Sphere), and Current Library "render" containing: 3D CEL TEXMAP, 4WAY BAR PATTERN, AMOEBA PATTERN, APE, APE BUMP, AQUA GLAZE, BEIGE MATTE, BEIGE PATTERN, BEIGE PLASTIC, BLACK MATTE, BLACK PLASTIC, BLUE GLASS. Buttons: Preview, <-Import, Export->, Open..., Save, Delete, Save As..., Purge, Save As..., OK, Cancel, Help]

DIALOG BOX OPTIONS

Import   Brings a material definition into the drawing; when there is a conflict, displays **Reconcile Imported Material Names** dialog box.

Preview   Previews the selected material mapped to a sphere object.

Export   Adds material definition to MLI library file; if there is a conflict, displays the **Reconcile Exported Material Names** dialog box, which is identical to **Reconcile Imported Material Names** dialog box.

Purge   Deletes unattached material definitions from the **Materials** list.

Save   Saves to an MLI file.

Delete   Deletes selected material definitions from the **Materials** or **Library** lists.

Open   Loads material definitions from an MLI file; displays file dialog box.

A variety of materials applied to a sphere.

Reconcile Imported Material Names dialog box:

Options options:

Overwrite Existing Material
> Overwrites existing material definition with selected material definition.

Transfer Attachments
> Keeps objects attached to material definition.

Material Names options:

Old Material in List
> Allows you to edit the name of the material.

New Material from Library
> Allows you to edit the name of the material.

RELATED COMMAND

RMat   Attaches a material definition to objects, colors, and layers.

RELATED FILE

Render.Mli   Material library; contains the material definitions.

TIPS

■ **MatLib** only loads and purges material definitions; use the **RMat** command to attach the definitions to objects.

■ A *material* defines the look of a rendered object: coloring, reflection or shine, roughness, and ambient reflection.

■ Materials do not define the density of 3D solids and bodies.

■ By default, a drawing contains a single material definition, called *GLOBAL*, with the default parameters for color, reflection, roughness, and ambience.

Measure

V. 2.5 Divides lines, arcs, circles, and polylines into equidistant segments, placing a point or a block at each segment.

Command	Alias	Ctrl+	F-key	Alt+	Menu Bar	Tablet
measure	me	...	...	DOM	Draw	V12
					↳Point	
					↳Measure	

```
Command: measure
Select object to measure: [pick]
Specify length of segment or [Block]: [enter option]
```

Polyline (left); measured with ten points (right).

COMMAND LINE OPTIONS

Select object Selects a single object for measurement.
Specify length of segment
   Indicates the distance between markers.

Block options:
```
Enter name of block to insert: [enter name]
Align block with object? [Yes/No] <Y>: ENTER
Specify length of segment: [enter value]
```

Enter name of block
   Indicates the name of the block to use as a marker; the block must already exist in the drawing.
Align block with object?
   Aligns the block's x axis with object.

RELATED COMMANDS

Block Creates blocks that can be used with the **Measure** command.
Divide Divides an object into a number of segments.

RELATED SYSTEM VARIABLES

PdMode Controls the shape of a point.
PdSize Controls the size of a point.

TIPS

■ You must define the block before it can be used with this command.

■ The **Measure** command does not place a point or block at the beginning of the measured object.

 **MeetNow**

2000i Allows two or more users to collaborate on a drawing.

Command	Alias	Ctrl+	F-key	Alt+	Menu Bar	Tablet
meetnow	...	...	...	...	...	...

Command: **meetnow**
Launching MeetNow...
Displays toolbar:

Remove participants   Allow others to edit   Display chat window   Display whiteboard

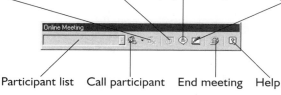

Participant list   Call participant   End meeting   Help

TOOLBAR OPTIONS

Participant List
Lists the names of current participants.
Call Participant
Contacts other users to invite them to meet now.
Remove Participants
Removes one or more participants.
Allow Others to Edit
Allows participants to edit the drawing.
Display Chat Window
Allows participants to exchange text messages.
Display Whiteboard
Displays whiteboard, a simple paint program.
End Meeting Disconnects all participants, and closes the dialog box.
Help Displays the **AutoCAD 2002 Help User Documentation** window.

RELATED COMMANDS

ETransmite Sends the drawing as an email message.
PublishToWeb Exports the drawing as a Web page.

TIPS

■ If NetMeeting is not installed, displays error dialog box: "Net Meeting version *n.nn* is not installed." Download a free copy from <u>windowsupdate.microsoft.com</u>.

■ The first time you run **MeetNow**, you are prompted for information about yourself:

Second, you register yourself with Autodesk's server. You have the option to not allow your personal information to be made public.

You specify the speed at which you will be connecting with other **MeetNow** users.

Select the video capture device; if your computer lacks video capability, the dialog box is not displayed.

Next, the software checks your computer's audio capabilities; the computer may lock up at this point.

Press the **Test** button to hear a repeating musical pattern, and adjust the volume if necessary. When done, click the **Done** button.

If necessary, plug in a microphone, and read the test sentence.

Click **Finish** to end the setup procedure.

Menu

V. 1.0   Loads MNS, MNL, and MNU menu files.

Command	Alias	Ctrl+	F-key	Alt+	Menu Bar	Tablet
menu	...	...	...	...	...	...

Command: **menu**
*Displays the **Select Menu File** dialog box.*

When FileDia = 0:
Command: **menu**
Enter menu file name or [. (for none)] <\support\acad>: **ENTER**
Menu loaded successfully. MENUGROUP: ACAD
AutoCAD menu utilities loaded.

COMMAND LINE OPTIONS

Enter menu file name
        Specifies the name of the menu file to load.
. for none   *(Dot)* Removes current menu from AutoCAD.
ENTER   Reloads current menu.

RELATED COMMANDS

MenuLoad   Loads a partial menu file.
Tablet   Configures digitizing tablet for use with overlay menus.

RELATED SYSTEM VARIABLES

MenuName   Specifies the name of the currently-loaded menu file.
MenuEcho   Suppresses menu echoing.
ScreenBoxes   Specifies the number of menu lines displayed on the side menu.

RELATED FILES

*.MNC   Compiled menu file; stored in binary format.
*.MNS   Source menu file; stored in ASCII format.
*.MNU   Menu template file; stored in ASCII format.

TIPS

- AutoCAD automatically compiles MNS and MNU files into MNC files for faster loading.

- The MNU file defines the function of the screen menu, menu bar, cursor menu, icon menus, digitizing tablet menus, pointing device buttons, and the **AUX:** device.

MenuLoad

Rel.13 Loads a part of a menu file.

Command	Alias	Ctrl+	F-key	Alt+	Menu Bar	Tablet
menuload	...	...	...	TC	Tools	Y9
					⸂Customize Menus	

Command: **menuload**
Displays tabbed dialog box:

*When **FileDia** = 0:*
Command: **menuload**
Enter name of menu file to load: **acad**
Menu loaded successfully. MENUGROUP: ACAD

DIALOG BOX OPTIONS

Menu Groups Lists the names of loaded menu groups and files.
Unload   Unloads selected menu group.

Replace All Replaces all currently-loaded menus with the newly-loaded menu.
Load   Loads the selected menu group into AutoCAD.
File Name   Displays the name of the menu file.
Browse   Displays the **Select Menu File** dialog box.

Close   Closes the dialog box.
Help   Provides context-sensitive help.

Menu Bar tab:

Menu Group	Selects a menu group or file.
Menus	Provides the names of the menu items in the selected menu group.
Insert	Inserts a menu item on the menu bar, immediately above the selected item.
Remove	Removes a menu item from the menu bar.
Remove All	Removes all menu items from the menu bar.
Menu Bar	Provides the names of menu items on the menu bar.

RELATED COMMANDS

Menu	Loads a full menu file.
MenuUnload	Unloads part of the menu file.
Tablet	Configures digitizing tablet for use with overlay menus.

RELATED SYSTEM VARIABLES

MenuName	Specifies the name of the currently-loaded menu file.
MenuEcho	Suppresses menu echoing.
ScreenBoxes	Specifies the number of menu lines displayed on the side menu.

RELATED FILES

*.MNC	Compiled menu file; stored in binary format.
*.MNS	Source menu file; stored in ASCII format.
*.MNU	Menu template file; stored in ASCII format.

TIP

- The **MenuLoad** command allows you to add *partial* menus to the menu bar, without replacing the entire menu structure.

MenuUnLoad

Rel.13 Unloads a partial menu file.

Command	Alias	Ctrl+	F-key	Alt+	Menu Bar	Tablet
menuload	...	...	...	TC	Tools	Y9
					ⓎCustomize Menus	

Command: **menuunload**
Displays tabbed dialog box:

```
Menu Customization                              [?][X]

 [ Menu Groups ] Menu Bar

      Menu Groups:
      ┌─────────────────────────────┐   ┌──────────┐
      │ ACAD                        │   │  Unload  │
      │ EXPRESS                     │   └──────────┘
      │                             │
      │                             │
      │                             │
      │                             │
      └─────────────────────────────┘
                        □ Replace All    ┌──────────┐
      File Name:                         │   Load   │
      ┌─────────────────────────────┐   └──────────┐
      │                             │   │ Browse... │
      └─────────────────────────────┘   └──────────┘

                          ┌────────┐  ┌────────┐
                          │ Close  │  │  Help  │
                          └────────┘  └────────┘
```

*When **FileDia** = 0:*
Command: **menuunload**
Enter the name of the MENUGROUP to unload: **acad**
Menu unloaded successfully. MENUGROUP: acad

DIALOG BOX OPTIONS

Menu Groups Lists the names of loaded menu groups and files.
Unload   Unloads selected menu group.

Replace All Replaces all currently-loaded menus with the newly-loaded menu.
Load   Loads selected menu group into AutoCAD.
File Name   Displays the name of the menu file.
Browse   Displays the **Select Menu File** dialog box.

Close   Closes the dialog box.

Help   Provides context-sensitive help.

TIPS

- See the **MenuLoad** command for **Menu Bar** tab options.

- The **MenuUnload** command allows you to remove partial menu files, such as *Db_Con.Mnu* and *AcCov.Mns*.

MInsert

V. 2.5 Inserts an array of blocks as a single block (*short for Multiple INSERT*).

Command	Alias	Ctrl+	F-key	Alt+	Menu Bar	Tablet
minsert	...	...	...	...	...	...

```
Command: minsert
Enter block name or [?]: [enter name]
Specify insertion point or [Scale/X/Y/Z/Rotate/PScale/PX/
   PY/PZ/PRotate]: [pick]
Enter X scale factor, specify opposite corner, or [Corner/
   XYZ] <1>: ENTER
Enter Y scale factor <use X scale factor>: ENTER
Specify rotation angle <0>: ENTER
Enter number of rows (---) <1>: [enter value]
Enter number of columns (|||) <1>: [enter value]
Enter distance between rows or specify unit cell (---):
   [enter value]
Specify distance between columns (|||): [enter value]
```

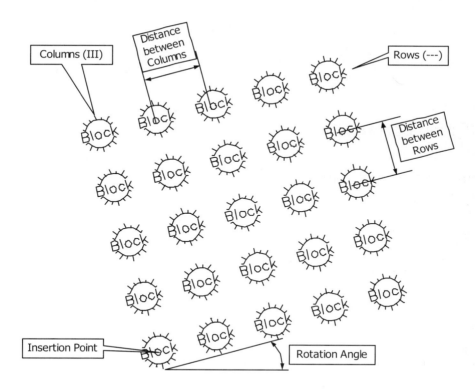

COMMAND LINE OPTIONS

Enter block name

Indicates the name of the block to be inserted; the block must already exist in the drawing.

?   Lists the names of blocks stored in the drawing.

Specify insertion point

Specifies the x,y coordinates for the first block.

P   Supplies predefined scale and rotation values.

X scale factor   Indicates the x scale factor.

Specify opposite corner

Specifies a second point that indicates the x,y-scale factor.

Corner   Indicates the x and y scale factors by picking two points on the screen.

XYZ   Specifies x, y, and z scaling.

Specify rotation angle

Specifies the angle for the array.

Number of rows

Specifies the number of horizontal rows.

Number of columns

Specifies the number of vertical columns.

Distance between rows

Specifies the distance between rows.

Specify unit cell

Shows the cell distance by picking two points on the screen.

Distance between columns

Specifies the distance between columns.

RELATED COMMANDS

3dArray   Creates 3D rectangular and polar arrays.

Array   Creates 2D rectangular and polar arrays.

Block   Creates a block.

TIPS

■ The array placed by the **MInsert** command is a single block.

■ You *cannot* explode the block created by the **MInsert** command.

■ You may redefine the block created by the **MInsert** command.

Mirror

V. 2.0   Creates a mirror copy of a group of objects in 2D space.

Command	Alias	Ctrl+	F-key	Alt+	Menu Bar	Tablet
mirror	mi	...	...	MI	Modify ⌐Mirror	V16

```
Command: mirror
Select objects: [pick]
Select objects: ENTER
Specify first point of mirror line: [pick]
Specify second point of mirror line: ENTER
Delete source objects? [Yes/No] <N>: [Enter]
```

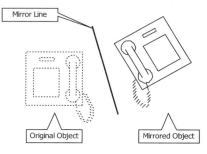

COMMAND LINE OPTIONS

Select objects   Selects the objects to mirror.
First point   Specifies the starting point of the mirror line.
Second point   Specifies the end point of the mirror line.
Delete source objects
       No: Does not delete selected objects.
       Yes: Deletes selected objects.

RELATED COMMANDS

Array   Mirrors object around a circle.
Copy   Creates a non-mirrored copy of a group of objects.
Mirror3d   Mirrors objects in 3D-space.

RELATED SYSTEM VARIABLE

MirrText   Determines whether text is mirrored by the **Mirror** command.

TIPS

■ The **Mirror** command is excellent for cutting your drawing work in half for symmetrical objects. For double-symmetrical objects, use **Mirror** twice.

■ Although you can mirror a viewport in paper space, this does not mirror the model space objects inside the viewport.

■ Turn on **Ortho** mode to ensure that the mirror is perfectly horizontal or vertical.

■ The mirror line become a mirror plane in 3D; it is perpendicular to the x,y plane of the UCS containing the mirror line.

Mirror3d

Rel. 11 Mirrors objects about a plane in 3D space.

Command	Alias	Ctrl+	F-key	Alt+	Menu Bar	Tablet
mirror3d	...	...	...	M3M	Modify	W21
					⌐3D Operation	
					⌐Mirror 3D	

```
Command: mirror3d
Select objects: [pick]
Select objects: ENTER
Specify first point of mirror plane (3 points) or
[Object/Last/Zaxis/View/XY/YZ/ZX/3points] <3points>: [enter
   option]
Delete old objects? <N> ENTER
```

COMMAND LINE OPTIONS

Select objects Selects the objects to be mirrored in space.

Specify first point
Specifies the first point of the mirror plane.

Object Selects a circle, arc or 2D polyline segment as the mirror plane.

Last Selects last-picked mirror plane.

View Specifies that the current view plane is the mirror plane.

XY Specifies that the x,y plane is the mirror plane.

YZ Specifies that the y,z plane is the mirror plane.

ZX Specifies that the z,x plane is the mirror plane.

Zaxis Defines mirror plane by a point on the plane and the normal to the plane; i.e., the z axis.

3 points Defines three points on mirror plane.

RELATED COMMANDS

Align Translates and rotates objects in 2D planes and 3D space.

Mirror Mirrors objects in 2D space.

Rotate3d Rotates objects in 3D space.

RELATED SYSTEM VARIABLE

MirrText Determines whether text is mirrored by the **Mirror** command:

MirrText	Meaning
0	Text is not mirrored about the horizontal axis (default).
1	Text is mirrored.

MIEdit

<u>Rel.13</u> Edits multiline vertices (*short for MultiLine EDITor*).

Command	Alias	Ctrl+	F-key	Alt+	Menu Bar	Tablet
mledit	...	...	...	...	Modify ↳Multiline	Y19
-mledit						

Command: **mledit**
Displays dialog box:

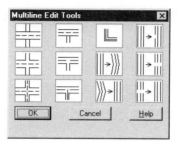

DIALOG BOX OPTIONS

Closed Cross Closes the intersection of two multilines.

Open Cross Opens the intersection of two multilines.

Merged Cross Merges a pair of multilines: opens exterior lines; closes interior lines.

Closed Tee Closes a T-intersection.

Open Tee Opens a T-intersection.

Merged Tee Merges a T-intersection: opens exterior lines; closes interior lines.

Corner Joint Creates a corner joint of a pair of intersecting multilines.

Add Vertex Adds a vertex (*joint*) to a multiline segment.

Delete Vertex Removes a vertex from a multiline segment.

Cut Single Places a gap in a single line of a multiline.

Cut All Places a gap in all lines of a multiline.

Weld All Removes a gap in a multiline.

-MLEDIT COMMAND

Command: **-mledit**

Enter mline editing option [CC/OC/MC/CT/OT/MT/CJ/AV/DV/CS/
   CA/WA]: **[enter option]**

COMMAND LINE OPTIONS

A V	Adds a vertex.
D V	Deletes a vertex.
C C	Closes a cross.
O C	Opens a cross.
M C	Merges a cross.
CT	Closes a tee.
OT	Opens a tee.
MT	Merges a tee
CJ	Creates a corner joint.
CS	Cuts a single line.
C A	Cuts all lines.
W A	Welds all lines.
U	Undoes the most-recent multiline edit.

RELATED COMMANDS

MLine	Draws up to 16 parallel lines.
MlStyle	Defines the properties of a multiline.

RELATED SYSTEM VARIABLES

CMlJust Specifies the current multiline justification mode:

CMlJust	Meaning
0	Top (default).
1	Middle.
2	Bottom.

CMlScale	Specifies the current multiline scale factor (default = 1.0).
CMlStyle	Specifies the current multiline style name (default = " ").

RELATED FILE

*.MLN Multiline style definition file in *Acad 2002**Support*.

TIPS

- Use the **Cut All** option to open up a gap before placing door and window symbols in a multiline wall.

- Use the **Weld All** option to close up a gap after removing the door or window symbol in a multiline.

- Use the **Stretch** command to move a door or window symbol in a multiline wall.

- When you open a gap in a multiline, AutoCAD does not cap the sides of the gap. You may need to add the endcaps with the **Line** command.

MLine

Rel.13 Draws up to 16 parallel lines (*short for Multiple LINE*).

Command	Alias	Ctrl+	F-key	Alt+	Menu Bar	Tablet
mline	ml	...	...	DM	Draw ⤷Multiline	M10

```
Command: mline
Current settings: Justification = Top, Scale = 1.00,
    Style = STANDARD
Specify start point or [Justification/Scale/STyle]: [pick]
Specify next point: [pick]
Specify next point or [Undo]: [pick]
Specify next point or [Close/Undo]: ENTER
```

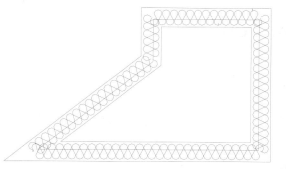

COMMAND LINE OPTIONS

Specify start point
> Indicates the start of the multiline.

Specify next point
> Indicates the next vertex.

Undo   Removes most recently-added segment.

Close   Closes the multiline to its start point.

Justification options:
```
Enter justification type [Top/Zero/Bottom] <top>: [enter option]
```

Top   Draws top line of multiline at cursor; remainder of multiline is "below" cursor.

Zero   Draws center (*zero offset point*) of multiline at cursor.

Bottom   Draws bottom of multiline at cursor; remainder of multiline is "above" cursor.

Scale options:
```
Enter mline scale <1.00>: [enter value]
```

Enter mline scale
> Specifies the scale of the width of the multiline; see Tips for examples.

STyle *options:*
```
Enter mline style name or [?]: [enter style name]
```

Enter mline style name
>Specifies the name of the multiline style.

?
>Lists names of the multiline styles defined in drawing:
```
Loaded mline styles:
      Name              Description
---------------- ------------------
STANDARD
```

RELATED COMMANDS

MlEdit   Edits multilines.
MlProp   Defines the properties of a multiline.

RELATED SYSTEM VARIABLES

CMlJust   Specifies the current multiline justification:

CMlJust	Meaning
0	Top (default).
1	Middle.
2	Bottom.

CMlScale   Specifies the current multiline scale factor (default = 1.0).
CMlStyle   Specifies the current multiline style name (default = "").

RELATED FILE

*.MLN   Multiline style definition file in *Acad 2002**Support*.

TIPS

- Multiline styles are stored in MLN files in DXF-like format.

- Examples of scale factors:

Scale	Meaning
1.0	Default scale factor.
2.0	Draws multiline twice as wide
0.5	Draws multiline half as wide.
-1.0	Flips multiline.
0	Collapses multiline to a single line.

MlStyle

Rel.13   Defines the characteristics of multilines (*short for MultiLine STYLE*).

Command	Alias	Ctrl+	F-key	Alt+	Menu Bar	Tablet
mlstyle	...	...	...	OM	Format	V5
					↳Multiline Style	

Command: **mlstyle**
Displays dialog box:

DIALOG BOX OPTIONS

Multiline Style *options:*

Current	Lists the currently-loaded multiline style names (default = STANDARD).
Name	Gives a new multiline style a name, or renames an existing style.
Description	Describes the multiline style, with up to 255 characters.
Load	Loads style from the multiline library file *Acad.Mln* or another MLN file; displays the **Load Multiline Styles** dialog box.
Save	Saves a multiline style or renames a style; displays dialog box.
Add	Adds the multiline style from the **Name** box to the **Current** list.
Remove	Removes the multiline style from the **Current** list.

Element Properties
Specifies properties of multiline elements; displays the **Element Properties** dialog box.

Multiline Properties
Specifies additional properties for multilines; displays the **Multiline Properties** dialog box.

Load Multiline Styles dialog box:

```
┌─────────────────────────────────────┐
│ Load Multiline Styles           [X] │
│                                      │
│       File ...  │  acad.mln          │
│   ┌──────────────────────────────┐   │
│   │ STANDARD                     │   │
│   │                              │   │
│   └──────────────────────────────┘   │
│                                      │
│     ┌───────┐                        │
│     │  OK   │   Cancel      Help    │
│     └───────┘                        │
└─────────────────────────────────────┘
```

File   Selects an MLN (multiline definition) file.

Element Properties dialog box:

```
┌─────────────────────────────────────────┐
│ Element Properties                  [X] │
│  Elements:   Offset   Color   Ltype     │
│           ┌─────────────────────────┐   │
│           │ 0.5    BYLAYER  ByLayer │   │
│           │ -0.5   BYLAYER  ByLayer │   │
│           └─────────────────────────┘   │
│                                          │
│   ┌─────┐  ┌────────┐          ┌───────┐│
│   │ Add │  │ Delete │  Offset  │ 0.500 ││
│   └─────┘  └────────┘          └───────┘│
│  ┌────────┐ ┌──┐   ┌──────────────┐     │
│  │ Color..│ │██│   │ BYLAYER      │     │
│  └────────┘ └──┘   └──────────────┘     │
│  ┌──────────┐        ByLayer            │
│  │ Linetype.│                           │
│  └──────────┘                           │
│       ┌───────┐                          │
│       │  OK   │   Cancel      Help      │
│       └───────┘                          │
└─────────────────────────────────────────┘
```

Add   Adds an element (line).
Delete   Deletes an element.
Offset   Specifies the distance from origin to element.
Color   Specifies the element color; displays **Select Color** dialog box.
Linetype   Specifies the element linetype; displays **Select Linetype** dialog box.

Multiline Properties dialog box:

```
┌─────────────────────────────────────────┐
│ Multiline Properties                [X] │
│  ☐ Display joints                        │
│  ┌─ Caps ─────────────────────────────┐ │
│  │           Start      End           │ │
│  │  Line      ☐         ☐             │ │
│  │  Outer arc ☐         ☐             │ │
│  │  Inner arcs ☐        ☐             │ │
│  │  Angle   ┌────────┐ ┌────────┐     │ │
│  │          │ 90.000 │ │ 90.000 │     │ │
│  │          └────────┘ └────────┘     │ │
│  └────────────────────────────────────┘ │
│  ┌─ Fill ─────────────────────────────┐ │
│  │  ☐ On    ┌──────┐ ┌──┐             │ │
│  │          │Color.│ │██│  BYLAYER    │ │
│  │          └──────┘ └──┘             │ │
│  └────────────────────────────────────┘ │
│       ┌───────┐                          │
│       │  OK   │   Cancel      Help      │
│       └───────┘                          │
└─────────────────────────────────────────┘
```

Display Joints Toggles the display of joints (miters) at vertices; affects all multiline
                    segments.

Caps *options:*

Line   Draws a straight line start and/or end cap.
Outer Arc   Draws an arc to cap the outermost pair of lines.
Inner Arcs   Draws an arc to cap all inner pairs of lines.
Angle   Specifies the angle for straight line caps.

Fill *options:*
On   Specifies the fill color.
Color   Displays the **Select Color** dialog box.

RELATED COMMANDS
MlEdit   Edits multilines.
MLine   Draws up to 16 parallel lines.

RELATED SYSTEM VARIABLES
CMlJust   Specifies the current multiline justification:

CMlJust	Meaning
0	Top (default).
1	Middle.
2	Bottom.

CMlScale   Specifies the current multiline scale factor (default = 1.0).
CMlStyle   Specifies the current multiline style name (default = " ").

RELATED FILE
Acad.Mln   Multiline style definition file in *Acad 2002**Support*.

TIPS
- Use the **MlEdit** command to create (or close up) gaps to place door and window symbols in multiline walls.

- The multiline scale factor has the following effect on the look of a multiline:

Scale	Meaning
1.0	The default scale factor.
0.5	Draws multiline half as wide.
2.0	Draws multiline twice as wide, not twice as long.
-1.0	Flips multiline about its origin.
0.0	Collapses multiline to a single line.

- The MLN file describes multiline styles in a DXF-like format.

- You cannot change the element or multiline properties once the drawing contains an multiline using the style.

Model

Switches to the model tab.

Command	Alias	Ctrl+	F-key	Alt+	Menu Bar	Tablet
model	...	...	...	...	...	...

Command: **model**
Switches to the model tab.

COMMAND LINE OPTIONS
None.

RELATED COMMANDS
Layout	Creates layouts.
MSpace	Switches to model space.

RELATED SYSTEM VARIABLE
Tilemode	Switches between model tab and layout tab.

TIPS
■ This command automatically sets **TileMode** to 1.

■ As an alternative to this command, you can select the **Model** tab:

■ The **Model** tab replaces the **TILE** button on the status bar of AutoCAD Release 13 and 14.

Move

V. 1.0 Moves a group of objects to a new location.

Command	Alias	Ctrl+	F-key	Alt+	Menu Bar	Tablet
move	m	...	...	MV	Modify ↳Move	V19

```
Command: move
Select objects: [pick]
Select objects: ENTER
Specify base point or displacement:  [pick]
Specify second point of displacement or
<use first point as displacement>: [pick]
```

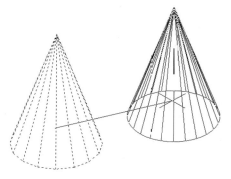

COMMAND LINE OPTIONS

Select objects Selects the objects to copy.

Specify base point
Indicates the starting point for the move.

Displacement Specifies relative x,y,z displacement when you press ENTER at the next prompt.

Specify second point of displacement
Indicates the distance to move.

RELATED COMMANDS

Copy   Makes a copy of the selected objects.

MlEdit   Moves the vertices of a multiline.

PEdit   Moves the vertices of a polyline.

MSlide

V. 2.0 Saves the current viewport as an SLD slide file on disk (*short for Make SLIDE*).

Command	Alias	Ctrl+	F-key	Alt+	Menu Bar	Tablet
mslide	...	...	...	...	...	...

Command: **mslide**
*Displays **Create Slide File** dialog box.*

When FileDia = 0:
Command: **mslide**
Enter name of slide file to create <C:\ACAD 2002\Drawing1.sld>:
   [enter filename]

COMMAND LINE OPTIONS
Enter name of slide file to create
Specifies the name of the file; press **Enter** to accept the default file name shown in angle brackets.

RELATED COMMANDS
Save	Saves the current drawing as a DWG-format drawing file.
SaveImg	Saves the current view as a TIFF, Targa, or GIF-format raster file.
VSlide	Displays an SLD-format slide file in AutoCAD.

RELATED AUTODESK PROGRAM
Slidelib.Exe   Compiles a group of slides into an SLB-format slide library file.

TIPS
- You view the slide with the **VSlide** command.

- Slide files are used to create the images in palette dialog boxes.

MSpace

Rel.11 Switches the drawing from paper space to model space (*short for Model SPACE*).

Command	Alias	Ctrl+	F-key	Alt+	Menu Bar	Tablet
mspace	ms	. . .	. . .	. . .	. . .	L4

Command: **mspace**
AutoCAD switches from paper space to model space in layout mode:

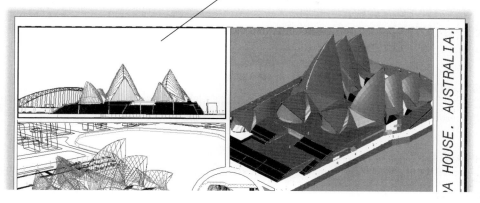

COMMAND LINE OPTIONS
None.

RELATED COMMANDS
PSpace Switches from model space to paper space.
Model Switches from layout mode to model mode.
Layout Switches from model mode to layout mode.

RELATED SYSTEM VARIABLES
MaxActVp Specifies the maximum number of viewports with visible objects; default=64.
TileMode Specifies the current setting of tiled viewports.

TIPS
■ To switch quickly between paper space and model space, click the **MODEL** and **PAPER** buttons on the status bar:

4.0679, 0.4813, 0.0000		SNAP GRID ORTHO POLAR OSNAP OTRACK LWT MODEL

4.0679, 0.4813, 0.0000		SNAP GRID ORTHO POLAR OSNAP OTRACK LWT PAPER

Click ***PAPER*** *to switch from* ***paper space*** *to* ***model space***.

■ The old restrictions, from AutoCAD Release 14 and earlier, no longer apply. You no longer need to set **TileMode** to zero (this is done automatically); one viewport is already active in a new layout.

■ AutoCAD clears the selection set when moving between paper space and model space.

MTEdit

Rel.13 Edits an mtext object (*short for Multiline Text EDITor; an undocumented command*).

Command	Alias	Ctrl+	F-key	Alt+	Menu Bar	Tablet
mtedit	...	...	...	...	...	...

Command: **mtedit**
Select an MTEXT object: **[pick]**
*Display **Mutiline Text Editor** dialog box; see **MText** command.*

COMMAND LINE OPTION
Select an MTEXT object
Selects one paragraph text object for editing.

RELATED COMMANDS
DdEdit Displays the text editor appropriate for the text object.
Properties Changes the properties of an mtext object.
MtProp Specifies the properties of an mtext object.

RELATED SYSTEM VARIABLE
MTextEd Specifies the name of the external text editor to place and edit multiline text.

TIPS
■ This command displays the same dialog box as the **DdEdit** command when an mtext object is selected.

MText

Rel.13 Creates a multiline, or paragraph, text object that fits the width defined by a boundary box (*short for Multline TEXT*).

Command	Alias	Ctrl+	F-key	Alt+	Menu Bar	Tablet
mtext	t	...	...	DXM	Draw	J8
	mt				ⓉText	
					ⓈMultiline Text	
-mtext	-t					

```
Command: mtext
Current text style:  "Standard"  Text height:  3/16"
Specify first corner: [pick]
```

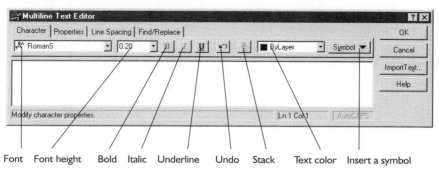

The mtext bounding box.

```
Specify opposite corner or [Height/Justify/Line spacing/
    Rotation/Style/Width]: [pick]
```
Displays tabbed dialog box.

DIALOG BOX OPTIONS

Import Text   Imports text from an ASCII file; displays **Open** dialog box.
Caution! The maximum size of text file is limited to 16KB.

Character tab:

Font   Selects a TrueType (TTF) or AutoCAD (SHX) font name (default=TXT).
Font height   Specifies the height of the text (default = 0.2 units).
Bold   Boldfaces the text, if the font allows.

Italic	Italicizes the text, if the font allows.
Underline	Underlines the text, if the font allows.
Undo	Undoes the last action.
Stack	Stacks a pair of characters to create a fraction.
Text Color	Selects color for text; click **Other Color** to display **Select Color** dialog box.
Insert Symbol	Inserts one of three common symbols or a non-breaking space:

Symbol	Meaning
%%d	Degree — °
%%p	Plus-minus — ±
%%c	Diameter — ∅

Click **Other** for **Character Map** dialog box.

Character Map dialog box:

Font	Selects the TTF TrueType font.
Characters to copy	
	Lists the characters that will be copied to the Clipboard.
Close	Dismisses the dialog box.
Select	Selects a character from the font.
Copy	Copies the selected character(s) to the Clipboard.

Properties tab:

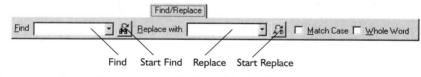

Style   Selects the text style (default = STANDARD).
Justification Selects the bounding box justification (default = Top Left).
Width   Selects the width of the bounding box.
Rotation   Sets the rotation angle of the bounding box (default = 0 degrees).

Line Spacing tab:

Line Spacing	
Line spacing	At Least ▾	Single (1.0x) ▾

Line spacing   Specifies the spacing between lines of text:
- **At least** adds space between lines of text, based on the largest character.
- **Exactly** spaces lines of text at an exact distance. *Caution*! This option may cause lines of text to overlap.

Spacing   Provides three standard line spacings; you may also indicate a custom spacing:
- **Single (1.0x)** applies normal (single-line) spacing.
- **1.5 Lines (1.5x)** applies one-and-a-half line spacing.
- **Double (2.0x)** applies double spacing.

Find/Replace tab:

Find/Replace	
Find [   ] ▾ 🔍 Replace with [   ] ▾ ⚎ ☐ Match Case ☐ Whole Word

                  Find   Start Find   Replace   Start Replace

Find   Enters the text to search for; click the **Find** icon to start finding.
Start Find   Starts the find process.
Replace With Enters the text to replace; click the **Replace** icon to start replacing.
Start Replace Starts the replace process.
Match Case   Matches the case of the text.
Whole Word   Looks for whole words, not partial words.

-MTEXT COMMAND

```
Command: -mtext
Current text style: STANDARD. Text height: 0.2000
Specify first corner: [pick]
Specify opposite corner or [Height/Justify/Rotation/Style/
   Width]: [pick]
MText: [enter text]
MText: ENTER
```

COMMAND LINE OPTIONS

Height   Specifies the height of UPPERCASE text (*default = 0.2 units*).

Justify options:

TL	Top left (default).
TC	Top center.
TR	Top right.
ML	Middle left.
MC	Middle center.
MR	Middle right.
BL	Bottom left.
BC	Bottom center.
BR	Bottom right.

Rotation	Specifies the rotation angle of the boundary box.
Style	Selects the text style for multiline text (default = STANDARD).
Width	Sets the width of the boundary box; a width of 0 eliminates the boundary box.

RELATED COMMANDS

Properties	Changes all aspects of mtext.
MtProp	Changes properties of multiline text.
MtEdit	Edits mtext.
PasteSpec	Pastes formatted text from the Clipboard into the drawing.
Style	Creates a named text style from a font file.

RELATED SYSTEM VARIABLE

MTextEd   Names the external text editor for placing and editing multiline text.

TIPS

- Use the **MTextEd** system variable to define a different text editor.

- The **Import Text** option is limited to ASCII (unformatted) text files no more than 16KB in size.

- To import formatted text, copy text from the word processor to the Clipboard, then use AutoCAD's **PasteSpec** command.

- To link text in the drawing with a word processor, use the **InsertObj** command. When the word processor updates, the linked text is updated in the drawing.

MtProp

Rel.13 Changes the properties of multiline text (*short for Multline Text PROPerties; an undocumented command*).

Command	Alias	Ctrl+	F-key	Alt+	Menu Bar	Tablet
mtprop	...	...	...	...	...	...

Command: **mtprop**
Select an MText object: **[pick]**
Displays **Multiline Text Editor** *dialog box; see the* **MText** *command.*

COMMAND LINE OPTIONS
See the **MText** *command.*

RELATED COMMANDS
DdEdit   Edits multiline text.
MText   Places multiline text.
Style   Creates a named text style from a font file.

Multiple

V. 2.5 Automatically repeats a command that does not repeat on its own.

Command	Alias	Ctrl+	F-key	Alt+	Menu Bar	Tablet
multiple	...	...	...	...	...	...

Command: **multiple**
Enter command name to repeat: **[enter command name]**

This command can be used as a command modifier:
Command: **multiple circle**
3P/2P/TTR/<Center point>: **[pick]**
Diameter/<Radius>: **[pick]**
circle 3P3P/2P/TTR/<Center point>: **[pick]**
Diameter/<Radius>: **[pick]**
circle 3P3P/2P/TTR/<Center point>: **Esc**

COMMAND LINE OPTIONS

Enter command name to repeat
        Specifies the name of the command to repeat.
Esc   Stops the command from automatically repeating itself.

COMMAND INPUT OPTIONS

Space   Repeats the previous command.
Click   Repeats a command by clicking on any blank spot of the tablet menu.

RELATED COMMANDS

Redo   Undoes an undo
U   Undoes the previous command; undoes one multiple command at a time.

RELATED COMMAND MODIFIERS

'   *(Apostrophe)* Allows the use of some commands within another command.
.   *(Period)* Forces the use of an undefined command.
-   *(Dash)* Forces the display of prompts on the command line for some commands.
+   *(Plus)* Prompts for the tab number of tabbed dialog box.
_   *(Underscore)* Uses the English command in an international version of AutoCAD.
(*(Open parenthesis)* Executes an AutoLISP function on the command line.
$(*(Dollar and parenthesis)* Executes a Diesel function on the command line.

TIPS

- Use the **Multiple** command to repeat commands that do not repeat on their own.

- **Multiple** repeats the command name only ; it does not repeat command options.

- Some commands automatically repeat, including **Point** and **Donut**.

MView

Rel.11 Creates and manipulates overlapping viewports (*short for Make VIEWports*).

Command	Alias	Ctrl+	F-key	Alt+	Menu Bar	Tablet
mview	mv	R	. . .	. . .	. . .	M4

```
Command: mview
Specify corner of viewport or
[ON/OFF/Fit/Hideplot/Lock/Object/Polygonal/Restore/2/3/4]
   <Fit>: [pick]
Specify opposite corner: [pick]
Regenerating drawing.
```

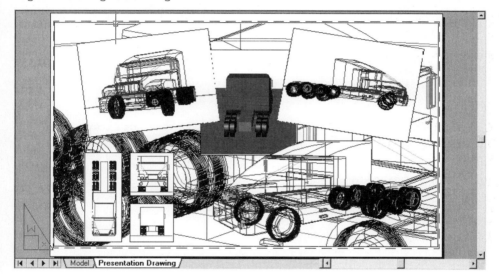

COMMAND LINE OPTIONS

Specify corner of viewport
    Indicates the first point of a single viewport (default).

Fit   Creates a single viewport that fits the screen.

Hideplot   Creates a hidden-line view during plotting and printing.

Lock   Locks the selected viewport.

Object   Converts a circle, closed polyline, ellipse, spline, or region into a viewport.

OFF   Turns off a viewport.

ON   Turns on a viewport.

Polygonal   Creates a multisided viewport of straight lines and arcs.

Restore   Restores a saved viewport configuration.

2 options:

```
Enter viewport arrangement [Horizontal/Vertical]
    <Vertical>:[enter option]
Specify first corner or [Fit] <Fit>: [enter option]
```
Horizontal   Stacks two viewports.
Vertical   Places two viewports side-by-side (default).

3 options:
```
[Horizontal/Vertical/Above/Below/Left/Right]<Right>:
    [enter option]
Specify first corner or [Fit] <Fit>: [enter option]
```
Horizontal   Stacks the three viewports.
Vertical   Places three side-by-side viewports.
Above   Places two viewports above the third.
Below   Places two viewports below the third.
Left   Places two viewports to the left of the third.
Right   Places two viewports to the right of the third (*default*).

4 options:
```
Specify first corner or [Fit] <Fit>: [enter option]
Regenerating model.
```

Fit   Creates four identical viewports that fit the viewport.
First Point   Indicates the area of the four viewports (default).

RELATED COMMANDS
Ctrl+R   Switches to the next viewport.
Layout   Creates new layouts.
MSpace   Switches to model space.
PSpace   Switches to paper space before creating viewports.
RedrawAll   Redraws all viewports.
RegenAll   Regenerates all viewports.
VpLayer   Controls the visibility of layers in each viewport.
VPorts   Creates tiled viewports in model space.
Zoom   Zooms a viewport relative to paper space via the **XP** option.

RELATED SYSTEM VARIABLES
CvPort   Specifies the number of the current viewport.
MaxActVp   Controls the maximum number of visible viewports:

MaxActVP	Meaning
1	Minimum.
64	Default.
32767	Maximum.

TileMode   Controls the availability of overlapping viewports.

TIPS

- Although the system variable **MaxActVp** limits the number of simultaneously-visible viewports, the **Plot** command plots all viewports.
- **TileMode** must be set to zero to switch to paper space and use the **MSpace** command.
- **Snap**, **Grid**, **Hide**, **Shade**, et cetera, can be set separately in each viewport.
- Press **CTRL+R** to switch between viewports.
- The preset viewports created by the **MView** command have these shapes:

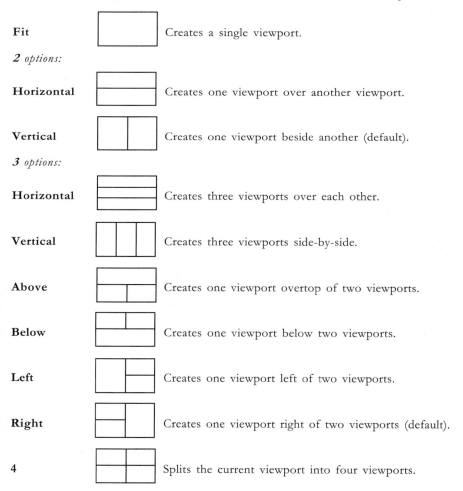

Fit   Creates a single viewport.

2 options:

Horizontal   Creates one viewport over another viewport.

Vertical   Creates one viewport beside another (default).

3 options:

Horizontal   Creates three viewports over each other.

Vertical   Creates three viewports side-by-side.

Above   Creates one viewport overtop of two viewports.

Below   Creates one viewport below two viewports.

Left   Creates one viewport left of two viewports.

Right   Creates one viewport right of two viewports (default).

4   Splits the current viewport into four viewports.

MvSetup

Rel. 11 Quickly sets up a drawing, complete with a predrawn border. Optionally sets up multiple viewports, sets the scale, and aligns views in each viewport (*short for Model View SETUP*).

Command	Alias	Ctrl+	F-key	Alt+	Menu Bar	Tablet
mvsetup	mvs	...	...	...	...	...

```
Command: mvsetup
Enable paper space? [No/Yes] <Y>: y
```

Command prompts in model tab (not paper space):
```
Enter units type [Scientific/Decimal/Engineering/
   Architectural/Metric]: [select an option]
Enter the scale factor: [enter value]
Enter the paper width: [enter value]
Enter the paper height: [enter value]
```

Command prompts in paper space:
```
Enter an option [Align/Create/Scale viewports/Options/Title
   block/Undo]: [select an option]
```

COMMAND LINE OPTIONS

Align options:
Pans the view to align a base point with another viewport.
```
Enter an option [Angled/Horizontal/Vertical alignment/
   Rotate view/Undo]: [enter an option]
```
Angled Specifies the distance and angle from a base point to a second point.

Horizontal Aligns views horizontally with a base point in another viewport.
Vertical alignment
Aligns views vertically with a base point in another viewport.
Rotate view Rotates the view about a base point.
Undo Undoes the last action.

Create options:
```
Enter option [Delete objects/Create viewports/Undo] <Create>:
   [enter an option]
```

Delete objects Erases existing viewports.
Create viewports
Creates viewports in these configurations:

Layout	Meaning
0	No layout.
1	Single viewport.
2	Standard engineering layout.
3	Array viewports along x and y axes.

Undo Undoes the last action.

Scale viewports options:
```
Select the viewports to scale...
Select objects: [pick a viewport]
1 found Select objects: ENTER
Set the ratio of paper space units to model space units...
Enter the number of paper space units <1.0>: [enter value]
Enter the number of model space units <1.0>: [enter value]
```

Select objects Selects one or more viewports.
Enter the number of paper space units
> Scales the objects in the viewport with respect to drawing objects.

Enter the number of model space units
> Scales the objects in the viewport with respect to drawing objects.

Options options:
```
Enter an option [Layer/LImits/Units/Xref] <exit>: [enter option]
```

Layer	Specifies the layer name for the title block.
Limits	Specifies whether to reset limits after title block insertion.
Units	Specifies inch or millimeter paper units.
Xref	Specifies whether title is inserted as a block or as an external reference.

Title block options:
```
Enter title block option [Delete objects/Origin/Undo/
    Insert] <Insert>: [enter option]
```

Delete objects	Erases an existing title block from the drawing.
Origin	Relocates the origin.
Undo	Undoes the last action.
Insert	Displays the available title blocks.

RELATED SYSTEM VARIABLE
TileMode   Specifies the current setting of **TileMode**.

RELATED FILES
MvSetup.Dfs The **MvSetup** default settings file.
AcadIso.Dwg Prototype drawing with ISO defaults.
Plus all title block drawings.

RELATED COMMANDS
LayoutWizard Sets up the viewports via a "wizard."

TIPS

■ When option **2 (Std. Engineering)** is selected at the **Create** option, the following views are created (counterclockwise from upper left):

    Top view.
    Isometric view.
    Front view.
    Right view.

■ To create the title block, **MvSetup** searches the path specified by the **AcadPrefix** variable. If the appropriate drawing cannot be found, **MvSetup** creates the default border.

■ **MvSetup** makes use the following predefined title blocks:

    0: None
    1: ISO A4 Size(mm)
    2: ISO A3 Size(mm)
    3: ISO A2 Size(mm)
    4: ISO A1 Size(mm)
    5: ISO A0 Size(mm)
    6: ANSI-V Size(in)
    7: ANSI-A Size(in)
    8: ANSI-B Size(in)
    9: ANSI-C Size(in)
    10: ANSI-D Size(in)
    11: ANSI-E Size(in)
    12: Arch/Engineering (24 x 36in)
    13: Generic D size Sheet (24 x 36in)

■ The metric A0 size is similar to the imperial E-size, while the metric A4 size is similar to A-size.

■ You can add your own title block with the **Add** option. Before doing so, create the title block as an AutoCAD drawing.

■ This command provides the following preset scales (scale factor shown in parentheses):

Architectural Scales		Scientific Scales		Decimal Scales		Engineering Scales		Metric Scales	
(480)	1/40"=1'	(4.0)	4 TIMES	(4.0)	4 TIMES	(120)	1"=10'	(5000)	1:5000
(240)	1/20"=1'	(2.0)	2 TIMES	(2.0)	2 TIMES	(240)	1"=20'	(2000)	1:2000
(192)	1/16"=1'	**(1.0)**	**FULL**	**(1.0)**	**FULL**	(360)	1"=30'	(1000)	1:1000
(96)	1/8"=1'	(0.5)	HALF	(0.5)	HALF	(480)	1"=40'	(500)	1:500
(48)	1/4"=1'	(0.25)	QUARTER	(0.25)	QUARTER	(600)	1"=50'	(200)	1:200
(24)	1/2"=1'					(720)	1"=60'	(100)	1:100
(16)	3/4"=1'					(960)	1"=80'	(75)	1:75
(12)	1"=1'					(1200)	1"=100'	(50)	1:50
(4)	3"=1'							(20)	1:20
(2)	6"=1'							(10)	1:10
(1)	**FULL**							(5)	1:5
								(1)	FULL

Using MvSetup

MvSetup has many options, but does not present them in a logical fashion. To set up a drawing with **MvSetup**, follow these basic steps:

Step 1: MVSETUP COMMAND

Start the **MvSetup** command:

```
Command: mvsetup
Enter an option [Align/Create/Scale viewports/Options/
      Title block/Undo]: o
```

Step 2: SELECT OPTIONS

```
Enter an option [Layer/LImits/Units/Xref] <exit>: l
```
1. Decide on the layer for the title block with the **Layer** option.

2. Specify the paper space units with the **Units** option.

Step 3: PLACE TITLE BLOCK

```
Enter title block option [Delete objects/Origin/Undo/
   Insert] <Insert>: ENTER
```
1. Place the title block with the **Title block** option's **Insert** option.

Step 4: CREATE VIEWPORTS

```
Enter option [Delete objects/Create viewports/Undo]
   <Create>: ENTER
```
1. Set up the viewports with the **Create** option's **Create viewports** option.

2. For standard drawings, select option #2, **Std. Engineering**.

Step 5: SCALE VIEWPORTS

1. Make the object the same size in all four viewports with the **Scale viewports** option.

2. When you are prompted to 'Select objects', select the four *viewports*, not the objects in the viewports.

Step 6: ALIGN VIEWS

1. Align the views in each viewport with the **Align** option.

2. You can interrupt the **MvSetup** command at any time with the **Esc** key, then resume the command to complete the setup.

3. Save your work when done!

New

Starts a new drawing from scratch, from a template drawing, or via a step-by-step drawing setup "wizard."

Command	Alias	Ctrl+	F-key	Alt+	Menu Bar	Tablet
new	...	N	...	FN	File ⤷New	T24

Command: **new**

*Display depends on the setting in the **Startup** option found in the **General Options** section of the **System** tab in the **Options** dialog box:*

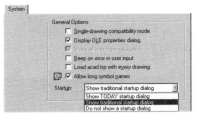

Startup
* **Show TODAY startup dialog** displays **AutoCAD 2002 Today** window; see the **Today** command.
* **Show traditional startup dialog box** displays one of two nearly identical dialog boxes: **Startup** dialog box when AutoCAD launches; or **Create New Drawing** dialog box when AutoCAD is already running.
* **Do not show a startup dialog** displays command line prompt; sets **FileDia** system variable to 0.

COMMAND LINE OPTIONS

*When **FileDia** = 0:*

Command: **new**

Enter template file name or [. (for none)]
   <C:\ACAD 2002\template\acad.dwt>: **[enter filename]**

Enter template file name

Specifies the name of a template file, or specifies another action:

Character	Meaning
. (*period*)	AutoCAD uses the default *Acad.Dwt* template file.
~ (*tilde*)	Displays the **Select template** dialog box.
Esc	Cancels the command.

COMMAND LINE SWITCHES

The switches used by the **Target** *filed in the* **Shortcut** *tab of AutoCAD 2002 desktop icon's* **Properties** *dialog box:*

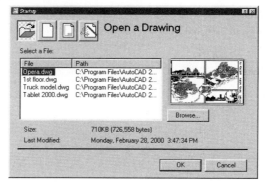

Shortcut	
AutoCAD 2000	
Target type:	Application
Target location:	ACAD 2000
Target:	acad.exe filename.dwg /b filename.scr

/b	Runs a script file after AutoCAD starts; uses the following format: acad.exe "the file name.dwg" /b "file name.scr"
/c	Specifies the path for alternative hardware configuration file; default = *Acad2002.Cfg.*
/nologo	Supresses the display of the AutoCAD logo screen.
/p	Specifies a user-defined profile to customize AutoCAD's user interface.
/r	Restores the default pointing device.
/s	Specifies additional support folders; maximum is 15 folders, with each folder name separated by a semicolon.
/t	Specifies the DWT template drawing to use.
/v	Specifies the named view to display upon startup of AutoCAD.

DIALOG BOX OPTIONS

Open a Drawing options

This option is not available in the **Create New Drawing** *dialog box:*

Select a File Selects one of the four drawings listed.

Browse Displays the **Select File** dialog box; see the **Open** command.

Startup		
	Open a Drawing	
Select a File:		
File	Path	
Opera.dwg	C:\Program Files\AutoCAD 2...	
1st floor.dwg	C:\Program Files\AutoCAD 2...	
Truck model.dwg	C:\Program Files\AutoCAD 2...	
Tablet 2000.dwg	C:\Program Files\AutoCAD 2...	
		Browse...
Size:	710KB (726,558 bytes)	
Last Modified:	Monday, February 28, 2000 3:47:34 PM	
		OK Cancel

Start from Scratch options

English   Creates a new drawing based on the *Acad.Dwt* (English units) template file.

Metric   Creates a new drawing based on the *AcadIso.Dwt* (metric units) template file.

Use a Template options

Select a Template

Creates a new drawing based on the selected DWT template file.

Browse   Display the **Select a template file** dialog box.

Use a Wizard options

Select a Wizard

- **Advanced Setup** sets up a new drawing in several steps.
- **Quick Setup** sets up a new drawing in two steps.

Quick Setup — Units page:

Decimal	Displays units in decimal (or "metric") notation (default): 123.5000.
Engineering	Displays units in feet and decimal inches: 10'-3.5000".
Architectural	Displays units in feet, inches, and fractional inches: 10' 3-1/2".
Fractional	Displays units in inches and fractions: 123 1/2.
Scientific	Displays units in scientific notation: 1.235E+02.

Cancel	Cancels the wizard, and returns to the previous drawing.
Back	Moves back one step.
Next	Moves forward one step.

Area page:

Width	Specifies the width of drawing in real-world (not scaled) units; default = 12 units.
Length	Specifies the length or depth of drawing in real-world units; default = 9 units.

Advanced Setup — Units page:

Decimal   Displays units in decimal (or "metric") notation (default): 123.5000.
Engineering   Displays units in feet and decimal inches: 10'-3.5000".
Architectural Displays units in feet, inches, and fractional inches: 10' 3-1/2".
Fractional   Displays units in inches and fractions: 123 1/2.
Scientific   Displays units in scientific notation: 1.235E+02.
Precision   Selects the precision of display up to 8 decimal places or $^1/_{256}$.

Angle page:

Decimal Degrees
                Displays decimal degrees (default): 22.5000.
Deg/Min/Sec Displays degrees, minutes, and seconds: 22 30.
Grads   Displays grads: 25g.
Radians   Displays radians: 25r.
Surveyor   Displays surveyor units: N 25d0'0" E.
Precision   Selects a precision ranging up to 8 decimal places.

Angle Measure page:

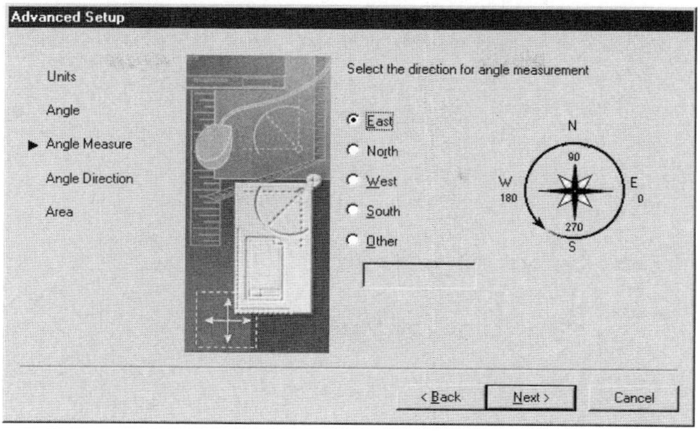

East	Specifies that zero degrees points East (default).
North	Specifies that zero degrees points North.
West	Specifies that zero degrees points West.
South	Specifies that zero degrees points South.
Other	Specifies any of the 360 degrees as zero degrees.

Angle Direction page:

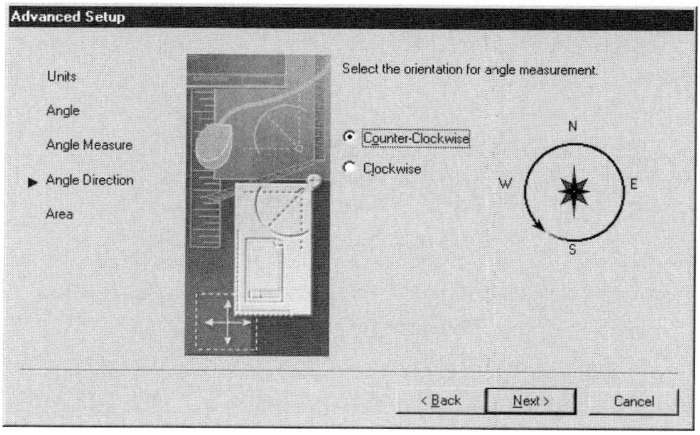

Counter-Clockwise

Measures positive angles counterclockwise from 0 degrees (default).

Clockwise Measures positive angles clockwise from 0 degrees.

Area page:

Width	Specifies the width of drawing in real-world (not scaled) units; default = 12 units.
Length	Specifies the length or depth of drawing in real-world units; default = 9 units.

RELATED COMMAND

SaveAs	Saves the drawing in DWG or DWT formats; allows the saving of template files.

RELATED SYSTEM VARIABLES

DbMod	Indicates whether the drawing has changed since being loaded.
DwgPrefix	Indicates the path to the drawing.
DwgName	Indicates the name of the current drawing.
FileDia	Displays prompts at the 'Command' prompt.

RELATED FILES

Wizard.Ini	Names and descriptions of template files.
*.DWT	Template files; stored in DWG format.

TIPS

■ Until you give the drawing a name, AutoCAD names it *Drawing1.Dwg*.

■ The default prototype drawing is *Acad.Dwg*.

■ Edit and save DWT template drawings to change the defaults for new drawings.

■ When you press **CTRL+N**, AutoCAD's behavior differs from Microsoft Office programs: AutoCAD displays either the **Today** window or the **Startup** dialog box; Office programs display a new document that takes on the properties of the current document.

Offset

V. 2.5 Draws parallel lines, arcs, circles and polylines; repeats automatically until cancelled.

Command	Alias	Ctrl+	F-key	Alt+	Menu Bar	Tablet
offset	o	...	...	MS	Modify ⤷Offset	V17

Command: **offset**
Specify offset distance or [Through] <Through>: **[enter number]**
Select object to offset or <exit>: **[pick]**
Specify point on side to offset: **[pick]**
Select object to offset or <exit>: **Esc**

Original objects (above) and offset objects (below).

COMMAND LINE OPTIONS

Offset distance Specifies the perpendicular distance to offset.
Through   Indicates the offset distance.
Esc   Exits **Offset**.

RELATED COMMANDS

Copy   Creates one of more copies of a group of objects.
Mirror   Creates a mirror copy of a group of objects.
MLine   Draws up to 16 parallel lines.

RELATED SYSTEM VARIABLE

OffsetDist Specifies the current offset distance.

OleLinks

Rel.13 Changes, updates, and cancels OLE links between the drawing and other Windows applications *(short for Object Linking and Embedding LINKS)*.

Command	Alias	Ctrl+	F-key	Alt+	Menu Bar	Tablet
olelinks	...	...	...	EO	Edit	...
					↳OLE Links	

Command: **olelinks**
When no OLE links are in the drawing, the command does nothing.
When at least one OLE object is in the drawing, displays dialog box:

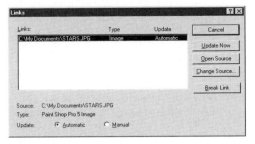

DIALOG BOX OPTIONS

Links   Displays a list of linked objects: source filename, type of file, and update mode: automatic or manual.

Update   Selects either automatic or manual updates.

Update Now   Updates selected links.

Open Source   Starts the source application program.

Break Link   Cancels the OLE link; keeps the object in place.

Change Source
                   Displays **Change Source** dialog box:

RELATED COMMANDS

InsertObj   Places an OLE object in the drawing.

PasteSpec   Places objects from the Clipboard as linked objects in the drawing.

RELATED WINDOWS COMMANDS

Edit | Copy   Copies objects from the source application to the Clipboard.

File | Update Updates the linked object in the source application.

OleScale

Modifies the properties of an OLE object.

Command	Alias	Ctrl+	F-key	Alt+	Shortcut Menu	Tablet
olescale	...	...	...	...	...	...

Command: **olescale**
Displays dialog box:

DIALOG BOX OPTIONS

Size options:

Height	Changes the height of the OLE object; displays the current height.
Width	Changes the width of the OLE object; displays the current width.
Reset	Resets the OLE object to its original size when first inserted into the drawing.

Scale options:

Height	Changes the height of the OLE object by a percentage of the original height.
Width	Changes the width of the OLE object by a percentage of the original width.
Lock Aspect Ratio	Changes the **Width** size and ratio to match the **Height**, and vice versa.

Text Size options:

Font	Displays the fonts used by the OLE object, if any.
Point Size	Displays the text height in point sizes; limited to the point sizes available for the selected font, if any (1 point = $^1/_{72}$ inch).
Text Height	Specifies the text height in drawing units.

OLE Plot Quality

Determines the quality of the pasted object when plotted:

Plot Quality	Meaning
Line Art	Text is plotted as text; no colors or shading are preserved; some graphical images are not plotted, while others are plotted as monochrome images (black and white only, no shades of gray).
Text	All text formatting is preserved; text is plotted as graphics, which plots less cleanly than the **Line Art** setting; graphics are plotted less cleanly and at reduced colors than at **Graphics** and **Photograph** settings.
Graphics	Graphics are plotted at a reduced number of colors (fewer shades of gray or "posterization"); all text formatting is preserved; text is plotted as graphics, but more cleanly than at **Text** and **Photograph** settings.
Photograph	Graphics are plotted at reduced resolution and colors; all text formatting is preserved; text is plotted as graphics.
High Quality	Graphics are plotted at full resolution and colors.
Photograph	All text formatting preserved; text plotted more cleanly than wiht **Text** and **Photograph** settings.

Display dialog when pasting new OLE object

On: Displays the **OLE Properties** dialog box automatically when you insert an OLE object in the drawing; the default.

Off: Does not dialog box.

RELATED SYTSTEM VARIABLES

OleHide	Toggles the display of OLE objects in the drawing and in plots.
OleQuality	Specifies the quality of display and plotting of embedded OLE objects.
OleStartup	Loads the source application of an embedded OLE object for plots.

RELATED COMMANDS

InsertObj	Inserts an OLE object into the drawing.
OleLinks	Modifies the link between the object and its source.
PasteSpec	Allows you to paste an object with a link.

TIPS

- The **U** and **Undo** commands do not reverse the effect of changes made by the **OLE Properties** dialog box. Instead, right-click the OLE object and select **Undo** from the shortcut menu.

- Change **OleStartup** to 1 to load the OLE source application, which may help improve the plot quality of OLE objects.

- The **OLE Plot Quality** list box determines the quality of the pasted object when plotted. I recommend the **Line Art** setting for text, unless the text contains shading and other graphical effects.

Oops

V. 1.0 Restores the last-erased group of objects; restores objects removed by the **Block** and **-Block** commands.

Command	Alias	Ctrl+	F-key	Alt+	Menu Bar	Tablet
oops	. . .	. . .	. . .	. . .	. . .	. . .

Command: **oops**

COMMAND LINE OPTIONS
None.

RELATED COMMANDS
Block   Use **Oops** after the **Block** command to return erased objects.

Erase   Use **Oops** after the **Erase** command to return erased objects.

U   Undoes the most recent command.

TIPS
■ **Oops** only restores the most-recently erased object; use the **Undo** command to restore earlier objects.

■ Use **Oops** to bring back objects after turning them into a block with the **Block** and **WBlock** commands.

 # Open

Loads one or more drawings and DXF files into AutoCAD.

Command	Alias	Ctrl+	F-key	Alt+	Menu Bar	Tablet
open	openurl	O	...	FO	File ⮩Open	T25

Command: **open**
Displays dialog box:

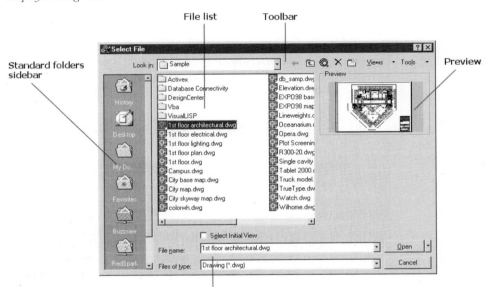

When FileDia=0:
Command: **open**
Enter name of drawing to open <.>: **[enter filename]**
Opening an AutoCAD 2000 format file.
Regenerating layout.
Regenerating model.
AutoCAD menu utilities loaded.

COMMAND LINE OPTION

Enter name of drawing to open

Specifies the name of a drawing file, or specifies another action:

Character	Meaning
. *(period)*	Option has no meaning!
~ *(tilde)*	Displays the **Select file** dialog box.
Esc	Cancels the command.

DIALOG BOX OPTIONS

Look in   Selects the network drive, hard drive, or folder (a.k.a. subdirectory).

Preview   Displays the preview image of AutoCAD drawings.

Select initial view

Selects a named view from a dialog box, if the drawing has saved views.

Displays dialog box listing named views after drawing is loaded:

Select Initial View	✕
[last view]	
isometric from NE	M
isometric low from SE	M
perspective from E at parking level	M
perspective from NW showing downtown	M
perspective from SW at water level	M
isometric from NW	M
plan--opening	M
perspective from SW through bridge	M
plan--region	M

OK   Cancel

M indicates a view created in model space;
P indicates a view was created in paper space (layout mode).

File name   Specifies the name of the drawing.

Files of type   Specifies the type of file:

- **Drawing (*.dwg)** AutoCAD drawing file.
- **Standard (*.dws)** drawing standards file; see the **Standards** command.
- **DXF (*.dxf)** drawing interchange file; see the **DxfIn** command.
- **Drawing Template File (*.dwt)** template drawing file; see **New** command.

Open   Opens the selected drawing file(s); to open more than one drawing at a time, hold down the **SHIFT** or **CTRL** keys:

- In the files list, hold down the **SHIFT** key to select a continuous range of files:

1st floor lighting.dwg	colorwh.dwg
1st floor plan.dwg	db_samp.dwg
1st floor.dwg	Drawing1.dwg
Campus.dwg	Elevation.dwg
City base map.dwg	EXPO Headquarters model.dwg
City map.dwg	EXPO98 base.dwg
City skyway map.dwg	EXPO98 maps.dwg

- Hold down the **CTRL** key to select two or more non-continuous files:

1st floor lighting.dwg	colorwh.dwg
1st floor plan.dwg	db_samp.dwg
1st floor.dwg	Drawing1.dwg
Campus.dwg	Elevation.dwg
City base map.dwg	EXPO Headquarters model.dwg
City map.dwg	EXPO98 base.dwg
City skyway map.dwg	EXPO98 maps.dwg

Cancel   Dismisses the dialog box without opening a file.

Open options:

Open	Opens the drawing.

Open as read-only

Loads drawing, but you cannot save changes to the drawing except by another filename. AutoCAD displays "Read Only" on the title bar:

Read Only warning

Partial Open Loads selected layers or named views; displays **Partial Open** dialog box; not available for DXF and template files.

Partial Open Read-Only

Partially loads the drawing in read-only mode.

Partial Open dialog box:

View geometry to load

Selects the model space views to load; paper space views are not available for partial loading.

Layer geometry to load options:

Load Geometry

Selects the layers to load.

Load All	Loads all layers.
Clear All	Deselects all layer names.

Index status options:
Available only when the drawing was saved with spatial indices.
Use spatial index
Determines whether to use the spatial index for loading, if available.
Spatial Index   Indicates whether the drawing contains the spatial index.
Layer Index   Indicates whether the drawing contains the layer index.

Unload all xrefs on open
Loads an externally-referenced drawing when opening the drawing.
Open   Opens the drawing and partially loads the geometry.

TOOLBAR ICONS

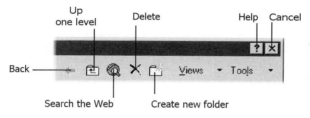

Back   Returns to the previous folder (keyboard shortcut **ALT+1**).
Up one level   Moves up one level, up to the next folder or drive (**ALT+2**).
Search the Web Displays the **Browse the Web** window (**ALT+3**); see **Browser** command.
Delete   Removes the selected file(s); does not delete folders or drives (**DEL**).
Create new folder
Creates a new folder a.k.a. subdirectory (**ALT+5**).
Views   Provides display options:
• **List** displays the file and folder names only.
• **Details** displays file and folder names, type, size, and date.
• **Preview** toggles display of the preview window.
Tools   Provides file-oriented tools:
• **Find** displays the **Find** dialog box for seaching files.
• **Locate** searches for the file along AutoCAD's search paths.
• **Add/Modify FTP Locations** displays the **Add/Modify FTP Locations** dialog box for specifying logon name and password for FTP sites.
• **Prompt for Point A Logon** prompts for your logon name when you click the Point A folder in the standard folders sidebar.
• **Add Current Folder to Places** adds the selected folder to the standard folder sidebar.
• **Add to Favorites** adds the selected file or folder to the Favorites list.

STANDARD FOLDERS

Also known as the Places List.

History displays files opened by AutoCAD during the last four weeks.
My Documents displays files and folders in the *My Documents* folder.
Favorites displays files and folders in the *\Windows\Favorites* folder.
Point A goes to the pointa.autodesk.com Web site.
Buzzsaw.com goes to the www.buzzsaw.com Web site.

RedSpark goes to the www.redspark.com Web site.
FTP displays the **FTP Locations** list.
Desktop displays the contents of the *\Windows\Desktop* folder

Remove removes a folder from the list.
Add Current Folder adds the selected folder to the list.
Add displays the **Add Places Item** dialog box.
Properties displays the **Places Item Properties** dialog box.
Restore Standard Folders restores the folders shown at the left.

SHORTCUT MENUS

Right-click in the file list window (without selecting a file or folder):

| View ▶ |
| Arrange Icons ▶ |
| Line Up Icons |
| Refresh |
| Paste |
| Paste Shortcut |
| Undo Copy |
| New ▶ |
| Properties |

View   Switches betwen filename views: large icons, small icons, list, and details.
Arrange Icons Arranges icons by name, type, size, and date.
Line Up Icons Places icons in an orderly pattern.
Refresh   Updates the folder listing.
Paste   Pastes a file from the Clipboard.
Paste Shortcut Pastes a file from the Clipboard as a shortcut.
Undo Copy   Undoes the copy-paste operation; available only after a copy or paste.
New   Creates a new folder (subdirectory) or shortcut.
Properties   Displays the **Properties** dialog box for this folder for the item selected in the Look in list.

Right-click a file or folder name:

Select	Opens the drawing in AutoCAD.
Open	Opens the drawing in AutoCAD.
Print	Does not print the drawing; you must **Open** the drawing, then use the **Plot** command inside of AutoCAD.
Send To	Copies the file to another drive; may not work with some software.
Cut	Cuts the file to the Clipboard.
Copy	Copies the file to the Clipboard.
Create Shortcut	Creates a shortcut icon for the selected file.
Delete	Erases the file; displays a warning dialog box.
Rename	Renames the file; displays a warning dialog box if you change the extension.
Properties	Displays the **Properties** dialog box in read-only mode; use the **DwgProps** command within AutoCAD to change the settings.

RELATED SYSTEM VARIABLES

DbMod	Indicates whether the drawing has been modified.
DwgCheck	Checks if the drawing was last edited byAutoCAD.
DwgName	Contains the drawing's filename.
DwgPrefix	Contains the drive and folder of the drawing.
DwgTitled	Indicates whether the drawing has a name other than *Drawingn.Dwg*.
FullOpen	Indicates whether the drawing is fully or partially opened.

RELATED COMMANDS

FileOpen	Opens a drawing without a dialog box.
SaveAs	Saves drawing with a new name.
PartiaLoad	Loads additional portions of a partially-opened drawing.

TIPS

- A drawing can be opened by dragging its filename from Explorer into AutoCAD. When the filename is into an open drawing, it is inserted as a block; when dragged to AutoCAD's titlebar, it is opened as a drawing.

- DXF and template files cannot be partially opened.

- After a drawing is partially opened, use **PartiaLoad** to load additional portions of the drawing.

- When a partially-opened drawing contains a bound xref, only the portion of the xref defined by the selected view is bound to the partially-open drawing.

Options

Sets system and user preferences; replaces the **Preferences**, **DdGrips**, and **DdSelect** commands.

Command	Alias	Ctrl+	F-key	Alt+	Menu Bar	Tablet
options	op	...	...	TN	Tools	Y10
	pr				⌐Options	
	preferences					
	ddgrips					
	ddselect					

+options

Command: **options**
Displays Options dialog box.

+OPTIONS COMMAND
Command: **+options**
Tab index <0>: ᴇɴᴛᴇʀ

COMMAND LINE OPTION
Tab index   Specifies the tab to display:

Tab Index	Meaning
0	Files tab.
1	Display tab.
2	Open and Save tab.
3	Plotting tab.
4	System tab.
5	User Preferences tab.
6	Drafting tab.
7	Selection tab.
8	Profiles tab.

DIALOG BOX OPTIONS
O K   Applies the changes, and closes the dialog box.
Cancel Cancels the changes, and closes the dialog box.
Apply   Applies the changes, and keeps the dialog box open.

REMOVED COMMAND
OpenUrl was removed from AutoCAD 2000; it was replaced by **Open**.

Files tab:

Search paths, file names, and file locations

        Specifies the folders and support files used by AutoCAD.

Browse   Displays the **Browse for Folder** dialog box when a folder is selected, or the **Select a File** dialog box when a file is selected.

Add   Adds an item below the currently-selected path or filename.

Remove   Removes the selected item without warning; click **CANCEL** to undo the removal.

Move Up   Moves the selected item above (or before) the preceding item; applies to search paths only.

Move Down   Moves the selected item below the following item; applies to search paths only.

Set Current   Makes the selected item current; applies to project names and spelling dictionaries only.

Display tab:

Window Elements *options:*

Display scroll bars in drawing window
>   Toggles the presence of the horizontal and vertical scroll bars; default = on.

Display screen menu
>   Toggles the presence of the screen menu; default = off.

Text lines in command line window
>   Specifies the number of lines of text in the docked command line window; range is 1 to 100 lines; default = 3.

Colors   Displays the **Color Options** dialog box to specify the colors of the AutoCAD graphics and text windows.

Fonts   Displays the **Command Line Window Fon**t dialog box to specify the font for text on the command line.

Layout Elements *options:*

Display Layout and Model tabs
>   Toggles the presence of the Model and Layout tabs.

Display margins Toggles the display of dashed margin lines in layout modes.

Display paper background
>   Toggles the presence of the page in layout modes.

Display paper shadow
>   Toggles the presence of the drop shadow under the page in layout modes.

Show Page Setup dialog for new layouts
>   Specifies whether the **Page Setup** dialog box is displayed when you create a new layout. Use this dialog box to set options related to paper and plot settings.

Create viewport in new layouts
>   Toggles the automatic creation of a single viewport for new layouts.

Crosshair size Specifies the size of the crosshair cursor; range is 1% to 100% of the viewport (stored in system variable **CursorSize**); default = 5%.

Display Resolution options:

Arc and circle smoothness
>   Controls the displayed smoothness of circles, arcs, and other curves; range is 1 to 20000 (**ViewRes**); default = 100.

Segments in a polyline curve
>   Specifies the number of line segments used to display polyline curves; range is -32767 to 32767 (**SplineSegs**); default = 8.

Rendered object smoothness
>   Controls the displayed smoothness of shaded and rendered curveds; range is 0.01 to 10 (**FaceTRes**) default = 0.5.

Contour lines per surface
>   Specifies the number of contour lines on ACIS solid 3D objects; range is 0 to 2047 (**IsoLines**); default = 4.

Display Performance options:

Pan and zoom with raster image
>   Toggles the display of raster images during realtime pan and zoom (**RtDisplay**); default = off.

Highlight raster image frame only
>   Highlights only the frame, and not the entire raster image, when on (**ImageHlt**); default = off.

True color raster images and rendering
>   Toggles between displaying raster images and renderings at True Color — 24-bit color or 16.7 million colors — or at the highest number of colors available with your computer; default = off.

Apply solid fill Toggles the display of solid fills in multilines, traces, solids, solid fill, and wide polylines; this option does not come into effect until you click **OK**, then use the **Regen** command (**FillMode**); default = on.

Show text boundary frame only
>   Toggles the display of rectangles in place of text this option does not come into effect until you click **OK**, then use the **Regen** command (**QTextMode**); default = off.

Show silhouettes in wireframe
>   Toggles the display of silhouette curves for ACIS 3D solid objects; when off, isolines are drawn when hidden-line removal is applied to the 3D object (**DispSilh**); default = off.

Reference fading intensity
>   Specifies the amount of fading during in-place reference editing; range is 0% to 90% (**XFadeCtl**); default = 50%.

Open and Save tab:

File Save *options:*

Save as   Specifies the default file format used by the **Save** and **SaveAs** commands; default = AutoCAD 2000 Drawing (*.dwg).

Save a thumbnail preview image

Saves a thumbnail preview image with the drawing (**RasterPreview**); default = on.

Incremental save percentage

Indicates the percentage of wasted space allowed in a drawing file before a full save is performed; range is 0% to 100% (**ISavePercent**); default = 50.

File Safety Precautions *options:*

Automatic save Automatically saves the drawing at prescribed time intervals (**SaveFile** and **SaveFilePath**); default = on.

Minutes between saves

Specifies the duration between automatic saves (**SaveTime**); default = 120 minutes.

Create backup copy with each save

Creates a backup copy of the drawing when saved; (**ISavBak**); default = on.

Full-time CRC validation

Performs the cyclic redundancy check (*CRC*) error-checking each time an object is read into the drawing.

Maintain a log file

Saves the Text window text to a log file (**LogFileMode**); default = off.

File extension for temporary files

Specifies the filename extension for temporary files created by AutoCAD (**NodeName**); default = .ac$.

File Open *options:*

Number of recently-used files to list
> Specifies the number of recently-opened filenames to list in the **Files** menu; default = 4; maximum = 9.

Display full path in title
> Displays the drawing file's path in AutoCAD's titlebar.

External References (Xrefs) *options:*

Demand load Xrefs
> Specifies the style of demand loading of externally-referenced drawings a.k.a. xrefs (**XLoadCtl**):
> • **Disabled** turns off demand loading.
> • **Enabled** turns on demand loading to improve performance, but the drawing cannot be edited by another user; default.
> • **Enabled with copy** turns on demand loading; loads a copy of the drawing so that another user can edit the original.

Retain changes to Xref layers
> Saves changes to properties for xref-dependent layers (**VisRetain**); default = on.

Allow other users to Refedit current drawing
> Allows another user to edit in-place the current drawing when referenced by another drawing (**XEdit**); default = on.

ObjectARX Applications *options:*

Demand load ObjectARX apps
> Demand-loads an ObjectARx application when the drawing contains proxy objects (**DemandLoad**):
> • **Disable load on demand** turns off demand loading.
> **Custom object detect** demand-loads the application when the drawing contains proxy objects.
> • **Command invoke** demand-loads the application when a command of the application is invoked.
> • **Object detect and command invoke** demand-loads the application when the drawing contains proxy objects, or when one of the application's commands is invoked; default.

Proxy images for custom objects
> Specifies how proxy objects are displayed:
> • **Do not show proxy graphics** does not display proxy object.
> • **Show proxy graphics** displays proxy objects.
> • **Show proxy bounding box** displays a rectangle instead of the proxy object.

Show Proxy Information dialog box
> Displays a warning dialog box when a drawing contains proxy objects; (**ProxyNotice**); default = on.

Plotting tab:

Default plot settings for new drawings *options:*

Use as default output device
> Selects the default output device, from the list of PC3 plotter configuration files.

Use last successful plot settings
> Reuses the plot settings from the last successful plot.

Add or configure plotters
> Displays **Autodesk Plotter Manager** window; see the **PlotterManager** command.

General plot options options:

When changing the plot device
> • **Keep the layout paper size if possible** uses the paper size specified by the **Page Setup** dialog box's **Layout Settings** tab, provided the output device can handle the paper size (**PaperUpdate**); default = on.
> • **Use the plot device paper size** uses the paper size specified by the PC3 plotter configuration file (**PaperUpdate**); default = off.

System printer spool alert
> Displays an alert when a spooled drawing has a conflict:
> • **Always alert (and log errors)** displays alert, and logs the error message.
> • **Alert first time only (and log errors)** displays the alert once, but logs all error messages.
> • **Never alert (and log first error)** does not display an alert, but logs the first error message.
> • **Never alert (do not log errors)** displays neither an alert, nor logs any error messages.

OLE plot quality
> Determines the quality of OLE objects when plotted (**OleQuality**); default = text; see the **OleScale** command.

Use OLE application when plotting OLE objects
> Launches the application that created OLE object when plotting a drawing with an OLE object (**OleStarup**); default = off.

Hide system printers
> Hides the names of Windows system printers, which are not specific to CAD.

Default plot style behavior for new drawings options:

Use color dependent plot styles
> Uses color-dependent plot styles, which use the AutoCAD color index ranging from 1 to 255 (**PStylePolicy**); default = 1.

Use named plot styles
> Uses plot property settings specified in the plot style definition (**PStylePolicy**); default = 0.

Default plot style table
> Names the default plot style table to attach to new drawings; default = None.

Default plot style for layer 0
> Specifies the default plot style for layer 0 (**DefLPlStyle**); default = ByColor.

Default plot style for objects
> Specifies the name of the default plot style assigned to new objects (**DefLPlStyle**); default = ByColor.

Add or Edit Plot Style Tables
> Displays the **Autodesk Plot Style Table Manager** window; see the **StylesManager** command.

System tab:

Current 3D Graphics Display *options:*
Current 3D Graphics Display

Selects the 3D graphics display driver (*default* = *GSHEIDI10*).

Properties   Displays the **3D Graphics System Configuration** dialog box.

Current Pointing Device *options:*
Current Pointing Device

Selects the pointing device driver.

• **Current System Pointing Device** selects the pointing device used by Windows.

• **Wintab Compatible Digitizer** selects a Wintab-compatible digitizer driver.

Accept input from

• **Digitizer only** reads input from the digitizer, and ignores the mouse.

• **Digitizer and mouse** reads input from the digitizer and the mouse.

Layout Regen *options:*
Regen when switching layouts

Regenerates the drawing each time layouts are switched.

Cache model tab and last layout

Saves the display list of the model tab and last layout accessed; default.

Cache model tab and all layouts

Saves the display list of model tab and all layouts.

dbConnect Options *options:*

Store links index in drawing file
> Stores the database index in the drawing file; default = on.

Open tables in read-only mode
> Opens database tables in read-only mode; default = off.

General Options *options:*

Single-drawing compatibility mode
> Forces the Single-drawing Interface (SDI), which limits AutoCAD to opening a single drawing at a time; this may be required for compatibility with some third-party applications (**SDI**); default = off.

Display OLE Properties dialog
> Displays the **OLE Properties** dialog box after an OLE object is inserted in the drawing; see the **OleScale** command; default = on.

Show all warning messages
> Displays all dialog boxes with the **Don't Display This Warning Again** option; default = on.

Beep on error in user input
> Forces the computer to sound a beep when AutoCAD detects a user error.

Load acad.lsp with every drawing
> Loads the *Acad.Lsp* file with every drawing (**AcadLspAsDoc**); default = off.

Allow long symbol names
> Allows symbol names — layers, dimension styles, blocks, linetypes, text styles, layouts, UCS names, views, and viewport configurations — to be up to 255 characters long, and to include letters, numbers, blank spaces, and most punctuation; when off, names are limited to 31 characters, and spaces may not be used (**ExtNames**); default = on.

Show Startup dialog
> • **Show TODAY startup dialog** displays **AutoCAD 2002 Today** window; see the **Today** command.
> • **Show traditional startup dialog box** displays **Startup** dialog box when AutoCAD launches or **Create New Drawing** dialog box when AutoCAD is already running.
> • **Do not show a startup dialog** displays command line prompt; sets **FileDia** system variable to 0.

Live Enabler Options *options:*

Check Autodesk Point A for Live Enablers
> **Never**: AutoCAD does not check for object enablers.
> **When Autodesk Point A is available in Today**: checks when Point A is available in the **Today** window, and an Internet connection is present; default
> **Always**: checks whenever an Internet connection is present.

Maximum number of unsuccessful checks
> Default = 5.

User Preferences tab:

Windows Standard Behavior options:
Windows standard accelerator keys

On: uses Windows' keyboard accelerators (default).

Off: uses DOS-based AutoCAD keyboard accelerators. Differences are:

Accelerator	On	Off
CTRL+C	CopyClip	Cancel command.
CTRL+O	Open	Ortho toggle.
CTRL+V	Paste	Viewports switch.

Shortcut menus in drawing area

On: right-click in the drawing area displays a shortcut menu.

Off: right-click is equivalent to pressing the ENTER key (**ShortCutMenu**); default = on.

Right-click customization

Displays the **Right-Click Customization** dialog box (**ShortCutMenu***)*.

AutoCAD DesignCenter options:
Source content units

Specifies the default units when an object is inserted into the drawing from AutoCAD DesignCenter; **Unspecified-Unitless** means the object is not scaled when inserted (**InsUnitsDefTarget**); default = inches or mm.

Target drawing units

Specifies the default units when "insert units" are not specified by the **InsUnits** system variable (**InsUnitsDefTarget**); default = inches or mm.

Hyperlink *options:*
Display hyperlink cursor and shortcut menu
> Displays the hyperlink cursor — looks like chain links and the planet earth — when the cursor passes over an object containing a hyperlink; displays the **Hyperlink** option when right-clicking an object containing a hyperlink; see the **HyperlinkOptions** command; default = on.

Display hyperlink tooltip
> Displays a tooltip when the cursor pauses over an object containing a hyperlink; default = on.

Priority for Coordinate Data Entry *options:*
Running object snap
> Osnap overrides coordinates entered at the keyboard (**OSnapCoord**); default = off.

Keyboard entry
> Coordinates entered at the keyboard override osnaps (**OSnapCoord**); default = off.

Keyboard entry except scripts
> Coordinates entered at the keyboard override running object snaps, except for coordinates provided in a script (**OSnapCoord**); default = on.

Object Sorting Methods *options:*

Object selection	Sorts objects in the drawing for selection from first to last created (**SortEnts**); default = off.
Object snap	Sorts objects in the drawing for selection from first to last created during object snap (**SortEnts**); default = off.
Redraws	Sorts objects in the drawing from first to last created for display during commands that cause a redraw, such as the **Redraw** command (**SortEnts**); default = off.
Regens	Sorts objects in the drawing from first to last created for display during commands that cause a regeneration, such as **Regen** (**SortEnts**); default = off.
Plotting	Sorts objects in the drawing from first to last created for plotted output to file or printer (**SortEnts**); default = on.

PostScript output
> Sorts objects in the drawing from first to last created for output to PostScript file or printer (**SortEnts**); default = on.

Associative Dimensioning *options:*
Associate new dimension with objects
> **Yes**: dimensions are associated with objects.
> **No**: dimensions are associated with defpoints.

Lineweight Settings
> Displays the **Lineweight Settings** dialog box; see the **LWeight** command.

Drafting tab:

| Drafting |

AutoSnap Settings
- ☑ Marker
- ☑ Magnet
- ☑ Display AutoSnap tooltip
- ☐ Display AutoSnap aperture box

AutoSnap marker color:
▉ Blue

AutoSnap Marker Size

AutoTrack Settings
- ☑ Display polar tracking vector
- ☑ Display full-screen tracking vector
- ☑ Display AutoTrack tooltip

Alignment Point Acquisition
- ◉ Automatic
- ○ Shift to acquire

Aperture Size

AutoSnap Settings *options:*

Marker   Displays the AutoSnap icon (**AutoSnap**); default = on.
Magnet   Turns on the AutoSnap magnet (**AutoSnap**); default = on.
Display AutoSnap tooltip
                  Displays the AutoSnap tooltip (**AutoSnap**); default = on.

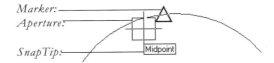

Marker:
Aperture:

SnapTip: — Midpoint

Display AutoSnap aperture box
                  Displays the AutoSnap aperture box (**ApBox**); default = off.
AutoSnap marker color
                  Specifies the color of the AutoSnap icons; choose from seven colors;
                  default = yellow.
AutoSnap marker size
                  Sets the size for the AutoSnap icon; range is 1 to 20 pixels.

□ Endpoint	귿 Insertion
△ Midpoint	┞ Perpendicular
○ Center	⟲ Tangent
⊠ Node	⊠ Nearest
◇ Quadrant	⊠ Apparent intersection
✕ Intersection	∕∕ Parallel
⋯ Extension	

The AutoSnap icons (markers).

AutoTrack Settings options:
Display polar tracking vector
> Displays the Polar Tracking vectors at specific angles (**TrackPath**); default = on.

Polar tracking vector (dotted line) and AutoTrack tootip.

Display full-screen tracking vector
> Displays the tracking vectors (**TrackPath**); default = on.

Full-screen tracking vector and AutoTrack tooltip.

Display AutoTrack tooltip
> Displays the AutoTrack tooltip (**AutoSnap**); default = on.

Alignment Point Acquisition options:

Automatic   Displays tracking vectors automatically when the aperture moves over an object snap.

Shift to acquire Displays tracking vectors when pressing SHIFT and moving the aperture over an object snap.

Aperture Size Sets the display size for the aperture; range is 1 to 50 pixels (**Aperture**); default = 10.

Selection tab:

Selection Modes options (replaces the **DdSelect** command):

Noun/verb selection

Allows you to select an object before executing an editing command (**PickFirst**); default = on.

Use Shift to add to selection

Allows you to press **SHIFT** to add or remove objects from the selection set (**PickAdd**); default = off.

Press and drag Allows you to create the selection window by dragging (**PickDrag**); default = off.

Implied windowing

Creates a selection window when you pick a point in the drawing that does not pick an object (**PickAuto**); default = on.

Object grouping

Selects the entire group when an object in the group is selected (**PickStyle**); default = off.

Associative hatch

Selects boundary object, along with the associative hatch pattern (**PickStyle**); default = off.

Pickbox Size   Specifies the size of the pickbox; range is 1 to 20 pixels (**PickBox**); default = 3.

Grips options (replaces the **DdGrips** command):

Enable grips   Displays grips on selected objects (**Grips**); default = on.

Enable grips within blocks

Displays all grips for every object in the selected block; when off, a single grip at the block's insertion point is displayed (**GripBlock**); default = off.

Unselected grip color

Specifies the color of an unselected — cold – grip (**GripColor**); default = blue.

Selected grip color

Specifies the color of a selected — hot – grip (**GripHot**); default = red.

Grip size   Specifies the size of grips; range is from 1 to 20 pixels (**GripSize**); default = 3.

Profiles tab:

Available Profiles

Lists available profiles, which customize the AutoCAD user interface.

Set Current   Sets the selected profile as the current profile.

Add to List   Displays the **Add Profile** dialog box; allows you to enter a name and description for the new profile.

Rename   Displays the **Change Profile** dialog box; allows you to change the name and the description of the selected profile.

Delete   Erases the selected profile; the current profile cannot be erased.

Export   Exports a profile as an ARG file.

Import   Imports an ARG profile into AutoCAD.

Reset   Resets the values of the selected profile to AutoCAD's default settings.

TIPS

- *Grips* are small squares that appear on an object when the object is selected at the 'Command' prompt. In other Windows applications, grips are known as *handles*.

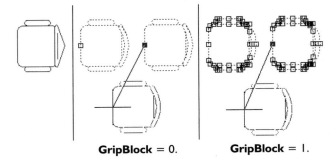

GripBlock = 0.   **GripBlock = 1.**

- When an object is first selected, the grips are blue, and are called *unselected* or *cold* grips.

- When a grip is selected, it turns into a solid red square; this is called a *hot* grip.

- Press **Esc** to turn off unselected grips; press **Esc** twice to turn off hot grips.

- A larger pickbox makes it easier to select objects, but also makes it easier accidentally to select unintended objects.

- Use **Object Sort Method** if the drawing requires objects to be processed in the order they appear in the drawing, such as for NC applications.

- **Plotting** and **PostScript Output** are turned on, by default; setting more sort methods increases processing time.

- The first time you use the **DrawOrder** command, it turns on all object sort method options.

'Ortho

<u>V. 1.0</u> Constrains drawing and editing commands to the vertical and horizontal directions only (*short for ORTHOgraphic*).

Command	Alias	Ctrl+	F-key	Alt+	Status Bar	Tablet
'ortho	...	L	F8	...	ORTHO	...

```
Command: ortho
Enter mode [ON/OFF] <OFF>: on
```

COMMAND LINE OPTIONS
OFF   Turns off ortho mode.
ON   Turns on ortho mode.

STATUS BAR OPTIONS
Ortho mode is toggled on and off by clicking **ORTHO** *on the status bar:*

| 10.1046, 0.9275 , 0.0000 | SNAP GRID ORTHO POLAR OSNAP OTRACK LWT MODEL |

| 7.3372, 0.2001 , 0.0000 | SNAP GRID ORTHO POLAR OSNAP OTRACK LWT MODEL |

RELATED COMMANDS
DSettings   Toggles ortho mode via a dialog box.
Snap   Rotates the ortho angle.

RELATED SYSTEM VARIABLES
OrthoMode   The current state of ortho mode.
SnapAng   Rotation angle of ortho mode.

TIPS
- Use ortho mode when you want to constrain your drawing and editing to right angles.

- Rotate the angle of ortho with the **Snap** command's **Rotate** option

- In isoplane mode, ortho mode constrains the cursor to the current isoplane.

- AutoCAD ignores ortho mode when you enter coordinates by keyboard, and in perspective mode; ortho is also ignored by object snap modes.

- Ortho is not necessarily horizontal or vertical; its orientation is determined by the current UCS and snap alignment.

'-OSnap

V. 2.0 Sets and turns on and off object snap modes at the command line
(*short for Object SNAP; note that the* **OSnap** *command displays the
Drafting Settings dialog box*).

Command	Alias	Ctrl+	F-key	Alt+	Status Bar	Tablet
'-osnap	-os	...	F3	...	OSNAP	T15 - U22

The **OSnap** *command displays the* **Drafting Settings** *dialog box; see the* **DSettings** *command.*

```
Command: -osnap
Current osnap modes: Ext
Enter list of object snap modes:
```

COMMAND LINE OPTIONS

You only need enter the first three letters as the abbreviation for each option:

APParent Snaps to the the intersection of two objects that don't physically cross, but appear to intersect on the screen, or would intersect if extended.

CENter Snaps to the center point of arcs and circles.

ENDpoint Snaps to the endpoint of lines, polylines, traces, and arcs.

EXTension Snaps to the extension path of objects.

FROm Extends from a point by a given distance.

INSertion Snaps to the insertion point of blocks, shapes, and text.

INTersection Snaps to the intersection of two objects, or to a self-crossing object, or to objects that would intersect if extended.

MIDpoint Snaps to the middle point of lines and arcs.

NEArest Snaps to the object nearest to the crosshair cursor.

NODe Snaps to a point object.

NONe Turns off all object snap modes temporarily.

OFF Turns off all object snap modes.

PARallel Snaps to a parallel offset.

PERpendicular Snaps perpendicularly to objects.

QUAdrant Snaps to the quadrant points of circles and arcs.

QUIck Snaps to the first object found in the database.

TANgent Snaps to the tangent of arcs and circles.

STATUS BAR OPTIONS

Right-click OSNAP on the status bar:

On Turns on previously-set object snap modes.

Off Turns off all running object snaps.

Settings Displays the **Object Snap** tab of the **Drafting Settings** dialog box.

SHORTCUT MENU

*Hold down the **CTRL** key and right-click:*

```
Temporary track point
From
Point Filters          ▶

Endpoint
Midpoint
Intersection
Apparent Intersect
Extension

Center
Quadrant
Tangent

Perpendicular
Parallel
Node
Insert
Nearest
None

Osnap Settings...
```

RELATED SYSTEM VARIABLES

Aperture	Specifies the size of the object snap aperture in pixels.
AutoSnap	Controls the display of AutoSnap (default = 63):

AutoSnap	Meaning
0	Turns off marker, SnapTip, and magnet.
1	Turns on the marker.
2	Turns on the SnapTip.
4	Turns on the magnet.
8	Turns on polar tracking.
16	Turns on object snap tracking.
32	Turns on polar and object snap tracking tooltips.

OsMode   The current object snap mode(s):

OsMode	Meaning
0	NONe (default)
1	ENDpoint
2	MIDpoint
4	CENter
8	NODe
16	QUAdrant
32	INTersection
64	INSertion
128	PERpendicular
256	TANgent
512	NEArest
1024	QUIck
2048	APParent intersection
4096	EXTension
8192	PARallel

OsnapCoord Overrides object snaps when entering coordinates at 'Command' prompt.

OsnapCoord	Meaning
0	Object snap overrides keyboard.
1	Keyboard overrides object snap settings.
2	Keyboard overrides object snap settings, except during a script (default).

TIPS

■ The **Aperture** command controls the drawing area AutoCAD searches through.

■ If AutoCAD finds no snap matching the current modes, the pick point is selected.

■ The **APPint** and **INT** object snap modes should not be used together.

■ To turn on more than one object snap at a time, use a comma to separate mode names:

```
Command: -osnap
Enter list of object snap modes: int,end,qua
```

■ The location of all object snaps:

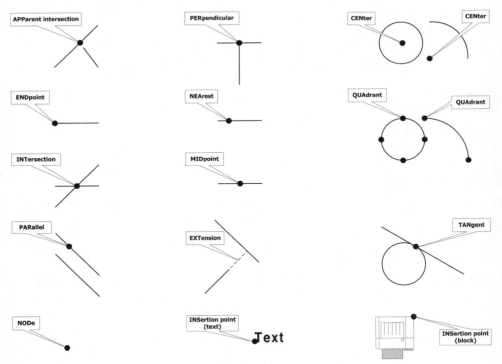

PageSetup

2000 Sets up model and layout views for plotting.

Command	Alias	Ctrl+	F-key	Alt+	Menu Bar	Tablet
pagesetup	. . .	. . .	. . .	FG	File ↳Page Setup	V25

Command: **pagesetup**
Displays dialog box:

DIALOG BOX OPTIONS
See **Plot** *command.*

RELATED COMMANDS
Layout   Creates new layouts.
Plot   Plots the drawing based on the settings of the **PageSetup** command.

RELATED SYSTEM VARIABLE
CTab   Contains the name of the current model or layout tab; default = "Model".

TIPS
■ The **Page Setup** dailog box is automatically displayed when you create a new layout, or when you execute the **Plot** command.

■ Right-click the **Model** or **Layout** tabs to display a shortcut menu; select **Page Setup**.

'Pan

V. 2.0 Moves the view in the current viewport to a different position.

Command	Alias	Ctrl+	F-key	Alt+	Menu Bar	Tablet
'pan	p	...	...	VPT	View	N11-
	rtpan				⌐Pan	P11
					⌐Realtime	
-pan	-p			VPP	View	
					⌐Pan	
					⌐Point	

Command: **pan** *or* **rtpan**
Press Esc or Enter to exit, or right-click to activate
    pop-up menu. **[move cursor]**
Enters real-time panning mode; displays hand cursor:

As you drag the hand cursor, the drawing pans in the viewport. Press **ENTER** *or* **ESC** *to return to the 'Command' prompt.*

-PAN COMMAND

Command: **-pan**
Displacement: **[pick]**
Second point: **[pick]**

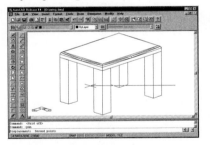

Before panning to the left: *After panning to the left:*

COMMAND LINE OPTIONS

ENTER	Exits real-time panning mode.
ESC	Exits real-time panning mode.
Displacement	Specifies the distance and direction to pan the view.
Second point	Pans to this point.

SHORTCUT MENU OPTIONS

During real-time pan mode, right-click the drawing to display shortcut menu:

Exit real-time pan mode ——— Exit
Real-time pan ——— ✓ Pan
Real-time zoom ——— Zoom
3D orbit ——— 3D Orbit
Zoom window ——— Zoom Window
Previous view ——— Zoom Original
Zoom to drawing extents ——— Zoom Extents

Exit	Exits real-time pan mode; returns to the 'Command' prompt.
Pan	Switches to real-time pan mode, when in real-time zoom mode.
Zoom	Switches to real-time zoom mode; see the **Zoom** command.
3D Orbit	Switches to 3D orbit mode; see the **3dOrbit** command.
Zoom Window	Prompts you to "Press pick button and drag to specify zoom window."
Zoom Original	Returns to the view when you first started the **Pan** command.
Zoom Extents	Displays the entire drawing.

RELATED COMMANDS

DsViewer	Displays the **Aerial View** window, which pans in an independent window.
RegenAuto	Determines how regenerations are handled.
View	Saves and restores named views.
Zoom	Pans with the **Dynamic** option.
3dOrbit	Pans during perspective mode.

RELATED SYSTEM VARIABLES

MButtonPan	Determines the action of a mouse's third button or wheel.
ViewCtr	Specifies the x,y-coordinate of the view's center.
ViewDir	Specifies the view direction relative to UCS.
ViewRes	Turns off real-time pan off when **FastZoom** is disabled.
ViewSize	Specifies the height of view.

TIPS

- You pan in each viewport independently.

- You can use the **'Pan** command transparently to start drawing an object in one area of the drawing, pan over, then continue working in another area of the drawing.

- Change the **Static** button (of the **Aerial View** window) to **Dynamic** to perform real-time panning; the drawing pans as quickly as you move the mouse.

- You cannot use transparent pan during: paper space, perspective mode, **VPoint** command, **DView** command, or another **Pan**, **View**, or **Zoom** command.

- You can use the horizontal and vertical scroll bars to pan the drawing.

- When the drawing no longer moves during real-time panning, you have reached the panning limit; AutoCAD changes the hand icon to show the limit:

PartiaLoad

<u>2000</u>   Loads additional views and layers of a partially-loaded drawing; this
command works only with drawings that have been partially loaded.

Command	Alias	Ctrl+	F-key	Alt+	Menu Bar	Tablet
partiaload	...	...	...	FR	File	
					⤷Partial Load	

-partiaload

Command: **partiaload**

If the drawing has not been partially opened (via the **Open** *command's* **Partial Open**
option), AutoCAD reports:

Command not allowed unless the drawing was partially opened.

Otherwise, displays dialog box:

DIALOG BOX OPTIONS

View geometry to load
> Selects the model space views to load; paper space views are not available
> for partial loading.

Pick a Window Dismisses the dialog box temporarily to allow you specify an area that
> becomes the view to load; prompts you:
> > Specify first corner: **[pick]**
> > Specify opposite corner: **[pick]**
> When the **Partial Load** dialog box returns, ***New View*** is listed in the
> **View Geometry to Load** list.

Layer geometry to load options:

Load Geometry Selects the layers to load.

Load All   Loads all layers.

Clear All   Deselects all layer names.

-PARTIALOAD COMMAND

```
Command: -partiaload
Specify first corner or [View]: v
Enter view to load or [?] <*Extents*>: ENTER
Enter layers to load or [?] <none>: ENTER
```

COMMAND LINE OPTIONS

Specify first corner

> Specifies a corner to create a new view.

Specify opposite corner:

> Specifies the second corner; causes geometry in the new view to be loaded into the drawing.

View options:

Enter view to load

> Loads the geometry found in view into the drawing.

?

> List the names of views in the drawing:
>
> ```
> Enter view name(s) to list <*>: ENTER
> ```
> *Sample display:*
> ```
> Saved model space views:
> View name"1"
> "Plot"
> ```

Extents   Loads all geometry into the drawing.

Enter layers to load

> Loads geometry on the layers in the drawing.

?

> List the names of layers in the drawing:
>
> ```
> Enter layers to list <*>: ENTER
> ```
> *Sample display:*
> ```
> Layer names:
> "0"
> "3"
> ```

None   Loads no layers.

RELATED COMMANDS

Open   Partially opens a drawing via a dialog box.
PartialOpen   Partially opens a drawing via the command line.

RELATED SYSTEM VARIABLE

FullOpen   Indicates whether the drawing is fully or partially opened.

-PartialOpen

2000 Opens a drawing and loads selected layers and views.

Command	Alias	F-key	Alt+	Menu Bar	Tablet
-partialopen	partialopen ...	...	...	...	...

```
Command: -partialopen
Enter name of drawing to open <C:\autocad 2002\sample\
   filename.dwg>: [enter filename]
Enter view to load or [?]<*Extents*>: ENTER
Enter layers to load or [?]<none>: ENTER
Unload all Xrefs on open? [Yes/No] <N>: ENTER
Opening an AutoCAD 2000 format file.
Regenerating model.
Regenerating model.
AutoCAD menu utilities loaded.
```

COMMAND LINE OPTIONS

Enter name of drawing to open
Specifies the name of the DWG file.
Enter view to load
Loads the geometry found in the view into the drawing.
? List the names of the views in the drawing.
Extents Loads all geometry into the drawing.
Enter layers to load
Loads geometry on the layers into the drawing.
? List the names of layers in the drawing.
None Loads no layers.
Unload all Xrefs on open
Yes: Does not load externally-referenced drawings.
No: Loads all externally-referenced drawings.

RELATED COMMANDS

Open Displays the **Select Drawing** dialog box; includes the **Partial Open** option.
PartiaLoad Loads additional views or layers of a partially-opened drawing.

RELATED SYSTEM VARIABLES

FullOpen Indicates whether the drawing is fully or partially opened.

TIPS

■ **PartialOpen** is an alias for the **-PartialOpen** command.

■ As an alternative, you may use the the **Partial Open** option of the **Open** command's **Select File** dialog box.

PasteAsHyperlink

2000 Pastes object as a hyperlink in the drawing; works only if the Clipboard contains appropriate data (*an undocumented command*).

Command	Alias	Ctrl+	F-key	Alt+	Menu Bar	Tablet
pasteashyperlink	...	...	...	EH	Edit	...
					⇘Paste as Hyperlink	

```
Command: pasteashyperlink
Select objects: [pick]
Select objects: ENTER
```

COMMAND LINE OPTION

Select objects Selects the objects that have the hyperlink added.

RELATED COMMANDS

CopyClip   Copies a hyperlink to the Clipboard.
Hyperlink   Adds hyperlinks to selected objects.

RELATED SYSTEM VARIABLES

None.

PasteBlock

<u>**2000**</u>   Pastes an object as a block in the drawing; works only when the Clipboard contains an AutoCAD block object.

Command	Alias	Ctrl+	F-key	Alt+	Menu Bar	Tablet
pasteblock	...	...	...	EK	Edit ⤷Paste as Block	...

Command: **pasteblock**
Duplicate definition of block direct ignored.
Specify insertion point: **[pick]**

COMMAND LINE OPTION

Specify insertion point
Specifies the position for the block.

RELATED COMMANDS

Insert   Inserts blocks in the drawing.
CopyClip   Copies a block to the Clipboard.

RELATED SYSTEM VARIABLES

None.

TIPS

■ This command does not work when the Clipboard contains data that cannot be pasted as a block.

■ This command pastes any AutoCAD object as a block, generating a block name similar to "A$C65D94228".

■ If the Clipboard contains a block, the block is nested by this command.

PasteClip

Rel.13 Places an object from the Clipboard in the drawing (*short for PASTE CLIPboard*).

Command	Alias	Ctrl+	F-key	Alt+	Menu Bar	Tablet
pasteclip	...	V	...	EP	Edit ⌐Paste	U13

```
Command: pasteclip
Specify insertion point: [pick]
```

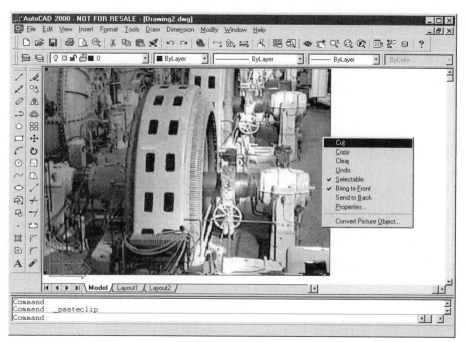

When the Clipboard contains a non-AutoCAD object,
it is pasted into the upper-left corner of the current viewport.

COMMAND LINE OPTION

This prompt does not appear when pasting a non-AutoCAD object into the drawing.
Specify insertion point
Specifies the position for the AutoCAD object.

SHORTCUT MENU OPTIONS

After pasting, right-click to display shortcut menu. Not all of these options appear with every pasted object.

Cut	Cuts the object from drawing to the Clipboard.
Copy	Copies the object to the Clipboard.
Clear	Erases the pasted object.
Undo	Undoes the last action.
Selectable	Toggles the selectability of the object; the handles disappear.
Bring to Front	Displays object as topmost in the drawing.
Send to Back	Displays objects as lowermost in the drawing.
Properties	Displays the **OLE Properties** dialog box; see the **OleScale** command.
Convert	Converts (or, in some cases, does not convert) the object to another format; displays dialog box:

RELATED COMMANDS

CopyClip	Copies drawing to the Clipboard.
Insert	Inserts an AutoCAD drawing in the drawing.
InsertObj	Inserts an OLE object in the drawing.
PasteSpec	Places the Clipboard object as pasted or linked object.

RELATED SYSTEM VARIABLE

OleHide	Toggles the display of the OLE object (1 = off).

TIPS

- The **PasteClip** command places all objects in the upper-left corner of the current viewport, unless they are AutoCAD objects.

- Graphical objects are placed in the drawing as OLE objects.

- Text is usually — but not always — placed in the drawing as an Mtext object.

- Use the **PasteSpec** command to paste the object as an AutoCAD block.

REMOVED COMMAND:

PcxIn was removed from AutoCAD Release 14. Use the **ImageAttach** command instead.

PasteOrig

<u>2000</u> Pastes a block from the Clipboard into another drawing as a block at the block's insertion point *(short for PASTE at ORIGin)*.

Command	Alias	Ctrl+	F-key	Alt+	Menu Bar	Tablet
pagesetup	...	...	...	ED	Edit	
					↳Paste to Original Coordinates	

Command: **pasteorig**

COMMAND LINE OPTIONS
None.

RELATED COMMANDS
CopyClip   Copies drawing to the Clipboard.
Insert   Inserts an AutoCAD drawing in the drawing.
PasteBlock   Pastes AutoCAD objects as a block.

RELATED SYSTEM VARIABLES
None.

TIPS
■ Use this command to copy objects from one drawing to another.

■ This command cannot be used to paste objects into the drawing from which they come.

'PasteSpec

Rel.13 Places the Clipboard object in the drawing as an embedded, linked, pasted, or converted object (*short for PASTE SPECial*).

Command	Alias	Ctrl+	F-key	Alt+	Menu Bar	Tablet
'pastespec	pa	...	...	ES	Edit ↳Paste Special	...

```
Command: pastespec
```
Displays dialog box:

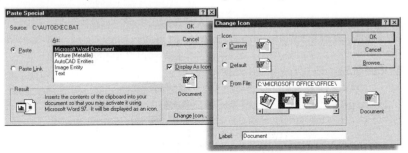

Paste (left) and Paste Link (right).

DIALOG BOX OPTIONS

Paste Pastes the object as an embedded object.
Paste Link Pastes the object as a linked object.
Display as Icon Displays the object as an icon from the originating application.
Change Icon Allows you to select the icon; displays dialog box:

RELATED COMMANDS

CopyClip Copies the drawing to the Clipboard.
InsertObj Inserts an OLE object in the drawing.
OleLinks Edits the OLE link data.
PasteClip Places the Clipboard object as a pasted object.

RELATED SYSTEM VARIABLE

OleHide Toggles the display of OLE objects (1 = off).

PcinWizard

<u>2000</u> Converts PCP and PC2 plot configuration files to PC3 format.

Command	Alias	Ctrl+	F-key	Alt+	Menu Bar	Tablet
pcinwizard	...	...	...	TZI	Tools	...
					↳Wizard	
					↳Import R14 Plot Settings	

Command: **pcinwizard**
Displays dialog box.

DIALOG BOX LINE OPTIONS

Back   Returns to the previous step.
Next   Continues to the next step.
Cancel   Cancels the wizard.

Introduction dialog box:

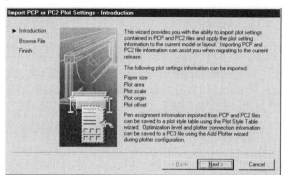

Browse File dialog box:

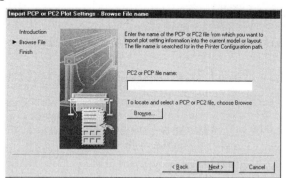

PCP or PC2 filename
            Specifies the name of a PCP or PC2 name.
Browse Displays the **Import** dialog box.

Finish dialog box:

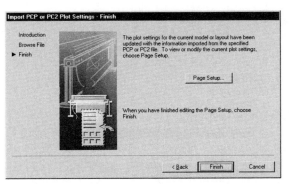

Page Setup   Displays the **Page Setup** dialog box; see the **PageSetup** command.
Finish   Completes the importation process.

RELATED COMMAND
Plot   Uses PC3 files to control the plotter configuration.

RELATED SYSTEM VARIABLES
None.

TIPS
■ PCP is short for "plotter configuration parameters"; PCP files are used by AutoCAD Release 13.

■ PC2 files are used by AutoCAD Release 14.

■ PC3 files are used by AutoCAD 2000, 2000i, and 2002.

■ This command imports PCP and PC2 files and applies them to the current layout or model tab.

■ You would only use this command if you created PCP or PC2 files with earlier versions of AutoCAD.

■ AutoCAD 2002 imports the following information from PCP and PC2 files: paper size, plot area, plot scale, plot origin, and plot offset.

■ To import color-pen mapping, use the **Plot Style Table** wizard, run by the *StyShWiz.Exe* program.

■ To import the optimization level and plotter connection, use the **Add-a-Plotter** wizard, run by the *AddPlWiz.Exe* program.

PEdit

V. 2.1 Edits one or more 2D polylines, 3D polylines, or 3D meshes — depending on which type of object is picked (*short for Polyline EDIT*).

Command	Alias	Ctrl+	F-key	Alt+	Menu Bar	Tablet
pedit	pe	...	...	MP	Modify ⬥Polyline	Y17

Command: **pedit**
Options vary, depending whether a 2D polyline, 3D polyline, or polymesh is picked:

2D polyline options:
```
Select polyline or [Multiple]: [pick a 2D polyline]
Enter an option [Open/Join/Width/Edit vertex/Fit/Spline/
    Decurve/Ltype gen/Undo]: [enter an option]
```

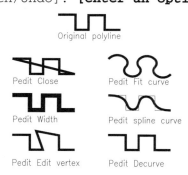

COMMAND LINE OPTIONS

Multiple Selects more than one polyline to edit.
Close Closes an open polyline by joining the two endpoints with a single segment.
Decurve Reverses the effects of a **Fit** or **Spline** operation.

Edit vertex options:
```
Enter a vertex editing option
[Next/Previous/Break/Insert/Move/Regen/Straighten/Tangent/
    Width/eXit] <N>: [enter an option]
```

Break Removes a segment or breaks the polyline at a vertex.
  Next Moves the x-marker to the next vertex.
  Previous Moves the x-marker to the previous vertex.

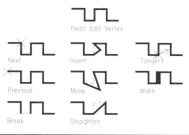

Go	Performs the break.
eXit	Exits the **Break** sub-submenu.
Insert	Inserts another vertex.
Move	Relocates a vertex.
Next	Moves the x-marker to the next vertex.
Previous	Moves the x-marker to the previous vertex.
Regen	Regenerates the screen to show the effect of the **PEdit** command.
Straighten	Draws a straight segment between two vertices:
Next	Moves the x-marker to the next vertex.
Previous	Moves the x-marker to the previous vertex.
Go	Performs the straightening.
eXit	Exits the **Straighten** sub-submenu.
Tangent	Shows the tangent to current vertex.
Width	Changes the width of a segment.
eXit	Exits the **Edit-vertex** submenu.
Fit	Fits a curve to the tangent points of each vertex.
Ltype gen	Specifies the linetype generation style.
Join	Adds other polylines to the current polyline.
Open	Opens a closed polyline by removing the last segment.
Spline	Fits a splined curve along the polyline.
Undo	Undoes the most-recent **PEdit** operation.
Width	Changes the width of the entire polyline.
eXit	Exits the **PEdit** command.

3D polyline options:

```
Command: pedit
Select polyline or [Multiple]: [pick a 3D polyline]
Enter an option [Open/Edit vertex/Spline curve/Decurve/Undo]:
```

COMMAND LINE OPTIONS

Multiple	Selects more than one 3D polyline to edit.
Close	Closes an open polyline.
Decurve	Reverses the effects of a **Fit-curve** or **Spline-curve** operation.

Edit vertex options:

```
Enter a vertex editing option
[Next/Previous/Break/Insert/Move/Regen/Straighten/eXit] <N>:
```

Break	Removes a segment or breaks the polyline at a vertex.
Next	Moves the x-marker to the next vertex.
Previous	Moves the x-marker to the previous vertex.
Go	Performs the break.
eXit	Exits the **Break** sub-submenu.
Insert	Inserts another vertex.

Move	Relocates a vertex.
Next	Moves the x-marker to the next vertex.
Previous	Moves the x-marker to the previous vertex.
Regen	Regenerates the screen to show the effect of **PEdit** options.

Straighten	Draws a straight segment between two vertices:
Next	Moves the x-marker to the next vertex.
Previous	Moves the x-marker to the previous vertex.
Go	Performs the straightening.
eXit	Exits the **Straighten** sub-submenu.
eXit	Exits the **Edit-vertex** submenu.

Open	Removes the last segment of a closed polyline.
Spline curve	Fits a splined curve along the polyline.
Undo	Undoes the most-recent **PEdit** operation.
eXit	Exits the **PEdit** command.

3D mesh options:
```
Select polyline or [Multiple]: [pick a 3D mesh]
Enter an option [Edit vertex/Smooth surface/Desmooth/
   Mclose/Nclose/Undo]: [enter option]
```

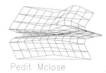
Pedit Mclose

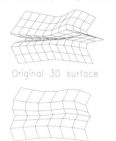
Original 3D surface

Pedit Smooth surface

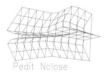
Pedit Nclose

COMMAND LINE OPTIONS

Multiple	Selects more than one 3D mesh to edit.
Desmooth	Reverses the effect of the **Smooth** surface options.

Edit vertex *options:*
```
Current vertex (0,0).
Enter an option [Next/Previous/Left/Right/Up/Down/Move/
   REgen/eXit] <N>: [enter option]
```

Down	Moves the x-marker down the mesh by one vertex.
Left	Moves the x-marker along the mesh by one vertex left.
Move	Relocates the vertex to a new position.
Next	Moves the x-marker along the mesh to the next vertex.
Previous	Moves the x-marker along the mesh to the previous vertex.

REgen	Regenerates the drawing to show the effects of the **PEdit** command.
Right	Moves the x-marker along the mesh by one vertex right.
Up	Moves the x-marker up the mesh by one vertex.
eXit	Exits the **Edit-vertex** submenu.

Mclose	Closes the mesh in the m-direction.
Mopen	Opens the mesh in the m-direction.
Nclose	Closes the mesh in the n-direction.
Nopen	Opens the mesh in the n-direction.
Smooth surface	Smooths the mesh with a Bezier-spline.
Undo	Undoes the most recent **PEdit** operation.
eXit	Exits the **PEdit** command.

RELATED COMMANDS

Break	Breaks a 2D polyline at any position.
Chamfer	Chamfers all vertices of a 2D polyline.
Convert	Converts older polylines to the new lwpolyline format.
EdgeSurf	Draws a 3D mesh.
Fillet	Fillets all vertices of a 2D polyline.
PLine	Draws a 2D polyline.
RevSurf	Draws a 3D surface of revolution mesh.
RuleSurf	Draws a 3D ruled surface mesh.
TabSurf	Draws a 3D tabulated surface mesh.
3D	Draws a 3D surface objects
3dPoly	Draws a 3D polyline.

RELATED SYSTEM VARIABLES

SplFrame Determines the visibility of a polyline spline frame:

SplFrame	Meaning
0	Do not display control frame (default).
1	Display control frame.

SplineSegs Specifies the number of lines used to draw a splined polyline (default = 8).
SplineType Determines the Bezier-spline smoothing for 2D and 3D polylines:

SplineType	Meaning
5	Quadratic Bezier spline.
6	Cubic Bezier spline.

SurfType Determines the smoothing using the **Smooth** option:

SurfType	Meaning
5	Quadratic Bezier spline.
6	Cubic Bezier spline.
7	Bezier surface.

TIP

■ During vertex editing, button #2 moves the x-marker to the next or previous vertex, whichever was used last.

PFace

Rel.11 Draws multisided 3D meshes; meant for use by AutoLISP, ADS, and ARx programs (*short for Poly FACE*).

Command	Alias	Ctrl+	F-key	Alt+	Menu Bar	Tablet
pface	...	...	...	...	...	...

```
Command: pface
Specify location for vertex 1: [pick]
Specify location for vertex 2 or <define faces>: ENTER
Face 1, vertex 1:
Enter a vertex number or [Color/Layer]:  1
Face 1, vertex 2:
Enter a vertex number or [Color/Layer] <next face>: 2
```
Etc.

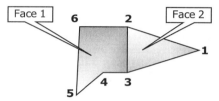

COMMAND LINE OPTIONS
Vertex   Defines the location of a vertex.
Face   Defines the faces, based on vertices.
Color   Gives the face a different color.
Layer   Places the face on a different layer.

RELATED COMMANDS
3dFace   Draws three- and four-sided 3D meshes.
3dMesh   Draws a 3D mesh with polyfaces.

RELATED SYSTEM VARIABLE
PFaceVMax   Maximum number of vertices per polyface (default = 4).
SplFrame   Controls the display of invisible faces (default = 0, not displayed).

TIPS
■ **3dFace** creates 3- and 4-sided meshes, while **PFace** creates meshes of an arbitrary number of sides, and can control the layer and the color of each face.

■ The maximum number of vertices in the m- and n-direction is 256 vertices when entered from the keyboard, and 32767 vertices when entered from a DXF file or created by programming.

■ Make an edge invisible by entering a negative number for the beginning vertex of the edge.

■ **PFace** is meant for programmers; to draw 3D surface objects, use these commands instead: **3d, 3dMesh, RevSurf, RuleSurf, EdgeSurf**, or **TabSurf**.

Plan

Rel.10 Displays the plan view of the WCS or the UCS.

Command	Alias	Ctrl+	F-key	Alt+	Menu Bar	Tablet
plan	...	...	...	V3P	View	N3
					⌐3D Views	
					⌐Plan View	

Command: **plan**
Enter an option [Current ucs/Ucs/World] <Current>: **ENTER**
Regenerating model.

Example of a 3D view.

*After using the **Plan World** command.*

COMMAND LINE OPTIONS

Current UCS Shows the plan view of the current UCS.
Ucs   Shows the plan view of a named UCS.
World   Shows the plan view of the WCS.

RELATED COMMANDS

UCS   Creates new UCS views.
VPoint Changes the viewpoint of 3D drawings.

RELATED SYSTEM VARIABLES

UcsFollow Display automatically the plan view for UCS or WCS.
ViewDir   Contains the x,y,z coordinates of the current view direction.

TIPS

- Entering **VPoint 0,0,0** is an alternative to the **Plan** command.

- The **Plan** command turns off perspective mode and clipping planes.

- **Plan** does not work in paper space; AutoCAD complains, "** Command only valid in Model space **".

- The **Plan** command is an excellent method for turning off perspective mode.

PLine

V. 1.4 Draws a complex 2D line made of straight and curved sections of constant and variable width; treated as a single object (*short for Poly LINE*).

Command	Alias	Ctrl+	F-key	Alt+	Menu Bar	Tablet
pline	pl	...	...	DP	Draw ⬐Polyline	N10

```
Command: pline
Specify start point: [pick]
Current line-width is 0.0000
Specify next point or [Arc/Halfwidth/Length/Undo/Width]: ENTER
Specify next point or [Arc/Close/Halfwidth/Length/Undo/Width]:
    [enter option]
```

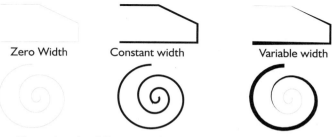

Zero Width   Constant width   Variable width

*Examples of polylines created with the **PLine** command.*

COMMAND LINE OPTIONS

Specify start point
> Indicates the start of the polyline.

Close   Closes the polyline with a line segment.

Halfwidth   Indicates the half-width of the polyline.

Length   Draws a polyline tangent to the last segment.

Undo   Erases the last-drawn segment.

Width   Indicates the width of the polyline.

Endpoint of line
> Indicates the endpoint of the polyline.

Arc options:
```
Specify endpoint of arc or
[Angle/CEnter/CLose/Direction/Halfwidth/Line/Radius/Second
   pt/Undo/Width]: [enter option]
```

Endpoint of arc
> Indicates the arc's endpoint.

Angle   Indicates the arc's included angle.

CEnter   Indicates the arc's center point.

CLose   Uses an arc to close a polyline.

Direction   Indicates the arc's starting direction.

Halfwidth   Indicates the arc's halfwidth.

Line	Switches back to the menu for drawing lines.
Radius	Indicates the arc's radius.
Second pt	Draws a three-point arc.
Undo	Erases the last drawn arc segment.
Width	Indicates the width of the arc.

RELATED COMMANDS

Boundary	Draws a polyline boundary.
Donut	Draws solid-filled circles as polyline arcs.
Ellipse	Draws ellipses as polyline arcs when **PEllipse** = 1.
Explode	Reduces a polyline to lines and arcs with zero width.
Fillet	Fillets polyline vertices with a radius.
PEdit	Edits the polyline's vertices, widths, and smoothness.
Polygon	Draws polygons as polylines of up to 1024 sides.
Rectang	Draws a rectangle out of a polyline.
Sketch	Draws polyline sketches, when **SkPoly** = 1.
Xplode	Explodes a group of polylines into line and arcs of zero width.
3dPoly	Draws 3D polylines.

RELATED SYSTEM VARIABLES

PLineGen Style of linetype generation:

PlineGen	Meaning
0	Vertex to vertex (default).
1	End to end (compatible with Release 12).

PLineType Controls the conversion of old (pre-R14) polylines and the creation of lwpolyline objects by the **PLine** command:

PLineType	Meaning
0	Old polylines not converted; old-format polylines created.
1	Not converted; lwpolylines created.
2	Polylines in pre-R14 drawings converted on open; **PLine** command creates lwpolyline objects (default).

PLineWid Current width of polyline (default = 0.0).

TIPS

- **Boundary** uses a polyline to outline a region automatically; use the **List** command to find its area.

- If you cannot see a linetype on a polyline, change system variable **PlineGen** to 1; this regenerates the linetype from one end of the polyline to the other.

- If the angle between a joined polyline and polyarc is less than 28 degrees, the transition is chamfered; at greater than 28 degrees, the transition is not chamfered.

- Use the object snap modes **INTersection** or **ENDpoint** to snap to the vertices of a polyline.

Plot

V.1.0   Creates a copy of the drawing on a vector, raster, and PostScript plotter or printer via the serial and other ports; also plots to file on disk.

Command	Alias	Ctrl+	F-key	Alt+	Menu Bar	Tablet
plot	print	P	...	FP	File 🖑Plot	W25

Command: **plot**
Displays dialog box:

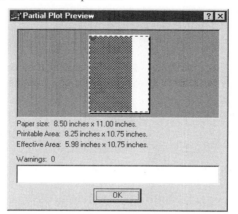

DIALOG BOX OPTIONS

Save changes to layout
       Toggles the saving of the settings in this dialog box.
Page setup name
       Specifies the name of the page setup.
Add   Displays the **User Defined Page Setup** dialog box.

Full Preview   Displays a detailed preview of the drawing; see the **Preview** command.
Partial Preview Displays an overview preview:

O K   Begins the plot.
Cancel   Dismisses the dialog box without plotting the drawing.

Plot Device tab:

Plotter Configuration *options:*

Name   Selects a system printer, or a named plotter configuration.
Properties   Displays the **Plotter Configuration Editor**; see **PlotterManager** command.
Hints   Displays an **AutoCAD Help** dialog box containing specific information about plotting with AutoCAD plotter configurations, or general information about plotting with the Windows system printer.

Plot style table (pen assignments) *options:*

Name   Selects a plot style table assigned to the current tab; see the **PlotStyle** command.
Edit   Displays the **Plot Style Table Editor** dialog box.
New   Displays the **Add Plot Style Table** wizard.

What to plot *options:*

   • **Current tab** plots the current model or layout tab; see the **Layout** command.
   • **Selected tabs** plots all selected tabs; hold down **CTRL** key to select more than one tab.
   • **All Layout Tabs** plots all layout tabs.

Number of copies
                 Specifies the number of copies to be plotted.

Plot to file *options:*

Plot to file Sends the plots to a file on disk.
File name   Specifies the file name for the plot (default = *filename-tab.plt*).
Location   Specifies the folder in which to place the plot file.
...   Displays a standard **Browse for Folder** dialog box.
Browse   Displays the **Browse the Web** window; see the **Browser** command.

Plot Settings tab:

Paper size and paper units options:

Paper size   Displays paper sizes supported by the selected output device.

Printable area Selects inches or mm as the plotting units; raster images show the size in pixels.

Drawing orientation options:
- **Portrait** plots with the long edge at the side of the page.
- **Landscape** plots with the long edge at the top of the page.

Plot upside-down
     Plots the drawing upside down, rotated by 180 degrees.

Plot area options:
- **Layout** plots all parts of the drawing within the margins of the specified paper size; the origin is calculated from 0,0 in the layout.
- **Limits** plots all parts of the drawing in model tab within the rectangle defined by the **Limits** command.
- **Extents** plots the entire drawing.
- **Display** plots all parts of the drawing within the current viewport.
- **View** plots a view saved with the **View** command.
- **Window** plots all parts of the drawing within a picked rectangle.

Plot Scale options:

Scale   Specifies the plotting scale; select **Scaled to Fit** to plot the entire drawing to fit the page.

Custom   Specifies a user-defined scale.

Scale lineweights

Scales lineweights proportionately to the plot scale.

Plot Offset *options:*

Center the plot

Centers the plot on the paper.

X   Specifies the plot origin offset from x = 0.

Y   Specifies the plot origin offset from y = 0.

Plot Options *options:*

Plot with lineweights

Plots objects with lineweights.

Plot with plot styles

Plots objects using the plot styles.

Plot paperspace last

Plots the model space objects first, followed by paper space objects.

Hide objects   Removes hidden lines before plotting.

RELATED COMMANDS

PageSetup   Selects one or more plotter devices.

Preview   Goes directly to the plot preview screen.

PsOut   Saves a drawing in EPS format.

RELATED SYSTEM VARIABLES

PlotId   (*Obsolete*) Specifies the currently-selected plotter number.

Plotter   (*Obsolete*) Specifies the currently-selected plotter name.

TextFill   Toggles the filling of TrueType fonts.

TextQlty   Specifires the quality of TrueType fonts.

RELATED FILES

*.PC3   Plotter configuration parameter files.

*.PLT   Plot files created with the **Plot** command.

TIPS

■ As of AutoCAD Release 12, the **Plot** command replaces the **PrPlot** command.

■ As of AutoCAD Release 13, the freeplot feature, which starts AutoCAD to plot with the **-p** parameter (without using up a network license) is no longer available.

■ AutoCAD cannot plot perspective view to scale, only to fit.

PlotStamp

2000i Adds information about the drawing to a plot.

Command	Alias	Ctrl+	F-key	Alt+	Menu Bar	Tablet
plotstamp	...	...	...	FPS	File	...
					⤷Plot	
					⤷Settings	

-plotstamp

Command: **plotstamp**
Displays dialog box:

DIALOG BOX OPTIONS

Plot Stamp Fields options:

Drawing name Adds the path and name of the drawing.

Layout name Adds the layout name.

Date and time Adds the date (short format) and time of the plot.

Login name Adds the Windows login name, as stored in the AutoCAD **LogInName** system variable.

Device name Adds the plotting device's name.

Paper size Adds the paper size, as currently configured.

Plot scale Adds the plot scale.

User Defined Fields options:

Add/Edit Displays the **User Defined Fields** dialog box.

Plot Stamp Parameter File options:

Load/Save Displays the **Plotstamp Parameter File Name** dialog box for opening (or saving) PSS files.

Advanced Displays the **Advanced Options** dialog box.

Advanced dialog box:

Location and Offset options:

Location   Specifies the location of the plotstamp: Top Left, Bottom Left (default), Bottom Right, or Top Right — relative to the orientation of the drawing on the plotted page.

Stamp upside down
              Yes: Draws the plot stamp upside down.
              No: Draws the plot stamp rightside up.

Orientation   Rotates the plot stamp relative to the page: Horizontal or Vertical.

X offset   Distance from the corner of the printable area or page; default = 0.1.

Y offset   Distance from the corner of the printable area or page; default = 0.1
              • **Offset relative to printable area.**
              • **Offset relative to paper border.**

Text Properties options:

Font   Selects the font for the plotstamp text.

Height   Specifies the height of the plotstamp text.

Single line plot stamp
              Yes: Plotstamp text is placed on a single line.
              No: Plotstamp test is placed on two lines.

Plot Stamp Units options:

Units   Selects either inches, millimeters, or pixels.

Log File Location options:

Create a log file
              Saves the plotstamp text to a text file.

Browse   Displays the **Log file name** dialog box.

-PLOTSTAMP COMMAND

Command: -plotstamp
Current plot stamp settings:
Displays current setting of nearly 20 plot stamp settigs.
Enter an option [On/OFF/Fields/User Fields/Log file/LOCation/
   Text Properties/UNits]: **[enter option]**

COMMAND LINE OPTIONS

On	Turns on plot stamping.
OFF	Turns off plot stamping.
Fields	Specifies plot stamp data: drawing name, layout name, date and time, login name, plot device name, paper size, plot scale, comment, write to log file, log file path, location, orientation, offset, offset relative to, units, font, text height, and stamp on single line.
User fields	Specifies two user-defined fields.
Log file	Writes the plotstamp data to a file instead of the drawing.
LOCation	Specifies the location and orientation of the plotstamp.
Text properties	Specifies the font name and height.
UNits	Specifies the units of measurement: inches, millimeters, or pixels.

RELATED COMMAND

Plot   Plots the drawing.

RELATED FILES

*.LOG   Plotstamp log file; stored in ASCII text format.
*.PSS   Plotstamp parameter file; stored in binary format.

TIPS

- When the options of the **Plot Stamp** dialog box are grayed out, or when the **-Plotstamp** command reports "Current plot stamp file or directory is read only," this means that the Inches.Pss or Mm.Pss file in the \Support folder is read-only. To change, in Explorer: (1) right-click the file; (2) select **Properties**; (3) uncheck **Read-only**; and (4) click **OK**.

- *Caution!* Too large of an offset value positions the plotstamp text beyond the plotter's printable area, which causes the text to be cut off. To prevent this, use the **Offset relative to printable area** option.

- You can access the **Plot Stamp** dialog box via the **Plot** dialog box's **Plot Device** tab:

PlotStyle

2000   Selects and assigns plot styles to objects.

Command	Alias	Ctrl+	F-key	Alt+	Menu Bar	Tablet
plotstyle	...	...	...	OY	Format ⌐Plot Style	...

-plotstyle

Command: **plotstyle**
When no objects are selected, displays the **Current Plot Style** *dialog box.*
When one or more objects are selected, displays the **Select Plot Style** *dialog box.*

DIALOG BOX OPTIONS

Plot styles   Lists the available plot styles.
Active plot style table
           Lists the available plot style tables.
Editor   Displays the **Plot Style Table Editor** dialog box; see the **StylesManager** command.
O K   Accepts the changes, and closes the dialog box.
Cancel   Cancels the changes, and closes the dialog box.

Select Plot Style dialog box:
Displayed when one or more objects are selected:

Plot styles   Lists the plot styles available in the drawing.
Active plot style table
           Selects the plot style table to attach to the current drawing.
Editor   Displays the **Plot Style Table Editor** dialog box; see the **StylesManager** command.

Current Plot Style dialog box:
Displayed when no objects are selected:

TOOLBAR OPTIONS

ByLayer	Applies the layer's plot style.
ByBlock	Applies the block's plot style.
Normal	Reverts to the object's default properties.
User-defined	Applies the plot style defined by user in a plot style table.
Other	Displays the **Current Plot Style** dialog box when no objects are selected; displays the **Select Plot Style** dialog box when one or more objects are selected.

LAYER DIALOG BOX OPTIONS

Plot Style	Displays the **Select Plot Styles** dialog box.

-PLOTSTYLE COMMAND

```
Command: -plotstyle
Current plot style is "Default"
Enter an option [?/Current] : c
Set current plot style : [enter name]
Current plot style is "plotstylename"
Enter an option [?/Current] : ENTER
```

COMMAND LINE OPTIONS

Current   Prompts you to change plot styles.

Set current plot style

     Specifies the name of the plot style.

ENTER   Exits the command.

?   Displays plot style names; sample output:

```
Plot Styles:
------------------

ByLayer
ByBlock
Normal
PLAN_ESTR
ARCH_Dimensions (COTAS)
ARCH_Dimensions for stairway
Current plot style is "PLAN_ESTR"
```

RELATED COMMANDS

Plot   Plots the drawing with plot styles.

PageSetup   Attaches plot style table to layouts.

StylesManager   Modifies a plot style table.

Layer   Specifies a plot style for each layer.

RELATED SYSTEM VARIABLES

CPlotStyle   Specifies the plot style for new objects; defined values include "ByLayer", "ByBlock", "Normal", and "User Defined".

DeflPlStyle   Specifies the current plot style name.

TIPS

- This command does not operate until a plot style table has been created for the drawing; the **PlotStyle** command displays this message box:

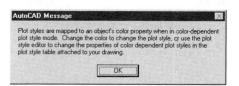

- Before you can use plot styles in a new drawing, you must turn on plot styles; notice that the **Plot Style Control** in the **Object Properties** toolbar is grayed out.

Follow these steps to turn on plot style:

1. From the menu bar, select **Tools | Options | Plotting**.

2. In the **Options** dialog box, click **Use named plot styles** to turn on the feature.

3. In the **Default** plot style list, select any plot style — *except* **Default R14 pen assignments.stb**, since it turns off plot styles.

4. Click **OK** to dismiss the **Options** dialog box. Notice that the **Plot Style Control** in the **Object Properties** toolbar is now available for use.

- A plot style can be assigned to any object and to any layer.

- A plot style can override the following plot settings: color, dithering, gray scale, pen assignment, screening, linetype, lineweight, end style, join style, and fill style.

- Plot styles are useful for plotting the same layout in different ways, such as emphasizing objects using different lineweights or colors in each plot.

- Plot style tables can be attached to the **Model** tab and layout tabs; attach different plot style tables to layouts, to create different looks for plots.

PlotterManager

Displays the **Plotters** window, the **Add-A-Plotter** wizard, and PC3 configuration **Editor**.

Command	Alias	Ctrl+	F-key	Alt+	Menu Bar	Tablet
plottermanager ...	...		...	FM	File ⮡Plotter Manager	Y24

Command: **plottermanager**
Displays window:

```
C:\CAD\ACAD 2000\PLOTTERS                                              _ □ ✕
 File   Edit   View   Go   Favorites   Help
 ⇦        ⇨         ⬆            ⬆            ✂       ▨       ▨        ↺        ✕         ☞
Back    Forward    Up     Map Drive Disconnect  Cut    Copy    Paste    Undo    Delete   Properties
Address  ☐ C:\CAD\ACAD 2000\PLOTTERS

  📁✏        📁          📁
Add-A-Plotter   DWF         DWF
  Wizard    Classic.pc3  ePlot.pc3

1 object(s) selected        1.22KB                          🖳 My Computer
```

WINDOW OPTIONS

Add-a-Plotter Wizard

Adds a plotter configuration; double-click to display the **Add Plotter** wizard.

.pc3

Specifies parameters for creating plotted output; double-click to display the **Plotter Configuration Editor**; see the **StylesManager** command.

HDI Driver	Supports
Raster	CALS MIL-R-28002A Type 1 Compressed JPEG Uncompressed BMP Compressed PNG Compressed and uncompressed TIF Uncompressed TGA Compressed PCX
Adobe PostScript	PostScript Level 1 Level 1Plus with color support Level 2
HP-GL and HP-GL/2	Hewlett-Packard 7475A, 7550A, 7580, 7585B, 7586 DraftPro, DXL, EXL, 24" Plus, 36" Plus DraftMaster I, II Roll Feed, Rx, Rx Plus, Mx, Mx Plus Draftmaster Sx Plus Sheet Feed 7586B Roll Feed
Optimized HP Windows System Printer	HP DesignJet 3500CP, 3000CP, 2500CP, 2000CP 1055CM, 1050C, 755CM, 750C Plus, 750C, 700 650C, 600, 488CA, 455CA, 450C, 430, 350C, 330, 250C, 230, 220, 200
Xerox	Xerox XES 8825 1 roll, 8825 2 roll, XES 8830
Océ	Océ G9034-S, G9035-S, G9054-S, 9055-S/95xx-S, 9400 with Scanner, 9700, 9800, 9600, 5104, 5105, 5100C A1 5100C A0, 5120 A1, 5120 A0, 5200, 4900

■ The Illustrated AutoCAD 2002 Quick Reference

ADD PLOTTER WIZARD

The following steps show how to create a PC3 plotter configuration for plotting drawings to an EPS (encapsulated PostScript) file; the steps are similar to create PC3 files for other types of plotters:

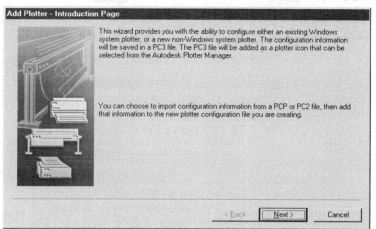

Next   Displays the next dialog box.
Cancel   Dismisses the dialog box.

Begin page:

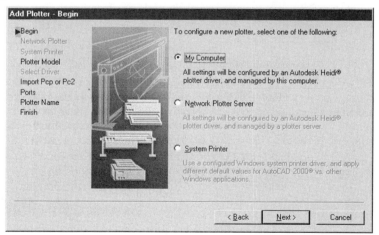

My Computer Configures a printer or plotter connected to your computer.
Network Plotter Server
                  Configures a printer or plotter connected to another computer on your
                  local network.
System Printer Configures the default Windows printer.

Plotter Model page:

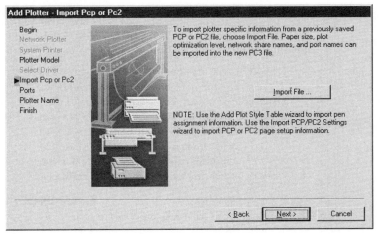

Manufacturer Selects a brand name of plotter.

Model Selects a specific model number.

Have Disk Allows you to select a plotter driver provided by another manufacturer; displays the **Open** dialog box.

Import Pcp or Pc2 page:

Import File Imports a PCP or PC2 plotter configuration file created by earlier versions of AutoCAD.

Ports page:

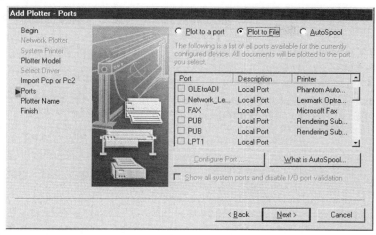

Plot to a port Sends the plot to an output port.

Port options:

Port   Lists the virtual ports defined by the Windows operating system:

Port	Meaning
USB	Universal serial bus.
COM	Serial port.
LPT	Parallel port.
HDI	Autodesk's Heidi Device Interface.

Description   Describes the type of port:

Description	Meaning
Local Port	Printer is connected to your computer.
Network Port	Printer is connected to another computer and is accessible via the network.

Printers   Describes the brand name of the printer connected to the port.

Configure Port Displays the **Configure Port** dialog box; allows you to specify parameters specific to the port, such as timeout and protocol.

Show all system ports and disable I/O port validation
Prevents AutoCAD from checking whether the port is valid.

Plot to File   Plots the drawing to a file with a user-definable filename; default filename is the same as the drawing name, with a PLT extension; PostScript plot files are given the EPS extension.

AutoSpool   Plots the drawing to a file with a filename generated by AutoCAD, then executes the command specified in the **Option** dialog box's **Files** tab:

Enter the name of the program that should process the AutoSpool file in **Print Spool Executable**. You may include these DOS command-line arguments:

Argument	Meaning
%s	Substitutes path, spool filename, and extension.
%d	Specifies the path, AutoCAD drawing name, and extension.
%c	Specifies the description for the device.
%m	Returns the plotter model.
%n	Specifies the plotter name.
%p	Specifies the plotter number.
%h	Returns the height of the plot area in plot units.
%w	Returns the width of the plot area in plot units.
%i	Specifies the first letter of the plot units.
%l	Specifies the login name (*LogInName* system variable).
%u	Specifies the user name.
%e	Specifies the equal sign (=).
%%	Specifies the percent sign (%).

What is AutoSpool?

Displays an explanatory dialog box:

Plotter Name page:

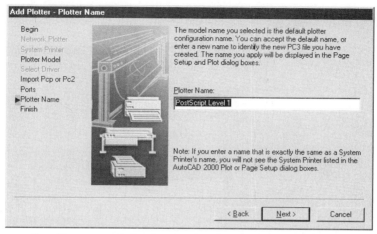

Plotter name   Specifies a user-defined name for the plotter configuration; you may have many different configurations for a single plotter.

Finish page:

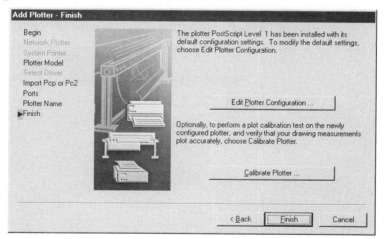

Edit Plotter Configuration
       Displays the **Edit Plotter Configuration** dialog box.
Calibrate Plotter
       Displays the **Calibrate Plotter** wizard.

Plotter Configuration Editor dialog box:

General tab:

Description   Allows you to provide a detailed description of the plotter configuration.

Ports tab:

Plot to the following port
    Sends the plot to an output port.

Plot to File   Plots the drawing to a file with a user-definable filename; default filename is the same as the drawing name, with a PLT extension; PostScript plot files are given the EPS extension.

AutoSpool   Plots the drawing to a file with a filename generated by AutoCAD, then executes the command specified in the **Option** dialog box's **Files** tab.

Show all ports Lists all ports on the computer.

Browse Network
    Displays the **Browse for Printer** dialog box; selects a printer on the network.

Configure Port
    Displays the **Configure Port** dialog box; allows you to specify the parameters specific to the port, such as timeout and protocol.

Device and Document Settings tab:

Media   Specifies the paper source, paper size, type, and destination.

Physical Pen Configuration (for pen plotters only)
         Specifies the physical pens in the pen plotter.

Graphics   Specifies settings for plotting vector and raster graphics and TrueType
         fonts.

Custom Properties
         Specifies settings specific to the plotter, printer, or other output device.

Initialization Strings (for non-system plotters only)
         Specifies the control codes for pre-initialization, post-initialization, and
         termination.

Calibration Files and Paper Sizes
         Calibrates the plotter by specifying the PMP file; adds and modifies
         custom paper sizes; see the **Calibrate Plotter** wizard.

Import   Imports PCP and PC2 plotter configuration files from earlier versions of
         AutoCAD.

Save As   Saves the plotter configyration data to a PC3 file.

Defaults   Resets the plotter configuration settings to the previously-saved values.

CALIBRATE PLOTTER WIZARD

Before using this wizard, use AutoCAD to draw and plot a rectangle — say, 11 inches by 8 inches — then use this wizard to check the accuracy of the plotted drawing:

Paper Size   Selects the size of media or paper.
Next   Displays the next dialog box.
Cancel   Dismisses the dialog box.

Rectangle Size page:

Length   Specifies the length of the calibration rectangle.
Width   Specifies the width of the calibration rectangle.
Units   Selects imperial inches or metric millimeters.

Measured Plot page:

Measured Length

Specifies the length of the rectangle, which is plotted by AutoCAD, then measured by you.

Measured Width

Specifies the width of the rectangle, which is plotted by AutoCAD, then measured by you.

File Name page:

PMP File name Specifies the name of the file in which to store the calibration data.

Finish page:

Check Calibration

Returns to the **Calibrate Plotter - Rectangle Size** dialog box.

Finish   Returns to the **Add Plotter - Finish** dialog box.

RELATED COMMANDS

Plot   Plots the drawing with plot styles.

PageSetup   Attaches a plot style table to layouts.

StylesManager Modifies a plot style table.

AddPlWiz.Exe Runs the **Add Plotter** wizard.

RELATED SYSTEM VARIABLES

PaperUpdate Toggles the display of a warning before AutoCAD plots a layout with a paper size different from the size specified by the plotter configuration file:

PaperUpdate	Meaning
0	Displays warning dialog box (default).
1	Changes paper size to match the size specified by the plotter configuration file.

PlotId (*Obsolete*) Holds the current plotter configuration ID number.

PlotRotMode Controls the orientation of plots:

PlotRotMode	Meaning
0	Aligns rotation icon with media at the lower left for 0 degrees; calculates x and y origin offsets relative to lower-left corner.
1	Aligns the lower-left corner of plotting area with lower-left corner of the paper.
2	Same as 0, except x and y origin offsets relative to the rotated origin position.

Plotter (*Obsolete*) Holds the current plotter name.

TIPS

■ The *DWF Classic.pc3* file specifies parameters for creating a DWF file via the Release 14-compatible **DwfOut** command.

■ The *DWF ePlot.pc3* file specifies parameters for creating a DWF file via the AutoCAD 2002-preferred **Plot** command.

■ You can create and edit PC3 plotter configuration files without AutoCAD. From the Start button on the Windows toolbar, select **Settings | Control Panel | Autodesk Plotter Manager**.

Point

<u>**V. 1.0**</u>   Draws a 3D point.

Command	Alias	Ctrl+	F-key	Alt+	Menu Bar	Tablet
point	po	. . .	. . .	DO	Draw	O9
					ᕴPoint	

```
Command: point
Current point modes:  PDMODE=0  PDSIZE=0.0000
Specify a point: [pick]
```

COMMAND LINE OPTION
Point   Positions a point, or enters a 2D or 3D coordinate.

RELATED COMMANDS
DdPType   Displays a dialog box for selecting **PsMode** and **PdSize**.
Regen   Generates the regeneration required to see the new point mode or size.

RELATED SYSTEM VARIABLES
PDMode   Determines the appearance of a point:

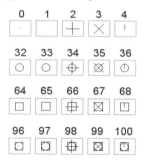

PDSize   Determines the size of a point:

PdSize	Meaning
0	5% of height of the **ScreenSize** system variable (default).
1	No display.
-10	(*Negative*) Ten percent of the viewport size.
10	(*Positive*) Ten pixels in size.

TIPS
■ The size and shape of the point is determined by **PdSize** and **PdMode**; changing these values changes the appearance and size of all points in the drawing with the next regeneration.

■ Entering only x,y coordinates places the point at a z coordinate of the current elevation; setting **Thickness** to a value draws the point as a line in 3D space.

■ Prefix the coordinate with * (*asterisk*) to place a point in the WCS, rather than the current UCS, such as *1,2,3.

■ Use the object snap mode **NODe** to snap to a point.

Polygon

V. 2.5 Draws a 2D polygon of between three to 1024 sides.

Command	Alias	Ctrl+	F-key	Alt+	Menu Bar	Tablet
polygon	pol	...	...	DY	Draw ↳Polygon	P10

```
Command: polygon
Enter number of sides <4>: ENTER
Specify center of polygon or [Edge]: [pick]
Enter an option [Inscribed in circle/Circumscribed about
    circle] <I>: ENTER
Specify radius of circle: [pick]
```

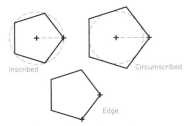

Inscribed   Circumscribed

Edge

COMMAND LINE OPTIONS

Center of polygon
  Indicates the center point of the polygon; then:
C   (*Circumscribed*) Fits the polygon outside a circle.
I   (*Inscribed*) Fits the polygon inside a circle.
Edge   Draws the polygon based on the length of one edge.

RELATED COMMANDS

PEdit   Edits polylines, include polygons.
PLine   Draws polylines and polyline arcs.
Rectang   Draws a rectangle from a polyline.

RELATED SYSTEM VARIABLE

PolySides   Specifiers the most-recently entered number of sides (default = 4).

TIPS

- Polygons are drawn as a polyline; use **PEdit** to edit the polygon, such as its width.
- The pick point determines the polygon's first vertex; polygons are drawn counterclockwise.
- Use the system variable **PolySides** to preset the default number of polygon sides.
- Use the **Snap** command to place the polygon precisely; use **INTersection** or **ENDpoint** object snap modes to snap to the polygon's vertices.

REMOVED COMMAND

Preferences was removed from AutoCAD 2000; it was replaced by **Options**.

◪ Preview

Rel.13 Displays plot preview; bypasses the **Plot** command.

Command	Alias	Ctrl+	F-key	Alt+	Menu Bar	Tablet
preview	pre	...	...	FV	File	X24
					⤷Plot Preview	

Command: **preview**
Press ESC or ENTER to exit, or right-click to display shortcut menu.
Displays preview screen:

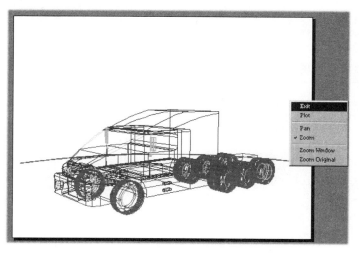

COMMAND LINE OPTION
Esc   Returns to the drawing window.

SHORTCUT MENU OPTIONS

Exit preview —
Plot drawing —
Pan view —
Zoom view —
Zoom window —
Original view —

(Exit / Plot / Pan / ✓ Zoom / Zoom Window / Zoom Original)

RELATED COMMANDS
Plot   Plots the drawing.
PageSetup   Enables plot preview once a plotter is assigned to the layout.

TIPS
■ This command does not operate when no plotter is assigned; use the **PageSetup** command to assign a plotter to the model and layout tabs.

■ Press **Esc** to exit preview mode.

'Properties

2000 Opens the **Properties** window for modifying the properties of selected objects.

Command	Alias	Ctrl+	F-key	Alt+	Menu Bar	Tablet
'properties	ch	1	...	TP	Tools	Y12-Y13
	props				⤷Properties	
	ddchprop			MP	Modify	
	ddmodify				⤷Properties	
	mo					

Command: **properties**
When no objects are selected, displays window with **Catagorized** *tab (left) or* **Alphabetic** *tab (right):*

Properties - Drawing1.dwg

No selection

Quick Select

Alphabetic | Categorized

General
Color	ByLayer
Layer	0
Linetype	ByLayer
Linetype scale	1.0000
Lineweight	ByLayer
Thickness	0.0000

Plot style
Plot style	ByColor
Plot style table	Default R14 pen assig
Plot table attached to	Model
Plot table type	Color dependent

View
Center X	8.0910
Center Y	4.5000
Center Z	0.0000
Height	18.0385
Width	32.4334

Misc
UCS icon On	Yes
UCS icon at origin	Yes
UCS per viewport	Yes
UCS Name	

Properties - Tablet 2000.dwg

No selection

Alphabetic | Categorized

Center X	10.8587
Center Y	7.0993
Center Z	0.0000
Color	ByLayer
Height	6.1504
Layer	0
Linetype	ByLayer
Linetype scale	1.0000
Lineweight	ByLayer
Plot style	ByColor
Plot style table	acad.ctb
Plot table attached to	Model
Plot table type	Color dependent
Thickness	0.0000
UCS icon at origin	Yes
UCS icon On	Yes
UCS Name	
UCS per viewport	Yes
Width	9.2485

Specifies the current view center x-coordinate

DIALOG BOX OPTIONS
Selection Lists the selected objects.
Alphabetic Displays the properties in alphabetical order.
Categorized Displays the properties in categories.
Quick Select Displays the **Quick Select** dialog box; see the **QSelect** command.

RELATED COMMANDS
ChProp Changes an object's color, layer, linetype, and thickness.
Style Creates and changes text styles.

RELATED SYSTEM VARIABLES

CeColor	Specifies the current color.
CeLtScale	Specifies the current linetype scale factor.
CeLtype	Specifies the current linetype.
CLayer	Specifies the current layer.
Elevation	Specifies the current elevation in the z-direction.
Thickness	Specifies the current thickness in the z-direction.

TIPS

- Use the **Selection** list to count objects in the drawing: first, use the cursor to select all objects — you *cannot* use the **Select All** command — then press **CTRL+1** to display the **Properties** window, and then click the **Selection** list:

- Double-click the title bar to dock and undock the window within the AutoCAD window.

- The **Properties** window can be dragged larger and smaller:

- When an item is displayed by gray text, it cannot be modified.
- Bodies, 3D solids, and 2D regions cannot be edited beyond the items in the **General** section.
- When one or more objects are displayed, the items displayed by the **Properties** window vary; here are three examples:

Arc	Mtext	Linear Dimension

Arc

Properties - Tablet 2000.dwg

Arc

Alphabetic	Categorized

⊞ **General**	
⊟ **Geometry**	
Start X	43.3417
Start Y	-2.6269
Start Z	0.0000
Center X	40.2690
Center Y	-3.2414
Center Z	0.0000
End X	37.1962
End Y	-2.6269
End Z	0.0000
Radius	3.1336
Start angle	11
End angle	169
Total angle	157
Arc length	8.6074
Area	11.5978
Normal X	0.0000
Normal Y	0.0000
Normal Z	1.0000

Specify the X, Y, Z coordinate of the start point of the arc

Mtext

Properties - Tablet 2000.dwg

MText

Alphabetic	Categorized

⊞ **General**	
⊟ **Text**	
Contents	This is a sample
Style	STANDARD
Justify	Top left
Direction	By style
Width	26.0000
Height	1.0000
Rotation	0
Line space facto	1.0000
Line space style	At least
⊟ **Geometry**	
Position X	65.0000
Position Y	-66.0000
Position Z	0.0000

Linear Dimension

Properties - Tablet 2000.dwg

Aligned Dimension

Alphabetic	Categorized

⊞ **General**	
⊟ **Misc**	
Dim style	STANDARD
⊟ **Lines & Arrow**	
Arrow 1	Closed filled
Arrow 2	Closed filled
Arrow size	0.1800
Dim line LW	ByBlock
Ext line LW	ByBlock
Dim line 1	On
Dim line 2	On
Dim line color	ByBlock
Dim line ext	0.0000
Ext line 1	On
Ext line 2	On
Ext line color	ByBlock
Ext line ext	0.1800
Ext line offset	0.0625
⊟ **Text**	
Fractional type	Horizontal
Text color	ByBlock
Text height	0.1800
Text offset	0.0900
Text outside alig	Off
Text pos hor	Centered
Text pos vert	Centered
Text style	STANDARD
Text inside align	Off
Text position X	-17.9421
Text position Y	-61.6567
Text rotation	0
Measurement	
Text override	
⊟ **Fit**	
Dim line forced	Off
Dim line inside	On
Dim scale overall	1.0000
Fit	Best fit
Text inside	Off
Text movement	Keep dim line wit
⊞ **Primary Units**	
⊞ **Alternate Unit**	
⊞ **Tolerances**	

Specifies the current dimension style by name (for DIMSTYLE system variable use SETVAR)

'PropertiesClose

2000 Closes the **Properties** window.

Command	Alias	Ctrl+	F-key	Alt+	Menu Bar	Tablet
'propertiesclose	prclose	1	...	TP	Tools ↳Properties	

Command: **propertiesclose**

COMMAND LINE OPTIONS
None.

RELATED COMMANDS

Properties	Displays the **Properties** window.
AdClose	Closes the AutoCAD DesignCenter.
Close	Closes the current drawing.
Exit	Closes AutoCAD.

RELATED SYSTEM VARIABLES
None.

TIPS
■ As an alternative to entering the **PropertiesClose** command, you can click the **x** button on the **Properties** window title bar:

```
Properties - Tablet 2000.dwg         [x]
                                       [Close]
Polyline (29)                  ▾   ▽
       Alphabetic    Categorized
```

DISCONTINUED COMMAND
The **PsDrag** command was discontinued with AutoCAD 2000i. It has no replacement.

PSetupin

Imports a user-defined page setup into the current drawing layout
(*short for Page SETUP IN*).

Command	Alias	Ctrl+	F-key	Alt+	Menu Bar	Tablet
psetupin	. . .	. . .	. . .	. . .	. . .	. . .
-psetupin						

Command: **psetupin**
*Displays the **Select File** dialog box; select a DWG, DWT, or DXF file.*
Select a file; AutoCAD displays dialog box:

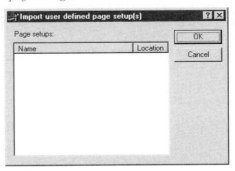

DIALOG BOX OPTIONS

Name	Lists the names of page setups.
Location	Lists the location of the setup.
OK	Closes the dialog box and loads the page setup.

-PSETUPIN COMMAND

Command: **-psetupin**
Enter filename: **[enter filename]**
Enter user defined page setup to import or [?]: **[enter name]**

COMMAND LINE OPTIONS

Enter filename
Enters the name of a drawing file.
Enter user defined page setup to import
Enters the name of a page setup.
? Lists the names of page setups in the drawing.

RELATED COMMANDS

PageSetup	Creates a new page setup configuration.
Plot	Plots the drawing.

RELATED SYSTEM VARIABLE

CTab	Contains the the name of the current model or layout tab in the drawing (default = "Model").

PsFill

Rel.12 Fills a 2D polyline outline with a raster PostScript pattern (*short for PostScript FILL; an undocumented command*).

Command	Alias	Ctrl+	F-key	Alt+	Menu Bar	Tablet
psfill	...	...	...	...	...	...

```
Command: psfill
Select polyline: [pick]
Enter PostScript fill pattern name (. = none) or [?] <.>:
   [enter pattern name]
```

COMMAND LINE OPTIONS

Select polyline
　　　　Selects the closed polyline to fill.

PostScript pattern
　　　　Specifies the name of the fill pattern.

.　　Selects no fill pattern.

?　　Lists the available fill patterns.

*　　Specifies to not outline the pattern with polyline.

RELATED COMMAND

BHatch　　Fills an area with a vector hatch pattern.

RELATED SYSTEM VARIABLE

PSQuality　　Specifies the display options for placing an EPS file:

PsQuality	Meaning
75	(*Positive*) Displays filled image at 75dpi (default)
0	Displays bounding box and filename; no image.
-75	(*Negative*) Displays image outline at 75dpi; no fill.

PsOut

Rel.12 Exports the current drawing as an encapsulated PostScript file (*an undocumented command*).

Command	Alias	Ctrl+	F-key	Alt+	Menu Bar	Tablet
psout	...	...	...	FE	File	...
				⌐EPS	⌐Export	
					⌐Encapsulated PS	

Command: **psout**
Specify filename in dialog box.
Select **Options** *to display dialog box:*

DIALOG BOX OPTIONS

Prolog Section Name

> (*Optional*) Specifies the name of the prolog section, which is read from the *Acad.Psf* file and customizes the PostScript output.

What to plot *options:*

Display	Selects the current display in the current viewport.
Extents	Selects the drawing extents.
Limits	Selects the drawing limits.
View	Selects a named view.
Window	Picks two corners of a window.

Preview *options*

None	Specifies no preview image (default).
EPSI	Specifies Macintosh preview image format.
TIFF	Specifies Tagged Image File Format.

Pixels *options:*

128	Specifies preview image size of 128x128 pixels (default).
256	Specifies preview image size of 256x256 pixels.
512	Specifies preview image size of 512x512 pixels.

Size Units *options:*

Inches   Specifies the plot parameters in inches.
MM   Specifies the plot parameters in millimeters.

Scale *options:*
Output Units Scales the output units.
Drawing Units Specifies the drawing units.
Fit to Paper   Forces the drawing to fit paper size.

Paper Size *options:*
Width   Enters a width for the output size.
Height   Enters a height for the output size.

RELATED COMMANDS

Plot   Exports the drawing in a variety of formats, including raster EPS.
PsIn   Imports EPS files into the drawing.

RELATED SYSTEM VARIABLE

PSProlog   Specifies the PostScript prologue information.

RELATED FILE

*.EPS   Extension of file produced by **PsOut**.

TIPS

■ The "screen preview image" is only used for screen display purposes, since graphics software generally cannot display PostScript graphic files.

■ When you select the **Window** option, AutoCAD prompts you for the window corners *after* you finish selecting options:

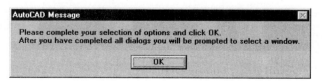

■ Although Autodesk recommends using the smallest screen preview image size (128x128), even the largest preview image (512x512) has a minimal effect on file size and screen display time.

■ Some software programs, such as those from Microsoft, might reject an EPS file when the preview image is larger than 128x128.

■ The screen preview image size has no effect on the quality of the PostScript output.

■ If you're not sure which screen preview format to use, select TIFF.

PSpace

Rel. I I Switches from model space to paper space (*short for Paper SPACE*).

Command	Alias	Ctrl+	F-key	Alt+	Menu Bar	Tablet
pspace	ps	...	...	...	...	L5

Command: **pspace**

COMMAND LINE OPTIONS
None.

RELATED COMMANDS
MSpace	Switches from paper space to model space.
MView	Creates viewports in paper space.
UcsIcon	Toggles the display of the paper space icon.
Zoom	Scales paper space relative to model space with the **XP** option.

RELATED SYSTEM VARIABLES
MaxActVP	Maximum number of viewports displaying an image.
PsLtScale	Linetype scale relative to paper space.
TileMode	Must equal 0 for paper space to work.

TIPS
- Use paper space to layout multiple views of a single drawing.

- Paper space is known as "drawing composition" in other CAD packages.

- You can switch to paper space by double-clicking the word **MODEL** on the status bar; switch back to model space by double-clicking the word **PAPER**.

| 4.0679, 0.4813, 0.0000 | SNAP | GRID | ORTHO | POLAR | OSNAP | OTRACK | LWT | MODEL |

| 4.0679, 0.4813, 0.0000 | SNAP | GRID | ORTHO | POLAR | OSNAP | OTRACK | LWT | PAPER |

- When a drawing is in paper space, AutoCAD displays **PAPER** on the status line and the paper space icon:

PublishToWeb

2000i

Exports the drawing as a DWF file embedded in a Web page.

Command	Alias	Ctrl+	F-key	Alt+	Menu Bar	Tablet
publishtoweb	...	...	...	FW	File	X25
					ᐂPublish to Web	

Command: **publishtoweb**
Displays wizard.

DIALOG BOX OPTIONS
Begin page:

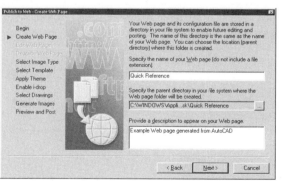

Create New Web Page
        Guides you through the steps in creating a new Web page from a drawing.
Edit Existing Web Page
        Guides you through the steps in editing an existing Web page.

Create Web Page page:

Specify the name of your Web page
        Allows you to enter a file name. To edit the Web page later, AutoCAD
        stores parameters in the file, and AutoCAD uses the name you enter here
        for the file. The name also appears at the top of the Web page.
Provide a description to appear on your Web page
        Enters a description, which appears below the name on the Web page.

Select Image Type page:

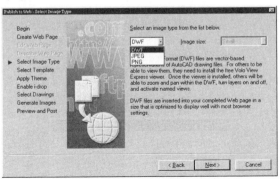

Select an image type from the list below

- **DWF** (drawing Web format) is a vector format that display cleanly, and can be zoomed and panned; not all Web browsers can display DWF.

- **JPEG** (joint photographic experts group) is a raster format that all Web browsers display; may create *artifacts* (details that don't exist).

- **PNG** (portable network graphics) is a raster format that does not suffer the artifact problem; some older Web browsers do not display PNG.

Image size   Selects a size of raster image (available fro JPEG and PNG only):

Image Size	Resolution	Approximate PNG Filesize
Small	789 x 610	60KB
Medium	1009 x 780	90KB
Large	1302 x 1006	130KB
Extra Large	1576 x 1218	170KB

Select Template page:

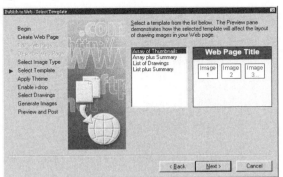

Select a template from the list below

Selects one of the pre-designed formats for the Web page.

Apply Theme page:
New to AutoCAD 2002:

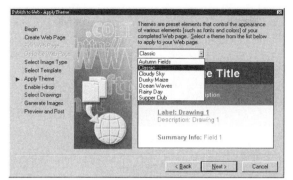

Select a theme from the list below
    Selects one of the pre-designed themes (colors and fonts) for the Web page.

Enable iDrop page:
New to AutoCAD 2002:

Enable i-drop Adds i-drop capability to the Web page.

Select Drawings page:

Drawing   Selects the drawing; the current drawing is the default.
Layout   Selects the name of a layout, or Model space.
Label   Specifies a name, such as the filename or a more descriptive name.
Description   Specifies a description that appears with the drawing on the Web page.

Add	Adds the image setting to the image list.
Update	Changes the image setting in the image list.
Remove	Removes the image setting from the image list.
Move up	Moves the image setting up the image list.
Move down	Moves the image setting down the image list.

Generate Images page:

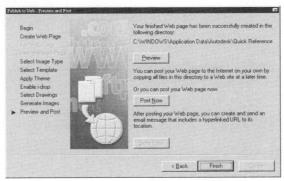

Regenerate images for drawings that have changed
> Updates images for those drawings that have been edited.

Regenerate all images
> Regenerates all images from all drawings; ensures all are up to date.

Preview and Post page:

Preview Launches the Web browser to preview the resulting Web page.
Post Now Uploads the files (HTML, JPEG, PNG, DWF, etc) to the Web site.
Send Email Sends an email to alert others of the posted Web page.

Example of the resulting Web page:

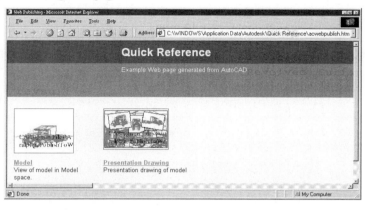

RELATED COMMANDS

DwfOut	Exports the drawing as a DWF file.
Plot	Exportsthe drawing as a DWF file via the ePlot option.
Hyperlink	Places hyperlinks in the drawing.

RELATED FILES

*.PTW	Publish to web parameter file; stores in tab-delimited ASCII file.
*.JS	JavaScript file.
*JPG	Joint photographic experts group (raster image) file.
*.PNG	Portable network graphics (raster image) file.
*.DWF	Drawing Web format (vector image) file.

TIPS

- Use the **Regenerate all images** option, unless you have an exceptionally slow computer or large number of drawings to process. The **Generate Images** step can take a long time.

- After you click **Preview** to see what the Web page will look like, and after AutoCAD launches the Web browser, you can click the **Back** button to make changes if the result is not to your liking.

- The image of the drawing in DWF format is displayed by the Web browser only if: (1) Autodesk's Whip plug-in has been installed; and (2) JaveScript is enabled.

- The **Post Now** option works only if you have correctly set up the FTP (file transfer protocol) parameters. If so, you can have AutoCAD directly upload the HTML files to your Web site. If not, use a separate FTP program to upload the files from the *\Windows\Applications Data\Autodesk*.

- You can customize the themes and templates by editing the *AcWebPublish.Css* (themes) and *AcWebPublish.Xml* (templates) files.

Purge

V. 2.1 Removes unused, named objects from the drawing: block, dimension style, layer, linetype, plot style, shape, text style, application ID table, and multiline style.

Command	Alias	Ctrl+	F-key	Alt+	Menu Bar	Tablet
purge	pu	...	...	FUP	File	X25
					⌐Drawing Utilities	
					⌐Purge	

-purge

Command: **purge**
Displays dialog box (new as of AutoCAD 2000i):

DIALOG BOX OPTIONS

View items you can purge
> Lists objects that can be purged from the drawing.

View items you cannot purge
> Lists objects that cannot be purged from the drawing.

Confirm each item to be purged
> Displays a confirmation dialog box for each object being purged.

Purge nested items
> Purges nested objects, such as an unused block within an unused block.

-PURGE COMMAND

Command: **-purge**

Enter type of unused objects to purge
[Blocks/Dimstyles/LAyers/LTypes/Plotstyles/SHapes/
    textSTyles/Mlinestyles/All]: **[enter option]**

Sample response:

No unreferenced blocks found.
Purge layer DOORWINS? <N> **y**
Purge layer TEXT? <N> **y**
Purge linetype CENTER? <N> **y**
Purge linetype CENTER2? <N> **y**
No unreferenced text styles found.
No unreferenced shape files found.
No unreferenced dimension styles found.

COMMAND LINE OPTIONS

Blocks	Purges named but unused (*not inserted*) blocks.
Dimstyles	Purges unused dimension styles.
LAyers	Purges unused layers.
LTypes	Purges unused linetypes.
Plotstyle	Purges unsed plot styles.
SHapes	Purges unused shape files.
STyles	Purges unused text styles.
APpids	Purges unused application ID tables of ADS and AutoLISP applications.
Mlinestyles	Purges unused multiline styles.
All	Purges drawing of all eight named objects, if necessary.

RELATED COMMAND

WBlock	Writes the current drawing to disk with the * option, and removes spurious information from the drawing.

TIPS

■ As of AutoCAD Release 13, the **Purge** command can be used at any time; it no longer must be used as the first command after a drawing is loaded.

■ It may be necessary to use the **Purge** command several times; follow each purge with the **Close** command, then open the drawing, and purge again. Repeat until the **Purge** command reports nothing to purge.

QDim

Draws continuous, baseline, ordindate, radius, diameter, or staggered dimensions with three picks (*short for Quick DIMensioning*).

Command	Alias	Ctrl+	F-key	Alt+	Menu Bar	Tablet
qdim	...	...	...	NQ	Dimension	W1
					↳QDIM	

```
Command: qdim
Select geometry to dimension: [pick]
1 found Select geometry to dimension: ENTER
Specify dimension line position, or
[Continuous/Staggered/Baseline/Ordinate/Radius/Diameter/
   datumPoint/Edit] <Continuous>: ENTER
```

COMMAND LINE OPTIONS

Select geometry to dimension
> Selects a single object to dimension.

Specify dimension line position
> Specifies the location of the dimension.

Continuous   Draws continuous dimensions.

Staggered   Draws staggered dimensions.

Baseline   Draws baseline dimensions.

Ordinate   Draws ordinate dimensions relative to the UCS origin.

Radius   Draws radial dimensions; prompts 'Specify dimension line position:'.

Diameter   Draws diameter dimensions; prompts 'Specify dimension line position:'.

datamPoint   Sets a new datum point for ordinate and baseline dimensions; prompts 'Select new datum point:'

Edit options:

```
Indicate dimension point to remove, or [Add/eXit] <eXit>: [pick]
```

Indicate dimension to remove
> Selects the dimension to remove from the continuous dimension.

Add   Adds a dimension to the continuous dimension.

eXit   Returns to dimension drawing mode.

RELATED COMMANDS

DimStyle   Creates dimension styles, which specify the look of a dimension.

Dim*xxx*   Draws other kinds of dimensions.

QLeader   Draws leaders.

RELATED SYSTEM VARIABLE

DimStyle   Specifies the current dimension style.

TIPS

■ Example of continuous dimensions:

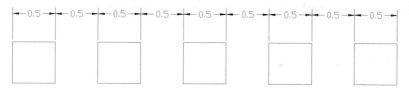

■ Example of staggered dimensions:

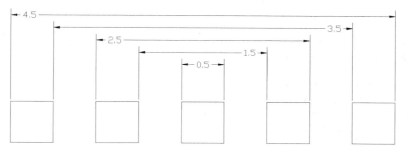

■ Example of ordinate dimensions:

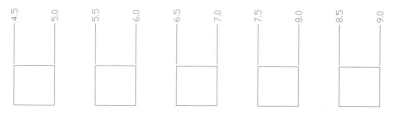

■ Example of radial dimensions:

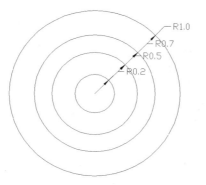

QLeader

Rel.14   Uses a dialog box to automate the creation of custom leaders and annotations (*short for Quick LEADER*).

Command	Alias	Ctrl+	F-key	Alt+	Menu Bar	Tablet
qleader	le	...	...	NE	Dimension ⤷ Leader	W2

Command: **qleader**
Specify first leader point, or [Settings]<Settings>: **ENTER**
Displays dialog box:

Click ***OK*** *to continue with the command; the prompts vary, depending on the options selected in the dialog box:*
Specify next point: **[pick]**
Specify next point: **ENTER**
Specify text width <0.0000>: **ENTER**
Enter first line of annotation text <Mtext>: **[enter text]**
Enter next line of annotation text: **ENTER**

COMMAND LINE OPTIONS

Specify first leader point
> Picks the location for the leader's arrowhead; press **ENTER** to display tabbed dialog box.

Specify next point
> Picks the vertices of the leader; press **ENTER** to end the leader line.

Specify text width
> Specifies the width of the bounding box for the leader text.

Enter first line of annotation text
> Specifies the text for leader annotation; press **ENTER** twice to end.

Enter next line of annotation text
> Specifies more text; press **ENTER** once to end.

DIALOG BOX OPTIONS
Annotation/Format tab:

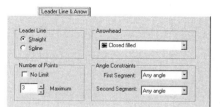

Annotation Type options:

MText   Prompts you to enter text for the annotation.

Copy an Object Attaches any object in the drawing as an annotation.

Tolerance   Prompts you to select tolerance symbols for the annotation.

Block Reference

        Prompts you to select a block for the annotation.

None   Attaches no annotation.

MText options options:

Prompt for width

        Displays the 'Specify text width' prompt.

Always left justify

        Forces the text to be left-justified, even when the leader is drawn to the right.

Frame text   Places a rectangle around the text.

Annotation Reuse options:

None   Does not retain annotation for next leader.

Reuse Next   Remembers the current annotation for the next leader.

Reuse Current Uses the last annotation for the current leader.

Leader Line & Arrow tab:

Leader Line options:

Straight   Draws the leader with straight lines.

Spline   Draws the leader as a spline curve.

Number of points options:

No limit   Keeps prompting for leader vertex points until you press **ENTER**.

Maximum   The **QLeader** command stops prompting for leader vertex points; default=3.

Arrowhead option:

Arrowhead   Selects the type of arrowhead, including **Closed filled** (default), **None**, and **User Arrow**.

Angle Constraints options:

First Segment Selects from **Any angle** (user-specified), **Horizontal** (0 degrees), **90**, **45**, **30**, or **15**-degree leader line, first segment.

Second Segment Selects from **Any angle** (user-specified), **Horizontal**, **90**, **45**, **30**, or **15**-degree leader line, second segment.

Attachment tab:

Left Side   Positions the annotation at one of five different locations relative to the last leader segment, when the annotation is located to the left of the leader.

Right Side   Positions the annotation at one of five different locations relative to the last leader segment, when the annotation is located to the right of the leader.

Underline bottom line
                  Underlines the last line of leader text.

RELATED COMMANDS

DdEdit   Edits leader text; see the **MText** command.
DimStyle   Sets dimension variables, including leaders.
Leader   Draws leaders without dialog boxes.
QLAttach   Attaches a leader to an annotation.
QLAttachSet   Attaches leaders globally to annotations.
QLDetachSet   Detaches leaders from annotations.

TIPS

■ The **QLeader** command draws leaders, just like the **Leader** command in AutoCAD Release 13 and 14. The difference is that it brings up a triple-tab dialog box for setting the leader options.

■ Some options have interesting possibilities, such as using any object in the drawing in place of the leader text.

■ This command was part of the Bonus CAD Tools collection in AutoCAD Release 14; the supplemental "QL" commands, such as **QLAttach**, was part of the Express Tools collection in AutoCAD 2000.

QSave

Saves the current drawing without requesting a filename (*short for Quick SAVE*).

Command	Alias	Ctrl+	F-key	Alt+	Menu Bar	Tablet
qsave	...	S	...	FS	File	U24-
					↳Save	U25

Command: **qsave**
*If the drawing has never been saved, displays the **Drawing Save As** dialog box.*

COMMAND LINE OPTIONS
None.

RELATED COMMANDS
Quit   Ends AutoCAD, with or without saving the drawing.
Save   Saves the drawing, after requesting the filename.
SaveAs   Saves the drawing with a different filename.

RELATED SYSTEM VARIABLES
DBMod   Indicates whether the drawing has changed since it was loaded.
DwgName   Specifies the current drawing filename (default = "Drawing1").
DwgTitled   Specifies the status of drawing's filename:

DwgTiled	Meaning
0	Drawing is named "Drawing1" (default).
1	Drawing was given another name.

TIPS
■ When the drawing is unnamed, the **QSave** command displays the **Save Drawing As** dialog box to request a file name; see the **SaveAs** command.

■ When the drawing file, its subdirectory, or drive (such as a CD-ROM drive) is marked read-only, use the **SaveAs** command to save the drawing by another filename, or to another subdirectory or drive.

QSelect

Creates a selection set of objects (*short for Quick SELECT*).

Command	Alias	Ctrl+	F-key	Alt+	Menu Bar	Tablet
qselect	...	...	...	TQ	Tools	X9
					⌐Quick Select	

Command: **qselect**
Displays dialog box:

DIALOG BOX OPTIONS

Apply to   Applies the selection criteria to the entire drawing or current selection set; click **Select Objects** to create a selection set.

Select Objects Allows you to select objects; AutoCAD prompts: 'Select objects:'. Right-click or press **ENTER** to return to this dialog box.

Object type   Lists the objects in the selection set; allows you to narrow the selection criteria to specific types of objects (default = Multiple).

Properties   Lists the properties valid for the selected object types; when you select more than one object type, only the properties in common are listed.

Operator   Lists logical operators available for the selected property; operators include:

Operator	Meaning
= Equals	Selects objects equal to the property.
<> Not Equal To	Selects objects different from the property.
> Greater Than	Selects objects greater than the property.
< Less Than	Selects objects less than the property.
* Wildcard Match	Selects objects with matching text.

Value Specifies the property value for the filter. If known values for the selected property are available, **Value** becomes a list from which you can choose a value. Otherwise, enter a value.

How to apply options:
Include in new selection set
Creates a new selection set.
Exclude from new selection set
Inverts the selection set, excluding all objects that match the selection criteria.
Append to current selection set
On: Adds to the current selection set.
Off: Replaces the current selection set.

RELATED COMMANDS

Select Selects objects on the command line.
Filter Runs a more sophisticated version of the **QSelect** command.

RELATED SYSTEM VARIABLES
None.

TIPS

■ This command works with the properties of proxy objects created by ObjectARX applications.

■ You may select objects before entering the **QSelect** command, then add or remove objects from the selection set with the **Quick Select** dialog box's options.

■ Since this command is not transparent, you cannot use it within other commands; instead, use the **'Filter** command.

QText

V. 2.0 Displays each line of text as a rectangular box (*short for Quick TEXT*).

Command	Alias	Ctrl+	F-key	Alt+	Menu Bar	Tablet
qtext	...	...	...	...	...	...

```
Command: qtext
Enter mode [ON/OFF] <OFF>: on
```
A regeneration is required before AutoCAD displays text in quick outline form:
```
Command: regen
Regenerating model.
```

Normal text (at left) and quick text after regeneration (at right).

COMMAND LINE OPTIONS

ON   Turns on quick text after the next **Regen** command.

OFF   Turns off quick text after the next **Regen** command.

RELATED COMMAND

Regen   Regenerates the screen; makes quick text take effect.

RELATED SYSTEM VARIABLE

QTextMode   Holds the current state of quick text mode.

TIPS

■ To reduce regen time, use qtext to turn lines of text into rectangles, which redraw faster.

■ The length of a qtext box does not necessarily match the actual length of text.

■ Turning on qtext affects text during plotting; qtext blocks are plotted as rectangles.

■ To find invisible text (such as text made of spaces), turn on qtext, thaw all layers, zoom to extents, and use the **Regen** command.

Quit

V. 1.0 Exits AutoCAD without saving changes to the drawing from the most recent **QSave** or **SaveAs** command.

Command	Alias	Ctrl+	F-key	Alt+	Menu Bar	Tablet
quit	exit	...	...	FX	File	Y25
				F4	↳Exit	

Command: **quit**
Displays dialog box:

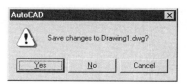

DIALOG BOX OPTIONS

Yes	Saves changes before leaving AutoCAD.
No	Doesn't save changes.
Cancel	Doesn't quit AutoCAD; returns to drawing.

RELATED COMMANDS

Close	Closes the current drawing.
SaveAs	Saves the drawing by another name or to another subdirectory or drive.

RELATED SYSTEM VARIABLE

DBMod   Indicates whether the drawing has changed since it was loaded.

RELATED FILES

*.DWG	AutoCAD drawing files.
*.BAK	Backup file.
*.BK*n*	Additional backup files.

TIPS

■ You can make changes to a drawing, yet preserve its original format: (1) use the **SaveAs** command to save the drawing by another name; and (2) use the **Quit** command to preserve the drawing in its original state.

■ Even if you accidently save over a drawing, you can recover the previous version: (1) use the Windows Explorer to rename the DWG file; and (2) use the Windows Explorer to rename the BAK (backup) extension to DWG — if you have AutoCAD set up to save backup files; see **Options** command.

■ You cannot save changes to a read-only drawing with the **Quit** command; use the **SaveAs** command instead.

R14PenWizard

2000 Helps you create a color-dependent plot style table (*an undocumented command*).

Command	Alias	Ctrl+	F-key	Alt+	Menu Bar	Tablet
r14penwizard	...	...	...	TZD	Tools ⬐Wizard ⬐Add Color-Dependent Plot Style Table	...

Command: **r14penwizard**
*Displays **Add Color-Dependent Plot Style Table** wizard.*

DIALOG BOX OPTIONS

Back   Goes back to the previous dialog box.
Next   Moves to the next dialog box.
Cancel   Exits the wizard process.

Begin page:

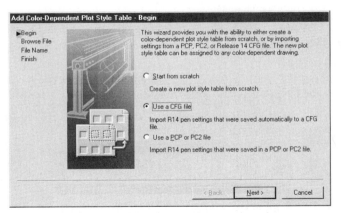

Start from scrach
       Creates a new color-dependent plot style table file.
Use a CFG file Converts the plotter pen settings stored in the AutoCAD Release 14
       Acad.Cfg file.
Use a PCP or PC2 file
       Converts the plotter pen settings stored in the plotter configuration
       parameter PCP and PC2 files of earlier versions of AutoCAD.

Browse File Name page:

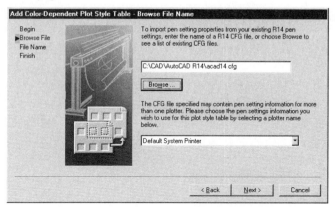

File name   Specifies the name of the file containing the plotter data.

Browse   Displays the **Open** dialog box.

Select printer Specifies the name of the printer whose configuration data should be
                 imported.

File Name page:

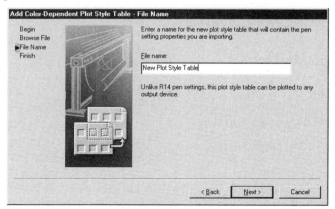

File name   Specifies the name of the file in which to store the new color-dependent
                 plot style table.

Finish page:

Plot Style Table Editor
> Displays the **Plot Style Table Editor** dialog box.

Use this plot style table for the current drawing
> Applies the plot style table to the current drawing.

Use this plot style table for new and pre-AutoCAD 2000 drawings
> Applies the plot style table to all new drawings and drawings created by versions of AutoCAD prior to 2000.

RELATED COMMANDS

PcinWizard   Imports PCP and PC2 configuration plot files into the current layout.

PlotterManager
> Accesses the **Add Plotter** wizard and **Assign Plot Style** wizard.

Plot   Plots the drawing.

RELATED SYSTEM VARIABLES

None.

TIP

■ This command makes AutoCAD 2002's **Plot** command compatible with versions of AutoCAD prior to 2000.

 # Ray

Rel.13 Creates a semi-infinite construction line.

Command	Alias	Ctrl+	F-key	Alt+	Menu Bar	Tablet
ray	...	...	...	DR	Draw ᑕRay	K10

```
Command: ray
Specify start point: [pick]
Specify through point: [pick]
Specify through point: ENTER
```

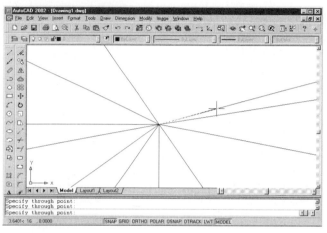

COMMAND LINE OPTIONS

Start point Specifies the starting point of the ray.
Through point Specifies the point through which the ray passes.

RELATED COMMANDS

Properties Modifies a ray.
Line Draws a finite line.
XLine Creates an infinite construction line.

TIPS

■ The *ray* object is semi-infinite in length.

■ A ray is a "construction line"; it displays and plots, but does not affect the extents.

■ A ray has all the properties of a line (including color, layer, and linetype), and can be used as a cutting edge for the **Trim** commmand.

REMOVED COMMAND

RConfig — render configuration — was removed from Release 14. It is no longer required.

Recover

Rel.12   Recovers a damaged drawing without user intervention.

Command	Alias	Ctrl+	F-key	Alt+	Menu Bar	Tablet
recover	...	...	...	FUR	File	...
					↳Drawing Utilities	
					↳Recover	

Command: **recover**
*Displays the **Select File** dialog box.*

Sample output:
Drawing recovery.
Drawing recovery log.
Scanning completed.
Validating objects in the handle table.
Valid objects 95   Invalid objects 0
Validating objects completed.
Used contingency data.
    Salvaged database from drawing.
Opening an AutoCAD 2000 format file.
 12   Blocks audited
Pass 1 13   objects audited
Pass 2 13   objects audited
Total errors found 0 fixed 0
Regenerating model.
AutoCAD menu utilities loaded.

COMMAND LINE OPTIONS
None.

RELATED COMMAND
Audit   Checks a drawing for integrity.

TIPS
- The **Recover** command does not ask permission to repair damaged parts of the drawing file; use the **Audit** command if you want control over the repair process.

- The **Quit** command discards changes made by the **Recover** command.

- If the **Recover** and **Audit** commands don't fix the problem, try using the **DxfOut** command, followed by the **DxfIn** command.

▢ Rectang

<u>Rel.12</u> Draws a rectangle out of a polyline.

Command	Alias	Ctrl+	F-key	Alt+	Menu Bar	Tablet
rectang	rec rectangle	...	...	DG	Draw ⎩Rectangle	Q10

```
Command: rectang
Specify first corner point or [Chamfer/Elevation/Fillet/
    Thickness/Width]: [pick]
Specify other corner point: [pick]
```

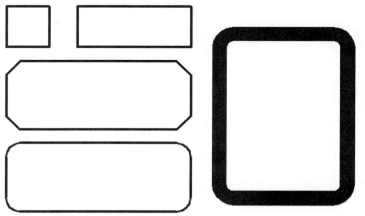

*Square and rectangles drawn with the **Rectangle** command's **Chamfer**, **Fillet**, and **Width** options.*

COMMAND LINE OPTIONS

Specify first corner point
> Picks the first corner of the rectangle.

Specify other corner point
> Picks the opposite corner of the rectangle.

Chamfer options:

```
Specify first chamfer distance for rectangles <0.0000>: [enter
value]
Specify second chamfer distance for rectangles <0.0000>: [enter
value]
```

First chamfer distance for rectangles
> Sets the first chamfer distance for all four corners.

Second chamfer distance for rectangles
> Sets the second chamfer distance for all four corners.

Elevation option:
```
Specify the elevation for rectangles <0.0000>: [enter value]
```

Elevation for rectangles
> Sets the elevation (*height of the rectangle in the z direction*).

Fillet option:
```
Specify fillet radius for rectangles <1.0000>: [enter value]
```
Fillet radius for rectangles
> Sets the fillet radius for all four corners of the rectangle.

Thickness option:
```
Specify thickness for rectangles <0.0000>: [enter vaaue]
```

Thickness for rectangles
> Sets the thickness of the rectangle's sides in the z direction.

Width option:
```
Specify line width for rectangles <0.0000>: [enter value]
```

Width for rectangles
> Sets the width of all segments of the rectangle's four sides.

RELATED COMMANDS

Donut	Draws solid-filled circles with a polyline.
Ellipse	Draws ellipsis with a polyline, when **PEllipse** = 1.
PEdit	Edits polylines, including rectangles.
PLine	Draws polylines and polyline arcs.
Polygon	Draws a polygon — 3 to 1024 sides — from a polyline.

RELATED SYSTEM VARIABLES
None.

TIPS

- Rectangles are drawn from polylines; use the **PEdit** command to change the rectangle, such as the width of the polyline.

- The values you set for the **Chamfer, Elevation, Fillet, Thickness**, and **Width** options become the default for the next execution of the **Rectangle** command.

- The pick point determines the location of the rectangle's first vertex; rectangles are drawn counterclockwise.

- Use the **Snap** command and object snap modes to place the rectangle precisely.

- Use object snap modes **ENDpoint** or **INTersection** to snap to the rectangle's vertices.

- This command ignores the settings in the **ChamferA, ChamferB, Elevation, FilletRad, PLineWid**, and **Thickness** system variables.

Redefine

Rel. 9 Restores the meaning of an AutoCAD command after being disabled by the **Undefine** command.

Command	Alias	Ctrl+	F-key	Alt+	Menu Bar	Tablet
redefine	...	...	...	...	...	...

Command: **redefine**
Enter command name:

COMMAND LINE OPTION
Enter command name
> Names the AutoCAD command to redefine.

RELATED COMMANDS
All commands Allows all AutoCAD commands to be redefined.
Undefine Disables the meaning of an AutoCAD command.

TIPS
■ You must undefine a command with the **Undefine** command before using the **Redefine** command.

■ Prefix any command with a . (*period*) to temporarily redefine the undefinition, as in:

> Command: **.line**

■ Prefix any command with an _ (*underscore*) to make an English-language command work in any linguistic version of AutoCAD, as in:

> Command: **_line**

Redo

V. 2.5 Reverses the effect of the most-recent **U** and **Undo** commands.

Command	Alias	Ctrl+	F-key	Alt+	Menu Bar	Tablet
redo	...	Y	...	ER	Edit	U12
					⌐Redo	

Command: **redo**

COMMAND LINE OPTIONS

None.

RELATED COMMANDS

Oops	Un-erases the most-recently erased objects.
U	Undoes the most-recent AutoCAD command.
Undo	Undoes the most-recent series of AutoCAD commands.

TIPS

■ The **Redo** command is limited to reversing a single undo, while the **Undo** and **U** commands undo operations all the way back to the beginning of the editing session.

■ The **Redo** command must be used immediately following the **U** or **Undo** command.

'Redraw

V. 1.0 Redraws the current viewport to clean up the screen.

Command	Alias	Ctrl+	F-key	Alt+	Menu Bar	Tablet
'redraw	r	. . .	. . .	. . .	. . .	. . .

Command: **redraw**

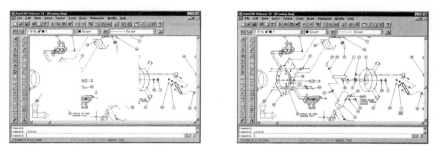

Before redraw, portions of the drawing are "missing" (at left);
the drawing is clean after the redraw (at right).

COMMAND LINE OPTION
Esc   Cancels the redraw.

RELATED COMMANDS
RedrawAll   Redraws all viewports.
Regen   Regenerates the current viewport.
Zoom   As of AutoCAD Release 14, most operations of the **Zoom** command no longer cause a regeneration.

RELATED SYSTEM VARIABLE
SortEnts   Controls the order of redrawing objects:

SortEnts	Meaning
0	Sorts by order in the drawing database.
1	Sorts for object selection.
2	Sorts for object snap.
4	Sorts for redraw.
8	Sorts for creating slides.
16	Sorts for regenerations.
32	Sorts for plotting.
64	Sorts for PostScript plotting.

TIPS
■ Use the **Redraw** command to clean up the screen after a lot of editing; some commands automatically redraw the screen when they are done.

■ **Redraw** does not affect objects on frozen layers.

■ Use the **RedrawAll** command to redraw all viewports.

'RedrawAll

Rel.10 Redraws all viewports to clean up the screen.

Command	Alias	Ctrl+	F-key	Alt+	Menu Bar	Tablet
'redrawall	ra	...	...	VR	View	Q11-
					⊾Redraw	R11

Command: **redrawall**

COMMAND LINE OPTION
Esc   Cancels the redraw.

RELATED COMMANDS
Redraw   Redraws only the current viewport.
RegenAll   Regenerates all viewports.

RELATED SYSTEM VARIABLE
SortEnts   Controls the order of redrawing objects:

SortEnts	Meaning
0	Sorts by order in the drawing database.
1	Sorts for object selection.
2	Sorts for object snap.
4	Sorts for redraw.
8	Sorts for creating slides.
16	Sorts for regeneration.
32	Sorts for plotting.
64	Sorts for PostScript plotting.

TIPS
- The **RedrawAll** command does not affect objects on frozen layers.
- Use the **Redraw** command to redraw a single viewport.

◪ 🖬 RefClose

2000 Saves or discards changes made to reference objects edited in-place (*short for REFerence CLOSE*).

Command	Alias	Ctrl+	F-key	Alt+	Menu Bar	Tablet
refclose	...	...	...	MBD	Modify ↳In-place Xref and Block Edit ↳Discard Changes to Reference	...
				MBS	Modify ↳In-place Xref and Block Edit ↳Save Changes Back to Reference	

Command: **refclose**
Enter option [Save/Discard reference changes] <Save>: ᴇɴᴛᴇʀ

COMMAND LINE OPTIONS
Save   Saves the editing changes made to the block or externally-referenced file.
Discard   Discards the changes.

RELATED COMMANDS
RefEdit   Edits blocks and externally-referenced files attached to the current drawing.
Insert   Inserts a block in the drawing.
XAttach   Attaches an externally-referenced drawing.

RELATED SYSTEM VARIABLE
RefEditName Specifies the filename of the referenced file being edited.

TIP
- AutoCAD prompts you with a warning dialog box to ensure you really want to discard or save the changes made to the reference:

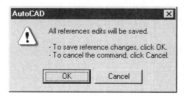

RefEdit

2000 Edits blocks and externally-referenced files attached to the current drawing (*short for REFerence EDIT*).

Command	Alias	Ctrl+	F-key	Alt+	Menu Bar	Tablet
refedit	...	...	...	MBE	Modify	...
					⌐In-place Xref and Block Edit	
					⌐Edit Block or Xref	

-refedit

Command: **refedit**
Select reference: **[pick]**
Displays dialog box:

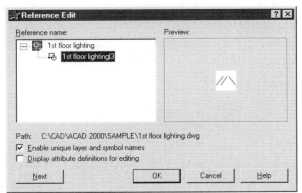

*Click **OK** to continue with the command:*
Select nested objects: **[pick]**
n items selected
Use REFCLOSE or the Refedit toolbar to end reference
   editing session.
Displays toolbar:

COMMAND LINE OPTIONS

Select reference Selects an externally-referenced drawing or inserted block for editing.
Select nested objects

Selects objects within the reference — this becomes the selection set of objects that you may edit; you may select all nested objects with the **All** option, with the exception of OLE objects and objects inserted with the **MInsert** command, which cannot be refedited.

DIALOG BOX OPTIONS

Reference name Lists a tree of the selected reference object and its nested references; a single reference can be edited at a time.

Preview Displays a preview image of the selected reference.

Enable unique layer and symbol names

> **On**: Prefixes layer and symbol names of extracted objects with **$*n*$**.
>
> **Off**: Retains the names of layers and symbols, as in the reference.

Display attribute definitions for editing

> **On**: Makes non-constant attributes invisible; attribute definitions can be edited. *Caution!* When edited attributes are saved back to the block reference, the attributes of the original reference are not changed; instead, the modified attribute definitions come into effect with the next insertion of the block.

Next Displays the next selected reference.

TOOLBAR OPTIONS

This toolbar appears autoamtically after you select nested objects to edit:

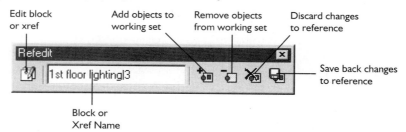

Edit block or xref
> Executes the **RefEdit** command.

Add objects to working set
> Executes the **RefSet Add** command.

Remove objects from working set
> Executes the **RefSet Remove** command.

Discard changes to reference
> Executes the **RefClose Discard** command.

Save back changes to reference
> Executes the **RefClose Save** command.

-REFEDIT COMMAND

Command: **-refedit**
Select nested objects: **[pick]**
n items selected
Select nesting level [Ok/Next] <Next>: **o**
Select nested objects: **[pick]**
n entities added Select nested objects: ENTER
Display attribute definitions [Yes/No] <No>: ENTER
Use REFCLOSE or the Refedit toolbar to end reference
    editing session.
*Displays **Refedit** toolbar.*

COMMAND LINE OPTIONS

Select reference Selects an externally-referenced drawing or inserted block for editing.

Select nested objects

> Selects objects within the reference — this becomes the selection set of objects that you may edit; you may select all nested objects with **All** with the exception of OLE objects and objects inserted with the **MInsert** command, which cannot be refedited.

Display attribute definitions

> **On**: Makes non-constant attributes invisible; attribute definitions can be edited. *Caution!* when edited attribute are saved back to the block reference, the attributes of the original reference are not changed; instead, the modified attribute definitions come into effect with the next insertion of the block.

RELATED COMMANDS

RefSet   Adds and removes objects from a working set.
RefClose   Saves or discards editing changes to the reference.

RELATED SYSTEM VARIABLES

RefEditName Stores the name of the externally-referenced file or block being edited.
XEdit   Determines whether the current drawing can be edited while being referenced by another drawing.
XFadeCtl   Specifies the amount of fading for objects not being edited in place.

TIPS

- OLE objects and objects inserted with the **MInsert** command cannot be refedited.

- AutoCAD identifies the "working set" as those objects that you have selected to edit in-place.

- Objects *not* selected to be edited have their layers locked.

⊞ ⊞ RefSet

2000 Adds and removes objects from a working set (*short for REFerence SET*).

Command	Alias	Ctrl+	F-key	Alt+	Menu Bar	Tablet
refset	...	...	...	MBA	Modify	...
					↳In-place Xref and Block Edit	
					↳Add Objects to Working Set	
				MBR	Modify	
					↳In-place Xref and Block Edit	
					↳Remove Objects from Working Set	

Command: **refset**
Transfer objects between the Refedit working set and host
   drawing...
Enter an option [Add/Remove] <Add>: ENTER
Select objects: **[pick]**

COMMAND LINE OPTIONS
Add   Prompts you to select objects to add to the working set.
Remove   Prompts you to select objects to remove from the working set.
Select objects Selects the objects to be added or removed.

RELATED COMMANDS
RefEdit   Edit reference objects in place.
RefClose   Saves or discards editing changes to the reference.

RELATED SYSTEM VARIABLES
RefEditName Stores the name of the external reference file or block being edited.
XEdit   Determines whether the current drawing can be edited while being
                 referenced by another drawing.
XFadeCtl   Specifies the amount of fading for objects not being edited in place.

TIPS
■ The purpose of this command is to add objects to — or remove them from — the
   "working set" of objects, while you are performing in-place editing of a block or an
   externally-referenced drawing.

■ When you select an object that cannot be added or removed from the working set,
   AutoCAD prompts: "** *n* selected objects are on a locked layer."

Regen

V. 1.0 Regenerates the current viewport to update the drawing.

Command	Alias	Ctrl+	F-key	Alt+	Menu Bar	Tablet
regen	re	...	...	VG	View ⸜Regen	J1

```
Command: regen
Regenerating model.
```

COMMAND LINE OPTION

Esc   Cancels the regeneration.

RELATED COMMANDS

Redraw   Cleans up the current viewport quickly.
RegenAll   Regenerates all viewports.
RegenAuto   Checks with you before doing most regenerations.
ViewRes   Controls whether zooms and pans are performed at redraw speed.

RELATED SYSTEM VARIABLES

RegenMode   Current setting of automatic regeneration:

RegenMode	Meaning
0	Off.
1	On (default).

WhipArc   Determines how circles and arcs are displayed:

WhipArc	Meaning
0	Circles and arcs displayed as vectors.
1	Circles and arcs displayed as true circles and arcs.

TIPS

■ Some commands automatically force a regeneration of the screen; other commands queue the regeneration.

■ The **Regen** command reindexes the drawing database for better display and object selection performance.

■ To save on regeneration time, freeze layers you are not working with, apply **QText** to turn text into rectangles, and place hatching on its own layer.

■ Use the **RegenAll** command to regenerate all viewports.

RegenAll

Rel.10 Regenerates all viewports.

Command	Alias	Ctrl+	F-key	Alt+	Menu Bar	Tablet
regenall	rea	...	...	VA	View	K1
					⬐Regen All	

```
Command: regenall
Regenerating model.
```

COMMAND LINE OPTION

Esc   Cancels the regeneration process.

RELATED COMMANDS

RedrawAll   Redraws all viewports.
Regen   Regenerates the current viewport.
RegenAuto   Checks with you before performing most regenerations.
ViewRes   Controls whether zooms and pans are performed at redraw speed.

RELATED SYSTEM VARIABLE

RegenMode   Current setting of automatic regeneration:

RegenMode	Meaning
0	Off.
1	On (default).

WhipArc   Determines how circles and arcs are displayed:

WhipArc	Meaning
0	Circles and arcs displayed as vectors.
1	Circles and arcs displayed as true circles and arcs.

TIPS

■ The **RegenAll** command does not regenerate objects on frozen layers.

■ Use the **Regen** command to regenerate a single viewport.

'RegenAuto

V. 1.2 AutoCAD asks you before performing a regeneration, when turned off (*short for REGENeration AUTOmatic*).

Command	Alias	Ctrl+	F-key	Alt+	Menu Bar	Tablet
'regenauto	...	...	...	...	...	...

```
Command: regenauto
Enter mode [ON/OFF] <ON>: off
```

Example:
```
Command: regen
About to regen, proceed? <Y>: ENTER
```

COMMAND LINE OPTIONS
OFF Turns on "About to regen, proceed?" message.
ON Turns off "About to regen, proceed?" message.

RELATED COMMANDS
Regen Forces a regeneration in the current viewport.
RegenAll Forces a regeneration in all viewports.

RELATED SYSTEM VARIABLES
Expert Suppresses "About to regen, proceed?" message when value is greater than 0
RegenMode Specifies the current setting of automatic regeneration:

RegenMode	Meaning
0	Off.
1	On (default).

TIPS
■ If a regeneration is caused by a transparent command, AutoCAD delays it and responds with the message, "Regen queued."

■ AutoCAD Release 12 reduces the number of regenerations by expanding the virtual screen from 16 bits to 32 bits.

Region

Rel.11   Creates a 2D region from closed objects (*an ACIS command*).

Command	Alias	Ctrl+	F-key	Alt+	Menu Bar	Tablet
region	reg	...	...	DN	Draw ↳Region	R9

```
Command: region
Select objects: [pick]
Select objects: ENTER
1 loop extracted.
1 region created.
```

Loop · Island · Loop · Island

COMMAND LINE OPTION

Select objects   Selects objects to convert to a region; AutoCAD discards unsuitable objects.

RELATED COMMANDS

All drawing commands.

RELATED SYSTEM VARIABLE

DelObj   Toggles whether objects are deleted during the conversion by the **Region** command.

TIPS

■ The **Region** command converts closed line sets, closed 2D and planar 3D polylines, and closed curves.

■ The **Region** command rejects open objects, intersections, and self-intersecting curves.

■ The resulting region is unpredictable when more than two curves share an endpoint.

■ Polylines with width lose their width when converted to a region.

■ An island can be considered a "hole" in the region.

DEFINITIONS

Curve   An object made of circles, ellipses, splines, and joined circular and elliptical arcs.

Island   A closed shape fully within (*not touching or intersecting*) another closed shape.

Loop   A closed shape made of closed polylines, closed lines, and curves.

Region   A 2D closed area defined as an ACIS object.

Reinit

Rel.12 Reinitializes the digitizer, display, plotter and input-output ports, and reloads the *Acad.Pgp* file (*short for REINITialize*).

Command	Alias	Ctrl+	F-key	Alt+	Menu Bar	Tablet
reinit	...	...	...	...	...	...

Command: **reinit**
Displays dialog box:

DIALOG BOX OPTIONS

I/O Port Initialization option:
Digitizer   Reinitializes ports connected to digitizer; grayed out if no digitizer configured.

Device and File Initialization options:
Digitizer   Reinitializes digitizer driver; grayed out if no digitizer configured.
PGP File   Reloads the *Acad.Pgp* file.

RELATED COMMAND
MenuLoad   Reloads menu files.

RELATED SYSTEM VARIABLE
Re-Init   Reinitializes via system variable settings.

RELATED FILES
Acad.Pgp   The program parameters file in *Acad 2002**Support* folder.
*.Hdi   Device drivers in *Acad 2002**Drv* folder.

TIPS
■ AutoCAD allows you to connect both the digitizer and the plotter to the same port, since you don't need the digitizer during plotting; use the **Reinit** command to reinitialize the digitizer after plotting.

■ AutoCAD reinitializes all ports and reloads the *Acad.Pgp* file each time another drawing is loaded.

Rename

<u>V.2.I</u>   Changes the names of blocks, dimension styles, layers, linetypes, plot styles, text styles, UCS names, views, and viewports.

Command	Alias	Ctrl+	F-key	Alt+	Menu Bar	Tablet
rename	ren	...	...	OR	Format ⌐Rename	V1
-rename	-ren					

Command: rename
Displays dialog box:

DIALOG BOX OPTIONS

Named Objects Lists the named objects in the drawing.
Items   Lists the names of named objects in the current drawing.
Old Name   Displays the current name of an object to be renamed.
Rename to   Allows you to enter a new name for the object.

-RENAME COMMAND
Command: **-rename**
Enter object type to rename
[Block/Dimstyle/LAyer/LType/Plotstyle/textStyle/Ucs/VIew/
    VPort]: **[enter option]**

Example usage:
Command: **-rename**
Enter object type to rename
[Block/Dimstyle/LAyer/LType/Plotstyle/textStyle/Ucs/VIew/
    VPort]: **B**
Enter old block name: **diode-20**
Enter new block name: **diode-02**

COMMAND LINE OPTIONS

Block	Changes the name of a block.
Dimstyle	Changes the name of a dimension style.
LAyer	Changes the name of a layer.
LType	Changes the name of a linetype.
Style	Changes the name of a text style.
Ucs	Changes the name of a UCS configuration.
VIew	Changes the name of a view configuration.
VPort	Changes the name of a viewport configuration.

RELATED COMMANDS

DimStyle	Changes the dimension style names.
Layer	Changes the layer names.
Style	Changes the the names of text styles.
UcsMan	Changes the name of UCS configurations.
View	Changes the names of views.
VPorts	Changes the viewport names.

RELATED SYSTEM VARIABLES

CeLType	Specifires the name of current linetype.
CLayer	Specifires the name of current layer.
CPlotStyle	Specifires the name of the current plot style.
DimStyle	Specifires the name of current dimension style.
InsName	Specifires the name of current block.
TextStyle	Specifires the name of current text style.
UcsName	Specifires the name of current UCS view.

TIPS

- You cannot rename layer "0", dimstyle "Standard", anonymous blocks, groups, or linetype "Continuous."

- To rename a group of similar names, use * (the wildcard for "all") and ? (the wildcard for a single character).

- Names can be up to 255 characters in length.

- The **Properties** command does *not* allow you to rename blocks.

- The **DdRename** command no longer works in AutoCAD 2000; use the **Rename** command instead.

- The **PlotStyle** option does not appear if the drawing contains no plot styles.

Render

Rel.12 Creates a rendering of 3D objects.

Command	Alias	Ctrl+	F-key	Alt+	Menu Bar	Tablet
render	rr	. . .	. . .	VER	View ⬑Render ⬑Render	M1

Command: **render**
Displays dialog box:

DIALOG BOX OPTIONS

Rendering Type

> Selects between basic **Render**, **Photo Real**, or **Photo Raytrace**; also lists installed third-party renderers.

Scene to Render

> Lists names of scenes defined by the **Scene** command; default = ***Current view***.

Rendering Procedure options:

Query For Selections

> **On**: Prompts you to select the objects to render; unselected objects appear in wireframe in the rendering only when you select the **Merge** option from the **Background** option.
>
> **Off**: Renders all objects in the current viewport.

Crop Window On: Prompts you to select a windowed area to render.

> **Off**: Renders the entire current viewport.

Skip Render Dialog

> Does not display the **Render** dialog box the next time you use the **Render** command.

Light icon scale
Sizes light blocks Overhead, Direct, and Sh_Spot.

Smoothing angle
Converts edges to smooth curves. For example, when the angle between two surfaces is greater than the default of 45 degrees, AutoCAD renders an edge; when less than 45 degrees, the edge is smoothed to a curve.

Rendering Options *options:*

Smooth shade Smooths the edges of multifaced surfaces.
Apply materials Applies surface materials defined by the **RMat** command.
Shadows Generates shadows when Photo Real and Photo Raytrace rendering modes are selected.
Render cache Caches the objects to help speed rendering.
More options Displays the **Render Options** dialog box, which varies according to rendering selected.

Destination *options:*

- **Viewport** displays the rendering in the current viewport.
- **Render Window** displays the rendering in a separate window.
- **File** saves the rendering to a file on disk; does not display the rendering on screen.

More Options When **File** is selected, displays **File Output Configuration** dialog box.

Sub Sampling Renders a fraction of pixels; ranges from 1:1 for best quality (default) to 8:1 for fastest.

Background Displays the **Background** dialog box; see the **Background** command.
Fog/Depth Cue
Displays the **Fog** dialog box; see the **Fog** command.
Render Renders the scene.

Render Options dailog box:

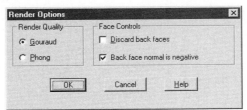

Render Quality *options:*

- **Gouraud:** Calculates light intensity at each vertex; faster.
- **Phong:** Calculates light intensity at each pixel; higher quality.

Face Controls options:

Discard back faces
> Speeds up rendering by ignoring the backs of objects.

Back face normal is negative
> Turn this option off if the rendering creates odd looking objects.

Photo Real Render Options dialog box:

Anti-Aliasing options:

- **Minimal** renders with analytical horizontal anti-aliasing; fastest rendering.
- **Low** renders with four samples per pixel.
- **Medium** renders with nine samples per pixel.
- **High** renders with 16 samples per pixel; best quality.

Face Controls options:

Discard back faces
> Speeds up rendering by ignoring the backs of objects.

Back face normal is negative
> Turn this option off if the rendering creates odd-looking objects.

Depth Map Shadow Controls options:

Minimum bias Adjusts the shadow map bias to prevent self-shadows and detached shadows; default = 2.0; ranges from 2.0 to 20.0.

Maximum bias Limited to 10 more than minimum bias; default = 4.0.

Texture Map Sampling options:

- **Point sample** renders the nearest pixel within a bitmap.
- **Linear sample** averages the four neighbor pixels pyramidically (default).
- **Mip map sample** averages pixels with the *mip* method, which pyramidically averages a square sample area.

Photo Raytrace Render Options dialog box:

Anti-Aliasing *options:*
- **Minimal** renders with analytical horizontal anti-aliasing; fastest rendering.
- **Low** renders with four samples per pixel.
- **Medium** renders with nine samples per pixel.
- **High** renders with 16 samples per pixel; best quality.

Adaptive Sampling *options:*

Enable   Toggles adaptive sampling; available when minimal anti-aliasing turned off.

Contrast Threshold

      Specifies the sensitivity of adaptive sampling; larger values increase rendering speed, but might reduce image quality; default = 0.03; ranges from 0.0 to 1.0.

Ray Tree Depth *options:*

Maximum Depth

      Limits the ray tree depth to track reflected and refracted rays; default = 3.

Cutoff Threshold

      Defines the percentage bounce cutoff; default = 0.03 means 3%.

Face Controls *options:*

Discard back faces

      Speeds up rendering by ignoring the backs of objects.

Back face normal is negative

      Turn this option off if the rendering creates odd looking objects.

Depth Map Shadow Controls *options:*

Minimum bias Adjusts shadow map bias to prevent self-shadows and detached shadows; default = 2.0; ranges from 2.0 to 20.0.

Maximum bias Limit to 10 more than minimum bias; default = 4.0.

Texture Map Sampling options:
- **Point sample** renders the nearest pixel within a bitmap.
- **Linear sample** averages the four neighbor pixels (default).
- **Mip map sample** averages pixels with the *mip* method, which pyramidically averages a square sample area.

RELATED COMMANDS

All rendering-related commands.

Hide	Removes hidden lines from wireframe view.
Replay	Displays a BMP, TIFF, or Targa raster (bitmap) file in the current viewport.
RPref	Sets up options for the **Render** command.
SaveImg	Saves the image in the current viewport to a raster file.
ShadEdge	Performs real-time shading of 3D objects.

TIPS

- If you do not place a light or define a scene, the **Render** command uses the current view and ambient light.

- If you do not select a light or scene, the **Render** command renders all objects using all lights and the current view.

- If you set up the **Render** command to skip the dialog box, use the **RPref** command to set rendering options.

- When outputting to a file, you have the following file format options: BMP, TGA, PCX, PostScript, and TIFF.

- You cannot create a rendering in paper space mode.

REMOVED COMMAND

RenderUnload was removed from Release 14. Use **Arx** to unload *Render.Arx* instead.

Your first rendering

■ *Basic rendering:*

Step 1: 3D DRAWING

Create a 3D drawing or select a 3D sample drawing.

Step 2: RENDER

Start the **Render** command, click the **Render** button, and wait a few seconds.

■ *Advanced Rendering:*

Step 1: 3D DRAWING

Create a 3D drawing or select a 3D sample drawing.

Step 2: MATLIB

Use the **MatLib** command to load material definitions into drawing.

Step 3: RMAT

Using the **RMat** command, assign materials to colors, layers, and/or objects.

Step 4: LIGHT

Use the **Light** command to place and aim lights: point, spot, and distant.

Step 5: SCENE

Use the **Scene** command to collect lights and a named view into a named object.

Step 6: RENDER

Render the named scene with the **Render** command.

Step 7: SAVEIMG

Use the **SaveImg** command to save the rendering to a TIFF, Targa, or GIF file on disk.

Step 8: REPLAY

View the saved rendering file with the **Replay** command.

RENDERING EFFECTS

Wireframe drawing:

Basic rendering; most options turned off:

Smooth Shading on:

Attach Materials on; requires Photo Real or Raytrace mode:

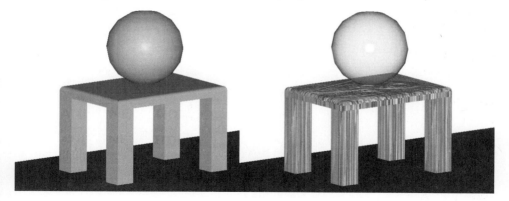

Background set to **Gradient**:

Background set to **Image**:

Fog set to white:

Fog set to black:

Shadows turned on:

Shadow Volumes turned off:

Sub Sampling set to **4:1**:

RendScr

Rel.12 Displays the most-recent rendering *(short for RENDer SCReen)*.

Command	Alias	Ctrl+	F-key	Alt+	Menu Bar	Tablet
rendscr	...	...	...	...	...	...

Command: **rendscr**

COMMAND LINE OPTIONS
None.

RELATED COMMANDS
Render   Creates a rendering of the current 3D viewport.

RELATED SYSTEM VARIABLES
None.

TIP
■ This command did not work during AutoCAD Release 14.

Replay

Rel.12 Displays a BMP, TIFF, or Targa file as a bitmap.

Command	Alias	Ctrl+	F-key	Alt+	Menu Bar	Tablet
replay	. . .	. . .	. . .	TDV	Tools	V8
					⤷Display Image	
					⤷View	

Command: **replay**
*Displays the **Select File** dialog box; select file.*
Displays dialog box:

DIALOG BOX OPTIONS

Image   Selects the displayed area by clicking on image tile.
Image Offset   Specifies the x,y coordinates of the image's lower-left corner.
Image Size   Specifies the size of the image in pixels.
Screen   Defines the maximum size of the image.
Screen Offset Specifies the x,y coordinates of the image's lower-left corner.
Reset   Restores the default values.

RELATED COMMANDS

Import   Displays a dialog-box frontend to loading some raster and vector files.
SaveImg   Saves a rendering as a GIF, TIFF, or Targa raster file.

RELATED FILES

*.BMP   Any Windows bitmap file.
*.TIF   Any RGBA TIFF file, up to 32-bits in color depth.
*.TGA   Any RGBA Targa v2.0 file, up to 32-bits in color depth.

In subdirectory \Acad 2002\Textures:
*.TGA   Contains many Targa-format images.

'Resume

V. 2.0 Resumes a script file after pausing it by pressing the **BACKSPACE** key.

Command	Alias	Ctrl+	F-key	Alt+	Menu Bar	Tablet
'resume	...	...	...	...	...	...

Command: **resume**

COMMAND LINE OPTIONS

BACKSPACE	Pauses the script file.
Esc	Stops the script file.

RELATED COMMANDS

RScript	Reruns the current script file.
Script	Loads and runs a script file.

Revolve

Rel.11 Creates a 3D solid object by revolving a closed 2D object about an axis *(formerly the **SolRev** command; an ACIS command).*

Command	Alias	Ctrl+	F-key	Alt+	Menu Bar	Tablet
revolve	rev	...	...	DIR	Draw	Q7
					⌐Solids	
					⌐Revolve	

```
Command: revolve
Current wire frame density:   ISOLINES=4
Select objects: [pick]
1 found Select objects: ENTER
Specify start point for axis of revolution or define axis
   by [Object/X (axis)/Y (axis)]: o
Select an object: [pick]
Specify angle of revolution <360>: ENTER
```

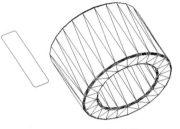

*The **REVOLVE** command uses the polyline rectangle (left) to create the solid object (right).*

COMMAND LINE OPTIONS

Select objects Selects a closed object to revolve: closed polyline, circle, ellipse, donut, polygon, closed spline, or a region.

Axis of revolution options:

Specify start point for axis of revolution
Indicates the axis of revolution; you must specify the endpoints.

Object Selects the object that determines the axis of revolution.

X Uses the positive x axis as axis of revolution.

Y Uses the positive y axis as axis of revolution.

Specify angle of rotation
Specifies the amount of rotation; full circle = 360 degrees.

RELATED COMMANDS

Extrude Extrudes 2D objects into a 3D solid model.

Rotate Rotates open and closed objects, forming a 3D surface.

TIPS

■ **Revolve** works with just one object at a time.

■ **Revolve** will not work with open objects, crossing, or self-intersecting polylines.

RevSurf

Rel.10 Generates a 3D surface of revolution defined by a path curve and an axis (*short for REVolved SURFace*).

Command	Alias	Ctrl+	F-key	Alt+	Menu Bar	Tablet
revsurf	...	...	...	DFS	Draw	O8
					⃰Surfaces	
					⃰Revolved Surface	

```
Command: revsurf
Current wire frame density: SURFTAB1=6  SURFTAB2=6
Select object to revolve: [pick]
Select object that defines the axis of revolution: [pick]
Specify start angle <0>: ENTER
Specify included angle (+=ccw, -=cw) <360>: ENTER
```

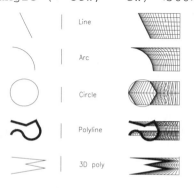

	Line	
	Arc	
	Circle	
	Polyline	
	3D poly	

Path Curve + Axis = Resulting Revolved Surface

COMMAND LINE OPTIONS

Select object to revolve
Selects the single object that will be revolved about an axis.

Select object that defines the axis of revolution
Selects the axis object.

Start angle Specifies the starting angle.

Included angle Specifies the angle to rotate about the axis.

RELATED COMMANDS

PEdit Edits revolved surfaces.

Revolve Revolves a 2D closed object into a 3D solid.

RELATED SYSTEM VARIABLES

SurfTab1 Specifies the mesh density in m-direction (default = 6).

SurfTab2 Specifies the mesh density in n-direction (default = 6).

TIPS

■ Unlike the **Revolve** command, **RevSurf** works with open and closed objects.

■ If a multi-segment polyline is the axis of revolution, the rotation axis is defined as the vector pointing from the first vertex to the last vertex, ignoring the intermediate vertices.

RMat

Rel.13 Applies material definitions to colors, layers, and objects; used by the **Render** command (*short for Render MATerials*).

Command	Alias	Ctrl+	F-key	Alt+	Menu Bar	Tablet
rmat	...	...	...	VEM	View	P1
					⬏Render	
					⬏Materials	

Command: **rmat**
Displays dialog box:

DIALOG BOX OPTIONS

Materials	Lists the names of materials loaded into drawing, by the **MatLib** command.
Preview	Previews the material mapped to a sphere or cube.
Materials Library	
	Displays the **Materials Library** dialog box; see the **MatLib** command.
Select	Selects the objects to which to attach the material definition.
Modify	Edits a material definition; displays a different **Modify Material** dialog box for standard, granite, marble and wood-based materials; see the **New** option.
Duplicate	Duplicates a material definition so that you can edit it; displays a different **Modify Material** dialog box for standard, granite, marble and wood-based materials; see the **New** option.
New	Creates a new material definition; displays a different dialog box for the four types of materials: standard, granite, marble, wood.
Attach	Selects the objects to which to attach the material definition.
Detach	Selects the objects from which to detach the material definition.

By ACI Attaches material via ACI number; displays dialog box:

By Layer Attaches material to a layer name; displays dialog box:

New Material options:

Material Name Names the material.

Value Adjusts the value of selected **Attributes** between 0 and a larger number.

Color options:

By ACI Specifies that the aterial's base color is the same as the object's color.

Lock Locks the ambient and reflective colors to the base color.

Mirror Allows mirrored reflection.

Color System Selects RGB or HLS color system:

- **HLS** specifies color by levels of Hue, Luminescence, and Saturation.

- **RGB** specifies color by levels of Red, Green, Blue.

Bitmap Blend Determines the degree the bitmap is rendered.

File Name Specifies the bitmap's filename.

Adjust Bitmap Displays the **Adjust Material Bitmap Placement** dialog box.

Find File Selects the bitmap file; displays the **Bitmap File** dialog box.

New Standard Material dialog box:

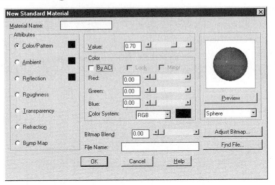

Attributes options:
- **Color/Pattern** sets the base color of the material.
- **Ambient** sets the ambient color shown in shadowed areas.
- **Reflection** sets the highlight color of the material.
- **Roughness** sets the size of the highlighted area; the higher the value of the roughness, the larger the highlight area.
- **Transparency** sets the amount of transparency of the material:

Transparency	Meaning
0.0	No transparency.
0.1 *through* 9.9	Increasing transparency with edge fall-off.
1.0	Perfect transparency.

- **Refraction** controls refraction of the material; Photo Raytrace rendering only.
- **Bump Map** attaches a bitmap to the material.

New Granite Material dialog box:

Attributes options:

- **First Color** sets the base color of the granite material.
- **Second Color** sets the second color of the granite material.
- **Third Color** sets the third color of the granite material.
- **Fourth Color** sets the fourth color of the granite material.
- **Reflection** sets the highlight color of the material.
- **Roughness** sets the size of the highlighted area; the higher the value of the roughness, the larger the highlighted area.
- **Sharpness** sets the sharpness of the four colors of the material:

Sharpness	Meaning
0.0	Complete blurring of colors.
0.1 *through* 9.9	Increasing sharpness of colors.
1.0	All four colors are perfectly distinct.

- **Scale** sizes the material relative to its attached object.
- **Bump Map** attaches a bitmap to the material.

New Marble Material dialog box:

Attributes *options:*
- **Stone Color** sets the base color of the marble material.
- **Vein Color** sets the secondary color of the marble material.
- **Reflection** sets the highlight color of the material.
- **Roughness** sets the size of the highlighted area; the higher the value of the roughness, the larger the highlighted area.
- **Turbulence** determines the swirling of the vein color.
- **Sharpness** sets the sharpness of the four colors of the material:

Sharpness	Meaning
0.0	Complete blurring of colors.
0.1 *through* 9.9	Increasing sharpness of colors
1.0	All colors are perfectly distinct.

New Wood Material dialog box:

Attributes options:
- **Light Color** sets the base color of the wood material.
- **Dark Color** sets the secondary color of the wood material.
- **Reflection** sets the highlight color of the material.
- **Roughness** sets the size of the highlighteded area; the higher the value of the roughness, the larger the highlight area.
- **Light/Dark** sets the amount of contrast between the two colors of the material:

Light/Dark	Meaning
0.0	Dark color.
0.1 *through* **9.9**	Increasing lightness of color.
1.0	Light color.

- **Ring Density** specifies the number of rings in the material definition.
- **Ring Width** specifies the variation in ring width; 0 = narrow rings; 1.0 = wide rings.
- **Ring Shape** specifies 0 = circular rings; 1.0 = irregular rings.
- **Scale** sizes the material relative to its attached object.
- **Bump Map** attaches a bitmap to the material.

RELATED COMMANDS

MatLib   Loads material definitions into the drawing.
Render   Renders drawing using material definitions.

TIPS

■ The **By ACI** option lets you attach a material definition to all objects of one color.

■ The **By Layer** option lets you attach a material definition to all objects on one layer.

RMLin

<u>2000i</u> Inserts a redline markup file from Autodesk Volo products (*short for Redline Markup Language INput*).

Command	Alias	Ctrl+	F-key	Alt+	Menu Bar	Tablet
rotate3d	...	...	...	IU	Insert ⬦Markup	...

Command: **rmlin**
Displays file dialog box; select .RML file, and click **OK**.

COMMAND LINE OPTIONS
None.

RELATED COMMANDS
DxfIn   Inserts a DXF file, which could contain redline markups from non-Autodesk viewer software.

TIPS
■ Redlines or markup are comments added to drawings; redlines are not normally part of the drawing. Redlines consists of notes, circles, arrows, hyperlinks, etc.

■ This command is meant for use with Autodesk's own viewing and redlining software, called Volo. It saves redlines in RML files.

■ When an RML file is inserted in the drawing, AutoCAD places it on a new layer called "Markup." This layer has the following properties that differ from the defaults:

Property	Value
Name	Markup.
Color	Red.
Locked/unlocked	Locked.

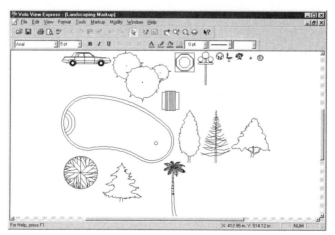

Volo View Express marks up AutoCAD drawing with "redlines."

⟳ Rotate

V. 2.5 Rotates objects about a base point in the 2D plane.

Command	Alias	Ctrl+	F-key	Alt+	Menu Bar	Tablet
rotate	ro	...	...	MR	Modify ⌐Rotate	V20

```
Command: rotate
Current positive angle in UCS: ANGDIR=counterclockwise  ANGBASE=0
Select objects: [pick]
1 found Select objects: ENTER
Specify base point: [pick]
Specify rotation angle or [Reference]: [pick]
```

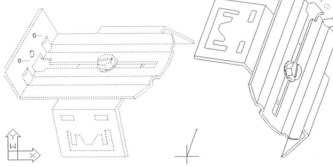

Base point

COMMAND LINE OPTIONS

Select objects Selects the objects to be rotated.

Specify base point
    Picks the point about which the objects will be rotated.

Specify rotation angle
    Specifies the angle by which the objects will be rotated.

Reference Allows you to specify the current rotation angle and new rotation angle.

RELATED COMMANDS

Rotate3D Rotates objects in 3D space.
UCS Rotates the coordinate system.
Snap Rotates the cursor.

TIPS

■ AutoCAD rotates the selected object(s) about the base point.

■ At the 'Specify rotation angle' prompt, you can show the rotation by moving the cursor. AutoCAD dynamically displays the new rotated position as you move the cursor.

■ Use object snap modes, such as INTersection, to position the base point accurately, as well as the rotation angle(s).

Rotate3D

Rel.11 Rotates objects about an axis in 3D space.

Command	Alias	Ctrl+	F-key	Alt+	Menu Bar	Tablet
rotate3d	...	...	...	M3R	Modify	W22
					⤷3D Operation	
					⤷Rotate 3D	

Command: **rotate3d**
Current positive angle: ANGDIR=counterclockwise ANGBASE=0
Select objects: **[pick]**
1 found Select objects: ENTER
Specify first point on axis or define axis by
    [Object/Last/View/Xaxis/Yaxis/Zaxis/2points]: **[pick]**
Specify second point on axis: **[pick]**
Specify rotation angle or [Reference]: **[pick]**
Specify second point: **[pick]**

COMMAND LINE OPTIONS

Select objects Selects the objects to be rotated.
Specify rotation angle
              Rotates objects by a specified angle: relative rotation.
Reference   Specifies starting and ending angle: absolute rotation.

Define axis by options:
Object   Selects object to specify the rotation axis.
Last   Selects the previous axis.
View   Specifies that the current view direction is the rotation axis.
Xaxis   Specifies that the x axis is the rotation axis.
Yaxis   Specifies that the y axis is the rotation axis.
Zaxis   Specifies that the z axis is the rotation axis.
2 points   Defines two points on the rotation axis.

RELATED COMMANDS

Align   Rotates, moves, and scales objects in 3D space.
Mirror3d   Mirrors objects in 3D space.
Rotate   Rotates objects in 2D space.

RPref

Rel.12 Specifies options for the **Render** command (*short for Render PREFerences*).

Command	Alias	Ctrl+	F-key	Alt+	Menu Bar	Tablet
rpref	rpr	...	...	VEP	View ↳Render ↳Preferences	R2

Command: **rpref**
Displays dialog box:

DIALOG BOX OPTIONS

Options are identical to the **Render** *command, with the exception of the* **OK** *button replacing the* **Render** *button.*

RELATED COMMANDS

All rendering-related commands.

Hide   Removes hidden lines from wireframe view.
Render   Renders the scene.
ShadEdge   Produces real-time shading of 3D objects.
3dOrbit   Creates perspective view.

TIP

■ If you set up the **Render** command to skip the dialog box, use the **RPref** command to set rendering options.

'RScript

<u>**V. 2.0**</u> Repeats the script file (*short for Repeat SCRIPT*).

Command	Alias	Ctrl+	F-key	Alt+	Menu Bar	Tablet
'rscript	...	...	...	...	...	...

Command: **rscript**

COMMAND LINE OPTIONS
None.

RELATED COMMANDS
Resume   Resumes a script file after being interrupted.
Script   Loads and runs a script file.

RuleSurf

Draws a 3D ruled surface between two objects (*short for RULEd SURFace*).

Command	Alias	Ctrl+	F-key	Alt+	Menu Bar	Tablet
rulesurf	...	...	...	DFR	Draw	Q8
					⬐Surfaces	
					⬐Ruled Surface	

```
Command: rulesurf
Select first defining curve: [pick]
Select second defining curve: [pick]
```

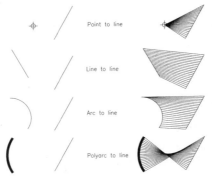

Point to line

Line to line

Arc to line

Polyarc to line

COMMAND LINE OPTIONS

Select first defining curve
> Selects the first object for the ruled surface.

Select second defining curve
> Selects the second object for the ruled surface.

RELATED COMMANDS

Edgesurf	Draws a 3D surface bounded by four edges.
Revsurf	Draws a 3D surface of revolution.
Tabsurf	Draws a 3D tabulated surface.

RELATED SYSTEM VARIABLE

SurfTab1   Determines the number of rules drawn.

TIPS

■ **RuleSurf** uses objects as the boundary curve: point, line, arc, circle, polyline, 3D polyline.

■ Both boundaries must either be closed or open; the exception is using the point object.

■ The **RuleSurf** command begins drawing its mesh as follows:

Object	RuleSurf
Open object	From the object's endpoint closest to your pick.
Circle	From the zero-degree quadrant.
Closed polyline	From the last vertex.

Save and SaveAs

V. 2.0 Saves the drawing to disk, after prompting for a filename.

Command	Alias	Ctrl+	F-key	Alt+	Menu Bar	Tablet
save	saveurl	...	...	...	...	...
saveas	...	...	...	FA	File ⮑Save As	V24

Command: **save** *or* **saveas**
Displays dialog box.

DIALOG BOX OPTIONS

Save in   Selects the folder, hard drive, or network drive in which to save the drawing.

File name   Names the drawing; maximum=255 characters; default=*Drawing1.Dwg*.

Save as type   Saves the drawing in a variety of DWG formats:

Save as type	Meaning
AutoCAD 2000 DWG	Saves the drawing in native format.
R14, LT 98/97 DWG	Exports the drawing in R14 DWG format.
R13, LT 95 DWG	Exports the drawing in R13 DWG format.
AutoCAD 2000 DXF	Exports the drawing in 2000 DXF format.
R14, LT 98/97 DXF	Exports the drawing in R14 DXF format.
R13, LT 95 DXF	Exports the drawing in R13 DXF format.
R12, LT 2 DXF	Exports the drawing in R12 DXF format.
Standard DWS	Saves the drawing as a CAD standard.
Template DWT	Saves the drawing in the *Template* folder.

Save   Saves the drawing and returns to AutoCAD. If a drawing of the same name already exists in the same subdirectory, displays dialog box:

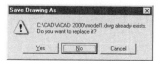

Cancel   Does not save the drawing.

Tools | Options dialog box:

O K   Accepts the changes and returns to the **Save Drawing** dialog box.

Cancel   Ignores the changes and returns to the **Save Drawing** dialog box.

DWG Options tab:

Save proxy images of custom objects

        On: Saves an image of the custom objects in the drawing file.

        Off: Saves a frame around each custom object.

Index type   Saves indices with drawing; useful only for xrefed and partially-loaded drawings:

Index type	Meaning
None	Creates no indices (default).
Layer	Loads layers that are on and thawed.
Spatial	Loads only the visible portion of a clipped xref.
Layer and Spatial	Combines the above two options.

DXF Options tab:

Select objects   Allows you to save selected objects to the DXF file; AutoCAD prompts you: "Select objects:"

Save thumbnail preview image

        Saves a thumbnail image of the drawing.

Decimal places of accuracy

        Specifies the number of decimal places for real numbers; range 0 to 16.

Format options:

ASCII   Saves the drawing in ASCII format, which can be read by humans – as well as common text editors – but takes up more disk space.

BINARY   Saves the drawing in binary format, which takes up less disk space, but cannot be read by some software programs.

Template Description dialog box:
Displayed when drawing is saved as a DWT template file:

Description   Describes the template file; stored in *Wizard.Ini*.
Measurement   Selects English or metric as the default measurement system.

RELATED COMMANDS

Export   Saves the drawing in a variety of raster and vector formats.
Plot   Saves the drawing in even more raster and vector formats.
Quit   Exits AutoCAD without saving the drawing.
QSave   Saves the drawing without prompting for a name.

RELATED SYSTEM VARIABLES

DBMod   Indicates that the drawing was modified since being opened.
DwgName   Specifies the name of the drawing; *Drawing1.Dwg* when unnamed.

TIPS

■ The **Save** and **SaveAs** command perform exactly the same function.

■ Use these commands to save the drawing by another name.

■ When a drawing is opened as read-only, use these commands to save the drawing to another filename.

■ To save a drawing without seeing the **Save Drawing As** dialog box, use the **QSave** command.

REMOVED COMMAND

SaveAsR12 was removed from AutoCAD Release 14. Use **SaveAs** instead, which saves drawings in Release 14, 13, and 12 formats.

Rel.12

DIALOG BOX OPTIONS

Format options:

- **BMP** saves in Windows bitmap format.
- **TGA** saves in Targa format.
- **TIFF** saves in Tagged image file format.

Options   Displays **Options** dialog box.

Portion options:

Active viewport Selects the area of the current viewport to save.
Offset   Specifies the lower-left x,y coordinates of the image area (default = 0,0).
Size   Specifies the upper-right x,y coordinates of the image area.

TGA Options dialog box:

- **None** saves TGA file with no file compression.
- **RLE** saves TGA file with run-length encoded compression.

TIFF Options dialog box:

- **None** saves TIFF file with no compression.
- **PACK** saves TIFF file with pack bits compression.

RELATED COMMANDS

Replay   Displays a raster image in the current viewport.
PRTSCR   Saves the entire screen to the Clipboard.

TIPS

■ The **SaveImg** command saves files in these formats:

Format	Specification
BMP	24-bit Windows bitmap.
TGA	32-bit RGBA TrueVision v2.0
TIFF	32-bit RGBA tagged image file.

■ The GIF format, which is used to display images on the Internet and was found in AutoCAD Release 12 and 13, was replaced by the less useful BMP format in AutoCAD Release 14.

REMOVED COMMAND

SaveUrl was removed from AutoCAD 2000; it was replaced by **Save** and **SaveAs**.

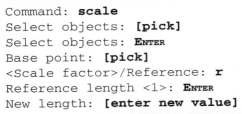

Scale

V. 2.5 Changes the size of selected objects, to make them smaller or larger.

Command	Alias	Ctrl+	F-key	Alt+	Menu Bar	Tablet
scale	sc	...	...	ML	Modify ⤷Scale	V21

```
Command: scale
Select objects: [pick]
Select objects: ENTER
Base point: [pick]
<Scale factor>/Reference: r
Reference length <1>: ENTER
New length: [enter new value]
```

Base point

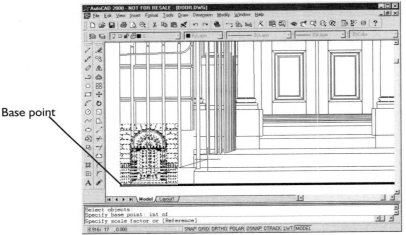

COMMAND LINE OPTIONS

Base point   Specifies the point from which scaling takes place.
Reference   Supplies a reference value, followed by a new value.
Scale factor   Indicates the scale factor, which applies equally in the x and y directions.

Scale Factor	Meaning
> 1.0	Enlarges the size of the object(s).
1.0	Makes no change.
> 0.0 *and* < 1.0	Reduces the size of the object(s).
0.0 *or negative*	Illegal values.

RELATED COMMANDS

Align   Scales an object in 3D space.
Insert   Allows a block to be scaled independently in the x, y, and z directions.
Plot   Allows a drawing to be plotted at any scale.

ScaleText

Changes the height of text relative to its insertion point..

Command	Alias	Ctrl+	F-key	Alt+	Menu Bar	Tablet
scaletext	...	...	...	MOTS	Modify ⤷Object ⤷Text ⤷Scale	...

```
Command: scaletext
Select objects: [pick]
Select objects: ENTER
Enter a base point for scaling
[Existing/Left/Center/Middle/Right/TL/TC/TR/ML/MC/MR/BL/BC/BR]
    <Existing>: ENTER
Specify new height or [Match object/Scale factor] <0.2000>:
    [enter option]
```

COMMAND LINE OPTIONS

Enter a base point for scaling
Specifies the point from which scaling takes place.
Existing Uses the existing insertion point.
Specify new height
Specifies the new height of the text.
Match object Matches the height of another text object.
Scale factor Scales the text by a factor:

Scale Factor	Meaning
> 1.0	Enlarges the size of the object(s).
1.0	Makes no change in size.
> 0.0 *and* < 1.0	Reduces the size of the object(s).
0.0 *or negative*	Illegal values.

RELATED COMMANDS

Justify	Changes the justification of the text.
Properties	Changes all aspects of the text.
Style	Creates text styles.

TIP

■ *Caution!* Scaling text larger may make it overlap nearby existing text.

Commands: S ■ 549

Scene

Rel.12 Collects lights and a viewpoint into a named scene prior to rendering.

Command	Alias	Ctrl+	F-key	Alt+	Menu Bar	Tablet
scene	. . .	. . .	. . .	VES	View	N1
					⤷Render	
					⤷Scene	

Command: **scene**
Displays dialog box:

DIALOG BOX OPTIONS

New	Creates a new named scene; displays the **New Scene** dialog box.
Modify	Changes an existing scene definition; displays the **Modify Scene** dialog box.
Delete	Deletes a scene from drawing; displays dialog box:

New Scene dialog box:

Scene Name	Allows you to enter a name for the scene; maximum = 8 characters.
Views	Selects one named view.
Lights	Selects one or more lights.

Modify Scene dialog box:

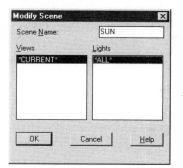

Scene name   Allows you to change the name for the scene; maximum = 8 characters.
Views   Selects one named view.
Lights   Selects one or more lights.

RELATED COMMANDS
Light   Places lights in the drawing for the **Scene** command.
Render   Uses scenes to create renderings.
RPref   Specifies options for renderings.
View   Creates named views for the **Scene** command.

TIPS
■ Before you can use the **Scene** command, you need to create at least one named view (with the **View** command), or place at least one light (with the **Light** command). Otherwise, there is no need to use the **Scene** command.

■ If you select no lights for a scene, **Render** uses ambient light.

■ Scene parameters are stored as attribute definitions in a block.

'Script

V. 1.4 Runs an ASCII file containing a sequence of AutoCAD instructions to execute a series of commands automatically.

Command	Alias	Ctrl+	F-key	Alt+	Menu Bar	Tablet
'script	scr	...	...	TR	Tools ↳Run Script	V9

Command: **script**
*Displays the **Select Script File** dialog box.*
Script file begins running as soon as it is loaded.

COMMAND LINE OPTIONS

BACKSPACE	Interrupts the script.
ESC	Stops the script.
~	Displays the file dialog box when **FileDia** is 0.

RELATED COMMANDS

Delay	Specifies the delay in milliseconds; pauses the script before executing the next command.
Resume	Resumes a script after a script was interrupted.
RScript	Repeats a script file.

TIPS

■ Since the **Script** command is transparent, it can be used during another command.

■ Prefix the **VSlide** command with * to preload it; this results in a faster slide show:

*vslide

■ You can make a script file more flexible — such as pause for user input, branch with conditionals — by inserting AutoLISP functions.

Writing your first script file

A script file consist of the exact keystrokes you enter for any command.

Step 1: START TEXT EDITOR

The script file must be plain ASCII text. Write the script using a text editor, such as Notepad, not a word processor.

Step 2: WRITE SCRIPT

Here is an example script that places a door symbol in the drawing:

```
; Inserts DOOR2436 symbol at x,y = (76,100)
; x-scale = 0.5, y-scale = 1.0, rotation = 90 degrees
insert door2436 76,100 0.5 1.0 90
```

In the script, these characters have special meaning:

Character	Meaning
	(*Space or end-of-line*) Equivalent to pressing the spacebar or ENTER key.
;	(*Semi-colon*) Include a comment in the script file.
*	(*Asterisk*) Prefix the **VSlide** command to preload the SLD file.

Step 3: SAVE FILE

Saves script file with any filename and the .SCR extension. For this example, use *InsertDoorBlock.Scr*.

Step 4: SCRIPT COMMAND

Return to AutoCAD, and run the script with the **Script** command:

```
Command: script
Script file: insertdoorblock.scr
Command: insert
Block name (or ?): door2436
Insertion point: 76,100
X scale factor <1>/Corner/XYZ: 0.5
Y scale factor (default = X):1.0
Rotation angle <0>:90
```

Step 5: RSCRIPT COMMAND

If required, you can rerun the script with the **RScript** command.

Section

Rel. 11 Creates a 2D region object from the intersection of a plane and a 3D solid (*an ACIS command*).

Command	Alias	Ctrl+	F-key	Alt+	Menu Bar	Tablet
section	sec	...	...	DIE	Draw ↳Solid ↳Section	...

```
Command: section
Select objects: [pick]
Select objects: ENTER
Section plane by Object/Zaxis/View/XY/YZ/ZX/<3 points>:
```

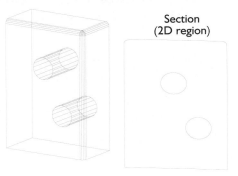

Section
(2D region)

COMMAND LINE OPTIONS

Select objects   Selects the 3D ACIS solid objects to be sectioned.

Section plane options:

Object	Aligns the section plane with an object: circle, ellipse, arc, elliptical arc, 2D spline, or 2D polyline.
Zaxis	Specifies the normal (*z axis*) to the section plane.
View	Uses the current view plane as the section plane.
XY	Uses the x,y plane of the current view.
YZ	Uses the y,z plane of the current view.
ZX	Uses the z,x plane of the current view.
3 points	Picks three points to specify the section plane.

RELATED COMMAND

Slice   Cuts a slice out of a solid model, creating another 3D solid.

TIPS

■ Section blocks are placed on the current layer, not the object's layer.

■ Regions are ignored.

■ One cutting plane is required for each selected solid.

■ The **Last** option was removed from AutoCAD Release 13.

Select

V. 2.5 Creates a selection set of objects before executing a command.

Command	Alias	Ctrl+	F-key	Alt+	Menu Bar	Tablet
select	...	...	...	...	...	...

```
Command: select
Select objects: [pick]
Select objects: ENTER
```

COMMAND LINE OPTIONS

[pick]	Selects a single object.
A U	Switches from [pick] to **C** or **W** modes, depending on whether an object is found at the initial pick point (*short for AUtomatic*).
ALL	Selects all objects in the drawing.
BOX	Goes into **C** or **W** mode, depending on how the cursor moves.
C	Selects objects in and crossing the selection box (*Crossing*).
CP	Selects all objects inside and crossing the selection polygon.
F	Selects all objects crossing a selection polyline (*short for Fence*).
G	Selects objects contained in a named group (*short for Group*).
M	Makes multiple selections before AutoCAD scans the drawing; saves time in a large drawing (*short for Multiple*).
SI	Selects only a single set of objects before terminating the **Select** command (*short for SIngle*).
W	Selects all objects inside the selection box (*short for Window*).
WP	Selects objects inside the selection polygon (*short for Windowed Polygon*).
L	Selects the last-drawn object still visible on the screen (*Last*).
P	Selects the previously-selected objects (*short for Previous*).
R	Removes objects from the selection set (*short for Remove*).
U	Removes the most-recently added selected objects (*short for Undo*).
A	Continues to add objects after using the **R** option (*short for Add*).
ENTER	Exits the **Select** command.
ESC	Aborts the **Select** command.

RELATED COMMANDS

All commands that prompt 'Select objects'.

Filter	Specifies objects to be added to the selection set.
QSelect	Selects objects via dialog box interface.

RELATED SYSTEM VARIABLES

PickAdd	Controls how objects are added to a selection set.
PickAuto	Controls automatic windowing at the 'Select objects' prompt.
PickDrag	Controls the method of creating a selection box.
PickFirst	Controls the command-object selection order.

TIPS

- **Select All** selects all objects in the drawing, except those on frozen and locked layers:

- **Select Crossing** selects objects within and crossing the selection rectangle (*shown in gray*):

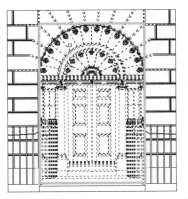

- **Select Window** selects objects within the selection rectangle (*shown in gray*):

■ **Select Fence** selects objects crossing the selection polyline (*shown in gray*):

■ **Select CPolygon** selects objects within and crossing the selection polygon (*shown in gray*):

■ **Select WPolygon** selects objects within the selection polygon (*shown in gray*):

SelectURL

Rel.14 Selects all objects and areas that have hyperlinks attached to them (*an undocumented command*).

Command	Alias	Ctrl+	F-key	Alt+	Menu Bar	Tablet
selecturl	. . .	. . .	. . .	. . .	. . .	. . .

Command: **selecturl**
Highlights all objects and areas with a hyperlink.

COMMAND LINE OPTIONS
None.

RELATED COMMANDS
AttachURL Attaches a URL to an object or an area.
Hyperlink Attaches URLs to objects via a dialog box.

TIPS
■ Examples of URLs include:

http://data.autodesk.com	Autodesk Data Publishing Web site.
http://www.autodesk.com	Autodesk primary Web site.
http://www.autodeskpress.com	Autodesk Press Web site.
news://adesknews.autodesk.com	Autodesk news server.
ftp://ftp.autodesk.com	Autodesk FTP server.
http://www.upfrontezine.com	Author Ralph Grabowski's Web site.

■ Don't delete layer URLLAYER.

■ The URL is stored as follows:

Attachment	URL
One object	Stored as xdata (extended entity data).
Multiple objects	Stored as xdata in each object.
Area	Stored as xdata in a rectangle object on layer URLLAYER.

DEFINITIONS
DWF Short for "drawing Web format," Autodesk's file format for displaying drawings on the Internet.

URL Short for "uniform resource locator," the universal file naming convention.

 # SetUV

Rel.14   Maps materials onto objects for rendering.

Command	Alias	Ctrl+	F-key	Alt+	Menu Bar	Tablet
setuv	• • •	• • •	• • •	VEA	View ↳Render ↳Mapping	R1

```
Command: setuv
Select objects: [pick]
Select objects: ENTER
Updating the Render geometry database...
```
Displays dialog box:

DIALOG BOX OPTIONS

Projection options:

- **Planar** specifies a plane for projecting the bitmap onto the selected object.
- **Cylindrical** specifies an axis of the cylindrical coordinate system and wrap line for projecting the bitmap onto the selected object.
- **Spherical** specifies the polar axis of the spherical coordinate system and wrap line for projecting the bitmap onto the selected object.
- **Solid** adjusts the coordinates to shift marble, granite, or wood materials.

Adjust Coordinates
Displays different dialog boxes, depending on the setting of **Projection**.

Acquire From Dismisses the dialog box temporarily allowing you to select a mapping object already existing in the drawing.

Copy To Dismisses the dialog box temporarily allowing you to select the objects to which to apply the mapping.

Adjust Planar Coordinates dialog box:

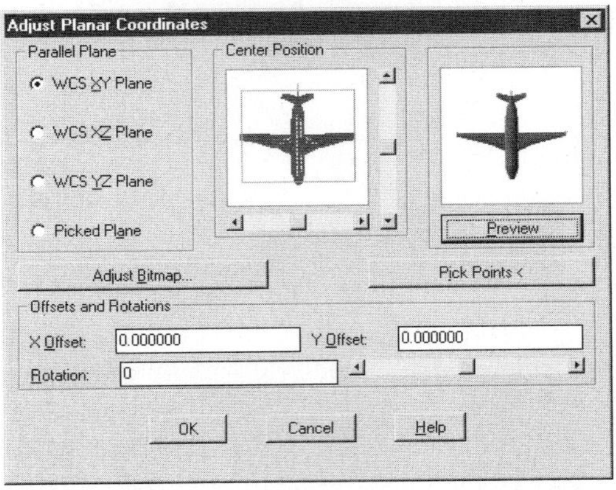

Parallel Plane Selects a WCS reference or picks a plane with the **Pick Points** radio button.
Center Position Shows a parallel projection of the selected object's mesh onto the current parallel plane:

Position	Meaning
Blue	Current projection square.
Blue tick mark	Top of the projection square.
Green	Projection square's left edge.

Adjust Bitmap Displays the **Adjust Object Bitmap Placement** dialog box.
Pick Points Specifies a projection plane by picking points in the drawing.
Offset Changes the x and y offset of the map.
Rotation Changes the rotation angle of the map.

Adjust Cylindrical Coordinates dialog box:

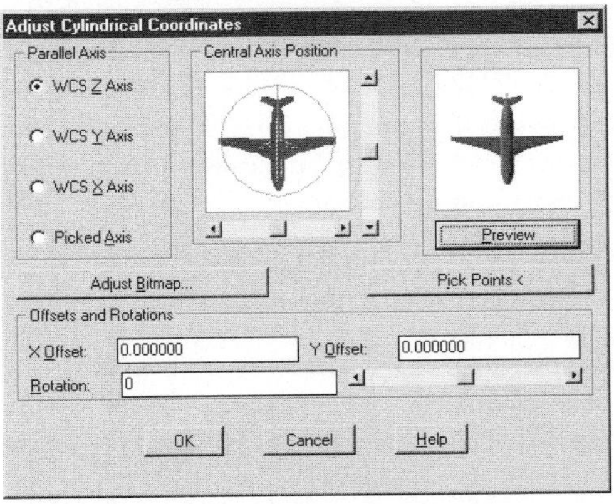

Parallel Axis Selects a WCS reference axis of the WCS, or picks an axis with the **Pick Points** radio button.

Central Axis Position

Displays a parallel projection of the object's mesh onto a plane perpendicular to the current axis.

Position	Meaning
Blue circle	Projection axis.
Green radius	Wrap line.

Adjust Bitmap Displays the **Adjust Object Bitmap Placement** dialog box.
Pick Points Specifies a projection axis by picking points in the drawing.
Offset Changes the x and y offset of the map.
Rotation Changes the rotation angle of the map.

Adjust Spherical Coordinates dialog box:

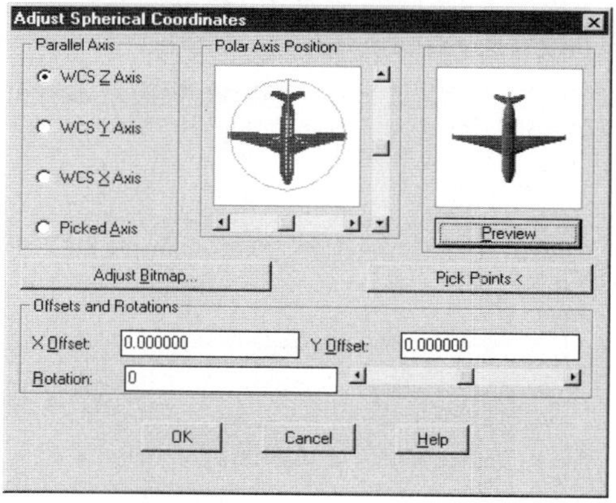

Parallel Axis Selects one of the three perpendicular axes of the WCS, or picks an axis with the **Pick Points** button.

Polar Axis Position

Displays a parallel projection of the object's mesh onto a plane perpendicular to the current axis.

Position	Meaning
Blue circle	Projection axis.
Green radius	Wrap line.

Adjust Bitmap Displays the **Adjust Object Bitmap Placement** dialog box.
Pick Points Specifies a projection axis by picking points in the drawing.
Offset Changes the x and y offset of the map.
Rotation Changes the rotation angle of the map.

Adjust Solid Coordinates dialog box:

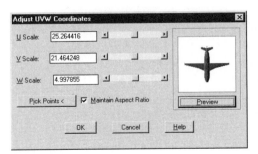

U Scale, V Scale, W Scale

Sets 3D projection coordinates.

Pick Points Specifies a projection axis by picking points in the drawing.

Adjust Object Bitmap Placement dialog box:

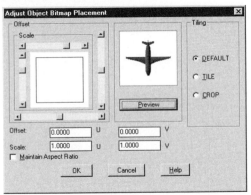

Offset Sets the u and v offset distances via slider bars interactively.

Scale Sets the u and v scale of the bitmap interactively.

Tiling options:

Tile Tiles the bitmap.

Crop Doesn't tile the bitmap.

TIPS

- The upper-left corner pixel of the bitmap defines the transparent color; to have no transparent colors in the bitmap, deliberately make that pixel a unique color.

- **Crop** tiling turns on transparent mode: all pixels have the same color as the upper-left pixel, which is treated as transparent.

- UV (and sometimes W) are equivalent to x,y,z coordinates; the letters U, V, W are used, however, because they are independent of the x,y,z coordinates.

'SetVar

V. 2.5 Lists the settings of system variables; allows you to change variables that are not read-only *(short for SET VARiable)*.

Command	Alias	Ctrl+	F-key	Alt+	Menu Bar	Tablet
'setvar	set	...	...	TQV	Tools ↳Inquiry ↳Set Variable	U10

```
Command: setvar
Enter variable name or [?]: [enter a name]
```

Example:
```
Command: setvar
Enter variable name or [?]: visretain
Enter new value for VISRETAIN <0>: 1
```

COMMAND LINE OPTIONS

Enter variable name
> Indicates the system variable name you want to access.

?   Lists the names and settings of system variables.

TIPS

■ See *Appendix A* for the complete list of all system variables found in AutoCAD 2002.

■ Almost all system variables can be entered without the **SetVar** command. For example:

```
Command: visretain
New value for VISRETAIN <0>: 1
```

REMOVED COMMAND

Shade was removed from AutoCAD 2000; it was replaced by **ShadeMode**.

ShadeMode

2000 Quickly generates renderings of 3D models in a variety of modes (*replaces the **Shade** command*).

Command	Alias	Ctrl+	F-key	Alt+	Menu Bar	Tablet
shademode	...	...	...	VS	View ⌐Shade	N2

```
Command: shademode
 Current mode: 2D wireframe
Enter option [2D wireframe/3D wireframe/Hidden/Flat/Gouraud/
    fLat+edges/gOuraud+edges] <2D wireframe>: [enter option]
```

COMMAND LINE OPTIONS

2D wireframe Displays wireframe models in 2D space.
3D wireframe Displays wireframe models in 3D space.
Hidden   Removes hidden faces.
Flat   Displays flat shaded faces.
fLat+edges   Displays flat shaded faces, with outlined faces of the background color.
Gouraud   Displays smooth shaded faces.
gOuraud+edges
                  Displays smooth shaded faces, with outlined faces of the background color.

RELATED COMMANDS

Hide   Performs a true hidden-line removal of 3D drawings.
MSlide   Saves a rendered view as an SLD-format slide file.
MView   Performs a hidden-line view of individual viewports during plotting.
Plot   Performs a hidden-line view during plotting.
Render   Performs a more realistic rendering.
3dOrbit Performs hidden-line removal of perspective views.

RELATED SYSTEM VARIABLES

None.

RELATED TOOLBAR

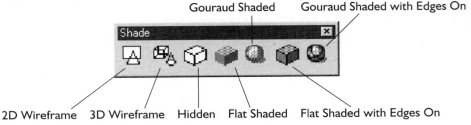

Gouraud Shaded   Gouraud Shaded with Edges On

2D Wireframe   3D Wireframe   Hidden   Flat Shaded   Flat Shaded with Edges On

TIPS

- As an alternative to the **ShadeMode** command, the **Render** module does high-quality renderings of 3D drawings, but takes somewhat longer to complete the rendering.

- The smaller the viewport, the faster the shading.

- This drawing is displayed in **ShadeMode**'s default **2D wireframe** mode; notice the standard 2D UCS icon.

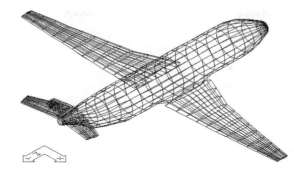

- This drawing is displayed in **3D wireframe** mode; notice the 3D UCS icon.

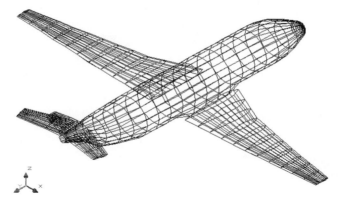

- This drawing is displayed in **Hidden** mode; notice that faces hidden by other faces are not displayed:

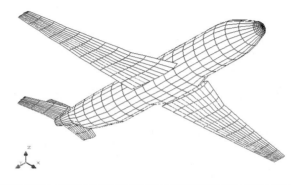

■ This drawing is displayed in **Flat** mode; notice that each face is filled with a shade of gray.

■ This drawing is displayed **Gouraud** mode; notice that the faces are smoothed.

■ This drawing is displayed in **fLat+edges** mode; notice that each face is outlined by the background color (*white*).

■ This drawing is displayed in **gOuraud+edges** mode; notice the outlining of each face.

Shape

V. 1.0 Inserts a predefined shape in the current drawing.

Command	Alias	Ctrl+	F-key	Alt+	Menu Bar	Tablet
shape	. . .	. . .	. . .	. . .	. . .	. . .

```
Command: shape
Enter shape name or [?]: [enter the name]
Specify insertion point: [pick]
Specify height <1>: ENTER
Specify rotation angle <0>: ENTER
```

COMMAND LINE OPTIONS

Enter shape name
  Indicates the name of the shape to insert.
? Lists the names of currently-loaded shapes.
Specify insertion point
  Indicates the insertion point of the shape.
Specify height Specifies the height of the shape.
Specify rotation angle
  Specifies the rotation angle of the shape.

RELATED COMMANDS

Load	Loads an SHX-format shape file into the drawing.
Insert	Inserts a block into the drawing.
Style	Loads SHX font files into the drawing.

RELATED SYSTEM VARIABLE

ShpName Specifies the current SHP file name.

TIPS

■ Shapes are defined by SHP files, which must first be compiled into SHX files before they can be loaded by the **Load** command. In addition, shapes must be loaded by the **Load** command before they can be inserted with the **Shape** command.

■ Compile an SHP file into an SHX file with the **Compile** command.

■ Shapes are used to define the text and symbols found in complex linetypes.

Some electronic shapes.

Shell

V. 2.5 Temporarily exits AutoCAD to the DOS compatibility mode; runs external commands defined in *Acad.Pgp*.

Command	Alias	Ctrl+	F-key	Alt+	Menu Bar	Tablet
shell	sh	...	...	...	...	...

Command: **shell**
OS Command: **[enter command]**

COMMAND LINE OPTIONS
OS Command Specifies an operating system command.
ENTER   Remains in the DOS compatibility mode for more than one command.
Exit   Returns to AutoCAD from the DOS compatibility mode.

RELATED COMMAND
Quit   Exits AutoCAD back to Windows.

RELATED FILE
Acad.Pgp   The external command definition file.

Adding commands to Acad.Pgp

Step 1: OPEN PGP FILE IN TEXT EDITOR

Load the *Acad.Pgp* file into a text editor.

Step 2: THE PGP FILE FORMAT

The PGP file uses this format to add a command:

```
CommandName, [OS request], MemoryReserve, [*]Prompt, ReturnCode
```

Meaning of the format:

Component	Meaning
CommandName	Specifies the name entered at AutoCAD prompt.
OS Request	Specifies the command sent to OS.
MemoryReserve	Always 0; heldover from old AutoCAD versions.
Prompt	Specifies the phrase to prompt user action.
*Prompt	Specifies that the user's response may contain spaces.

Meaning of the return code:

Return Code	Meaning
0	Returns to AutoCAD's text screen.
1	Loads *$Cmd.Dxb* file into drawing upon return.
2	Loads *$Cmd.Dxb* as a block into the drawing.
4	Returns to AutoCAD's previous screen mode, usually the graphics screen.

For example, add easy access to the WordPad word processor. Add the following line anywhere in the *Acad.Pgp* file. You may need to include the path to the *WordPad.Exe* file:

```
WP, wordpad.exe, 0, File to edit: ,4
```

Step 3: SAVE FILE

Save the file and return to AutoCAD.

Step 4: REINIT COMMAND

Use the **ReInit** command to reload the *Acad.Pgp* file.

Step 5: TRY IT OUT

Enter **WP** at the 'Command' prompt:

```
Command: wp
```

AutoCAD shells out to the operating system and prompts you:

```
File to edit:
```

Enter the name of a text file; AutoCAD launches WordPad with the file. To return to AutoCAD, you must exit WordPad.

ShowMat

Rel.13 Lists the rendering material attached to an object (*short for SHOW MATerial*).

Command	Alias	Ctrl+	F-key	Alt+	Menu Bar	Tablet
showmat	...	...	...	...	...	...

```
Command: showmat
Select object: [pick]
```

Example output:
```
Material BRONZE is explicitly attached to the object.
```

COMMAND LINE OPTION

Select object Selects the object to examine.

RELATED COMMANDS

MatLib Loads the material definitions into the drawing.
RMat Attaches the materials to objects, colors, and layers.

TIP

■ When no material is attached to the model, AutoCAD reports, "Material *GLOBAL* is attached by default or by block."

Sketch

V. 1.4 Allows freehand drawing as a series of lines or as a polyline, depending on the setting of system variable **SkPoly**.

Command	Alias	Ctrl+	F-key	Alt+	Menu Bar	Tablet
sketch	...	...	...	...	...	...

Command: **sketch**
Record increment <0.1000>: **ENTER**
Sketch. Pen eXit Quit Record Erase Connect .
Click pick button to begin drawing:
<Pen down>
Click pick button again to stop drawing:
<Pen up>
Press ENTER to record sketching and exit Sketch:
nnn lines recorded.

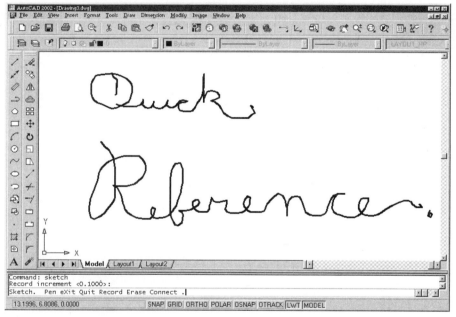

COMMAND LINE OPTIONS

Commands can be invoked by mouse and digitizer buttons:

Connect   Connects to the last drawing segment (*as an alternative, press button #6*).

Erase   Erases temporary segments as the cursor moves over them (*button #5*).

eXit   Records the temporary segments and exits the **Sketch** command (*button #3 or spacebar or ENTER*).

Pen   Lifts and lowers the pen (*pick button #1*).

Quit	Discards temporary segments, and exits the **Sketch** command (*button #4 or Esc*).
Record	Records the temporary segments as permanent (*button #2*).
.	(*Period*) Connects the last segment to the current point (*button #1*).

RELATED COMMANDS

Line	Draws line segments.
PLine	Draws polyline and polyline arc segments.

RELATED SYSTEM VARIABLES

SketchInc	Specifies the current recording increment for the **Sketch** command (default = 0.1).
SKPoly	Controls the type of sketches recorded:

SkPoly	Meaning
0	Record sketches as lines (default).
1	Record sketches as polylines.

TIPS

■ During the **Sketch** command, the definitions of the pointing device's buttons change to:

Button	Meaning	Keystroke
0	Raises and lowers the *p*en	P
1	Draws line to the current *point*	.
2	*R*ecords the sketch	R
3	Records the sketch and e*X*its	X *or* ENTER *or* spacebar
4	Discards the sketch and *Q*uits	Q *or* Esc
5	*E*rases the sketch	E
6	*C*onnects to last-drawn segment	C

■ Only the first several button commands are available on a mouse.

■ Pull-down menus are unavailable during the **Sketch** command.

Slice

Rel.11 Cuts a 3D solid with a plane, creating two 3D solids (*an ACIS command*).

Command	Alias	Ctrl+	F-key	Alt+	Menu Bar	Tablet
slice	sl	. . .	. . .	DIL	Draw	. . .
					⌐Solids	
					⌐Slice	

```
Command: slice
Select objects: [pick]
Select objects: ENTER
Specify first point on slicing plane by [Object/Zaxis/View/
    XY/YZ/ZX/3points] <3points>: [pick]
Specify a point on desired side of the plane or [keep
    Both sides]: b
```

Half a slice

COMMAND LINE OPTIONS

Select objects   Selects the 3D ACIS solid model to slice.

Slicing plane options:

Object   Aligns the cutting plane with a circle, ellipse, arc, elliptical arc, 2D spline, or 2D polyline.

View   Aligns the cutting plane with the viewing plane.

XY   Aligns the cutting plane with the x,y plane of the current UCS.

YZ   Aligns the cutting plane with the y,x plane of the current UCS.

Zaxis   Aligns the cutting plane with two normal points.

ZX   Aligns the cutting plane with the z,x plane of the current UCS.

3 points   Aligns the cutting plane with three points.

keep Both sides Retains both halves of the cut solid model.

Specify a point on the desired side of the plane
                Retains either half of the cut solid model.

TIP

■ This command cannot slice a 2D region, a 3D wireframe model, or other 2D shapes.

'Snap

V. 1.0 Sets the drawing "resolution," grid and hatch origin, isometric mode, and angle of grid, hatch, and ortho.

Command	Alias	Ctrl+	F-key	Alt+	Menu Bar	Tablet
'snap	sn	B	F9	. . .	. . .	. . .

```
Command: snap
Specify snap spacing or [ON/OFF/Aspect/Rotate/Style/Type]
   <0.5>: ENTER
```

COMMAND LINE OPTIONS

Snap spacing Sets the snap increment.
Aspect Sets separate x and y increments.
OFF Turns off snap.
ON Turns on snap.
Rotate Rotates the crosshairs for snap and grid.
Style Switches between standard and isometric style.
Type Switches between grid or polar snap.

STATUS BAR OPTION

Click SNAP to turn snap on and off:

Polar Snap On Turns on polar snap.
Grid Snap On Turns on snap.
Off Turns off snap.
Settings Displays the **Snap and Grid** tab of the **Drafting Settings** dialog box.

RELATED COMMANDS

DSettings Sets snap values via dialog box.
Grid Turns on the grid.
Isoplane Switches to a different isometric drawing plane.

RELATED SYSTEM VARIABLES

SnapAng Specifies the current angle of the snap rotation.
SnapBase Specifies the base point of the snap rotation.
SnapIsoPair Specifies the current isometric plane setting.
SnapMode Determines whether snap is on.
SnapStyl Determines the style of snap.
SnapUnit Specifies the current snap increment in the x and y directions.

TIPS

■ Setting the snap is setting the cursor resolution. For example, setting a snap distance of 0.1 means that when you move the cursor, it jumps in 0.1 increments. You can, however, still type in numerical values of greater resolution, such as 0.1234.

■ The **Aspect** option is not available when the **Style** option is set to **Isometric**; you may, howecer, rotate the isometric grid.

■ You can toggle snap mode by double-clicking the word **SNAP** on the status bar.

■ The options of the **Snap** command affect several other commands:

Command	Snap Option	Effect
Ellipse	Style	Adds **Isocircle** option to the **Ellipse** command.
Grid	Rotate	Rotates the grid display.
Hatch	Rotate	Rotates the hatching angle.
Hatch	SnapBase	Relocates the origin of the hatch pattern.
Ortho	Rotate	Rotates the ortho angle.

SolDraw

Rel.13 Creates profiles and sections in viewports created with the **SolView** command (*short for SOLids DRAWing; an ACIS command*).

Command	Alias	Ctrl+	F-key	Alt+	Menu Bar	Tablet
soldraw	...	...	...	DIUD	Draw	...
					⌖Solids	
					⌖Setup	
					⌖Drawing	

Command: **soldraw**
Select viewports to draw ...
Select objects: **[pick]**
Select objects: ENTER

COMMAND LINE OPTION

Select objects Selects a viewport; must be a floating viewport in model space (**Tilemode**=0).

RELATED COMMANDS

SolProf   Creates profile images of 3D solids.
SolView   Creates floating viewports.

TIPS

■ The **SolView** command must be used before this command.

■ This command performs the following actions:

   1. Creates visible and hidden lines representing the silhouette and edges of solids in the viewport.
   2. Projects to a plane perpendicular to the viewing direction.
   3. Silhouettes and edges are generated for all solids and portions of solids behind the cutting plane.
   4. Sectional views are crosshatched.

■ Existing profiles and sections in the selected viewport are erased.

■ All layers — except the ones needed to display the profile or section — are frozen in each viewport.

■ The following layers are used by **SolDraw**, **SolProf**, and **SolView**: *viewname*-**VIS**, *viewname*-**HID**, and *viewname*-**HAT**.

■ Hatching uses the values set in system variables **HpName**, **HpScale**, and **HpAng**.

Solid

V. 1.0 Draws solid-filled triangles and quadrilaterals; does *not* create a 3D solid.

Command	Alias	Ctrl+	F-key	Alt+	Menu Bar	Tablet
solid	so	...	...	DF2	Draw ↳Surfaces ↳2D Solid	L8

```
Command: solid
Specify first point: [pick]
Specify second point: [pick]
Specify third point: [pick]
Specify fourth point or <exit>: ENTER
```

Three-point solid.   *Pick order makes a difference for four-point solids.*

COMMAND LINE OPTIONS

First point   Picks the first corner.
Second point Picks the second corner.
Third point   Picks the third corner.
Fourth point Picks the fourth corner; or
                  Press **ENTER** to draw triangle.
ENTER   Draws quadilateral; ends **Solid** command.

RELATED COMMANDS

Fill   Turns object fill off and on.
BHatch   Fills any shape with a solid fill pattern.
Trace   Draws lines with width.
PLine   Draws polylines and polyline arcs with width.

RELATED SYSTEM VARIABLE

FillMode Determines whether solids are displayed filled or outlined.

SolidEdit

2000 Edits the faces and edges of 3D solids *(short for SOLids EDITor; an ACIS command).*

Command	Alias	Ctrl+	F-key	Alt+	Menu Bar	Tablet
solidedit	...	...	...	MN	Modify ↳Solids Editing	...

Command: **solidedit**
Solids editing automatic checking: SOLIDCHECK=1
Enter a solids editing option [Face/Edge/Body/Undo/eXit] <eXit>:
   [enter an option]

COMMAND LINE OPTIONS

Undo   Undoes the last editing actions, one at a time, up to the start of the **SolidEdit** command.

eXit   Exits body mode.

Face options:
Enter a face editing option
[Extrude/Move/Rotate/Offset/Taper/Delete/Copy/coLor/Undo/
   eXit] <eXit>: **[enter an option]**

Extrude   Extrudes one or more faces to the specified distance, or along a path; a positive value extrudes the face in the direction of its normal.

Move   Moves one or more faces the specified distance.

Rotate   Rotates one or more faces about an axis by a specified angle.

Offset   Offsets one or more faces by the specified distance, or through a specified point; a positive value increases the size of the solid, while a negative value decreases the size.

Taper   Tapers one or more faces by a specified angle; a positive angle tapers in, while a negative angle tapers out.

Delete   Removes the selected faces; also removes attached chamfers and fillets.

Copy   Copies the selected faces as a 3D region or a 3D body object.

Color   Changes the color of the selected faces.

Edge options:
Enter an edge editing option [Copy/coLor/Undo/eXit] <eXit>:
[enter an option]

Copy   Copies the selected 3D edges as a line, arc, circle, ellipse, or spline.

coLor   Changes the color of the selected edges.

Body *options:*
```
Enter a body editing option
[Imprint/sePalrate solids/Shell/cLean/Check/Undo/eXit] <eXit>:
```
   [enter an option]

Imprint	Imprints a selection set of arcs, circles, lines, 2D and 3D polylines, ellipses, splines, regions, bodies, and 3D solids on the face of a 3D solid.
sePalrate solids	Separates 3D solids into independent 3D solid objects; the solid objects must have disjointed volumes; this option does *not* separate 3D solids that were joined by a Boolean editing command, such as **Intersect**, **Subtract**, and **Union**.
Shell	Creates a hollowed, thin-walled solid of specified thickness; a positive thickness creates a shell toward the inside of the solid, while a negative value creates the shell on the outside of the solid.
cLean	Removes redundant edges and vertices, imprints, unused geometry, shared edges, and shared vertices.
Check	Checks whether the object is a 3D ACIS solid; duplicates the function of the **SolidCheck** system variable.

RELATED SYSTEM VARIABLE

SolidCheck   Toggles ACIS solid validation on and off (default = on).

RELATED COMMANDS

All commands related to creating and editing 3D solid models.

TIP

■ When working with the **SolidEdit** command, you can select a face, an edge, an internal point on a face, or use the **CP** (*crossing polygon*), **CW** (*crossing window*), **F** (*fence*) object selection options.

SolProf

Rel.13 Creates profile images of 3D solids (*short for SOLid PROFile; an ACIS command*).

Command	Alias	Ctrl+	F-key	Alt+	Menu Bar	Tablet
solprof	...	...	...	DIUP	Draw	...
					↳Solids	
					↳Setup	
					↳Profile	

Command: **solprof**
Select objects: **[pick]**
Select objects: ENTER
Display hidden profile lines on separate layer? [Yes/No] <Y> ENTER
Project profile lines onto a plane? [Yes/No] <Y>: ENTER
Delete tangential edges? [Yes/No] <Y>: ENTER
n solids selected.

COMMAND LINE OPTIONS

Select objects Selects the objects to profile.
Display hidden profile lines on separate layer?

> **No**: All profile lines are visible; a block is created for the profile lines for every selected solid.
> **Yes**: Generates just two blocks: one for visible lines, and one for hidden lines.

Project profile lines onto a plane?

> **No**: Creates profile lines with 3D objects.
> **Yes**: Creates profile lines with 2D objects.

Delete tangential edges?

> **No**: Does not display *tangential edges*, the transition line between two tangent faces.
> **Yes**: Displays tangential edges.

RELATED COMMANDS

SolDraw   Creates profiles and sections in viewports.
SolView   Creates floating viewports.

TIPS

- The **SolView** command must be used before the **SolProf** command.

- Solids that share a common volume can produce dangling edges, if you generate profiles with hidden lines. To avoid this, first use the **Union** command.

- AutoCAD must be in a layout before you can use the **SolProf** command.

SolView

Rel.13 Creates floating viewports in preparation for the **SolDraw** and **SolProf** commands *(short for SOLid VIEWs; an ACIS command).*

Command	Alias	Ctrl+	F-key	Alt+	Menu Bar	Tablet
solview	...	...	...	DIUV	Draw	...
					⤷Solids	
					⤷Setup	
					⤷View	

Command: **solview**
Enter an option [Ucs/Ortho/Auxiliary/Section]: **[enter option]**

COMMAND LINE OPTIONS

Ucs options:

Named	Creates the profile view using the x,y plane of a named UCS.
World	Creates the profile view using the x,y plane of the WCS
?	Lists the names of existing UCSs.
Current	Creates the profile view using the x,y-plane of the current UCS.

Ortho options:

Pick side of viewport to project
  Selects the edge of one viewport.

View center	Picks the center of the view.
Clip	Picks two corners for a clipped view.
View name	Names the view.

Auxiliary options:

Inclined plane's 1st point
  Picks the first point.
Inclined plane's 2nd point
  Picks the second point.
Side to view from
  Determines the view side.

Section options:

Cutting plane 1st point
  Picks the first point.
Cutting plane 2nd point
  Picks the second point.
Side to view from
  Determines the view side.

Viewscale	Specifies the scale of the new view.
eXit	Exits the **SolView** command.

RELATED COMMANDS

SolDraw	Creates profiles and sections in viewports.
SolProf	Creates profile images of 3D solids.

'SpaceTrans

Converts distances between model and space units (*short for SPACE TRANSlation*).

Command	Alias	Ctrl+	F-key	Alt+	Menu Bar	Tablet
'spacetrans	...	...	...	...	...	...

Command: **spacetrans**
This command does not operate in Model tab.

In model view of a layout tab:
Specify paper space distance <1.000>: **[enter value]**

In paper space of a layout tab:
Select a viewport: **[pick]**
Specify model space distance <1.000>: **[enter value]**

COMMAND LINE OPTIONS

Specify paper space distance
Specifies the paper space length to be converted to model space equivalent, usually the scale factor.

Select a viewport
Selects a paper space viewport.

Specify model space distance
Specifies the model space length to be converted to paper space equivalent, usually the scale factor.

RELATED COMMANDS

Text   Places text in the drawing.
SolProf   Creates profile images of 3D solids.

TIPS

■ This command is meant to be used transparently during another command.

 # Spell

Rel.13 Checks the spelling of text in the drawing.

Command	Alias	Ctrl+	F-key	Alt+	Menu Bar	Tablet
spell	sp	...	...	TE	Tools ↳Spelling	T10

```
Command: spell
Select objects: [pick]
Select objects: ENTER
```

When unrecognized text is found, displays dialog box:

```
┌─ Check Spelling ───────────────────────── [?][X]
│  Current dictionary:        American English
│  ┌─ Current word ──────────────┐    ┌─ Cancel ─┐
│  │ ("nullsurf"                 │    └──────────┘
│  └─────────────────────────────┘    ┌─ Help ───┐
│  Suggestions:                        └──────────┘
│  ┌─────────────────┐  ┌─ Ignore ─┐  ┌─ Ignore All ─┐
│  │ ("null surf"    │  └──────────┘  └──────────────┘
│  ┌─────────────────┐  ┌─ Change ─┐  ┌─ Change All ─┐
│  │ ("null surf"    │  └──────────┘  └──────────────┘
│  │ ("nulls"        │  ┌─ Add ────┐  ┌─ Lookup ─────┐
│  │                 │  └──────────┘  └──────────────┘
│  └─────────────────┘
│                      ┌─ Change Dictionaries... ─┐
│                      └──────────────────────────┘
│  ┌─ Context ──────────────────────┐
│  │ ("nullsurf" "")                │
│  └────────────────────────────────┘
└──────────────────────────────────────────────────┘
```

When selected text is recognized, or when spelling check is complete:

```
┌─ AutoCAD Message ─── [X]
│   Spelling check complete.
│      ┌──── OK ────┐
│      └────────────┘
└────────────────────────
```

DIALOG BOX OPTIONS

Ignore	Ignores the word, and goes on to the next word.
Ignore All	Ignores all words with this spelling.
Change	Changes the word to the suggested spelling.
Change All	Changes all words with this spelling.
Add	Adds the word to the user (custom) dictionary.
Lookup	Checks spelling of the word in **Suggestions** box.

Change dictionaries

Selects a different dictionary; displays the dialog box:

Change Dictionaries dialog box:

Main dictionary Selects a language for the dictionary.

Custom dictionary options:

Directory Specifies the drive, folder, and filename of the custom dictionary.

Browse Displays the **Select Custom Dictionary** dialog box.

Custom dictionary words options:

Add Adds a word.

Delete Removes a custom word from the dictionary.

RELATED COMMANDS

DdEdit Edits text.

MText Places paragraph text.

Text Places lines of text in the drawing.

RELATED SYSTEM VARIABLES

DctCust Specifires the name of custom spelling dictionary.

DctMain Specifires the name of main spelling dictionary.

RELATED FILES

Enu.Dct Dictionary word file.

*.Cus Custom dictionary files.

TIPS

■ A spell checker does *not* check your spelling; words that are spelled correctly but used incorrectly (such as *its* and *it's*) are not flagged. Rather, a spell checker looks for words that it does not recognize, which are words not in its dictionary file.

■ As of AutoCAD 2002, the **Spell** command also checks words in blocks.

Sphere

Rel.II Draws a 3D sphere as a solid model (*an ACIS command*).

Command	Alias	Ctrl+	F-key	Alt+	Menu Bar	Tablet
sphere	...	...	...	DIS	Draw ⟍Solids ⟍Sphere	K7

```
Command: sphere
Current wire frame density:  ISOLINES=4
Specify center of sphere <0,0,0>: [pick]
Specify radius of sphere or [Diameter]: [pick]
```

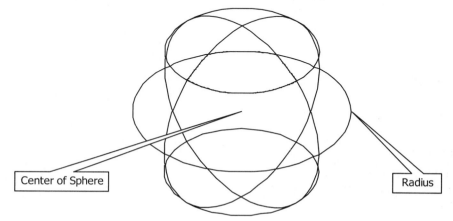

Center of Sphere   Radius

COMMAND LINE OPTIONS

Specify center of sphere
        Locates the center point of the sphere.

Diameter   Specifies the diameter of the sphere.

Radius   Specifies the radius of the sphere.

RELATED COMMANDS

Box   Draws solid boxes.

Cone   Draws solid cones.

Cylinder   Draws solid cylinders.

Torus   Draws solid tori.

Wedge   Draws solid wedges.

Ai_Sphere   Draws a surface meshed sphere.

RELATED SYSTEM VARIABLES

DispSilh   Specifies the silhouette display of 3D solids:

DispSilh	Meaning
0	Off.
1	On.

IsoLines   Specifies the number of tessellation lines that define the surface of the 3D solid:

IsoLines	Meaning
0	Minimum.
4	Default.
2047	Maximum.

TIPS

■ The **Sphere** command places the sphere's central axis parallel to the z axis of the current UCS, with the latitudinal isolines parallel to the x,y plane.

■ You must use the **Regen** command after changing the **DispSilh** and **IsoLines** system variables.

■ Notice the effect of the **DispSilh** system variable, which toggles the silhouette display of 3D ACIS solids, after executing the **Hide** command:

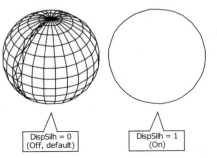

■ Notice the effect of the **IsoLines** system variable, which controls the number of tessellation lines used to define the surface of a 3D solid:

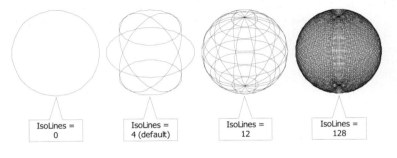

Spline

Rel.13 Draws NURBS (short for non-uniform rational Bezier spline) curves (*an ACIS command*).

Command	Alias	Ctrl+	F-key	Alt+	Menu Bar	Tablet
spline	spl	...	...	DS	Draw ⌐Spline	L9

```
Command: spline
Specify first point or [Object]: [pick]
Specify next point: [pick]
Specify next point or [Close/Fit tolerance] <start tangent>: [pick]
Specify next point or [Close/Fit tolerance] <start tangent>: ENTER
Specify start tangent: [pick]
Specify end tangent: [pick]
```

Open spline   Closed spline

COMMAND LINE OPTIONS

Specify first point
Picks the starting point of the spline.
Object Converts 2D and 3D splined polylines into a NURBS spline.
Specify next point
Picks the next tangent point.
Close Closes the spline at the start point.
Fit Changes the spline tolerance; 0 = curve passes through fit points.
Specify start tangent
Specifies the tangency of the starting point of the spline.
Specify end tangent
Specifies the tangency of the endpoint of the spline.

RELATED COMMANDS

PEdit Edits a splined polyline.
PLine Draws a splined polyline.
SplinEdit Edits a NURBS spline.

RELATED SYSTEM VARIABLE

DelObj Toggles whether the original polyline is deleted with the **Object** option.

TIP

■ A closed spline has the same start and end tangent.

SplinEdit

Rel.13 Edits a NURBS spline (*an ACIS command*).

Command	Alias	Ctrl+	F-key	Alt+	Menu Bar	Tablet
splinedit	spe	...	...	...	Modify ⮑Spline	Y18

```
Command: splinedit
Select spline: [pick]
Enter an option [Fit data/Close/Move vertex/Refine/rEverse/
    Undo]: [enter option]
```

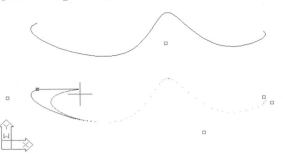

COMMAND LINE OPTIONS

Close	Closes the spline, if open.
Move vertex	Moves a control vertex.
Open	Opens the spline, if closed.
Refine	Adds a control point; changes the spline's order or weight.
rEverse	Reverses the spline's direction.
Undo	Undoes the most-recent edit change.
eXit	Exits the **SplinEdit** command.

Fit data options:
```
Enter a fit data option
[Add/Close/Delete/Move/Purge/Tangents/toLerance/eXit] <eXit>:
    [enter option]
```

Add	Adds fit points.
Close	Closes the spline, if open.
Delete	Removes fit points.
Move	Moves fit points.
Open	Opens the spline, if closed.
Purge	Removes fit point data from the drawing.
Tangents	Edits the start and end tangents.
toLerance	Refits spline with the new tolerance value.
eXit	Exits suboptions.

RELATED COMMANDS

PEdit	Edits a splined polyline.
PLine	Creates polylines, including splined polylines.
Spline	Draws a NURBS spline.

TIPS

- The spline loses its fit data when you use the following **SplinEdit** command options: **Refine**; **Fit Purge**; **Fit Tolerance** followed by **Fit Move**; and **Fit Tolerance** followed by **Fit Open** or **Fit Close**.

- The maximum order for a spline is 26; once the order has been elevated, it cannot be reduced.

- The larger the weight, the closer the spline is to the control point.

- This command automatically converts a spline-fit polyline to a Spline object, even if you don't edit the polyline.

Standards

Loads standards into the current drawing.

Command	Alias	Ctrl+	F-key	Alt+	Menu Bar	Tablet
standards	...	...	...	TSC	Tools	...
					⌐CAD Standards	
					⌐Configure	

Command: **standards**
Displays tabbed dialog box:

DIALOG BOX OPTIONS

+	Adds a standards file (**F3**); displays the **Select standards file** dialog box.
Move up	Moves a standards file higher in the list.
Move down	Moves a standards file lower in the list.
X	Remove the selected standards file (**DEL**).

Check Standards

Displays the **Check Standards** dialog box; see the **CheckStandards** command.

Plug-ins tab:

Displays information about each item in the CAD standard.

RELATED COMMAND

CheckStandards Checks the drawing against standards loaded by the **Standards** command.

RELATED FILE

*.STD CAD Standards file; stored in DWG format.

Stats

Rel.12 Lists statistics of the most-recent rendering *(short for STATisticS)*.

Command	Alias	Ctrl+	F-key	Alt+	Menu Bar	Tablet
stats	...	...	...	VET	View ↳Render ↳Statistics	...

Command: **stats**
Displays dialog box:

```
Statistics                                                    [x]
 ┌─────────────────────────────────────────────────────────┐ ▲
 │ Rendering Type:        Photo Raytrace                     │
 │ Scene Name:            "current view"                     │
 │                                                           │
 │ Total Time:            8 Seconds                          │
 │                                                           │
 │ Shadow Map Time:       0 Seconds                          │
 │ Initialization Time:   0 Seconds                          │
 │ Traversal Time:        0 Seconds                          │
 │ Render + Display Time: 8 Seconds                          │
 │ Cleanup Time:          0 Seconds                          │
 │                                                           │
 │ Total Faces:           196                                │
 │ Total Triangles:       196                                │
 │                                                           │
 │ Width:                 1024                               │
 │ Height:                768                                │
 │ Colors:                24-bits                            │ ▼
 └─────────────────────────────────────────────────────────┘
  ☐ Save Statistics to File:      ┌─────────────┐  [ Find File... ]
                                  └─────────────┘
           [   OK   ]     [ Cancel ]    [ Help ]
```

DIALOG BOX OPTION
Save Statistics to File
Saves the rendering statistics to the file specified in the adjacent text entry box.

RELATED AUTOCAD COMMAND
Render   Creates renderings.

DEFINITIONS
Scene name   Name of the currently-selected scene; when no scene is current, displays "(none)."

Last Rendering Type
Name of currently-selected renderer; default is AutoCAD Render.

Rendering Time Time required to create most-recent rendering; reported in HH:MM:SS *(hours, minutes, seconds)* format.

Total Faces   Number of faces processed in most-recent rendering; a single 3D object consists of many faces.

Total Triangles Number of triangles processed in most-recent rendering; a rectangular face is typically divided into two triangles.

'Status

Displays information about the current drawing and environment.

Command	Alias	Ctrl+	F-key	Alt+	Menu Bar	Tablet
'status	...	...	...	TYS	Tools	...
					⤷Inquiry	
					⤷Status	

Command: **status**
Example output for the Acad.Dwg prototype drawing:

```
42 objects in Drawing3.dwg
Model space limits are X:     0.0000   Y:      0.0000   (Off)
                       X:    12.0000   Y:      9.0000
Model space uses         *Nothing*
Display shows          X:     0.0000   Y:      0.0000
                       X:    16.1820   Y:      9.0000
Insertion base is      X:     0.0000   Y:      0.0000   Z:      0.0000
Snap resolution is     X:     0.5000   Y:      0.5000
Grid spacing is        X:     0.5000   Y:      0.5000

Current space:           Model space
Current layout:          Model
Current layer:           "0"
Current color:           BYLAYER -- 7 (white)
Current linetype:        BYLAYER -- "Continuous"
Current lineweight:      BYLAYER
Current plot style:      ByLayer
Current elevation:       0.0000   thickness:      0.0000
Fill on  Grid off  Ortho off  Qtext off  Snap off  Tablet off
Object snap modes:       None
Free dwg disk (C:) space: 2047.7 MBytes
Free temp disk (C:) space: 2047.7 MBytes
Free physical memory: 7.5 Mbytes (out of 191.3M).
Free swap file space: 1743.1 Mbytes (out of 1856.7M).
```

COMMAND LINE OPTIONS

ENTER   Continues the listing.
F2   Returns to the graphics screen.

RELATED COMMANDS

DbList   Lists information about all the objects in the drawing.
List   Lists information about the selected objects.
Stats   Lists information about the most-recent rendering.

DEFINITIONS

Model Space limits, Paper Space limits
>The x,y coordinates stored in the **LimMin** and **LimMax** system variables; 'Off' indicates limits checking is turned off (**LimCheck**).

Model Space use, Paper Space use
>The x,y coordinates of the lower-left and upper-right extents of objects in the drawing; 'Over' indicates drawing extents exceed the drawing limits.

Display shows   The x,y coordinates of the lower-left and upper-right corners of the current display.

Insertion base is The x,y,z coordinates stored in system variable **InsBase**.

Snap resolution is, Grid spacing is
>The snap and grid settings, as stored in the **SnapUnit** and **GridUnit** system variables.

Current space   Indicates whether model space or paper space is current.

Current layout Indicates the name of the current layout.

Current layer, Current color, Current linetype, Current lineweight, Current plot style, Current elevation, Thickness
>The current values for the layer name, color, linetype name, elevation, and thickness, as stored in system variables **CLayer**, **CeColor**, **CeLType**, **CeLweight**, **CPlotSytle**, **Elevation**, and **Thickness**.

Fill, Grid, Ortho, Qtext, Snap, Tablet
>The current settings for the fill, grid, ortho, qtext, snap, and tablet modes, as stored in the system variables **FillMode**, **GridMode**, **OrthoMode**, **TextMode**, **SnapMode**, and **TabMode**.

Object Snap modes
>The currently-set object modes, as stored in system variable **OsMode**.

Free disk (dwg + temp = C)
>The amount of free disk space on the drive storing AutoCAD's temporary files, as held by by system variable **TempPrefix**.

Free physical memory
>The amount of free RAM.

Free swap file space
>The amount of free space in AutoCAD's swap file on disk.

StlOut

Rel.12 Exports 3D solids and bodies in binary or ASCII SLA format (*short for STereoLithography OUTput; an ACIS command*).

Command	Alias	Ctrl+	F-key	Alt+	Menu Bar	Tablet
stlout	...	...	...	FE	File	...
				⬐STL	⬐Export	
					⬐Lithography	

```
Command: stlout
Select a single solid for STL output...
Select objects: [pick]
Select objects: ENTER
Create a binary STL file? [Yes/No] <Y>: ENTER
```

COMMAND LINE OPTIONS

Select objects Selects a single 3D ACIS solid object.
Y Creates a binary-format SLA file.
N Creates an ASCII-format SLA file.

RELATED COMMANDS

All solid modeling commands.
AcisOut Exports 3D solid models to an ASCII SAT-format ACIS file.
AmeConvert Converts AME v2.x solid models into ACIS models.

RELATED SYSTEM VARIABLE

FaceTRes Determines the resolution of triangulating solid models.

RELATED FILE

*.STL The SLA-compatible file with STL extension created by this command.

TIPS

- The solid model must lie in the positive x,y,z-octant of the WCS.

- The **StlOut** command exports a single 3D ACIS solid; it does not export ACIS regions or any other AutoCAD object.

- Even though this command prompts you twice to 'Select objects', selecting more than one solid causes AutoCAD to complain, "Only one solid per file permitted."

- The resulting STL file cannot be imported back into AutoCAD.

DEFINITIONS

STL Stereolithography data file, which consists of a faceted representation of the ACIS model.
SLA StereoLithography Apparatus.

⬛ Stretch

V. 2.5 Stretches objects to lengthen, shorten, or distort them.

Command	Alias	Ctrl+	F-key	Alt+	Menu Bar	Tablet
stretch	s	...	...	MH	Modify ⮡Stretch	V22

```
Command: stretch
Select objects to stretch by crossing-window or
    crossing-polygon...
Select objects: c
Specify first corner: [pick]
Specify opposite corner: [pick]
Select objects: ENTER
Specify base point or displacement: [pick]
Specify second point of displacement or <use first point as
displacement>: [pick]
```

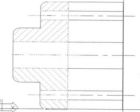

COMMAND LINE OPTIONS

First corner Selects object; must be **CPolygon** or **Crossing** object selection.
Select objects Selects other objects using any selection mode.
Base point Indicates the starting point for stretching.
Second point Stretches the object larger or smaller.

RELATED COMMANDS

Change Changes the size of lines, circles, text, blocks, and arcs.
Scale Increases or decreases the size of any object.

TIPS

■ The effect of the **Stretch** command is not always obvious; be prepared to use the **Undo** command.

■ The first time you select objects for the **Stretch** command, you must use **Crossing** or **CPolygon** object selection; objects entirely within the selection window are moved.

■ The **Stretch** command will not move a hatch pattern unless the hatch's origin is included in the selection set.

■ Use the **Stretch** command to update associative dimensions automatically by including the dimension's endpoints in the selection set.

Style

V. 2.0 Creates and modifies a text style via a dialog box.

Command	Alias	Ctrl+	F-key	Alt+	Menu Bar	Tablet
style	st	...	...	OS	Format	U2
	ddstyle				⌦Text Style	

-style

Command: **style**
Displays dialog box:

DIALOG BOX OPTIONS

Style Name options:

Style Name   Selects an existing text style.

New   Creates a new text style; displays dialog box:

Rename   Renames an existing text style; displays dialog box:

Delete   Deletes a text style.

Font *options:*

Font Name   Specifies the name of the AutoCAD SHX or TrueType TTF font.

Font Style   Selects from available font styles, such as Redgular, **Bold**, *Italic*, and ***Bold Italic***.

Height   Specifies the text height.

Use Big Font   Specifies the use of a big font file, typically for Asian alphabets.

Effects *options* *(not available for all fonts):*

Upside Down   Draws text upside down: Ɐ° BρϹᏟD

Backwards   Draws text backwards: ᗡϽqᗺoA

Vertical   Draws text vertically.

Width Factor   Changes the width of characters.

Width factor = 0.5 (left) and 2.0 (right):

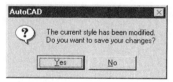

Oblique Angle Slants characters forward or backward:

Oblique angle = 30 (left) and -30 (right):

Preview   Previews the effects on the style.

Apply   Applies the changes to the style.

Close   Closes the dialog box; in some cases, you can click the **Close** button before clicking the **Apply** button; then AutoCAD displays the following warning dialog box:

-STYLE COMMAND

Command: **-style**
Enter name of text style or [?] <STANDARD>: **ENTER**
Specify full font name or font filename (TTF or SHX)
   <txt>: **ENTER**
Specify height of text <0.0000>: **ENTER**
Specify width factor <1.0000>: **ENTER**
Specify obliquing angle <0>: **ENTER**
Display text backwards? [Yes/No] <N>: **ENTER**
Display text upside-down? [Yes/No] <N>: **ENTER**
Vertical? <N> **ENTER**
"STANDARD" is now the current text style.

COMMAND LINE OPTIONS

Enter name of text style
> Names the text style; maximum = 31 characters (default = "STAN-DARD").

?   Lists the names of styles already defined in the drawing.

Specify full font name or font filename
> Names the font file (SHX or TTF) from which the style is defined (default = Txt.Shx).

Specify height of text
> Specifies the height of the text (default = 0 units**).**

Specify width factor
> Specifies the width factor of the text (default = 1.00).

Specify obliquing angle
> Specifies the obliquing angle or slant of the text (default = 0 degrees).

Display text backwards
> **Yes**: Text is printed backwards — mirror writing.
> **No** (default): Text is printed forwards.

Display text upside-down
> **Yes**: Text is printed upside-down.
> **No:** Text is printed rightside-up (default).

Vertical   **Yes**: Text is printed vertically; not available for all fonts.
> **No:** Text is printed horizontally (default).

RELATED COMMANDS

Change	Changes the style assigned to selected text.
Purge	Removes any unused text style definitions.
Rename	Renames a text style name.
DText	Places a single line of text.
MText	Places paragraph text.
Text	Places a single line of text.

RELATED SYSTEM VARIABLES

TextStyle   Specifies the current text style.

TextSize   Specifies the current text height.

RELATED FILES

*.SHP   Autodesk's format for vector source fonts.

.SHX   Autodesk's format for compiled vector fonts; stored in *Acad 2002*Fonts* folder.

.TTF   TrueType font files; stored in *Windows*Fonts* subdirectory.

TIPS

- A **Width Factor** of 0.85 fits in 15% more text without sacrificing legibility.

- An **Obliquing Angle** of +15% can sometimes enhance the look of a font.

- The **Obliquing Angle** can be positive (forward slanting) or negative (backward slanting).

- As of Release 14, AutoCAD no longer works with PostScript fonts.

- You can use any TrueType font with AutoCAD.

- The **Style** command affects the font used with the **Text**, **DText**, **MText**, and dimensioning commands, including **Leader** and **Tolerance**.

- A text height of 0 lets you specify the text height while you are adding text with the **Text**, **DText**, and **MText** commands. If you specify a text height other than 0 in the **Style** command, that height is always used with that particular style name.

- Some of the fonts included with AutoCAD 2002:

©®®®™™ @%%‖ ±°′″∅＋ − × ÷ ＝•●◗■▣○○□☐□□♣□□♦∅☒☑

abcdefghijABCDEFGHIJ123456789!@#$%^&*()

abcdefghijABCDEFGHIJ123456789!@#$%^&*()

ABCDEFGHIJABCDEFGHIJ123456789!@#$%^&*()

abcdefghijABCDEFGHIJ123456789.@#$%^&()*

ABCDEFGHIJABCDEFGHIJ123456789!@#$%^&*()

αβψδεφγηιξΑΒΨΔΕΦΓΗΙΞ＋ − × ÷ ＝± ∓°′/□□ >□□∅≦×ς

▥ StylesManager

2000 Displays the **Plot Styles** window.

Command	Alias	Ctrl+	F-key	Alt+	Menu Bar	Tablet
stylesmanager	...	...	...	FY	File ⤷Plot Style Manager	Y24

Command: **stylesmanager**
Displays window:

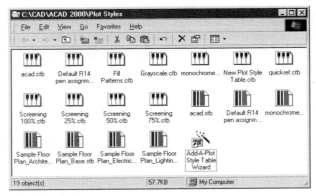

WINDOW OPTIONS

Open .ctb   Opens the **Plot Style Table Editor** dialog box.
Open .stb   Opens the **Plot Style Table Editor** dialog box, as well.
Open Add-A-Plot Style Table Wizard
　　　　　　　　Opens **Add Plot Style Table** wizard; see the **R14PenWizard** command.

SHORTCUT MENU OPTIONS

Open   Opens file.
Send To   Copies the file to another drive, or to your computer's communications
                  software; may not work with some software.
Cut   Cuts the file to the Clipboard.
Copy   Copies the file to the Clipboard.
Create Shortcut Creates a shortcut icon for the selected file.
Delete   Erases the file; displays a warning dialog box.
Rename   Renames the file; displays a warning dialog box if you change the exten-
                  sion.
Properties   Displays the **Properties** dialog box in read-only mode; use the **DwgProps**
                  command within AutoCAD to change the settings.

DIALOG BOX OPTIONS

Save and Close Saves the changes, and closes the dialog box.
Cancel   Cancels the changes, and closes the dialog box.

General tab:

Description   Allows you to describe the plot style.
Apply global scale factor to non-ISO linetypes and fill patterns
                  Applies the scale factor to all non-ISO linetypes and hatch patterns in the plot.
Scale factor Specifies the scale factor.

CBT File **Table View** tab:

See the following pages for options.

CBT File **Form View** tab:

See the following pages for options.

STB File **Table View** tab:

Name	Normal	PLAN_1F	PLAN_1FIN	PLAN_2F	PLAN_2FIN	PLAN_CAI	PLAN_CAIX
Description							
Color	Use object color	Use object color	Use object color	Use object color	Use object color	Use object color	Use object color
Enable dithering	☑	☑	☑	☑	☑	☑	☑
Convert to grayscale	☐	☑	☑	☑	☑	☑	☑
Use assigned pen #	Automatic	Automatic	Automatic	Automatic	Automatic	Automatic	Automatic
Virtual pen #	Automatic	Automatic	Automatic	Automatic	Automatic	Automatic	Automatic
Screening	100	100	100	100	100	100	100
Linetype	Use object linetype	Use object linetype	Use object linetype	Use object linetype	Use object linetype	Use object linetype	Use object linetype
Adaptive adjustment	☑	☑	☑	☑	☑	☑	☑
Lineweight	Use object lineweight	Use object lineweight	Use object lineweight	Use object lineweight	Use object lineweight	Use object lineweight	Use object lineweight
Line End Style	Use object end style	Use object end style	Use object end style	Use object end style	Use object end style	Use object end style	Use object end style
Line Join Style	Use object join style	Use object join style	Use object join style	Use object join style	Use object join style	Use object join style	Use object join style
Fill Style	Use object fill style	Use object fill style	Use object fill style	Use object fill style	Use object fill style	Use object fill style	Use object fill style

See the following pages for options.

STB File **Form View** tab:

See the following pages for options.

The options for **Table View** *and* **Form View** *are identical:*

Object color Specifies the color of the object.

Description Allows you to describe the plot style.

Color Specifies the plotted color for the objects.

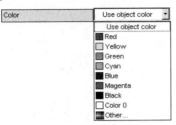

Enable dithering

Toggles dithering, if the plotter is supports dithering, to generate more colors than the plotter is capable of; this setting should be turned off for ploting vectors, and turned on for plotting renderings.

Convert to grayscale

Converts colors to shades of gray, if the plotter supports gray scale.

Use assigned pen #

Specifies the pen number of pen plotters; range is 1 to 32.

Use assigned pen #	Automatic ⬍

Virtual pen number

Specifies the virtual pen number (default = Automatic); range is 1 to 255. A value of 0 (or Automatic) tells AutoCAD to assign virtual pens from ACI (AutoCAD Color Index); this setting is meant for non-pen plotters that can make use of virtual pens.

Virtual pen #	Automatic ⬍

Screening Specifies the intensity of plotted objects; range is 0 (plotted "white") to 100 (full density):

Screening	100 ⬍

Linetype Specifies the linetype with which to plot the objects:

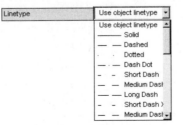

Adaptive adjustment

Adjusts linetype scale to prevent the linetype from ending in the middle of its pattern; keep off when the plotted linetype scale is crucial.

Lineweight   Specifies how wide lines are plotted, in millimeters:

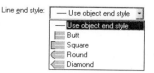

Line end style Specifies how the ends of lines are plotted:

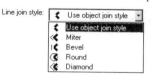

Line join style Specifies how the intersections of lines are plotted:

Fill style   Specifies how objects are filled:

Add Style   Adds a plot style.
Delete Style   Removes a plot style.
Edit Lineweights

           Displays the **Edit Lineweights** dialog box.
Save As   Displays the **Save As** dialog box.

TIPS

- **CTB** is short for "color dependent style table" file, which is compatible with earlier versions of AutoCAD.

- **STB** is short for "style table" file.

- To configure a printer or plotter for *virtual pens*, open the **PC3 Editor** dialog box on the **Device and Document Settings** tab; in the **Vector Graphics** section, select **255 Virtual Pens** from Color Depth.

Subtract

Rel. II Removes the volume of one 3D model or 2D region from another (*an ACIS command*).

Command	Alias	Ctrl+	F-key	Alt+	Menu Bar	Tablet
subtract	su	...	...	MNS	Modify ⬫Solids Editing ⬫Subtract	X16

```
Command: subtract
Select objects: [pick]
Select objects: ENTER
1 solid selected.
Objects to subtract from them...
Select objects: [pick]
Select objects: ENTER
1 solid selected.
```

COMMAND LINE OPTION

Select objects   Selects the objects to be subtracted.

RELATED COMMANDS

Intersect   Removes all but the intersection of two solid volumes.

Union   Joins two solids.

SysWindows

Rel.13 Controls multiple windows (*short for SYStem WINDOWS*).

Command	Alias	Ctrl+	F-key	Alt+	Menu Bar	Tablet
syswindows	...	F6	...	W	Windows ↳*varies*	...

Command: **syswindows**
Enter an option [Cascade/tile Horizontal/tile Vertical/
   Arrange icons]: **[enter option]**

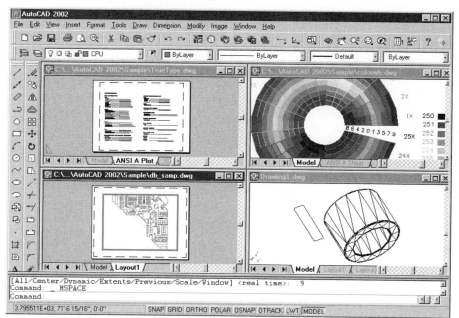

COMMAND LINE OPTIONS

Cascade   Cascades the window.
tileHorizontal Tiles the window horizontally.
tileVertical   Tiles the window vertically.
Arrange icons Arranges icons in an orderly fashion.

TITLE BAR OPTIONS

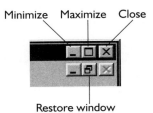

Restore	Restores the window to its "windowized" size.
Move	Moves the window.
Size	Resizes the window.
Minimize	Minimizes the window.
Maximize	Maximizes the window.
Close	Closes the window.
Next	Switches the focus to the next window.

RELATED COMMANDS

Close	Closes a window.
Open	Opens one or more drawings, each in its own window.
MView	Creates paper space viewports in a window.
Vports	Creates model space viewports in a window.

TIPS

■ The **SysWindows** command had no practical effect until AutoCAD 2000, since AutoCAD Release 13 and 14 supported only a single window.

■ Press **CTRL+F6** to switch quickly between currently-loaded drawings.

■ Window control icons:

'Tablet

V. 1.0 Configures, calibrates, and toggles the digitizing tablet.

Command	Alias	Ctrl+	F-key	Alt+	Menu Bar	Tablet
'tablet	ta	T	F4	TT	Tools ↳Tablet	X7

Command: **tablet**
Enter an option [ON/OFF/CAL/CFG]: **[enter an option]**

COMMAND LINE OPTIONS
CAL   Calibrates the coordinates for the tablet.
CFG   Configures the menu areas on the tablet.
OFF   Turns off the tablet's digitizing mode.
ON   Turns on the tablet's digitizing mode.

RELATED SYSTEM VARIABLE
TabMode   Toggles use of the tablet:

TabMode	Meaning
0	Tablet mode disabled.
1	Tablet mode enabled.

RELATED FILES
Acad.Mnu   Menu source code that defines functions of tablet menu areas.
Mc.Exe   Menu compiler; semi-automates the creation of a tablet menu.
Tablet14.Dwg AutoCAD drawing of the printed template overlay.

TIPS
■ AutoCAD includes a plastic tablet overlay in the package.

■ To change the tablet overlay, edit the *Tablet.Dwg* file, then plot it to fit your digitizer.

■ **Tablet** does not work if a digitizer has not been configured with the **Options** command.

■ AutoCAD supports up to four independent menu areas; macros are specified by the ***TABLET1 through ***TABLET4 sections of the *Acad.Mnu* menu file.

■ Menu areas may be skewed, but corners must form a right angle.

■ Projective transformation is a limited form of "rubber sheeting": straight lines remain straight, but not necessarily parallel.

DEFINITIONS
Affine transformation
            Requires three pick points; sets an arbitrary linear 2D transformation with independent x,y scaling and skewing.
Orthogonal transformation
            Requires two pick points; sets the translation; the scaling and rotation angle remain uniform.

Residual Error Is largest is where mapping is least accurate; second largest is where mapping is second-least accurate.

Outcome of fit Reports on the results of transformation types:

Outcome	Meaning
Exact	Enough points to transform data.
Success	More than enough points to transform data.
Impossible	Not enough points to transform data.
Failure	Too many colinear and coincident points.
Cancelled	Fitting cancelled during projective transform.

Projective transformation

Maps a perspective projection from one plane to another plane.

RMS error Root mean square error; smaller is better; measures closeness of fit.

Standard deviation

When near zero, residual error at each point is roughly the same.

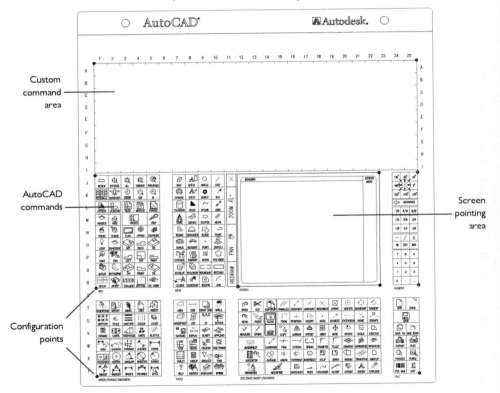

Custom command area

AutoCAD commands

Configuration points

Screen pointing area

TabSurf

Rel.10 Draws a tabulated surface as a 3D mesh; defined by a path curve and a direction vector (*short for TABulated SURFace*).

Command	Alias	Ctrl+	F-key	Alt+	Menu Bar	Tablet
tabsurf	...	...	...	DFT	Draw	P8
					⤷Surfaces	
					⤷Tabulated Surface	

```
Command: tabsurf
Select object for path curve: [pick]
Select object for direction vector: [pick]
```

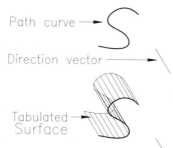

COMMAND LINE OPTIONS

Select object for path curve
Selects the object that defines the tabulation path.
Select object for direction vector
Selects the vector that defines the tabulation direction.

RELATED COMMANDS

Edge	Changes the visibility of 3D face edges.
Explode	Reduces a tabulated surface into 3D faces.
PEdit	Edits a 3D mesh, such as a tabulated surface.
EdgeSurf	Draws a 3D mesh surface between boundaries.
RevSurf	Draws a revolved 3D mesh surface around an axis.
RuleSurf	Draws a 3D mesh surface between open or closed boundaries.

RELATED SYSTEM VARIABLE

SurfTab1 Defines the number of tabulations drawn by **TabSurf** in n-direction.

TIPS

- The path curve can be open or closed: line, 2D polyline, 3D polyline, arc, circle, or ellipse.

- The direction vector defines the direction and length of extrusion.

- The number of m-direction tabulations is always 2 and lies along direction vector.

- The number of n-direction tabulations is determined by system variable **SurfTab1** (default = 6) along curves only.

 **Text**

V. 1.0 Places text, one line at a time, in the drawing.

Command	Alias	Ctrl+	F-key	Alt+	Menu Bar	Tablet
text	dtext	...	...	...	Draw	K8
	dt				⤷Text	
					⤷Single Line Text	

```
Command: text
Current text style:  "Standard"  Text height:  0.2000
Specify start point of text or [Justify/Style]: [pick]
Specify height <0.2000>: ENTER
Specify rotation angle of text <0>: ENTER
Enter text: [enter text]
Enter text: ENTER
```

COMMAND LINE OPTIONS

Specify start point of text
> Indicates the starting point of the text.

ENTER Continues text one line below previously-placed text line.

Specify height Indicates the height of the text; this prompt does not appear if the style has set the height to a value other than 0.

Specify rotation angle of text
> Indicates the rotation angle of the text.

Enter text Specifies the text; press **Enter** twice to end the command.

Justify options:
```
Enter an option [Align/Fit/Center/Middle/Right/TL/TC/TR/ML/
    MC/MR/BL/BC/BR]: [enter an option]
```

Align	Aligns the text between two points with adjusted text height.
Fit	Fits the text between two points with fixed text height.
Center	Centers the text along the baseline.
Middle	Centers the text horizontally and vertically.
Right	Right justifies the text.
TL	Top-left justification.
TC	Top-center justification.
TR	Top-right justification.
ML	Middle-left justification.
MC	Middle-center justification.
MR	Middle-right justification.
BL	Bottom-left justification.
BC	Bottom-center justification.
BR	Bottom-right justification.

Style options:
```
Enter style name or [?] <Standard>: ENTER
```
Style name Indicates a different style name.

? Lists the currently-loaded styles.

TEXT MODIFIERS

%%c	Draws diameter symbol: Ø.
%%d	Draws degree symbol: °.
%%o	Starts and stops overlinning.
%%p	Draws the plus-minus symbol: ±.
%%u	Starts and stops <u>underlining</u>.
%%%	Draws the percent symbol: %.

RELATED COMMANDS

DdEdit	Edits the text.
Change	Changes the text height, rotation, style, and content.
Properties	Changes all aspects of text.
Style	Creates new text styles.
MText	Places paragraph text in drawings.

RELATED SYSTEM VARIABLES

TextSize	The current height of text.
TextStyle	The current style.
ShpName	The default shape name

TIPS

■ Use the **Text** command to place text easily in many locations in the drawing. It displays text on screen as you type.

■ You can erase text by pressing the **BACKSPACE** key while at the 'Text' prompt.

■ *Warning*: the spacing between lines of text does not match the current snap spacing.

■ Transparent commands do not work during the **Text** command.

■ You can enter any justification mode at the 'Start point' prompt.

■ The 'Enter text' prompt repeats until cancelled with **ENTER**.

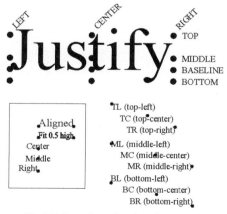

The dot indicates the text insertion point.

'TextScr

V. 2.1   Switches from the AutoCAD window to the Text window (*short for TEXT SCReen*).

Command	Alias	Ctrl+	F-key	Alt+	Menu Bar	Tablet
'textscr	...	...	F2	VLT	View ⤷Display ⤷Text Window	...

Command: **textscr**
Displays the Text window:

COMMAND LINE OPTIONS

Command window navigation:

Key	Meaning
←	Moves the cursor left by one character.
→	Moves the cursor right by one character.
↑	Displays the previous line in the command history.
↓	Displays the next line in the command history.
Page Up	Displays the previous screen of text.
Page Down	Moves to the next screen of text.
Home	Moves the cursor to the start of the line.
End	Moves the cursor to the end of the line.
Insert	Toggles insert mode.
Delete	Deletes the character to the right of the cursor.
BACKSPACE	Deletes the character to the left of the cursor.

EDIT MENU OPTIONS

Paste to CmdLine

        Pastes text from the Clipboard to the command line; available only when the Clipboard contains text.

Copy   Copies selected text to the Clipboard.

Copy History Copies all text to the Clipboard.

Paste   Pastes text from the Clipboard into text window; available only when the Clipboard contains text.

Options   Displays **Options** dialog box; see the **Options** command.

SHORTCUT MENU OPTIONS

Paste To CmdLine
Copy
Copy History
Paste
Options...

Paste to CmdLine

        Pastes text from the Clipboard to the command line; available only when the Clipboard contains text.

Copy   Copies selected text to the Clipboard.

Copy History Copies all text to the Clipboard.

Paste   Pastes text from the Clipboard into text window; available only when the Clipboard contains text.

Options   Displays the **Options** dialog box; see the **Options** command.

RELATED COMMANDS

GraphScr   Switches from the **Text** window to the AutoCAD drawing window.

F2   Toggles between text and graphics widows.

RELATED SYSTEM VARIABLE

ScreenMode Reports whether the screen is in text or graphics mode:

ScreenMode	Meaning
0	Text screen.
1	Graphics screen.
2	Dual screen displaying both text and graphics.

REMOVED COMMAND

TiffIn was removed from AutoCAD Release 14. Use the **ImageAttach** command instead.

'Time

V. 2.5 Displays time-related information about the current drawing.

Command	Alias	Ctrl+	F-key	Alt+	Menu Bar	Tablet
'time	...	...	...	TQT	Tools ↳Inquiry ↳Time	...

```
Command: time
Display/ON/OFF/Reset: ENTER
```

Example output:
```
Current time:            Saturday, June 19, 1999 at 11:17:39:310 AM
Times for this drawing:
  Created:               Saturday, April 11, 1992 at 8:47:04:940 PM
  Last updated:          Saturday, August 06, 1994 at 5:33:43:850 PM
  Total editing time:    0 days 18:15:42.260
  Elapsed timer (on):    0 days 18:15:42.310
  Next automatic save in: <no modifications yet>
Enter option [Display/ON/OFF/Reset]: [enter an option]
```

COMMAND LINE OPTIONS
Display Displays the current time and date.
OFF Turns off the user timer.
ON Turns on the user timer.
Reset Resets the user timer.

RELATED COMMANDS
Status Displays information about the current drawing and environment.
Preferences Sets the automatic back-up time.
F2 Returns to graphics screen.

RELATED SYSTEM VARIABLES
CDate The current date and time.
Date The current date and time in Julian format.
SaveTime The automatic drawing save interval.
TDCreate Date and time the drawing was created.
TDInDwg The time the drawing spent in AutoCAD.
TDUpdate The last date and time the drawing was changed.
TDUsrTimer The current user timer setting.

TIP
■ The time displayed by the **Time** command is only as accurate as your computer's clock; unfortunately, the clock in some personal computers can stray by several minutes per week.

Today

2000i
Displays the **AutoCAD 2002 Today** window, which can replace the **Create New Drawing** dialog box (see **New** Command).

Command	Alias	Ctrl+	F-key	Alt+	Menu Bar	Tablet
today	. . .	. . .	. . .	TT	Tools ⤷Today	. . .

Command: **today**
Displays window:

DIALOG BOX OPTIONS

My Drawings Lists the names of recently-used drawings, template files, new drawing wizards, and symbol libraries.

The Web Provides access to Autodesk's "Point A" Web site; requires a connection to the Internet.

Bulletin Board Displays customizable content.

Open Drawings tab:

Select how to begin

- Most recently used.
- History (by date).
- History (by filename).
- History (by location).

Create Drawings tab:

Select how to begin
- Template.
- Start from scratch.
- Wizards.

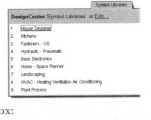

Symbol Libraries tab:

Symbol Libraries

DesignCenter Symbol Libraries or Edit...

1	House Designer
2	Kitchens
3	Fasteners - US
4	Hydraulic - Pneumatic
5	Basic Electronics
6	Home - Space Planner
7	Landscaping
8	HVAC - Heating Ventilation Air Conditioning
9	Plant Process

Edit   Displays dialog box:

Allows you to add, remove, rename, and reorder the names of symbol libraries; does not edit symbols.

RELATED COMMANDS

EndToday   Closes the **AutoCAD Today** window.
New   Displays the **Create New Drawing** dialog box when **Today** is turned off.
Options   Determines whether **Today** is displayed when AutoCAD starts.

TIPS

■ The **Today** window is actually a mini Web browser containing HTML code. The foundation is found in *AcToday.Htm*.

■ Before doing an update, you must have the AutoCAD serial number ready.

Tolerance

Rel.13   Places geometric tolerancing symbols and text.

Command	Alias	Ctrl+	F-key	Alt+	Menu Bar	Tablet
tolerance	tol	...	...	NT	Dimension	X1
					↳Tolerance	

Command: **tolerance**
Displays dialog box.

Clicking a symbol displays this dialog box:

Enter tolerance location: **[pick]**

Orientation symbols:

⊕	Position.	//	Parallelism.
◎	Concentricity and coaxiality.	⊥	Perpendicularity.
=	Symmetry.	∠	Angularity.

Form symbols:

	Cylindricity.
	Flatness.
	Circularity and roundness.
	Straightness.

Profile symbols:

	Profile of the surface.
	Profile of the line.
	Circular runout.
	Total runout.

DIALOG BOX OPTIONS

Sym	Specifies the geometric characteristic symbol.
Tolerance	Specifies the first tolerance value.
Dia	Specifies the places optional Ø (diameter) symbol.
Value	Specifies the tolerance value.
Datum	Specifies the datum reference.
Height	Specifies the projected tolerance zone value.

Projected Tolerance Zone
> Places the projected tolerance zone symbol.

Datum Identifier
> Creates the datum identifier symbol, such as -A-

MC	Displays **Material Condition** dialog box:

Material Condition dialog box:

Ⓜ	Maximum material condition.
Ⓛ	Least material condition.
Ⓢ	Regardless of feature size.

RELATED FILES

Gdt.Shp	Tolerance symbol definition source file.
Gdt.Shx	Compiled tolerance symbol file.

TIP

- You can use the **DdEdit** command to edit tolerance symbols and feature control frames.

DEFINITIONS

Datum	A theoretically-exact geometric reference that establishes the tolerance zone for the feature. These objects can be used as a datum: point, line, plane, cylinder, and other geometry.
Material condition	These symbols modify the geometric characteristics and tolerance values (modifiers for features that vary in size).
Projected tolerance zone	Specifies the height of the fixed perpendicular part's extended portion; changes the tolerance to positional tolerance.
Tolerance	Indicates the amount of variance from perfect form.

-Toolbar

<u>Rel.13</u> Displays or hides one or all toolbars via the command line.

Command	Alias	Ctrl+	F-key	Alt+	Menu Bar	Tablet
-toolbar	...	...	...	...	...	...

*Note: the **Toolbar** and **TbConfig** commands are aliases for the **Customize** command.*

```
Command: -toolbar
Enter toolbar name or [ALL]: ALL
Enter an option [Show/Hide]: s
```

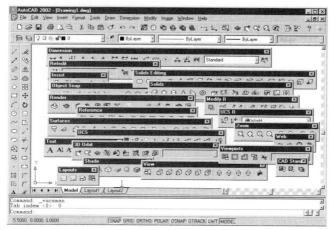

Opening all of AutoCAD's toolbars with the -Toolbar All Show command.

COMMAND LINE OPTIONS

Toolbar name Specifies the name of the toolbar.
ALL Works with all toolbars; must be entered in all capital letters.
Show Displays the toolbar.
Hide Dismisses the toolbar.

RELATED COMMANDS

Customize Customizes toolbars via a dialog box.
MenuLoad Loads a partial menu file, including toolbar definitions.
Tablet Configures the tablet.

RELATED SYSTEM VARIABLE

ToolTips Toggles the display of tooltips.

RELATED FILES

*.Mnc Compiled menu file.
*.Mns AutoCAD source menu file.
*.Bmp BMP bitmap files, which define custom icon buttons.

 # Torus

Rel.11 Draws a 3D torus as a solid model (*an ACIS command*).

Command	Alias	Ctrl+	F-key	Alt+	Menu Bar	Tablet
torus	tor	...	...	DIT	Draw ⤷Solids ⤷Torus	O7

```
Command: torus
Current wire frame density:  ISOLINES=4
Specify center of torus <0,0,0>: [pick]
Specify radius of torus or [Diameter]: [pick]
Specify radius of tube or [Diameter]:[pick]
```

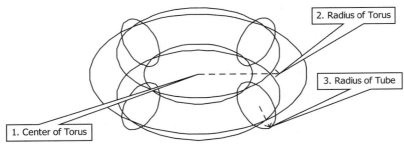

2. Radius of Torus

3. Radius of Tube

1. Center of Torus

COMMAND LINE OPTIONS

Center of torus   Indicates the center of the torus.
Diameter   Indicates the diameter of the torus and the tube.
Radius   Indicates the radius of the torus and the tube.

RELATED COMMANDS

Ai_Torus   Creates a torus from 3D polyfaces.
Cone   Draws solid cones.
Cylinder   Draws solid cylinders.
Sphere   Draws solid spheres.

TIPS

■ When the torus radius is negative, the tube radius must be a larger positive number; for example, with torus radius of -1.99, the tube radius must be greater than +1.99.

■ A negative torus radius creates a football shape.

Football: *Hole-less torus:*

■ Specify a tube diameter larger than the torus diameter to create a hole-less torus.

Trace

V. 1.0 Draws lines with width.

Command	Alias	Ctrl+	F-key	Alt+	Menu Bar	Tablet
trace	...	...	...	...	...	...

```
Command: trace
Specify trace width <0.050>: ENTER
Specify start point: [pick]
Specify next point: [pick]
Specify next point: ENTER
```

COMMAND LINE OPTIONS

Trace width Specifies the width of the trace.
Start point Picks the starting point.
Next point Picks the next vertex.
ENTER Exits the **Trace** command.

RELATED COMMANDS

Line Draws lines with zero width.
MLine Draws up to 16 parallel lines.
PLine Draws polylines and polyline arcs with varying widths.
LWeight Gives every object a width.

RELATED SYSTEM VARIABLES

FillMode Toggles display of fill or outline traces (default = 1, on).
TraceWid Specifies the current width of the trace (default = 0.05).

TIPS

■ Traces are drawn along the centerline of the pick points.

■ Display of a trace segment is delayed by one pick point.

■ During the drawing of traces, you cannot back up since an **Undo** option is missing; if you require this feature, draw wide lines with the **PLine** command, setting the **Width** option.

■ There is no option for controlling joints (always bevelled) or endcapping (always square); if you require these features, draw wide lines with the **MLine** command, setting the solid fill, endcap, and joint options with the **MlStyle** command.

Tracking

Rel.14 Locates x or y points visually, relative to other points in the command sequence; *not* a command but a command modifier.

Modifer	Alias	Ctrl+	F-key	Alt+	Menu Bar	Tablet
tacking	tk	...	...	...	...	T15
	track					

Example usage:
Command: **line**
Specify first point: **[pick]**
Specify next point or [Undo]: **tk**
First tracking point: **[pick]**
Next point (Press ENTER to end tracking): **[pick]**
Next point (Press ENTER to end tracking): ENTER
Specify next point or [Undo]: **[pick]**
Specify next point or [Close/Undo]: ENTER

COMMAND LINE OPTIONS
First tracking point
            Picks the first tracking point.
Next point   Picks the next tracking point.
ENTER   Exits tracking mode.

RELATED COMMANDS
Any command that prompts for a point, such as 'Specify first point' and 'Specify next point.'

TIPS
■ **Tracking** is not a command, but a command option modifier.

■ **Tracking** can be used in conjunction with direct distance entry.

■ In tracking mode, AutoCAD automatically turns on **Ortho** mode to constrain the cursor vertically and horizontally.

■ If you start tracking in the x direction, the next tracking direction is y, and vice versa.

■ You can use tracking as many times as you need to at 'Specify first point' and 'Specify next point' prompts.

Transparency

<u>Rel.14</u> Toggles the transparency of background pixels in a raster image.

Command	Alias	Ctrl+	F-key	Alt+	Menu Bar	Tablet

transparency	...	...	...	MOIT	Modify
					  ↳Object
					    ↳Image
					      ↳Transparency
						X21

Command: **transparency**
Select image(s): **[pick]**
Select image(s): ENTER
Enter transparency mode [On/Off] <Off>: **on**

COMMAND LINE OPTIONS
Select image(s)

        Selects the objects whose transparency to change.
ON   Makes the background pixels transparent.
OFF   Makes the background pixels opaque.

RELATED COMMANDS
ImageAttach Attaches a raster image as an externally-referenced file.
ImageAdjust Changes the brightness, contrast, and fading of a raster image.

'TreeStat

Rel.12 Displays the status of the drawing's spatial index, including the number and depth of nodes (*short for TREE STATistics*).

Command	Alias	Ctrl+	F-key	Alt+	Menu Bar	Tablet
'treestat	...	...	...	...	...	...

Command: **treestat**

COMMAND LINE OPTIONS
None.

RELATED SYSTEM VARIABLES

TreeDepth Specifies the size of the tree-structured spatial index in *xxyy* format:

Depth	Meaning
xx	Number of model space nodes (default = 30).
yy	Number of paper space nodes (default = 20).
-xx	2D drawing.
+xx	3D drawing (default).
3020	Default value of **TreeDepth**.

TreeMax Maximum number of nodes (default = 10,000,000).

TIPS

■ Better performance occurs with fewer objects per oct-tree node.

■ When redraws and object selection seem slow, increase the value of system variable **TreeDepth**.

■ Each node consumes 80 bytes of memory.

DEFINITIONS

Oct tree The model space branch of the spatial index, where all objects are either 2D or 3D. *Oct* comes from the eight volumes in the x,y,z coordinate system of 3D space.

Quad tree The paper space branch of the spatial index, where all objects are two-dimensional. *Quad* comes from the four areas in the x,y coordinate system of 2D space.

Spatial index Objects indexed by oct-region to record their position in 3D space; has a tree structure with two primary branches: oct tree and quad tree. Objects are attached to *nodes*; each node is a branch of the *tree*.

Trim

V. 2.5 Trims lines, arcs, circles, and 2D polylines back to a real or projected cutting line or view.

Command	Alias	Ctrl+	F-key	Alt+	Menu Bar	Tablet
trim	tr	...	...	MT	Modify ⤷Trim	W15

```
Command: trim
Current settings: Projection=UCS Edge=None
Select cutting edges ...
Select objects: [pick]
1 found Select objects: ENTER
Select object to trim or [Project/Edge/Undo]: [pick]
Select object to trim or [Project/Edge/Undo]: ENTER
```

COMMAND LINE OPTIONS

Select objects Selects the cutting edges.
Select object to trim
              Picks the object at the trim end.
Undo Untrims the last trim action.

Edge options:
```
Enter an implied edge extension mode [Extend/No extend]
   <No extend>: e
```
Extend Extends the cutting edge to trim object.
No extend Trims only at an actual cutting edge.

Project options:
```
Enter a projection option [None/Ucs/View] <Ucs>: ENTER
```
None Uses only objects as cutting edge.
Ucs Trims at the x,y plane of current UCS.
View Trims at the current view plane.

RELATED COMMANDS

Change	Changes the size of lines, arcs and circles.
Extend	Lengthens lines, arcs and polylines.
Lengthen	Lengthens open objects.
PEdit	Changes polylines.
Stretch	Lengthens or shortens lines, arcs, and polylines.

U

V. 2.5 Undoes the most recent AutoCAD command (*short for Undo*).

Command	Alias	Ctrl+	F-key	Alt+	Menu Bar	Tablet
u	...	Z	...	EU	Edit ↳Undo	T12

Command: **u**

COMMAND LINE OPTIONS
None.

RELATED COMMANDS
Oops	Unerases the most-recently erased object.
Quit	Exits the drawing, undoing all changes.
Redo	Reverses the most-recent undo, if **U** or **Undo** was the previous command.
Undo	Allows more sophisticated control over undo.

RELATED SYSTEM VARIABLE
UndoCtl Determines the state of undo control:

UndoCtrl	Meaning
0	Undo disabled.
1	Undo enabled.
2	Undo limited to one command.
4	Auto-group mode.
8	Group currently active.

TIPS
- The **U** command is convenient for stepping back through the design process, undoing one command at a time.

- The **U** command is the same as the **Undo 1** command; for greater control over the undo process, use the **Undo** command.

- The **Redo** command redoes the one most-recent undo only.

- The **Quit** command, followed by the **Open** command, restores the drawing to its original state, if not already saved.

- Since the undo mechanism creates a mirror drawing file on disk, disable the **Undo** command with system variable **UndoCtl** (set to 0) when your computer is low on disk space.

- Commands that involve writing to file, plotting, and some display functions (such as **Render**, **Shade**, and **Hide**) are not undone.

Ucs

Rel.10 Defines a new coordinate plane, and restores existing UCSs (*short for User-defined Coordinate System*).

Command	Alias	Ctrl+	F-key	Alt+	Menu Bar	Tablet
ucs	...	...	...	TW	Tools ↳New UCS	W7
				TH	Tools ↳Orthographic UCS	...

```
Command: ucs
Current ucs name:   *TOP*
Enter an option [New/Move/orthoGraphic/Prev/Restore/Save/
    Del/Apply/?/World] <World>: [enter option]
```

COMMAND LINE OPTIONS

New Creates a new user-defined coordinate system.
Move Moves the UCS along the z axis.
orthoGraphic Selects a standard orthographic UCS: top, bottom, front, back, left, and right.
Prev Restores the previous UCS orientation.
Restore Restores a named UCS.
Save Saves the current UCS by name.
Del Deletes the name of a saved UCS.
Apply Applies the UCS setting to a selected viewport, or all active viewports.
? Lists the names of saved UCS orientations.
World Aligns the UCS with the WCS.

New options:
For compatibility with earlier versions of AutoCAD, you may enter any of these options at the earlier 'Enter an option' prompt.
```
Specify origin of new UCS or [ZAxis/3point/OBject/Face/View/X/Y/
    Z] <0,0,0>: [enter option]
```
Specify origin of new UCS
  Moves the UCS to a new origin point.
ZAxis Aligns the UCS with a new origin and z axis.
3point Aligns the UCS with a point on the positive x-axis and positive x,y plane.
OBject Aligns the UCS with a selected object.
Face Aligns the UCS with the face of a 3D ACIS solid object.
View Aligns the UCS with the current view.
X Rotates the UCS about the x axis.
Y Rotates the UCS about the y axis.
Z Rotates the UCS about the z axis.

RELATED TOOLBARS
UCS toolbar:

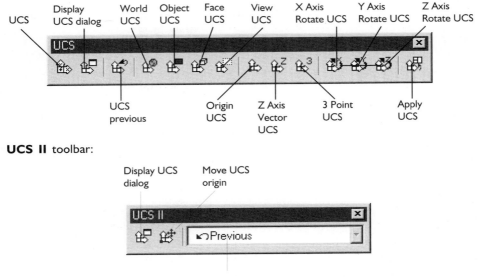

UCS | Display UCS dialog | World UCS | Object UCS | Face UCS | View UCS | X Axis Rotate UCS | Y Axis Rotate UCS | Z Axis Rotate UCS

UCS previous | Origin UCS | Z Axis Vector UCS | 3 Point UCS | Apply UCS

UCS II toolbar:

Display UCS dialog | Move UCS origin

UCS Name

RELATED SYSTEM VARIABLES

UcsAxisAng   Specifies the default rotation angle when the UCS is rotated around an axis using the **X, Y,** or **Z** option of this command

UcsBase   Specifies the UCS that defines the origin and orientation of orthographic UCS settings.

UcsFollow   Shows the plan view in new UCS automatically:

UcsFollow	Meaning
0	No change in view (default).
1	Displays plan view of new UCS.

UcsIcon   Determines visibility and location of UCS icon:

UcsIcon	Meaning
0	UCS icon not displayed.
1	UCS icon displayed in lower-right corner.
2	UCS icon displayed at the UCS origin, when possible.
3	UCS icon displayed at UCS always (default).

UcsOrg   Specifires the WCS coordinates of UCS icon (default = 0,0,0).

UcsOrtho   Specifies whether the related UCS is automatically displayed when an orthographic view is restored.

UcsView	Specifies whether the current UCS is saved when a view is created with the **View** command.
UcsVp	Specifies that the UCS reflects the UCS of the currently active viewport.
UcsXdir	Specifies the X direction of current UCS (default = 1,0,0).
UcsYdir	Specifires the Y direction of current UCS (default = 0,1,0).
WorldUcs	Correlates the WCS to the UCS:

WorldUcs	Meaning
0	Current UCS is WCS.
1	UCS is same as WCS (default).

RELATED COMMANDS

UcsMan	Modifies the UCS via a dialog box.
UcsIcon	Controls the visibility of the UCS icon.
Plan	Changes the view to the plan view of the current UCS.

TIPS

- Use the **UCS** command to draw objects at odd angles in 3D space.

- Although you can create a UCS in paper space, you cannot use 3D viewing commands.

- A UCS can be aligned with these objects: point, line, trace, 2D polyline, solid, arc, circle, text, shape, dimension, attribute definition, 3D face, and block reference.

- A UCS will *not* align with these objects: mline, ray, xline, 3D polyline, spline, ellipse, leader, viewport, 3D solid, 3D mesh, region.

DEFINITIONS

UCS	User-defined 2D coordinate system oriented in 3D space; sets a working plane, orients 2D objects, defines the extrusion direction, and the axis of rotation.
WCS	World coordinate system is the default 3D x,y,z coordinate system.

UcsIcon

Rel.10   Controls the location and display of the UCS icon.

Command	Alias	Ctrl+	F-key	Alt+	Menu Bar	Tablet
ucsicon	...	...	...	VLU	View	L2
					⍉Display	
					⍉UCS Icon	

Command: **ucsicon**
Enter an option [ON/OFF/All/Noorigin/ORigin] <ON>:
   [enter option]

COMMAND LINE OPTIONS

All   Forces the changes of this command effective in all viewports.
Noorigin   Always displays the UCS icon in lower-left corner.
OFF   Turns off the display of the UCS icon.
ON   Turns on the display of the UCS icon.
ORigin   Displays the UCS icon at the current UCS origin.

RELATED SYSTEM VARIABLE

UcsIcon   Determines the visibility and location of UCS icon:

UcsIcon	Meaning
0	UCS icon not displayed.
1	UCS icon displayed in lower-right corner.
2	UCS icon displayed at the UCS origin, when possible.
3	UCS icon displayed at UCS always (default).

RELATED COMMAND

UCS   Creates and controls user-defined coordinate systems.

TIPS

■ The UCS icon varies, depending on the current viewpoint relative to the active UCS:

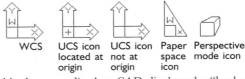

WCS | UCS icon located at origin | UCS icon not at origin | Paper space icon | Perspective mode icon

■ When you cannot reliably draw or edit, AutoCAD displays the "broken pencil" icon (left):

■ When AutoCAD 2002 switches from 2D wireframe mode to one of the **ShadeMode** command's options, such as 3D wireframe and flat rendered, the UCS icon changes to a 3D icon (above, right).

UcsMan

<u>**2000**</u>   Displays the UCS dialog box (*formerly the **DdUcs** and **DdUcsP** commands*).

Command	Alias	Ctrl+	F-key	Alt+	Menu Bar	Tablet
ucsman	dducs ...	...	...	Tools ⌐Named UCS	W8
	dducsp				Tools ⌐Orthographic UCS ⌐Preset	W9

+ucsman

Command: **ucsman**
Displays dialog box.

DIALOG BOX OPTIONS
Named UCSs tab:

Named UCSs   Lists the names of the AutoCAD-generated and user-defined coordinate systems of the current viewport in the active drawing; the arrowhead points to the current UCS.

Set Current   Restores the selected UCS.

Details   Displays the **UCS Details** dialog box:

Orthographic UCSs tab:

Name	Lists the six standard orthographic UCS views: top, bottom, front, back, left, and right.
Depth	Specifies the height of the UCS above the x,y plane.
Relative to	Specifies the orientation of the selected UCS relative to the WCS or to a customized UCS.
Set Current	Activates the selected UCS.
Details	Displays the **UCS Details** dialog box.

Settings tab:

UCS icon settings options:

On	Displays the UCS icon in the current viewport; each viewport can display the UCS icon independently.

Display at UCS origin point

> **On**: Displays the UCS icon at the origin of the current UCS.
>
> **Off**: Displays the UCS icon at the lower-left corner of the viewport.

Apply to all active viewports

> Applies these UCS icon settings to all active viewports in the current drawing.

UCS settings options:

Save UCS with viewport

> **On**: Saves the UCS setting with the viewport.
>
> **Off**: Current viewport determines UCS settings.

Update view to Plan when UCS is changed

> Restores plan view when the UCS changes.

SHORTCUT MENU OPTIONS

*Right-click the list in the **Named UCSs** tab:*

> Set Current
> Rename
> Delete
> Details...

Set Current	Sets the selected UCS as active.
Rename	Renames the selected UCS; you cannot rename the World UCS.
Delete	Erases the selected UCS; you cannot delete the World UCS.
Details	Displays the **UCS Details** dialog box.

*Right-click the list in the **Orthographic UCS** tab:*

> Set Current
> Reset
> Depth
> Details...

Set Current	Sets the selected UCS as active.
Reset	Restores the origin of the selected UCS.
Depth	Moves the UCS in the z direction.
Details	Displays the **UCS Details** dialog box.

+UCSMAN COMMAND

Command: **+ucsman**
Tab index <0>: **ENTER**

COMMAND LINE OPTION

Tab index   Displays the tab related to the tab number:

Index	Meaning
0	**Named UCS** tab.
1	**Orthographic UCS** tab.
2	**Settings** tab.

RELATED SYSTEM VARIABLES

UcsAxisAng	Specifies the default rotation angle when the UCS is rotated around an axis using the **X**, **Y**, or **Z** option of this command
UcsBase	Specifies the UCS that defines the origin and orientation of orthographic UCS settings.
UcsFollow	Shows the plan view in new UCS automatically:

UcsFollow	Meaning
0	No change in view (default).
1	Displays plan view of new UCS.

UcsIcon	Determines the visibility and location of UCS icon:

UcsIcon	Meaning
0	UCS icon not displayed.
1	UCS icon displayed in lower-right corner.
2	UCS icon displayed at the UCS origin, when possible.
3	UCS icon displayed at UCS always (default).

UcsOrg	Specifies the WCS coordinates of UCS icon (default = 0,0,0)
UcsOrtho	Specifies whether the related UCS is automatically displayed when an orthographic view is restored.
UcsView	Specifies whether the current UCS is saved when a view is created with the **View** command.
UcsVp	Specifies that the UCS reflects the UCS of the currently-active viewport.
UcsXdir	Specifies the X direction of current UCS (default = 1,0,0).
UcsYdir	Specifies the Y direction of current UCS (default = 0,1,0).
WorldUcs	Correlates the WCS to the UCS:

WorldUcs	Meaning
0	Current UCS is WCS.
1	UCS is same as WCS (default).

RELATED COMMANDS

UCS	Displays the UCS options at the command line.
UcsIcon	Changes the display of the UCS icon.
Plan	Displays the plan view of the WCS or a UCS.

TIPS

■ **Unnamed** is the first entry, when the current UCS is unnamed.

■ **World** is the default for new drawings; it cannot be renamed or deleted.

■ **Previous** is the previous UCS; you can move back through several previous UCSs.

Undefine

Rel. 9 Makes an AutoCAD command unavailable.

Command	Alias	Ctrl+	F-key	Alt+	Menu Bar	Tablet
undefine	...	...	...	...		

```
Command: undefine
Enter command name: [enter name]
```

Example usage:
```
Command: undefine
Enter command name: line
Command: line
Unknown command.  Type ? for list of commands.
Command: .line
From point:
```

COMMAND OPTIONS

Enter command name
> Specifies the name of the command to make unavailable.

. > (*Period*) Precede undefined command with a period to redefine it temporarily.

RELATED COMMAND

Redefine   Redefines an AutoCAD command.

TIPS

■ Commands created by programs cannot be undefined, including the following programming interfaces:

> AutoLISP and Visual LISP.
> ObjectARx.
> Visual Basic for Applications.
> External commands.
> Aliases.

■ In menu macros written with international language versions of AutoCAD, precede command names with an underscore character (_) to translate the command name into English automatically.

Undo

V. 2.5   Undoes the effect of previous commands.

Command	Alias	Ctrl+	F-key	Alt+	Menu Bar	Tablet
undo	...	...	...	...	...	...

```
Command: undo
Enter the number of operations to undo or [Auto/Control/
    BEgin/End/Mark/Back] <1>: [enter option]
```

COMMAND LINE OPTIONS

Auto	Treats a menu macro as a single command.
Control	Limits the options of the **Undo** command:
All	Toggles on full undo.
None	Turns off undo feature.
One	Limits the **Undo** command to a single undo.
BEgin	Groups a sequence of operations (formerly the **Group** options).
End	Ends the group option.
Mark	Sets a marker.
Back	Undoes back to the marker.
number	Indicates the number of commands to undo.

RELATED COMMANDS

Oops	Unerases the most-recently erased object.
Quit	Leaves the drawing without saving changes.
Redo	Undoes the most recent undo.
U	Undoes a single step.

RELATED SYSTEM VARIABLES

UndoCtl   Determines the state of undo control:

UndoCtrl	Meaning
0	Undo disabled.
1	Undo enabled.
2	Undo limited to one command.
4	Auto-group mode.
8	Group currently active.

UndoMarks   Number of undo marks placed in the **Undo** control stream.

TIP

- Since the undo mechanism creates a mirror drawing file on disk, disable the **Undo** command with system variable **UndoCtl** (set it to 0) when your computer is low on disk space.

- There are a number of commands and system variables that cannot be undone, including: **About, Area, AttExt, CvPort, DbList, Delay, Dist, DxfIn, DxfOut, GraphScr, Help, Hide, Id, List, New, Open, Plot, PsOut, QSave, Quit, Recover, Redraw, RedrawAll, Regen, RegenAll, ReInit, Resume, Save, SaveAs, Shade, Shell, Status, TextScr,** and others.

Union

Joins two or more solids and regions together into a single model (*an ACIS command*).

Command	Alias	Ctrl+	F-key	Alt+	Menu Bar	Tablet
union	uni	...	...	MNU	Modify ↳Solids Editing ↳Union	X15

```
Command: union
Select objects: [pick]
Select objects: [pick]
```

Before Union   *After Union*

COMMAND LINE OPTION

Select objects Selects the objects to join into a single object; you must select at least two ACIS objects.

RELATED COMMANDS

Intersect Creates a solid model from the intersection of two objects.

Subtract Creates a solid model by subtracting one object from another.

TIPS

■ You must select at least two ACIS solid or coplanar region objects.

■ The two objects need not overlap for this command to operate.

'Units

V. 1.4 Controls the display and format of coordinates and angles.

Command	Alias	Ctrl+	F-key	Alt+	Menu Bar	Tablet
'units	**un**	...	...	**OU**	**Format**	**V4**
	ddunits				**⇘Units**	
-units	**-un**					

```
command: units
```
Displays dialog box:

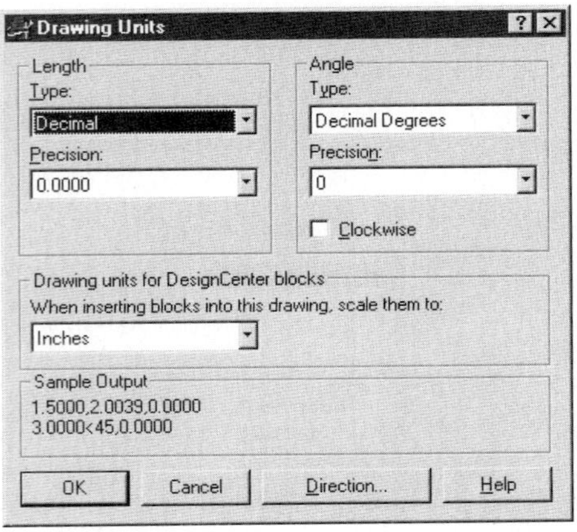

DIALOG BOX OPTIONS

***Length** options:*

Type Sets the format for units of linear measure displayed by AutoCAD: Architectural, Decimal, Engineering, Fractional, and Scientific.

Precision Specifies the number of decimal places or fractional accuracy.

***Angle** options:*

Type Sets the current angle format.

Precision Sets the precision for the current angle format.

Clockwise Calculates positive angles in the clockwise direction.

Drawing units for AutoCAD DesignCenter blocks

Specifies the units when blocks are inserted from the AutoCAD DesignCenter.

Direction Displays dialog box.

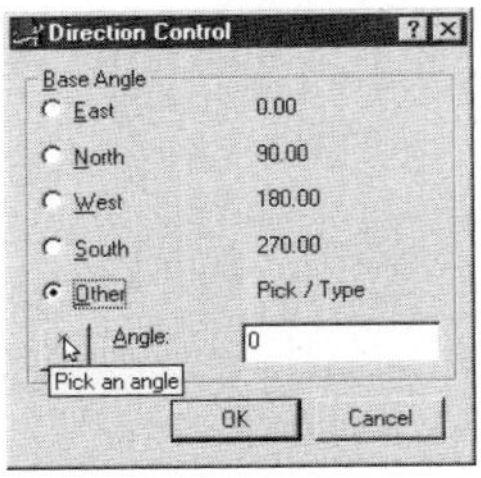

Base Angle *options:*

East	Sets the base angle to 0 degrees (default).
North	Sets the base angle to 90 degrees.
West	Sets the base angle to 180 degrees.
South	Sets the base angle to 270 degrees.
Other	Turns on the **Angle** option.
Angle	Sets the base angle to any direction.
Pick an angle	Dismisses the dialog box temporarily, and allows you to define the base angle by picking two points in the drawing; AutoCAD prompts you 'Pick angle' and 'Specify second point'.

-UNITS COMMAND

```
Command: -units
Report formats:        (Examples)

  1.  Scientific      1.55E+01
  2.  Decimal         15.50
  3.  Engineering     1'-3.50"
  4.  Architectural   1'-3 1/2"
  5.  Fractional      15 1/2
```

With the exception of Engineering and Architectural formats, these formats can be used with any basic unit of measurement. For example, Decimal mode is perfect for metric units as well as decimal English units.

```
Enter choice, 1 to 5 <2>: ENTER
Enter number of digits to right of decimal point
    (0 to 8) <4>: ENTER
Systems of angle measure:       (Examples)

  1.  Decimal degrees             45.0000
  2.  Degrees/minutes/seconds     45d0'0"
  3.  Grads                       50.0000g
  4.  Radians                     0.7854r
  5.  Surveyor's units            N 45d0'0" E

Enter choice, 1 to 5 <1>: ENTER
Enter number of fractional places for display of angles
    (0 to 8) <0>: ENTER

Direction for angle 0:
   East    3 o'clock  =  0
   North  12 o'clock  =  90
   West    9 o'clock  =  180
   South   6 o'clock  =  270
Enter direction for angle 0 <0>: ENTER

Measure angles clockwise? [Yes/No] <N> ENTER
```

COMMAND LINE OPTIONS

Report formats Selects scientific, decimal, engineering, architectural, or fractional format for length display.

Number of digits to right of decimal point
Specifies the number of decimal places between 0 and 8.

Systems of angle measure
Selects decimal degrees, degrees/minutes/seconds, grads, radians, or surveyor's units for angle display.

Denominator of smallest fraction to display
Specifies the denominator of faction displays, such as 1/2 or 1/128.

Number of fractional places for display of angles
Specifies the number of decimal places between 0 and 8.

Direction for angle 0
Selects the direction for 0 degrees as east, north, west, or south.

Do you want angles measured clockwise?
Yes: measures angles clockwise.
No: measures angles counterclockwise.

F2   Returns to graphics screen.

RELATED SYSTEM VARIABLES

AngBase   Specifies the direction of zero degrees.
AngDir   Specifies the direction of angle measurement.
AUnits   Specifies the units of angles.
AuPrec   Specifies the displayed precision of angles.
InsUnits   Specifies the drawing units for blocks dragged from AutoCAD DesignCenter:

InsUnits	Meaning
0	Unitless.
1	Inches.
2	Feet.
3	Miles.
4	Millimeters.
5	Centimeters.
6	Meters.
7	Kilometers.
8	Microinches.
9	Mils.
10	Yards; 3 feet.
11	Angstroms; 0.1 nanometers.
12	Nanometers; 10E-9 meters.
13	Microns; 10E-6 meters.
14	Decimeters; 0.1 meter.
15	Decameters; 10 meters.
16	Hectometers; 100 meters.
17	Gigameters; 10E9 meters.
18	Astronomical Units; 149.597E8 kilometers.
19	Light Years; 9.4605E9 kilometers.
20	Parsecs; 3.26 light years.

InsUnitsDefSource
          Specifies that source units that should be used.
InsUnitsDefTarget
          Specifies that target units that should be used.
LUnits   Specifies the unit of measurement.
LuPrec   Specifies the displayed precision of coordinates.
UnitMode   Toggles the type of display units.

RELATED COMMAND

New   Sets up a drawing with Imperial or metric units.

TIPS

- Since **'Units** is a transparent command, you can change units during another command.

- The 'Direction Angle' prompt lets AutoCAD start the angle measurement from any direction.

- AutoCAD accepts the following notations for angle input:

Notation	Meaning
<	Specify an angle based on current units setting.
<<	Bypass angle translation set by **Units** command to use 0-angle-is-east direction and decimal degrees.
<<<	Bypass angle translation; use angle units set by **Units** command and 0-angle-is-east direction.

- The system variable **UnitMode** forces AutoCAD to display units in the same manner that you enter them.

- Do not use a suffix — such as 'r' or 'g' — for angles entered as radians or grads; instead, use the **Units** command to set angle measurement to radians and grads.

- The **Drawing units for AutoCAD DesignCenter blocks** option is for inserting blocks from AutoCAD DesignCenter, and especially for when the block was created in other units.

- To not scale a block when dragged from the AutoCAD DesignCenter window, select **Unitless**.

Vbaide

2000 Displays the **Visual Basic** window (*short for Visual Basic for Applications Integrated Development Environment*).

Command	Alias	Alt+	F-key	Alt+	Menu Bar	Tablet
vbaide	...	F11	...	TMB	Tools	...
					↳Macro	
					↳Visual Basic Editor	

Command: **vbaide**
Displays window:

MENU BAR OPTION
*Select **Help | Microsoft Visual Basic Help** for assistance in using this VBA IDE window.*

RELATED COMMANDS
VbaLoad	Loads a VBA project; displays the **Open VBA Project** dialog box.
VbaMan	Displays the **VBA Manager** dialog box.
VbaRun	Displays the **Macros** dialog box.
VbaStmt	Executes a VBA expression at the command line.
VbaUnload	Unloads a VBA project.

RELATED SYSTEM VARIABLES
None.

TIPS

■ VBA is short for "Visual Basic for Applications," a macro programming language common to a number of Windows applications; it is based on the Visual Basic programming language.

■ AutoCAD 2002 contains sample VBA projects in the *Acad 2002**Sample**VBA* folder.

■ For more information about Visual Basic for Applications, read the *ActiveX and VBA Developer's Guide* included with AutoCAD.

■ Since loading a macro from other sources into AutoCAD can also expose your computer to malicious viruses, AutoCAD displays the following warning:

More Info   Displays AutoCAD's on-line help window.
Always ask before opening projects with macros
                     On: Displays this dialog box.
                     Off: Prevents this dialog box from being displayed; to turn back on, use the **VbaRun** command' s **Options** dialog box; see **VbaRun** command.
Disable Macros   Loads VBA project file, but disables macros; you can view, edit, and save the macros. To renable the macros, close the project and open it again with **Enable Macros**.
Enable Macros   Loads the project file with macros enabled.
Do Not Load   Prevents the project file from being loaded.

■ Since many viruses can be spread via VBA macros, I strongly recommend that your computer have real-time virus protection to prevent infection.

VbaLoad

<u>**2000**</u>   Loads a VBA project into AutoCAD (*short for Visual Basic for Applications LOAD*).

Command	Alias	Ctrl+	F-key	Alt+	Menu Bar	Tablet
vbaload	...	...	...	TML	Tools ⤷Macro ⤷Load Project	...

-vbaload

Command: **vbaload**
*Displays the **Open VBA Project** dialog box.*
*When the project contains macros, the **AutoCAD** dialog box is displayed; see the **Vbaide** command.*

DIALOG BOX OPTIONS

Open   Opens the VBA project into AutoCAD; use the **VbaMan** command to run the macros found in the project.

Open Visual Basic Editor
              Displays the Visual Basic Editor; see the **Vbaide** command.

-VBALOAD COMMAND

Command: **-vbaload**
Open VBA project <*projectname*>: **[enter project name]**

COMMAND LINE OPTION

Open VBA project
              Specifies the project path and filename.

RELATED COMMANDS

Vbaide	Displays the Visual Basic for Applications development environment window.
VbaMan	Displays the **VBA Manager** dialog box.
VbaRun	Displays the **Macros** dialog box.
VbaStmt	Executes a VBA expression at the command line.
VbaUnload	Unloads a VBA project.

RELATED SYSTEM VARIABLES

None.

TIPS

- You may load one or more VBA projects; there is no practical limit to the number.

- To unload a VBA project, use the **VbaUnload** command.

- This command does not load embedded VBA projects; these projects are automatically loaded with the drawing.

- When the project contains macros, AutoCAD displays the AutoCAD dialog box to warn you about protection against macro viruses; see the **Vbaide** command.

- For more information about Visual Basic for Applications, read the *ActiveX and VBA Developer's Guide* included with AutoCAD.

VbaMan

Displays the **VBA Manager** dialog box (*short for Visual Basic for Applications MANager*).

Command	Alias	Ctrl+	F-key	Alt+	Menu Bar	Tablet
vbaman	...	...	...	TMV	Tools	...
					↳Macro	
					↳VBA Manager	

Command: **vbaman**
Displays dialog box:

DIALOG BOX OPTIONS

Drawing options:

Drawing   Lists the names of drawings currently loaded in AutoCAD.

Embedded Project
        Specifies the name of the embedded project.

Extract   Moves the embedded project from the drawing to a global project file.

Projects options:

Embed	Embeds the project in the drawing.
New	Creates a new project; default name = **Global** *n*.
Save as	Saves a global project.
Load	Displays the **Open VBA Project** dialog box; see the **VbaLoad** command.
Unload	Unloads the global project.
Macros	Displays the **Macros** dialog box; see the **VbaRun** command.

Visual Basic Editor
        Displays the Visual Basic Editor; see the **Vbaide** command.

▶ VbaRun

2000 Displays the **Macros** dialog box (*short for Visual Basic for Applications RUN*).

Command	Alias	Alt+	F-key	Alt+	Menu Bar	Tablet
vbarun	...	F8	...	TMM	Tools	...
					⁴Macro	
					⁴Macros	

-vbarun

Command: **vbarun**

DIALOG BOX OPTIONS

Macro name	Specifies the name of the macro; enter a name or select one from the list.
Macros in	Specifies the projects and drawings containing macros from: all active drawings and projects; all active drawings; all active projects; and any single drawing or project currently open in AutoCAD.
Description	Describes the macro; you may modify the description.

Run	Runs the macro.
Close	Closes the dialog box.
Help	Displays context-sensitive on-line help.
Step into	Displays the **Visual Basic Editor** and executes the macro, pausing at the first executable line of code.
Edit	Displays the **Visual Basic Editor** with the macro; see the **Vbaide** command.
Create	Displays the **Visual Basic Editor** with an empty procedure.
Delete	Erases the selected macro.
VBA Manager	Displays the **VBA Manager** dialog box; see the **VbaMan** command.

Options   Displays the **VBA Options** dialog box:

Enable auto embedding

Creates an embedded VBA project for all drawings when you open the drawing:

Allow Break on errors

On: Stops the macro, and displays the **Visual Basic Editor** with the code, showing the error in the macro.
Off: Displays an error message, and stops the macro.

Enable macro virus protection

Enables virus protection, which displays a dialog box when VBA macros are loaded; see **Vbaide** command.

-VBARUN COMMAND

Command: **-vbarun**
Macro name: **[enter macro name]**

COMMAND LINE OPTION

Macro name   Treats a menu macro as a single command.

RELATED COMMANDS

Vbaide   Displays the **Visual Basic for Applications** integrated development environment window.
VbaLoad   Loads a VBA project; displays the **Open VBA Project** dialog box.
VbaMan   Displays the **VBA Manager** dialog box.
VbaStmt   Executes a VBA expression at the command line.
VbaUnload   Unloads a VBA project.

RELATED SYSTEM VARIABLES

None.

TIPS

- A *macro* is an executable subroutine; each project can contain one or more macros.
- When the macro's name is not unique among loaded projects, include the module's project and names in this format: **Project.Module.Macro**
- When the macro is not yet loaded, include the DVB filename using this format: **Filenamedvb!Project.Module.Macro**

VbaStmt

Executes a single line VBA expression at the command prompt (*short for Visual Basic for Applications StaTeMenT*).

Command	Alias	Ctrl+	F-key	Alt+	Menu Bar	Tablet
vbastmt	...	...	...	...	...	...

```
Command: vbastmt
Statement: [enter VBA statement]
```

COMMAND LINE OPTION

Statement   Specifies the VBA statement for AutoCAD to execute.

RELATED COMMANDS

Vbaide   Displays the **Visual Basic for Applications** integrated development environment window.

VbaLoad   Loads a VBA project; displays the **Open VBA Project** dialog box.

VbaMan   Displays the **VBA Manager** dialog box.

VbaRun   Displays the **Macros** dialog box.

VbaUnload   Unloads a VBA project.

RELATED SYSTEM VARIABLES

None.

TIPS

■ A VBA *statement* is a complete instruction containing keywords, operators, variables, constants, and expressions.

■ A VBA *macro* is an executable subroutine.

■ At the 'Statement' prompt, enter a single line of code; use the colon (:) to separate multiple statements on the single line.

VbaUnload

Unloads a VBA project (*short for Visual Basic for Applications UNLOAD*).

Command	Alias	Ctrl+	F-key	Alt+	Menu Bar	Tablet
vbaunload	...	...	...	...	...	...

Command: **vbaunload**
Unload VBA Project: **[enter project name]**

COMMAND LINE OPTION
Unload VBA Project
Specifies the name of the VBA project to unload.
ENTER   Unloads the active global project.

RELATED COMMANDS
Vbaide   Displays the **Visual Basic for Applications** integrated development environment window.
VbaLoad   Loads a VBA project; displays the **Open VBA Project** dialog box.
VbaMan   Displays the **VBA Manager** dialog box.
VbaRun   Displays the **Macros** dialog box.
VbaStmt   Executes a VBA expression at the command line.

RELATED SYSTEM VARIABLES
None.

TIPS
■ When you do not enter a project name, AutoCAD unloads the active global project.

■ To load a VBA project, use the **VbaLoad** command.

View

V. 2.0 Saves and displays the view in the current viewport by name.

Command	Alias	Ctrl+	F-key	Alt+	Menu Bar	Tablet
view	v	. . .	. . .	VN	View Named Views	M5
+view						
-view	-v			V3	View 3D Views	O3-Q5

Command: view
Displays dialog box.

DIALOG BOX OPTIONS
Named Views tab:

Name	Lists the names of saved views in the current drawing.
Location	Locates the view in Model or a Layout.
UCS	Names the UCS saved with the view.
Perspective	Specifies whether the view was saved in perspective view, was clipped, or neither.
Set Current	Restores the named view.
New	Displays the **New View** dialog box.
Details	Displays the **View Details** dialog box.

Orthographic & Isometric Views tab:

Names	Lists the names of standard orthographic and isometric views; an arrowhead points to the current view.
Relative to	Sets the selected view relative to the WCS or a named UCS.
Restore orthographic UCS with View	
	Restores the associated UCS.
Set Current	Sets the selected view; after clicking **OK**, AutoCAD automatically zooms to the extents of the view.

New View dialog box:

View name	Specifies the view name; up to 255 characters long.
Current display	
	Stores the current viewport as the named view.
Define window	Stores a windowed area as the named view.
Define View Window	
	Dismisses the dialog box temporarily, and prompts you to pick two corners that define the view.

UCS Settings options:
Save UCS with view
> Toggles the option to save a UCS with the named view.

UCS name   Selects the name of a UCS to store with the named view.

View Details dialog box

Relative to   Sets the selected view relative to the WCS or a named UCS.

SHORTCUT MENU OPTIONS

Right-click the list in the **Named Views** *tab:*

Set Current   Sets the selected view as active.

Rename   Renames the selected view; you cannot rename the Current view.

Delete   Erases the selected view; you cannot delete the Current view.

Details   Displays the **View Details** dialog box.

+VIEW COMMAND

Command: **+view**
Tab index <0>: ENTER

Tab index   Specifies the tab of the **View** dialog box to display:

Index	Meaning
0	Named Views tab (default).
1	Orthographic & Isometric Views tab.

-VIEW COMMAND

```
Command: -view
Enter an option [?/Orthographic/Delete/Restore/Save/Ucs/
   Window]: [enter an option]
```

COMMAND LINE OPTIONS

?	Lists the names of views saved in the current drawing.
Delete	Deletes a named view.
Restore	Restores a named view.
Save	Saves the current view with a name.
Ucs	Saves the current UCS with the view.
Window	Saves a windowed view with a name.

Orthographic options:

```
Enter an option [Top/Bottom/Front/BAck/Left/Right] <Top>:
   [enter an option]
Restoring Model space view.
Select Viewport for view: [pick]
Regenerating model.
```

Enter an option Selects a standard orthographic view for the current viewport: Top, Bottom, Front, BAck, Left, or Right.

Select Viewport for view
Selects the viewport — in either Model or layout tab — in which to apply the orthographic view.

RELATED COMMANDS

Rename	Changes the name of views via a dialog box.
UCS	Creates and displays user-defined coordiante systems.
PartialLoad	Loads a portion of a drawing, based on view names.
Open	Opens a drawing and optionally starts with a named view.
Plot	Plots a named view.

RELATED SYSTEM VARIABLES

ViewCtr	Specifies the coordinates of the center of the view.
ViewSize	Specifies the height of the view.

TIPS

- Name views in your drawing to move quickly from one detail to another.

- The **Plot** command plots named views of a drawing.

- Objects outside of the window created by the **Window** option may be displayed, but are not plotted.

- You create separate views in model and paper space; when listing named views with ?, AutoCAD indicates an 'M' or 'P' next to the view name.

ViewRes

V. 2.5 Controls the roundness of curved objects; determines whether zooms and pans are performed as redraws or regens (*short for VIEW RESolution*).

Command	Alias	Ctrl+	F-key	Alt+	Menu Bar	Tablet
viewres	...	...	...	...	...	...

```
Command: viewres
Do you want fast zooms? [Yes/No] <Y>: ENTER
Enter circle zoom percent (1-20000) <100>: ENTER
```

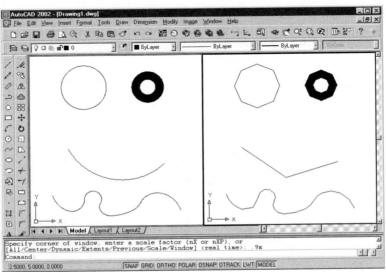

Circle zoom percent = 100 (at left) and 1 (at right).

COMMAND LINE OPTIONS

Do you want fast zooms?

> **Yes**: AutoCAD tries to make every zoom and pan a redraw (faster).
>
> **No**: Every zoom and pan causes a regeneration (slower).

Enter circle zoom percent

> Smaller values display faster, but make circles look less round (see figure); default = 100.

RELATED SYSTEM VARIABLE

WhipArc Toggles the display of circles and arcs as vectors or as true, rounded objects.

RELATED COMMAND

RegenAuto Determines whether AutoCAD uses redraws or regens.

REMOVED COMMAND

VlConv was removed from AutoCAD Release 14; use **3dsIn** and **3dsOut** instead.

VLisp

Opens the VLisp integrated development environment *(short for Visual LISP)*.

Command	Alias	Ctrl+	F-key	Alt+	Menu Bar	Tablet
vlisp	vlide ...		...	TSV	Tools	...
					⌐AutoLISP	
					⌐Visual LISP Editor	

vlide

Command: **vlisp**
Displays window:

MENU BAR OPTION
Select **Help | Visual LISP Help Topics** *for assistance in using this VLISP window.*

RELATED COMMAND
AppLoad   Loads Visual LISP applications, as well as programs written in AutoLISP and other APIs.

TIP
■ Sample VLisp code can be found in the *\Acad 2002\Sample\Vlisp* folder.

VpClip

2000 Clips a layout viewport (*short for ViewPort CLIPping*).

Command	Alias	Ctrl+	F-key	Alt+	Menu Bar	Tablet
vpclip	...	...	...	...	Modify ⌐Clip ⌐Viewport	...

```
Command: vpclip
Select viewport to clip: [pick]
Select clipping object or [Polygonal] <Polygonal>: [pick]
```
The selected viewport disappears, and is replaced by the new clipped viewport.

COMMAND LINE OPTIONS

Select viewport to clip
> Selects the viewport that will be clipped.

Select clipping object
> Selects the object that defines the clipping boundary: closed polyline, circle, ellipse, closed spline, or region.

Polygonal options:
```
Specify start point: [pick]
Specify next point or [Arc/Close/Length/Undo]: [pick]
Specify next point or [Arc/Close/Length/Undo]: c
```
Specify start point
> Specifies the starting point for the polygon.

Arc   Draws an arc segment; see the **Arc** command.

Close   Closes the polygon.

Length   Draws a straight segment of specified length.

Undo   Undoes the previous polygon segment.

RELATED COMMAND

Mview   Creates rectangular and polygonal viewports in paper space.

TIPS

■ This command does not operate in Model tab.

■ An example of clipped viewports:

VpLayer

V. 2.1 Controls the visibility of layers in viewports, when **TileMode** is turned off (*short for ViewPort LAYER*).

Command	Alias	Ctrl+	F-key	Alt+	Menu Bar	Tablet
vplayer	...	...	...	...	...	...

```
Command: vplayer
Enter an option [?/Freeze/Thaw/Reset/Newfrz/Vpvisdflt]:
   [enter an option]
Select a viewport: [pick]
```

COMMAND LINE OPTIONS

Freeze   Indicates the names of layers to freeze in this viewport.

Newfrz   Creates new layers which will be frozen in all newly-created viewports (short for NEW FReeZe).

Reset   Resets the state of layers based on the **Vpvisdflt** settings.

Thaw   Indicates the names of layers to thaw in this viewport.

Vpvisdflt   Determines which layers will be frozen in a newly-created viewport and default visibility in existing viewports (short for ViewPort VISibility DeFauLT).

?   Lists the layers frozen in the current viewport.

RELATED COMMANDS

Layer   Creates and controls layers in all viewports.

MView   Creates and joins viewports when tilemode is off.

RELATED SYSTEM VARIABLE

TileMode   Controls whether viewports are tiled or overlapping.

VPoint

Rel.10 Changes the viewpoint of a 3D drawing *(short for ViewPOINT)*.

Command	Alias	Ctrl+	F-key	Alt+	Menu Bar	Tablet
vpoint	-vp	...	...	V3V	View	N4
					⌐3D Views	
					⌐VPOINT⌐	

```
Command: vpoint
Current view direction:  VIEWDIR=0.0000,0.0000,1.0000
Specify a view point or [Rotate] <display compass and
   tripod>: ENTER
```

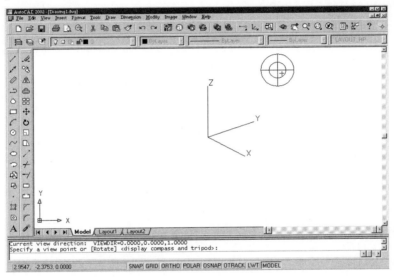

COMMAND LINE OPTIONS

Specify a view point
Indicates the new 3D viewpoint by coordinates.

Rotate   Indicates the new 3D viewpoint by angle.

ENTER   Brings up visual guides (see figure).

RELATED COMMANDS

DdVpoint   Adjusts the viewpoint via a dialog box.

DView   Changes the viewpoint of 3D objects, and allows perspective mode.

3dOrbit   Rotates the viewpoint in real-time.

RELATED SYSTEM VARIABLES

VpointX   X coordinate of current 3D view.

VpointY   Y coordinate of current 3D view.

VpointZ   Z coordinate of current 3D view.

WorldView   Determines whether **VPoint** coordinates are in WCS or UCS.

TIPS

- The *compass* represents the globe, flattened to two dimensions:

  - The north pole (0, 0, z) is in the center.

  - The equator (x, y, 0) is the inner circle

  - The south pole (0, 0, -z) is the outer circle.

- As you move the crosshair on the compass, the *axis tripod* rotates to show the 3D view direction.

- To select the view direction, pick a location on the globe and press the pick button.

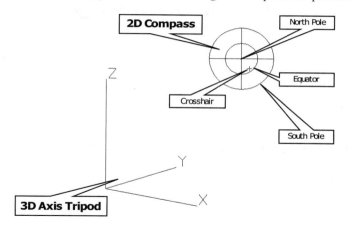

VPorts *and* Viewports

V. 2.0 Creates viewports of the current drawing when **TileMode** is on (*short for ViewPORTS*).

Command	Alias	Ctrl+	F-key	Alt+	Menu Bar	Tablet
vports	viewports	R	...	VV	View ⌐Viewports	M3-4
+vports						
-vports				VV1	View ⌐Viewports 　⌐1 Viewport	

Command: **vports**
Displays tabbed dialog box.

DIALOG BOX OPTIONS
New Viewports tab:

In Model tab:

New name   Specifies the name for the viewport configuration; name can be up to 255 characters long.

Standard viewports

Lists the available viewport configurations.

Preview   Displays a preview of the viewport configuration.

Apply to   Applies the viewport configuration to:
* Display.
* Current Viewport.

Setup	Selects 2D or 3D configuration; the 3D option applies orthogonal views, such as top, left, and front.
Change view to	Selects the type of view; in 3D mode, selects a standard orthoganal view.

In Layout tab:
Viewport spacing

Specifies the spacing between the floating viewports; default = 0 units.

Named Viewports tab:

Named viewports

Lists the names of saved viewport configurations.

+VPORTS COMMAND
```
Command: +vports
Tab index <0>: ENTER
```

Tab index   Specifies the tab to display:

Index	Meaning
0	New Viewports tab (default).
1	Named Viewports tab.

-VPORTS COMMAND

Command: **-vports**

In layout mode, displays **MView** *command prompts. In model space, prompts:*

Enter an option [Save/Restore/Delete/Join/SIngle/?/2/3/4] <3>:

ENTER

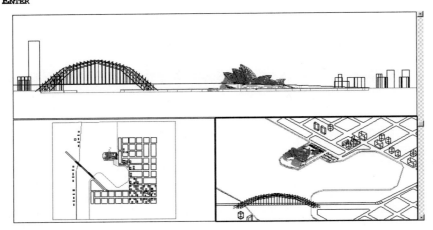

COMMAND LINE OPTIONS

In model tab:

Delete	Deletes a viewport definition.
Join	Joins two viewports together as one when they form a rectangle.
Restore	Restores a viewport definition.
Save	Saves the settings of a viewport by name.
SIngle	Joins all viewports into a single viewport.
2	Divides the curent viewport into two:
Horizontal	Creates one viewport over another.
Vertical	Creates one viewport beside another (default).
3	Divides the curent viewport into three:
Horizontal	Creates three viewports over each other.
Vertical	Creates three viewports beside each other.

Above	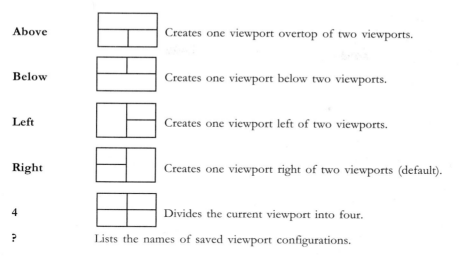	Creates one viewport overtop of two viewports.
Below		Creates one viewport below two viewports.
Left		Creates one viewport left of two viewports.
Right		Creates one viewport right of two viewports (default).
4		Divides the current viewport into four.
?		Lists the names of saved viewport configurations.

In layout tab:
```
Specify corner of viewport or
[ON/OFF/Fit/Hideplot/Lock/Object/Polygonal/Restore/2/3/4]<Fit>: ENTER
```
ON   Turns on the viewport; the objects in the viewport become visible.
OFF   Turns off the viewport; the objects in the viewport become invisible.
Fit   Creates one viewport that fills the display area.
Hideplot   Removes hidden lines when plotting in layout mode.
Lock   Locks the viewport, so that no editing can take place.
Object   Converts a closed polyline, ellipse, spline, region, or circle into a viewport.
Polygonal   Creates an non-rectangular viewport
Other options are identical to those displayed in model tab.

RELATED COMMANDS
MView   Creates viewports in paper space.
RedrawAll   Redraws all viewports.
RegenAll   Regenerates all viewports.
VpClip   Clips a viewport.

RELATED SYSTEM VARIABLES
CvPort   The current viewport number.
MaxActVp   The maximum number of active viewports.
TileMode   Controls whether viewports can be overlaped or tiled.

TIPS
- The **Join** option joins two viewports only when they form a rectangle.
- You can restore saved viewport arrangements in paper space using the **MView** command.
- Many display-related commands (such as **Redraw** or **Grid**) affect the current viewport only.
- The **CTRL+R** shortcut moves the *focus* to the next viewport.

VSlide

V. 2.0 Displays an SLD-format slide file in the current viewport (*short for View SLIDE*).

Command	Alias	Ctrl+	F-key	Alt+	Menu Bar	Tablet
vslide	...	...	...	...	...	...

Command: **vslide**
*Displays **Select Slide File** dialog box.*

COMMAND LINE OPTIONS
~   Displays the file dialog box when **FileDia** = 0.

RELATED COMMANDS
MSlide   Creates an SLD-format slide file of the current viewport.
Redraw   Erases the slide from the screen.

RELATED AUTODESK PROGRAM
SlideLib.Exe   Creates an SLB-format library file of a group of slide files.

RELATED AUTOCAD FILES
*.Sld   Stores individual slide files.
*.Slb   Stores a library of slide files.

TIPS
■ For faster viewing of a series of slides, placing an asterisk proceeding the **VSlide** commands preloads the SLD slide file, as in:

  Command: ***vslide filename**

■ Use the following format to display a specific slide stored in an SLB slide library file:

  Command: **vslide**
  Slide file: **acad.slb(slidefilename)**

WBlock

V. 1.4 Writes a block or the drawing to disk; exports the drawing in XML format (*short for Write BLOCK*).

Command	Alias	Ctrl+	F-key	Alt+	Menu Bar	Tablet
wblock	w	...	...	FE	File	...
				⌂DWG	⌂Export	
					⌂Block	
-wblock	-w					

Command: **wblock**
Displays dialog box:

DIALOG BOX OPTIONS

Source options:

Block   Specifies the name of a block to save as a DWG file.

Entire drawing

      Selects the current drawing to save as DWG file.

Objects   Specifies objects from the drawing to be saved as a DWG file.

Base point options:

Pick Insertion Base Point

      Dismisses the dialog box temporarily to allow you to select the insertion base point.

X   Specifies the x coordinate of the insertion point.

Y   Specifies the y coordinate of the insertion point.

Z   Specifies the z coordinate of the insertion point.

Objects *options:*

Select Objects Dismisses the dialog box temporarily to allow you to select one or more objects.

Quick Select   Displays the **Quick Select** dialog box; see the **QSelect** command.

Retain   Retains the selected objects in the current drawing after saving them as a file.

Convert to block
Converts the selected objects to a block in the drawing, after saving them as a DWG file; names the block under **File name** in the **Destination** section.

Delete from drawing
Deletes the selected objects from the drawing, after saving them as a DWG file.

Destination *options:*

File name   Specifies a file name for the block or objects; to export in XML format, change filename extension to .xml (new to AutoCAD 2002).

Location   Specifies a path.

...   Displays the **Browse for Folder** dialog box.

Insert units   Specifies the units when the DWG file is inserted as a block.

Browse for Folder dialog box

Create Drawing File
Selects the drive and folder in which to store the DWG file extracted from the current drawing.

-WBLOCK COMMAND

Command: **-wblock**

*Displays the **Create Drawing File** dialog box.*

```
Enter name of existing block or
[= (block=output file)/* (whole drawing)] <define new
    drawing>: [enter name]
```

COMMAND LINE OPTIONS

Enter name of existing block

Specifies the name of a block that already exists in the drawing; to export the drawing in XML format, specify the filename extension as .xml.

=   (*Equals*) Writes block to disk using block's name as filename.

*   (*Asterisk*) Writes the entire drawing to disk.

ENTER   Creates a block on disk of the selected objects.

SPACEBAR   Moves the selected objects to the specified drawing.

RELATED COMMANDS

Block   Creates a block of a group of objects.

Insert   Inserts a block or another drawing into the drawing.

RELATED SYSTEM VARIABLES

None.

TIPS

- Use the **WBlock** command to extract blocks from the drawing and store them on a disk drive. This allows the creation of a block library.

- This command exports the drawing in XML format; to import a compatible XML file, use the **Insert** command.

- XML is short for eXtended Markup Language, and is based on HTML, the format used to create Web pages. The XML schema used by AutoCAD is called DesignXML. The first DesignXML channel, AcDbXM, describes the content of the DWG file; it features 100% accurate round-tripping of DWG data.

 # Wedge

Rel.11 Draws a 3D wedge as a solid model (*an ACIS command*).

Command	Alias	Ctrl+	F-key	Alt+	Menu Bar	Tablet
wedge	we	...	...	DIW	Draw	N7
					⌖Solids	
					⌖Wedge	

```
Command: wedge
Specify first corner of wedge or [CEnter]  <0,0,0>: [pick]
Specify corner or [Cube/Length]: [pick]
Specify height: [pick]
```

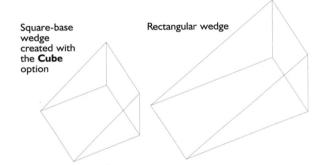

Square-base wedge created with the **Cube** option

Rectangular wedge

COMMAND LINE OPTIONS

Corner   Draws the wedge's base between two pick points.
CEnter   Draws the wedge's base about the center of the sloped face.
Cube   Draws a cubic wedge.
Length   Specifies the length, width, and height of the wedge.

RELATED COMMANDS

Ai_Wedge   Draws a wedge as a 3D surface model.
Box   Draws solid boxes.
Cone   Draws solid cones.
Cylinder   Draws solid cylinders.
Sphere   Draws solid spheres.
Torus   Draws solid tori.

WhoHas

Determines which computer has a drawing open.

Command	Alias	Ctrl+	F-key	Alt+	Menu Bar	Tablet
whohas	...	...	...	...	...	...

Command: **whohas**
*Displays the **Select Drawing to Query** dialog box.*

When the drawing is open, reports:
Owner: ralphg
Computer's Name : HEATHER
Time Acessed : Sunday, May 20, 2002 11:27:28 AM

When the drawing is not open, reports:
No owner information available.

COMMAND LINE OPTIONS
None.

RELATED COMMANDS
Open   Opens a drawing.
XAttach   Attaches a drawing, which can be opened by another user.

Wmfln

Rel.12 Imports a WMF vector file (*short for Windows MetaFile IN*).

Command	Alias	Ctrl+	F-key	Alt+	Menu Bar	Tablet
wmfin	...	...	...	IW	Insert	...
					⌐Windows Metafile	

Command: **wmfin**
Displays the **Import WMF** *dialog box.*
Specify insertion point or [Scale/X/Y/Z/Rotate/PScale/PX/
    PY/PZ/PRotate]: **[pick]**
Enter X scale factor, specify opposite corner, or
    [Corner/XYZ] <1>: ENTER
Enter Y scale factor <use X scale factor>: ENTER
Specify rotation angle <0>: ENTER

COMMAND LINE OPTIONS

Insertion point   Picks the insertion point of the lower-left corner of the WMF image.
X scale factor   Scales the WMF image in the x direction (default = 1).
Corner   Scales the WMF image in the x and y directions.
XYZ   Scales the image in the x, y, and z directions.
Y scale factor   Scales the image in the y direction (default = x scale).
Rotation angle Rotates the image (default = 0).

RELATED COMMANDS

WmfOpts   Controls the importation of WMF files.
WmfOut   Exports selected objects in WMF format.

TIPS

■ The WMF is placed as a block with the name **WMF0**; subsequent placements of a
   WMF file increment the digit: **WMF1**, **WMF2**, etcetera.

■ Exploding the WMF*n* block results in polylines; even circles, arcs, and text are
   converted to polylines; solid-filled areas are exploded into solid triangles.

WmfOpts

<u>Rel.12</u> Controls the importation of WMF files (*short for* *Windows Meta File OPTionS*).

Command	Alias	Ctrl+	F-key	Alt+	Menu Bar	Tablet
wmfopts	...	...	...	IWP	Insert ⁿWindows Metafile ⁿOptions	...

Command: **wmfopts**
Displays dialog box:

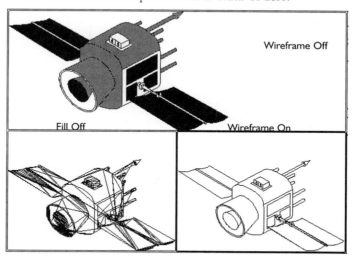

DIALOG BOX OPTIONS

Wire Frame **On**: The WMF file is displayed with lines only, no filled areas (default).
Off: The WMF file is imported with area fills.

Wide Lines **On**: Wide lines are imported as is (default).
Off: Wide lines are imported with a width of zero.

Wireframe Off

Fill Off

Wireframe On

RELATED COMMANDS

WmfIn   Imports WMF files.
WmfOut   Exports selected objects in WMF format.

WmfOut

Rel.12   Exports a WMF vector file (*short for Windows MetaFile OUTput*).

Command	Alias	Ctrl+	F-key	Alt+	Menu Bar	Tablet
wmfout	...	...	...	FE	File	...
				⌑WMF	⌑Export	
					⌑Metafile	

Command: **wmfout**
*Displays the **Create WMF File** dialog box.*
Select objects: **[pick]**
Select objects: ENTER

COMMAND LINE OPTION
Select objects   Selects objects to export.

RELATED SYSTEM VARIABLE
WmfBkgnd   Toggles the background color of an exported WMF file:

WmfBkgnd	Meaning
0	Transparent background.
1	AutoCAD background color.

WmfForegnd   Switches the foreground and background colors of an exported WMF file:

WmfFoegnd	Meaning
0	Foreground is darker than background color.
1	Bckground is darker than foreground color.

RELATED COMMANDS
WmfOpts   Controls the importation of WMF files.
WmfIn   Imports files in WMF format.
CopyClip   Copies selected objects to the Clipboard in several formats, including WMF, also called "picture" format.

TIPS
■ WMF files created by AutoCAD are resolution-dependent; small circles and arcs lose their roundness.

■ The **All** selection does not select all objects in the drawing; instead, the **WmfOut** command selects all objects *visible* in the current viewport.

XAttach

Rel.14 Attaches an externally-referenced drawing to the current drawing (*short for eXternal reference ATTACH*).

Command	Alias	Ctrl+	F-key	Alt+	Menu Bar	Tablet
`xattach`	`xa`	...	...	IX	`Insert` ↳`External Reference`	...

Command: **xattach**

Displays the ***Select File to Attach*** *dialog box.*

After you select a DWG file, displays dialog box:

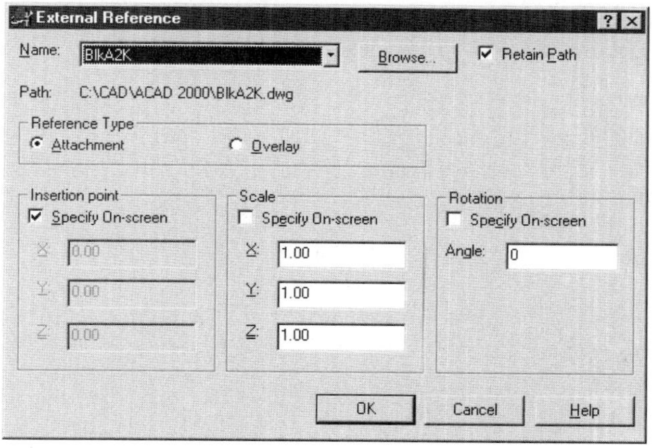

After you click ***OK****, AutoCAD prompts at the command line:*

```
Attach Xref FILENAME: C:\filename.dwg
FILENAME loaded.
```

DIALOG BOX OPTIONS

Name Specifies the name the filename of the external DWG to be attached; the drop list shows the names of currently-attached externally-referenced files.

Browse Displays the **Select File To Attach** dialog box.

Retain Path **Yes**: Saves the xref's filename and full path in the DWG file.
No: Saves only the filename of the xref; when the xref cannot be found, AutoCAD searches the **Support File Search Path** and the **ProjectName**.

Reference Type *options:*

Attachment Attaches the xref.

Overlay Overlays the xref.

Insertion point *options:*

Specify On-screen

Specifies the insertion point of the xref in the drawing, after you click **OK** to dismiss the dialog box; AutoCAD prompts you:

```
Specify insertion point or [Scale/X/Y/Z/Rotate/PScale/
PX/PY/PZ/PRotate]: [enter option]
```

Scale	Sets the scale factor for the x, y, and z axes.
X	Sets the x-scale factor.
Y	Sets the y-scale factor.
Z	Sets the z-scale factor.
Rotate	Specifies the rotation angle.
PScale	Presets the scale factor for the x, y, and z axes.
PX	Presets the x-scale factor.
PY	Presets the y-scale factor.
PZ	Presets the z-scale factor.
PRotate	Presets the rotation angle.

Scale *options:*

Specify On-screen

Specifies the scale of the xref in the drawing, after you click **OK** to dismiss the dialog box; AutoCAD prompts you:

```
Enter X scale factor, specify opposite corner,
  or [Corner/XYZ] <1>:  [enter option]
Enter Y scale factor <use X scale factor>: [enter option]
```

X	Scales the xref in the x direction.
Y	Scales the xref in the y direction.
Z	Scales the xref in the z direction.

Rotation Angle *options:*

Specify On-screen

Specifies the rotation of the xref in the drawing, after you click **OK** to dismiss the dialog box; AutoCAD will prompt you: 'Specify rotation angle <0>'.

Angle   Specifies the rotation angle of the xref.

RELATED SYSTEM VARIABLES

DemandLoad Specifies if and when AutoCAD demand loads a third-party application if a drawing contains custom objects created in that application:

DemandLoad	Meaning
0	Turns off demand loading.
1	Loads app when drawing contains proxy objects.
2	Loads app when the app's command is invoked.
3	Loads app when drawing contains proxy objects or when the app"s command is invoked.

IdxCtl	Controls the creation of layer and spatial indices:

IndexCtl	Meaning
0	Creates no indices (default).
1	Creates layer index.
2	Creates spatial index.
3	Creates both layer and spatial indices.

ProjectName Holds the project name for the current drawing (default = "").

VisRetain Specifies how the layer settings — on-off, freeze-thaw, color, and linetype — in xref drawings are defined by the current drawing:

VisRetain	Meaning
0	Xref layer definition in the current drawing takes precedence.
1	Settings for xref-dependent layers take precedence over xref layer definition in the current drawing.

XEdit Determines whether the drawing may be edited in-place, when being referenced by another drawing:

XEdit	Meaning
0	Cannot be edited in-place.
1	Can be edited in-place.

XLoadCtl Controls the loading of xref drawings:

XLoadCtl	Meaning
0	Loads the entire xref drawing.
1	Demand loading; xref is opened.
2	Demand loading; copy of the xref is opened.

XLoadPath Stores the path of temporary copies of demand-loaded xref drawings.

XRefCtl Controls whether XLG external reference log files are written:

XRefCtl	Meaning
0	XLG file not written (default).
1	XLG log file written.

RELATED COMMANDS

RefEdit	Edits an externally-referenced drawing.
XBind	Binds portions of an externally-referenced drawing to the current drawing.
XClip	Inserts an externally-referenced block.
XRef	Attaches another drawing to the current drawing.

XBind

Rel.11 Binds portions of an externally-referenced drawing to the current drawing (*short for eXternal BINDing*).

Command	Alias	Ctrl+	F-key	Alt+	Menu Bar	Tablet
xbind	xb	...	...	MOEB	Modify ⤷Object ⤷External Reference ⤷Bind	X19
-xbind	-xb					

Command: **xbind**
Displays dialog box:

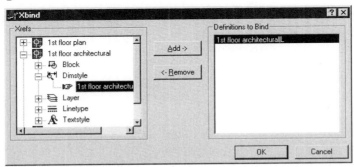

DIALOG BOX OPTIONS

Xrefs Lists xrefs, along with their bindable objects: blocks, dimension styles, layer names, linetypes, and text styles.

Add Adds a definition to the binding list.

Remove Removes a definition from the binding list.

Definitions to Bind
  Lists definitions that will be bound.

-XBIND COMMAND

Command: **-xbind**
Enter symbol type to bind [Block/Dimstyle/LAyer/LType/Style]: **b**
Enter dependent Block name(s): **[enter name]**

COMMAND LINE OPTIONS

Block Binds the blocks to the current drawing.

Dimstyle Binds the dimension styles to the current drawing.

LAyer Binds the layer names to the current drawing.

LType Binds the linetype definitions to the current drawing.

Style Binds the text styles to the current drawing.

RELATED TOOLBAR ICONS

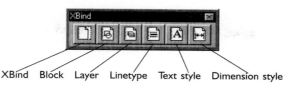

XBind   Block   Layer   Linetype   Text style   Dimension style

RELATED SYSTEM VARIABLES
None.

RELATED COMMANDS
RefEdit   Edits an externally-referenced drawing.
XRef   Attaches another drawing to the current drawing.

TIPS

- The **XBind** command lets you copy named objects from another drawing to the current drawing.

- Before you can use the **XBind** command, you must first use the **XAttach** command to attach an xref to the current drawing.

- Blocks, dimension styles, layer names, linetypes, and text styles are known as "dependent symbols."

- When a dependent symbol is part of an xrefed drawing, AutoCAD uses a vertical bar (|) to separate the xref name from the symbol name, as in *filename* | *layername*.

- After you use the **XBind** command, AutoCAD replaces the vertical bar with **0**, as in *filename***0***layername*. The second time you bind that layer from that drawing, **XBind** increments the digit, as in *filename***1***layername*.

- When the **XBind** command binds a layer with a linetype (other than Continuous), it automatically binds the linetype.

- When the **XBind** command binds a block — with a nested block, dimension style, layer, linetype, text style, and/or reference to another xref — it automatically binds those objects as well.

XClip

Rel. 12 Clips a portion of a block or an externally-referenced drawing (*short for eXternal CLIP; formerly the **XRefClip** command*).

Command	Alias	Ctrl+	F-key	Alt+	Menu Bar	Tablet
xclip	xc	...	...	...	Modify	X18
					⌖Clip	
					↳Xref	

```
Command: xclip
Select objects: [pick]
Select objects: ENTER
Enter clipping option
[ON/OFF/Clipdepth/Delete/generate Polyline/New boundary]
    <New>: ENTER
```

Clipping boundary

Clipping turned off | Clipping turned on

COMMAND LINE OPTIONS

Select objects Selects the xref or block, *not* the clipping polyline.

ON	Turns on clipped display.
OFF	Turns off clipped display; displays all of the xref or block.
Clipdepth	Sets front and back clipping planes for 3D xrefs and blocks.
Delete	Erases the clipping boundary.

generate Polyline
Draws a polyline over top of the clipping boundary.

New Boundary
Places a new rectangular or irregular polygon clipping boundary, or creates an irregular clipping boundary from an existing polyline.

RELATED COMMANDS

XBind Bind parts of the externally-referenced drawing to the current drawing.
Xref Displays an externally-referenced drawing in the current drawing.

RELATED SYSTEM VARIABLE

XClipFrame Toggles the display of the clipping boundary.

TIPS

■ While the old **XRefClip** command could not create an irregularly clipped xref, the new **XClip** command is able to create an arbitrary clipping boundary.

■ The **XClip** command works for both blocks and xrefs.

■ A spline-fit polyline results in a curved clip boundary, but a curve-fit polyline does not.

XLine

Rel.13 Places an infinitely long construction line.

Command	Alias	Ctrl+	F-key	Alt+	Menu Bar	Tablet
xline	xl	...	...	DT	Draw	L10
					Construction Line	

```
Command: xline
Specify a point or [Hor/Ver/Ang/Bisect/Offset]: [pick]
Through point: [pick]
Through point: ENTER
```

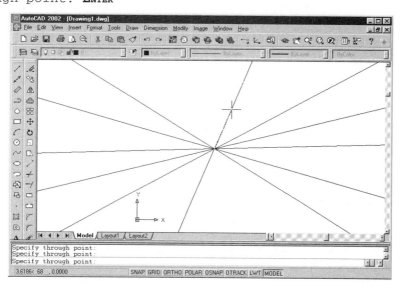

COMMAND LINE OPTIONS

Ang	Places the construction line at an angle.
Bisect	Bisects an angle with the construction line.
From point	Places the construction line through a point.
Hor	Places a horizontal construction line.
Offset	Places the construction line parallel to another object.
Ver	Places a vertical construction line.
ENTER	Exits **XLine**.

RELATED COMMANDS

Properties	Modifies characteristics of xline and ray objects.
Ray	Places a semi-infinite construction line.

RELATED SYSTEM VARIABLE

OffsetDist	Specifies the current offset distance.

TIP

■ ay and xline construction lines do plot, but do not affect the extents.

Xplode

Rel.12 Explodes complex objects into simpler objects, with user control (*short for eXPLODE*).

Command	Alias	Ctrl+	F-key	Alt+	Menu Bar	Tablet
xplode	xp	...	...	...	...	...

```
Command: xplode
Select objects to XPlode.
Select objects: [pick]
n found Select objects: ENTER
n objects found.
Enter an option [Individually/Globally] <Globally>: ENTER
Enter an option [All/Color/LAyer/LType/Inherit from parent
    block/Explode] <Explode>: ENTER
```

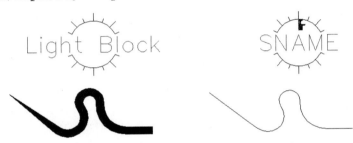

Block and polyline (at left); exploded (at right).

COMMAND LINE OPTIONS

Select objects Selects objects to be exploded.
Individually Allows you to specify options for each selected object.
Globally Applies options to all selected objects.
All Displays all the prompts individually with the **Color, LAyer,** and **LType** options.
Color Allows you to specifiy a single color for all objects after they are exploded: red, yellow, green, cyan, blue, magenta, white, bylayer, byblock, or any color number.
LWeight Allows you to specify a lineweight.
LAyer Allows you to specify the layer name for the exploded objects.
LType Allows you to specify any loaded linetype name for the exploded objects.
Inherit from parent block
      Assigns the color, linetype, lineweight, and layer to the exploded objects, based on the original object.
Explode Reduces the complex object into its components.

RELATED COMMANDS

Explode Explodes the object without options.
U Reverses the explosion.

682 ■ The Illustrated AutoCAD 2002 Quick Reference

RELATED SYSTEM VARIABLES

None.

TIPS

- Examples of complex objects include blocks and polylines; examples of simple objects include lines, circles, and arcs.

- Blocks with unequal scale factors cannot be exploded with this command; in its place, use the **Explode** command.

- Mirrored blocks can be exploded.

- The **LWeight** option is not displayed when the lineweight is off.

- The 'Enter an option [Individually/Globally]' option appears only when more than one valid object is selected for explosion.

- Specifying **BYLayer** for the color or linetype means that the exploded objects take on the color or linetype object's original layer.

- Specifying **BYBlock** for the color or linetype means that the exploded objects take on the color or linetype of the original object.

- The default layer is the current layer, not the exploded object's original layer.

- The **Inherit** option works only when the parts were originally drawn with color, linetype, and lineweight set to BYBLOCK, and drawn on layer 0.

- The **XPlode** command breaks down complex objects as follows:

Object	Exploded into
Block	Component objects.
Attributes	Attribute values are deleted; displays attribute definitions.
2D polyline	Line and arc segments; width and tangency are lost.
3D polyline	Line segments.
Leaders	Line segments, splines, mtext, and tolerance objects; arrowheads become solids or blocks.
Mtext	Text.
Multiline	Line and arc segments.
Polyface mesh	Point, line, or 3D faces.
Region	Lines, arcs, and splines.
3D ACIS solid	Planar surfaces become regions; nonplanar surfaces become bodies.
3D ACIS body	Single-surface body, regions, or curves.

XRef

Rel.11 Attaches an externally-referenced drawing to the current drawing (*short for eXternal REFerence*).

Command	Alias	Ctrl+	F-key	Alt+	Menu Bar	Tablet
xref	xr	...	...	IR	Insert	T4
					ⵈXref Manager	
-xref	-xr					

Command: **xref**
Displays dialog box:

DIALOG BOX OPTIONS

Attach Attaches a drawing as an external reference; displays the **Attach Xref** dialog box — see **XAttach** command.

Detach Detaches an externally referenced (xref) file.

Reload Reloads and displays the most-recently saved version of the xref.

Unload Unloads the xref; does not remove it permanently; rather it does not display the xref.

Bind Binds named objects — blocks, dimension styles, layer names, linetypes, and text styles — to the current drawing; displays the **Bind Xrefs** dialog box — see **XBind** command.

Xref Found At Displays the path to the xref file.

Browse Selects a path or filename; displays the **Select New Path** dialog box.

Save Path Saves the path displayed by the **Xref Found At** option.

-XREF COMMAND

Command: **-xref**

Enter an option [?/Bind/Detach/Path/Unload/Reload/Overlay/
    Attach] <Attach>: ᴇɴᴛᴇʀ

COMMAND LINE OPTIONS

?	Lists the names of externally-referenced drawings.
Bind	Makes the externally-referenced drawing part of the current drawing.
Detach	Removes the externally-referenced drawing.
Path	Respecifies the path to the externally-referenced drawing.
Unload	Unloads the xref.
Reload	Updates the externally-referenced drawing.
Overlay	Overlays the externally-referenced drawing.
Attach	Attaches another drawing to the current drawing.

RELATED TOOLBAR ICONS

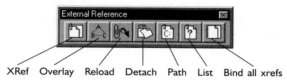

XRef Overlay Reload Detach Path List Bind all xrefs

RELATED COMMANDS

Insert	Adds another drawing to the current drawing.
RefEdit	Edits an xref'ed drawing.
XBind	Binds parts of the xref to the current drawing.
XClip	Lets you clip portions of an xref.

RELATED SYSTEM VARIABLES

DemandLoad Specifies if and when AutoCAD demand loads a third-party application, if a drawing contains custom objects created in that application:

DemandLoad	Meaning
0	Demand loading turned off.
1	Loads app when drawing contains proxy objects.
2	Loads app when the app's command is invoked.
3	Loads app when drawing contains proxy objects or when the app's command is invoked.

VisRetain   Specifies the layer settings — on-off, freeze-thaw, color, and linetype — in xref drawings:

VisRetain	Meaning
0	Xref layer definition in the current drawing takes precedence.
1	Settings for xref-dependent layers take precedence over xref layer definition in the current drawing.

XEdit   Determines whether the drawing may be edited in-place, when being referenced by another drawing:

XEdit	Meaning
0	Cannot be edited in-place.
1	Can be edited in-place.

XLoadCtl   Controls the loading of xref drawings:

XLoadCtl	Meaning
0	Loads entire xref drawing.
1	Demand loading; xref is opened.
2	Demand loading; copy of the xref is opened

XLoadPath   Stores the path of temporary copies of demand-loaded xref drawings.
XRefCtl   Controls whether XLG external reference log files are written:

XRefCtl	Meaning
0	XLG file not written (default).
1	XLG log file written.

TIPS

■ *Caution!* Nested xrefs cannot be unloaded.

■ Tree view shows how the xrefs are nested:

'Zoom

V. 1.0   Displays a drawing larger or smaller in the current viewport.

Command	Alias	Ctrl+	F-key	Alt+	Menu Bar	Tablet
'zoom	z	...	...	VZ	View	K11
	rtzoom				⌐Zoom	

```
Command: zoom
Specify corner of window, enter a scale factor (nX or nXP),
    or [All/Center/Dynamic/Extents/Previous/Scale/Window]
    <real time>: ENTER
Press ESC or ENTER to exit, or right-click to display
    shortcut menu.
```

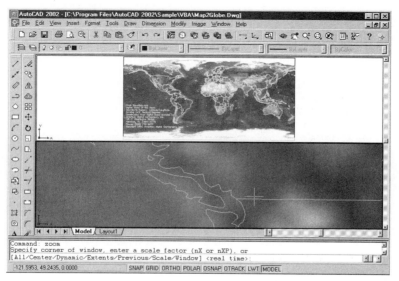

COMMAND LINE OPTIONS

realtime	Press ENTER to start real-time zoom.
All	Displays the drawing limits or extents, whichever is greater.
Dynamic	Brings up the dynamic zoom view.
Extents	Displays the current drawing extents.
Previous	Displays the previous view generated by **Pan**, **View**, or **Zoom**.
Vmax	Displays the current virtual screen limits (short for Virtual MAXimum; an undocumented option).
Window	Indicates the two corners of the new view.

Center *options:*

```
Specify center point: [pick]
Enter magnification or height <>: [enter value]
```

Center point   Indicates the center point of the new view.
Enter magnification or height
                    Indicates a magnification value or height of view.

Left *options (an undocumented option):*
Lower left corner point: **[pick]**
Enter magnification or height <>: **[enter value]**
Lower left corner point
           Indicates the lower-left corner of the new view.
Enter magnification or height
           Indicates a magnification value or height of view.

Scale(X/XP) *options:*
n **X**   Displays a new view as a factor of the current view.
n **X P**   Displays a paper space view as a factor of model space.

[pick]   Begins the window option.
ENTER *or* **ESC**   Ends real-time zoom.

RIGHT-CLICK OPTIONS

Exit real-time zoom mode:
Real-time pan:
Real-time zoom:
3D orbit mode:
Zoom window:
Original view:
Zoom to drawing extents:

| Exit |
| Pan |
| ✓ Zoom |
| 3D Orbit |
| Zoom Window |
| Zoom Original |
| Zoom Extents |

RELATED TOOLBAR ICONS

Window Dynamic Scale Center

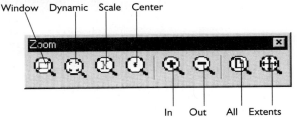

In   Out   All Extents

RELATED COMMANDS
DsViewer   Displays **Aerial View** window.
Limits   Specifies the limits of the drawing.
Pan   Moves the view to a different location.
View   Saves zoomed views by name.

RELATED SYSTEM VARIABLES
ViewCtr   Specifies the coordinates of the current view's center point.
ViewSize   Specifies the height of the current view.

TIPS
■ A zoom factor of 1 displays the entire drawing as defined by the limits; a zoom factor of 2 enlarges objects (zooms in), while 0.5 makes objects smaller (zooms out).

■ Transparent zoom is *not* possible during the **VPoint, Pan, DView,** and **View** commands.

3D

Rel.11   Draws 3D primitives with polymeshes (*short for three Dimensions*).

Command	Alias	Ctrl+	F-key	Alt+	Menu Bar	Tablet
3d	...	...	...	DF3	Draw	N8
					⌐Surfaces	
					⌐3D Surfaces	

Command: **3d**
Enter an option
[Box/Cone/DIsh/DOme/Mesh/Pyramid/Sphere/Torus/Wedge]: **[enter
an option]**
*See the **Ai_** commands for more details.*
*Selecting **Draw | Surfaces | 3D Surfaces** from the menu bar displays the dialog box:*

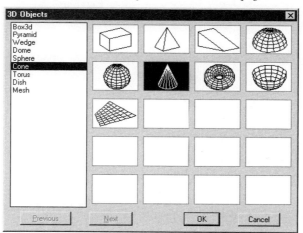

ICON MENU OPTIONS

Box	Draws a 3D box or cube.
Cone	Draws a cone shape.
DIsh	Draws a dish — bottom-half of a sphere.
Dome	Draws a dome — top-half of a sphere.
Mesh	Draws a 3D mesh.
Pyramid	Draws a pyramid shape.
Sphere	Draws a sphere.
Torus	Draw a torus — 3D donut — shape.
Wedge	Draws a wedge shape.

RELATED COMMANDS

Ai_Box	Draws a 3D surface box or cube.
Ai_Cone	Draws a 3D surface cone shape.
Ai_Dish	Draws a 3D surface dish.
Ai_Dome	Draws a 3D surface dome.
Ai_Mesh	Draws a 3D mesh.

Ai_Pyramid	Draws a 3D surface pyramid.
Ai_Sphere	Draws a 3D surface sphere.
Ai_Torus	Draws a 3D surface torus.
Ai_Wedge	Draws a 3D surface wedge.
Box	Draws a 3D solid box or cube.
Cone	Draws a 3D solid cone.
Cylinder	Draws a 3D solid cylinder.
Sphere	Draws a 3D solid sphere.
Torus	Draws a 3D solid torus.
Wedge	Draws a 3D solid wedge.

RELATED TOOLBAR ICONS

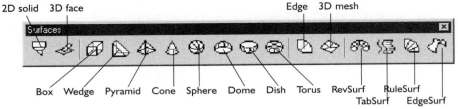

TIPS

■ The **3D** command creates 3D objects made of 3D meshes and *not* 3D solids.

■ To draw a cylinder, apply thickness to a circle.

■ You *cannot* perform Boolean operations on 3D surface models.

■ To convert a 3D solid model to a 3D surface model, export the drawing with the **3dsOut** command, then import with the **3dsIn** command.

■ Use the **Ucs** command to place 3D surface models in space; use the **VPoint** and **Dview** commands to view surface models from different 3D viewpoints.

■ You can apply the **Hide**, **Shade,** and **Render** commands to 3D surface models.

3dArray

Rel.11 Creates 3D rectangular and polar arrays .

Command	Alias	Ctrl+	F-key	Alt+	Menu Bar	Tablet
3darray	...	...	...	M33	Modify ↳3D Operation ↳3D Array	W20

```
Command: 3darray
Select objects: [pick]
Select objects: ENTER
Enter the type of array [Rectangular/Polar] <R>: ENTER
```

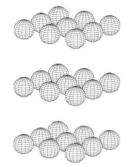

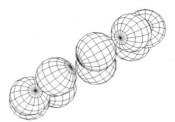

3D rectangular array   3D Polar array.

Rectangular array options:
```
Enter the number of rows (---) <1>: [enter a number]
Enter the number of columns (|||) <1>: [enter a number]
Enter the number of levels (...) <1>: [enter a number]
Specify the distance between rows (---) <1>: [enter a number]
Specify the distance between columns (|||) <1>: [enter a number]
Specify the distance between levels (...) <1>: [enter a number]
```

COMMAND LINE OPTIONS

Rectangular array options:

R   Creates a rectangular 3D array.

Enter the number of rows
         Specifies the number of rows in the x direction.

Enter the number of columns
         Specifies the number of columns in the y direction.

Enter the number of levels
         Specifies the number of levels in the z direction.

Specify the distance between rows
         Specifies the distance between objects in the x direction.

Specify the distance between columns
         Specifies the distance between objects in the y direction.

Specify the distance between levels

        Specifies the distance between objects in the z direction.

Polar array options:

```
Enter the number of items in the array: [enter a number]
Specify the angle to fill (+=ccw, -=cw) <360>: ENTER
Rotate arrayed objects? [Yes/No] <Y>: ENTER
Specify center point of array: [pick]
Specify second point on axis of rotation: [pick]
```

COMMAND LINE OPTIONS

Polar array options:

P   Creates a polar array in 3D space.

Enter the number of items

        Specifies the number of objects to array.

Specify the angle to fill

        Specifies the distance along the circumference that objects are arrayed (default = 360 degrees).

Rotate arrayed objects?

        Yes: objects are rotated so that they face the central axis (default).

        No: objects are not rotated.

Specify enter point of array

        Specifies the x,y,z coordinates for one end of the axis for the polar array.

Specify second point on axis of rotation

        Specifies the x,y,z coordinates for the other end of the array axis.

Esc   Interrupts drawing of the array.

RELATED COMMANDS

Array   Creates a rectangular or polar array in 2D space.

Copy   Creates one or more copies of the selected object.

MInsert   Creates a rectangular block-array of blocks.

3dClip

2000 Performs real-time front and back clipping (*short for three Dimensional CLIPping*).

Command	Alias	Ctrl+	F-key	Alt+	Menu Bar	Tablet
3dclip	...	...	...	...	...	...

Command: **3dclip**
Displays window:

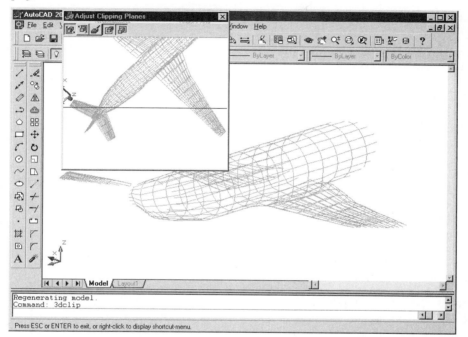

TOOLBAR OPTIONS

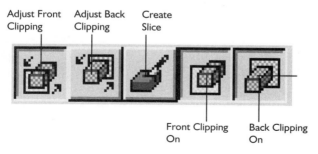

Adjust Front Clipping   Adjust Back Clipping   Create Slice

Front Clipping On   Back Clipping On

SHORTCUT MENU OPTIONS

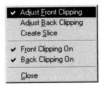

Adjust Front Clipping
> Switches to front clipping mode.

Adjust Back Clipping
> Switches to back clipping mode.

Create Slice   Switches to slicing — ganged front and back clipping — mode.

Front Clipping On
> Toggles on and off front clipping.

Back Clipping On
> Toggles on and off back clipping.

Close   Closes the **Adjust Clipping Planes** window.

RELATED COMMANDS

Vpoint	Creates a static 3D viewpoint.
3dCOrbit	Places the drawing into real-time, 3D, continuous orbit mode.
3dDistance	Performs real-time 3D forward and backward panning.
3dOrbit	Provides real-time 3D viewing of the drawing.
3dPan	Performs real-time 3D sideways panning.
3dSwivel	Tilts the 3D view.
3dZoom	Performs real-time 3D zooming.

TIP

■ Use this command to remove objects in the front of a 3D scene, or to expose the interior of a 3D model, such as this airplane.

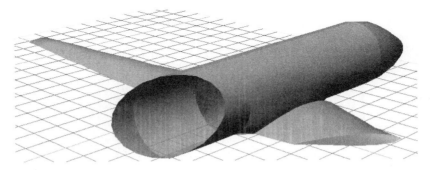

3dCOrbit

2000 Places the drawing into real-time, 3D, continuous orbit mode (*short for three Dimensional Continuous ORBIT*).

Command	Alias	Ctrl+	F-key	Alt+	Menu Bar	Tablet
3dcorbit	...	...	...	...	...	...

Command: **3dcorbit**
Press ESC or ENTER to exit, or right-click to display
   shortcut-menu.

COMMAND LINE OPTIONS
Esc   Exits the command.
ENTER   Exits the command.

SHORTCUT MENU OPTIONS
See the **3dOrbit** *command.*

RELATED COMMANDS
Vpoint   Creates a static 3D viewpoint.
3dClip   Performs real-time 3D front and back clipping.
3dDistance   Performs real-time 3D forward and backward panning.
3dOrbit   Provides real-time 3D viewing of the drawing.
3dPan   Performs real-time 3D sideways panning.
3dSwivel   Tilts the 3D view.
3dZoom   Performs real-time 3D zooming.

TIP
■ To set the 3D model to continuous orbit mode, drag the cursor across the drawing.

3dDistance

<u>**2000**</u> Performs real-time 3D forward and backward panning by dragging the cursor.

Command	Alias	Ctrl+	F-key	Alt+	Menu Bar	Tablet
3ddistance	...	...	...	...	...	...

Command: **3ddistance**
Press ESC or ENTER to exit, or right-click to display shortcut-menu.

COMMAND LINE OPTIONS

Esc   Exits the command.
Enter   Exits the command.

SHORTCUT MENU OPTIONS

See the ***3dOrbit*** *command.*

RELATED COMMANDS

Vpoint   Creates a static 3D viewpoint.
3dClip   Performs real-time 3D front and back clipping.
3dCOrbit   Places the drawing in real-time, 3D, continuous orbit mode.
3dOrbit   Provides real-time 3D viewing of the drawing.
3dPan   Performs real-time 3D sideways panning.
3dSwivel   Tilts the 3D view.
3dZoom   Performs real-time 3D zooming.

3dFace

V. 2.6 Draws a 3D face with three or four corners.

Command	Alias	Ctrl+	F-key	Alt+	Menu Bar	Tablet
3dface	3f	...	...	DFF	Draw ⇃Surfaces ⇃3D Face	M8

```
Command: 3dface
Specify first point or [Invisible]: [pick]
Specify second point or [Invisible]: [pick]
Specify third point or [Invisible] <exit>: [pick]
Specify fourth point or [Invisible] <create three-sided
    face>: [pick]
Specify third point or [Invisible] <exit>: ENTER
```

COMMAND LINE OPTIONS

First point Picks the first corner of the face.
Second point Picks the second corner of the face.
Third point Picks the third corner of the face.
Fourth point Picks the fourth corner of the face; or press ENTER to create a triangular face.
Invisible Makes the edge invisible.

RELATED COMMANDS

3D Draws a 3D object: box, cone, dome, dish, pyramid, sphere, torus, or wedge.
Properties Modifies the 3d face, including visibility of edges.
Edge Changes the visibility of the edges of 3D faces.
EdgeSurf Draws 3D surfaces made of 3D meshes.
PEdit Edits 3D meshes.
PFace Draws generalized 3D meshes.

RELATED SYSTEM VARIABLE

SplFrame Controls the visibility of edges.

TIPS

- A 3D face is the same as a 2D solid, except that each corner can have a different z-coordinate.

- Unlike the procedure for **Solid**, corner coordinates are entered in natural order.

- The **i** (short for invisible) suffix must be entered before object snap modes, point filters, and corner coordinates.

- Invisible 3D faces, where all four edges are invisible, do not appear in wireframe views; however, they hide objects behind them in hidden-line mode, and are rendered in shaded views.

- 3D faces cannot be extruded.

- The **Properties** and **Edge** commands can be used to change the visibility of 3D faces.

3dMesh

Rel.10 Draws an open 3D rectangular mesh made of 3D faces.

Command	Alias	Ctrl+	F-key	Alt+	Menu Bar	Tablet
3dmesh	...	...	...	DFM	Draw ↳Surfaces ↳3D Mesh	...

```
Command: 3dmesh
Enter size of mesh in M direction: [enter a number]
Enter size of mesh in N direction: [enter a number]
Specify location for vertex (0, 0): [pick]
Specify location for vertex (0, 1): [pick]
Specify location for vertex (1, 0): [pick]
Specify location for vertex (1, 1): [pick]
```

COMMAND LINE OPTIONS

Enter size of mesh in M direction
> Specifies the m-direction mesh size (between 2 and 256).

Enter size of mesh in N direction
> Specifies the n-direction mesh size (between 2 and 256).

Specify location for vertex (*m,n*)
> Enter a 2D or 3D coordinate for each vertex.

RELATED COMMANDS

3D	Draws a variety of 3D objects.
3dFace	Draws a 3D face with three or four corners.
Explode	Explodes a 3D mesh into individual 3D faces.
PEdit	Edits a 3D mesh.
PFace	Draws a generalized 3D face.
Xplode	Explodes a group of 3D meshes.

TIPS

- It is more convenient to use the **EdgeSurf**, **RevSurf**, **RuleSurf**, and **TabSurf** commands than the **3dMesh** command. Instead, the **3dMesh** command is meant for use by AutoLISP and other programs.

- The range of values for the m- and n-mesh size is 2 to 256.

- The number of vertices = **m** x **n**.

- The first vertex is at (0,0). The vertices can be any distance from each other.

- The coordinates for each vertex in row **m** must be entered before starting on vertices in row **m+1**.

- Use the **PEdit** command to close the mesh, since it is always created open.

- The **SurfU** and **SurfV** system variables do not affect the 3dmesh object.

3dOrbit

2000 Provides real-time 3D viewing of the drawing.

Command	Alias	Ctrl+	F-key	Alt+	Menu Bar	Tablet
3dorbit	orbit ...	...		VB	View 3D Orbit	R5

Command: **3dorbit**
Press ESC or ENTER to exit, or right-click to display
   shortcut-menu.

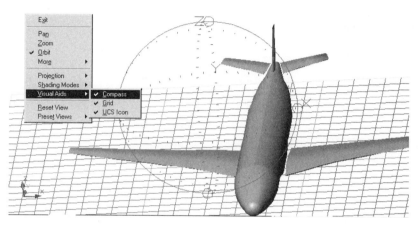

COMMAND LINE OPTIONS

Esc   Exits the command.
Enter   Exits the command.

SHORTCUT MENU OPTIONS

Right-click the drawing:

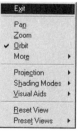

Exit   Exits the command.
Pan   Pans the view in real-time; see the **3dPan** command.
Zoom   Zooms the view in real-time; see the **3dZoom** command.
Orbit   Rotates the view in real-time.
More   Displays a submenu with additional view controls.

Projection Displays a submenu for toggling between parallel and perspective projection.

Shading Modes Displays a submenu for selecting the type of wireframe or shaded modes; see the **ShadeMode** command.

Visual Aids Displays a submenu of visual aids for navigating in 3D space.

Reset View Resets to the original view when you first began the command.

Preset Views Displays a submenu of standard views.

More options:

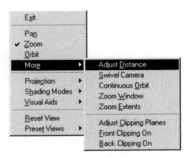

Adjust Distance
Moves the view closer and further away; see the **3dDistance** command.

Swivel Camera Rotates the view; see the **3dSwivel** command.

Continuous Orbit
Continously rotates the model; see the **3dCOrbit** command.

Zoom Window Performs a windowed zoom; see the **Zoom** command.

Zoom Extents Displays the entire drawing.

Adjust Clipping Planes
Sets the front and back clipping planes; see the **3dClip** command.

Front Clipping On
Toggles the front clipping plane.

Back Clipping On
Toggles the back clipping plane.

Projection options:

Parallel Displays the view in orthoganal view.

Perspective   Displays the view in one-point perspective view; some commands do not work in perspective mode, such as the **Pan** and **Zoom** commands.

Shading Modes options (see the ShadeMode command):

Wireframe   Displays the model in wireframe mode.
Hidden   Removes hidden lines from the view.
Flat Shaded   Flat shades the model.
Gouraud Shaded
    Smooth shades the model.

Flat Shaded, Edges On
    Flat shades the model, and outlines faces with the background color.
Gouraud Shaded, Edges On
    Smooth shades the model, and outlines faces with the background color.

Visual Aids options:

Compass   Toggles the display of the compass to help you navigate in 3D space.

| **Grid** | Toggles the display of the grid as lines, to help you see the x,y-plane; see the **Grid** command. |
| **UCS Icon** | Toggles the display of the 3D UCS icon; see the **UcsIcon** command. |

Preset Views options:

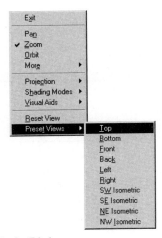

Top, Bottom, Front, Back, Left, Right
Displays the standard orthogonal views.
SW Isometric, SE Isometric, NW Isometric, NW Isometric
Displays the standard isometric views.

RELATED COMMANDS

Vpoint	Creates a static 3D viewpoint.
3dClip	Performs real-time 3D front and back clipping.
3dCOrbit	Places the drawing in real-time, 3D, continuous orbit mode.
3dDistance	Performs real-time 3D forward and backward panning.
3dPan	Performs real-time 3D sideways panning.
3dSwivel	Tilts the 3D view.
3dZoom	Performs real-time 3D zooming.

TIP
■ This command replaces the **DView** command.

3dPan

2000 Performs real-time 3D sideways panning.

Command	Alias	Ctrl+	F-key	Alt+	Menu Bar	Tablet
3dpan	...	...	...	...	...	...

Command: **3dpan**
Press ESC or ENTER to exit, or right-click to display
    shortcut-menu.

COMMAND LINE OPTIONS
Esc   Exits the command.
ENTER   Exits the command.

SHORTCUT MENU OPTIONS
See the **3dOrbit** *command.*

RELATED COMMANDS
Vpoint   Creates a static 3D viewpoint.
3dClip   Performs real-time 3D front and back clipping.
3dCOrbit   Places the drawing in real-time, 3D, continuous orbit mode.
3dDistance   Performs real-time 3D forward and backward panning.
3dOrbit   Provides real-time 3D viewing of the drawing.
3dSwivel   Tilts the 3D view.
3dZoom   Performs real-time 3D zooming.

TIP
■ You must use this command when the current drawing is in perspective mode; when
you try to use the **Pan** command, AutoCAD complains, '** That command may not
be invoked in a perspective view **'.

3dPoly

<u>Rel.10</u> Draws 3D polylines (*short for 3D POLYline*).

Command	Alias	Ctrl+	F-key	Alt+	Menu Bar	Tablet
3dpoly	...	...	...	D3	Draw ⌐3D Polyline	O10

```
Command: 3dpoly
Specify start point of polyline: [pick]
Specify endpoint of line or [Undo]: [pick]
Specify endpoint of line or [Undo]: [pick]
Specify endpoint of line or [Close/Undo]: ENTER
```

COMMAND LINE OPTIONS

Specify start point
    Indicates the starting point of the 3D polyline.
Close   Joins the last endpoint with the start point.
Undo   Erases the last-drawn segment.
Specify endpoint of line
    Indicates the endpoint of the current segment.
ENTER   Ends the **3dPoly** command.

RELATED COMMANDS

Explode   Reduces a 3D polyline into lines and arcs.
PEdit   Edits 3D polylines.
PLine   Draws 2D polylines.

TIPS

■ Since 3D polylines are made of straight lines, use the **PEdit** command to spline the polyline as a curve.

■ 3D polylines do not support linetypes and widths.

■ You may use lineweights to fatten up a 3D polyline.

3dsin

Rel.13 Imports a 3DS file created by 3D Studio (*short for 3D Studio IN*).

Command	Alias	Ctrl+	F-key	Alt+	Menu Bar	Tablet
3dsin	...	...	...	I3	Insert	...
					↳3D Studio	

Command: **3dsin**

Displays the **3D Studio File Import** *dialog box.*
After you select a 3DS file, AutoCAD displays dialog box:

DIALOG BOX OPTIONS

Available and Selected Objects options:

Object Name   Names the object.
Type   Specifies the type of object.
Add   Adds the object to the **Selected Objects** list.
Add All   Adds all objects to the **Selected Objects** list.
Remove   Removes the object from **Selected Objects** list.
Remove All   Removes all objects from **Selected Objects** list.

Save to Layers options:

By Object   Places each object on its own layer.
By Material   Places the objects on layers named after materials.
By Object Color
  Places the objects on layers named "Color*nn*."
Single Layer   Places all objects on layer "AvLayer."

Multiple Material Objects options:

Always Prompt   Prompts you for each material.

Split by Material

> Splits objects with more than one material into multiple objects, each with one material.

Assign First Material

> Assigns the first material to the entire object.

Don't Assign to a Material

> Removes all 3D Studio material definitions.

RELATED COMMAND

3dsOut   Exports drawing as a 3DS file.

RELATED FILES

*.3DS   3D Studio files.

*.TGA   Converted bitmap and animation files.

TIPS

- You are limited to selecting a maximum of 70 3D Studio objects.

- Conflicting object names are truncated and given a sequence number.

- The **By Object** option gives the AutoCAD layer the name of the object.

- The **By Object Color** option places all objects on layer "ColorNone" when no colors are defined in the 3DS file.

- 3D Studio assigns materials to faces, elements, and objects; AutoCAD only assigns materials to objects, colors, and layers.

- 3D Studio bitmaps are converted to TGA (Targa format) bitmaps.

- Only the first frame of an animation file (CEL, CLI, FLC, and IFL) is converted to a Targa bitmap file.

- Converted TGA files are saved to the 3DS file's subdirectory.

- 3D Studio ambient lights lose their color.

- 3D Studio "omni lights" become point lights in AutoCAD.

- 3D Studio cameras become a named view in AutoCAD.

3dsOut

Rel.13 Exports the AutoCAD drawing as a 3DS file for 3D Studio (*short for 3D Studio OUT*).

Command	Alias	Ctrl+	F-key	Alt+	Menu Bar	Tablet
3dsout	...	...	...	FE	File	...
				⌐3DS	⌐Export	
					⌐3D Studio	

```
Command: 3dsout
Select objects: [pick]
Select objects: ENTER
```
Displays **3D Studio File Export** *dialog box.*
After specifying a 3DS filename, displays dialog box:

After you select options, the **3dsOut** *command exports selected objects:*
```
Generating objects
Writing preamble
Converting and writing material definitions
UCSVIEW = 1   UCS will be saved with view
Collecting geometry
Converting object BODY
Unifying normals
Assigning smoothing
3D Studio file output completed
```

COMMAND LINE OPTION

Select objects Selects objects to export; note that **3dsOut** exports only objects with a surface.

DIALOG BOX OPTIONS

Derive 3D Studio Objects From options:

Layer	All objects on an AutoCAD layer become a single 3D Studio object (default).
ACI	All objects of an ACI color become a single 3D Studio object.
Object Type	All objects of an AutoCAD object type become a single 3D Studio object.

AutoCAD Blocks option:

Override	Each AutoCAD block becomes a single 3D Studio object; overrides the **Derive 3D Studio Objects From** options.

Smoothing options:
Auto-Smoothing

	Yes: Creates a 3D Studio smoothing group (default).
	No: No smoothing assigned to new 3D Studio objects.
Degrees	Smoothes the face normals, when the angle between two face normals is equal to or less than this value (default = 30 degrees).

Welding options:
Auto-Welding Yes: Creates a 3D Studio welded vertex (default).

	No: Vertices remain unwelded upon export.
Threshold	Welds two vertices into a single vertex when their interdistance is less than or equal to this value (default = 0.001).

RELATED AUTOCAD COMMAND

3dsIn	Imports a 3DS file to the drawing.

RELATED FILE

*.3DS	3D studio files.

TIPS

- AutoCAD objects with 0 thickness are not exported, with the exception of circles, polygons, and polyface meshes.

- Solids and 3D faces must have at least three vertices.

- 3D solids and bodies are converted to meshes.

- AutoCAD blocks are exploded unless the **Override** option is turned on.

- The weld threshold distance ranges from 0.00 000 001 to 99,999,999.

- AutoCAD named views become 3D Studio cameras.

- AutoCAD point lights become 3D Studio "omni lights."

3dSwivel

<u>**2000**</u> Tilts the 3D view based on cursor movement.

Command	Alias	Ctrl+	F-key	Alt+	Menu Bar	Tablet
3dswivel	...	...	...	...		...

Command: **3dswivel**
Press ESC or ENTER to exit, or right-click to display
  shortcut-menu.

COMMAND LINE OPTIONS

Esc   Exits the command.
ENTER   Exits the command.

SHORTCUT MENU OPTIONS

See the **3dOrbit** *command.*

RELATED COMMANDS

Vpoint   Creates a static 3D viewpoint.
3dClip   Performs real-time 3D front and back clipping.
3dCOrbit   Places the drawing in real-time, 3D, continuous orbit mode.
3dDistance   Performs real-time 3D forward and backward panning.
3dOrbit   Provides real-time 3D viewing of the drawing.
3dPan   Performs real-time 3D sideways panning.
3dZoom   Performs real-time 3D zooming.

3dZoom

2000 Performs real-time 3D zooming based on cursor movement.

Command	Alias	Ctrl+	F-key	Alt+	Menu Bar	Tablet
3dzoom	...	...	...	...	...	...

Command: **3dzoom**
Press ESC or ENTER to exit, or right-click to display shortcut-
menu.

COMMAND LINE OPTIONS

Esc   Exits the command.
ENTER   Exits the command.

SHORTCUT MENU OPTIONS

See the **3dOrbit** *command.*

RELATED COMMANDS

Vpoint   Creates a static 3D viewpoint.
3dClip   Performs real-time 3D front and back clipping.
3dCOrbit   Places the drawing in real-time, 3D, continuous orbit mode.
3dDistance   Performs real-time 3D forward and backward panning.
3dOrbit   Provides real-time 3D viewing of the drawing.
3dPan   Performs real-time 3D sideways panning.
3dSwivel   Tilts the 3D view.

TIP

■ You must use this command when the current drawing is in perspective mode; when
you try to use the **Zoom** command, AutoCAD complains, '** That command may not
be invoked in a perspective view **'.

System Variables

AutoCAD stores information about its current state, the drawing and the operating system in 400 *system variables*. The variables help programmers — who often work with menu macros and AutoLISP — determine the state of the AutoCAD system.

The following pages list all documented system variables, plus several more not documented by Autodesk. The listing uses the following conventions:

CONVENTIONS

Bold   System variable is documented in AutoCAD 2002.

Italicized   System variable is not listed by the **SetVar** command.

~~Strikethru Italic~~   System variable was removed from AutoCAD.

⌨   System variable must be accessed via the **SetVar** command.

▣   System variable is new to AutoCAD 2002.

COLUMN HEADINGS

Default   Default value, as set in the *Acad.Dwg* prototype drawing.

R/O   Read-only; cannot be changed by the user or by a program.

Loc   Location where the value of the system variable is saved:

Location	Meaning
ACAD	Set by AutoCAD.
DWG	Saved in current drawing.
REG	Saved globally in Windows registry.
...	Not saved.

TIPS

■ The **SetVar** command lets you change the value of all variables, except those marked read-only (R/O).

■ You can get a list of most system variables at the 'Command' prompt with the **?** option of the **SetVar** command:

```
Command: setvar
Variable name or ?: ?
Variable(s) to list <*>: ENTER
```

■ When a system variable is stored in the Windows registry, it affects all drawings.

■ When a system variable is stored in the drawing, it affects the current drawing only.

■ When a system variable is not stored, the variable is set when AutoCAD loads. The value of the variable is either read from the operating system, or set to a default value.

Variable	Default	R/O	Loc	Meaning
~~_LInfo~~				*Removed from AutoCAD 2002.*
_PkSer	*varies*	R/O	*ACAD*	*Software package serial number, such as "117-69999999".*
_Server	*0*	R/O	*REG*	*Network authorization code.*
_VerNum	*varies*	R/O	*REG*	*Internal program build number, such as "T.0.98".*

A

Variable	Default	R/O	Loc	Meaning
AcadLspAsDoc	0	...	REG	Acad.Lsp is loaded into: **0** Just the first drawing. **1** Every drawing.
AcadPrefix	*varies*	R/O	...	Path spec'd by ACAD environment variable, such as "d:\acad 2002\support; d:\acad 2002\fonts".
AcadVer	"15.06"	R/O	...	AutoCAD version number.
AcisOutVer	40	R/O	...	ACIS version number, such as 15, 16, 17, 18, 20, 21, 30, or 40.
AFlags	0	...	...	Attribute display code: **0** No mode specified. **1** Invisible. **2** Constant. **4** Verify. **8** Preset.
AngBase	0	...	DWG	Direction of zero degrees relative to UCS
AngDir	0	...	DWG	Rotation of angles: **0** Clockwise **1** Counterclockwise
ApBox	0	...	REG	AutoSnap aperture box cursor: **0** Off. **1** On.
Aperture	10	...	REG	🖻 Object snap aperture in pixels: **1** Minimum size. **50** Maximum size.
Area	0.0000	R/O	...	🖻 Area measured by the last **Area**, **List**, or **Dblist** commands.
AttDia	0	...	DWG	Attribute entry interface: **0** Command-line prompts. **1** Dialog box.
AttMode	1	...	DWG	Display of attributes: **0** Off. **1** Normal. **2** On.
AttReq	1	...	REG	Attribute values during insertion are: **0** Default values. **1** Prompt for values.

Variable	Default	R/O	Loc	Meaning
AuditCtl	0	...	REG	Determines creation of ADT audit log file: **0** File not created. **1** ADT file created.
AUnits	0	...	DWG	Mode of angular units: **0** Decimal degrees. **1** Degrees-minutes-seconds. **2** Grads. **3** Radians. **4** Surveyor's units.
AUPrec	0	...	DWG	Decimal places displayed by angles.
AutoSnap	63	...	REG	Controls AutoSnap display: **0** Turns off all AutoSnap features. **1** Turns on marker. **2** Turns on SnapTip. **4** Turns on magnetic cursor. **8** Turns on polar tracking . **16** Turns on object snap tracking . **32** Turns on tooltips for polar tracking and object snap tracking .
AuxStat	*0*	...	DWG	*-32768 Minimum value.* *32767 Maximum value.*
~~AxisMode~~	*0*	...	DWG	*Removed from AutoCAD 2002.*
AxisUnit	*0.0000*	...	DWG	*Obsolete system variable.*

■ B

Variable	Default	R/O	Loc	Meaning
BackZ	0.0000	R/O	DWG	Back clipping plane offset.
BindType	0	...	...	When binding an xref or editing an xref, xref names are converted from: **0** xref|name to xref\$0\$name. **1** xref|name to name.
BlipMode	0	...	DWG	▦ Display of blip marks: **0** Off. **1** On.

■ C

Variable	Default	R/O	Loc	Meaning
CDate	*varies*	R/O	...	Current date and time in the format YyyyMmDd.HhMmSsDd, such as 20001503.18082328
CeColor	"BYLAYER"	...	DWG	Current color.
CeLtScale	1.0000	...	DWG	Current linetype scaling factor.
CeLType	"BYLAYER"	...	DWG	Current linetype.

Variable	Default	R/O	Loc	Meaning
CeLWeight	-1	...	DWG	Current lineweight in millimeters; valid values are 0, 5, 9, 13, 15, 18, 20, 25, 30, 35, 40, 50, 53, 60, 70, 80, 90, 100, 106, 120, 140, 158, 200, and 211, plus the following: **-1** BYLAYER. **-2** BYBLOCK. **-3** DEFAULT as defined by **LwDdefault**.
ChamferA	0.5000	...	DWG	First chamfer distance.
ChamferB	0.5000	...	DWG	Second chamfer distance.
ChamferC	1.0000	...	DWG	Chamfer length.
ChamferD	0	...	DWG	Chamfer angle.
ChamMode	0	...	...	Chamfer input mode: **0** Chamfer by two lengths. **1** Chamfer by length and angle.
CircleRad	0.0000	...	...	Most-recent circle radius.
CLayer	"0"	...	DWG	Current layer name.
CmdActive	1	R/O	...	Type of current command: **1** Regular command. **2** Transparent command. **4** Script file. **8** Dialog box. **16** AutoLISP is active .
CmdDia	1	...	REG	Formerly determined whether the **Plot** command displayed at the command line prompt or via a dialog box; no longer has an effect in AutoCAD 2000; replaced by **PlQuiet**.
CmdEcho	1	...	...	AutoLISP command display: **0** No command echoing. **1** Command echoing.
CmdNames	*varies*	R/O	...	Current command, such as "SETVAR".
CMLJust	0	...	DWG	Multiline justification mode: **0** Top. **1** Middle. **2** Bottom.
CMLScale	1.0000	...	DWG	Scales width of multiline: **-*n*** Flips offsets of multiline. **0** Collapses to single line. **1** Default. ***n*** Scales by a factor of *n*.
CMLStyle	"STANDARD"	...	DWG	Current multiline style name.
Compass	0	...	...	Toggles display of the 3D compass: **0** Off. **1** On.
Coords	1	...	DWG	Coordinate display style: **0** Updated by screen picks. **1** Continuous display. **2** Polar display upon request.

Variable	Default	R/O	Loc	Meaning
CPlotStyle	"ByColor"	...	DWG	Current plot style; values defined by AutoCAD are: "ByLayer" "ByBlock" "Normal" "User Defined"
CProfile	"<<Unnamed Profile>>"	R/O	REG	Current profile.
CTab	"Model"	R/O	DWG	Current tab.
~~*CurrentProfile*~~	*"<<UnnamedProfile>>"*	*...*	*...*	*Removed from AutoCAD 2000; replaced by* **CProfile.**
CursorSize	5	...	REG	Cursor size, in percent of viewport: **1** Minimum size. **100** Full viewport.
CVPort	2	...	DWG	Current viewport number: **2** Minimum (default).

D

Variable	Default	R/O	Loc	Meaning
Date	*varies*	R/O	...	Current date in Julian format, such as 2448860.54043252
~~*DBGListAll*~~	*0*	*...*	*ACAD*	*Removed from AutoCAD 2002.*
DBMod	4	R/O	...	Drawing modified, as follows: **0** No modification since last save. **1** Object database modified. **2** Symbol table modified. **4** Database variable modified. **8** Window modified. **16** View modified.
DctCust	"d:\acad 2002\support\sample.cus"	...	REG	Name of custom spelling dictionary.
DctMain	"enu"	...	REG	Code for spelling dictionary: **ca** Catalan. **cs** Czech. **da** Danish. **de** German; sharp 's'. **ded** German; double 's'. **ena** English; Australian. **ens** English; British 'ise'. **enu** English; American. **enz** English; British 'ize'. **es** Spanish; unaccented capitals. **esa** Spanish; accented capitals. **fi** Finish. **fr** French; unaccented capitals. **fra** French; accented capitals. **it** Italian. **nl** Dutch; primary. **nls** Dutch; secondary. **no** Norwegian; Bokmal. **non** Norwegian; Nynorsk.

Variable	Default	R/O	Loc	Meaning
				pt Portuguese; Iberian.
				ptb Portuguese; Brazilian.
				ru Russian; infrequent 'io'.
				rui Russian; frequent 'io'.
				sv Swedish.
DefLPlStyle	"ByColor"	R/O	REG	Default plot style for new layers.
DefPlStyle	"ByColor"	R/O	REG	Default plot style for new objects.
DelObj	1	...	REG	Toggle source objects deletion:
				0 Objects deleted.
				1 Objects retained.
DemandLoad	3	...	REG	When drawing contains proxy objects:
				0 Demand loading turned off.
				1 Load app when drawing opened.
				2 Load app at first command.
				3 Load app when drawing opened or at first command.
DiaStat	1	R/O	...	User exited dialog box by clicking:
				0 Cancel button.
				1 OK button.

DIMENSION VARIABLES

Variable	Default	R/O	Loc	Meaning
DimADec	0	...	DWG	Angular dimension precision:
				-1 Use **DimDec** setting (default).
				0 Zero decimal places (minimum).
				8 Eight decimal places (maximum).
DimAlt	Off	...	DWG	Alternate units:
				On Enabled.
				Off Disabled.
DimAltD	2	...	DWG	Alternate unit decimal places.
DimAltF	25.4000	...	DWG	Alternate unit scale factor.
DimAltRnd	0.0000	...	DWG	Rounding factor of alternate units.
DimAltTD	2	...	DWG	Tolerance alternate unit decimal places.
DimAltTZ	0	...	DWG	Alternate tolerance units zeros:
				0 Zeros not suppressed.
				1 All zeros suppressed.
				2 Include 0 feet, but suppress 0 inches .
				3 Includes 0 inches, but suppress 0 feet.
				4 Suppresses leading zeros .
				8 Suppresses trailing zeros .
DimAltU	2	...	DWG	Alternate units:
				1 Scientific.
				2 Decimal.
				3 Engineering.
				4 Architectural; stacked.
				5 Fractional; stacked.
				6 Architectural.
				7 Fractional.
				8 Windows desktop units setting.

Variable	Default	R/O	Loc	Meaning
DimAltZ	0		DWG	Zero suppression for alternate units: **0** Suppress 0 ft and 0 in. **1** Include 0 ft and 0 in. **2** Include 0 ft; suppress 0 in. **3** Suppress 0 ft; include 0 in. **4** Suppress leading 0 in dec dim. **8** Suppress trailing 0 in dec dim. **12** Suppress leading and trailing zeroes.
DimAPost	""	...	DWG	Prefix and suffix for alternate text.
DimAso	On	...	DWG	Toggle associative dimensions: **On** Dimensions are created associative. **Off** Dimensions are not associative.
DimAssoc	2	...	DWG	▦ Controls creation of dimensions: **0** Dimension elements are exploded. **1** Single dimension object, attached to defpoints. **2** Single dimension object, attached to geometric objects.
DimASz	0.1800	...	DWG	Arrowhead length.
DimAtFit	3	...	DWG	When insufficient space between extension lines, dimension text and arrows are fitted: **0** Text and arrows outside extension lines. **1** Arrows first outside, then text. **2** Text first outside, then arrows. **3** Either text or arrows, whichever fits better.
DimAUnit	0	...	DWG	Angular dimension format: **0** Decimal degrees. **1** Degrees.Minutes.Seconds. **2** Grad. **3** Radian. **4** Surveyor units.
DimAZin	0	...	DWG	Supress zeros in angular dimensions: **0** Display all leading and trailing zeros. **1** Suppress 0 in front of decimal. **2** Suppress trailing zeros behind decimal. **3** Suppress zeros in front and behind the decimal.
DimBlk	""	R/O	DWG	Arrowhead block name: Architectural tick: "Archtick" Box filled: "Boxfilled" Box: "Boxblank" Closed blank: "Closedblank" Closed filled: "" (default) Closed: "Closed" Datum triangle filled:"Datumfilled" Datum triangle: "Datumblank" Dot blanked: "Dotblank"

Variable	Default	R/O	Loc	Meaning
				Dot small: "Dotsmall"
				Dot: "Dot"
				Integral: "Integral"
				None: "None"
				Oblique: "Oblique"
				Open 30: "Open30"
				Open: "Open"
				Origin indication: "Origin"
				Right-angle: "Open90"
DimBlk1	""	R/O	DWG	Name of first arrowhead's block; uses same list of names as under **DimBlk**. . No arrowhead.
DimBlk2	""	R/O	DWG	Name of second arrowhead's block; uses same list of names as under **DimBlk**. . No arrowhead.
DimCen	0.0900	...	DWG	Center mark size: -*n* Draws center lines. 0 No center mark or lines drawn. +*n* Draws center marks of length *n*.
DimClrD	0	...	DWG	Dimension line color: 0 BYBLOCK (default) 1 Red. ... 255 Dark gray. 256 BYLAYER.
DimClrE	0	...	DWG	Extension line and leader color.
DimClrT	0	...	DWG	Dimension text color.
DimDec	4	...	DWG	Primary tolerance decimal places.
DimDLE	0.0000	...	DWG	Dimension line extension.
DimDLI	0.3800	...	DWG	Dimension line continuation increment.
DimDSep	"."	...	DWG	Decimal separator (must be a single char.)
DimExe	0.1800	...	DWG	Extension above dimension line.
DimExO	0.0625	...	DWG	Extension line origin offset.
~~*DimFit*~~	*3*	...	*DWG*	*Obsolete: Autodesk recommends use of* **DimATfit** *and* **DimTMove** *instead.*
DimFrac	0	...	DWG	Fraction format when **DimLUnit** is set to 4 or 5: 0 Horizontal. 1 Diagonal. 2 Not stacked.
DimGap	0.0900	...	DWG	Gap from dimension line to text.
DimJust	0	...	DWG	Horizontal text positioning: 0 Center justify. 1 Next to first extension line. 2 Next to second extension line. 3 Above first extension line. 4 Above second extension line.

Variable	Default	R/O	Loc	Meaning
DimLdrBlk	""	...	DWG	Block name for leader arrowhead; uses same name as **DimBlock**. . Supresses display of arrowhead.
DimLFac	1.0000	...	DWG	Linear unit scale factor.
DimLim	Off	...	DWG	Generate dimension limits.
DimLUnit	2	...	DWG	Dimension units (except angular); replaces **DimUnit**: **1** Scientific. **2** Decimal. **3** Engineering. **4** Architectural. **5** Fractional. **6** Windows desktop.
DimLwD	-2	...	DWG	Dimension line lineweight; valid values are BYLAYER, BYBLOCK, or an integer multiple of 0.01mm.
DimLwE	-2	...	DWG	Extension lineweight; valid values are BYLAYER, BYBLOCK, or an integer multiple of 0.01mm.
DimPost	""	...	DWG	Default prefix or suffix for dimension text (maximum 13 characters): "" No suffix. **< > m m** Millimeter suffix. **< > Å** Angstrom suffix.
DimRnd	0.0000	...	DWG	Rounding value for dimension distances.
DimSAh	Off	...	DWG	Separate arrowhead blocks: **Off** Use arrowhead defined by **DimBlk**. **On** Use arrowheads defined by **DimBlk1** and **DimBlk2**.
DimScale	1.0000	...	DWG	Overall scale factor for dimensions: **0** Value is computed from the scale between current modelspace viewport and paperspace. **> 0** Scales text and arrowheads.
DimSD1	Off	...	DWG	Suppress first dimension line: **On** First dimension line is suppressed. **Off** Not suppressed.
DimSD2	Off	...	DWG	Suppress second dimension line: **On** Second dimension line is suppressed. **Off** Not suppressed.
DimSE1	Off	...	DWG	Suppress the first extension line: **On** First extension line is suppressed. **Off** Not suppressed.
DimSE2	Off	...	DWG	Suppress the second extension line: **On** Second extension line is suppressed. **Off** Not suppressed.
DimSho	On	...	DWG	Update dimensions while dragging: **On** Dimensions are updated during drag. **Off** Dimensions are updated after drag.

Variable	Default	R/O	Loc	Meaning
DimSOXD	Off	...	DWG	Suppress dimension lines outside extension lines: **On** Dimension lines not drawn outside extension lines. **Off** Are drawn outside extension lines.
DimStyle	"STANDARD"	R/O	DWG	🔲 Current dimension style.
DimTAD	0	...	DWG	Vertical position of dimension text: **0** Centered between extension lines. **1** Above dimension line, except when dimension line not horizontal and **DimTIH** = 1. **2** On side of dimension line farthest from the defining points. **3** Conforms to JIS.
DimTDec	4	...	DWG	Primary tolerance decimal places.
DimTFac	1.0000	...	DWG	Tolerance text height scaling factor.
DimTIH	On	...	DWG	Text inside extensions is horizontal: **Off** Text aligned with dimension line. **On** Text is horizontal.
DimTIX	Off	...	DWG	Place text inside extensions: **Off** Text placed inside extension lines, if room. **On** Force text between the extension lines.
DimTM	0.0000	...	DWG	Minus tolerance.
DimTMove	0	...	DWG	Determines how dimension text is moved: **0** Dimension line moves with text. **1** Adds a leader when text is moved. **2** Text moves anywhere; no leader.
DimTOFL	Off	...	DWG	Force line inside extension lines: **Off** Dimension lines not drawn when arrowheads are outside. **On** Dimension lines drawn, even when arrowheads are outside.
DimTOH	On	...	DWG	Text outside extension lines: **Off** Text aligned with dimension line. **On** Text is horizontal.
DimTol	Off	...	DWG	Generate dimension tolerances: **Off** Tolerances not drawn. **On** Tolerances are drawn.
DimTolJ	1	...	DWG	Tolerance vertical justification: **0** Bottom. **1** Middle. **2** Top.
DimTP	0.0000	...	DWG	Plus tolerance.
DimTSz	0.0000	...	DWG	Size of oblique tick strokes: **0** Arrowheads. **> 0** Oblique strokes.

Variable	Default	R/O	Loc	Meaning
DimTVP	0.0000	...	DWG	Text vertical position when **DimTAD**=0: **1** Turns **DimTAD** on. **>-0.7** *or* **<0.7** Dimension line is split for text.
DimTxSty	"STANDARD"	...	DWG	Dimension text style.
DimTxt	0.1800	...	DWG	Text height.
DimTZin	0	...	DWG	Tolerance zero suppression: **0** Suppress 0 ft and 0 in. **1** Include 0 ft and 0 in. **2** Include 0 ft; suppress 0 in. **3** Suppress 0 ft; include 0 in. **4** Suppress leading 0 in decimal dim. **8** Suppress trailing 0 in decimal dim. **12** Suppress leading and trailing zeroes.
~~DimUnit~~	*2*	...	*DWG*	*Obsolete; replaced by **DimLUnit** and **DimFrac.***
DimUPT	Off	...	DWG	User-positioned text: **Off** Cursor positions dimension line **On** Cursor also positions text
DimZIN	0	...	DWG	Suppression of 0 in feet-inches units: **0** Suppress 0 ft and 0 in. **1** Include 0 ft and 0 in. **2** Include 0 ft; suppress 0 in. **3** Suppress 0 ft; include 0 in. **4** Suppress leading 0 in decimal dim. **8** Suppress trailing 0 in decimal dim. **12** Suppress leading and trailing zeroes.
DispSilh	0	...	DWG	Silhouette display of 3D solids: **0** Off. **1** On.
Distance	0.0000	R/O	...	Distance measured by last **Dist** command.
~~Dither~~				*Removed from Release 14.*
DonutId	0.5000	...	...	Inside radius of donut.
DonutOd	1.0000	...	...	Outside radius of donut.
DragMode	2	...	REG	▦ Drag mode: **0** No drag. **1** On if requested. **2** Automatic.
DragP1	10	...	REG	Regen drag display.
DragP2	25	...	REG	Fast drag display.
DwgCheck	0	...	REG	Toggles checking if drawing was edited by software other than AutoCAD: **0** Supresses dialog box. **1** Displays warning dialog box.
DwgCodePage	*varies*	R/O	DWG	Drawing code page, such as "ANSI_1252"

ariable	Default	R/O	Loc	Meaning
DwgName	*varies*	R/O	...	Current drawing filename, such as "Drawing1.dwg".
DwgPrefix	*varies*	R/O	...	Drawing's drive and subdirectory, such as "d:\acad 2002\".
DwgTitled	0	R/O	...	Drawing has filename: **0** "Drawing1.Dwg". **1** User-assigned name.
~~DwgWrite~~				*Removed from AuoCAD Release 14.*

E

EdgeMode	0	...	REG	Toggle edge mode for **Trim** and **Extend** commands: **0** No extension. **1** Extends cutting edge.
Elevation	0.0000	...	DWG	Current elevation, relative to current UCS.
EntExts	*1*	...	...	*Controls how the drawing extents are calcualted:* *0 Extents calculated every time; slows down AutoCAD but uses less memory.* *1 Extents of every object is cached as a two-byte value (default).* *2 Extents of every object is cached as a four-byte value (fastest but uses more memory).*
EntMods	*0*	R/O	...	*Increments by one each time an object is modified to indicate that an object has been modified since the drawing was opened; value ranges from 0 to 4.29497E9.*
ErrNo	*0*	...	...	*Error number from AutoLISP, ADS, & Arx*
~~ExeDir~~				*Removed from Release 14.*
Expert	0	...	...	Suppresses the displays of prompts: **0** Normal prompts **1** "About to regen, proceed?" and "Really want to turn the current layer off?" **2** "Block already defined. Redefine it?" and "A drawing with this name already exists. Overwrite it?" **3** **Linetype** command messages. **4** **UCS Save** and **VPorts Save**. **5** **DimStyle Save** and **DimOverride**.
ExplMode	1	...	...	Toggle whether **Explode** and **Xplode** commands explode non-uniformly scaled blocks: **0** Does not explode. **1** Explodes.
ExtMax	-1.0000E+20, -1.0000E+20, -1.0000E+20	R/O	DWG	Upper-right coordinate of drawing extents.

Variable	Default	R/O	Loc	Meaning
ExtMin	1.0000E+20, 1.0000E+20, 1.0000E+20			
		R/O	DWG	Lower-left coordinate of drawing extents.
ExtNames	1	...	DWG	Format of named objects: **0** Names are limited to 31 characters, and can include A - Z, 0 - 9, dollar ($), underscore (_), and hyphen (-). **1** Names are limited to 255 characters, and can include A - Z, 0 - 9, spaces, and any characters not used by Microsoft Windows or AutoCAD for special purposes.

F

Variable	Default	R/O	Loc	Meaning
FaceTRatio	0	...	...	Controls the aspect ratio of facets on cylinder and cone ACIS solids: **0** Creates an *n* by 1 mesh. **1** Creates an *n* by *m* mesh.
FaceTRres	0.5000	...	DWG	Adjusts smoothness of shaded and hidden-line objects: **0.01** Minimum value. **10.0** Maximum value.
FfLimit	...	...	...	*Removed from AutoCAD Release 14.*
FileDia	1	...	REG	User interface: **0** Command-line prompts. **1** Dialog boxes, when available.
FilletRad	0.5000	...	DWG	Current fillet radius.
FillMode	1	...	DWG	Fill of solid objects: **0** Off. **1** On.
Flatland	*0*	R/O	...	*Obsolete system variable.*
FontAlt	"simplex.shx"	...	REG	Name for substituted font.
FontMap	"acad.fmp"	...	REG	Name of font mapping file.
Force_Paging	*0*	...	...	*0 Minimum (default).* *4.29497E9 Maximum.*
FrontZ	0.0000	R/O	DWG	Front clipping plane offset.
FullOpen	1	R/O	...	Drawing is: **0** Partially loaded. **1** Fully open.

G

Variable	Default	R/O	Loc	Meaning
GlobCheck	*0*	...	...	*Reports statistics on dialog boxes:* *-1 Turn off local language.* *0 Turn off.* *1 Warns if larger than 640x400.* *2 Also reports size in pixels.* *3 Additional info.*

Variable	Default	R/O	Loc	Meaning

GridMode	0	...	DWG	Display of grid:
				  0 Off.
				  1 On.

GridUnit	0.5000,0.5000	...	DWG	X,y-spacing of grid.

GripBlock	0	...	REG	Display of grips in blocks:
				  0 At insertion point.
				  1 At all objects within block.

GripColor	5	...	REG	Color of unselected grips:
				  1 Minimum color number; red.
				  5 Default color; blue.
				  255 Maximum color number.

GripHot	1	...	REG	Color of selected grips:
				  1 Default color, red.
				  255 Maximum color number.

Grips	1	...	REG	Display of grips:
				  0 Off.
				  1 On

GripSize	3	...	REG	Size of grip box, in pixels:
				  1 Minimum size.
				  255 Maximum size.

H

Variable	Default	R/O	Loc	Meaning
HaloGap	0	...	DWG	Distance to shorten a haloed line; specified as the percentage of 1".
Handles	1	R/O	...	Obsolete system variable.

HidePrecision	0	...	DWG	Controls the precision of hide calculations:
				  0 Single precision, less accurate, faster.
				  1 Double precision, more accurate, but slower.

HideText	0	...	...	Determines whether text is hidden during the **Hide** command:
				  0 Text is not hidden nor hides other objects, unless text object has thickness.
				  1 Text is hidden and hides other objects.

Highlight	1	...	...	Object selection highlighting:
				  0 Disabled.
				  1 Enabled.

HPAng	0	...	...	Current hatch pattern angle.

HPBound	1	...	...	Object created by **BHatch** and **Boundary** commands:
				  0 Reegion.
				  1 Polyline.

HPDouble	0	...	...	Double hatching:
				  0 Disabled.
				  1 Enabled.

Variable	Default	R/O	Loc	Meaning
HPName	"ANSI31"	...	...	Current hatch pattern name "" No default. . Set no default.
HPScale	1.0000	...	...	Current hatch scale factor; cannot be zero.
HPSpace	1.0000	...	...	Current spacing of user-defined hatching; cannot be zero.
HyperlinkBase	""	...	DWG	Path for relative hyperlinks.

■

I

Variable	Default	R/O	Loc	Meaning
ImageHlt	0	...	REG	When a raster image is selected: 0 Image frame is highlighted. 1 Entire image is highlighted.
IndexCtl	0	...	DWG	Creates layer and spatial indices: 0 No indices created. 1 Layer index created. 2 Spatial index created. 3 Both indices created.
InetLocation	"www.autodesk.com"	...	REG	Default browser URL.
InsBase	0.0000,0.0000,0.0000	...	DWG	Insertion base point relative to the current UCS for **Insert** and **DdInsert**.
InsName	""	...	...	Current block name: . Set to no default.
InsUnits	1	...	...	Drawing units when a block is dragged into drawing from DesignCenter: 0 Unitless. 1 Inches. 2 Feet. 3 Miles. 4 Millimeters. 5 Centimeters. 6 Meters. 7 Kilometers. 8 Microinches. 9 Mils. 10 Yards. 11 Angstroms. 12 Nanometers. 13 Microns. 14 Decimeters. 15 Decameters. 16 Hectometers. 17 Gigameters. 18 Astronomical Units. 19 Light Years. 20 Parsecs.
InsUnitsDefSource	1	...	REG	Source drawing units value; ranges from 0 to 20; see above.

Variable	Default	R/o	Loc	Meaning
InsUnitsDefTarget				
	1	...	REG	Target drawing units value; ranges from 0 to 20.
ISaveBak	1	...	REG	Controls whether BAK file is created: 0 No BAK file created. 1 BAK backup file created.
ISavePercent	50	...	REG	Percentage of waste in DWG file before cleanup occurs: 0 Every save is a full save.
IsoLines	4	...	DWG	Isolines on 3D solids: 0 No isolines; minimum. 16 Good-looking. 2,047 Maximum.

L

Variable	Default	R/o	Loc	Meaning
LastAngle	0	R/O	...	Ending angle of last-drawn arc.
LastPoint	*varies*	...	...	Last-entered point, such as 15,9,56.
LastPrompt	""	R/O	...	Last string on the command line; includes user input.
LazyLoad	*0*	...	...	*Toggle: 0 or 1.*
LayoutRegenCtl				
	2	...	REG	▦ Controls display list for layouts: 0 Display list is regenerated with each tab change. 1 Display list is saved for model tab and last layout tab. 2 Display list is saved for all tabs.
LensLength	50.0000	R/O	DWG	Perspective view lens length, in mm.
LimCheck	0	...	DWG	Drawing limits checking: 0 Disabled. 1 Enabled.
LimMax	12.0000,9.0000	...	DWG	Upper right drawing limits.
LimMin	0.0000,0.0000	...	DWG	Lower left drawing limits.
LispInit	1	...	REG	AutoLISP functions and variables are: 0 Preserved from drawing to drawing. 1 Valid in current drawing only.
Locale	"enu"	R/O		ISO language code.
LogFileMode	0	...	REG	Text window written to log file: 0 No. 1 Yes.
LogFileName	"d:\acad 2002\Drawing1_1_1_0000.log"			
		R/O	DWG	Filename and path for log file.
LogFilePath	"d:\acad 2002\"	...	REG	Path for the log file.
LogInName	""	R/O	...	User's login name; max = 30 chars.
~~LongFName~~				*Removed from AutoCAD Release 14.*
LTScale	1.0000	...	DWG	▦ Current linetype scale factor; cannot be 0.

Variable	Default	R/O	Loc	Meaning
LUnits	2	...	DWG	Linear units mode: 1 Scientific. 2 Decimal. 3 Engineering. 4 Architectural. 5 Fractional.
LUPrec	4	...	DWG	Decimal places of linear units.
LwDefault	25	...	REG	Default lineweight, in millimeters; must be one of the following values: 0, 5, 9, 13, 15, 18, 20, 25, 30, 35, 40, 50, 53, 60, 70, 80, 90, 100, 106, 120, 140, 158, 200, or 211.
LwDisplay	0	...	DWG	Toggles whether lineweight is displayed; setting is saved separately for Model space and each layout tab. 0 Not displayed. 1 Displayed.
LwUnits	1	...	REG	Determines units for lineweight: 0 Inches. 1 Millimeters.

M

Variable	Default	R/O	Loc	Meaning
MacroTrace	*0*	...	...	*Diesel debug mode:* *0 Off.* *1 On.*
MaxActVP	64	...	...	Maximum viewports to regenerate: 2 Minimum. 64 Maximum (increased from 48 in R14).
MaxObjMem	*0*	...	...	*Maximum number of objects in memory; object pager is turned off when value = 0, <0, or 2,147,483,647.*
MaxSort	200	...	REG	Maximum names sorted alphabetically.
MButtonPan	1	...	REG	Determines behavior of wheelmouse: 0 As defined by AutoCAD menu file. 1 Pans when dragging with wheel.
MeasureInit	0	...	REG	Drawing units: 0 English. 1 Metric.
Measurement	0	...	DWG	Drawing units (overrides **MeasureInit**): 0 English. 1 Metric.
MenuCtl	1	...	REG	Submenu display: 0 Only with menu picks. 1 Also with keyboard entry.
MenuEcho	0	...		Menu and prompt echoing: 0 Display all prompts. 1 Suppress menu echoing. 2 Suppress system prompts. 4 Disable ^P toggle. 8 Display all input-output strings.

Variable	Default	R/O	Loc	Meaning
MenuName	"acad"	R/O	REG	Current menu filename.

MirrText	1	...	DWG	Text handling during **Mirror** command:
				  0 Retain text orientation.
				  1 Mirror text.

ModeMacro	""	...	...	Invoke Diesel programming language.

MTextEd	"Internal"	...	REG	Name of the **MText** editor:
				  . (Use default editor.
				  0 Cancel the editing operation.
				  -1 Use the secondary editor.
				  "blank" MTEXT internal editor.
				  "Internal" MTEXT internal editor.
				  "Notepad" Windows Notepad editor.
				  ":lisped" Built-in AutoLISP function.
				*string*Name of editor; must be less than 256 characters long and use this syntax:
				:AutoLISPtextEditorFunction#TextEditor

N

Variable	Default	R/O	Loc	Meaning
NodeName	*"AC$"*	R/O	REG	*Name of network node; range is one to three characters.*

NoMutt	0	...	...	Suppresses the display of message (a.k.a. muttering) during scripts, LISP, macros:
				  0 Display prompt, as normal.
				  1 Suppress muttering.

O

Variable	Default	R/O	Loc	Meaning

ObscureColor	0	...	DWG	▓ Color of objects obscured by **Hide** command:
				  0 Invisible
				  1 - 255 Color number.

ObscureLtype	0	...	DWG	▓ Linetype of objects obscured by **Hide** command:
				  0 Invisible.
				  1 Solid.
				  2 Dashed.
				  3 Dotted.
				  4 Short dash.
				  5 Medium dash.
				  6 Long dash.
				  7 Double short dash.
				  8 Double medium dash.
				  9 Double long dash.
				  10 Medium long dash.
				  11 Sparse dot.

OffsetDist	1.0000	...	...	Current offset distance: < 0 Offsets through a specified point. > 0 Default offset distance.

Variable	Default	R/o	Loc	Meaning
OffsetGapType	0	...	REG	Determines how to reconnect polyline when individual segments are offset: 0 Extend segments to fill gap. 1 Fill gap with fillet (arc segment). 2 Fill gap with chamfer (line segment).
OleHide	0	...	REG	Display and plotting of OLE objects: 0 All OLE objects visible. 1 Visible in paper space only. 2 Visible in model space only. 3 Not visible.
OleQuality	1	...	REG	Quality of display and plotting of embedded OLE objects: 0 Line art quality. 1 Text quality. 2 Graphics quality. 3 Photograph quality. 4 High quality photograph.
OleStartup	0	...	DWG	Loading OLE source application improves plot quality: 0 Do not load OLE source app. 1 Load OLE source app when plotting.
OrthoMode	0	...	DWG	Orthographic mode: 0 Off. 1 On.
OSMode	4133	...	REG	Current object snap mode: 0 NONe. 1 ENDpoint. 2 MIDpoint. 4 CENter. 8 NODe. 16 QUAdrant. 32 INTersection. 64 INSertion. 128 PERpendicular. 256 TANgent. 512 NEARest. 1024 QUIck. 2048 APPint. 4096 EXTension. 8192 PARallel. 16383 All modes on. 16384 Object snap turned off via **OSNAP** on the status bar.
OSnapCoord	2	...	REG	Keyboard overrides object snap: 0 Object snap override keyboard. 1 Keyboard overrides object snap. 2 Keyboard overrides object snap, except in script.

Variable	Default	R/O	Loc	Meaning

P

PaperUpdate 0 ... REG Determines how AutoCAD plots a layout with paper size different from plotter's default:
   0 Displays a warning dialog box.
   1 Changes paper size to that of the plotter configuration file.

PDMode 0 ... DWG Point display mode:
   0 Dot.
   1 No display.
   2 +-symbol.
   3 x-symbol.
   4 Short line.
   32 Circle.
   64 Square.

0 1 2 3 4
32 33 34 35 36
64 65 66 67 68
96 97 98 99 100

PDSize 0.0000 ... DWG Point display size, in pixels:
   > 0 Absolute size.
   0 5% of drawing area height.
   < 0 Percentage of viewport size.

PEllipse 0 ... DWG Toggle **Ellipse** creation:
   0 True ellipse.
   1 Polyline arcs.

Perimeter 0.0000 R/O ... Perimeter calculated by the last **Area**, **DbList**, and **List** commands.

PFaceVMax 4 R/O ... Maximum vertices per 3D face.

PHandle *0* ... *ACAD* *Ranges from 0 to 4.29497E9.*

PickAdd 1 ... REG Effect of **SHIFT** key on selection set:
   0 Adds to selection set.
   1 Removes from selection set.

PickAuto 1 ... REG Selection set mode:
   0 Single pick mode.
   1 Automatic windowing and crossing.

PickBox 3 ... REG Object selection pickbox size, in pixels:
   0 Minimum size.
   50 Maximum size.

PickDrag 0 ... REG Selection window mode:
   0 Pick two corners.
   1 Pick a corner; drag to second corner.

PickFirst 1 ... REG Command-selection mode:
   0 Enter command first.
   1 Select objects first.

Variable	Default	R/O	Loc	Meaning
PickStyle	1	...	REG	Include groups and associative hatches in selection: **0** Neither included. **1** Include groups. **2** Include associative hatches. **3** Include both.
Platform	"Microsoft Windows Version 4.10 (x86)"	R/O	...	AutoCAD platform (name of the operating system).
PLineGen	0	...	DWG	Polyline linetype generation: **0** From vertex to vertex. **1** From end to end.
PLineType	2	...	REG	Automatic conversion and creation of 2D polylines by **PLine**: **0** Not converted; old-format polylines created. **1** Not converted; optimized polylines created. **2** Polylines in older drawings are converted on open; **PLine** creates optimized polylines with Lwpolyline object.
PLineWid	0.0000	...	DWG	Current polyline width.
PlotId	""	...	REG	Obsolete; has no effect in AutoCAD 2002.
PlotRotMode	1	...	DWG	Orientation of plots: **0** Lower left = 0,0. **1** Lower left plotter area = lower left of media. **2** X, y-origin offsets calculated relative to the rotated origin position.
Plotter	0	...	REG	Obsolete; has no effect in AutoCAD 2002.
PlQuiet	0	...	REG	Toggles display during batch plotting and scripts (replaces **CmdDia**): **0** Plot dialog boxes and nonfatal errors are displayed. **1** Nonfatal errors are logged; plot dialog boxes are not displayed.
PolarAddAng	""	...	REG	Contains a list of up to 10 user-defined polar angles; each angle can be up to 25 characters long, each separated with a semicolon (;). For example: 0;15;22.5;45.
PolarAng	90	...	REG	Specifies the increment of polar angle; contrary to Autodesk documentation, you may specify any angle.
PolarDist	0.000	...	REG	The polar snap increment when **SnapStyl** is set to 1 (isometric).

Variable	Default	R/o	Loc	Meaning
PolarMode	0	...	REG	Settings for polar and object snap tracking: **0** Measure polar angles based on current UCS (absolute), track orthogonally; don't use additional polar tracking angles; and acquire object tracking points automatically. **1** Measure polar angles from selected objects (relative). **2** Use polar tracking settings in object snap tracking. **4** Use additional polar tracking angles (via **PolarAng**). **8** Press **SHIFT** to acquire object snap tracking points.
PolySides	4	...	...	Current number of polygon sides: **3** Minimum sides. **1024** Maximum sides.
Popups	1	R/O	...	Display driver support of AUI: **0** Not available. **1** Available.
Product	*"AutoCAD"*	R/O	ACAD	*Name of the software.*
Program	*"acad"*	R/O	ACAD	*Name of the software's executable file.*
ProjectName	""	...	DWG	Project name of the current drawing; searches for xref and image files.
ProjMode	1	...	REG	Projection mode for **Trim** and **Extend** commands: **0** No projection. **1** Project to x,y-plane of current UCS. **2** Project to view plane.
ProxyGraphics	1	...	REG	Proxy image saved in the drawing: **0** Not saved; displays bounding box. **1** Image saved with drawing.
ProxyNotice	1	...	REG	Display warning message: **0** No. **1** Yes.
ProxyShow	1	...	REG	Display of proxy objects: **0** Not displayed. **1** All displayed. **2** Bounding box displayed.
ProxyWebSearch	0	...	REG	Object enablers are checked: **0** AutoCAD does not check for object enablers. **1** AutoCAD checks for object enablers if Point A window is open in **Today**, and Internet connection is present. **2** AutoCAD limits the number of times it checks for object enablers.

Variable	Default	R/o	Loc	Meaning
PsLtScale	1	...	DWG	Paper space linetype scaling: **0** Use model space scale factor. **1** Use viewport scale factor.
PsProlog	""	...	REG	PostScript prologue filename
PsQuality	75	...	REG	Resolution of PostScript display, in pixels: **< 0** Display as outlines; no fill. **0** Not displayed. **> 0** Display filled.
PStyleMode	1	...	DWG	Toggles the plot color matching mode of the drawing: **0** Use named plot style tables. **1** Use color-dependent plot style tables.
PStylePolicy	1	...	REG	Determines whether the object color is associated with its plot style: **0** Color and plot style not associated. **1** Object's plot style is associated with its color.
PsVpScale	0	...	...	Sets the view scale factor (the ratio of units in paper space to the units in newly created model space viewports) for all newly-created viewports: **0** Scaled to fit.
PUcsBase	""	...	DWG	Name of UCS defining the origin and orientation of orthographic UCS settings in paper space only.

▬ Q

Variable	Default	R/o	Loc	Meaning
QAFlags	0	...	...	*Quality assurance flags:* **0** *Turned off.* **1** *The ^C metacharacters in a menu macro cancels grips, just as if user pressed* **Esc**. **2** *Long text screen listings do not pause.* **4** *Error and warning messages are displayed at the command line, instead of in dialog boxes.* **128** *Screen picks are accepted via the AutoLISP (command) function.*
QTextMode	0	...	DWG	Quick text mode: **0** Off. **1** On.

▬ R

Variable	Default	R/o	Loc	Meaning
RasterPreview	1	R/O	REG	Preview image: **0** None saved. **1** Saved in BMP format.

Variable	Default	R/O	Loc	Meaning
RefEditName""		...	...	The reference filename when it is in reference-editing mode.
RegenMode	1	...	DWG	Regeneration mode: **0** Regen with each view change. **1** Regen only when required.
Re-Init	*0*	...	...	*Reinitialize I/O devices:* *1 Digitizer port.* *2 Plotter port.* *4 Digitizer.* *8 Plotter.* *16 Reload PGP file.*
RememberFolders	1	...	REG	🔲 Controls path search method: **0** Path specified in desktop AutoCAD icon is default for file dialog boxes. **1** Last path specified by each file dialog box is remembered.
~~RIAspect~~				*Removed from AutoCAD Release 14.*
~~RIBackG~~				*Removed from AutoCAD Release 14.*
~~RIEdge~~				*Removed from AutoCAD Release 14.*
~~RIGamut~~				*Removed from AutoCAD Release 14.*
~~RIGrey~~				*Removed from AutoCAD Release 14.*
~~RIThresh~~				*Removed from AutoCAD Release 14.*
RTDisplay	1	...	REG	Raster display during real-time zoom and pan: **0** Display the entire raster image. **1** Display raster outline only.

■
S

Variable	Default	R/O	Loc	Meaning
SaveFile	"auto.sv$"	R/O	REG	Automatic save filename.
SaveFilePath	"d:\temp\"	...	REG	Path for automatic save files.
SaveName	""	R/O	...	Drawing save-as filename.
SaveTime	120	...	REG	Automatic save interval, in minutes: **0** Disable auto save.
ScreenBoxes	0	R/O	ACAD	Maximum number of menu items **0** Screen menu turned off.
ScreenMode	3	R/O	...	State of AutoCAD display screen: **0** Text screen. **1** Graphics screen. **2** Dual-screen display.
ScreenSize	*varies*	R/O	...	Current viewport size, in pixels, such as 719.0000,381.0000.
SDI	0	...	REG	Toggles multiple-document interface (SDI is "single document interface"): **0** Turns on MDI. **1** Turns off MDI (only one drawing may be loaded into AutoCAD). **2** MDI disabled for apps that cannot support MDI; read-only.

Variable	Default	R/O	Loc	Meaning
				3 MDI disabled for apps that cannot support MDI, even when **SDI** set to 1; R/O.
ShadEdge	3	...	DWG	**Shade** style: **0** Shade faces; 256-color shading. **1** Shade faces; edges background color. **2** Hidden-line removal. **3** 16-color shading.
ShadeDif	70	...	DWG	Percent of diffuse to ambient light: **0** Minimum. **100** Maximum.
ShortcutMenu	11	...	REG	Toggles availability of shortcut menus: **0** Disables all default, edit, and command shortcut menus. **1** Enables default shortcut menus. **2** Enables edit shortcut menus. **4** Enables command shortcut menus whenever a command is active. **8** Enables command shortcut menus only when command options are available at the command line.
ShpName	""	...	...	Current shape name: . Set to no default.
SketchInc	0.1000	...	DWG	**Sketch** command's recording increment.
SkPoly	0	...	DWG	Sketch line mode: **0** Record as lines. **1** Record as a polyline.
SnapAng	0	...	DWG	Current rotation angle for snap and grid.
SnapBase	0.0000,0.0000	...	DWG	Current origin for snap and grid.
SnapIsoPair	0	...	DWG	Current isometric drawing plane: **0** Left isoplane. **1** Top isoplane. **2** Right isoplane.
SnapMode	0	...	DWG	Snap mode: **0** Off. **1** On.
SnapStyl	0	...	DWG	Snap style: **0** Normal. **1** Isometric.
SnapType	0	...	REG	Toggles between standard or polar snap for the current viewport: **0** Standard snap. **1** Polar snap.
SnapUnit	0.5000,0.5000	...	DWG	X,y-spacing for snap.
SolidCheck	1	...	...	Toggles solid validation: **0** Off. **1** On.

Variable	Default	R/o	Loc	Meaning
SortEnts	96	...	DWG	Object display sort order: **0** Off. **1** Object selection. **2** Object snap. **4** Redraw. **8** Slide generation. **16** Regeneration. **32** Plot. **64** PostScript output.
SplFrame	0	...	DWG	Polyline and mesh display: **0** Polyline control frame not displayed; display polygon fit mesh; 3D faces invisible edges not displayed **1** Polyline control frame displayed; display polygon defining mesh; 3D faces invisible edges displayed.
SplineSegs	8	...	DWG	Number of line segments that define a splined polyline.
SplineType	6	...	DWG	Spline curve type: **5** Quadratic Bezier spline. **6** Cubic Bezier spline.
StartupToday	1	...	REG	▦ AutoCAD starts with: **0** Startup dialog box. **1** **Today** window.
SurfTab1	6	...	DWG	Density of surfaces and meshes: **5** Minimum. **32766** Maximum.
SurfTab2	6	...	DWG	Density of surfaces and meshes: **2** Minimum. **32766** Maximum.
SurfType	6	...	DWG	Pedit surface smoothing: **5** Quadratic Bezier spline. **6** Cubic Bezier spline. **8** Bezier surface.
SurfU	6	...	DWG	Surface density in m-direction: **2** Minimum. **200** Maximum.
SurfV	6	...	DWG	Surface density in n-direction: **2** Minimum. **200** Maximum.
SysCodePage	"ANSI_1252"	R/o	...	System code page.

▬ T

Variable	Default	R/o	Loc	Meaning
TabMode	0	...	...	Tablet mode: **0** Off. **1** On.
Target	0.0000,0.0000,0.0000	R/o	DWG	Target in current viewport.
TDCreate	*varies*	R/o	DWG	Time and date drawing created, such as 2448860.54014699.

Variable	Default	R/O	Loc	Meaning
TDInDwg	*varies*	R/O	DWG	Duration drawing loaded, such as 0.00040625.
TDuCreate	*varies*	R/O	DWG	The universal time and date the drawing was created, such as 2451318.67772165.
TDUpdate	*varies*	R/O	DWG	Time and date of last update, such as 2448860.54014699.
TDUsrTimer	*varies*	R/O	DWG	Time elapsed by user-timer, such as 0.00040694.
TDuUpdate	*varies*	R/O	DWG	The universal time and date of the last save, such as 2451318.67772165.
TempPrefix	"d:\temp"	R/O	...	Path for temporary files.
TextEval	0	...	...	Interpretation of text input: **0** Literal text. **1** Read (and ! as AutoLISP code.
TextFill	1	...	REG	Toggle fill of TrueType fonts: **0** Outline text. **1** Filled text.
TextQlty	50	...	DWG	Resolution of TrueType fonts: **0** Minimum resolution. **100** Maximum resolution.
TextSize	0.2000	...	DWG	Current height of text.
TextStyle	"Standard"	...	DWG	Current name of text style.
Thickness	0.0000	...	DWG	Current object thickness.
TileMode	1	...	DWG	View mode: **0** Display layout tab. **1** Display model tab.
ToolTips	1	...	REG	Display tooltips: **0** Off. **1** On.
TraceWid	0.0500	...	DWG	Current width of traces.
TrackPath	0	...	REG	Determines the display of polar and object snap tracking alignment paths: **0** Display object snap tracking path across the entire viewport. **1** Display object snap tracking path between the alignment point and "From point" to cursor location. **2** Turn off polar tracking path. **3** Turn off polar and object snap tracking paths.
TreeDepth	3020	...	DWG	Maximum branch depth in *xxyy* format: *xx* Model-space nodes. *yy* Paper-space nodes. *> 0* 3D drawing. *< 0* 2D drawing.
TreeMax	10000000	...	REG	Limits memory consumption during drawing regeneration.

Variable	Default	R/O	Loc	Meaning
TrimMode	1	...	REG	Trim toggle for **Chamfer** and **Fillet** commands: **0** Leave selected edges in place. **1** Trim selected edges.
TSpaceFac	1.0000	...	...	Mtext line spacing distance; measured as a factor of text height; valid values range from 0.25 to 4.0.
TSpaceType	1	...	...	Type of mtext line spacing: **1** At Least: adjust line spacing based on the height of the tallest character in a line of mtext. **2** Exactly: use the specified line spacing; ignores character height.
TStackAlign	1	...	DWG	Vertical alignment of stacked text. **0** Bottom aligned. **1** Center aligned. **2** Top aligned.
TStackSize	70	...	DWG	Sizes stacked text as a percentage of the selected text height: **1** Minimum %. **127** Maximum %.

Ū
U

Variable	Default	R/O	Loc	Meaning
UcsAxisAng	90	...	REG	Default angle for rotating the UCS around an axes (via the **UCS** command using the **X**, **Y**, or **Z** options; valid values are limited to: 5, 10, 15, 18, 22.5, 30, 45, 90, or 180.
UcsBase	""	...	DWG	Name of the UCS that defines the origin and orientation of orthographic UCS settings.
UcsFollow	0	...	DWG	New UCS views: **0** No change. **1** Automatic display of plan view.
UcsIcon	3	...	DWG	▣ Display of UCS icon: **0** Off. **1** On. **2** Display at UCS origin, if possible. **3** On, and displayed at origin.
UcsName	""	R/O	DWG	Name of current UCS view: "" Current UCS is unnamed.
UcsOrg	0.0000,0.0000,0.0000	R/O	DWG	Origin of current UCS relative to WCS.

Variable	Default	R/o	Loc	Meaning
UcsOrtho	1	...	REG	Determines whether the related orthographic UCS setting is restored automatically: **0** UCS setting remains unchanged when orthographic view is restored. **1** Related orthographic UCS setting is restored automatically when an orthographic view is restored.
UcsView	1	...	REG	Determines whether the current UCS is saved with a named view: **0** Not saved. **1** Saved.
UcsVp	1	...	DWG	Determines whether the UCS in active viewports remains fixed (locked) or changes (unlocked) to match the UCS of the current viewport: **0** Unlocked. **1** Locked.
UcsXDir	1.0000,0.0000,0.0000	R/O	DWG	X-direction of current UCS relative to WCS.
UcsYDir	0.0000,1.0000,0.0000	R/O	DWG	Y-direction of current UCS relative to WCS.
UndoCtl	5	R/O	...	State of undo: **0** Undo disabled. **1** Undo enabled. **2** Undo limited to one command. **4** Auto-group mode. **8** Group currently active.
UndoMarks	0	R/O	...	Current number of undo marks.
UnitMode	0	...	DWG	Units display: **0** As set by **Units** command. **1** As entered by user.
UserI1 thru UserI5 *0*		...	...	*Five user-definable integer variables.*
UserR1 thru UserR5 *0.0000*		...	...	*Five user-definable real variables.*
UserS1 thru UserS5 *""*		...	...	*Five user-definable string variables.*

▬ V

Variable	Default	R/o	Loc	Meaning
ViewCtr	*varies*	R/O	DWG	X,y,z-coordinate of center of current view, such as 6.2433,4.5000,0.0000.
ViewDir	*varies*	R/O	DWG	Current view direction relative to UCS, such as 0.0000,0.0000,1.0000.

Variable	Default	R/O	Loc	Meaning
ViewMode	0	R/O	DWG	Current view mode: **0** Normal view. **1** Perspective mode on. **2** Front clipping on. **4** Back clipping on. **8** UCS-follow on. **16** Front clip not at eye.
ViewSize	9.0000	R/O	DWG	Height of current view.
ViewTwist	0	R/O	DWG	Twist angle of current view.
VisRetain	1	...	DWG	Determines xref drawing's layer settings — on-off, freeze-thaw, color, and linetype: **0** Xref layer settings in the current drawing takes precedence for xref-dependent layers. **1** Settings for xref-dependent layers take precedence over the xref layer definition in the current drawing.
VSMax	*varies*	R/O	DWG	Upper-right corner of virtual screen, such as 37.4600,27.0000,0.0000.
VSMin	*varies*	R/O	DWG	Lower-left corner of virtual screen, such as -24.9734,-18.0000,0.0000.

W

Variable	Default	R/O	Loc	Meaning
WhipArc	0	...	REG	Display of circlular objects: **0** Displayed as connected vectors. **1** Displayed as true circles and arcs.
WhipThread	*3*	...	REG	*Controls multithreaded processing on two CPUs (if present) during drawing redraw and regeneration:* *0 Single-threaded calculations.* *1 Regenerations multi-threaded.* *2 Redraws multi-threaded.* *3 Regens and redraws multi-threaded.*
WmfBkgnd	1	...	...	Controls background of WMF files: **0** Background is transparent. **1** Background has same as AutoCAD's background color.
WmfForegnd	0	...	...	Controls foreground colors of exported WMF images: **0** Foreground is darker than background. **1** Foreground is lighter than background.
WorldUcs	1	R/O	...	Matching of WCS with UCS: **0** Current UCS is not WCS. **1** UCS is WCS.

Variable	Default	R/O	Loc	Meaning
WorldView	1	...	DWG	Display during **3dOrbit**, **DView**, and **VPoint** commands: **0** Display UCS. **1** Display WCS. **2** UCS changes relative to the UCS specified by the **UcsBase** system variable.
WriteStat	1	R/O	...	Indicates whether drawing file is read-only: **0** Drawing cannot be written to. **1** Drawing can be writen to.

▬ X

Variable	Default	R/O	Loc	Meaning
XClipFrame	0	...	DWG	Visibility of xref clipping boundary: **0** Not visible. **1** Visible.
XEdit	0	...	DWG	Toggles whether drawing can be edited in-place when referenced by another drawing: **0** Cannot in-place refedit. **1** Can in-place refedit.
XFadeCtl	50	...	REG	Fades objects not being edited in-place: **0** No fading; minimum value. **90** 90% fading; maximum value.
XLoadCtl	1	...	REG	Controls demand loading: **0** Demand loading turned off; entire drawing is loaded. **1** Demand loading turned on; xref file opened. **2** Demand loading turned on; a *copy* of the xref file is opened.
XLoadPath	"d:\temp"	...	REG	Path for loading xref file.
XRefCtl	0	...	REG	Determines creation of XLG xref log files: **0** File not written. **1** XLG file written.

▬ Z

Variable	Default	R/O	Loc	Meaning
ZoomFactor	40	...	REG	Controls the zoom level via mouse wheel; valid values range between 3 and 100.

Obsolete & Removed Commands

The following commands have been removed from AutoCAD since v 2.5.

Command	Introduced	Removed	Replacement	Reaction
3Dline	R9	R11	Line	"Line"
AmeLite	R11	R12	Region	"Unknown command"
AscText	R11	R13	MText	"Unknown command"
Ase...	R12	R13	ASE...	"Unknown command"
(Most R12 ASE commands were combined into ASE commands with R13.)				
Ase...	R13	2000	dbConnect	"Unknown command"
AseUnload	R12	R14	Arx Unload	"Unknown command"
Axis	v1.4	R12	*none*	"Discontinued command"
BMake	R12	2000	Block	Displays **Block Definition** dialog.
CConfig	R13	2000	PlotStyle	"Discontinued command"
Config	R12	R14	Options	Displays **Options** dialog.
DdAttDef	R12	2000	AttDef	Displays **Attribute Def** dialog.
DdAttE	R9	2000	AttEdit	Displays **Edit Attributes** dialog.
DdAttExt	R12	2000	AttExt	Displays **Attribute Ext** dialog.
DdChProp	R12	2000	Properties	Displays **Properties** window.
DdColor	R13	2000	Color	Displays **Select Color** dialog.
DdEModes	R9	R14	Object Properties	"Discontinued command"
DdGrips	R12	2000	Options	Displays **Options** dialog.
DDim	R12	2000	DimStyle	Displays **Dim Style Mgr** dialog.
DdInsert	R12	2000	Insert	Displays **Insert** dialog.
DdLModes	R9	R14	Layer	Displays **Layer Manager** dialog.
DdLType	R9	R14	Linetype	Displays **Linetype Mgr** dialog.
DdModify	R12	2000	Properties	Displays **Properties** window.
DdOSnap	R12	2000	DSettings	Displays **Drafting Settings** dialog.
DdRename	R12	2000	Rename	"Unknown command"
DdRModes	R9	2000	DSettings	Displays **Drafting Settings** dialog.
DdSelect	R12	2000	Options	Displays **Options** dialog.
DdUcs	R10	2000	UcsMan	Displays **UCS** dialog.
DdUcsP	R12	2000	UcsMan	Displays **UCS** dialog.
DdUnits	R12	2000	Units	Displays **Units** dialog.
DdView	R12	2000	View	Displays **View** dialog.
DText	v2.5	2000	Text	Executes **Text** command.
DL, DLine	R11	R13	MLine	"Unknown command"
DwfOutD	R14	2000	DwfOut	"Unknown command"

Command	Introduced	Removed	Replacement	Reaction (con't)
End	R11	R13	Quit	"Discontinued command"
EndRep	v1.0	v2.5	Minsert	"Discontinued command"
EndSv	v2.0	v2.5	End	"Discontinued command"
ExpressTools	2000	2002	*none*	"Unknown command"
Files	v1.4	R14	*Explorer*	"Discontinued command"
FilmRoll	v2.6	R13	*none*	"Unknown command"
FlatLand	R10	R11	*none*	"Cannot set Flatland to that value"
GifIn	R12	R14	ImageAttach	"No longer supported"
HpConfig	R12	2000	PlotStyle	"Discontinued command"
IgesIn, IgesOut	v2.5	R13	*none*	"Discontinued command"
InetCfg	R14	2000	*none*	"Unknown command"
InetHelp	R14	2000	Help	"Unknown command"
InsertUrl	R14	2000	Insert	Displays **Insert** dialog.
ListUrl	R14	2000	QSelect	"Unknown command"
MakePreview	R13	R14	*none*	"Discontinued command"
OceConfig	R13	2000	PlotStyle	"Discontinued command"
OpenUrl	R14	2000	Open	Displays **Select File** dialog.
OSnap	v2.0	2000	DSettings	Displays **Drafting Settings** dialog.
PcxIn	R12	R14	ImageAttach	"No longer supported"
PsDrag	R12	2000i	*none*	"Unknown command"
PsIn	R12	2000i	*none*	"Unknown command"
Preferences	R11	2000	Options	Displays Options dialog.
PrPlot	v2.1	R12	Plot	"Discontinued command."
QPlot	v1.1	v2.0	SaveImg	"Unknown command"
RConfig	R12	R14	*none*	"Unknown command"
RenderUnload	R12	R14	Arx Unload	"Unknown command"
Repeat	v1.0	v2.5	Minsert	"Discontinued command"
SaveAsR12	R13	R14	SaveAs	"Unknown command"
SaveUrl	R14	2000	SaveAs	Displays **Save Drawing As** dialog.
Snapshot	v2.0	v2.1	Saveimg	"Unknown command"
Sol...	R11	R13	*(AME commands lost their SOL-prefix.)*	
TbConfig	R12	R14	Toolbar	Displays **Customize** dialog box.
TiffIn	R12	R14	ImageAttach	"No longer supported"
TbConfig	R14	2000i	Customize	Displays **Customize** dialog box.
Toolbar	R13	2000i	Customize	Displays **Customize** dialog box.
VlConv	R13	R14	*none*	"Unknown command"